TH

M.

Also by Freda Warrington

The Amber Citadel
The Sapphire Throne
The Obsidian Tower

Books One, Two and Three of *The Jewelfire Trilogy*

THE COURT OF THE
MIDNIGHT KING

Freda Warrington

POCKET
BOOKS

LONDON · SYDNEY · NEW YORK · TOKYO · SINGAPORE · TORONTO

First published in Great Britain by Pocket Books, 2003
An imprint of Simon & Schuster UK Ltd
A CBS Company

1 3 5 7 9 10 8 6 4 2

Simon & Schuster UK Ltd
1st Floor, 222 Gray's Inn Road
London WC1X 8HB

www.simonandschuster.co.uk

Simon & Schuster Australia
Sydney

A CIP catalogue record for this book is available
from the British Library

ISBN 978-0-7434-1567-5

Typeset by Palimpsest Book Production Limited,
Polmont, Stirlingshire

Printed and bound by CPI Group (UK) Ltd, Croydon, CR0 4YY

This book is dedicated to the memory of my father
Stanley Cecil Warrington
1916–2000

Richard is gone from us, yet his name fascinates every tongue.

Rosemary Hawley Jarman

Prelude 1485:
'The truth that none dares utter.'

Above Redmore Plain the sky darkened. It glowed violet, bluest violet, smudged with bars of cloud. On the humped back of Ambion Hill the encampment slept, waiting; the wind dropped and banners hung as ragged and as blue as the night. Silence rolled in.

So complete was the stillness that Raphael could hear the chirrup of frogs down in the marsh. He heard the rasp of the horned toad and the owl's fluting cry. Around him the land felt deserted. Even the slow spirits of the stones and the mercurial beings of the hedgerows were absent. Had they deserted in terror of the battle to come? Men feared the denizens of the twilight, not realizing that those spirits were more afraid of humans by far.

In the great, hushed darkness, he thought he could hear the voices of the enemy; snapping fragments of sound, far away. The usurper, flaunting his rose-red dragon and claiming to be sent by heaven to destroy the Adversary. Raphael spat a quiet curse in his direction, and slipped back into the King's pavilion.

A lamp burned inside, glimmering on the cloth-of-gold walls, its flame as pallid as the gaunt face that reflected it. The King could not sleep. He had tried, only to wake with a shuddering gasp, complaining of dreadful nightmares, wraiths with pale fingers and yellow eyes waiting for him just below the surface of sleep. Recovering himself, he'd sent his concerned lieutenants away to their rest. Only Raphael remained, wide awake and glad to keep the vigil with him.

'Is anything stirring out there?' asked the King. He was

1

as Raphael had left him – sitting with his arms folded upon the table, gazing at the lamp.

'The sentries report that all is quiet.'

'Then it must be my own ghosts I can hear.'

'Sire, won't you try to have an hour or two's rest, at least?' Raphael spoke quietly, trying not to disturb the pages asleep in the outer chamber of the tent.

'It's too late,' the King answered. 'I'll not sleep again tonight. All I can do is wait for the dawn. Fate must be telling me I need a time of reflection.'

His face was a shell with light shining through it; frail and pearly like that of a heavenly messenger, but more eerie than saintly. Raphael could imagine the same luminous face belonging to the most beautiful of the angels, the morning star, Lucifer. The King's hair was feathered shadow around his shoulders. His eyes were grey and shrouded, like twilight.

'Do you think that I am wicked, my friend?' he asked.

Raphael sat down on a canvas stool, facing him across the table. 'No, sire, of course not!'

'I have been accused of poisoning, infanticide and incest, among other crimes. You know this full well.'

'Lies.'

'Have I been so bad a king?' His voice sounded thin and distant, as if it already came from beyond the veil of death. 'The tales they tell of me run like fire from mouth to mouth, so that I must deny them even to my friends. I'm sick to the stomach with denial. After all, how honestly can I say that there is no truth at all in any of the stories?'

'They are only words, rumours . . .' Raphael trailed off, helpless.

'On the strength of rumours, a nonentity named Henry Tudor fashions himself as the revolving sword of God, come to slay the Devil. And look! My kingdom is sinking into the marsh.'

'No!' Raphael was fierce with denial. 'That is utterly untrue. I can't bear to see you so disheartened.'

The King shook his head, his hair moving softly, like crow's wings. 'No, I'm not disheartened, don't think that. I'm thinking aloud to get at the truth. You've always helped me in that. You know more of my secrets that any other being, and this could be the last chance I have.'

A shuddering fear went through Raphael, from the soles of his feet to the roots of his hair. His mouth was thick. He tried to go on breathing.

'It seems every weapon I ever used has been turned back upon me,' King Richard went on. 'Myths are more enduring than truth, you have told me so yourself.'

'I shouldn't have said anything. Ever.'

'No.' Richard spoke gently. 'What, endured that on your own? You were right to tell me all. If you'd kept such matters to yourself, you would have failed me indeed. As it is, I am prepared for the worst.'

Raphael had run out of answers. He wished himself anywhere but sitting in the midst of this quiet nightmare. 'Dearest lord, don't. You should rest, not think about—'

'My death?' Richard said calmly.

'I was going to say, my dream. It was only . . .'

'Perhaps real, and perhaps not. I know that. Well, in the morning this humour will be gone from me and I'll go into battle roaring, a black dragon to affright the red. But now, Raphael, tell me . . .'

The merest slide of light could change Richard's face from frail pearl to chiselled marble. He looked straight at Raphael and his expression was terrible, like that of a demon who had passed through storms of madness to chilling serenity on the far side. 'Is the Tudor right? Is his tight little Beaufort mother right, all of them right? That I have been used as an instrument of Satan to bring the downfall of a rotten dynasty – while God has chosen to press his holy sword of vengeance into the paw of one Welsh–French nobody?'

'I'm surprised Tudor didn't style himself with the name of an archangel,' said Raphael so venomously that Richard laughed.

'Gabriel, or Michael . . . or Raphael. So, even the Devil's chosen has an angel to comfort him through the longest night.'

Raphael poured wine for the King as a diversion from his own brimming misery. His hand shook as he passed the cup; Richard took it, and kept his hand on Raphael's for a moment. The King's flesh felt as cold, clammy and steady as a dolmen.

'I don't seem to be comforting you very well,' Raphael said.

'But you are.' Richard glanced behind him, where a small altar had been set up near his bed. Candles fluttered around a small figure of the Virgin. 'Given a choice between spending this night praying to a Creator who turned his back on me in childhood, and talking to a flesh and blood friend, I know which is more likely to save my soul.'

The wine was heavily watered, and tasted flat and ghostly. 'I don't care what you say, sire. There are souls in Tudor's camp in far worse danger than yours.'

Richard only grimaced. 'I have done wrong, but what could I have done otherwise?' he said quietly. 'Nothing. Thus I am condemned not only for what I did, but for what I am. Thus is the Devil condemned for being what his Creator made him.'

'Sire, you mustn't listen to their rumours and slanders. You can't let yourself believe their lies.'

'I am not talking about the views of others,' Richard answered. 'I'm talking about what I know of myself. For there is a shadow in me, a great and dreadful shadow that would blot out the entire world with its clawed wings if it were left unchecked. And this has not been planted in me by enemies. They've glimpsed it, and that's why they are afraid of me, but they didn't put it there. It was born within me, and awoken when I was a child. We were at Ludlow . . .'

His voice was soft and calm. The lamp burned blue. So intense was the hush outside that Raphael feared they had

4

slipped into the hidden world. 'Sire, you are low in spirits. This is nothing, a waking nightmare.'

'And you, an experienced walker in waking nightmares,' Richard retaliated. Suddenly he sounded weirdly cheerful. 'Asleep or awake, I can't escape hideous visitations tonight, but at least I have you at my side. I have never told this to anyone in my life before. Let me tell you about the waking of the shadow.'

He ran through the wildwood, deeper and deeper. Vibrant images haunted him, of his father and brothers fighting a battle far away. It would be days before he knew whether they had lived or died. No one even cared to tell a boy of seven; he would be the last to know. Distraught with frustration, he had evaded tutors and guardians and escaped the castle walls, and now he ran and ran.

At first he was bold, striking out at bushes and shadows with a twig sword. One day his weapons would be true metal and the shadows would be enemies of flesh and armour. He would fight alongside his brothers, turning the red rose crimson with blood.

It was survival he dreamed of, more than glory. His family's survival.

But for now he was only a child, suddenly lost and cold. The shadows began to move and whisper. Looking back the way he had come, he saw no path, only the gnarled gloom of the woods enclosing him. The moss-green eyes of elementals were staring at him from behind heavy, wet canopies of leaves. He saw their thin long limbs, like folded brambles. They stared at him, pointing, whispering.

Richard let the sword fall to his side and backed away.

Dark blue twilight dripped through the trees. There was only one way to go, a thread of a path taking him even further from safety. Ahead shone a gap in the trees, a patch of slaty sky in which a single bright star hung like a white rose. He fled towards it, feet and heart pounding.

Where the trees ended there lay a marsh, stretching away

into a blue mist. Two herons started up at his approach and flapped away, luminous in the dusk, their long legs stirring layers of vapour. The boy swallowed a cry of shock. He stood trapped between the wildwood and the marsh. Water gleamed in the saturated sapphire light. Tussocks crouched in the turbid water. Like ghosts the herons were gone and nothing moved, yet everything watched him, breathing.

Richard knew then that he'd made a dreadful mistake. He'd strayed out of the real world and into the netherworld, the dread place that only came to life while God-fearing men slept. He breathed hard, clutching his sword. The damp, rank air filled his lungs. Away to his left he saw an arch of rock at the wood's edge, and behind it a mound of rock containing the slit of a cave mouth. If only he could reach it, he could shelter there and set up his sword at the entrance like a cross to ward off the famished shadows. God the Creator would protect him until morning. So his mother had always told him.

His feet slid on the tussocks. The cave was further away and bigger than it had seemed. The entrance looked threatening, not a refuge but the mouth of the demon-realm. An eerie tongue of light lapped within it. There was something alive in there, moving, chanting.

The fog thickened. He could see barely an arm-span ahead. He stopped, shivering, tasting blood. He'd bite his tongue to ribbons before he would let himself cry.

A woman took shape out of the mist like the prow of a ship.

He stood rooted and helpless as she sailed towards him. She might have come out of the cave or formed from the fog itself; he couldn't tell. He glimpsed dangling sleeves of charcoal velvet, a tissue of black silk stiffly framing her head, a terrible, stern white face with gold eyes boring into his.

A sorceress.

'Child, how did you come here?' she said.

Richard couldn't speak. Petrified, he watched her long

pale hands coming towards him. The fingers touched him, moving over his shoulders, his cheeks, into his hair. The touch felt light and waxen, like mouse feet.

'It is late for you to be out alone. You strayed too far from the path. You trespass where you do not belong.'

He nodded, trying to say, *Your pardon, my lady, I meant no harm.* At last he managed a whisper. 'The path brought me here.'

'And so it did. Therefore you must have been called. No one comes among us without a reason. Would you walk the spiral chambers with us to the innermost heart of the shell?'

Her eyes frightened him. She looked mad, or in a trance. He tried to back away but her hands closed tight on his skull. The pressure made his bones ache, brought red fire behind his eyes – and then a grotesque vision.

His mouth fell open. He was looking at a severed head. The head of a robust man with greying hair and the plain weathered face of a foot soldier, stuck on a spike beneath a market cross. The parchment skin was yellow and the lips hung slack. The eyes looked sideways at Richard, as if in deadly warning.

The face was dead and yet alive, animated by the leaping light of a hundred candles. An old woman was in the act of lighting them. She rose and lifted the head off its spike, cradled it for a moment, then set it down amid the candles. She began to comb the grey hair and wash the blood-daubed cheeks, all the while sobbing and singing and murmuring to the head.

'Your sons will avenge you,' she lamented. 'Your grandson will avenge you.'

It was not only the head that horrified Richard, but the pointless desperation of the old woman.

He cried out. The vision vanished. The witch had removed her hands from his hair and now gazed at him with her unhuman eyes.

'With every step the path divides,' she said.

7

'The path divides,' echoed a high voice.

The voice came not from the sorceress but from some-where near her hip. Richard saw that she had a small companion, a familiar that lurked behind her, peering round her skirts. It had wild black hair and eyes like marsh-fire. An elf-child. The words issuing from the child-ish mouth made the creature seem more terrifying than its mistress.

'What did you see?' asked the sorceress.

'What does it mean?' asked her familiar.

Richard shook his head mutely. Their faces shone with witch-light, mocking, demanding. He was sure he'd wan-dered into hell.

'I don't know. A man beheaded. Is it . . .' He struggled for the right word. 'Is it a prophecy?'

The elf-child's eyes rolled back in its head, showing two moon-white crescents. Imp and witch spoke in unison. 'There is no such thing as prophecy. No such thing as destiny. This is the truth that none dares utter.'

The sorceress raised her hand to his shoulder and went on, 'This is the truth. With every step, you weave the spider's web for yourself. Shall you weave a great web or a small? One of shining dew colours or one of soot and barbs? None can tell. Your future is all darkness.'

She meant, he was sure, that he was going to die.

'No,' he said.

'Come in with us,' said the witch. She half-turned, her hand sweeping towards the cave entrance. The mouth glimmered and smoked through the fog.

'In there?'

'Yes. Come into the labyrinth of the shell. The meaning of your vision will become clear. Some of your questions will be answered. The serpent's bite brings wisdom, if you can bear the pain. Come with us.'

He stared at the terrible cave and felt his stomach turn liquid with terror.

'No!'

Panicking, he stumbled out of her grasp, twisted round and began to run. His feet splashed into water, mud sucked at his boots. He floundered. Death sighed and clawed him down with famished hands. Deep inside himself he felt a shadow waking and flapping anguished wings, and it was not fear of death but something far darker. Something that recognized this place and wanted to keep him there.

'That way.'

He glanced round. The sorceress was pointing, a wing of velvet hanging from her outstretched arm, back towards the wildwood. A wide, clear path had opened between the trees.

At the far end – another illusion, surely – he could see Ludlow Castle standing upon its hill. Home.

'Take that path, child,' said the sorceress. 'No creature of the twilight will harm you while you are under our protection. They'll not dare. You'll come back when you are ready.'

With those last ominous words chasing him, Richard pulled free of the marsh, and fled. He clutched his flimsy sword for all he was worth, teeth bared against green-eyed sprites that chittered in the undergrowth as he passed. The castle at the end of the starlit path stood aloof, never drawing any closer.

That was not my father's head I saw, he told himself. *Not my father's.* Yet still the tears of dread choked him.

He ran. He left the netherworld behind but it tried to pull him back. Wraiths tugged at his heels with cold blue fingers. Blanched and staring faces swam before his blurred eyes. However far, however hard he fled, the terror rushed along with him.

Inside him, the shadow stretched fledgling wings and made its claim.

'She spoke the truth,' said the King, pacing slowly in the dim light of the tent. 'My future was darkness. Almost everyone I have ever loved is dead. That was the head of

9

Owen Tudor she showed me. He was the Welsh squire who married Henry the Fifth's widow. Their son Edmund Tudor spawned my enemy, the pretender who waits for me now. But Owen Tudor did not lose his head until two years or more *after* I met the witches. When I heard the story of the madwoman lighting the candles I knew I'd seen a glimpse of the future and I cannot describe the fear that this hellish netherworld struck into me. I don't envy you your dreams, my friend.'

'I think that I would have gone into the cave,' Raphael said.

'Then you would have been braver than me.'

'No. Just too afraid to refuse.'

'I knew – not thought, *knew* – that if I entered that cave, my soul would be lost for all time.'

'But you might have understood what it all meant.'

'Yes, perhaps I would, and perhaps it would have given me undreamed-of power – but at the cost, as I said, of my soul. All my life, the shadow within me has been trying to drag me back there. The temptation has been almost unbearable, sometimes. But I've fought it. If I lose my soul anyway, no one can say I haven't battled to the death for it.' Richard turned, his face aglow and ghastly. 'I've never spoken of this to anyone. I could never admit the terror I felt, not to my brothers, not even to my mother. She would only have told me to pray, pray for redemption. How could I explain what I had seen, what horror had been shown to me, still less explain that I knew this darkness to be so interwoven with my soul that an eternity of praying and an army of priests could never exorcise it? They'd have thought me bewitched. All I've done to avert this destiny has been in vain. I might as well have torn down the altar, burned my prayer books, ripped out my own heart and offered it to Satan.'

His voice rose, making Raphael start. He was suddenly alight with controlled, incandescent passion. 'Well, let Tudor come! Let them have the apocalypse they want.

10

I shall fight as I have lived, and take as many with me as I may to the pits of hell.'

Outside, Raphael could hear the first sounds of the camp coming to life.

King Richard rose, moved towards the pavilion's entrance and lifted the flap. The first indigo glimmer of dawn brushed Redmore Plain. In the gloom, Raphael saw tiny figures toiling up the hill.

Very quietly, Richard said, 'For all I've done, for all I am, and for all the sins of my family, I am punished. I am punished. I've spun a web of soot and barbs. And now, the final act.'

The battlefield of Bosworth always feels bleak, even at the height of summer. Imagine away the midge-clouded heat and the visitors, and just beneath the surface there's a harder, darker reality. King Richard was piteously betrayed and slain here. The land has never forgotten.

It happens once in a lifetime that you encounter someone who goes straight into you, like a laser. You can't explain why it's that person and not another, or what it means. But in they go, directly into your soul and they are locked there forever, dark and sweet and painful. Even when, as often happens, they don't know you exist.

For some it's a god or a guru, for others a lover, a film star, an absent father. And for me – what? A villain? A hero? An enigma. A man who died more than five hundred years ago.

I remember the moment. I was new at university, studying medieval history and already wondering if I'd made a mistake. I'd come back to the halls of residence, tired. My tutor didn't like me, I thought, and was already giving me a hard time. The girl across the hall from me, Fin, came out at just the right moment and said, 'We're watching a video, Gus. I've opened a bottle of wine. Come and join us.'

She's a rare one, Fin. Easy to be with, open and kind. I was so glad that afternoon, new and uncertain, to curl up on her sofa, accept a glass of merlot, and forget everything.

There were a couple of other students there, sprawled

on the floor smoking. The film they were watching was *Richard III*. It wasn't the period I was studying and all I knew was the wisdom received from Shakespeare, now laid before me in 1950's technicolour, with gorgeous costumes, pageantry, a rainbow of banners and, at the centre, holding the attention like a dark star, the ravishingly handsome Laurence Olivier, trying to convince us he was an ugly hunchback.

'Since I cannot prove a lover . . . I am determined to prove a villain.'

The room was dark, bathed in the flickering colours of the tragedy. No villain was ever more attractive. At times gleeful, at others flatly chilling, slaughtering his way through brother, friends, nephews and wife to gain the throne, and doing so with such wit, sharp self-awareness and panache that we cheered him on even as we recoiled. Entranced, I watched him weave a web of deadly charm and throw it over the Lady Anne, turning her in minutes from venomous hatred to love with his honeyed lies; and I believed it completely. If I'd been her, I would have fallen too.

It wasn't the actor. It wasn't the real Richard III. I don't know what it was that lashed from the screen, from a film a half-century old . . . An entity, a delicious shadow.

When the hero, Henry Tudor, Earl of Richmond, arrived to defeat him, I was dismayed. The others booed. Who could celebrate the triumph of bland conformity over such ruthless, wild creativity?

'It's all cobblers, of course,' said one of the others, a Yorkshire lass. Fin poured more wine into my glass and sat smiling, inscrutable.

'A ton of dramatic licence,' I said, 'but why is it cobblers?'

'I thought you were doing medieval history, August?'

'Twelfth century.' I pulled a face without meaning to. I was thinking of my tutor's demolition of my essay;

13

I'd focused on the wrong aspects, he'd said, and I disagreed, but my feeble attempts to put my case had been crushed flat by his superior insights, blah blah.

'Bloody good play, not much resemblance to reality,' the Yorkshire lass stated flatly. 'Best king we ever had, Richard the Third.'

'Shakespeare never let facts stand in the way of a good story,' said Fin. 'It's a morality story. Higher truth. Triumph of good over evil.'

'Except he wasn't evil!' said her friend.

They went on arguing with half-remembered facts. I picked up the remote and rewound to the wooing scene. God, he was convincing; Olivier, or Richard, or the Entity. Seducing his victim with all the dark charisma of a vampire. It was spellbinding. It was the beginning.

That night, as I lay down to sleep, he came to me.

Chapter One 1460: Eleanor

RICHARD
The curse my noble father laid on thee,
When thou didst crown his warlike brows with paper,
And with thy scorns drew'st rivers from his eyes;
And then, to dry them, gav'st the Duke a clout
Steeped in the faultless blood of pretty Rutland –
His curses then, from bitterness of soul
Denounced against thee, are all fallen upon thee;
And God, not we, hath plagued thy bloody deed.

Richard III Act I scene 3

White-gold light flooded a frieze of snow. Katherine played in white enchantment, on her knees in a drift, squeezing snowballs between her palms and pressing them into small figures, naming each one as she set it down. Her own king, queen and court. She wondered at the sensation of snow compacting and the ice-water running between her fingers. Strange it should be so cold and yet burn like flame. Her wet, burning fingers were as red as strawberries.

Other children played around her in the courtyard garden, hurling snow. Kate ignored them, even when a stray snowball burst on her shoulder and trickled its chill down her neck. Their babbling laughter was a vague background. The friar who had been set to supervise them stood blowing on his hands, his long nose scarlet.

From within the house – that of her mother's friend, Dame Eylott – she could still hear the low chanting of the priestesses. From the street beyond the courtyard wall carried the sharper sound of raised voices, the quick tramp of boots muffled in the snow. Tension fogged the air. One boy stood apart, waiting anxiously at the closed, solid gate that led onto the street. Now and then Kate sat back, cushioned by the thick wool of her skirts, to see if he was still there.

She knew the boy only by sight. The custom was for the priestesses to include their sons and daughters in the early part of the meeting, to dance a circle in the incense-wreathed light of the cellar temple. Then the adults would proceed to their own secret business, while the children were turned loose to play. The boy had gone straight to the gate and had waited there ever since. She'd asked him why, but he hadn't answered, so she'd left him alone.

Kate began to build an ice palace for her courtiers. It would be large and fantastical with spires of ice, as she imagined the great ice palaces in the sparkling lands of the north.

The courtyard gate was flung back. The boy was knocked flying. Thomas Copper, her mother's steward, came running through, yelling. 'The battle's lost, York is dead!' He rushed straight past and into the house until his shouts were swallowed within it. 'My Lady Lytton, Dame Eylott, Dame Marl . . .'

Kate glanced down at her snow figures and found them ruined. She had struck off their heads with her sleeve.

Seconds later, women came pouring out of the house, nobles and servants mingling together. Across the courtyard and out into the street they went, gathering children in their wake. Katherine found herself swung up into her mother's arms and carried along, into a river of people. Nan, the little maid, only a few years older than Kate herself, ran at their side.

Winter had transformed the city of York, turning its walls to sparkling veils. All dirt and imperfection lay smothered in white drifts, goosedown-thick and achingly cold. The tall

16

houses glittered under deep caps of snow. Underfoot, slush lay rutted and churned brown.

'Ma'am, what's happened?' Nan cried, her white breath curling in wisps.

'The Duke of York is dead,' answered Lady Eleanor Lytton, Kate's mother. Her voice sounded sad and remote. 'The battle went against them. This time, the Lancastrians triumphed.'

Slowed to a walk by the press of people, they reached the city gate. Before them rose the crenellated bulk of Micklegate Bar, black against the bright sky. A great crowd had gathered around it, stamping and breathing fog into the air, and staring up at the parapet that arched above the gate.

'Oh, Great Goddess,' said Lady Eleanor.

Katherine squinted against brightness and shaded her eyes with a chilled hand. Atop the gate, framed against the glaring acid-gold of the sky, were three heads. Three severed heads, stuck on spikes, staring across the city.

Their faces were vague in silhouette but the look of them was ragged and bruised. The sight filled Kate with an immense, nebulous sense of tragedy.

'Mama, who are they?' Katherine asked after a while.

'She shouldn't see this,' said Nan. Tears were rolling down her cheeks and nose.

'No, she *should* see it,' Eleanor answered. She had begun to chafe Kate's numb fingers with hands that felt like fire. 'Let her see the ways of men. The fewer illusions she grows up with, the better.' Her voice was low, calm, but full of passion. 'Look well, sweetheart. The head in the centre is that of the Duke of York. He quarrelled with King Henry and tried to claim the throne. Some say his claim was better than Henry's, but that only made him too troublesome; and this is where it has got him. The head on his right is that of his friend, the Earl of Salisbury. The one on his left is his son, Edmund of Rutland.'

'The boy was only seventeen,' said Thomas Copper. He'd

shouldered his way to them and stood hunched under his thick fleece-lined coat, looking up at the trophies. 'It's being said that the Lancastrians attacked during a truce, while the Duke was still at Sandal Castle, celebrating Christmas. He stood no chance. Edmund fled, but the Queen's men chased him and slaughtered him even while he was pleading for mercy. Massacre!'

He went on, grumbling about the atrocities perpetrated on the battlefield by the House of Lancaster. Slaughter, mutilation, vengeful cruelty beyond belief. Kate's rich imagination conjured its own images and wove them into a crimson nightmare.

'Is this the end, then?' asked Eleanor. 'Gentle Harry has destroyed his enemies. We might see peace at last.'

'Not a chance,' Thomas Copper replied. 'York still has three sons living. Edward, George and Richard.'

'Yes. Naturally it will never end.'

'Why?' asked Kate.

Her mother didn't answer for a time. Katherine looked closely at her, at her strong, gentle, troubled face, her kind hazel eyes, her hair showing coppery beneath a covering of umber velvet. Her outwards appearance of demure graciousness was deceptive, Kate knew. As her other-self, her hidden self, Eleanor was unrecognizable.

Around them, the crowd murmured with outrage and wonder. Eventually she said under her breath, 'White rose and red rose, Kate; different shoots of the same thorny bush. They're like two brothers who have become the deadliest rivals.'

Kate had a clear view through the open gates of Micklegate Bar to the road beyond. She saw a cloud of ice crystals, whirling and billowing along the road towards them. In an ecstasy of terror, she clutched her mother.

'Are they coming to kill us?'

'Of course not. Why, Kate?'

'Because Father loved the Duke of York.'

Eleanor bit her lip. There was a hard shine in her eyes.

'They won't kill us for that. One king is much the same as another. Whoever wins, we'll swear loyalty to the crown and keep our heads down, as we've always done. There's nothing to fear, love.'

Closer the glittering diamond cloud came, and Katherine saw what it was. A swirl of winter spirits, roused by some disturbance and now cavorting joyously in a mad dance. Through the cloud appeared the grey silhouettes of six priests, flaunting huge crosses with dagger-pointed ends and scattering holy water. They were trying to drive the elementals away. They looked like wizards, ridiculously fighting an invisible enemy.

Kate's mother gave a small, tight gasp. Exorcism. Such rituals always made her sigh in contempt. The holy men went on chanting and the elementals went on playing. Suddenly – of its own mischievous will, not the priests' – the silver cloud twisted upon itself, veered into the air and vanished in a shower of snow-mist. The exorcists were slow to cease their ritual, looking around bewildered, as if unsure of their success. Kate realized she could see more clearly than them.

She saw the road beyond and the hard white land-scape around it. A long column of mounted knights was approaching, thunderous and magnificent. Kate's heart thumped. The priests, half-running to avoid being ridden down, formed two hasty lines to flank the column. Their cloaks flapped in the chill air. They'd been frantic to drive the mischievous snow spirits out of the path; it almost looked as if the elementals had been trying to bar their way into the city. Perhaps, thought Kate, Mama and her friends had summoned them.

The riders reached the gate and came rumbling through. The ground shook. The crowd split and peeled back and between them a great procession came riding. Huge horses breathing steam like dragons. Men in armour, their sur-coats torn and bloodied, amid a forest of banners stiff with ice. Ten couple of graylix on chains: great charcoal creatures with almost-human faces, snarling and snapping at the onlookers, straining to escape the pages who fought to hold them. A sigh of fear went through the onlookers. On every surcoat the red rose glistened like a burst heart.

Eleanor and Katherine were jostled as the people around them pushed backwards and forwards. Kate was afloat on a sea of florid, staring faces.

In centre of the army rode a woman. A slender, blade-straight woman, armoured beneath a golden cloak. Her face was all hard planes, pale and keen, with eyes of colourless ice. Hair as straight and pale as straw fell from beneath her crowned helm.

'Queen Marguerite,' whispered Eleanor. The whisper ran through the crowd all around them. *Queen Marguerite. Henry sits like a monk in a cell while she fights his battles for him! She's a monster. Slew a boy of seventeen. Poor Edmund!* From some throats came a hiss that she must have heard. Others bent a reluctant knee as she passed.

The Queen pulled up her horse hardly two yards from where Kate and her mother stood, and looked back at Micklegate Bar. Her chestnut mount danced on the spot, half-rearing. Its thick neck was bent, foam dripping from its open mouth.

'Regard!' Marguerite cried, pointing upwards, her arm straight as a spear. 'York looks out over York.' Her voice was harsh, sharply accented. 'He strove to be king; so let him be crowned indeed. With straw!'

And all her knights and supporters roared with laughter.

The image of the Queen, silver and gold and terrible, struck Katherine to the heart with excitement. She hated her on sight. Yet she was magnificent.

'Mama,' she whispered. 'Is she one of ours?'

'No,' Eleanor said quickly. 'Shush, child!' Then, 'No, my chick. Hush. You'll learn how to tell, in time.'

The royal party surged onwards in all their victorious arrogance. They passed along the curve of the street, and were swallowed by the city.

When the Queen had gone, the crowd loosened and moved off in her wake. Eleanor set Katherine down and they walked hand in hand back to the house of Dame Eylott, Nan scurrying beside them and Thomas Copper following.

The courtyard garden lay iced and silent, its whiteness barely marked by the children's games. The falling sun flushed the tops of snow-laden bushes with gold, but the rest had turned coldly blue. The women regathered there, shivering, the hems of their cloaks and skirts heavy with wetness. An air of shock hung over them; no one seemed glad that King Henry had won. Three of the women came to greet Eleanor. One was Dame Eylott, a sweet-faced old woman with a pointed chin and silver hair. The second, small and wrapped in a green velvet cloak, was Edith, Lady Hart. Much younger than the Dame, she still appeared ancient to Kate, with a perpetual air of frailty and worry about her.

The third was a statuesque woman in a close-fitting gown of midnight blue. Her height was all the more imposing for a hennin of the same blue, sewn all over with tiny pearls. Within the enclave, their identities were discretely shed and ignored. But Kate knew that this was Anne Beauchamp, the Countess of Warwick.

The four talked softly, heads bent together. Eleanor and the Countess looked pale and serious. Lady Hart was crying.

Kate remembered that the boy who had stood by the gate was Edith Hart's son. She looked around for him and saw him kneeling in the drift where she had made her snow figures. He was a sapling, very slender and dressed in brown; fine garments that were faded with wear. His head was bowed, chestnut hair hiding his face. He was either weeping or praying.

Katherine went to him, light-footed and hesitant.

'Are you crying?' she asked.

He started, jumped to his feet and stared at her. His eyes

21

were dry but edged with redness; burning, shocked eyes in a blank face. He wasn't much older than her. Seven at the most.

'Did you see the heads?' she asked, cradling her snow-bitten hands under her armpits. 'I did. Is that why you're upset?'

'My father died.' The words fell out of him, rough and bitter. 'He was in the battle. A man came and told my mother that he was killed, trying to protect Edmund of Rutland.'

Kate looked at him, not knowing what to say. 'Is his head on the gate?' she asked at last.

'No. He wasn't a high enough lord for that, not one of the leaders.' The boy wiped his red eyes and sniffed. 'I don't think I'd know his face, even if he was. He was always away fighting. He was a brave, noble lord and he was loyal to Richard of York and the Lancastrian fiends killed them.'

'Are they fiends?' Katherine asked, going closer. 'My mother says they're all as bad as each other.'

'They're fiends all right. Savages.' His voice was shaky, gravel-rough. 'We're not allowed to see his body because it was so badly chopped up. The Lancastrians went on killing even when the battle was over. They killed prisoners – people who'd surrendered. They'd kill you if you stood in their way! That's what they're like.'

Katherine stepped back from his vehement grief, shocked. She wanted to put her arms round him but dared not – he was too prickly with grief. She looked up at the courtyard wall and realized that, above it, she could just see the top of Micklegate Bar. Behind its stark grey fortifications, the sky was cold pink, streaked with clouds like sword blades. The heads were tiny. Puppet heads. Crows and petitmorts were already squabbling for their flesh, squawking black darts.

Winter wind bit through her. It seemed that the scene was shifting, changing.

'There will be different heads there soon,' she said.

'Lancastrian heads?' She nodded. 'I hope so. Are you a seer?'

She didn't answer the question, wasn't sure what it meant. There were no words to explain about the paths and webs that people made. 'What's your name? I'm Katherine Lytton.'

'Raphael Hart,' he said. He bowed and kissed her hand, and she curtseyed, as if they were grown-ups. It made them both giggle. His eyes were very green, like jade.

'Now your father is dead, where will you live?' she asked. 'With your mother?'

He shook his head. 'I'll be sent as a ward with my brother Simon. He's two years older than me. We'll learn Greek and Latin, and we'll train to be knights.'

Katherine imagined draughty castle corridors, sour-faced tutors droning on and on. 'That sounds boring. Why don't you come and live with us?'

He laughed. 'You are strange, Lady Katherine.'

'Why? I would like a brother. I'd be a very good sister.'

'You look as if you would be.' His agreement warmed her. She grinned, but he wore that shocked, remote look again. 'I'd like that, but I can't. I must learn to bear arms, so I can avenge my father.'

Abruptly his face lengthened, and he bowed. A long shadow fell. Katherine realized her mother was standing over them.

'And that's why this will never end,' Eleanor said, tight and angry. 'I am so sorry about your father, Raphael. But remember this, which I tell my daughter: neither side is more virtuous than the other; either may bear a gift in one hand and a dagger in the other. Whichever rose you support, you might as well throw dice for your survival!'

Eleanor's face was transformed, as luminous as Queen Marguerite's had been. Raphael looked startled. His mother Edith was behind her, crimson-faced from cold and grief.

'I believe in loyalty, my lady,' he said, his childish

23

voice dignified. 'I am loyal to my father, who was ever loyal to the white rose of York. Have you no loyalty, madam?'

Eleanor glared. Then her face softened. She said over her shoulder, 'Your son is very pert, Edith.'

'He speaks out of grief,' Lady Hart said quietly. 'Raphael, show respect to my dear friend, Lady Eleanor.'

Raphael dropped his gaze, but his eyes glittered. Eleanor said, 'Loyalty and bravery, sir, have left an endless line of weeping widows and orphans. They have destroyed your father and my husband. I know you'll forget my words, and act as you must, and I don't blame you, but one day, the son of some Lancastrian knight you slew will come to avenge himself upon *you*. And on it goes. Is this the only path we can make for ourselves?'

'Eleanor,' said Anne Beauchamp, touching her elbow. 'It's not the easiest way we've chosen. We each have to be two separate people. Look at these women; some are Yorkists, some Lancastrians. Within our Motherlodge, there are no divisions between us, and our only loyalty is to the Serpent Mother Auset. But we can't separate ourselves from the outer world. Don't ask this boy to end a ten-year war!'

'It would be a start.' Eleanor folded her arms and exhaled. 'Forgive me. It's been a terrible day.'

'The Duke of York did nothing wrong,' said Anne Beauchamp. 'He constantly swore fealty to King Henry, only to be used and cast aside each time. His quarrel was not with Henry, but with Marguerite and the corrupt influence of her councillors. In the end, he had no choice but to make his rightful claim to the throne. My father-in-law Salisbury also died today.'

'Yes. I'm sorry.'

'Richard failed, however, because he was not the right one. He was making the path for his son. My husband will not let this rest. There is a chosen king, and it is not Henry! My husband – may the Creator strengthen his arm

– will put young Edward upon the throne. Then we'll have peace.'

Eleanor's face was thoughtful, closed. 'I don't wish to argue with you, Anne, but you know I don't believe any king is divinely appointed. There's only the best appointed, the one most suited to the position at the time.'

'Divinely chosen, best appointed,' the Countess of Warwick said dismissively. 'There is always one who is meant to be king. Otherwise, our work within there' – she swept a hand at the house, her finger dropping to indicate the cellar meeting place – 'is wasted.'

'My dear, it's never wasted,' said Dame Eylott. Her heart-shaped face was gentle, her voice steel. 'When I summoned the sisters to this meeting, I didn't know there was going to be a battle, yet a battle there was.'

'Nothing is foretold, but certain things are as predictable as sunrise,' said Eleanor.

'We work for knowledge and for healing, not for the triumph of one side against the other,' the Dame went on.

'It follows, therefore, that we work to support the chosen king who may best bring that healing,' said Anne. 'Knowledge, as we saw, that the land is in turmoil and must change.'

Kate saw the quick glance that passed between Dame Eylott and Eleanor. She wondered what they meant by it. It was hard to follow their arguments sometimes, even to tell if they were actually arguing at all. She would ask her mother later.

'None of us can disagree with you there,' said the Dame. 'Come in now and warm yourselves. You'll rest here tonight, of course.'

'Thank you, but I cannot,' said Edith. She took Raphael's hand. He stood close against her, looking very young and delicate for all his brave words. 'My elder son, Simon, is being brought to me at the Augustinian Friary. We must go to meet him. Then I am taking the boys home with me, at least until the spring. Simon is heir to what little land we gratefully possess.'

'May he guard the Hollow well, and the Great Mother aid him,' Dame Eylott said darkly. She kissed Edith. Other women came to embrace her. Farewells were said. Kate kept her eyes on Raphael.

He stared back, his green eyes lost, bereft. She didn't want him to go but it was too late. Edith was trudging away. Kate watched as they passed through the courtyard gate and into grey-white gloom beyond, drinking in her last glimpse of the boy, who – if fortune had taken a different path – should have been her dear friend. They hadn't even said goodbye.

The way back to their demesne in Derbyshire was long. Rutted roads twisted south and west of York, taking Eleanor, Kate and their party through bleak hills. The small line of humans and horses was tiny beneath the vast winter caul of the sky.

With them rode Thomas Copper and his son Tom, Eleanor's servants Martha and Nan, and her friend Friar Bungay. Thomas had scratched his head and grumbled that she should not go to York at all, should not take the child; but in the end he had done Eleanor's bidding as always. Dame Eylott, the *Mater Superior* of the Motherlodge, had summoned her. Eleanor must attend to her business in the hidden world, as did any abbot or bishop in the open world.

They had left York early and now night was coming down, wet and chill. A few disconsolate foot soldiers wandered down the road, but left the party unmolested. Raising her head and scenting the air like a hound, Eleanor fancied she could hear distant voices and smell the bitter smoke of campfires. Fools, these warring men, she thought, such fools.

They broke their journey at Eriswater, where Lady Lytton was well known and always welcome at the Crescent Moon

Inn. Thomas and Tom slept above the stables, Friar Bungay in a downstairs room, Eleanor and Katherine in the best apartments on the top floor, with Nan and Martha in an adjoining chamber at the head of the narrow, creaking stairs. As always, the flustered landlady apologized for everything: the poor chambers, the poor food, even the weather. As always, Eleanor assured her that all was satisfactory, and everything they needed was here: a bed, some bread and ale for their supper, and a roaring fire to ease their chilled limbs.

Eleanor slept soundly, with her daughter soft and warm in her arms. Kate, with her wild black hair and bright cornflower-blue eyes, already knew far more than any six-year-old should. She was a strange and remarkable gift.

In the night the clouds cleared. Dawn came early, sharp and frost bright. The thin light roused Eleanor. A strange sound brought her fully awake, a distant rushing noise like a stream in flood, louder and louder, breaking up into staccato fragments. Voices. Men shouting. Like the steady flow of a river, closer and closer the sounds came and she was aware of them washing along the lanes outside, breaking on the walls of the inn. War-cries, violent laughter.

The pounding of fists on timber, right below their window, brought her leaping out of bed.

Tangling with the sound of male exuberance were other cries, ones of distress. The commotion seemed to be both outside and inside their lodging; she couldn't make a distinction. Eleanor clasped her robe around her. As she did so she heard a great pounding of feet up the stairs and then Martha shrieking through the door.

'My lady – oh, my lady—'

The door flew open, shuddering. Framed in the gap, Martha was falling awkwardly as a brute of a man knocked her aside. She landed on her backside, tears of pain streaking her face. Eleanor caught the barest sight of Nan, huddling behind her, still wrapped in bedclothes.

27

The man stepped over Martha. There was another behind him. Not men but beasts, with wild beards, sagging trews under layers of filthy ragged cloth, glittering berry eyes like blood drops. They stank. The foul waft of their sweat and dirt and ale-sour breath made her gag.

Eleanor put herself in the doorway to block them. A huge hand struck her in the breastbone. The blow took all her breath, sent her reeling, and the man was through the door and seizing her daughter from the bed.

Eleanor fell, striking her head on the thick corner of a table. Through a cloud of black stars she saw the beasts above her, grasping her squirming child in their paws. They grinned and leered and spoke a thick dialect she barely understood.

'This one's vurra young,' said the man who had Katherine. He was huge and dark, his companion a comparative runt with greasy orange curls.

'Old enough,' sneered the other. 'She's female wi' a slit, aye?'

And they laughed, while the giant threw Katherine onto the bed, pulled up her nightdress, and began to fumble with the laces of his grimy trews. She looked as tiny as a kitten beneath him.

'No!' Eleanor roared.

She was on her feet, her head a vortex of pain. The two stared at her, faces cruel within their bramble manes. They grinned, showing broken teeth.

'Do what you want to me, only leave her alone!'

The dark one crooked a thick finger at her. 'Wait yer turn, yer whore. We'll have the both of ye. This one can't wait, eh!' And the two savages roared their mirth.

The carrot-haired one came towards Eleanor. Although a runt beside his comrade, he was still bigger than her, a squat red bull. She could hear Katherine whimpering, terrified but too young to understand. Eleanor put her hands up to stop him but he was hideously strong. His

28

stench made her retch. His fingers felt fat and hot on her skin, polluting her. Pain flamed in her wrists as he grabbed her, held her one-handed, and tore open the front of her night robe.

And saw the symbol lying between her breasts. The black serpent crowned with the moon, curved like a leech and glistening on its leather cord.

He dropped her hands. He blasphemed. He backed away, crossing himself, cursing so vehemently that his companion stopped his struggle with Katherine. Eleanor saw her daughter, wriggling like a fish, her feet braced against the pig's broad stomach to fend him off. Brave, strong girl. His small cock bobbed ridiculously in mid-air.

'What?' snarled the pig.

The red-haired savage pointed wordlessly. Eleanor clutched the torn side of her gown but made sure they both saw the symbol, the crowned serpent. She drew deeply on the air, enduring the miasma of their steaming bodies and stale breath. Softly, she began to chant.

'Stop that,' said the dark one. 'Make the bloody witch stop!'

She paused. 'Put down the child,' she said.

As she spoke, Katherine bit her captor in the fleshy side of his hand. He swore and dropped her. Katherine bounced off the bed and crouched beside it, peering over the edge with bright, watchful eyes.

Eleanor was trembling violently. Yet she forced a frigid smile onto her face and let desperation give her the aspect of a priestess. The beasts saw the terrible ice-light shine from her face and the gold fire in her eyes. It was as if they shrank. They were not, after all, as big as they'd first seemed.

'You can force us, if you will,' she said, her voice quick and fierce. 'Being but women, like your own mothers and sisters, we cannot stop you. Before you continue, be warned. Lay another finger upon us and you shall be cursed. The vengeance of Black Auset is terrible. And her shadow will follow you from this place to the end of your days.'

'Wurrds,' snarled the darker beast. The red one went sickly white and crossed himself. They glared from slitted wet eyes at Eleanor and she thought that her threat had failed. She could smell burning. She closed her eyes, shuddering in horror, her lips moving in a plea to the hidden powers: *Spare my daughter, spare my daughter. Let them know that I speak the truth.*

There was a soft scuffling sound, thick breathing. She heard the distressed voices of Martha and Nan very faint then rushing closer. When she opened her eyes again, her women were there, and the beast-men had fled.

Wind blew veils of snow off the trees. Over ground as hard as iron their horses toiled, their breath fogging the air. Eleanor and Katherine were almost home.

Silent as a funeral procession they had ridden away from Eriswater, leaden-eyed. Thomas Copper rode with Katherine clasped on the saddle in front of him, a bundle that was more wool and fur than child: untouched, safe. Martha and Nan, both badly shaken, let their horse be led along by the lanky young groom, Tom. Friar Bungay shook his head and muttered prayers to himself as he rode. His arm was in a sling, his lean body bowed in the saddle; he'd taken some bad blows, trying to keep the invaders out of the house.

Eleanor's party had survived the raid upon the village; others had been less fortunate. The mercenaries had left the place scoured raw; stripped of food and drink, stripped even of animals and firewood. Women had been raped, their menfolk slain or wounded. All they could not remove or despoil they had set afire, leaving barns and thatches to choke the air with black ash.

Only the cold and wet had saved the village from destruction. Eleanor was exhausted from binding wounds and soothing distress. She swore privately that she would make amends somehow. She had little money to do so; but she could at least send sheep, fresh fish and wine, and men to help repair the damage.

After a long, wretched tract of silence, Thomas spoke. 'They were Queen Marguerite's mercenaries. It's said she gathered that rabble in the north, and threw them against the Duke of York while he was celebrating Yule at Sandal Castle. Now they're on their way to London to claim victory. Drunk on their own glory.'

'Then may the Dark Mother and all the denizens of the hidden world help the poor souls who happen to dwell in their path!' cried Eleanor.

'So much for the red rose of Lancaster,' Martha said bitterly. Small, dark and quiet, she was a shrewd woman; Eleanor's lady-in-waiting in the outer world, her equal in the hidden. 'They recruit barbarians who think nothing of raping children!'

Eleanor caught her breath, thinking of her own manor. Did Lytton Dale lie in their way? No, no, it lay far from any route they might take to the capital. And Edith, freshly widowed, her sons too young to protect her? What would she find? Eleanor chewed her lip. We must hold firm, she told herself. We must be rocks in the turmoil of a flood.

Eleanor looked at Friar Bungay. His long, kindly face was drawn, the tip of his nose cherry-red from the cold. 'Was I wrong to believe we shouldn't take sides?' she asked. 'I even had the nerve to lecture the Countess of Warwick.'

The friar gave her a sharp look. He frowned. 'My lady, it's human nature to take sides which means it should probably be resisted. That our Creator favours one side above the other, and will ensure their victory, is a claim common to both. And he has not revealed his will to me.'

He spoke sardonically. Eleanor gave a hard smile. 'Judging by his past record, he's as likely to confide in a humble friar as in anyone.'

'Henry should have been a monk, not a king,' said

31

Thomas Copper in disgust. 'It's a weak king that has brought us all this trouble.'

Eleanor thought of Edith's son Raphael, proud and grief-stricken in the snow, lecturing her about loyalty. 'How can I give support to either? I can never pay lip service to Lancaster, who unleash hoards of savages upon us.'

'And think how popular it will make them,' put in Friar Bungay.

'Still, to bind myself to York, just when Marguerite is victorious, would be utter folly.'

'And I wouldn't dare to suggest that you abide by your husband's counsel,' said the friar. He said it lightly, but she gave him a glance that might have blasted the flesh from his bones.

'I would, gladly, if it weren't my husband's counsel that brought us to this sorry state.' Her words condensed on the air. 'Since we have no money, no arms and few men, we're of no consequence to either faction. All I want, all I want is to hold on to what is ours! John's devotion to York has all but ruined us, and yet I don't blame him, I understand ... Yesterday I believed the Motherlodge could keep itself aloof. Now, I don't know. I was annoyed with Anne; she would gladly turn our sacred meetings to political ends to aid the Earl of Warwick, even though she knows full well that it's not our purpose. That, apart from the fact we're forbidden to practise magic. Yet I can't say she was wrong.'

Kate stirred. 'Why are we forbidden to practise magic, Mama?' Her dark blue eyes were bright, polished marbles within the fur hood.

'Because certain ignorant people believe us to be danger-ous. Unfortunately, those people are part of government and we have to do what they say. Perhaps they're right to fear us. There are those who would like to ban the Motherlodge entirely; but they can't have things all their own way. We're still here.'

'And we do practise magic,' said Kate.

32

'Only for healing.' Eleanor put a finger to her lips. 'Kate, you must never say such a thing in front of a priest.'

The girl glanced at the friar, confused. 'Sorry, Mama, I thought—'

'It's all right. I know of two who are safe: one is our village priest, and the other is Friar Bungay. Creator knows how he manages it, but he walks in both worlds.'

'And will one day get my tail burned by both, no doubt,' Bungay said. 'I see no reason why different ways can't coexist, as they used to.' He tended to mumble, half-swallowing his words, Eleanor strained to hear him above the clatter of hooves and moan of the wind. 'Mine is not a popular view with the church hierarchy, however.'

'Do they know you live a dual life?'

'It hasn't been discussed. I'm tolerated as long as I do nothing blatant.'

'Such as sorcery to aid one side in battle?' said Eleanor. 'I think that's what Anne Beauchamp would have liked.'

They all looked at her: Martha and Nan, Thomas Copper and the Friar. Hurt eyes, thirsty . . . not for revenge, Eleanor thought, but for survival.

'If we pressed for it, it would change the nature of the Motherlodge,' said Martha.

Eleanor thought of their Goddess, Great Mother Auset, the Serpent of Wisdom whose body was the earth. The night sky was her cloak, the moon and sun her crown. No God stood above her. Auset was life and death, mercy and vengeance; everything. Why would she care about the petty politics of humans? Yet a little of her serpent power lies coiled in each of us, Eleanor thought, and that makes us her avatars.

'Things must change, though,' she said. 'The Serpent Mother showed us that, if nothing else. She doesn't show us the future, only glimpses of things that *might* be. Perhaps we should try to influence the branches of the paths, instead of merely observing. Perhaps that's what Auset was showing us. In which case, Anne Beauchamp was right.'

Survival. That was everything.

Close behind came all the other matters: status, power, wealth, dignity. For Eleanor, power meant the ability to hold on to her demesne unmolested. Wealth meant enough to feed and clothe her household; it meant healthy sheep, with good grassland on which their fleeces would grow thick and white as curds. Status must be upheld to keep away those who might covet her lands. Dignity came from her endless struggle to maintain all this, day after day.

She was Lady Lytton by birth, an only child of parents who'd died young. Her husband John was lord only in right of his wife. Without a husband or father it was nearly impossible for a woman to hold what was hers, especially in this warlike time when any victorious lord might seize an estate in passing as his by right of conquest. She had male relatives who would swoop like petitmorts if she revealed the slightest weakness.

Only as long as her husband lived was she safe.

She sighed through her teeth. The breath-cloud curled like an elemental. The rutted path bent and gave her, at last, a sight of the familiar beloved landscape.

Her demesne, the manor of Lytton Dale. To the east curved the distant, ghostly arm of the high moors, and closer at hand the familiar hump of the hill, Bride Cloud. To the west stood Mag Tor and other peaks crowned with limestone, hard and pale against the snow-choked sky. White-crusted grassland pleated down into deep sheltered valleys where her sheep huddled. The river Melandra, with its many tributaries flowing down from the moors, now lay silent under clouded glass. Her wildwoods, bare and uninviting at this season, were a tangle of bones in the chill twilight, keeping her secrets.

There was the village, nested in the deepest folds and strung along the banks of the river. And at the heart, Lytton

Hall itself, a great rambling place of soft red stone, glowing against the stony greys of winter. Smoke was curling above the slate roof. All the windows shone with firelight.

Eleanor's heart lifted.

'This is our whole world, Kate. Ours,' she said softly. 'Yours.'

Katherine remembered the attack on the village in fragments. She remembered fear – a sickening smell of foul breath and bodies, a whiskered face thrust into hers – but it seemed distant. Her most vivid impression was of her mother, fragile and yet unconquerable, in her most fearsome aspect. The chant hissing from her mouth. The serpent curling between her breasts. Her strength, shining so powerfully that her whole body seemed encased in a halo of fire. The beast-men falling away from the light, dark and insubstantial as ash.

And then her mother catching her up in her arms, shouting for Martha, for Thomas and the others, to come to her and tell her they were safe. Outside, uproar in the streets; barns and cottages on fire. The wildmen rampaging onwards, leaving the villagers stunned and despairing.

Katherine knew this terrible event had changed everything. There was a grim light in her mother's eyes, and an anger that hadn't been there before. She thought of Raphael, mourning his father.

Pain balled in her chest. When they reached the house, she was on the ground and flying into the great hall while the others were still alighting from the saddle. Heat enveloped her.

There was her father on his couch by the huge firegrate, woollen blankets wrapped around him. He was weaker. She saw that at once, in the parchment pallor of his face. But he roused from his doze and greeted her with a smile as bright as the fire and with outstretched arms. Katherine ran, and threw herself upon him.

Her mother came in more slowly. Softly gliding, and

unwrapping layers of wool and leather as she came, she knelt by her husband and bent to kiss his hand.

'John,' she said. 'Dearest John.' And then, 'Kate, don't be so rough.'

He laughed. 'It will take more than my daughter's love to harm me. How went your stay in York?'

'Ah, terrible, terrible.' Eleanor sighed.

She told him about the battle of Wakefield, the heads on Micklegate Bar, Marguerite's triumphal entry, the raid on Eriswater. She spared him nothing. Katherine only half-listened, clinging to the feverish warmth of her father's body. She saw how his face grew grey and lined as her mother spoke, and how his blue eyes flickered with frustration, and she hugged him all the harder.

'Richard . . . dead,' he whispered.

After a long time, he spoke again. 'Eleanor,' he said softly, clasping her hand. His voice was frail. 'I am so sorry. I would not have brought you this trouble for anything.'

Her mother's eyes blazed with fire and tears. 'I don't blame you. I blame only these warring dukes and their houses.'

Katherine wanted to tell her father about Raphael, but he and her mother forgot she was there. They pressed their hands to each other's cheeks and looked only at each other. Their wools and furs steamed in the heat. Thomas, Martha and the others blurred back into the steam and the fireglow as if they had no more substance than elementals.

Kate's father had been ill for a long time. He was going to die; they all knew that, and lived with it every day. It made every moment with him quiet and precious. So they clung to him, and poured the power of Blue Mother Mary and Dark Mother Auset into him, and willed him to stay alive.

Eleanor was glad of the winter in the weeks that followed. While curtains of snow folded over the moors and muffled the paths, no unwelcome strangers would come. There was pleasure in sitting with her husband and daughter at the fireside, retelling their stories until they took on the quality of legend. John demanded every detail.

There was no pleasure, though, in watching him shed tears for the Duke of York. Eleanor half-hated the Duke for commanding her husband's devotion. He and John had almost bankrupted themselves fighting King Henry's wars in France, only to receive no thanks or recompense from the jealous Queen. When the Duke had finally risen up against the Queen's faction – and at last, against the King himself – John had fought unquestioningly beside him. Thus he had received the wound that crippled him. It had seemed to destroy his heart and his mind along with his spine, and turned him from a spirited knight into this dozing, fading invalid.

Eleanor cursed John's loyalty, and loved him for it. For months she had been preparing herself for the inevitable parting and the peril it would bring. Winter felt safe, a suspended time when nothing could penetrate the thick soft veils of snow.

She started up from a reverie, one dark afternoon when no one should be abroad in the deep blue cold. Something was pounding and scratching at the outer door. It was a fluttering, desperate sound. Eleanor had been reading to John, chanting the words so gently that she'd almost sent herself into a trance. Now the book slid off her knee and hit the flagstones. Katherine was already at the door. Eleanor rushed to stop her opening it, too late.

There was a beggar woman there, so Eleanor thought, as the poor creature struck out with a bony arm to stop herself falling. She half-collapsed across the threshold into Eleanor's arms. A dead weight of bones, sparrow-thin. Clouds of snow billowed in around her. Eleanor was about to call Martha to help her when Katherine cried out.

'Mama? It's Lady Hart, Raphael's mother.'

It was only then, in horror, that Eleanor recognized her.

'Sanctuary,' gasped Edith. Tears began to roll down the wax of her face. 'Sanctuary, Eleanor, I beg you.'

Chapter Two 1461: Edith

RICHARD
> I'll drown more sailors than the Mermaid shall;
> I'll slay more gazers than the basilisk . . .
> I can add colours to the chameleon,
> Change shapes with Proteus for advantages,
> And set the murderous Machiavel to school.
> Can I do this, and cannot get a crown?
> Tut! were it further off, I'll pluck it down.

Henry VI Part 3 Act III scene 2

Raphael was dreaming. His body lay inert, heavy with the weight of sleep. In his deep torpor, the chill ache of damp chained him, weeds licked his hands like cold flames, rusty saws carved at his chest. Yet it was happening to someone else, a distant irritation. He was in two places at once, memories assaulting him like shouts. The layers of reality were double-woven together. His body was lying cushioned in rank green undergrowth yet his real self was riding with the winter wind in his face, dreaming one dream inside another . . .

As they drew close to the grey house, Raphael was nodding on his pony, eyelids weighed down with weariness and twilight. The snow had fallen only lightly here, a lichen crust of white on grey. In his mind stood the crow-child, the little girl who'd spoken to him. Somehow she'd comforted him when he'd thought comfort was impossible. Now he was only half aware of climbing the hill towards his house, a stone shadow poised bleakly amid wind-blown trees. Home, home. Soon he would lie in his own bed with his tabby kitten purring on his chest, Simon beside him, and the crackle of the fire lulling them to sleep. No father – but then their father had rarely been at home. It would feel no different.

One of his mother's servants spoke, an indistinct sound of puzzlement. Raphael barely heard it through the fleece of sleep. He heard his mother answering, then his brother piping a question.

'Who are they?'

Raphael came awake, cold and confused. The twilight was busy with shadows.

At first the bustle was part of his dream – meaningless. Then he heard his mother cry out, Simon shouting, 'Hey!' and angry voices raised all around them.

He heard the creak of armour, the stomping of horse's hooves, saw white surcoats glowing pale with the dark stain of a rose upon them. A huge bearded knight on a brown charger was confronting Edith and her small entourage.

'Forfeit to Lancaster, madam,' he was saying. 'Forfeit to the Crown.'

Behind the knight was their household steward, moving restlessly from foot to foot, whey-faced with misery. 'I'm sorry, my lady, so sorry, there was nothing we could do.'

Raphael was sharply awake now. He felt exhausted, vulnerable. Simon was flushed with anger. Raphael had thought him so grown-up, but now he looked hopelessly small, just a child after all.

Edith said nothing, but her face was a soundless wail. Her mouth hung open, like a tear in paper. Beyond the armoured knight and the trembling steward, Raphael saw the door to the house standing open, and figures moving in the orange glow of the great hall. They seemed to be carrying objects: furniture, tapestries. Their household servants stood in postures of helplessness, watching.

Simon rode his pony forward. 'Mama, what is he saying?' Raphael hurried to join him, to show he was no less brave.

'That our estate is confiscated in the name of the Crown,' Edith answered in a small, dry voice, 'because your father fought against King Henry. We are attainted of treason. We have no home.'

'They cannot!' Raphael cried.

He drew his small sword. Simon looked at him in shock, and Raphael realized that his brave, grown-up brother was terrified.

The Lancastrian knight laughed. 'We can, young knave. This land is mine. It was taken from my family a century since and awarded to yours for some trivial favour your great-grandsire did the third Edward. Queen Marguerite promised it back to me in reward for my loyal service. I am only claiming what is mine.'

'No!' Raphael cried, but his mother's arm swung out and locked across his ribs, restraining him.

'As a landless widow, madam, you will find many a kind sanctuary willing to shelter you and your boys. A nunnery will suit you, I think. My squires will accompany you to the nearest.'

The world stood cruelly still. The Lancastrian glowered and grinned in triumph; Raphael raged silently, waiting for a saviour to burst out of the darkness. Some faceless armoured knight with the white rose shining like a beacon on his breast, setting the conquerors to flight. His father, back from the dead! But the night betrayed them. No one came.

He heard his mother draw a heavy, trembling breath. Her eyes were distant, as if she were not even thinking of the house. One soft word she uttered under her breath, and then she swung her palfrey around on its haunches, nearly knocking her sons off their own mounts.

Raphael's pony spun round and bolted, following hers. Raphael heard mocking male laughter behind them. Simon

41

was riding alongside him, overtaking, his face dark with fear and anger, his curls flying. There was only the drum of hooves, the rush of air.

The night whirled past in a blue spiral of fear. Raphael realized that, in her despair, his mother had gone mad.

A couple of Edith's esquires were galloping in pursuit. Down into the narrow valley called the Sheepfold she rode, down towards the spring that bubbled slow and glassy from a cluster of rocks. Memory danced through his mind. This place in summer sunlight, cupped beneath the green shimmer of hawthorns. Only last summer – which seemed so long ago – his mother had brought him here many times to lay flowers upon the rocks, telling him to bless and thank the kind spirits. She so loved the spring, her special sacred place. The Green Hollow, she called it.

Now the valley lay frozen and leafless.

Raphael saw men standing around the spring. The rocks were splashed with the gold of so many lanterns and rushlights that it seemed they must be very afraid of the dark. There were a few soldiers in leather brigandines, standing around leaning on pikes. The heart of the little gathering was a knot of five priests with numerous attendants.

'Who are they?' demanded Simon. His voice, fierce but small, was swallowed by the wind. 'How dare they?'

Raphael saw the silver and saffron of their robes, the glitter of pearls, the imposing arch of a bishop's mitre. Each cleric wore on his chest the badge of the white Lamb, and the spindle-limbed cross with its dagger points. The intense monotone of their prayers thrummed like a leaden bell.

There was a thickness in the air; a pall of solemnity. Raphael didn't understand what was happening but he sensed the deadly seriousness of their purpose. They were trespassing on Edith's beloved Green Hollow.

Sometimes she had brought Raphael and Simon with her; at others she came here alone, or at night with other women. Raphael and Simon had never been allowed to attend these mysterious night meetings, but on one occasion they had followed, and spied. They'd watched the women dancing in a circle, speaking and singing in soft chorus, like nuns in a secret church. A few of them had gone to stand in the spring itself and had appeared – Raphael was sure he hadn't imagined it – to waver into watery mist, even to vanish completely. The whole valley had been enveloped in an unearthly cobalt glow. Raphael had been transported, terrified. Edith was no longer his mother but another being entirely. From the closed enigma of the circle the women had sung of hidden mysterious joy, and summoned a power that was subtle, beautiful and weird beyond his experience.

He and Simon had fled in fear of discovery, but they'd never forgotten.

This was Edith's place. These men had no right here. Their ceremony was crude and heavy with authority, devoid of understanding. They reeked of contemptuous arrogance. And his mother, mad, was rushing to stop them like a hare throwing herself among graylix.

'In the name of the Creator, the Son, the Holy Lamb, we exorcise thee,' the Bishop uttered in a high, thin voice. He spoke in Latin, but Raphael had learned well. 'With holy water we purge thee. With the cross of the Lamb we bind thee. Demons of the dark, we cast thee into that darkness forever, no more to haunt this place. By the light of the Holy Lamb let this gate be sealed for eternity!'

'No,' cried Edith. 'No!'

She rode her horse in among the priests. They scattered with oaths. The two esquires who'd followed shouted in dismay for her to come away, to stop. With a cry, Simon galloped after her. Raphael's pony stood on end, spiralling on the spot with fear. He fought for control.

Edith was shouting, 'You don't know what you do – you don't understand – violation—' and the Bishop was yelling in righteous rage, his voice roaring above hers, complaining of witchcraft and blasphemy.

One of the clerics seized the palfrey's reins. Edith was pulled from her horse and fell amid the priests, her skirts billowing like a cloud brought to earth. Her esquires plunged in after her and then the foot soldiers sprang into the fray. The struggle was wild and violent. Raphael saw the esquires – his friends, his companions, hardly more than boys themselves – unhorsed and cut down. He saw blood spraying in the rushlight. Shouts and the screams of horses filled his head.

Simon was in the midst of the melee, his little sword shining, his mouth square with fear and war-fury. Raphael spurred his pony to his brother's side. He saw the rosy face turn to him in despair and even as their eyes locked, he saw the sword knocked from Simon's hand and a big, heavy blade slicing the thin abdomen. His brother slid from sight. Raphael heard his mother wail.

Furious white faces surrounded him. Mouths oblong with rage, yelling. Raphael was disorientated. He felt a crushing blow across his back and, as he doubled over, his pony reared and threw him.

As he fell, a vision rushed in upon him. Above the spring he saw a tunnel of blue twilight winding through trees to some strange realm where marsh birds uttered lonely cries and mists were alive and watchful and full of alien passions. A wonderful, terrible place. But now, across the subtle unguarded entrance to the hidden realm, there stood a portcullis of white fire, blocking the way. Elementals fled, melting into the water, vanishing on the wind, diving deep into the earth. Priests with pearly halos of authority looked with satisfaction on the results of their work: a dead Hollow.

The vision was cut short as he hit the ground.

Lying stunned on the frosted grass, Raphael saw through a burst of stars his mother trying to rise, falling again with a red wound on her temple. He saw his brother lying in a dark lake, staring up at the sky. He heard the sharp snorting breath of horses. He could smell blood and earth. Sounds rattled in his skull: the clack of weapons beating in a triumphant rhythm; the voices of the priests uttering grunts of indignation, then of satisfaction.

Through the roar of black fire in his head, Raphael began to crawl away. He shook and sobbed as he went. The dry-eyed anger he'd felt at his father's death was seared away, forgotten. That had been childish emulation of his elders' behaviour, without true understanding. But this – this was hell.

Mindless and weeping, he crawled. No one came after him. Through lightless wilderness, over sharp stones and thorns and snow he went on, never daring to stop, onwards down into oblivion.

Raphael relived all this. Lying in a ditch he relived it endlessly, that he was still crawling, stabbed by his own short breath. Still in the dark, still pursued, still watching his mother fall and his brother lying in the lake of his own blood.

And more. Inexplicable memories of sitting outside a cottage with a mouth full of milk and his mind as empty as the sky.

At some point between one thick heartbeat and the next, he began to come back to himself. Sharp pain and disturbance roused him. One reality receded and let him go. Now there was only a single reality, which was that he lay at the bottom of a hedge. Grass and weeds held him in their slimy embrace. His skin was ice-blanched, his clothes damp rags on his bones. Some boys stood over him, poking him with sticks. Rosy faces, gap-toothed mouths, eyes round with curiosity.

'Is he dead?' one said.

'Near as,' said another, jabbing at him as if he were a fledgling fallen naked from a nest. Harder they poked him until he reacted, jerking around the pain with a moan. The boys shrieked their triumph. Raphael was too confused even to be afraid.

'Anything in his pockets?'

'Nah.'

And then something happened, utterly bizarre, yet logical in his dream state. A clamour in the distance, like a hundred wagons trundling over cobblestones. One of the boys yelled, 'The King's coming! The King!'

Raphael flung his arms over his head. He'd been wicked, he'd committed treason. Of course King Henry would hunt him down wherever he went; he and his terrifying wife, Queen Marguerite.

'Hoy!' The shout, loud and imperious, rang out a few yards away. 'Leave him be!'

Raphael lay dazzled. Like a tortoise on its back he tried feebly to rise. With sneers the boys turned to see who had shouted, but as they saw, a change came over them. Suddenly they were all nervous bravado, pups caught in mischief.

'They're coming,' one said, fresh excitement in his voice. He flung up a hand, pointing at something Raphael couldn't see. 'He's there, look, he's there!'

'Shush!' said another. 'Look at the jewels on this lord!'

It was a boy who'd shouted and he was striding towards them. Raphael saw that he had a sword, clothes of rich dark velvet, a chain of sparkling gems in gold. He was leading a glossy bay pony clothed in heraldry. Although he looked much younger than Raphael's tormentors, he fingered the hilt of his sword and stood looking at them with calm, storm-coloured eyes. The eyes gave Raphael a flash of vision, of rain running over a standing stone in the dark.

'Leave him be,' the young noble said again. He strode forward, fearless, as if no one had ever disobeyed him.

The boys sneered nervously. 'Who says?'

The lordling said nothing. He drew his sword only a hand's width from its sheath and the tormentors fled.

They ran whooping with exhilaration, as if they'd won a game, towards a blur of colour that came rumbling slowly along the road towards them. Raphael, though, could look at nothing but the child with ancient eyes.

The boy came forward and knelt on the grass, oblivious to the dew and the mud caking his splendid boots. His face was fine ivory, luminous; Raphael was sure he was an apparition. Did angels appear as children? Awe made a speechless idiot of him. The boy put out his hand and was solid flesh after all. He pulled Raphael up, out of the ditch, onto his shaking legs, where he swayed, and promptly sat down again.

'What happened to you?' the boy said kindly.

'I don't know,' whispered Raphael, and felt a white worm of panic in his heart, growing as the rumbling procession on the road drew closer. 'I can't remember.'

Eleanor sat tending Lady Hart, who lay blanched against the rough pillows. Katherine watched, taking in everything her mother did. First the administration of bitter herbs, sweetened with honey, spoon by spoon into Edith's trembling mouth. The mingled scents of herbal sap and flowery nectar, of rushlights and the stale breath of illness, were so familiar to Katherine that she barely noticed them. Then with bunches of sage and bloodroot set alight, Eleanor cleansed the room with smoke, pacifying the sour-humoured foggy elementals that always gathered to feed on illness.

At last, Edith was able to speak.

'A Lancastrian knight came, claiming rights to my demesne now my lord is dead and attainted. That I could have borne, but the Hollow, the Green Hollow . . .'

Katherine saw her mother's face set bone-solid with rage and suppressed fear.

'What knight?'

'It doesn't matter; I don't care. If not him, it would have been another. But my sacred spring . . . The priests were there already with their accursed crosses, their blind and foolish arrogance. They were despoiling it.' She struggled, as if palsy had seized her mouth.

'You tried to stop them?' Eleanor asked.

'Yes, I fought. I ran at them like an enraged pard.' Edith coughed out a dry laugh.

'Oh, Edith!'

'You would have done the same! A great armoured man brought his pike down upon my head. They slew my sons in front of me, my two dear knaves . . .' a long, shuddering pause, a battle agonizing to watch.

Katherine cried out. 'Raphael?'

'Yes, Raphael is dead, Simon is dead.'

'Oh, God,' breathed Eleanor. 'Oh dear Auset, Mother of God.'

They were silent for a time. Katherine felt grief squeezing her throat and pushing tears from her eyes. Raphael, whom she'd befriended less than a month ago. The slender dark boy stood in her memory, full of anger and life. How could he be dead? It wasn't real.

Eventually Edith went on. 'I got up somehow, and ran for my life. I must have hidden in the woods for a while, out of my mind. But I wish they had killed me too.' Edith was weeping, shuddering on Eleanor's shoulder. 'I could think of nothing to do but come to you.'

'All this way, on foot, in the snow?'

'If the cold had finished me, I wouldn't have cared. I wish it had.'

'We shall appeal to the King,' said Eleanor. 'He must grant you back your manor!'

'What shall a mad, beleaguered king do to bring back my sons?' Edith cried. 'No, no, Eleanor, I can't fight this. Without my sons, property means nothing to me.'

'Another of the old ways stolen and sealed against us,' Eleanor said grimly.

'But if I had not foolishly tried to protect the Green Hollow, my sons would not have died! Even my sacred spring wasn't worth that. We can't stand against the Church, Eleanor.'

'You weren't to know.' Eleanor said against Edith's grimy hair, rocking her. Timidly, Katherine held one of Edith's narrow, limp hands. 'You acted bravely. We mustn't give up. Surrender to barbarians who think nothing of raping children or destroying our ancient ways? Surrender, just because they have the upper hand? Never. This must not happen here!'

She turned glaring marsh-light eyes onto her daughter, and Katherine was afraid. She felt her mother was laying a compulsion upon her, some great burden under which they might all fall, as Edith had.

'But it will,' Edith said softly, as if from a deep, dry well. 'We're too few to hold back the tide. We have no bishops, no armies. The world is ever more blind and deaf to us. I beg you, let me stay here, dear friend, and may I die long before they come to desecrate your sweet demesne also. And Auset judge them.'

The heavy gold collar around the boy's neck glinted with sapphires and rubies, rich against plum velvet. 'Were you hit on the head?' he asked, as serious as a physician. 'Is that why you can't remember? I saw those knaves at something. Did they knock you down and rob you?'

'No. They only found me,' whispered Raphael. He wished his mind would clear; afraid that if it did, the boy would vanish. Visions, reality and all sense of time were hopelessly entangled. The background was filled with flashing colours and the soft thunder of horsemen. Dozens of voices, far away.

'Are you ill, then? I was often ill as a child. It gave me such dreams.'

'Yes, dreams . . .' Raphael shuddered. He was mortified as the boy fingered his ragged doublet with long pale fingers.

'You've worn these same garments a long, long time, from the look of them.'

'I don't know,' Raphael said, looking down at himself in horror. How, in one night, had his clothes become so thin and shiny grey with grime? How many nights?

'Look, here come my companions. They'll help you.'

A handful of riders appeared behind the young lord. Raphael had never seen esquires so splendidly attired. He stared until his eyes blurred at their bright armour, shining horses, and the devices upon their surcoats.

The world had turned upon its head. Everywhere he saw the White Rose of York. Not the red rose but the *white*.

The boy stood up and turned, calling out, 'Ho! I've found a child, half dead! Bring him some ale, quick!'

One of the esquires dismounted and hurried to obey. He was smiling. 'Your Grace.'

Raphael's sight cleared by degrees. He saw the cavalcade on the road, burning white and gold. His heart caught the rhythm of panic.

'What is it?' he gasped. 'Is the King going to kill me?'

The dark eyebrows lifted. 'You must have had a *very* bad dream. Of course he isn't.'

'How do you know?'

'He's my brother. I think he would have told me.'

Raphael coughed. 'If you're the King's brother, I'm still dreaming.'

'You're not, and I am. He's just made me the Duke of Gloucester. You can ask him yourself, if you like. I'm Richard. What's your name?'

The procession was flowing past at a rolling walk; a great array of lords, knights, esquires, followers. Children ran alongside, waving and shouting. A menagerie flaunted against the sky: swan and griffin, graylix and silver pard and bear, each sewn upon its own bright pennant. Heraldry dazzled him. He saw the white rose everywhere, snowy as the Holy Lamb.

Leading the procession was a great banner, a joyful sunburst of gold on gold. Among the leading riders Raphael saw among them an amazingly tall man, his bronze hair blazing like a halo. His mouth opened. The light burned his eyes. The Sun in Splendour. This was no grim ride to battle, but a victory progress.

Had he walked out of winter into full summer? In one night?

The young Duke was kneeling beside him, one arm round his shoulders, holding a flask of musky, honeyed ale to his lips. Raphael took a swallow, gagging on its richness. Richard watched him seriously. Behind him, his esquires were murmuring and shaking their heads in good humour.

'What . . . what king?' he asked stupidly.

'King Edward, of course. How can you not know that? Where have you been?'

'I – I don't know,' he said miserably.

'I knew you were an angel who had tumbled out of heaven,' said the child, smiling. 'This proves it.'

Fringing the top edge of Raphael's vision, the procession had halted. He didn't realize, at first, that they had stopped for him; or, rather, to wait for the young Duke who had run to help him. He was awash in memory, but the memories were flickering shades, torn scraps of nightmare. Running, crawling. A helm of pain squeezing his head. Brambles slithering beneath his palms, clawing and cutting. Dead leaves pressing their pattern like red lace into his cheek. An old woman, spooning milk into his mouth.

Raphael's reality jumped again.

A man and a woman in a solid round cottage. The man thatched and mended and built for a living; the woman was a weaver, her skin and clothes oily with lanolin. Half a dozen rosy-faced children always yelling and bouncing around him. They called him lackwit. Everywhere he went, lackwit, idiot, moon-gazer. A strange boy who couldn't speak, and who woke every night screaming.

It had all happened on some strange canvas far away from him. In the abyss of winter, for no reason, he had left the cottage and walked, insensible, to the next settlement, and the next. The impartial kindness of strangers had sustained him. He had sleepwalked his way through two seasons, not speaking, not remembering, not thinking. Now the fog had begun to lift and the memories scalded like frostbite.

All that brought him back to life and held him there was the face of this strange, graceful, dark-haired boy. His eyes, the grey-blue-violet of rain, held Raphael enthralled.

'Can you remember your name?' the boy probed. He seemed so fascinated by Raphael's state that he'd forgotten all else. 'Try.'

'Raphael,' he managed. 'I'm Raphael Hart.'

Richard continued his intense scrutiny. 'My father had a knight called Hart.'

A tall fair boy came up behind, splendidly dressed, all of ten years old and full of himself. He must be sweating hard under all that purple velvet and cloth of gold, Raphael thought. So warm, the day, and everything green. The last I remember was hard winter. I've gone mad, I am mad.

'Lamb's blood, Dickon, get back on your horse,' said the older boy. 'Only you could stop a royal procession to pick up a beggar out of a ditch.'

'He's not a beggar, George. He's ill.'

The fair boy took an exaggerated step back. He waved his hand in front of his face. 'Then he could have the plague for all you know! Leave him. You can't keep Edward waiting.'

'He won't mind,' the dark one said mildly, turning to Raphael again. 'Where are you from, Raphael Hart?'

Raphael shook his head. His skull ached and see-sawed. Motes of memory leapt screaming at him.

'I was in York,' he said. 'I saw the heads above the gate. The Duke of York, and Edmund of Rutland . . . I saw the Queen ride in and mock them. All her men had red roses splashed upon them like blood.'

As he spoke, the young noble's face paled horribly. He looked, for the first time, like the child he was, and about to collapse with grief or fear. 'That was my father, the Duke of York, and my brother . . .'

'My father died with yours at Wakefield,' Raphael whispered. 'The Lancastrians killed my mother and brother a few days later. I ran away. I went mad. That's all I know.'

'You have been ill a long time,' Gloucester said very softly. 'That happened last December. It's June. There have been other battles since then. York has triumphed. Edward is King, Edward the Fourth.'

'Thank the Creator,' said Raphael. Strange, dry sobs came out of him. Emotion and memory were unbearable. He felt like some shrivelled new-born thing dropped onto the earth, without identity.

'You're safe now.' Richard clasped his hand, gave him a long, serious look. 'Our fathers died together. We'll never forget that.'

Abruptly he coloured, and jumped to his feet. A man, all blue and gold with flowing brown hair, strode up to stand beside the fair boy, and as he came all the esquires bent their knees, as did the Duke of Gloucester and his brother George. Raphael suddenly wished the earth would gulp him down. Edward was a gilded giant, laughing, shedding radiance around him like manna from heaven. Raphael could only sit open-mouthed and stare at him.

'What are you at, Dickon?' the King laughed. 'Up, up.'

'He's trying to heal a plague-ridden idiot he found in the hedge,' said George.

'He's no idiot,' Richard said sharply. 'His father was a Yorkist knight. The Lancastrians killed his family. He's been ill, and didn't know you were king.'

'Then I hope the good news returns him swiftly to good health,' Edward said heartily. 'Go on with your ministry, give him every comfort.'

So Richard continued, while tears of embarrassment, grief and joy ran from Raphael's eyes. Having to be lectured like a four-year-old in front of the King, yet hearing that his father was avenged was too much to bear.

'Two months after Wakefield, York had its revenge. We won. And they took down the heads of my father and brother and placed the heads of the traitors in their stead.'

Raphael remembered then the words of the crow-haired child, her pale and sombre face. 'Other heads will take their place.' Impossibly, she had known.

He saw a brief vision of a sour pink sky, grisly heads gawping at drunken angles, crows and petitmorts dropping through the bloody glare to peck indiscriminately at the heads of York or Lancaster alike. His head rang. He lurched to one side, throwing up bile over Edward's fancy boot. When the faintness passed, he found Richard kneeling beside him, stroking his forehead.

'Sorry, Your Grace. Sorry,' he rasped, shivering.

Edward crouched on muscular haunches and touched his cheek. 'Worse has happened to me, lad. You are in truth a victim of Lancaster's cruelty. I must make amends. Let me think.'

Raphael waited, looking sideways at Richard, whose eyes were on his magnificent brother. It was only then that it sank in. Here was the King of England and the two greatest dukes in the land, and he was the centre of their attention. It couldn't be real.

'I have it,' said Edward, rising.

'He could . . .' Richard began, but Edward was already walking away, and signalling to someone in the royal party.

Two esquires got Raphael to his feet. Edward returned with a wiry, upright little man, all in red velvet. He had the look of a terrier, Raphael thought, bright-natured, eager to please, smug.

'Here is Lord Lykenwold of Glastonbury,' said Edward. 'William, here is a good Yorkist boy who has fallen on unfortunate times. He is orphaned, and in need of a home.

He'll make you a good page, and in time a good knight. A small token of my thanks for your steadfast service. What do you say?'

'I'd be honoured to take him,' the terrier answered. He gave a deep bow. 'I ask no reward from you, my liege, but I give you my deepest and most heartfelt thanks. The boy shall make a splendid ward.'

The deed was done.

Raphael found himself lifted up onto an esquire's horse and carried off in the train of William Lykenwold. He caught one last glimpse of Richard, Duke of Gloucester, swept away into the river of the royal progress. Never to be seen again except in the furthest distance.

Returning to his place near his brother at the front of the procession, Richard of Gloucester glanced back, haloed by a glitter of reflected glory. He was like a piece of jet against flowing gold cloth. Raphael stared, helpless.

For what had passed between them today, Richard had his heart forever. All Raphael wanted was to stay at Richard's side, to serve him as loyally as his father had served the Duke of York. And he'd thought, for a few moments, that it would happen.

From the procession an exuberant, deafening roar peeled into the air. *'God save King Edward!'*

As I lay in that strange, seductive half-state between waking and sleeping, Richard seemed to whisper to me. 'You think you know me, but you don't. No one ever can. Would you even dare to try?'

He was so close to me – I thought I could feel the softness of his hair, the velvet of his cloak, his warmth on my neck – but untouchable. If I tried to encompass him with my mind he slipped away and became a distant figure seen through layers of frosted glass. And yet he came to me at night, dark and irresistible, urging me to pass through those layers and see him clearly. It was a challenge.

I got up and went from velvety dreams to stark facts.

There was the campus, spread out in formal squares, its beautiful old buildings covered in red vines, trees everywhere in their stately, restful dance. An enchanted place, out of time. And there was me: one ordinary, wispy young woman, long mouse-brown hair, gold-rimmed glasses (fashionable for once), a bit shy and serious and slightly out of my depth. And now, with poor timing, under a spell.

I was in the library, wreathed in the mustiness of old books; supposedly studying the twelfth century. Books of the fifteenth strayed into my hands instead.

Just as Fin's friend had said, Shakespeare had played fast and loose with the truth; or rather, his sources had. Henry Tudor arrived to depose Richard on the most tenuous grounds, and it was a heinous matter, to overthrow an anointed king. It had to be justified.

The Tudor historians had done so, by heaping every physical and mental deformity they could imagine upon Richard. In doing so, they had made him immortal.

So, the bare bones: King Richard III, king for only two years, and yet up there among the most famous, certainly the most infamous, of all monarchs. Born in 1452 at Fotheringhay Castle, Northamptonshire, youngest son of Richard Plantagenet, Duke of York, and Cecily Neville. The Duke's claim to the throne, arguably stronger than that of the monarch, Henry VI, led to conflict. The wars between the rival houses of York and Lancaster shaped Richard's life. He faithfully served his brother, Edward IV, helping him to win the throne. He became Duke of Gloucester and lord of the north of England; and when their other brother, George, Duke of Clarence, was executed for treachery, it only emphasized Richard's own impeccable loyalty. Then, in 1483, without warning, Edward died. Richard struggled with the Queen's family, the Woodvilles, for control of his young nephew, Edward V. Within weeks, he'd had Edward V and his younger brother declared bastards and confined in the Tower, and had taken the throne himself. The boys disappeared. In 1484 Richard's own son died; the following year, his wife. His unpopularity grew, his supporters leached away. In 1485, Henry Tudor challenged him upon Bosworth Field and Richard lost his life; the last English king to die in battle.

At first, I was almost disappointed by the facts. I couldn't find the glittering villain or anti-hero of Shakespeare's creation. Instead I found a conscientious man, pious, unswervingly loyal to his brother Edward IV until that brother died. Then with the same single-mindedness he imprisoned Edward's sons, disinherited them and probably – but might not have – murdered them.

At first he seemed less interesting; then more intriguing

than ever. Because the evidence was inconclusive, the interpretations came in scores of shades and hues. I couldn't stop reading.

One of the most recent authors called Richard a 'puritan martinet' and suggested we should all be jolly grateful that Henry Tudor came along when he did. It seemed a strange judgement upon a man who loved music and luxurious clothes, and who insisted on equal justice for everyone.

Other books spoke of the betrayal of Richard III. The *betrayal*. And I read that he wasn't the ambitious scheming malefactor I'd been led to believe in. He'd been let down by those he trusted at every turn. Crucially, he did not kill his nephews, the Princes. Even they had been murdered by someone else with motives of their own.

Each book told me something different. Each book told me more about the author than it did about Richard III.

I couldn't leave him alone. All the time I should have been reading for my next essay, I was drawn to him instead.

Richard, the ultimate wicked uncle.

Richard, the unjustly maligned hero.

The Tudors won, and the Tudors rewrote history to shine the best light upon themselves. Oh no, they didn't, other historians said sternly. All the rumours and slanders against him were in place long before he died.

I was lost in confusion. I emerged from the library with my arms full of books, dazed. I couldn't force Richard out of my mind. He was there constantly, posing endless questions, answering none. Looking back, I was obsessed; and it felt wonderful, delicious.

I walked to meet Fin at our favourite coffee shop and I think it was then, as I floated through the lovely autumn-veiled misty cloisters of the campus, that I first saw in my mind's eye the gentle face of a young man. I knew he was not Richard. He wore clothes I didn't recognize and snow blew hard around him and he was looking back at me over his shoulder, inviting me to share something no one else had ever seen. He looked desperate. There was a woman with him, some way ahead of him so I could see her less clearly. It was only a flash, that first vision, but I felt the most incredible wave of excitement, of recognition.

It had begun. A story was unfolding to me, one not found in any book. It might hold an answer. Richard, who were you, who are you?

Chapter Three 1468–9: Richard

And curst be trolls, elves, goblins and fairies upon the
earth, and hypogriffs and Pegasus in the air, and all the
tribes of mer-folk under the sea. Our holy rites forbid
them. And cursed be all doubts, all singular dreams, all
fancies. And from magic may all true folk be turned
away. Amen.

Lord Dunsany, *The King of Elfland's Daughter*

Katherine's father lived longer than any could have pre-
dicted. Sustained on the fire of his household's love he
lingered, opening his eyes each new morning to smile at
his wife and daughter.

There came a day when Katherine was fifteen and John
died at last. He had endured the chill hardships of winter,
only to cease in the face of a full-throated May morning.
Stillness lay on the house; wordless shock. The eyes of
Thomas Copper, Martha, Nan, Tom and all the servants
hung with tears. The villagers came weeping to the hall
to pay their respects.

Eleanor alone was calm. She ministered to the others,
her face the mask of a painted apostle, her pale hands
betraying only the slightest tremor.

The tiny village church stood in a circular churchyard,
upon a far more ancient site where five old tracks of power
met and crossed. Within, Father Dunstan, the priest, kept
two altars: the Christian one was of mint gold with an
image of Iesu on the cross; the older one was a block of
pitted stone, engraved with spirals. Eleanor was determined that the old altar would not be destroyed as long

as she lived. Statues of the Blue Virgin and the Dark Mother faced each other across the dusty space. Here John was entombed beneath a stone effigy of himself in armour. Friar Bungay, Dame Eylott and Bridget Marl – the priestess of the London Motherlodge – attended the service, the only outsiders Eleanor had wanted. Christian prayers were said, blessings of divine Auset given. The villagers trod both paths as it suited them and saw no conflict in it.

'He said it was King Edward's triumph that kept him alive so long,' Eleanor told Katherine later, when all the mourners had gone. Kate saw the stiffness of grief and suppressed fear in every line of her body. 'If Henry and Marguerite had won, so John said, his spirit would have faded and died with Henry's wits. Instead, Edward came from heaven to breathe life back into the land. Is it so, Kate? Did your father truly think life issued from the King's divine appointment, and not from the earth, the heartbeat, the Serpent Mother? He was my soul's companion, ah, but still a man.'

She stared without focus at the arched brightness of a window. Something broke inside Kate. She flung herself out of the house, away from the oppressive atmosphere, out into the push of wild cool air in the herb garden. There she fell behind banks of feverfew and wept her heart out.

A year passed. Eleanor sent out no messengers, so the news that Lady Lytton was widowed, her only heir a daughter, travelled slowly. Indomitable, she continued to nurture her estate as she always had. Like the abbess of a holy house, with a great bunch of keys at her waist, she was constantly busy with every matter of the estate and village. No concern was too small for her attention.

Lytton Hall had always been a sanctuary for waifs: peasant girls who found themselves with child; nuns outcast from their order for some transgression; Eleanor turned no one away. Nan had been an unwanted infant. Martha, a healer driven from a village near Nottingham with accusations of witchcraft. And then Edith Hart, a grey spectre haunting the house.

Edith was gone now. She had survived four years after coming to them. The Lancastrian who'd confiscated her estate had smartly switched allegiance the moment King Edward took the throne. Since Edith refused to challenge him, her lands were lost. She no longer cared. Eleanor's attempts to rally her were disregarded. All Edith wanted was peace, to mourn in the safe solitude of her friend's domain until she faded away.

She was gone, but Katherine often saw her ghost wandering the corridors of the house, or sitting in corners like a mass of cobwebs. She still heard Edith's soft voice whispering the unpalatable truths that she and Eleanor wanted to deny.

'The only sure way to protect this place is for Katherine to marry,' she would say. 'She must find a good strong lord who will support you and keep you safe. She needs sons to secure the title and estate for all time. Otherwise the jewel will be snatched from you, as mine was.'

'I do not wish to marry,' Katherine had answered, then nine or ten years old. She tried not to lose her temper with Edith, who was sad and frail. 'Good lady, I want no husband to command and order me. My mother and I do perfectly well as we are.'

Eleanor had also reacted with fire. 'Edith, I know of no such "good lords". I was lucky with John, for we loved each other and he respected my path. But husbands die. Sons guarantee nothing – yours did not!'

Edith's face had turned to ash. Eleanor had caught her hand and said, 'I'm sorry. Forgive me. But it's the truth. Our only certainty is the sacred earth, our secret ways into the hidden world. That's where our strength is found. Not from self-seeking arrogant nobles who would buy and sell us like sheep!'

Katherine was watchful and perceptive. Even at ten,

she suspected her mother's anger was because Edith had touched a raw truth. Now, at sixteen, the ghostly warnings were ever more insistent. However steadfastly she and Eleanor ignored the problem, it would not go away. Without a husband, she thought, without his shield and his armour, his title and his knights, we are naked . . . and Mama hates this, hates it! And so do I.

Among the sisterhood of Auset, most of Eleanor's friends kept silent on the matter. They, of all people, appreciated Eleanor's stance. Only Anne Beauchamp, the Countess of Warwick, had the nerve to confront her.

'You should think about a husband for Katherine,' she would tell Eleanor in front of a seething Kate, at every gathering of the Motherlodge. When Eleanor objected, the Countess overrode her, unmoved. 'You have your principles, but we must be realistic. We can't live entirely in the hidden realm. Unless we conform to the outer world, we won't survive. *My* daughters know that. Choose her a husband, before one is imposed upon you!'

There was turmoil in the outer world, as always. Edward's victory hadn't stopped the fighting. Marguerite, in exile, had not ceased trying to reinstate Henry on the throne, and she also had a half-grown son to promote, Edouard of Lancaster, whom many suspected was not Henry's offspring at all. When he was told of his son's birth, so the story went, Henry was astonished and remarked that the conception must have been effected by an angel, since he had no recollection of it.

Kate still laughed delightedly every time she thought of this.

The conflict grew worse. The Countess had not appeared at the last two gatherings of the sisterhood. On their travels to York and to Nottingham for the meetings, Eleanor and Katherine gathered news. King Edward and the Earl of Warwick – the Kingmaker who had placed Edward on the throne – had quarrelled.

Kate asked her mother what the quarrel was about.

'Jealousy,' Eleanor answered flatly. 'I like the Countess well enough; I don't like her husband, at least not from anything I've heard of him. He thought he could manipulate Edward like a puppet, but Edward has a mind of his own. So now Warwick probably thinks he will make a different king instead, one who is more easily bullied.'

'Who?' Kate asked in amazement.

'I don't know,' Eleanor said thinly. 'The one woman who might know the truth of it, the Countess, has not shown her face since this began.'

'There'll be more fighting, I suppose,' said Kate.

'Dear, it's never really stopped.'

Within her mother's demesne, it was hard to imagine nobles at war in the outside world. Here, everything was peaceful. Spring was in full, lush bloom, warm as summer, dew heavy and brilliantly green. Kate rode her young dapple-grey mare Mab up to Lytton Edge, where lines of rock swept above them like the crumbled ruins of a Roman fortress; over the heathery slopes of Bride Cloud and down into the oak-veiled chasm of Lytton Griffe. Along the banks of the surging Melandra she went, across the Sheepwash Bridge, through heavily scented avenues of may trees. It was impossible to imagine anything disturbing this sweetness.

On this morning, she'd been to visit a sick villager, a man who'd fallen from a cart and impaled himself on a stake. The wound was healing now, thanks to the skills Kate had absorbed from her mother. Brews of certain herbs for cleansing, others to ease pain, honey ointment for healing. Incense to draw kind elementals and repel the less savoury ones. The man had joked about battle wounds, and she wondered how she would feel if it was a sword thrust she was tending. She thought about Raphael.

'There is something worse than having to be married,' she said to her mare. 'What if you married a man you loved, and he went off to be killed in battle?'

Sweat prickled her skin, made her head itch under her hennin of green silk. Impatiently she tore it from her head and the fluttering of the veil made the mare dance. Kate let her gallop.

Arriving at the house in disarray with her hair loose, the mare skittish and sweat-hot beneath her, she was shocked to find visitors in the stable yard. There were a dozen horses, clad in bright leather and silver. What did this mean? Conquest? Theft?

A handful of men stood about, as magnificently clad as princes in violet and gold and green; and those only the esquires of the party, she suspected, from the way they were joking with Eleanor's grooms. They were bawling with laughter, but as she rode into the yard they all stopped and stared at her.

Katherine bristled. She'd meant to walk Mab around to cool her down but she couldn't do so under their scrutiny and it would look peculiar if she rode away again. Tom was already there, waiting to take the mare from her.

'Who are they?' she whispered.

He shook his head, nervously excited. 'Lady Lytton's asking for you, my lady.'

'Cool Mab down, will you?' she said, slipping from the saddle. The esquires were bowing to her, but there seemed a sarcastic quality to the gesture. Scorched by their burning stares, their apparent judgement, she gave Mab to Tom and passed, with head high, into the coolness of the house.

Inside, Martha and Nan intercepted her, and rushed her up the servants' stairs to her own bedchamber. Nan was guilelessly excited, Martha tense. They undressed her, sluiced her hot body with rose-water and stuffed her into the best dress she had, a gown of deep blue velvet embellished with gold net. A hennin was pressed on her head, her black hair tucked away beneath its structure of golden satin and lace froth. The two little horns, Kate thought, shown her reflection in a glass, gave her a devilish aspect. Her eyes looked storm-blue and furious. She was hardly the demure gentlewoman the visitors would be expecting.

'Martha, who are they?' she asked impatiently for the third time. 'Why must I be trussed up to meet them?'

'Lady Lytton will tell you. It's not my business.'

'Don't slide out of this. You must know!'

'Your distant cousin,' Martha whispered, thin-lipped. 'Thomas, Lord Stanley. But I didn't tell you.'

When Katherine entered the great hall, she found her mother entertaining in high estate – as high as they could manage. The four visitors were grouped in chairs around the fire, the table being readied for the noon meal. She'd thought their house luxurious, with its softly faded glow of red and bronze, tapestries and a firegrate the size of a small kitchen. Now, as a backdrop to the visitors' glory, she realized how shabby it was. The tableware was dark with age and dented, and there were tapers instead of good candles on the board. She noticed the mended patches of her mother's brown velvet gown. All their finery had long ago been sold, at first to finance the late Duke of York's armies, later to support her mother's waifs – her guests, Eleanor called them, affording them more respect than these intrusive lords could conceive.

'Here is my daughter Katherine,' said Eleanor, rising. 'She shares my duties, ministering to the sick.'

'A worthy cause of delay,' said one of the visitors as they rose.

Eleanor was encased in an aura of grandeur and ice, almost her priestess-self. Katherine felt foolish, annoyed and apprehensive. Her eyes blazed upon each man in turn. There was an older lord with black hair, a neat moustache and beard. His face was narrow but handsome and pleasant enough. The younger one had unkempt curly hair and a rosy, eager face that shone in the firelight. They wore the finest materials, cream and blue and red, slashed and shaped in fashions she'd never seen before. Gold chains hung upon them, bearing the white rose and other emblems. They dripped riches like honey from the comb.

They'd brought a cleric with them; a bishop dressed quietly in earth colours rather than the ceremonial silver and saffron. He had a neat little face in a round head and a neck so short and broad that his double chin rested directly on his chest. The thin dark hair was oiled to a high shine. He smiled, appraising her from small brilliant eyes like a polecat's. Although his garb was modest, there were jewels on his fingers, and the Lamb on his chest was made of pearl and diamond, with rubies for the blood.

He had a companion, a thin stooped priest in ochre. An expression of well-intentioned interest sat strangely on the priest's cadaverous face.

'Your daughter's virtues, my lady, are highly praised and praiseworthy,' said the senior lord. 'As are yours.'

'It is flattering of you to say so,' Eleanor said stiffly. 'Katherine, greet kindly your cousin Thomas, Lord Stanley, to whom we have the honour to be related on my father's side.'

As the older lord kissed her hand, she sensed his condescension. He was beautifully groomed, and smelled of an exotic but subtle perfume.

'Our dear friend, Bishop Morton,' said Stanley, stepping aside to present her.

As protocol required, Kate kissed the Lamb with thin, dry lips. 'Your Grace.'

'His assistant, Dr Fautherer . . .'

The man in ochre only grasped her fingertips for a brief moment. The touch sent a shudder through her. His hands were parchment-dry, like lizard skin.

'And allow me to present my son, George Stanley.'

The son, like his father, was huge in his puffed and padded finery. His fingers were hot and soft on hers as he bowed low, pressing clammy lips to the back of her hand. He smelled of sweat, as if radiating nervous heat. At least he wasn't condescending. Rather, he regarded her with a wide-eyed eagerness that, after a while, she found worse.

'We are honoured,' said Kate, not knowing what else to say.

She exchanged glances with her mother. Eleanor's face was drum-tight. They both knew who these men were, the danger they represented, and the utter presumption of their visit; but there was no choice but to present a gracious facade.

It had been easy to believe that their small estate, their minor title, tucked in a lush fold of the Derbyshire Peaks, was unknown beyond its boundaries. So easily was the illusion shattered.

'Come, you must be hungry after your journey,' said Eleanor. 'It's been too long.'

'Indeed, I would have come to pay my respects before now,' Stanley said in a flat tone, 'if the news of your husband's demise had reached me sooner.'

Roast capon and goose were brought to the table while her mother's musicians played – a rough country affair it must have seemed. A drum tapped gently beneath the sound of reed pipes. The bagpipes' two chanters played in thin, haunting harmony.

At first the conversation was of generalities: what a fine small church the village had; such a splendid tomb to honour John; the excellent grazing afforded by Eleanor's demesne; the special softness and quality of the wool from her sheep. They spoke of trade, land management and music. Only Dr Fautherer said little. His bulbous pale eyes flicked back and forth as if he were committing every word to memory.

Lord Stanley and his son were personable enough, if dull. Katherine forgot her unease and longed to ask a series of babbling questions. How many times had they been at court, and what happened there? What was King Edward like in person? If she saw him, would she fall in love with him, as all women were said to do? Was his wife, the Widow Grey, Queen Elizabeth, as beautiful as everyone claimed? She bit back the rude, ridiculous questions.

'A fine little church,' said Bishop Morton, 'but the arrangement is somewhat . . . old-fashioned. If you wish, I could send some men to aid your priest to effect the, ah, improvements.'

Katherine saw her mother stiffen from head to foot, as if she'd turned to glass. 'I appreciate your kind offer, Your Grace, but we are quite happy with our church.'

'The pagan remains can draw negative influences,' Morton said off-handedly. 'Where the Devil can find a crack in the door, he'll be in. That old stone – I won't grace it with the term altar – it ought to go, really. I'll send someone; it's no trouble.'

Kate thought her mother was going to explode.

'Truly, Your Grace, there's no need,' she said, delicately polite. 'The villagers would be extremely upset if anything were to be disturbed. The church has served us well for hundreds of years. The old altar has always been there. No good could come of removing it.'

'I understand.' Morton acquiesced, raising plump neat hands. 'It's your demesne, of course, my lady. I was not suggesting that you are anything but a devout believer.'

He backed down, but the damage was done, the threat made. Morton sat, serene, watching Eleanor silently fuming. Kate was outraged. Her mother would never pretend to be something she wasn't, just to appease this man; nor did she see why she should defend her own beliefs, which were not forbidden. There was nothing she could say.

Delicately the conversation pressed onwards. Surely the management of an estate was a difficult matter for a woman alone, Lord Stanley suggested. It was a tragedy that she had been widowed, and was without a son and heir. Her mother neatly deflected each question, but the insinuations kept coming; all disguised as concern for her future.

Throughout the ordeal, George Stanley's stare never left Katherine's breasts.

He spoke to her breathlessly. He seemed good-natured,

clumsy as a calf. His father exchanged narrow smiles with Morton, as if to say, 'He's well pleased.'

'Gentlemen, my husband – may his soul rest in peace – was the devoted servant of the King's father,' Eleanor said coolly. 'If a single one of the misfortunes you suggest should threaten us, the King himself would not refuse me his protection.'

That halted them in their tracks.

'Indeed, we're all devoted servants of the King,' Stanley countered. 'He would not deny you *our* protection. In these uncertain times, if anything were to happen to King Edward – which God forbid – you might find you have dire need of us.'

Eleanor paled. Katherine chewed at the cushion of her lip. There was a fog of deceit and compulsion in their honeyed words but she couldn't tease out the true meaning. Or if she could, she feared to believe it. In dread, she sat watching her mother's face.

'Katherine, would you leave us now?' Eleanor said.

'What?' Kate was taken by surprise.

'Go up to the solar and wait for me there.'

'But Mama—'

'Katherine.' The word hit her, precise as an arrow head. Kate could not be seen to defy her mother in front of visitors. Defeated, she feigned subservience and left with all the grace she could muster.

Nan came running after her, but Kate, brusquely, sent her away.

In the solar, her mother's private chamber, she sat watching the sunlight flooding through the stained-glass windows, filling the room with a watery red-gold glow. She pulled off the stifling head-dress and shook her hair loose. What a waste of a glorious afternoon, when she had so much to do. She bitterly resented the visitors for intruding on them. What did they want?

Perhaps all was innocent: Eleanor was alone and they genuinely wanted to help her.

George Stanley's young face glimmered in front of her, beads of sweat on his lip. Earnest, eager, made almost stupid by that eagerness. Many would have called him handsome. He was pleasant enough in his way, but there was nothing about him that attracted her. She had often wondered about love but it was not nervous, moist-eyed and sweaty; love did not wear the face of Lord Stanley's son.

The idea of marrying him . . .

A thread of panic startled her. Katherine sat amazed at the strength of her disgust. It wasn't so much the suitor himself as the idea of compulsion. Should I be expected to take the first man who is offered to me? she wondered. Does it matter, will anyone care that I can't love him, or even tolerate him? Does anything matter at all, except that he wants me and that's an end of it?

No, no, she thought. My mother would never do that to me. She promised.

Edith was dust moving through the sunbeams, saying nothing.

After an hour or so, the door was thrust open and her mother came in.

Eleanor looked stern, her eyes bruised with anxiety. In her hand was a parchment, folded in three and sealed with a thick clot of wax.

'They have left,' she said.

Kate jumped up. 'Already? Thank goodness!'

'They will return in ten days to hear our answer.'

'What answer, Mama?'

'I don't know what I'm going to do.' Eleanor's voice was low, her eyes molten iron. Kate had never seen her like this before. '"Might I remind you, madam," Lord Stanley said to me, "that when your father died, without sons or nephews, that left me his closest male heir. That gives me a claim upon this land. I have so far chosen not to pursue it." As if I should be grateful to him!' Eleanor cried.

'Mama . . .'

'He wants my land. He means to take it. He will generously let us stay in a small corner of the house, while he moves in his own household, takes control of my estate, my Cauldron Hollow—'

'The Hollow?'

'The Church has an interest, too. Although the Motherlodge is lawful and permitted, they're desperate to end that. Another sacred place quietly destroyed would be a great satisfaction to them.'

'They can't! You laughed at them and threw them out, didn't you?'

Her mother's lack of response chilled her.

'I don't know what I'm going to do,' Eleanor repeated. 'If Stanley chooses to fight me in court, with the Church's backing, he could well win. Corruption, favouritism . . .'

Katherine drew herself up, trembling like a birch. The shuddering rushed through her until it felt as if the house itself were shaking. 'He has swathes of land! Why does he need ours?'

'It's a place of rare beauty. Why would he not take every morsel, if he can?' She struck her palm with the parchment in a slow, sinister rhythm.

'What's in the letter?' Kate asked.

'Our way out. He offered me a compromise. I know I said this would never happen, but it might be the best answer after all. The only answer.'

'Oh, no.'

Her mother's eyes were blank with shock. Now they turned ruthless. 'Stanley's son is a decent man, not at all in the mould of his father. He would be gentle, and cherish you. It would not be the worst thing in the world to marry him. That is Stanley's offer. The only way for us to keep our demesne is for you to marry George.'

Katherine cried, 'So he makes it a wedding present to his son, with me thrown in! I was right, then! All the time they were looking me over as if I were a mare at market!

72

I wonder he didn't thrust his fingers in my mouth and examine my teeth.'

A frown creased Eleanor's forehead. She looked dangerous. 'Did you find him offensive?'

'I'd sooner marry Tom in the stables!' Tears of rage rolled down her face. 'You promised! You promised you would never do this to me!'

'I know, Kate. But it may be the only way. Calm yourself and think! Yes, if you marry George, Stanley's descendants will inherit our demesne but so will *ours*. Thomas Stanley himself will rarely be here, and George will prove malleable. We can ease him into our ways, make him a good lord. The land, then, will pass to your children.'

'Are the Stanleys Yorkists?' Kate demanded.

'When it suits them.'

'Lancastrians the rest of the time? Father would never forgive you!'

'Don't you dare throw your father's name at me! I cannot lose this land! I know it's hard, but for once in your life you are going to do as I say. Read it.'

Eleanor held out the letter. Her daughter glared at it, recoiling. 'What's in it?'

'George Stanley's proposal. He insisted I read over his shoulder as he wrote it, and it's surprisingly sincere and touching. Otherwise I would not have considered it.'

Kate snatched the parchment, crying, 'I will not read it! How can you consider it, even for a moment? How can you just give in without a fight? You're not my mother! After all you've said, all my life – this! I'll not be bought and sold like a sheep, I'll die before I marry that sweating overdressed oaf!'

Dramatically she tore the letter in half and threw it in the grate. She pushed past her mother and fled the room, driven harder by the imperious roar that followed.

'*Kate!*'

She'd never known such rage. It was a black flurry, almost blinding her. After all her mother had said, year after year: 'We need no lord to protect us, we are strong, we can survive, Auset is our protection,' on and on.

Kate ran from fear as much as from anger. Denial pushed hot heavy fingers through her. If she only fled hard and fast enough, she could prevent the whole thing from ever having happened.

Still in her best dress, she ran to the stables and bridled Mab. Ignoring Tom's pleas to step aside, he would do it for her, and why the hurry, she fastened the buckles with trembling fingers, led the mare outside and vaulted on bareback, sitting astride like a boy. Tom's face became a fading blur. Mab loved to gallop and she flowed like silk between Kate's thighs. They were running away.

Deep in the countryside, Kate felt free. Her fury cooled. She dismounted and looked up at the sky of the sweetest blue. A valley cupped her, with green meadows folding around her, a narrow stream chiming along its lowest crease to feed the Melandra. On her left was a steep rise of woodland; on all sides stood oak, ash and birch, rustling endlessly in the warm breeze, lush and dewy and limpidly green. Tethering Mab to a branch, she scratched the mare's neck affectionately and left her to graze.

Kate sat down in her favourite place, a spread of grass within a loop of the little stream, with an oak tree at her back. This was her retreat, Blackthorn Griffe. Her meadow, wholly secluded by the trees and bushes growing along the curves of the stream. There was such a feeling of enchantment here that it could well be another Hollow, a sacred way to the hidden world; one even her mother hadn't found. Hers.

A bee bumped against her face and she felt the velvet of its body. All her senses were alive. The grass was thick with buttercups. A layer of shimmering air peeled up from the bank and tumbled, full of flashes and rippling laughter, into the water. Kate glimpsed the forms of naiads, transparent and laced with rainbows, like bubbles. She felt the intense shimmer of the hidden world. The veil between her and the faerie realm seemed so thin she was certain she could pass through as if through a cobweb.

Here it seemed possible that nothing else existed. She could simply stay here, or just run and run, and never go back. And then?

Kate didn't want to run away. She wanted to go home, and everything to be as it always had been. Perhaps if she'd been brought up in an ordinary household, taught to bend to the will of men, she would have accepted her fate. But she had not, and she felt utterly betrayed. My mother is not Edith, she thought. How has Mama become so worn down by struggle that she would go against all our principles and sell her only daughter?

Kate was cut adrift, and felt wretched. She half thought of killing herself. No, she was too full of life to martyr herself like that. Too angry. There was something wild and desperate boiling up inside her, impelling her to take drastic action; but not suicide, and certainly not a nunnery, Auset help her.

She closed her eyes. Her lips moved in a plea to the great Serpent Mother.

'Sweet Auset, Mother of All, please help me. I beg you, show me what to do. If not an answer, give me a sign, a clue, anything. Whatever path you show me when I open my eyes, I will take it.'

Beyond the red wall of her eyelids the world grew loud, the rustle of trees, the hum of insects and birdsong blending in one vibrating roar, drowning her.

Her eyes snapped open. Nothing had changed. The meadow was just as it had been; exquisite, serene, revealing nothing.

Kate sighed. She should have known better than to expect an easy answer from the Goddess. She leaned back against the warm trunk, sunning her face. She'd have to go home eventually, but not yet. At this moment, she couldn't bear the thought.

A noise startled her. Animals running about in the trees ... and then a steadier noise. Hoofbeats on dry earth.

She sat up, infuriated. Had someone been sent to look for her?

Through the trees on her left she saw a man on horseback, following the narrow path that ran along the foot of the slope. It was a magnificent horse, a glossy bay with an arched neck and a high-stepping gait. No one she knew, at least. If she sat still, he would go straight past and not see her.

Then Mab put up her head and whickered.

The man turned his head and looked straight at her.

Kate cursed. No one ever came here! Why today? The last thing she wanted was an encounter with a stranger, whether he offered a threat or protection. She wanted neither. His intrusion was an echo of the Stanleys' visit, a reminder of her powerlessness in the outer world.

Then something extraordinary happened. A furious growling broke out, issuing from a copse that lay behind and to her right. A feline squawling, tangling with darker snarls. Kate leapt up and ran to quiet Mab who was dancing from side to side in alarm.

She saw, striped by tree shadow, two astonishing beasts. One had stepped out of heraldry: a small lithe leopard, pure white with blue eyes. Silver dapples ruffled its coat and there was an aura around its head, like a sun. Light shone through a stiff mane raised in aggression; it looked like a crown of spiked silver. The leopard was growling, swishing its tail.

Its adversary was a heavy, charcoal-grey beast, all bunched muscles. A lion's mane, black; an ugly, furious face, all fangs. Not much bigger than the pard but three times its weight. A graylix.

Kate had never seen one loose before. She felt sick with terror. They could bite a small child in half. They could bring down a fleeing horse and lame it for life. Nothing frightened them, and they attacked anything that moved.

The two beasts stood face to face, roaring threats. She saw the brave leopard crouch, ready to spring. It stood no chance. With a flurry of snarls both creatures leapt and clashed.

There was a whirr, a dull thud. The graylix twisted in mid-air and fell, squealing like a boar, with an arrow in its ribs. Kate glanced round and saw the man riding towards her and jumping the stream, the bow still in his hand. Halfway across the meadow he leapt off his horse and ran onwards into the copse. He threw his bow aside as he went, and drew a broadsword.

Kate lifted her heavy skirts and ran after him. Twigs cracked under her embroidered slippers. As she entered the edge of the trees, she saw him pierce the graylix through the heart. The terrible noise ceased. The creature lay still, its thin dark-grey coat turning black with blood. Kate stood there, panting, watching the man carefully wipe and sheath the sword. He was slim and raven-haired, and no older than her. He turned and looked at her. Neither spoke. There seemed nothing to be said.

Then another extraordinary thing happened that convinced her she must have crossed into the hidden world, or at least be standing on its borders.

The snowy pard came to her, just as her mother's cats would. Although it was another dangerous creature, a hunter, it didn't occur to her to be frightened. The pard reared up, placed its big paws on her shoulders and touched its tongue to the tip of her nose. The tongue was edged with purple-black, like an orchid. It held her gaze for a moment with eyes as blue as her own. Then it jumped softly down, slipped away through the trees, and vanished.

'It was a silver pard,' said the young man, very quietly. 'I've never seen one before. Not even in the royal menagerie.'

'Neither have I,' said Kate.

'I thought they only existed in myths, like the unicorn.'

'There's something strange about the unicorn,' she said. 'My mother has the horn of one, but she says it came out of the sea, far up in the northern lands. They're shaped like horses, but they live in the sea. How is that possible?' She shook her head, feeling she was talking nonsense and was suddenly tongue-tied. 'Still, if they can exist, so can the silver pard.'

He was staring at her. She stared back, seeing him properly at last. He was lean, very graceful, only a few inches taller than her, and wearing clothes of dark hues, midnight blue and mulberry, beautifully sewn. The doublet was cut into long, curved points over slim velvet trousers, and edged with jet beads. He had high boots of umber leather, fine but well-worn, and the sword in a sombre sheath inlaid with dull gold. He had a subtle air of confidence.

A nobleman, obviously. Kate thinned her lips, out of humour with nobles. But he wasn't like Lord Stanley or his son. Nothing overbearing or self-important about him. His presence was a relief; slender and quiet. His face was very fair, she noticed. Fine-boned, like ivory, with dark soft eyes: the brows and lashes black, the irises crystalline grey. His thick dark hair shone in the sun.

He looked like someone who would not be easy to befriend. His eyes managed to be gentle and remote at the same time. But he appeared captivated by her, or at least mystified. She found it oddly pleasing.

'Who are you?' he asked. 'Apart from an enchantress of animals.'

'Kate.'

'That doesn't tell me much. I'm Richard.' Hesitantly he took her hand, and kissed it. 'I'm sorry, my lady. You must be shaken. I didn't mean to startle you, but I had to . . .'

He waved a hand at the fallen graylix. In curiosity she went to it and stroked the fur of the strange half-lion, half-human face. In death it still looked defiant.

When she rose, he was regarding her in even greater astonishment.

'It's probably the only chance I'll ever have to touch one,' she explained. 'It's a shame you had to kill it, but you saved the pard's life, and that of my mare, and probably mine as well. Thank you, Sir Richard.'

He gave a diffident smile. 'You're welcome, my lady. You seem very calm.'

'I'm not, I assure you.' She laughed, placing a hand over her bodice. She could feel the gold-thread device of lilies under her fingers, and remembered that it was coming unpicked and needed repair, yet again. She became aware that her hair was loose and wild, her sapphire velvet covered in horse hair. Did she look like an enchantress to him, or merely bizarre?

'I have a flask of wine,' he said. He caught his horse and tied up the glossy beast next to Mab, who looked tiny next to the huge gelding. Kate walked back to her oak and Richard reappeared with the leather flask, uncorked it and offered it to her.

She drank gratefully. The wine was delicious, tasting of elderflowers.

'Thank you, sir. My mouth was very dry.'

'You should sit down and rest for a while.'

'Yes, if you'll sit with me.'

'Gladly,' he said, and they sat next to each other on the warm, smooth roots of the oak. They passed the wine back and forth, taking sips, which seemed unnervingly intimate. His hands were beautiful: long and silken. 'Are you alone?'

'Obviously,' she said. 'It's my mother's demesne. I always come here alone.'

'I think I have got lost,' he said. 'I thought I knew where I was, but this all looks different. Er . . . I should be on my way, my lady, but I don't like to leave you.'

A small, thrilling pang; she didn't want him to leave. 'And I don't want to keep you from your destination, but if you can stay a little while, I'd be grateful.'

'I was only riding around, trying to clear my thoughts,' he said quickly. 'I've nowhere to go.'

'Nor have I.' She sat with her knees raised, her hands dangling loosely between them over the folds of her skirt. Leaning her head back, she felt her hair sliding over her shoulders, and was aware of him watching her. It felt delicious, like being stroked. 'It's such a beautiful afternoon. I've never had anyone to share it with before. Let's hope nothing else disturbs us.'

'No wolves or wild boars.' He passed her the wine again. It was going to her head.

His eyes were serious and watchful. Wounded eyes. She saw a guarded intelligence in them and something else, unreadable. Her mother had taught her well how to read people but this man was elusive, as if there was a veil over him, dark and silver. He unnerved her. Never in her life had she felt so powerfully, physically drawn to someone. She wanted to sit closer. It would have seemed natural to touch him. The thought shocked and excited her.

He frowned suddenly. 'Have we met before?'

'I don't think so,' she said. 'I think I would have remembered.'

A smile flickered. 'So would I. Still, you remind me of someone, my lady, but I don't know who, or why.'

'You can call me Kate.'

'Katherine, after the saint? It means pure.'

'I doubt my mother was thinking of saints when she named me. And Richard, that means hard rule, or something of the sort, doesn't it?'

It was a little sword-thrust, to show her knowledge was equal to his. His smile thinned. 'I was named for my father. If he had ruled, I suppose he would have been hard, but certainly fair. There must be something in names.'

His remark about his father seemed off-hand; she read nothing into it. 'So you're hard, and I'm pure,' she said, then laughed, her cheeks heating with embarrassment.

He laughed with her, his gaze dropping under long eyelashes, then meeting hers again.

'I thought I was dreaming when I saw you,' he said. 'Do you always ride about on your own?'

'All the time. I go wherever I wish.'

'But it's not safe, Kate.'

'Usually it is. I have never seen a graylix or a pard here before, and I doubt I ever will again.'

'There may be boars in the woods, horned toads . . .'

'A horned toad lives in our garden,' she smiled. 'I think of it as a pet.'

'A witch's pet. They're poisonous!'

'Only if threatened. You were riding alone too. Is it less dangerous for you?'

'I have a sword.'

'And know how to use it, clearly.'

His laugh had a sour edge. 'As I've been taught by the greatest master in England, I hope so.'

'And you defended me well, Richard, but all my life these woods and their inhabitants have been my dear friends. One incident won't stop me going where I please.'

'But friends can turn on you,' he flashed back, and his eyes were all shadow and smoke from a bitter fire. 'The dearest and best will betray you. You can know and love a wolfhound all your life but there's no guarantee it won't turn and savage you!'

Katherine drew back from his outburst. She waited; he rested his elbows over his knees, and stared at the stream.

'What's wrong?' she asked. 'Someone has hurt you.'

'Ah, well. Not me, but my brother, which is the same as betraying me. Someone who was dearer to us than our own father . . . dearer to me, at least. If I talk about this, you'll know who I am.'

'Will that matter?' Kate placed her hand along his arm, just below the shoulder. He didn't shake her off, rather he seemed to move closer.

81

'I don't know. It's pleasant to talk with someone who doesn't know me, and has no ideas about me, and doesn't want me to petition the King for them.'

'You're obviously not a shepherd, Richard,' she said. 'Tell me whatever you want, or not, as you wish. I won't tell a soul.'

'And you won't treat me any differently?'

'No,' she said, with gentle conviction. 'You're in my demesne. The enchantment won't be lost.'

'This man who betrayed us, he's one of the most powerful in the land. I grew up in his household. He helped my brother to achieve his high estate but now he's turned against us and sided with our enemies. He tried to persuade me to join him in betraying Edward! So I've had to choose between them. If I seem distracted, and poor company, Kate, that's why. I'll soon be required to take up arms against a man that I used to love like a father.'

'You are not poor company.' Kate felt a flare of pain. Ridiculous, since she didn't know him. But it had been easier not to know who he was. Anonymous, he'd been hers alone; now he had a weight of responsibilities about him, a whole life that had nothing to do with her. He was on his way into battle. 'I'm sorry.'

'Thank you. Tomorrow I'll be angry about it. Today I was riding alone to exorcise the sadness without anyone seeing.'

'Are you talking about the Earl of Warwick? And King Edward?'

'So it was that obvious.'

'We hear rumours, even here.' She touched the white boar pin on his shoulder. A haunting excitement went through her, which was, she sensed, the last response he wanted. She kept her voice even. 'You're the King's brother, Richard – Duke of Gloucester? Or it could just be something you tell unsuspecting maidens.'

'Yes.' He looked at her with warmth. 'That's all it is.'

'I won't tell a soul. Why did they quarrel?'

A hardness came into his face that made him look older. 'They're two highly ambitious men who are never content. Edward is King, but Warwick still only the Kingmaker and he can't be satisfied with that. He's a great man, Kate, but driven. It was mostly over Edward's marriage. You must have heard something of it? Edward embarrassed Warwick horribly. Warwick went to immense trouble to negotiate an important foreign union for him, only for Edward to tell him, "Oh, did I forget to mention that I am already married to this Lancastrian widow?" I don't blame Warwick for being angry. They are as bad as each other, in some respects. But at least I know where my loyalty lies.'

'With Edward.'

'I don't know how they can question it.' He pushed a hand through his hair. 'He's the King, for God's sake! But Warwick will use anybody in the slightest bit vain or malleable to further his ambitions and George . . .' His eyes were flint. 'My stupid brother George is jealous of Edward and I'm sure Warwick has seduced him with some ludicrous promise of getting him on the throne. Warwick wants his daughter Isabel to marry George; Edward won't permit it. It would make Warwick even more powerful. He's done nothing but cause trouble this past year and he has got to be stopped. I don't know that it's entirely the Queen's fault, but it all went wrong when Edward met her.'

'What's she like?' Kate asked, fascinated.

Richard's face hardly moved, yet a look of poisonous hatred flickered over it as clear as light across water. 'She's very, very fair, Elizabeth Woodville or Dame Grey,' he said diplomatically. 'If only Edward had married just her and not her entire family. It's hard for the old nobility to see a great clan of Lancastrian commoners receiving so many rewards; high positions and marriages they don't deserve. Warwick has a right to be angry; but not to commit treason. Not that. I can't forgive him for what he's doing. He promised me the earth to go with him. He couldn't believe it when I said no, I know what loyalty is and there's no reward under heaven that would induce me to betray Edward. And I'm sick of thinking about it all.'

Where her hand rested on his arm, she gave it a quick, gentle squeeze. 'Don't, then. Forget about it for a while and be comforted. That's why we met.'

He smiled at her. 'And you? You had a face like a storm when I first saw you. Aren't we meant to comfort each other?'

She drew a breath. Strong instinct warned her not to tell him her own troubles. She would only hold him as long as she seemed unreal to him. 'Nothing. Just a quarrel with my mother. I assure you I have no identity to guess.'

'Good. As long as your name isn't Woodville. The Queen has dozens of sisters, and they lie in wait everywhere.'

'It isn't, I promise,' Kate answered, amused.

Her fingertips were still touching the boar badge. His hand slid up and closed around hers. Her breathing grew quicker and deeper. The sun-warmed velvet of his doublet smelled delicious, fragrant like cedarwood. The scent was on his skin. Beneath the doublet, his linen shirt was white and crisp as may blossom.

'I'm glad I met you, Kate. You're so pretty.'

He kissed her, his lips light and sweet on hers. His arms went round her and she was pressed against him, certain he must feel her heartbeat shaking her whole body. Then she knew that her fear of marriage was not a fear of men. In the space of a day she'd discovered the difference between a man who repulsed her, and one who drew her in like a bee to nectar.

Kate hadn't planned it, but she saw the path in all its shining glory and ruin. A way to ensure that no marriage would be forced upon her. Drastic and wild, but that was the action she must take.

She felt him exhale. 'I ought to go,' he said, reluctantly. 'This isn't right. I didn't mean to take advantage of you, Kate.' She felt him trembling, his young body taut against hers. There were too many layers of clothes between them. Her own hunger startled her, a sensation of dissolving heat. 'I'll ride with you back to your house.'

He spoke without conviction, but he gave her a choice. He was a gentleman. If she said, yes, escort me home, he would do so without argument. Her choice. She stood poised on the fork of the path and her heart was pounding.

There was only this cocoon of time, suspended on the fringe of the hidden world. Nothing else existed. The world breathed around them, as rich and iridescent as a dragonfly.

'No, don't go,' she said, laying her hand along his cheek.

He stared at her with intense dark eyes, torn. 'Kate, if we stay here . . .'

'I know.'

'It isn't right.'

'Yes, it is,' she breathed, her mouth almost touching his. 'It is.'

'But I may never see you again.'

'Yes, that's it!' She kissed his neck, and he gasped. 'We are never going to see each other again. This is our only chance.'

'Oh, Kate.' He groaned, surrendering.

She expected to be frightened and wasn't. It was easy. Awkward, for they both suffered the clumsiness of inexperience. If he'd done this before, she was sure it wasn't many times, if at all. They laughed at their ineptness and then it didn't matter. There was only a slight pain, nothing she couldn't bear, and soon the pain eased into a richer sensation. Yes, the easiest thing in the world. It wasn't terrible but sweet, as her mother had told her it could be, ineffably delicious, gentle and transporting, a flight through the mysteries of the hidden world.

And forbidden. She could not possibly be doing this with someone she had met barely an hour ago, a stranger . . . but she was, and exaltation filled her. They laughed together. The green world trembled.

*   *   *

85

There was a spring nearby. Kate went to refill the empty flask with water and brought it back to him. He took the saddle from his horse; she watched the care with which he tended the animal. Then they quenched their thirst, twined their bodies together joyfully, and made love again. Dusk fell. The world turned blue and the denizens of the hidden world whispered around them. Kate saw their firefly eyes over her lover's shoulder, and smiled.

Eventually, forgetting themselves, they slept.

Kate woke suddenly to a cold, dewy dawn and found herself looking at a stranger.

They'd loosely pulled their clothes back on for warmth and the night had not been cold, but now, without his arms around her, she was freezing. Her dress was soaked. Richard was kneeling, dishevelled and trying to lace his shirt with shaking hands. As she rose, he regarded her with a wary look, bordering on accusation. All enchantment had gone.

Kate sat up in sharp dread. 'Oh, dear Iesu, my mother will be going out of her mind.'

He said nothing. He looked very young, grim and almost frightened.

'Richard?' She tried to shift her dress into a more comfortable shape, shaking out the damp underskirts. 'Are you all right? You're looking at me as if you'd seen a ghost.'

He took a deep breath. He was as white as the dawn. 'I've remembered where I've seen you before.'

'Oh? Are you going to tell me?'

'I think you know.'

'Really, I don't.'

He rose, fastening his doublet and making a poor job of it. When she went to help him, he stepped back.

'What have I done?' she said, frowning.

'I should have realized.' He glanced around him. His face had the hardness she'd seen when he had been talking about the Earl of Warwick. 'It's obvious you're a witch. I shouldn't have been taken in.'

'Taken in?'

'I recognize this . . . otherworld. I've been here before. Yesterday, too beautiful to be real, and then spectres all around us, demons in my dreams all night.'

Kate's face gave her away. What he said was true, at least in part. 'It's not what you think.'

'You don't deny it, then! No doubt you thought I'd have no idea what was happening, and you lying in wait to ensorcell any unsuspecting knight who happens to be passing.'

'Ensorcell you? Don't flatter yourself! Great Goddess, you make me sound like Morgana lying in wait for King Arthur! Richard, don't be angry. It wasn't that at all.'

'I thought it was something beautiful and innocent but it was all a deceit. They warn us against demonesses who lie in wait to tempt men into sin. I should have known. Iesu's blood, what have I done?'

He went to saddle his horse. She followed him. 'I suppose they've told you that the otherworld is evil. They know nothing about it.'

'And I know too much,' he said. 'It's profane, it's outside the realm of God, it's full of horrors – and deceitful enchantments. The world is a battleground of light and dark and I won't be dragged into the dark!'

Kate stood hugging herself against the cold. She was hurt and offended. To her the hidden world was a place of wonder. Yet she couldn't summon the strength to argue. If that was what he'd been taught, she was unlikely to change his mind. The shock of what she had done was setting in.

Suddenly she wished it had been a lad like Tom, after all, and not this guarded, difficult nobleman.

She couldn't argue with Richard, because he was right. She'd asked Auset for a sign, and he had come; but Auset had still given her a choice. Kate had drawn him into the hidden world and enchanted him.

Other men might have been grateful.

'You should know, I don't make a habit of it,' she said tightly. 'It was my first time.'

He stopped buckling straps, and gazed at her across the bay's saddle. His eyes were like ice. She began to hate him for looking at her like that.

She added, 'You must have realized.'

The flicker in his eyes was guilt. Of course he'd realized. 'How could you do that? Just – give yourself to a stranger?' he exclaimed.

Kate arched her eyebrows. 'How could *you*, gentle knight?'

He was almost speechless. She could imagine that, when he grew older, his severity would be frightening. 'That's different. That's utterly different!'

'Why?'

'It's obvious. How could you give a stranger your virginity, which should have been for your husband?'

'Because they were forcing me to marry a man I found loathsome! So I set out to ruin myself, so that no one would want me!'

If she'd meant to prove she was human, and not a succubus, she had failed. He looked horrified.

'And you thought you'd use me in this monstrous scheme?'

'It wasn't a scheme.' She wanted to pacify him, so they could part with affection, not angry words, but he'd gone too far. If he wanted a witch, he would get one. 'My poor suitor shall be ten times more outraged than you, and I shall laugh in his face. And be careful whom you call monstrous. It will come back to haunt you.'

He finished saddling the bay, checked its legs and hooves, and flung the reins over its wide neck. Mab's nostrils flared and she shifted, eager to follow.

When Richard spoke again, some of the zeal seemed to have gone out of him. 'How shall I find my way out of here?'

'The hidden world is everywhere,' said Kate. 'Tell the

King that the faeries abducted you, and you woke up a hundred miles away.'

'Haven't you had enough sport with me?'

'You wandered into the hidden world and you've been here a day and a night. I could keep you here forever. Didn't they teach you not to offend the faerie folk?'

He led his fidgeting horse in a half-circle, which brought him face to face with her. 'Please, Kate.' The intense sombre radiance of his face struck unexpected pain through her. She recalled the silk of his hair under her fingers. 'I didn't mean to offend you. Is there a correct way to behave? If I give you a gift, will you tell me the path?'

'Something to remember you by?' She thought of asking for a lock of his hair; then he'd fear her witchcraft for the rest of his life. She wanted to ask for a kiss, but pride wouldn't let her. 'Give me your white boar.'

He hesitated.

'I'll keep it close and secret,' she said. 'I won't use it for sorcery against you, on the word of a witch. I'll look at it and never forget you.'

'I don't suppose this will be easy to forget,' he said thinly. He unpinned the jewel and pressed it into her palm without touching her skin. 'Which way?'

His eagerness to leave hardened her heart. Disillusioned, all she wanted now was for him to go. He'd served his purpose. Did people always feel guilt after lust and turn the blame on each other? If so, it was hateful.

'That way,' she said, pointing to the track on which he'd first appeared. 'You'll see your path. You may see many paths, so choose the right one.' She heard her mother's voice coming out of her, and it made her feel powerful. 'No creature of the twilight will harm you while you are under our protection. Go.'

He gave her a last glance, grim and fearful. Then the big bay carried him off through the trees in plunging leaps. Katherine stood and watched him until he was out of sight.

Once he was gone, her heart sank. Now she must go back and face her mother's anguish. It had been a mad act of defiance, coldly regretted in the dregs of dawn. And now, because of the way he had reacted, she couldn't even remember her lover fondly. She was no sorceress, just an unhappy girl; but neither aspect, apparently, could please the Duke of Gloucester.

Kate went and put her arms around her mare's neck. 'Nothing I've done has made anything better,' she said against the damp mane. 'All I've done is make it worse, Mab. Come on. I'll go back and face my punishment with my chin in the air.'

Arriving home, she ran up the stairs into the solar and collided with her mother, who'd come rushing to the doorway to meet her. Katherine braced herself for loud fury, even for a blow. Instead, Eleanor threw her arms around her, and held her so close she couldn't breathe. She didn't even mention her ruined dress.

'Kate, where have been? Thomas has men riding over the whole demesne, looking for you! Thank Auset you're all right.'

'I've done something terrible,' said Kate. Her voice came out rough with regret. 'I'm sorry, but I'd rather die than have a husband forced upon me. I met a man in Blackthorn Griffe and I let him . . .'

'What? Kiss you? What?'

Kate shook her head, and held her mother's horrified gaze. 'Everything. I lay with him all night. So that George Stanley wouldn't want me, and no one else would want me either. With any luck, I'm with child. If not, I shall stuff a bolster under my dress and moan and sigh and have Martha help me out of my seat to greet him!'

Eleanor gaped at her. Never before had Kate managed to place such astonishment in her mother's eyes. And then such complete agony that Kate would have done anything to take back all her words and actions.

In the dreadful silence, a shape moved in the shadows on the far side of the firegrate. A broad silhouette, sheathed in plum damask, was rising from a chair.

Too late, Kate saw Anne Beauchamp, the Countess of Warwick. The last person in the world she would have wished to overhear her confession.

'Eleanor, perhaps I had better leave you and your daughter alone?'

Chapter Four 1469: Katherine

I am the Queen of war
I am the Queen of the thunderbolt
I stir up the sea and I calm it.
I am in the rays of the sun . . .
I set free those in bonds . . .
I overcome Fate.

Aretalogy of Isis

Katherine waited for the firmament to fall. Eleanor stood rigid, with flooded eyes. The Countess was a statue in the background.

Waves of regret were flowing through her, becoming more intense by the second. She'd meant to outrage her mother, to show how desperate she was; not to break her heart. Then, incredibly, her mother began to laugh.

'Kate, please tell me you are joking. What am I going to do with you?'

Slowly, she shook her head. 'Mother, every word of what I've told you is true. I met a young man I had never seen before and I deliberately gave myself to him. I set out to make myself unfit for marriage. And I'm sorry.'

Eleanor's laughter stopped. She groaned, and stood regarding her as if weighing up whether to believe her or not. Her daughter had never been a liar, and she knew it. Kate saw the shadow-play of thoughts behind her eyes. There was no anger, only intense mortification, which was worse.

'Oh, love, have you really done this? There was no need for you to go to such an extreme! I'd rather we had argued all night, than this. Of course I won't make you marry against your will.'

Heat pricked Katherine's eyes. 'That's not what you said yesterday.'

Eleanor put her arms tight around her daughter. 'I was beleaguered. In a moment of complete desperation, I thought we must give up the fight and play by their rules instead. Adopt a more subtle game, not wage a war we couldn't win. I never thought you would react so wildly!' She looked into Kate's eyes, and smoothed the hair off her forehead. 'You're in disarray. He didn't hurt you, did he?'

'No, he didn't. And I can save the dress; it's only damp.' Kate gave a few quiet sobs. Light flushed the windows; another beautiful May day, cruelly echoing the one before. 'I'm so sorry, Mama.'

'And so am I, love. I shouldn't have considered Stanley's proposal for a moment.'

'But *I* should have done. I've been utterly selfish.'

The Countess of Warwick stirred, her skirts sighing on the floor. 'Eleanor, I'll leave you to resolve this . . . painful matter.'

'No, no, Anne, don't go,' Eleanor said over Kate's shoulder. 'You've heard the worst – I hope. Your counsel on this disaster would be welcomed, with all my heart.' She held Kate away from her and looked intently into her eyes. 'We can't afford to make enemies, especially not of men who could take everything from us. I have to think of another way to appease them.'

'Come, sit down,' said the Countess. Eleanor led Kate to a settle with a red tapestry seat, and their guest returned to her tall chair beside the fire. Her face was stern, but warmer than Kate would have expected. 'Katherine, I don't need to point out how shocking your confession has been. If one of my own daughters had behaved in this way I don't know how I would have begun to deal with her. In fact, it's impossible to imagine such a course of action even entering their minds.'

Eleanor acknowledged this dig with a slow, cool blink.

'However, let's be pragmatic. It's not the end of the world.'

Kate started. 'Isn't it?'

'Why does young Stanley need to know you are not a virgin? Worse indiscretions than yours have been overlooked. Whatever the Church says, when it comes to the point, the quality most valued in a potential wife is not virtue, but land. Of course you can still marry.'

Katherine was both relieved and dismayed. 'Can I?'

Eleanor snorted. 'Oh, that will look fine, if her belly swells up with another man's child!'

'Then let them marry quickly, and he'll never know.'

'I'll do it,' Kate said quickly, catching her mother's eye. 'Without a word of complaint.'

'No. You won't.'

'Mama, to save Lytton Dale. Nothing else matters!'

'But you were right to be furious at me! I promised we would hold our manor in our own right and I won't go back on that. I'll think of another way.'

Kate had meant what she'd said, but her mother's response filled her with utter relief. She tried to hide it.

'Risky,' said the Countess. 'What if she is with child?'

Eleanor sighed. 'Anne, it was only once.'

Three times, actually, thought Kate. Or was it four?

'Once is sufficient,' Anne Beauchamp replied crisply.

'Well, then, I'll do what I've done for a dozen other girls. We'll keep it secret, bring a girl here to look after the babe and say it is hers. It won't be the first time . . . although I never dreamed I might have to do it for *you*, Lady Katherine.'

Her mother's blunt practicality shocked Kate. She turned faint with remorse.

'Mama, I'm truly sorry. I was distraught. I asked Auset to show me a way out, and he appeared.'

The older women exchanged a look. The Countess said, 'Well, there's a lesson in the danger of taking the Dark

Mother's signs too literally. You can see why so many are against us. It's a tortuous path, not for the simple-minded.'

'I hope you don't think I'm simple-minded, madam,' Kate said delicately. 'I'm not blaming Auset. She gave me a choice. There was a point when I could have left and come home untouched. I chose to go on.'

Anne Beauchamp's crêpey, deep-lidded eyes flared with disapproval. 'You're certainly candid, child. Others might have denied everything, or claimed to have been ravished.' Her gaze fell, fixing on Kate's waist.

'I brought her up to be honest,' Eleanor put in. 'An essential quality in a priestess.'

'Who was he?' The Countess looked up. Her eyebrows rose in a firm arch, prompting her.

'No one,' said Kate, taken aback. 'I don't know.'

'He must have told you his name.'

'I don't wish to lie. I can't say.'

Anne leaned forward suddenly, plucking at something in a fold of Kate's bodice. 'Where did you get this? From him?'

It was the white boar, of nacre and diamond set in heavy silver. Kate had pinned it there for safekeeping, and forgotten it. She watched, helpless, as the Countess removed the jewel and examined it. 'Do you know whose badge this is?'

'No.' She exhaled. 'Yes, of course I do.'

'So he was a servant of the Duke of Gloucester. That narrows the field.'

They were both looking hard at her. She flushed with heat. 'Does this matter?'

'It might,' said Eleanor. 'I could half believe this was a figment of your imagination, until I saw he gave you a token. Is Anne right?'

'Not a servant,' Kate breathed. 'He *was* the Duke of Gloucester.'

Outside, she could hear birdsong, the bleating of sheep,

a horse neighing. She wished she could be out there riding Mab . . . to turn back time by a day.

Eventually the Countess spoke. 'It's highly unlikely he would be near here; not impossible, of course. The jewel is fine enough to belong to him, but might be stolen.'

'He was a true nobleman, not a thief.' Now her pride wanted them to believe her.

'What did he look like?'

Kate described him. She watched the Countess turn grey, and drape her hands over her eyes. 'He should be brought to task for this.'

'No!' Kate cried, horrified. 'I promised him I wouldn't tell a soul I'd met him!'

'But he's behaved disgracefully. It must have been apparent to him that you were of good breeding, not some dairymaid, or—'

'Madam, I know dairymaids who would not have behaved as badly as I have done. What recompense do you expect him to make? Money, as if I were a whore?'

'Katherine.' The Countess sat upright, fixing her with a firm stare. 'I feel half to blame. You do realize, don't you, that he grew up in our household? He is to me, if not a son, at least very close to it. I'm ashamed. An apology and some recognition of his own transgression would be something.'

'No,' Kate said emphatically. 'I want no apology. As things stand, he doesn't even know who I am. If you said something, he would know. Others would be bound to find out, gossip would spread, and I'd be utterly humiliated. If he thinks of me as a witch, at least he'll remember me with a little healthy fear. If I present myself as a victim, he'll see me in a different light, of pity, or even contempt. I couldn't bear that. Let it be forgotten!'

The two women looked at each other. 'She has a point,' said Eleanor.

Kate stood up and went to the window, her arms folded, while her elders went on arguing. This fuss was hateful.

She felt like diving headfirst through the glass into the herb garden.

Eventually the Countess sighed. 'It's a mystery to me how one so sharp can at the same time be given to such rash idiocy. Very well, Kate. It's your choice. The next time I see him I shall bite my tongue – for your sake.'

'Promise me!'

'I promise. On my life, on the holy book, and on the cauldron of the sacred Serpent.'

'Thank you, madam.' She came back and curtseyed. 'And I don't mean to be so rude.'

'I'm growing quite used to you,' the Countess said with a dry smile. 'You put me in mind of my Isabel – your pertness, not your behaviour.'

'This is awful,' Kate said, sitting down again with her head in her hands. 'Why did it have to be him, someone my lady the Countess knows in person? How did my path manage to cross with his, and not with that of some shepherd, or saddler, or a half-witted farm boy—'

'Katherine!' Eleanor snapped. 'Must I point out that you should not have been out there trying to cross paths with anyone?'

'You had better keep this,' said the Countess. She held out the badge. Kate reached out and received it in her damp palm. The small tusks of the boar were sharp, and dug into her. 'Did he . . . speak of the King's troubles at all?'

Kate looked up, wary. 'A little. He seemed upset.'

'You are probably aware that my good husband, the Earl of Warwick, has certain differences with King Edward.'

Eleanor's eyebrows flicked in surprise. 'If you can call stirring up actual rebellions and spreading seditious rumours about him differences. To be honest, I'm very surprised to see you, Anne.'

There was no change in the Countess's stately visage. 'You see how hard it is not to take sides and become involved. My husband has a genuine grievance. Not least, having his hard work of diplomacy spat back at him with the news that Edward had already married the Woodville woman. In secret, as though even he acknowledged it was something to be ashamed of!'

Kate wondered what was wrong with the Queen's pedigree. She knew how imperative bloodlines, land and titles were to the nobility, for they shed each other's blood over it constantly; but in her heart, she couldn't see why it actually *mattered*. Aware of sounding naive, she asked, 'Was it wrong for the King to marry for love?'

'Certainly it was silly of him to marry for lust,' Anne Beauchamp said shortly. 'Still, that's not the issue. It was a tactless, wasteful union that's brought the kingdom near ruin and, in the process, he made my husband look a fool.'

'This must be difficult for you,' Eleanor said mildly. Her hand rose to play absently with Kate's hair.

'Well, yes, it is; but in what sense?'

'Your husband's strength put Edward upon the throne. You wanted the Motherlodge to bend their energies to help him. You told us he was chosen and divinely appointed. Have you and your noble husband now changed your minds? It's one thing to fall out with someone, quite another to claim that a king is divine, and then to rescind that claim.'

Anne Beauchamp's strong face was stormy. 'I'm aware of that.'

'So which line do you take now? That your husband is right and your own instincts were wrong? Or do you claim that Edward was only best appointed, and now another might be better appointed, or just more usefully appointed?'

The Countess stared at her. 'Eleanor, what have I said to deserve this outburst? This is my husband's quarrel, not mine. I am bound to support him, of course. In the outer world, a wife has no voice but her husband's—'

'Anne!' Eleanor lifted her hands, exasperated. 'You are talking to a sister, not to a bishop! What do *you* think?'

Her voice fell. 'I don't know. Edward has shown foolishness and impulsiveness, but that does not make him a bad king. I would rather this had never begun. I'm as uneasy about the Earl's actions as you are, but I can't stop him. He never listens to me.'

'Anne, I can't get involved. If you now want the Motherlodge to work *against* Edward, it's impossible. If he was best appointed before, he still is. If anything, the lodge has swayed in his favour. It's in our interests to support him.'

'So, the keepers of the cauldron are becoming partial, after all?'

'It's been happening for quite some time. Since the Duke of York died and Marguerite's mercenaries were let loose upon us. Henry attracts the pious; the sort of churchmen who most want to destroy us. King Edward is a kinder master. He couldn't care less about us, which isn't ideal, but better than an active drive to remove us. I need his protection now, more than ever. Even Dame Eylott and Dame Marl agree. We need Edward's protection.'

The Countess breathed out through her nose. 'Dear, you've quite misunderstood me. I didn't come here to persuade you against the King. I came to say that I most fervently hope and desire that these surface quarrels will not affect our friendship. Must they?'

'Well, no,' Eleanor said, sitting forward. 'As long as we don't bring them to meetings.'

'It's not a good idea for me to appear at the Motherlodge until the quarrel is over. But it could be settled in a month, and everyone amicable again. You know how they are: at each other's throats one moment, swearing undying love and fealty the next.'

'That's true enough.' Eleanor looked relieved.

The Countess leaned forward and took Eleanor's hands. 'The bonds between us are deep and secret, and cannot be uprooted by the surface bickering of men.'

'Yes. The circle cannot be broken. Furthermore, we shall feel free to argue about politics, or any other subject, without it undermining our friendship. I don't want to lose your friendship, Anne.'

Katherine looked at the two women making peace, and felt a pang of unease. She didn't dislike the Countess of Warwick – she'd proved sensible and kind, despite her forbidding demeanour. It was her duality that was worrying, the way she moved through two worlds at once. Beside her husband, she was the perfect Christian wife, grand yet mild and pious. In secret, she was someone else entirely. A high priestess, a sinuous channel of earthly powers. She could slip from one masque to another in a blink, and for that Kate admired her but didn't trust her.

Eleanor had never lived that dual life. She didn't broadcast what she was, but neither did she hide it. So churchmen such as Bishop Morton looked at her through slitted eyes, and dropped insinuations about hellfire and repentance that made Kate want to punch them; but at least she was honest.

Kate placed her palm over her stomach, and wondered if anything had taken inside, or if her blood would flow again with the moon. She felt an echo of tingling pleasure between her thighs. She remembered his long gentle hands on her body and his mouth on hers, the scent of sun-warmed velvet . . . his lean body hard with muscle and marked with the scars of hard training. His gentleness, and the long dark hair brushing her breasts . . . gods, the heart-stopping strangeness and enchantment of it. She was sorry it had ended badly, but that didn't take away the sweetness of the memory. No, she refused to regret it.

'Kate, are you listening?'

'Your pardon, Mama. What did you say?'

Anne Beauchamp replied patiently, 'I was saying to your good mother that I'll lend what little help I can: protection against Lord Stanley, should he choose to press his claim. And she agrees it would benefit you to enter a different household for a time.'

Katherine was startled. 'I don't especially want to leave here, madam.'

'It's the tradition for ladies of lesser nobility to wait on the greater. It wouldn't be seen as anything out of the ordinary. Besides, it's time you learned something of the world beyond this demesne. Despite the Earl's disputes, our household is perfectly secure and peaceful. I think you'd be happy with us. Perhaps we might even find a husband to content you, in time.'

'I – I don't know,' Kate whispered. A little fire of excitement ran through her. Adventure. 'I thank you most kindly, but I can't leave Mama.'

'Don't be ridiculous,' said Eleanor. 'Anne is right. It would take you out of George Stanley's way. It would distance you from any other, er, consequences you might have brought on yourself. You can't hide here all your life. It would certainly extend your education. And before you say anything, I can handle Lord Stanley perfectly well without you.'

'I've no doubt,' said Kate. It would be a wrench to leave, but it felt like salvation. She turned to the Countess and answered demurely, 'Very well, I'll go with you, madam, and gladly. Thank you. I'll write a letter to Lord Stanley's son, so mild and regretful that he's bound to forgive me.'

Katherine sat in a bath lined with white satin and full of violet petals. The fragrant heat was exquisite. Eleanor came in with an armful of towels and a fresh russet-brown dress for her.

'Well?' she said, sitting on a stool beside her. 'What was he like, really?'

Kate gasped. 'Mama! Don't ask me that!'

Eleanor gave a thin but affectionate smile. 'The trouble is that we try to live in two worlds. The outer world teaches that you have committed a mortal sin and should spend several weeks on your knees in penance, followed by entrance to a nunnery. However, in the eyes of the

Dark Mother, you have committed no sin, only made full sacred use of the body with which she blessed you. You've done nothing deserving of punishment. I believe this, yet I still react like any horrified mother of the outer world. It's unspeakably difficult.'

'So I see.'

'I can't bear to think that you endured a wretched time, just to spite me.'

Kate reached out and put a dripping hand on her mother's sleeve. 'I didn't.'

'Truly?'

'Mama, Auset sent him. She wouldn't send me anyone vile. He was charming, gentle and beautiful. I would have done the same if I *hadn't* been trying to spite you. I don't think anything that magical will ever happen to me again.'

'Magical?' Eleanor said, one eyebrow tilting. 'You're making me envious.'

'I didn't mean to stay out all night. We fell asleep, and then it was dawn.'

'A little dew is good for the complexion.'

Kate grinned. 'We saw a graylix and a silver pard in the woods, fighting.'

Her mother's expression darkened as Kate described what had happened.

'If you really saw a silver pard it was a manifestation of the hidden world.'

'I know,' said Kate. 'We were there all night, on the borders. I didn't take him there knowingly. It just happened. The enchantment was part of it, I couldn't have helped it. Unfortunately, it alarmed him. He was upset when he realized. Quite angry. Then he couldn't get away fast enough. He'd got it into his head I was an enchantress or some wicked faerie lying in wait for him.' Her mouth soured as she spoke.

Eleanor sighed through her teeth. 'Typical. Did you try to explain?'

'Not really,' said Kate. 'I played up to it. I wanted to see how fast his horse could go.'

Her mother burst out laughing.

'You would have been proud of me,' Kate added.

'I'm sure.'

She rose and stepped from the water, steam rising from her shining body. Eleanor wrapped towels around her and rubbed briskly.

'Mama,' Kate asked after a moment. 'When I was a child, I remember something happening . . . I would have been about six, I think. We were in the hidden world and a little boy came out of nowhere. You gave him a vision and he said he'd seen a man beheaded. I was in a trance and repeating everything you said. It was as if I wasn't a child but a thousand years old, and knew everything. You spoke about paths; you told him he was going into darkness unless he chose the way very carefully. Then you asked him to come into the cave-circle with us to learn more, but he was terrified, and ran as if the Devil were after him. Did that really happen, or was it a dream I had?'

Eleanor spoke softly, her mouth next to Kate's ear. 'It really happened.'

'It was him.'

'Who?'

'The boy was the man, my magical lover. Richard of Gloucester.'

'Ahh.'

'I didn't recognize him, but he recognized me. Then I remembered.'

'You have to understand, love, that most people are taught all their lives that anything outside the Church is to be reviled. We are witches, and witches are tools of the Devil. That's their belief. Richard will have been brought up to think that, of course. Don't blame him.'

'I don't. I'm just sad about it.'

'Some are more relaxed about it than others. However,

from what I have heard, his mother Cecily Neville is a pious woman, and he's very close to her.'

'So virtuous that he had the nerve to lecture me about the folly of giving my virginity to a passing stranger!' said Kate. 'But not virtuous enough to refuse me in the first place!'

'That's a man for you. Drawn to us twice, though . . . that's interesting. It probably has more significance for him than it has for us.'

'Mama, why are people frightened of us?'

'Because they think we're evil.'

'And they think we're evil . . .'

'Because they're frightened of us.'

Kate groaned. 'So we can't win! Anyway, it doesn't matter. I'll never see him again.'

'No. I suppose he's unlikely to visit Warwick's household, as things stand.'

The thought gave Kate a twinge of apprehension. 'I hope not. I don't want to see him. It would be unbearable.' She was quiet, drying her hair. 'Does he know that the Countess of Warwick follows the hidden path? He must.'

'Not necessarily. That is another story.' She turned Kate to face her, pushing back her tangled hair. 'When you go to her, you will find life somewhat different. Just do as she instructs, yes? However hard you must bite your tongue at times. You'll learn a lot.'

In a murmuring procession the celebrants trod barefoot along the path. All the maidens and women of Eleanor's household, all the boys and men too, whispering excitedly, bearing torches and lanterns, their hair streaming like smoke. Even Father Dunstan was there, the priest of their little church, who led Christian rituals and deferred to the old ways in his heart. In the twilight all were equal. Their gowns were of thin linen, their heads crowned with buttercups and ivy.

Many of them had come to Eleanor in the direst state

of wretchedness. She observed their rosy, joyful faces and was content.

Flanks of limestone curved up to enclose the demesne in protective walls. Close around them, trees swayed and the grass was moist between their toes. Down to the sacred Melandra they went, paddled through the swift-running shallows and over glassy pebbles to the far bank. Beneath the shadow of Mag Tor they climbed up to Briganta's Cave; passing under the arch where the roof of a greater cave had long since collapsed, leaving a stand of rock like a huge gateway framing the smaller cavern beyond.

There, on the luscious apron of grass that lay before the cavern, they formed a mirthful, shifting circle, and in its centre were Eleanor, Katherine, Martha and Nan.

Martha began the chant. Laughter faded and voices rose in a soft, eerie chorus. This was Katherine's rite of adulthood, a blessing to empower her before she stepped into the outer world.

Her daughter looked extraordinary in the wavering lantern glow. Slim, shapely, pure of purpose in her white gown; her hair was a black flow over her shoulders, her face a clear bright oval. Eleanor felt proud of her. Girls who were born into the old ways – as Kate had been, and Martha, and Eleanor herself – had something about them, a certain confidence, a swing in their step and a light in the eyes that commanded respect. Women who lived in the conventional world looked on them with envy. The authorities, naturally, were at pains to discourage such envy with savage reminders of damnation.

Eleanor had no patience with the warnings and admonishments that frothed from the pulpits. If women – and men – were drawn to the Serpent Mother, they would come.

She foresaw danger. Their worship was not forbidden – yet. The path of Auset was immeasurably old. It had survived the onslaughts of the Church thanks to a law created for its protection, in gratitude – so the legend went – after a priestess had saved the life of Henry II. No monarch, so far, had dared overturn it.

Even Henry VI, admired for his piety, hadn't summoned the will to challenge them. But the bishops were narrow-eyed and jealous of their power. They missed no opportunity to corrode the sisterhood. There were controls on the Motherlodge. They were forbidden to practise sorcery, which was like forbidding Christians to pray. Magic was practised anyway, in secret, as it had been for eons. Influence, the sisters preferred to call it, since it did not work in quite the supernatural way people liked to imagine.

As long as we are quiet, and make no waves, Eleanor thought, we are tolerated. However much our rulers dislike us, they know that people need us. But if we threw our weight around – as we could – it would give them just the excuse they need. It might only take a change of king for the flood to break, and every last sister of Auset to be hunted, persecuted, slain . . .

Eleanor turned her mind towards summoning strength and protection. Kate was all that mattered now. She was the future.

At the north, east, south and west of the circle, a man or a woman stood facing outwards, calling upon the elemental powers to protect them. Eleanor felt the deep vibration of the earth beneath her feet, the air breathing around them, the crystal rush of the stream. The lantern flames flared brightly. The celebrants danced in a slow circle, parting to let Eleanor and Martha through. Together they led Katherine into Briganta's Cave: the Cauldron Hollow.

The night became a blue funnel, turning slowly about them. Inside the cave they knelt before the statue, the weather-worn and primal form of the Black Mother. There Eleanor offered up perfumed oil for blessing. She slipped Kate's gown from her shoulders, dipped her finger and anointed Katherine upon her forehead, palms and breast. A cross contained within a circle, for the elements. A serpent crowned with a crescent, for the Goddess. A pentagram, the footprint of the Queen of Sheba, for wisdom.

'Great Mother of Darkness, we call your blessing upon Katherine our daughter. Let her go out into the world in safety. Let her walk in wisdom. Pour over her the light of your protection. Open to her your mysteries.'

Katherine felt the cave spinning. A terrible joy rose in her and threatened to burst whirling out of her chest. Everything was blue. The air shimmered. It seemed to her that she was alone, and in the trance she rose, and stepped out of the cave, and found the world changed.

She stood upon the edge of a marsh, where rushes bent to a soft breeze and herons flew silent and luminous into the twilight. A forest fringed the marsh, a tangled and hag-haunted place. The hidden world. Some said it only came into being while the outer world slept, but Kate knew it was always there.

'Great Serpent of the Earth, we bring you our faithful daughter . . .'

Now she remembered the time that the boy had appeared from nowhere. She remembered perfectly his brave, terrified face. She saw in it the older Richard, who had learned to conceal his fear beneath armour.

She was sure she'd understood more as a child than she did now, that she'd somehow forgotten too much and must become that other-self again if she was ever to understand the mysteries.

'Katherine, your daughter and sister, offers herself to your service. Fill her with your power, your healing power and your wisdom . . .'

Something stirred in the marsh. Fear thrilled through her. She had a sudden violent fear that she was to be sacrificed, thrown into the swamp like a maiden into the jaws of a great rumbling dragon. The ground shook.

Katherine cried out.

A huge, stinking man clasped her and she beat against

him like a bird, not knowing what unspeakable act he planned, but knowing it was something worse than nightmare. Then her mother was standing there, filling the air with her chill laughter, and the brute backed away, shrinking as he went.

Eleanor whispered in her ear. *'The power I hold over them is only the power they choose to give me.'*

Her mother was powerful. Kate wanted to be like her. But it was a strange power; not like that of the Earl of Warwick, who could make or break kings as if he were a god. It was a subtle strength that kept them on a knife-edge of survival.

'The fear that gives us our power is the fear that may make them destroy us. Hold it delicately, like fire.'

Katherine's eyes rolled back in her head. A force was winding around her, a huge muscular serpent with endless coils. She was being stripped naked, heart, mind and soul.

She cried out, 'Auset, Great One, behold your servant and lover, behold your vessel Katherine, bearer of your hidden flame. Your blessing on me, for I am worthy, being clothed in the sacred shape you gave me, the sacred flesh and hidden fire. And I go forth in your protection, to do your work.'

'This is the work of Auset, our purpose.' Her mother's voice came from everywhere. *'To heal the sick and ease the dying. To embrace the reviled. To tend your flame and keep open your channels in the earth.'*

Kate saw the pard and the graylix fighting again. They changed, flowing together in something other than hatred and she felt a sharp, transporting pleasure, the pulse of life.

Then she saw, winding away as far as she could see, dozens of Hollows: caves, spings and wells. Some were dark and peaceful, alive with elementals. Others were desolate and barred with cold silver. From every sacred way that had been desecrated, she sensed the Dark Mother's energy pulling away, deep into the earth, lost. And it was not a potential path of the future but one that was already, hideously, unfolding.

Kate moaned aloud.

The serpent-power surged around her, raging and pushing like a wild boar. It flung her to the ground and she thought she was going to die. Then it was gone, sucked away, down into the silent marsh.

She found herself on the floor of the cave, supported by her mother and Martha. Nan was there, holding a chalice of red wine to her lips.

'I saw what's happening,' she said hoarsely. 'I never knew. Something terrible.'

'It's all right,' said Eleanor. 'Breathe deeply. Can you stand up?'

'Yes. Yes, I'm all right.'

Outside stood the glowing, chanting circle of her friends, waiting to embrace her. The chalice was taken from her and passed around, Thomas Copper following with a wine skin to keep it full. Katherine felt elated but shaken. Her innocence had been stripped away.

Eleanor was looking closely at her, concerned. 'What did you see?'

'The Serpent Mother's power is the life energy of the land,' she whispered.

'Yes. And?'

'I felt her anguish. I saw winter falling. The more Hollows we lose, the further away she grows.'

'I know this, I know.' There were tears on Eleanor's face.

'Our enemies don't understand and don't care. But if we cease to tend her spirit, she will withdraw completely. The land will go cold and dry and abandon us, as we've abandoned her.' Kate's passion subsided, leaving her drained, cynical, but steady upon the ground. 'I see that the outer world doesn't care. They think the earth is just cold clay. And I must go out into that, do what little I can to remind them otherwise and be reviled for it.'

'Welcome to the sisterhood,' said Eleanor.

*   *   *

Nan was upset. Her tears brought Kate back to cold reality. 'Why must you leave?'

So Kate told her. They were alone in the meadow plucking wild herbs in the dawn, their skirts silver with dew. Kate went on working as she spoke, to avoid looking at Nan, at the square, almost pretty, open face surrounded by wispy hair, at the expression of concerned amazement. Eleanor's grey cat wove back and forth through Nan's hands, and Nan caressed it absently as she listened.

'May I go with you?' she said at last.

'Not this time,' said Kate.

'But I've always looked after you.'

'Exactly. It's time I learned to look after myself.'

'I see,' said Nan. People thought her simple, but Kate knew they were wrong. Nan's directness had a clarity that was close to pure wisdom. 'But if there is a child, you will not be able to stay with the Countess of Warwick, either.'

Kate sighed through her teeth. 'She and my mother have it all worked out. If that comes to pass, I shall be sent to Dame Eylott in York on some pretext. Once my embarrassment is over, I'll return to the Countess, as if nothing had happened. I shall not bring scandal upon her household. Don't worry. No one will know, neither in my house nor in hers.'

'It is said that the younger a woman is, the higher the babe is carried, so it does not show. Sometimes it may not show at all, right to the end.'

Her guileless reassurance was the one thing that brought Kate, unexpectedly, close to tears. She laughed to hide it. 'Thanks, Nan. That is a comfort.'

Nan frowned. 'And the child?'

Kate saw her anxiety. Nan, of all people, knew what it was to be abandoned. 'It will be brought back here, by some other woman, as if it's hers. Thus my mother will have the care and ordering of its life. It will want for nothing.'

Nan was looking at the sky, her eyes two crescent moons.

'Then he'll be fortunate, as I was. I wonder if my mother cried when she left me?'

Kate dropped her head onto the heel of her hand. 'Nan, there is no child.'

'You don't know that yet. Wouldn't it make you weep, to leave him?'

'No,' said Kate, her jaw set. 'I'll not shed a tear. I made a mistake that must be neatly tidied away. Once it's over I shall never think of it again.'

'You're not that hard-hearted!'

'Oh, but I am,' she answered quietly. 'To survive, I must be.'

This was very strange. I felt sick with fear for Kate, tainted with envy and touched by her courage. Where was the sense in feeling such strong emotions about events that existed purely inside my own daydreams? Still, the story was unrolling as if it had nothing to do with me. I couldn't stop it. I couldn't control which episodes I experienced. But it was awe-inspiring, and brought me closer to Richard than any book ever could.

There were three strands now. One was the story of Kate and Raphael. The second was reality: history books, the places where Richard had lived and the field where he died.

I walked across Bosworth battlefield for the first time; a plain green hump of a field, high and bleak. In winter the hedges looked black and the trees were skeletal. I'd read the arguments over the site of the battle: it was on Ambion Hill, it was further off at Dadlington, it was somewhere else . . . All I know is that the site, the official site, has an extraordinary atmosphere, a stark power, full of ghosts. There lay the dried-up marsh, there the well where Richard took his last drink. There was the stone to mark the place where he fell.

I wept. It seemed unfair. He barely had a chance to prove his worth as king. Why did it matter? It was only history. A cold wind blowing steadily across a Leicestershire field.

Visiting the battlefield unleashed streams of narrative in my imagination. I saw Raphael everywhere. He seems closer to me than Kate. She's oblivious of me, private, keeping her secrets to herself. Raphael, though, I often sense is searching for me, beckoning me with his eyes to come closer and help him. I thought I saw him on the battlefield and my heart nearly choked me. Almost all of Richard's men died with him.

It might be a sign of nascent madness, to see signs and symbols in everything, but I reflect that my name is the month he died: August.

In the visitor centre I bought a poster, a portrait of Richard in rich colours, red, gold and black. It shows a handsome man with a sensitive, serious face. He watches me now as I write.

I found myself looking forward eagerly to each new day, the unfolding of another chapter. I suppose it wasn't healthy that I detached myself from real life, neglected my studies, went into daydreams while people were speaking to me. Well, preferable to taking drugs, but not ideal. Still, there was no way round. I was on a wondrous journey. I could only reach my destination by going through everything with Kate and Raphael.

And the third strand: my night visitor.

My room in the hall of residence is basic: magnolia walls, grey lino, a sink, a lumpy single bed and a cheap melamine wardrobe. Even in the dark, it isn't sinister. A street light shines orange through the thin curtains. Not like my childhood bedroom, which was full of alcoves and mysterious shapeless shadows, ideal raw material for a dreamy child to spin terrors.

But now, caught in the spell, things change. The portrait has added atmosphere, a hovering presence. I lie awake, or imagine I do. I must be dreaming because the room seems dark, all pitch-black velvet. There is something in the shadows. A man is standing there, watching me.

I can't see his face. I'm not frightened because, in the back of my mind, I know he isn't real. If someone real had broken into my room I would have been out of bed yelling in raw panic. This isn't like that.

This is a trance, a half state between sleep and awareness. He comes to me, leans over me. Now a long gleaming face slides into the light. I see dark eyes and midnight hair flowing over him like the cloak of shifting darkness he wears. I can only stare up at him in an ecstasy of dread, not daring to speak in case he vanishes. He gazes back. There is warmth in his eyes, but also intentness, sharp as a sword.

Does he wear deformity as an outwards badge of evil, the shoulders of a vulture hunched above his victim? No. It is only the stoop of his posture as he leans down to me. His body is straight, perfect.

> *For never yet one hour in his bed,*
> *Did I enjoy the golden dew of sleep . . .*

There's no innocence about him. He looks fully self-aware, even self-mocking. He comes not to plead mitigation, but to challenge me. I can never truly know him, but he wants to watch me try, to watch me imagining I grasp the truth only to see it slide away again. I open my arms to the challenge, to him.

Without a word he kisses me, lies down and folds himself around me and into me, like a velvet cloak.

Chapter Five 1470: Isabel

RICHARD
> Ere you were queen, yea, or your husband king,
> I was a packhorse in his great affairs;
> A weeder-out of his proud adversaries,
> A liberal rewarder of his friends.
> To royalize his blood I spent mine own.

Richard III Act I scene 3

The falcon plunged, taking Raphael's heart with her down the arc of the sky. Nothing else existed. There was only the lethal, perfect stoop of the bird through a white crystal sky and the green slope beneath. A sharp cold wind blew, scented with spring and freedom. The falcon met her prey on the wind with a brief *thack* and a whirr of feathers.

A cheer rose from the hunting party. Raphael ran to retrieve the prey, rewarded the falcon with a sliver of meat, whirled the lure and watched her fly again. She was the most magnificent of his master's raptors: tawny-gold with great wings arched like an angel's. He loved the birds of prey: the huge black or white gyrfalcons of dukes, the fire hawk with its red-streaked tail, the dainty merlins that the ladies flew, common sparrowhawks, owls – Raphael worshipped them all.

Here he could forget himself.

Lords and ladies were arrayed against the curve of the hill, small and bright like figures in a tapestry with their birds of prey perched upon their wrists. Behind them rose Lykenwold Castle with the creamy veils of its walls falling from ragged battlements. The huge waterwheels beside it glistened black and bronze, filling the air with a constant plashing thunder as they drove fresh water up to the castle.

Lord Lykenwold was robin-bright among his guests, all laughter and good-humoured energy. The falcon flew low over their heads, drawing gasps. Raphael called her in and she swooped onto his raised gauntlet and settled there, claws cuffing his forearm, her weight perfectly balanced, fierce eyes flaming above the bloodied curve of her beak. The nobles, for whose pleasure he nurtured these birds, were a mere backdrop. The falcon held all his attention.

This had been Raphael's home for the past ten years. He'd led the typical life of a ward, set down among a dozen unknown boys in an icy castle and expected, like a puppy thrown into a torrent, to swim. Together they ate, slept and attended chapel, learned Latin and French, were drilled in the arts of riding, tilting, archery and warfare; and then literature and chivalry, dancing and music to civilize them for their noble families.

Raphael alone had no family to return to. He'd minded once, feeling an outcast, but the sadness had long faded. He was content here. Not happy, exactly – there were too many foggy stretches of nightmare in his memory – but content in his own quiet way. William Lykenwold was a kind lord. There were worse ways to live.

The wind was growing cold. Lord Lykenwold signalled an end to the afternoon's sport. Raphael bowed in acknowledgment, while pages ran forward to relieve the nobles of their various hawks and return them to their mews. The banquet tonight would include a delectable array of roasted songbirds and pigeon pies.

Will Shaw was toiling up the slope towards him, a stocky figure with two slim saluki hounds flowing at his heels. 'Hey, Raffel!' he called, hand raised in greeting. 'You impressed the ladies today.'

Raphael smiled and said nothing. He was tying a hood onto the falcon's tawny head.

Will smirked. 'Don't be coy. You heard the oohs and aahs.'

'That was for the hawks, not for me.'

'If you say so.' Will gave a loose-lipped grin, and winked.

Will Shaw was a few years older than Raphael, a rough and cheerful lad always in trouble of one sort or another. They made an odd pair, the slender taciturn boy and the robust stable hand. Yet Shaw was a good friend.

Raphael still couldn't clearly remember the death of his mother and brother, nor the six months he had lost. Or rather, he was afraid to try. He couldn't bear to be questioned. Nothing would induce him to delve back into that swirling horror. Scarred, he'd become withdrawn and wary, and because he wasn't boisterous like the other wards, he had been a natural target for bullying. He'd been an outcast among them until Will Shaw had befriended him. With his protection, Raphael had grown a tough cold shell to protect himself, which had eventually won the other boys' respect, if not their friendship.

He preferred the company of animals. In that, he and Will were alike.

Will Shaw was one for hounds and horses. Raphael liked all animals, even the graylix, ferocious and foul-smelling beasts that no one else loved. Their very fierceness had made them a status symbol among the aristocracy, reviled yet feared. Raphael thought they deserved higher regard; it was as if they raged against captivity out of sheer pride.

He'd found his place: falconer, groom and graylix-handler to Lord Lykenwold. One day he hoped he would rise to the highest position, Steward of Animals. Raphael accepted this, but there was a chasm inside him: regret for the life he might have had instead, but for a spur of the moment impulse on King Edward's part.

He had never forgotten Richard of Gloucester. Surfacing from his nightmare and looking into the eyes of his saviour, there had been a wonderful sense of recognition. A boy who should have been a lifelong friend, a lord he would have gladly served to the end of his days – and Richard had wanted that, too. All torn away by Edward's thoughtless generosity.

Raphael realized it had only been a boyish fantasy. Of course he could not share the life of the King's brother. Ridiculous idea.

Still, he treasured that image of Richard. A dark child dressed like a king . . . but something more. Serious, radiant eyes, a complex but gracious soul bending all his attention upon Raphael, as if he were the most important being in the world. There was a lot he tried to forget, but not that.

Raphael often wondered about the Duke of Gloucester. He was young and so little was heard of him. It was all King Edward and George of Clarence, their rivalry and their quarrels. They seemed a thousand miles away in their London palaces, simmering in the steamy breath of the great river Isis. But once, King Edward and his royal brothers had stood looking down on Raphael in a hedgerow, and wondered what to do with him. The memory made Raphael smile. He felt braided into history by it.

They touched me, he thought. It was only for a moment, and no one will record the event or remember it, but still, it happened.

'Raffel, a bunch of us are going down into the village tonight,' Will Shaw was saying as they walked towards the castle. 'There's a cask of ale with my name carved on it. I can fit two women apiece on these knees. I'll spare you one, if you behave. So don't tell me you're going early to bed with a posset of warm milk.'

Will had led him on several riotous nights that Raphael had always regretted, especially when he was standing shivering before the henxmaster's wrath the next dawn, his head pounding as if someone were striking his sallet with a hammer.

'Thanks, Will, but no. His lordship's beasts need *someone* sober around them.'

'What sort of excuse is that?' Shaw slapped Raphael on the back, nearly knocking him over. 'Come on, man!'

Raphael sighed. 'I don't want some girl I can't even remember meeting coming up here complaining I've got her with child.'

Shaw leered. 'That danger, mate, falls only to me.' He lowered his voice, oddly serious. 'You know why they're here, don't you?'

'Who?'

He tipped his large, curly-haired head towards the drawbridge. 'Those lords who've come to visit. They're talking about war. Know what a commission of array is?'

'Yes,' said Raphael. 'It means his lordship has to provide the King with a certain number of armed men.'

'Exactly. Lord William knows who salts his stew. He'll take every man who can stand up without a stick. He did last time. A fair few of 'em didn't come back.'

Raphael felt a dull unease. 'How long have we got?'

'A good question. How long have we got?' Shaw threw his arm over Raphael's shoulders. 'Only the Almighty has the answer to that one. We're going into battle, Raffel. We might get through it fine, but we might just as easily get an axe through the guts. That changed your mind about having fun while you still can?'

Katherine had expected an orderly life in the Earl of Warwick's household. After her initial excitement, it had occurred to her that this might be a subtle punishment on her mother's part: a round of prayers, embroidery, gentle duties, stifling boredom. She had not expected to find herself, almost exactly a year after meeting Richard, beleaguered on board ship in the company of his enemy, tossed by an angry sea in the English Channel.

Yet here she was. Cold and salt-soaked, but mercifully a good sailor.

The cabin was dark, washed in a ghastly swaying light. On the bunk, Isabel Neville groaned in childbirth. Her fox-pelt hair hung in strings and her sweat bled into her open, straining mouth. Around them the ship tipped and heaved upon the abyss. Katherine held Isabel's hand through each excruciating spasm, wiped away the sweat, trickling a concoction of raspberry leaf and clary sage onto Isabel's tongue and encouraging her to swallow.

Dull cannon fire drummed in the storm. The Earl of Warwick had brought them to Calais but the Captain of the town, Lord Wenlock – supposedly Warwick's ally – had panicked and would not let them land. Not even for Isabel's sake. The man, Kate decided, was a plain idiot with a heart of stone.

She had never been more frightened in her life. Isabel's maids and her midwife were prostrate with seasickness, fretting over their mistress's plight but too weak to do more than lie on their bunks and lip the ginger paste Kate had ground for them. Isabel's sister Anne was in her own cabin with their mother, exhausted and praying. As for the men – the Earl of Warwick and his son-in-law, George, Isabel's husband – they were barely worth thought. It's their fault, Kate thought angrily, that we are in this wretched mess in the first place.

Someone must be strong. At present there was only Kate.

'How is she?' Anne's long, pallid face appeared in the doorway. Behind her, a strip of sky wheeled and bucked. 'George is asking.'

'This has gone on too long,' said Kate. 'She will need a surrogate after all. Do you know what that means?'

Anne, luminous and unworldly in the doorway, shook her head. The timbers creaked. She staggered, pulling the door half-open and letting in a flurry of rain and spray.

'It means I need you to come in and shut the door!' Kate snapped. Anne obeyed quickly. 'I want you to watch over both Isabel and me. Will you do that?'

Hesitantly Anne nodded. Strange, Kate thought, that the Countess took me in in order to educate me, but here's her daughter Anne, not much younger than me, knowing almost nothing of matters that I've witnessed all my life. Witnessed . . . and, if they only knew it, experienced.

'No,' Isabel said through her teeth. 'I said, no surrogate. George wouldn't want me to. I can do this alone!'

Kate held her wrist so hard her nails bit in. 'If you go on alone, you will die. George isn't the one doing the work! There is a line between brave and stubborn, Bel.'

Another racking spasm. When Isabel could speak again, it was a rasp. 'All right. Enough. Help me, please.'

'Can you really do this?' Anne asked softly.

'I hope so,' Kate mouthed to herself. 'Breathe with me, Bel,' she said softly, sinking down onto the hard bunk beside her and holding Isabel's clammy hand. 'Relax and think of nothing but breathing – breathing. You're safe. I'm here. I'm with you now . . .'

Altered awareness came swiftly upon Kate. The roar of the sea dwindled. The violence of the waves became a gentle weightless rocking in a red mist. And then the first wave of pain came, making Kate tear her throat with cries. Dreadful piercing pain all through her womb and back and shoulders. There was no part of her that did not hurt as she bore down, as if some huge cannon-ball were trying to void itself from her body.

Gods, was it this bad for my mother? She never said, never complained.

As Kate laboured and strained and cried out, Isabel lay with closed eyes, her chest rising and falling with shallow breaths. A surrogate could not take all sensation away, but she could take the worst of it. As if her own body had become the mother's she could sense how the child lay and had the fresh strength to go on forcing it out when the mother's own vigour had failed.

Kate sank deeper into the red void. Deep enough even for the pain to become distant. She must push it away in order to endure it. Her mind reached out for echoes of

121

happier times. She sank into unreality and then into clear memory.

A year had passed since the Countess of Warwick had first taken her home, or rather, to one of the Earl's several impressive homes. Much had happened since then. The household was at Warwick Castle when Katherine had first arrived. A princely residence, into which her mother's house would fit ten times over. The family called it homely, the most comfortable of their castles, but to Kate it was too grand ever to seem friendly. There were great rooms like crimson caskets, guard chambers so full of weapons that they smelled of blood, a great hall lofty enough to befit a king. There were long galleries painted pale gold, where she and Isabel would chase each other like children, playing tag around the fat, enamelled columns.

The Countess had said that, despite her husband's troubles, her household was peaceful. She must have known it couldn't hold true.

Katherine and the Kingmaker's elder daughter had formed an instant bond. On the surface they were unalike: Kate was quiet and watchful, afraid to show anything of her true self in this unknown house; Isabel was noisy and mischievous, with fox-red hair, full of the fire of life. Anne, the younger sister, was self-contained, usually to be found reading, sewing, or in chapel. Kate wondered what went on beneath her serene features, but since Anne never solicited attention, Kate left her alone. That was what she seemed to wish.

Isabel doted on her little sister, but craved a friend in mischief. Kate was recruited. Isabel proved a demanding companion, always wanting games, music, escapades. She was childlike in that way, with too much energy craving release. Sometimes she could be stiffly imperious, at others vulnerable. Although they were close in age, Kate felt herself to be older.

At home, Kate had never been idle. There had always

been too much to do in her mother's demesne. Here, by contrast, the ladies lived like true gentlefolk. Anne Beauchamp had her dual life, which – Kate learned – her husband tolerated, as long as his attention was never drawn to it. Their daughters, though, had nothing to do but wait for husbands. They might sew, read their prayer books, pore over bolts of material for sumptuous new dresses, find a score of distractions, but, really, they were only marking time.

After a while, Kate realized it was more subtle than that and worse. They were waiting for their father to determine the course of their lives to his own best advantage. And all they wanted was to please him.

Most shocking of all, the Countess hadn't introduced them to the path of Auset. Kate had been strictly instructed never to broach such matters with them. From oblique probing she realized they knew nothing at all. All they had been taught was obedience to their father and to the Church. No barefoot walks in the moonlight, no aware-ness that everything around them had its own spirit, no wondrous encounters with those elementals. Their eyes had been sealed shut. Kate was outraged on their behalf, but dared do nothing.

The outer world, as her mother had warned, was an alien place. Larger and grander in every way, yet oddly stark.

'We are haunches of meat,' Isabel whispered once, in a rare reflective mood. She had one hand through Kate's arm, her body pressing slim and warm against Kate's. 'I love my father but I know his schemes. He's so disappointed that he has no sons. More than disappointed; it's a disaster for him. The only answer is for him to marry his daughters to the richest, most powerful men in the kingdom. He is determined to marry at least one of us to a king, and he'll gamble and barter with us until he does it.'

'What king?' said Katherine. 'Edward is taken.'

'And how my father has wept blood over that mar-riage!' Isabel's eyelids were half closed, brooding. 'I know who's intended for me. Edward's brother, the Duke of Clarence. He is fond of me, and a fine, handsome man, but . . .'

'Not a king?'

'He is Edward's heir, until Edward has a son,' Isabel said softly. 'That's why Edward has forbidden us to marry.'

'Will the Earl obey him?'

'I doubt it,' Isabel said, sanguine. 'My father's suffered too many wounds and insults at the King's hands. It's all the fault of the Woodville clan. This would never have happened, if not for them.' She made a noise of disgust. 'No doubt the Queen thought she'd chain George to yet another of her own relatives. But my father always gets his own way in the end.'

'What do *you* want?' Kate asked. The sacrilegious question. As the Countess had suggested, it was impossible to imagine Isabel rushing out and seducing a stranger in order to avoid a political marriage. The shame on the family, Isabel vanishing into some nunnery . . . it could never, ever happen.

Kate still turned hot with the memory of what she'd done. She clung to Nan's words of reassurance and they had proved true: under the full robes she wore, she still looked slim. Sometimes remorse seized her, and she could not believe she would ever get away with it; then her self-possession would return and she knew she would, she *must*.

Worse, Richard of Gloucester had been part of this family. He'd been the Earl of Warwick's ward until a year or two ago. Isabel knew him; Anne knew him. How would they view her behaviour, or his, from the strict cage of their lives?

Luckily, he'd gone to serve King Edward long before Kate arrived and he was unlikely to come again, given the animosity between Edward and Warwick. She was glad. The embarrassment of meeting him would have been excruciating. It would have ruined the wistful perfection of anonymity. Yet she sometimes imagined him walking these corridors, speaking courteously with Isabel or Anne.

If ever they mentioned him, she tried not to listen, although there was no avoiding the impression that their memories of him were fond. In fact, they couldn't find a bad word to say about him. For some reason, this discovery made Kate feel faintly jealous.

'I want to please my father,' said Isabel. 'And I do like George very, very much. But I can only wait, while they argue, and I am driven mad!'

The scarlet ship fell, fell. Lines of pain held Kate steady, like rope. *They argue, and no one wins, and we are brought to this.*

Isabel was running, her russet hair flying in front of Kate as they ran the length of the high gallery. Then she was turning suddenly to hush Kate, and they were colliding in suppressed laughter, their slippers noiseless on the polished boards.

Below, in the crimson light of the great hall, stood the Earl of Warwick and the Duke of Clarence with a dozen armed men around them. Kate had seen the Earl rarely, and always from a distance. No sooner did he arrive than he was leaving again.

Warwick was a blood-red man. So Katherine saw him, with his flushed meaty face, his sharp narrow eyes always observing, needling, brooding. He wore burgundy velvets the colour of clotted blood, and huge rubies on his fingers. His badge of a great black bear made her think of raw meat being torn. Blood and meat. He laughed a lot, and snapped from laughter to rage in the same hard, loud voice. His face was big, with bushy eyebrows that swept up like curved swords on either side, uneven and rogueish. Kate was nervous of him. He was so different from her own gentle father.

He wasn't as alarming as he looked, Isabel assured her. His charity and generosity were legend. But as Kate looked down that day he was every inch the patriarch, the warrior-leader she'd imagined.

He was raging about something, harsh yet controlled. 'It was I that put him on the throne, with my own sweat and wealth, and see how he has repaid me! Made a jackass of me with his marriage, dealing behind my back, removing my brother from his Chancellorship and replacing him with that doddering Stillington, and a dozen other exploits of idiocy. He has proved himself unfit to be king.' The voice fell to a purr. 'He will presently recall that all he has, he owes to me; by then it will be too late. If I can make one king, I can make another. He had better look to me, and tremble.'

All the men were talking at once. Warwick silenced them with one huge hand raised, the other resting on George of Clarence's shoulder. Kate couldn't see much more of the Duke than the top of his fair curly head but his posture was taut, proud, trembling with nervous aggression. 'I can prove that Edward is a bastard. I can prove that George here is the rightful heir to the throne of England.'

'You can prove that the moon is the sun, my liege,' said one of the men. Warwick took his admiring tone at face value, threw back his head and barked with mirth. The murmuring giggles of conspiracy ran among them.

Isabel's fingers dug into Kate's arm. Her eyes were bonfires. 'He is going to do it. He will make George king!'

Kate stared at her. All she felt was an oddly detached shock. 'Just a quarrel, your mother said to mine.'

Isabel shook her head, biting her lip magenta. 'No. It has been more than a quarrel for a long, long time.'

'It's treason, Bel. He can't unseat the King.'

'Why not? He's done it before. He unseated mad old Henry.'

Kate wondered if Warwick, too, were not mad. 'Then what?' she whispered.

'Then I shall be the Queen of England,' said Isabel.

Many things had happened since then. Kate had not

witnessed them all, but had swiftly gleaned the news of each event. In defiance of Edward, Warwick had taken George and Isabel to Calais and married them there. The next anyone knew, Warwick was invading England with an army. He won battles. Queen Elizabeth's own father and one of her brothers were killed upon Edgecote Field; some said by George of Clarence's own hand. Edward, astonishingly, gave himself up as a prisoner to Warwick's brother, George Neville, Archbishop of York. A crafty move. By placing himself under the protection of the Church, he avoided death in battle, or execution afterwards.

Katherine wondered where Thomas, Lord Stanley stood in all this. She wrote concerned letters to her mother and received strangely cryptic replies that all was well; he had not pressed his claim to their demesne. Too busy calculating which side to support, Kate guessed.

An astonishing thing had happened to Kate in those strange months. The news that Warwick had won and now held King Edward captive was unbelievable. Even the Countess and her daughters had been stunned by it. Then one day the castle was suddenly full of men and hounds and Warwick's triumphant blustering. Kate found herself on an errand, the Earl having instructed the Countess to send someone, anyone, to take books to a private chamber.

Warwick's men stood guard outside. Kate entered the room and he was there, the Earl's prisoner: King Edward.

Kate stood like dumb stone as she realized it was truly him, the caged king, so real she could smell his sweat. Even sitting in silence, he dominated the room. Not the ethereal gilded prince she'd imagined, but broader, heavier and overpoweringly real. Long legs with thickly muscled thighs and calves, resting at casual angles. He had dark brown hair shot with gold, restless eyes, and the whitest, most charming smile she had ever seen.

'Hello, who's this?' he said, standing up and dwarfing her.

'Katherine Lytton, Your Grace.' Flustered, she went on one knee to kiss his hand, dropped a book and almost fell over her own skirts. As he helped her up, she suddenly wondered how many women those warm fleshy hands had touched. Hundreds, from what they said of him. The thought was vaguely repellent.

'Considerate of the Earl to send me some entertainment.' He took the books from her and put them aside without a glance. Sitting down again, he cheerfully indicated a footstool, and she sat, condemned to stay and make a gibbering fool of herself.

Then, to her horror, he said lightly, 'Aren't you the Katherine Lytton who had the nerve to defy my Lord Stanley and refuse his son?'

Her mouth dropped open, then snapped shut. Edward grinned. 'That wasn't fair of me. I'm sorry, my lady. I'm too fond of watching people fall over their own feet with shock.'

Words fell from her bone-dry throat. 'I – I'm amazed that you should know about such a small matter, sire.'

'It's not a small matter. I take a keen interest in all my subjects, and I never forget anything. I thought it made me quite a good king, but my lord of Warwick seems to disagree. So, the Stanleys are not good enough for you?'

Kate looked down, acutely uncomfortable. 'I had my reasons,' she said in a small, tight voice, 'Your Grace.'

'And I applaud your bravery in upholding them.' She looked up and realized his amusement was warm, not malicious. 'It takes rare courage to defy a scorpion like Thomas Stanley, believe me. You're right; they're not good enough.' Edward's gaze travelled blatantly over her. 'Still, his poor, poor son. He must have been demented at losing you.'

'He took it very graciously.'

'I'm sure, but still, George Stanley – the most miserable wretch in Christendom!'

'I doubt it.' Kate felt as if she were glowing ruby-red with embarrassment. 'I was sent with books. Can I . . . may I do anything else to aid Your Grace's comfort?'

His eyes narrowed, cat-like, and his smile grew insinuating. 'Most certainly you can. My lord of Warwick is proving a more generous host than I'd given him credit for.'

Kate suspected, for one ghastly moment, that she had indeed been sent to Edward for that reason. She was suddenly too shocked to be afraid of him.

'Would you talk to Anne or Isabel Neville like that?' she said coldly.

Her outrage, and something darker, must have reached her eyes. He actually paled, and sat up straight to look at her.

'Not while their father has several hundred armed men standing around the place pointing spears at me. But if I caught them on their own, and didn't know them, of course I would. It's a terrible habit,' he said, contrite. 'Alas, my sense of humour grows coarse; blame it on the utter boredom of confinement. Please forgive me, Lady Katherine.'

She began to like him then and could see why almost everyone liked him.

'You are forgiven, sire.'

'Entertainment, then.' He sat back, resting one elbow on the chair arm. 'Can you play the psaltery, sing, or both?'

'Passing badly.'

'I'm certain there's no call for such modesty. Won't you play for me?'

It could happen so easily. She would play a song or three; he would be entertained, and ply her with wine, and make her laugh; at some stage he would pull her onto his knee, and there would be nothing she could do about it without causing a dreadful scene. He was attractive enough. She suspected that she would enjoy it. And no danger of pregnancy, since . . .

She swallowed and glanced down at herself. Even now, there was nothing much to see. But afterwards, there would be only the ashen knowledge that she was another conquest among hundreds. Such things never happened without consequences of some degree. Just to say she had bedded the King? It wasn't worth it.

'I don't think it would be a good idea, sire.'

'Is your singing that bad?'

'Truly appalling,' said Kate. 'Would you like me to read?'

'No.' The smile had softened now, and he looked serious. 'Just talk to me for a while. I promise to keep my hands in clerical mode.'

He rested them on one knee, fingers laced together. She laughed.

'So, am I still the King in your eyes?' he asked softly.

'Yes.'

'But not in the eyes of your master, my once-dear friend.'

'The Earl is not my master,' she replied. 'I'm the ward of his wife, and his daughter's companion. I am no one's servant and my opinions are my own.'

Edward's eyes were thoughtful. Warwick painted an increasingly elaborate picture of him as a lecherous buffoon, but the man who sat regarding her was no fool. His voice became very soft. 'Katherine, I know your mother, Lady Lytton. She wrote, appealing to me for help after your unfortunate experience with Lord Stanley. I met her in Northampton a few months ago with her friend, Friar Bungay.'

Kate was shocked. She hadn't known, but then realized it was something her mother might not have wanted to reveal to her in a letter. 'She said she was going to appeal to you, sire. I didn't know she had.'

'I try to help everyone I can, so far as it's in my power. And your mother is a special case. I know of her ... affiliations.'

She stiffened. 'I can't speak for my mother, sire.'

'Be at ease. I don't care what the Church says; I respect

130

what you are. There is a long Plantagenet tradition of association with the old ways for all our public face is painted to appease the Pope. Your mother offered, in return for my protection of her lands and title, her . . . influence. Can I rely on the same from you, my lady?'

Kate felt confident again, on firm ground.

'If you mean . . .' she delved in the front of her robe and brought out the symbol on its chain, the charcoal snake crowned with the moon. He held her eyes and nodded. She hid the symbol again between her breasts.

'Only call me, and I'll come,' she whispered. 'One condition my mother laid on the Countess, that I was to have leave to pass freely in and out of the household. That's my right as a priestess. None will stop me.'

She thought, with a chill, even though I have just agreed to betray my guardian and thus his family, and my dearest friend.

'I won't put you in any danger,' he said, as if he'd read her concern. 'I'll be as subtle as that serpent. But I am coming back, Kate.' He smiled again, and winked. Then, cutting the floor from under her again, 'Have you ever met my brother?'

'The Duke of Clarence?' She thought she was being recruited as a spy now. 'I see him. He never speaks to me.'

Edward was shaking his head. 'No, no, obviously you know George. I meant my youngest brother, Richard, the little dark one.'

Kate didn't know whether to curse Edward for mentioning Richard, or herself for being so transparent. Her face burned through several transitions of colour. 'I don't think so, sire.'

'I only wondered. He's the very devil for keeping things to himself. It took me a week to get this one out of him. Something to do with an exquisite young girl he'd met, who it transpired was a witch, and who frightened seven shades of hell out of him. Do you think he takes such things too seriously?'

'I don't know why you are asking me.'

'Her name was Kate. She had black hair and violet eyes that could light beacons. You look exactly as he described her. It must be a coincidence, of course.'

'What did he say?' she asked desperately.

Edward put back his head and laughed delightedly. 'So it was you! I half thought he'd made it all up, except he's never been one for such fantasies. Good for Dick, Creator bless him. Don't look so worried; your secret is safe with me. The lucky dog.'

Kate stood glaring at him. She wanted to be furious but had a dreadful feeling she was going to spoil it all by laughing. If Edward noticed anything now, it would be utter disaster; but he hadn't. Not a thing. Relief left her shaky. 'What did he say?' she asked again.

One of the guards hammered on the door, making her jump.

'I'll tell you tomorrow, sweetheart, if you promise to come to me again.'

'Yes.'

'Don't forget what I've said,' he added. 'When someone helps me, it's never forgotten. Thank you for the books.'

But she didn't see Edward again. By the next evening, Warwick had spirited him away to a new hiding place.

Shortly after this episode, the shrewdness of Edward's apparent surrender was revealed. While Warwick was drawn north to subdue a rebellion among his own relatives, Edward did some swift deals among the nobility and was restored to the throne. Whether her mother's influence played any part in his release, Kate doubted. The country itself would not endure the limbo in which the Kingmaker had placed it.

A short time later, Warwick and Clarence were pardoned, and everyone was friends again. It couldn't last.

Kate slipped away to York in late autumn of the same year, apprehensive and exhausted from fending off Isabel's protests with excuses and reassurances. Soon, she heard that

Warwick and his son-in-law were stirring fresh troubles. She resisted Isabel's pleading letters for as long as necessary, but the moment Kate could go back to her – two months into the new year, 1470 – she did so. She closed her mind to her own troubles and fled to her lady's side.

She didn't realize what she was going into. On this occasion Edward had gained the upper hand. Suddenly it was Warwick flying into exile with his wife, son-in-law, daughters and servants, this time to seek support in France. Kate found herself bundled along with them, unable to refuse because Isabel needed her. Careless that Isabel was pregnant and Anne often ill, Warwick hauled his daughters about like currency. And here was Isabel, wife of a throneless, disgruntled duke, close to dying of his ambition.

Kate swore to herself that she would never leave Isabel's side again. She was a dancing russet flame, Kate her shadow; they loved each other, failings and all. Now they had truly been through everything together, even the red hell of childbirth.

Memories faded. Reality congealed around Kate, unstable with pain. Isabel was quiet as Kate laboured in her place with steady, unrelenting determination. *You will be born, child, and as Auset is my teacher, I swear that your birth shall not kill your mother!*

Katherine felt something giving, sliding inside her. For a few moments she floated in delirium and was in another place, with the faces of Dame Eylott and her mother hovering over her. Then she snapped back to full consciousness to hear Anne crying out, urgently calling her name. 'Kate! Bel . . . oh, Kate, quickly!'

She was on her feet, dizzy, just in time to catch the babe that oozed slithering into her hands. Isabel uttered a groan and lay blinking tears. 'Is it over?' she asked.

Blue and sickly, the infant boy died within hours.

At last they landed further along the Normandy coast, and

dragged themselves in exhaustion through the steep dark streets of a harbour town. The sky arched grey and wind blown above their bedraggled party.

Kate's impression of the town was of dankness, of cobbled ways twisting between teetering houses, sometimes so steep that she had to grasp the slimy stone of house walls to help herself. They felt mouldering, mossy, all their corners rounded off by the weather. A goblin town from a fairy tale. There were petitmorts everywhere, bigger than those at home. Here they were called *les vulturs anglais*. They sat hunched along the rooftops waiting for fish to scavenge. Even the elementals she sensed or glimpsed seemed foreign, pale and slant-eyed in their hiding places. There were surprises, though. Tiny red flowers with whiskery tendrils growing in crannies, salamanders and little frogs like jewels.

Here Warwick brought them to the house of a friend: a teetering, damp place with warped floorboards, rich hangings that smelled of mildew and narrow pointed windows filled with red and green stained glass. He was busy at once, sending out letters and messengers, as if the nightmare voyage had not touched him. The letters were to arrange an audience with Louis XI. Warwick was begging ships, troops and money of the French king, offering him the earth in exchange.

The following days were dark with rain. Afterwards, Kate could never remember it growing light at all. If the sun had shone, her mind was shadowed with worry over Isabel's fever, George's disappointment, Anne's silent sorrow. Even the Countess had little to say. She had thanked Kate for aiding her daughter and that was all. Her thanks had been stiff, possibly from guilt that she'd been too ill to help, or from resentment that Kate was so healthy. Kate hated to see her powerless and without opinion; the opposite of her priestess-self. She supposed her family had never seen that side of her.

Kate went out into the eerie town, ostensibly searching

for food to tempt Isabel's appetite, but really as an excuse to escape the oppressive atmosphere of the house. Clarence and Warwick argued continually and the women sat tense and apprehensive. If not for Isabel, Kate would happily have abandoned them.

When she returned and went to their private chamber, Isabel came to greet her, rising from her chair with livid cheeks and feverish eyes. At first Kate thought she had been weeping over her baby's death again. The Countess wasn't there. Anne was sitting at the window, looking composed but ghostly, as if she'd had a shock.

'Where have you been?' Isabel demanded.

Kate placed her bundle on a table. 'Shopping, for you and Anne. Sugared pastries, cordials, wonderful herbs I've never seen before . . . What's happened?'

'George is furious. He was in here raving. I can't speak to him when he's like that, and it isn't my fault.' Isabel sat down on the edge of a chest, her shoulders bowed, head drooping. 'It's not my fault!'

'About the child? Of course it isn't.'

'No, not that.'

Kate sat beside her and Isabel moved close, slipping her hand through Kate's arm, as she always did. Her body no longer felt taut with energy against Kate's, but limp and weak. There were brown shadows under her eyes, a staleness on her breath.

'What is it, dear? What's upset you?'

'Father's plans. We suspected he had this in mind but I never, ever believed he'd go through with it. They say old Henry's as peaceful as a monk in the Tower. Why, why must they try to push him onto the throne yet again? It's plain cruel. That bloody woman!'

'Who?'

'Queen Margeurite. Have you any idea how much Father hates her? I shouldn't call her queen. Henry's wife, Margeurite. Her armies killed my grandfather and many other people we loved. He loathes her, despises her!'

'I saw Queen Marguerite once,' said Kate. 'She was all in gold, on a huge horse. I thought she was magnificent. I wanted to be like her.' She added quickly, seeing Isabel's expression of disbelief, 'But on the Yorkists' side, of course.'

Isabel gave an arid smile. 'She's in exile here, sheltered by King Louis.'

'I know.'

'Father means to go on his knees to her and forge an alliance.'

Kate thought of the promise she'd made King Edward. She felt slightly sick.

'Warwick and Marguerite? Would he really do that?'

'You wouldn't think it was physically possible to swallow that much pride,' Isabel said bitterly. 'But yes, he will truly do anything to get Edward off the throne. Even become a Lancastrian. If she and Louis support him, he promises to restore Henry the Sixth.'

Kate saw a long, gelid stare pass between Isabel and Anne.

'Oh, Mother of God,' said Kate. 'Then George won't be king after all?'

'What do you imagine he was ranting about?' Isabel sighed through her teeth. 'He was trying so hard to be calm and measured about it. Then one of us said something soothing, and he exploded.'

'You won't be queen, either.'

'I don't care about that.' She looked again at her sister. 'It seems Anne will be, instead.'

Anne stayed silent, biting her lip.

Isabel went on, 'Father plans to marry her to Marguerite's son, Prince Edouard. He's explaining everything to my mother now. I just feel sick. It's outrageous, but what can we do?'

'Anne?' said Kate. 'Do you want this?'

The younger girl exhaled and half-turned to face them. 'Have you two quite finished? I've told Bel, there is no point in her getting upset about it. We must accept what Father wants for us. You're looking in the wrong place for happiness. It's not about getting what we want, it's about submitting to the Creator's will.' Then she dropped her head. A sob broke out of her, and tears fell into her lap. 'The truth is, I would rather I'd drowned in that hellish storm than marry Marguerite's spoiled son.'

'Oh, dearest . . .' Isabel began, but Anne silenced her with a look, a rare flash of bright, cold determination.

'However, now it's said that's the end of it. I am going to do whatever Father wants with all the good grace and humility I can muster. We are Nevilles, Isabel. Of course we should marry kings.'

The cathedral was huge and flooded with pale gold light. Doves fluttered up through nets of sunlight. Katherine sat open-mouthed at the spectacle of the Lancastrian court in exile. Everyone wore glittering clothes patterned with red roses. French was murmured all around her. There was the Earl of Warwick in a position no one would ever have believed, standing alongside the Earl of Somerset and other men who'd been his bitter enemies on the battlefield. There was his daughter Anne, ethereal and dignified, being joined in marriage to a big, plain blond youth who seemed unreasonably fond of himself. The Bishop who conducted the service, adorned with saffron silks, gold and jewels, looked like an overdecorated vase. His mitre was so high that it put Kate in serious danger of being ejected from the cathedral for laughing.

And there was Queen Marguerite. Kate couldn't believe she was looking at her. She was an icon, unreal. Not as tall as Kate remembered, nor as majestic. In fact, she seemed a gaunt figure, ten years older, the glorious hair turned grey and the hard face sunken against the skull. Years of frustrated ambition sat in her expression. Yet she still looked like a goddess to Kate, but of the worst kind – one of war and cruelty.

There was little joy in the service. The smiles were strained. Isabel sometimes wore a look of plain incredulity at the fact that her father could have kissed Marguerite's slippers to seal this hellish bargain. George of Clarence looked murderous throughout. But there was an atmosphere of suppressed excitement. It was a new beginning. Enemies had become allies. Enemies would swallow their loathing and slide into bed together, if it brought the achievement of their dreams.

The music was exquisite, almost making Kate cry if she closed her eyes and forgot where she was. She made a quiet appeal to the magnificent statue of the Blue Virgin Mary, the only aspect of the Goddess that was acknowledged here. Sweet Mother, protect your daughter Anne, let her be happy. Forgive me for being here. Please don't let this hurt either Anne or King Edward.

A prayer was said in French, entreating Almighty God to let this divine union herald Lancastrian victory; and the capricious divinity smiled upon them.

Within months, Henry VI was back on the throne of England, and Edward had fled into exile.

Chapter Six 1471: Raphael

'What is your favourite weapon, Your Grace?' asked Ratcliffe.
'An axe,' the Duke told him. 'One so seldom has to hit twice with it.'

Patrick Carleton, *Under the Hog*

Along the slope of a hill the army waited, looking at a swirling white wall. Vapour came from Raphael's mouth to thicken the mist, yet he was sweating. His armour felt heavy, his skin soapy under its weight.

All night Warwick's cannon fire had shaken the ground, overshooting King Edward's troops but ensuring they had no sleep. Even then the mist had been gathering, wisps layering the air like summoned elementals. By dawn, the fields and woods lay submerged, a drowned valley under a lake of thick, wet vapour.

Somewhere in this sea of milk stood the enemy: the Earl of Warwick with his troops; his brother Marquis Montagu commanding the centre; their Lancastrian allies the Earl of Oxford and the Marquis of Exeter on the flanks. They were close, Raphael knew, but nothing could be seen. Both armies had taken up their positions in darkness but now the growing light gave them no help.

He was in half-armour for ease of movement, with one gauntleted hand on the harness of two graylix, Tyrant and Teaser. He wore a breastplate shaped long over the thighs for protection, sleeves of padding and chain mail, leather breeches and boots, a surcoat with Lykenwold's colours, or and azure. Hung about him he had his axe, sword, dagger and shield. Will Shaw was with him, and a couple of apprentice handlers, solid lads with cool nerves, each holding a couple of beasts. He envied their more basic garments, long padded jacks which, they claimed, were easier to move in and better protection against sword and arrow than armour. They were positioned just to one side of the front rank of archers, a poor place to be when arrows began flying.

The meaty, sweaty stench of the animals was strong and the archers nearby kept a cautious distance, averting their eyes from the nearly human, cruel and knowing faces of the graylix. In the unnatural fog, even the beasts were quiet.

Raphael's mouth was dry, his sallet heavy and confining upon his head. This was his first battle. He'd been nervous earlier, but now the marching and the waiting had gone on so long he felt merely uncomfortable, tired and impatient. All around him was a murmur of sound: the clatter of armour, men clearing their throats, horses fidgeting and pawing the ground. Far away to their left, King Edward commanded the centre and Lord Hastings the far flank, but they might as well have been in another county in the cold wreaths of fog.

Raphael roughly knew the disposition of troops on his own flank: the well-equipped archers in front; behind them the higher-ranked men-at-arms in full armour; bill-men and halberdiers in livery; down to the poorest foot soldiers who'd come in whatever padded jackets they could find, armed with cleavers or pitchforks. At present, though, he could see no further than the nearest three ranks of men. Their helmets gleamed dully under a coating of dew. Their longbows were a stiff winter forest. Occasionally one would cough or shift his weight, otherwise they were grimly silent.

Lord Lykenwold's men had been put on the right flank under Gloucester's command. Raphael was glad, although he'd only glimpsed the Duke at a distance, and knew he might be dead before he had a chance to see Richard again. Gloucester was inexperienced, and the blood-red Earl of Warwick was a terrifying opponent who had crushed Edward's supporters at Edgecote Field. Raphael imagined the crushing as literal. Armour smashed like snail-shells, blood trails silvering the grass around the broken bodies.

Edward had returned from exile and taken back the throne without resistance, while Warwick – caught unawares – had hidden himself in Coventry and waited for his supporters to regroup. It was said that poor King Henry had given up the throne graciously, even gratefully. Now Edward had intercepted Warwick at Barnet, forcing him to give battle before Marguerite arrived with reinforcements.

There was a muffled thump of hooves. Lord Lykenwold appeared through the mist, mounted on a huge black destrier with a long rippling mane and a tail that brushed the ground. Most of the lords and commanders would go into battle on foot, to reassure their men that they would not turn tail and flee if things went badly, that they would fight and die beside them. Lykenwold was one of the few who was mounted for the swift dispersal of commands.

His horse was caparisoned in blue and gold. It danced, nostrils flaring at the scent of graylix. Lord Lykenwold's armour, too, was blue and gold, the colours swirling like oil upon the metal plates. He was slender, bright and energetic, a dragonfly; beneath the raised visor his face looked small and pink.

'Not long, lads,' he said, reining in the horse. 'Courage. Remember who we're fighting for, even with this wretched weather.' His conversational manner always had a way of reassuring them. 'King Edward reckons this fog is worse for the enemy than it is for us.' He winked.

'How's he make that out, your lordship?' asked Will Shaw.

'God's on our side, of course. Also something to do with the fact that we've got an extra four thousand men, which Warwick's lost. We've the Duke of Gloucester to thank for that, though how he managed to persuade the Duke of Clarence back to Edward's side, I'll never know.'

'Well, Clarence just goes along with the last person who spoke to him, doesn't he?' said Will Shaw, with a smirk.

'Even Clarence isn't that feather-headed, Will,' said Lord Lykenwold. 'He's been made to see sense, that's all.'

One week ago, Lykenwold's army had reached the town of Warwick and Raphael had seen, at a distance, the brothers meeting. The two groups had met on the road, their great horses with their arched necks resembling creatures in a tapestry. Clarence had appeared as a bright and profligate figure, with white armour and a flying cloak of cream velvet resplendent with the tails of silver foxes. Gloucester was his opposite: dark and spare, a raven.

It was the first time Raphael had seen Richard since childhood. He hadn't expected the sight of him to rouse such a deep, powerful feeling of excitement. It was like the first glimpse of a legendary king or a saint, unbearably moving. He couldn't breathe. Clarence was the flamboyant one, but it was Richard of Gloucester who drew all Raphael's attention, as if he were some mysterious icon of shining black stone. The brothers had embraced and ridden away together.

'I wonder what they said to each other?' Raphael murmured.

'It's not hard to guess,' said Lykenwold. 'An appeal to brotherly love and solidarity.'

'More like the rewards Clarence'd get from Edward if he came back,' said Will.

Lykenwold grinned narrowly. 'Not to get his head struck off was reward enough, I'd say. They say that young Gloucester has a tongue of velvet that would charm the Devil himself into doing good.'

'I believe it,' said Raphael.

'May we be as glad of it as Warwick is miserable,' said Lykenwold, shortening the reins.

'Warwick the Kingshafter,' said Will, and Lykenwold

rode away laughing. Within two strides, he was lost in the pearly wall.

'Wonder if the other side have got graylix?' said one of the apprentices, high-voiced.

'They say not,' Raphael answered. 'Nobles can only keep them under royal licence, and the Lancastrians have all had theirs revoked. Warwick never used them anyway.'

'That's summat,' said Will.

Somewhere in the cloud, a trumpet spoke. Tyrant and Teaser rose on their haunches, growling. Raphael's arm ached from holding them.

'All right, lads,' he said, switching hands and rubbing the backs of their skulls to soothe them.

There was movement in the smothering greyness. Captains were shouting orders, their voices muffled. One of them must be Richard's, but he couldn't tell which. A shout sounded, closer, and a sudden storm of arrows was released by the archers beside him. The rattle and *whoosh* of them was startling; when it ended, there came no answering rain. A shiver went through him. Men muttered. Tension drew bow tight.

Tyrant stood on muscular hindlegs, froth dropping from his unmuzzled jaws.

Above the ranks of soldiers the mist thinned briefly and Raphael glimpsed King Edward's banner far away, the Sun in Splendour, swaying and moving uphill. Closer, a white boar ramped on a cobalt banner, then vanished.

The archers were dropping aside to let men-at-arms through. The trumpet sang the command Raphael had been waiting for.

'Now!' he said.

Harnesses were unclipped. Four couple of graylix went roaring into the fog, and were lost. Raphael, Will and the two lads stood undecided for a few moments, like archers who'd loosed all their arrows. Then Lykenwold was yelling, and the foot solders behind them were moving forward, and they were caught in the flow, running uphill over wet, ridged ground. Raphael positioned his buckler on his left arm, held his axe in his left hand and drew his sword with the right. His heart began to race, with either fear or exertion, he couldn't tell. All sensations slid into one.

There was nothing but milky cloud around them and confused shouts. The fog seemed full of elementals: eyes, or a hand, or half a face kept forming from vapour and vanishing again.

'Where the bloody hell's the enemy, then?' Will Shaw said through his teeth. 'Bloody Nottingham?'

They were running into nothingness. He saw the dim shapes of graylix, circling, confused. They were crude weapons, painstakingly trained to run among the enemy and cause havoc, terrifying horses and foot soldiers alike. They could have a devastating if brief effect. But they were only flesh and blood. Raphael knew that at least two-thirds of them would be slain.

'Christ,' Raphael panted. 'You know what's happened? Must've drawn up our troops too far over.'

The graylix were racing off to the left, and became swallowed in the fog again. There was a yell, 'Wheel left! Left!'

Lykenwold came galloping along the lines.

'Wheel around!' he shouted, enunciating carefully through laboured breaths. 'We've overlapped Exeter. Our forces are too far over to the right. We're going to manoeuvre left towards him and attack him in the flank. He'll not be expecting it. Follow Gloucester's banner!'

'I would if I could bloody see it,' said Will Shaw.

Raphael ran on, mouth sand-dry and his throat sore. Will was on his left, a man called John, whom he knew slightly, on his right. They were on the far fringe of the lines and had to sprint as the whole formation swept round into position. They were running through a gully, wet grass squelching underfoot, tussocks tripping them. Then uphill, steeper and steeper, towards noise.

He was more apprehensive than frightened, looking no

further into the future than the next few steps. He felt like throwing off his armour, just to feel cold air on his skin.

The screams of the horses and the shouts of the men brought down by his graylix pack were ghastly. He couldn't see them, could only see the surface writhing of helmeted heads and shoulders, billhooks slicing the sea of mist. A mass of men – Exeter's – were engaged with the edge of King Edward's vanguard. In dismay, they were turning to find Gloucester's men about to crash into the fray from the side.

All around Raphael, the sounds grew loud and harsh. Men were roaring battle cries, beating their weapons on their shields to affright the enemy. On his left, Will Shaw was yelling square-mouthed, unrecognizable, a berserker. On his right, John was also horribly transformed.

A few steps on, he saw the first dead graylix. It was curled up like a puppy and its wounds were crimson flaps in the mole-velvet of its coat. Raphael felt as though he'd been struck across the stomach. It was Teaser. Hideous, devilish beasts, most people thought them – respected, feared, but expendable. If Raphael survived today, he'd be going home to train a fresh pack of cubs to the same end.

'Raffel!' Will Shaw barked over the noise. 'Don't mind that. Reckon the Devil sent this fog? At least the Devil fights for York, so they say.'

Ghost-shapes turned solid. Huge, heavy, panicked soldiers were charging towards them, shoulder to shoulder, screaming from contorted faces. Raw fear was hammered into rage. Raphael began to scream too, tearing his throat, beating his sword upon his shield. The whole world roared. He was deafened, terrified, mindless.

Arrows thudded around them. He tripped over something on the ground and realized it was a dead man who'd nearly brought him down: one of Gloucester's, with an arrow stuck through his neck.

Three seconds later, the front lines clashed. A man came at Raphael out of the greyness like a bull, face bestial, sword swinging. Raphael's heartbeat was choking him. No time to think. He heard himself yelling as he parried, all his training forgotten yet still there by instinct. The sword swung over him as he ducked. He chopped upwards with the axe and the man fell, gurgling. Raphael stared at what he'd done, jumped over the man's feet, met the next. Beside him Will Shaw was grunting as he swung his axe. His opponent sprawled headlong. The jet of blood hit Raphael and two men next to him.

This was terrible. Worse than he'd ever expected. He was mad with fear and so were the soldiers he fought, but their madness was terrifying. The taste of blood caught in his throat. Pain lanced his arms but it was only the pain of fatigue, and they had barely begun.

The battle was ferocious. Gloucester's men were thrusting forward and Exeter's holding their ground, trying to force the Yorkists back into the gully that lay behind them. Raphael knew if they were pushed down there, they would be overwhelmed. It was hard to be sure who had the advantage in the clinging fog.

He heard Richard's voice, yelling hoarsely, rallying them to hold and not give ground. It held Raphael steady. He took blows on his sallet and shoulders. He was knocked over onto one knee and the man beside him leaned down to pull him back to his feet. Raphael looked up and saw John's face squashed and plum-red beneath his helmet.

'All right, mate?' he said. And fell, a stray arrow taking him straight through the centre of the face.

Raphael reeled back in horror, and at the same moment was defending himself again.

The fighting went on and on, lumbering, inescapable. Battle cries fragmented into shrieks of anguish. The world closed down to an amorphous grey sphere where one man after another, as desperate as himself, tried to kill him; and yet – more through their ineptness than his own skill – reeling, drinking his own sweat, he was still on his feet.

Shapes resolved in the murk. Raphael, alone for a

moment, saw Lord Lykenwold on his black destrier, assailed by Lancastrian foot soldiers. He was swinging wildly to either side of the saddle using an axe almost as big as himself. One man fell, clutching his face with bloodied hands. Raphael shoved past knots of fighting men to go to his aid too late. The dragonfly was unhorsed. Raphael saw him fall, his armour dented like tin and blood escaping at the joints. He heard the dull clank of blows rained upon Lykenwold even after he'd fallen. He heard the Lancastrians cheer.

A red rush of disbelief and panic seized him. He raised both sword and axe and ran yelling at his lord's killers. One turned to engage Lykenwold's esquires but the remaining two were ready for him. They had the hard faces of veterans. As Raphael planted his feet and swung at them, he felt he was about to die.

A dark bulk leapt in from the side. It took down the first Lancastrian and tore out his throat with a horrible crunch of bone and tendon. The second man saw the graylix and backed away in shock, his halberd lowered as if to spear the beast. The trembling point made figures of eight on the air.

'Come on, then, you bastard,' he snarled.

The graylix sprang clear over the weapon and brought him down. Its weight must have crushed the breath out of the man's chest because his screams were weak and muffled, and swiftly cut short. The graylix was still chewing a rag of flesh as it came towards Raphael. He saw then that it was Tyrant.

The beast circled him, keeping his face turned towards him, and proved to Raphael that what everyone believed of graylix was wrong: they did know loyalty. Tyrant had avenged Lykenwold and protected his handler.

The graylix's presence made a space around him. Raphael ran to his lord, raised the visor and found the bright eyes staring straight at him, lifeless in blood-drowned sockets. He recoiled, fighting for breath. Three of Lykenwold's esquires who'd survived shouldered him aside and made to carry their lord's corpse from the field. They were grim-faced with shock.

'And get that thing in harness!' snapped one, tilting his head at Tyrant.

Raphael had no chance. As he sheathed his sword, Lykenwold's horse came running straight at him, bolting in terror. By reflex, Raphael dropped his axe and caught the reins. The destrier was immensely strong, he couldn't hold it, and was dragged along for a hundred yards or more.

By the time Raphael managed to bring the horse to a halt, there was a hush around him, nothing but soaked grass, grey trees and wreathes of mist. He'd lost his bearings. He held the horse's reins and did his best to calm it as it swung in circles round him, eyes wild, rippling mane heavy with moisture. It responded to his touch as Raphael stood stroking the soft muzzle. Such a relief to be out of the battle. He could barely stand from exhaustion. The idea of going back in was unbearable. He thought he could hear trickling water, faint voices. The fog was beginning to drive him mad. To drink fresh running water, then to mount and flee . . .

He wasn't as far from the field as he'd hoped. Vague in the murk, he made out a knot of battle captains nearby, a white boar banner. A knight came running towards him, as if his full armour weighed nothing. The armour was made of bronze scales, each edged with gold, but it was black with dew and running with trails of water. As he reached Raphael, breathing hard, he put up his visor and revealed a savage, grim face.

It was Richard of Gloucester.

He spoke urgently, panting, 'The horse?'

'Yes, take it, sir,' said Raphael, but Richard was already mounting. The destrier plunged and leapt about despite Raphael's attempts to hold him steady.

'Exeter's fighting like a graylix,' Richard said quickly. 'I won't let him push us down into that gully.'

Raphael was sure Richard hadn't recognized him. No

time to ask. As Richard settled in the saddle and took control of the horse, the fog thinned briefly and revealed, where the meadow fell away into the steepness of the valley, a dip in the ground half-concealed by bushes. There were three figures there, a friar and two women kneeling before a mass of rocks. Sunlight washed the tableau. The three had their eyes closed, mouths moving in a whispered spell. A spring issued from the rock, and set into a niche above it was an idol: a grotesque stone goddess, fat and powerful.

It appeared as if mist was exhaling from the spring – if not from the mouth of the goddess figure itself. The illusion roused a powerful, eerie sense of fear within Raphael, and even more strongly, dismay that Richard had witnessed the ritual. No one was meant to see it.

Then one of the conjurers opened her eyes, and stared straight at Raphael. Her eyes were bright violet-blue. He knew her – and was certain she knew him.

The fog wreathed more thickly than before, and the sorcerers were gone behind an impenetrable curtain.

Raphael looked at Richard. The young Duke's face was severe and he gave Raphael the briefest glance as he slammed down his visor. 'God keep you,' he said. Then he was away, the magnificent black horse leaping off its haunches and kicking up clods of earth. In seconds, his silhouette had turned from dark to white in the fog veils.

Raphael ran after him. Every fibre of him protested. He was staggering with tiredness. Revulsion rose sourly in his throat and his sword felt too heavy to lift, but if Richard would not give up, neither would he.

Tyrant reappeared to shadow him and seconds later he was in the thick of the fighting again. He was beyond fear now, intent only on following the white boar banner. The fighting had gone on for over two hours now; men were falling on both sides from fatigue if not from wounds. Raphael pushed on and found Will Shaw, still in action, shaken, exhausted but not beyond a few sardonic quips.

Mounted, Richard rallied his fractured lines into a solid force. And at last, Exeter's onslaught began to collapse. His men were falling back, fleeing.

Close to Richard, Raphael gained a rise in the ground and saw, as if through watered milk, the spread of the battlefield. It was an astonishing sight. Thousands upon thousands of men clashing in shining waves. Banners swaying back and forth. Messengers from King Edward reached Richard, and the news spread through the ranks: Warwick's ally Oxford had overlapped Lord Hastings' flank – as Richard had overlapped Exeter's – and had put Hastings' forces to flight and pursued them into Barnet. In the centre, Edward and Clarence were holding firm against Montagu but Oxford was returning to add his weight to the Lancastrian side.

'Raffel, look at that!' said Will Shaw.

If King Edward had claimed that this fog was worse for the enemy than for him, it seemed he had occult knowledge after all. Sunlight silvered helms, spear tips and standards, while the soldiers themselves waded through shoulder-high vapour. The battle had shifted on its axis. Montagu's men were now positioned where Oxford had expected Edward's to be, and Oxford, not realizing, launched his attack upon the wrong side. In the haze, Oxford's streaming star banner was readily mistaken for Edward's sun. Montagu and Oxford, allies, turned blindly upon each other.

Raphael thought the fighting would end quickly when both sides realized, but it continued.

'They must each think the other has turned traitor,' he said. He was drunk with tiredness, mouth and throat and lungs as dry as fire.

'That's it, it's over!' Will said gleefully. 'The day is Edward's!'

Raphael had bent down to clip a chain onto Tyrant's harness when he felt a jag of fire searing his arm. Black and red stars sparked on the fog and through them he glimpsed the sheen of armour and weapons, the flutter of a Lancastrian surcoat as the mounted knight who'd struck him down fled the field. Stones flew from the horse's hooves and spattered him in vicious rain as he fell.

A young lad, Friar Bungay's servant, came skidding into the hollow to tell the sorcerers the news. The battle was reaching its end. Warwick's armies had collapsed and were retreating in disarray.

Kate kissed her mother, leaped to her feet and ran into the mist without explanation or permission. She had seen Raphael – or at least, a young man who looked uncannily like her memory of him. She had to find him. He had seen them at work. She knew what Eleanor would ask her to do; to silence him.

Minutes later, she wished she hadn't set out. The mist was still treacherous, even to her. She could hear men shouting, some in distress that was terrible to hear. Nervously she skirted the edge of the field, keeping her distance from the flitting shapes and sounds. As she angled further away from the battlefield towards Wrotham Wood, a thick silence enveloped everything. The pale broth was full of writhing spirits that seemed to beckon and reach out with smothering arms . . . but not to her.

Footsteps began to shake the ground. Kate froze. A man was running in her direction, so close she could hear his labouring breath. He came out of the chill whiteness, a big man, lumbering in his armour. His surcoat was torn, his helmet gone, his face crimson.

It was the Earl of Warwick.

His gaze clipped her. There was a flicker in his eyes, recognition or dumb fear, but he didn't pause and she wasn't sure he'd truly seen her at all. She stood dazed as he staggered past and vanished into the sheltering greyness of the woods.

Twenty yards behind him came a score of Yorkist soldiers on foot. They ran nimbly and their swords were drawn.

Half a minute later, she heard echoing from the woods a single, bellowing cry.

Pain brought Raphael awake. It was less sharp than the pain that had felled him but somehow deeper, more sickening. He was lying in a dark chamber with tallow light flickering off the walls. A thick odour of sweat, blood and damp stone filled the room but he'd been breathing it so long it was only a tang congealed in the back of his throat. Raising his head, he saw he was in what appeared to be a monk's dormitory with rushes strewn on the floor. Daylight gleamed through oiled cloth over a tiny window. There were three other men on pallets, their limbs wrapped in reddened bandages. Two were grumbling to each other, the third lay silent. Against the far wall, a friar sat chanting from a prayer book. He looked like a tiny lichened statue.

Raphael shifted and the pain in his left shoulder took his breath away. It was a crab-like mass of fire, spearing his neck and arm, which now rested in a sling. He tried to piece together what he could recall of the battle. Surreal chaos. Meeting Richard of Gloucester on the edge of the hollow where the sorcerers lurked and giving him the horse, his dead lord's horse . . .

The grinning face of Will Shaw loomed over him. Raphael reached up with his good hand and grabbed his arm. 'Lykenwold's dead,' he said.

'Yes, Raffel,' Will said gently, the grin extinguished. 'But you're all right, eh?'

'I think so. And you?'

'Not a scratch. I'm just born lucky, me.'

'And the graylix? Tyrant?'

'He's fine, the old bastard. Three out of the eight's not so bad; I got 'em back in cages. No one would even ask, except you.'

'You can't tell me you don't have just a little sneaking respect for them, Will.' Raphael's throat felt rusty.

'Well. Never mind that. You've got a visitor. Said he's

been looking for you all day.' The thick mousy eyebrows flicked up in dramatic astonishment.

'Who?'

Will slipped away without answering and another man came out of the shadows and sat down on a stool beside his pallet. Raphael started. It was Richard of Gloucester who sat there, looking as worn out and dispirited as Raphael felt. A gentle, ghost-like face smiled down at him, grey eyes tired amid the sooty darkness of brows and lashes. He looked serious even when he smiled. Thick sable hair exaggerated his pallor. He sat with his elbows on his knees, a coat thrown loosely over his arming doublet and hanging open. Only the richness of the coat, burgundy and black with a device of roses sewn in white and silver, made him look out of place.

'Iesu's blood, Raphael, it's really you. I knew I recognized you on the field.'

'Your Grace.' Raphael was overcome, couldn't find anything sensible to say. He tried to rise, but the fire in his shoulder made him gag.

'No. Rest.' The Duke put out a quick hand to stay him. 'They tell me it's a bad blow you've taken, but not an open wound. That bodes well. I hope you've been well-tended. If not, these friars will answer to me for it.'

Raphael had only the haziest memory of being carried here, three quarters unconscious with pain, and his armour being stripped from him. He wondered if he were dreaming with fever. It wouldn't be the first time his mind had played cruel tricks on him. He closed and opened his eyes, but Richard was still there, solid contours just visible in the darkness. The white boar badge on his shoulder seemed to float, detached. 'Thank you, my lord, but I'll be fit to get up as soon as this pain eases as little.'

'I hope so.' Richard looked intently at him. 'Gods, the day was witched.'

'In Edward's favour.'

'It would appear so. I came to thank you for the horse.

I can't claim it saved the day, but it certainly helped, more than you can know. I'm sorry about your Lord Lykenwold.'

The grey eyes cut into him and Raphael dropped his gaze, awkward and still half-choked with pain. 'He was a good man.'

'I'd hate to think that Edward had sent you to a lord you hated.'

'He didn't.'

'I'm glad, because I've often thought about you – the angel in the hedgerow.'

Raphael could barely answer, not without sounding an idiot. He managed to say with dignity, 'I never forgot. I didn't expect a duke, however kind, to remember me.'

Richard gave a long, slow sigh. 'Raphael, my brother has won the day, but at great cost. I have seen sights today I never thought to see. Half of my esquires, my dear friends, were cut down around me. The Earl of Warwick is dead. Edward had commanded him to be taken alive, but the command never reached the hot-blooded Yorkists who pursued and slaughtered him. I was fighting against him, I know, but that only seems to make his death less bearable.'

'Creator acquit him,' murmured Raphael.

Richard fell silent for a time, looking down at his hands. His posture was one of beaten, human despair. Raphael wanted to say something, to put a hand on his shoulder as any soldier might do to another. Instead he was paralysed.

Eventually Richard continued. 'You needn't be amazed that I came to find you, but since you are, that is why. I've been searching all afternoon for anyone I know who might be lying wounded, not dead.'

'Have you found any?'

'A fair few, Creator be blessed. And you say you'll be fit to rise when the pain eases?'

'Yes.'

'Good, because I would like you to come with me.'

Raphael gaped at him.

Richard rested his chin on his hand. 'Will you?'

'Your Grace, I'll rise from bed this minute, with all my heart, and follow you anywhere; but do you know how I served Lord Lykenwold?' The Duke waited for an answer, the sharp eyes demanding upon him. Raphael sensed he might not always be an easy master. 'I was his graylix handler.'

'Then you're a braver man than most.'

'Most seem to think there's disgrace in handling such rude beasts.'

'Do you?'

Raphael thought of Teaser and the other dead beasts, thrown in sacrifice to aid King Edward's victory, of Tyrant's courage. He hoped Will Shaw had recaptured all those that had lived. Running loose, they'd be shot or speared on sight – before they killed either sheep or child, he hoped. 'They have their own nobility of character, like the wolf . . . or the wild boar.'

Richard smiled again. His expression was tired, but warm. Raphael felt he was being tested, and didn't mind; he could only submit himself fatalistically to the Duke's scrutiny. 'That's well said. But you do yourself an injustice. You were also his falconer, I understand, and skilled with all animals. Yes, I have been making enquiries.'

'I love falcons above anything.' Raphael spoke with feeling. The powerful shadowy bonds between him and the Duke were irresistible.

'Well, so do I,' Richard said softly. 'From all accounts, you served your lord well.'

Raphael looked straight into his eyes. 'The only lord I was ever meant to serve pulled me out of a ditch when I was eight years old.'

Richard's forehead creased. 'Are you a believer in destiny? A sorceress told me once there was no such thing. We make our own fate. But sorcerers are deceivers.'

'I don't know, but I know a good friend when I see one,' said Raphael.

The Duke laughed. The rims of his eyes shone red. 'Indeed, so do I, for they are very rare. Well, you had better heal quickly, if you are going to come with me. There will be more battles yet. Warwick is dead, but Marguerite is on her way.'

The glitter of his eyes held determination as much as grief, Raphael thought. He could feel his injury burning, healing under the very force of his will to recover. He bent his head to hide his own tears and kissed the Duke of Gloucester's hand, swearing loyalty to the end of his life.

'There's Will Shaw,' he said, suddenly remembering. 'The man who brought you to me. He's been my only true friend.'

'Bring him with you. He can be your squire, as you are mine, if he's agreeable.'

'I think he will be. Thank you.'

'I have others to see. Sleep now, and I'll come back before nightfall,' Richard said quietly. 'I'm glad we met again.'

The Duke must have put the fear of God into the brothers, for they hovered solicitously over Raphael with broth and wine, with damp fragrant towels and herbal brews, as if he had been a duke himself. He slept in strange dreams of horror and bliss. When he woke again, with a start of obscure fear, he found a different face hovering over him.

A young woman. Her face was a cloud, bright as the cloth she'd folded nun-like over her head. She was one of the three sorcerers he'd seen on the battlefield. She had the self-sufficient bearing of a wise one, a member of the sisterhood who moved under the surface of the world, protected by occult armour. But he knew her from long before then, through other fogs too painful to penetrate. Her face had lengthened out of its childish roundness but it could never be forgotten. Her black hair was escaping wildly from underneath the cloth, her irises two butterfly-blue moons glaring down at him.

'Is your name Raphael Hart?' she whispered.

She had searched half the day, through tents and hovels where the wounded lay, passing weary soldiers all along the roads, common and noble alike not too weary to give her a crude compliment or an invitation as she passed.

The shock of Warwick's death had not sunk in. Later, she would go back to Isabel and find out, like the slow teasing of fleece into yarn, what it might mean. When she'd first been seduced by Edward into promising her aid, her immediate dread had been of betraying the Earl, and being found out. Since George of Clarence had returned to the King's party – taking his wife and household with him – that danger had been averted. Still, the shock of knowing Warwick was dead . . . how could such an immense character be dead, gone from the stage forever? She felt a mix of incredulity and unspeakable relief.

What if Warwick had won, and propped Henry up on the throne yet again? Perhaps it would not have made a great difference to most ordinary people, but Kate could only think of Eleanor's fears: the slow death of the Motherlodge. The danger wasn't over yet. The dreaded Queen Marguerite was on her way, with her Lancastrian lovers and a horde of foreign mercenaries.

Memories fade, but Kate had never forgotten the stink of the bearded man clasping her while she beat against him like a wren, not knowing what he intended but certain it was something unspeakably foul. Her mother standing there, filling the room with her chill laughter, and the brutes shrinking away as if they had literally, physically diminished. Kate had learned that day what power could be. She wanted to be like her mother. Yet it was a strange power, not like that of the Earl of Warwick or Thomas Stanley or the King lording it over others. It was a power that kept them on a knife-edge of survival, not trying to crush their enemies, only to slip out of their toils like trout slithering through the hands of boys.

Years after the events in Eriswater, Kate and Eleanor had talked about it. Eleanor had whispered, 'The power I held over those barbarians, to protect you and myself, was only the power they chose to give to me. The art is to keep them afraid of us, but never so afraid that they turn round and destroy us. We must keep the flame of power. We must keep it *secret*.'

An atmosphere hung over Barnet after the battle, like shimmering curtains of fire falling down from the heavens. She saw two men, one in Warwick's livery and one in Gloucester's, sitting on the side of the road together, sharing a flask of ale. Warwick's soldier was crying, the other was comforting him. Goddess, this was so exciting, if only you could stay alive. Exciting, unreal and horrific.

At last, halfway through the afternoon, she found him.

What a shock to see Raphael again, a grown man. His face was long and rather beautiful despite its weariness, with firm cheeks and restless green eyes. His hair was dark brown with a touch of gold fire in it, as if the sun had bleached the ends.

'Iesu,' he breathed. 'Am I fevered? Katherine . . .' He struggled for her name. 'Katherine Lytton.'

'Sweet Auset, it's really you!' she exclaimed, with all the astonishment she could put into a whisper. 'I saw you out there in the fog. I recognized you, but I wasn't sure . . . I didn't think it could be you. We thought you were dead!'

'It hurts as if my arm's been severed, but they tell me I'll live.' He managed a smile.

'No – no, I mean long before that.' Her eyes widened, liquid with tears. 'You don't know, do you? You can't have known. Years ago, your mother came to mine and told us you were dead, you and your brother, killed in a fight over your estate—'

His face lengthened so horribly that she stopped.

'I don't know anything of that,' he said, turning his face away on the pillow.

A silence. She knelt beside him and rested her fingers over his hand. 'What do you mean?'

'I don't remember it.'

'It's not surprising,' she said. 'You were very young. Horrible things happened to me and I only half remember them. Otherwise I suppose it would drive me mad. Raphael, the point is that everyone thought you were dead.'

He turned to look at her again. 'I believed my mother was dead. But you say she came to yours and . . . ?'

She hated to kill the hope in his eyes. 'She is gone now, I'm sorry. But yes, she fled to my mother and lived with us for four peaceful years. If only she'd known you were alive.'

'Oh, God.' He groaned, and put his hand over his eyes.

'I'm so sorry, Raphael. Where have you been all this time?'

'In the service of Lord Lykenwold, whom I've just seen hacked up like a haunch of venison. I was sent to him at the age of seven or eight. Before that, I remember two things from my childhood. One was being picked up out of a ditch by another child, who saved my life. The other was your face.'

'We met in York,' she said, prompting. 'We saw Marguerite ride through, and the heads over the gate.'

'I remember talking to you and being told my father was dead. That's all.'

'Can you really not remember what happened to you?'

'No,' he said, and now he was gripping her hand so hard she winced. 'Kate, I can see it if I try, but I don't want to. I was out of my mind. I ran away and lived like an animal for six months. A boy rescued me and that was when I began to live. All the time before was lost. You tell me my mother's dead and I really can't feel what it means.'

Kate paused, concerned. 'I didn't come here to distress

you, not with you lying here wounded. I'm just so glad to have found you.'

'You're not distressing me.' He smiled, and she smiled back. It was as if they were children again, holding hands. 'Katherine, my lady, this has been one of the worst days of my life and one of the sweetest.'

'Sweet? Lying in this miserable friary with your arm half-severed from your body?'

'It's not that bad. It was worth being wounded, for the miracles I've had today. You found me, for one.'

'Ah, but I had a pressing reason to find you.' She was serious again. 'Because of what you may or may not have seen upon the field of battle.' She looked meaningfully at him.

Raphael shared Kate's plain wonder at finding him, but her gaze made him hot with discomfort . . . and with feelings that would find no approval from the friars.

She prompted him. 'You know what I mean, don't you, Raphael?'

'I think so.'

'You seem to be quite good at forgetting certain things. Forget that you saw us in the mist, and tell no one.'

Burning silence. He felt afraid, touched by the raven's wings of the hidden world. 'Witchcra—'

She put her fingers to his lips. He tasted her sweat. 'Don't be simple. Your mother Edith, Auset give her rest, was one of our sisters. You must have learned something in your childhood.'

'I know that certain things went on, but I've had no contact with . . . with your sisterhood since.'

'You've not been poisoned against us? Oh, not you, Raphael, surely.'

He shook his head. 'No. I've no opinion, and nothing against you, truly. I'd be betraying my own mother.'

'I'm glad to hear it.' She whispered so low he could only just hear her. 'Our noble employer, although he set us on, knows that such intervention is forbidden. If we are found out, he may not protect us. Or, to put it another way, everyone suspects it goes on but they turn a blind eye. They don't want their faces rubbed in it. If it's brought into the open, we'll be the scapegoats. Therefore I was sent to warn you—'

'It's all right!' He clasped her wrist. 'I saw nothing. I was born into the old ways, as you were. I'm your friend, Lady Katherine, you don't need to threaten me.'

She sighed, tension fading. 'Thank you. Call me Kate.'

'And I thought you came to see me out of love, Kate.'

'That too.' Her eyes were tender. He didn't want her to leave. 'I'm sorry I even had to mention the other matter. Let me see this bruise.'

He submitted to her examination. Her fingers upon him felt exquisite, even where they caused agony. When she had finished, he could barely feel the pain any more. 'They seem to have put a good salve upon it,' she said grudgingly. 'I'll bring you better, and herbs to ease the ache.'

'Bless you,' Raphael said softly. 'And you were conjuring the fog for which side?'

A quick, warning glare. 'Hush. For Edward, of course. As he asked. But I'm concerned about the other man who saw us, the one who was with you—'

'No need to worry about him,' Raphael said quickly. 'It was the King's brother, Richard. Since you were working for Edward, he's hardly going to object, is he?'

Kate's face went oddly blank, her lips an acid line. 'Let us hope not.'

Around them the murmurs of the wounded went on in the sweaty half-light, but they didn't notice. Raphael felt a rush of joy. 'For all today has been horrific, it's been miraculous, too. The past doesn't matter any more. I know where I'm going.'

'Not holy orders!' she said, so loudly that a couple of brothers glanced her way, mouths folded as if around vinegar.

'What?'

'You said your lord was cut down. And yet there's a light shining out of you, as if you've had a vision. You can't become a priest, you're far too unworldly!'

He laughed. 'I'm happy, because seeing you is the second miracle today.'

'Only the second?'

'The boy I mentioned, who found me all those years ago, when I might have been dead within the day – I hadn't seen him since. I never stopped thinking of him, wondering if we'd meet again.'

Her mouth curved, anticipating. 'And today?'

'Yes, we met again, and the miracle was that he remembered me. Have you ever seen someone and thought, that is the person I will follow for the rest of my days?' He held her forearm, so full of excitement he no longer felt the slightest twinge from his shoulder. 'He's asked me to serve him. I suppose it's close to what monks must feel for God, though it's probably blasphemy to say so.'

'King Edward has that effect upon people. You're not going to tell me it's him?'

There was a small, cynical crease at each corner of her mouth. He pressed on, determined to share his pleasure. 'Close. His brother.'

'Ah.' She frowned. 'The one I saw you with?'

'Yes, him, Richard of Gloucester.'

Her expression turned rigidly glacial, then smoothed over again so quickly that he thought he had imagined the look. Kate had no reason to be dismayed. She didn't know Richard.

'That's wonderful,' she said thinly. 'So you will get up from one battle and go straight into another for him?'

In the archway that gave into the chamber there was a stir and the sound of voices. Raphael looked up and saw Richard coming in again, subtle as a shadow, as if in answer to a necromancer's summons. Kate was kneeling with her back to him. Raphael caught his breath, startled

162

by her acerbic tone and worried she'd say something angry in Richard's hearing.

'Excuse me, I didn't mean to interrupt,' said the Duke of Gloucester.

Kate didn't turn round, yet at the sound of his voice Raphael saw her body stiffen and the blood sink out of her face.

'It's all right, Your Grace, I'm leaving,' she said, rising.

'No, Kate, there's no need,' Raphael said quickly. 'Don't go yet. I don't know where to find you.'

She meant to turn and leave quickly, her head averted, so that Richard would not recognize her. The sound of his voice had turned her to cold wax. Somehow her manoeuvre failed, and brought her face to face with the man she hadn't seen for two years. He looked startled.

A strong, serious face, still with the porcelain clarity of youth. He'd be only eighteen now, though he spoke and moved with the authority of a man ten years older. They stood and looked at each other for long seconds. Richard bit the side of his lower lip but his eyes, unchanging, were ice-grey crystal.

Kate felt a stirring of discomfort, almost of humiliation. She read his expression as judgement. How dare he stand and judge her, when they'd both been equals in – no, she wouldn't call it sin – in impetuous misbehaviour. Her unease became anger. The injustice of his cold look made her harden in self-defence. She could feel herself becoming as imperious as Eleanor at her best.

'My lady, a word with you?' he said eventually.

From the corner of her eye, she saw Raphael's puzzlement. Understandably, he'd expected the Duke to speak to him, not to her. Richard drew her into a deep alcove a few feet from Raphael's pallet. There she could see nothing of him but points of rushlight in his eyes, a dusting of light on his black hair.

'Have you taken holy orders?' he asked, looking at her head-dress.

She gave a soft, grim laugh. 'No, Your Grace. It's so I can go about my business without being pestered quite so much.'

'Your business?'

'As a healer,' she said tersely.

'Then I'm glad of your attendance upon my friend Raphael. Do you know him well?'

'Only a little. Our mothers were friends.' She added, 'He tells me he has you to thank for saving his life when he was a child. For which I'm grateful.'

She heard him breathe in and out in the darkness. 'It was only what anyone would have done. I'm glad to have found him again, after all this time.'

'I hope these friars know what they are doing,' she said. 'The most trivial of wounds can turn mortal if treated wrongly.'

'He'll be taken from here on the morrow and given the best of care, as will all of my knights and esquires injured today,' Richard answered coolly, adding, 'my lady,' with frigid courtesy. She perceived no trace of the fear he'd shown the last time she'd met him; none of the tenderness either. He'd matured beyond recognition.

'Thank you for telling me,' she replied. 'Is it why you wanted to speak to me?'

Another pause. Then he said uncomfortably, 'I didn't expect to meet you again. I almost hoped you had not been real.'

'Likewise,' retorted Kate. 'I still have your white boar badge, if you want it back.'

'No, it was for you to keep,' he said, almost ruefully. 'I have others.'

'I'm quite sure you do.'

'Forgive me. This is unspeakably awkward. I would give anything to undo what happened, but I can't, so . . .'

'We shall conduct ourselves as if nothing happened,' Kate said firmly. 'I shall never refer to it again, if you do not.'

'Yes,' he said very quietly, and sighed. 'Thank you, Katherine of Lytton Dale.'

His use of her name was a shock. 'So you found out who I was, after all. You must have known I was not a fey of the woods, or—'

'Sometimes this entire kingdom seems no bigger than a gossiping market town. Edward met you, and couldn't resist telling me.'

'I knew I couldn't trust him!'

He gave her a sharp, sideways look. 'I'm aware that you are my sister-in-law's lady-in-waiting and I marvel that you are not at her side, rather than wandering upon a battlefield at great danger to your life. I know what you have been doing for my brother Edward.'

The last words held menace. 'Do you, my lord?'

She turned her face to his and he stared straight at her, his face all hard lines of disapproval. 'I saw you. Madam, it's no secret that my brother uses sorcerers. He's consorted with that damned Friar Bungay for years.'

'The gentle friar is a friend of my mother,' Kate said softly, but he went on as if she hadn't spoken.

'There are many evil influences around my brother. It's well known that Elizabeth Woodville snared him by witchcraft; he'd never have married her otherwise. The worst thing is that he knows it and doesn't care! They'll set him on the road to damnation and it's hard to watch, harder to bear. Their voices are louder than mine and I cannot make him hear me. But I would sell my own soul to save his.' His fierce whisper shocked her. She turned hot, as if overhearing his private thoughts. 'All I can do is fight for him.'

'You'd fight for him, yet deny him a little elemental influence to aid him?'

'I'll fight for him to the very death!' said Richard. 'Do you know what would happen if his enemies should triumph? They'd have grounds to execute him as a witch.'

'Edward?' Kate said, disbelieving.

'And the Friar, and you, and all his other sorcerers along with him.'

'Execution is not a penalty permitted for sorcery,' she said. 'We are protected by law. Since the time of Henry the Second—'

'Don't lecture me on the law. Sorcery is still forbidden. They won't scruple to change the penalty, believe me, to destroy him. It should have been changed long ago, then he might never have been tempted.'

A shiver of heat and anger went through her. 'Your loyalty to your brother does you credit, but you have absolutely no idea what you are talking about.'

'Have I not?' She saw his teeth, a white and dangerous gleam.

'You're making the same mistake as his enemies. This concept of evil is meaningless. Edward isn't evil. I've met him. No doubt he has his faults but he is a good-hearted, amiable man and at least my mother and our sisters know that we have nothing to fear from his rule!'

'All fair women find him amiable,' Richard said wearily. 'I didn't say he was evil. Only too susceptible to the honey voices that whisper in his ears, and to taking the easiest options. I would do anything to sever him from these vile influences before they destroy him.'

'So you begin with one inconsequential sorceress?' Kate folded her arms, and couldn't look at him. She was trembling with anger and nascent fear.

'I can't stop you, Kate. But if Edward goes on flaunting his necromancy, *someone* will stop all of you. Take it as a gentle warning.'

Kate stood rigid, so enraged she didn't trust herself to move. 'Good, well, thank you, Your Grace. Now it's clear why you wanted to speak to me, not to make peace but to make an enemy.'

'No. No,' he said, quiet as the darkness. 'I meant what I said but, Lamb's blood, I wish no harm against *you* . . . only against corruption. I can't bear to see the Devil using people

I love. Today . . .' he raised a hand to rub his forehead. 'Today a man was killed whom I loved as a father.'

'The Earl of Warwick,' she said.

Raw pain bled through Richard's mask of self-control, turning him grey and pallid. 'I loved him as a father, and had to help destroy him.'

Katherine was quiet. He would not want to know that she had heard the Earl's dying bellow. Had *he* seen a witch in the mist, and blamed her for the clawing elementals that sucked him into a smothering death? If this was power, it was perilous and not always welcome.

Part of her bled for Richard, but she had no inclination to offer him sympathy, any more than she would have put her arms round a wounded graylix.

'And I must go home and comfort Isabel for the same complaint,' she said.

Gloucester took a long breath, looked at her more calmly. 'How – how is her sister, Anne?'

'I don't know, my lord.' It was suddenly, unpleasantly easy to be as thorny to him as he'd been to her. 'We haven't seen her for several months. She's in the charge of Queen Marguerite, having been reluctantly married to Marguerite's son Prince Eduoard. I shouldn't imagine she knows much pleasure, but who can tell?'

Richard took himself out of the alcove without another word to her. Obviously he'd known about the marriage, but Katherine's words seemed to have rubbed venom into the wound. She watched as he exchanged a few words with Raphael then walked away, quick and pre-occupied. Taut with indignation, she went slowly back to Raphael's bedside. She hated being at odds with people, but surely even Richard's high birth did not give him the right to speak so brusquely to her, to utter threats and warnings.

What have I done to offend him, she thought, except generously offered him my body once? Ah, that must be my crime, then.

'What did you say to him?' Raphael asked. 'He looked like a ghost.'

'I didn't realize he was so fond of his cousin Anne.'

'I didn't know you knew him.' Raphael sounded indignant.

'I don't,' said Kate. 'But he saw me in the fog. He knew. He disapproves of Edward's methods and chose to berate *me* for them. Raphael, dear, are you really sure you want to serve him?'

His mouth dropped. 'Of course.'

'I'm the Duke of Clarence's wife's companion. Why not come to serve him instead? Then we would see each other. I know he'd be glad of you.'

She thought, and why couldn't it have been George you decided to worship? She had nothing against the Duke of Gloucester. Nothing except that he'd crossed her path like some dark spirit of the forest, then had the temerity to set himself apart from her, as absolutely as a priest from a witch. Nothing, except that he was now going to take Raphael away from her.

'Kate, I don't want us to be apart, but I can't change my mind. One lord isn't interchangeable for another. Clarence? You might as well say a mule is as fine as a destrier, or a petitmort a good substitute for a gyrfalcon. I'm sworn to the Duke of Gloucester and that will never change.'

'Why? I can't see it!'

A veil of estrangement fell between them, gossamer-thin. 'There's something about him,' said Raphael. 'A light. I can't explain. True and pure, like diamond. Did you not hear how valiantly he fought today? And yet he is the gentlest man I have ever met.'

'Well, if you feel this, you must follow your heart.'

'I don't know what he's done to offend you. He's concerned about King Edward, that's all.'

She rose, then bent, impulsively, to kiss his hand. 'Gods, Raphael, I hope you are right and he holds true to you. He needed someone to vent his feelings on today, and since our paths happened to cross, it was me. I'll survive. I will bring you that salve tomorrow.'

'I'll be gone tomorrow,' he said. 'Shall I see you again?'

'I hope so.' Katherine turned, wrapped the head cloth carefully to half-conceal her face, and ran out into the night.

It was less than a month later that they met again, and stood in Tewkesbury market-place to watch the beheading of the Lancastrian traitors.

Queen Marguerite had arrived with her dreaded army under her commander, Beaufort, Duke of Somerset. King Edward's forces had outwitted hers and rolled defeat into a massacre. They called it the Bloody Meadow, the place where most of her soldiers had been butchered. Edward and Clarence had made very sure that her precious son, Prince Edouard, was among the dead. As revenge for their own young brother, Edmund, it could not have been more silver-sharp.

Raphael had fought alongside Richard and had come through cut and bruised but whole, full of tales that Kate would have preferred not to hear.

The commanders who'd sought sanctuary in the abbey had been dragged out bodily and tried and condemned by the Duke of Gloucester. All Marguerite's dreams were dead. Kate had caught a glimpse of her, taken prisoner. She had been amazed at how tiny Marguerite looked, a birch twig, pride crushed to its raw, tough essence. She had no love for the ex-queen but sympathized with her all the same: she'd fought so passionately and still lost.

Crowds gathered to watch the axe fall. Great Lancastrian lords, one after another, trembling, eyes drooping, their hair darkly beaded with sweat. Their lips moved in prayer. Katherine wondered if any prayed secretly to Dark Mother Auset, there at the beginning and at the end, rather than to the distant Father. She watched transfixed, feeling all the fibres of her body would come apart in the horror of it; unable to spare herself.

Worst of all were the sounds. The thick gathered hush as the next one was hustled to the butcher's block. The grunt as he was pushed down, the ghastly marriage of dignity and terror. The heavy swish of iron through air and then the thick collision, like a cleaver into a joint of meat. One by one they were gone, the great lords: Beaufort, Duke of Somerset and the rest. The crowd gasped and uttered ragged, shocked cheers.

The Duke of Gloucester, judge and executioner, stood apart. He looked graceful, impassive, his dress and demeanour all economical restraint, the very image of Death. His soot-black cloak with sable edges hung like the folded wings of a raptor. His eyes looked black and calm, overseeing the event without emotion.

Kate stood with her hand through Raphael's arm. She was numb. There was horror in this and a hypnotic fascination. She couldn't take her eyes off Richard, could not believe she had ever been so close to him. She tried to hate him for this cold brutality, but failed.

She'd heard a tale from the battle: one of Somerset's commanders, Lord Wenlock, had failed to join battle, and Somerset had ridden across to him in fury and split his skull with an axe.

Lord Wenlock was the man who had refused to let their ship land at Calais even though Isabel had been in the most extreme and wretched straits. Now Kate couldn't condemn Richard or turn away from his severity. For when she'd heard of the manner of Wenlock's death, she had laughed.

I sat in the café with Fin, watching her play with the foam on her cappuccino, her teaspoon trailing marbled patterns. 'So what's with this fascination with old King Dick, then, Gus?' she said, flicking a glance at my stack of books.

'It's your fault.' I grinned. 'It started when we watched that film.'

'Oh, *my* fault? Hope it's not interfering with your course work.'

'Completely fucked it,' I said, very softly. 'But I can't stop, until I get to the end.'

'What d'you mean, the end?'

I couldn't explain about my encounters with people who were long dead, or perhaps had no existence at all, not even to Fin. I hoped the fact that I thought it would *sound* mad, proved that I was not yet *actually* mad.

I was looking for something I'd lost; that's how it felt.

A story was unfolding to me. The story of a young woman called Katherine and a young man called Raphael. I couldn't find their names in any history book but that wasn't to say they hadn't existed; how many other names have been lost?

It's hard to explain. I wasn't inventing it. I wasn't dreaming it. It came to me in episodes, in long waking daydreams as if I were watching a film, but more real, like being there on set as an invisible witness. The clothes weren't quite right for the period, not as I'd seen them portrayed in countless illustrations. They were more extravagant, more structured, more elegant.

The men wore tight-fitting trousers, not hose, that were sometimes laced down the sides. The women's headgear was flimsy, tantalizingly designed to reveal the hair rather than hide it. There were strange build-ings, strange animals I've never seen in any book, but still distinctly medieval in flavour.

It was deeper and more vivid than anything I could have invented. It was like suddenly remembering an evocative dream from years ago and trying to recapture it. Like a memory of a lost book.

When I'd gone home to visit my parents one weekend, I actually went searching their bookshelves and loft to find this phantom book. For a time I was convinced it had existed, frustrated when my family looked blank and shook their heads. I could almost recall how it had felt and looked, its weight in my hands and its musty odour, the magic it had contained. But the book itself was not to be found.

Or I might have mistaken it for a folk legend I'd learned, and always believed to be fact, but when I came to refresh my memory, I could find no reference to it anywhere, and anyone I asked denied all knowledge. Or a dusty old manuscript, miraculously rediscovered, full of wondrous revelation, and then misplaced.

Maddening.

Kate and Raphael would not tell me who they were, or had been. Still, I travelled with them blindly, gladly. I don't know why this channel opened up between me and Raphael, perhaps because we were both open and searching for an anchor and so found each other in the void? What convinced me it was real was this: there were many things the characters never revealed, either in action or in thought. Too much was going on beneath the surface. Kate's iron will; a child hinted at but never seen. In other words, I felt I was not making it up, but catching glimpses of other people's real lives.

'Trance alert,' said Fin. 'It must be absolutely fascinating in there.'

'Sorry,' I said, shaking myself. 'I was thinking. It's so unfair that Richard is still seen as this evil king. I was listing all the things he *hasn't* been accused of. Brutality, genocide: Henry the Fifth. Torture and attempted rape: Edward the Fourth. Cutting the heads off his wives: Henry the Eighth.'

'And red-hot pokers,' said Fin. 'Who was that?'

'The point is that those kings are still remembered in a heroic light. Richard was actually a good king. He did his job well. I'm not saying he was a saint, but why single him out as a particular example of evil?'

'Because we need a villain,' Fin said darkly. 'We love a villain.'

I thought she had put her finger on it precisely.

'Villains are interesting.'

'Villains are sexy!' Fin laughed. 'Admit it. Didn't Shakespeare do him a huge favour?'

'It's a point of view,' I said, and wondered again about Raphael. Kate needed nothing from me, but Raphael, I sensed, did. Raphael was descending into the vale of shadows and didn't even know it.

'August,' Fin said carefully, 'this happened over five hundred years ago, you know.'

'No. It's happening now.'

Chapter Seven 1471: Henry

RICHARD
   I cannot tell; the world is grown so bad
   That wrens make prey where eagles dare not perch:
   Since every Jack became a gentleman
   There's many a gentle person made a Jack.

Richard III Act I scene 3

London broke upon Raphael like some crazed demonic carnival out of a fog. Houses stood crammed together and teetering with the signs of merchants and alehouses thrust like a morass of banners into the steamy air. The streets glistened like stream beds. Pointed roofs ran with sunlight. And the crowds along the streets – never in his life had Raphael seen such an array of folk, such wealth and exuberance. Their clothes were like jewels, blue and red and green; their headgear was fashioned in ostentatious imitation of royalty, plump velvet cushions crowning the men, gossamer drapery flowing over the hair of the women. Gold glinted upon their hands as they waved. Their cheers deafened and thrilled him like the blare of battle horns.

They roared for King Edward, throwing white roses across his path all along streets that had been swept glass-clean for his arrival. Raphael remembered how it felt to watch such a procession pass by. He saw the same open-mouthed wonder in the children who were shouting and leaping through the crowds. Now he was part of it. Richard of Gloucester led the victory march and Raphael rode proudly in his retinue, only a few horses behind the

Duke himself. Will Shaw rode in happy bemusement at his elbow – his esquire. Richard's friends were around him and Raphael was counted one of them. It was the most precious feeling. The whole day was a swelling wave of joy. He wanted to capture the moment for eternity, as a painting: the dark shine of Gloucester's armour and hair, the proud gleam of his livery upon him and his followers, ruby and azure, and the white boar ramping on every surcoat like a mascot of the gods.

Raphael, with others, had been knighted after Tewkesbury.

The streets grew broader, the houses greater, showing high walls to the street and shining roofs in the oriental style. The sun had burned mists from the Isis to make the air soft and mysterious. Suddenly Raphael could smell the river: a green miasma of cold, fishy rot, rank, yet evocative. It thrilled him like the scent of the ocean.

'Have you never been to London before?' asked Francis, Lord Lovell beside him. 'You're head's swivelling about like an owl's.'

'Never,' said Raphael. He couldn't stop smiling. Francis grinned back. He was Richard's closest friend and he'd ridden at Raphael's side all the way, taking him under his wing. He was someone whom Raphael trusted without a qualm; an affable man with light gold-brown hair, a soft-skinned pleasant face and hazel eyes that looked directly and honestly at everyone.

'Ah, then you're in for fair times,' he said confidentially. 'The sumptuousness of Edward's court is like the lushest honeyed wine that could ever trickle over your tongue. Too much of it will make you sick.'

He laughed at Raphael's expression. 'I'm not one to gorge myself,' Raphael said, shaking his head.

'Some find it all too easy to slip into the habit, that's the trouble. I only advise that you keep close to our good Duke of Gloucester's side, and say nothing. Don't be dragged into arguments, it's safer that way.'

'I'll do as you do.'

'And keep your thoughts to the one you can trust, that is, yourself.'

Raphael stared at him. 'Stark advice.'

Francis raised an eyebrow, cynical but serious. 'D'you have a loved one to send letters to? Mother, sister, paramour?'

Heat suffused his face. 'There is someone . . . a friend. She's in the Duchess of Clarence's service.'

Lovell clapped his hand to his forehead. 'Clarence! Agh.' He whispered, 'Be careful anyway, but in that particular case be as close-lipped as a stone effigy upon a tomb. Never write a word that you wouldn't be happy for every single person at court to read, and especially Duke George himself.'

'Are you saying that someone might take my letters and open them?'

'Spies within the court?' His tone was low and amused. 'Heaven forbid. What do you think? Everyone has a dagger out for everyone else, it's part of the fun.'

A small black stone was forming in Raphael's stomach. He swallowed it away. 'I don't want to make enemies.'

'My dear, you already have them, by wearing the white boar upon your heart. So don't bother trying to ingratiate yourself with anyone. Whatever you do, you'll be painted as black as the rest of us.'

Raphael looked quizzically at Lord Lovell, who described a circle on the air with his finger, taking in Richard and his retinue. 'Dickon doesn't subscribe to the fawning, flattering manners at court. Some admire him for it, and some hate him. There it is. King Edward adores him, but it's another reason for certain parties to resent him bitterly. You'll see. But we have that to look forward to. Tonight we lodge at the Tower, dour old grandfather of a place.'

The Tower of London was a square, turreted mountain against the sky, grim and magnificent, standing aloof from admiration or hatred. The sheer walls were grey, mottled with a dark sheen of silver and scarred in places with cannon-shot. The scars were no more than flea bites upon its tough hide. Its towers rose, shadowy, into the river mist.

Raising his head, Francis said, 'Old Henry's up there somewhere.'

Raphael looked up at the blind slits of windows. It looked less a palace than a fortress. He hadn't thought of the Lancastrian king for a long time, not even to wonder if he still lived. It was weird and shocking to realize that he was still alive; Edward's prisoner.

'Poor wretch. What will become of him?'

'He'll remain King Edward's guest for the rest of his life. Harry should have been a monk, not a king, and how much happier for the rest of us if he had been. That was the cause of all our troubles: a child-king with quarrelsome uncles. I wonder if monarchs shouldn't be appointed with some degree of merit alongside the blood royal?'

'You're close to speaking treason,' Raphael said, with a quick grin.

'Well, we have both in Edward, and praise the Creator for it,' Lovell answered. 'Henry, they say, is happier in his cell than ever he was on the throne, and doesn't know much difference.' His tone was offhand.

'I feel sorry for him,' said Raphael.

'So do we all, but don't shed too many tears over him. Saint or holy idiot, he's still dangerous. As long as he lives, there'll be those who'll use him as a figurehead for another bloody rebellion, a puppet to get Lancaster back in the ascendant.'

Francis Lovell went quiet suddenly, the warm light leaving his eyes.

'What is it?' Raphael asked. He was unsure yet whether Francis trusted him enough to give an answer, but after a moment he spoke.

'I'm just praying that Henry's wretched twig of a son didn't get poor Anne Neville with child before he died. Christ knows, she doesn't deserve that.'

*   *   *

The great hall where they supped that night was as sombre as Raphael had expected, though more colourful: a great pillared space with the walls painted a cold blue and decorations of subdued silver. The yellow flare of fire and candlelight washed a greenish cast over the blue, giving the hall the feel of a drowned sepulchre. Banners floated down from the ceiling like waving sea-weed.

Lancaster was dead, finished. The triumphant Yorkists were loud with joy, reliving their battles with extravagant drama. To Raphael, though, it seemed as if the celebrations were muted under bubbling water. Lancaster was dead . . . except for the ghosts still haunting the tower rooms above them.

He was beginning to recognize Edward's circle now. Anthony Woodville, the most celebrated of the Queen's brothers, handsome, fair, smooth-mannered and exquisitely dressed. The Duke of Clarence, loud, flamboyant and sometimes desperate in his attempts to outshine Woodville. William Hastings, a broad dark man, solid and affable, who moved stiffly as if age or battle had got the better of him.

Later, all the lords – Edward and his brothers Clarence and Gloucester, Anthony Woodville and a number of others – left the feast and closeted themselves in a private meeting. Their knights and servants feasted riotously enough without them. Raphael wanted to join in but something held him back – a sense of oppression in the green, sinister light of the hall. Unused to anything stronger than ale, he tasted for the first time the peppery fire of hippocras, and got drunk so fast the whole evening rolled into unreality. There was the throb of voices, the endless sway and flutter of figures, faces lurching in and out of his vision, some smiling, some yelling in song. At one stage a woman was whirling him round and round in a dance, at another, Francis's face loomed flushed and sweaty in front of him, asking him with laughter if he was celebrating hard enough.

He had no memory of going to bed, but he was there, on a pallet in a dark room, vaguely aware of other sleeping shapes around him. All was sooty gloom. Tapestries flapped above in him a ghostly draught, seeming to rise forever into the dark. He felt ice-cold sober with no trace of a hangover.

Something moved, making him jump.

Richard was bending over him, his face lit from beneath by the candle he carried, and as pale as its flame. His hair winged around him, black like the fathomless centre of his pupils.

'Get up,' he whispered, so faintly Raphael could hardly hear him. 'An enterprise of the deepest dye, not for the faint-hearted.'

Raphael rose, and walked in silence beside his master, down stone staircases that folded round upon themselves. Outside, the bailey was cat-grey in a shimmer of starlight. The Tower stood solid all around them, its walls fading upwards into the night. He felt they were moving through water; he could hear nothing, not even their footsteps as they crossed to the Wakefield Tower. He was worried that Richard was speaking and he couldn't hear what was being said. But when he looked, Richard's lips were tightly closed in a face of carved limestone.

Queen Marguerite had been brought here and imprisoned after Tewkesbury, though kept apart from her husband. The thought of her presence was terrifying. They said she wailed like a *bain sidhe* for the loss of her son Edouard. The whole Tower was a casket of skeletons, spiders and horrors that would spring out at the touch of a lock.

They went in through the door of the tower and there were other shapes waiting in the shadows; faces he recognized but tried not to see, lest they murder him to keep his silence. Anthony Woodville. Sir John Fogge. Other close followers of the King. Edward himself was absent.

He could smell their soft-breathing excitement as they

climbed the stairs, their fear, but Richard was black ice, as he'd been in Tewkesbury market-place.

They found Henry VI, king no longer, sitting at a small table in the centre of his cell. He wore a plain robe of blue, worn and faded almost to grey. The room smelled of damp, of crushed reeds and candle fat. His hair and face, caught in the circle of candlelight, were the colour of bleached straw. A book shone bright with pigment between his hands, as if it had sucked all colour into itself, a casket of blue, red and gold. Henry was reading, his lips moving as he mouthed the text. The long curve of his skull and neck had a shapely nobility to them. He wasn't the shambling wreck Raphael had envisioned, nor did he look old. He was a man who could be imagined on the throne, even with his colourless eyes and his trembling chin. High on the wall behind him was a plaster Christ on the cross, with the slaughtered Lamb across his feet to symbolize his sacrifice.

Raphael pressed himself back against a wall, a horrified observer. None of the others spoke to him or looked at him, he might have been invisible.

Henry looked up, mild and friendly.

'Gentlemen, you are kind to visit me.' He looked about vaguely. 'I would offer you wine, but . . . the servants are gone. I never know where they are. Is my wife come to see me?'

'No, Your Grace, she is not,' said Anthony Woodville, and Henry's head dipped in plain relief.

'Must I be moved again?' His eyes, innocent and pleading, betrayed no understanding of where he was. Pain dragged at Raphael's throat and he saw the others glancing at each other with hesitant, reluctant expressions. All but Richard, who looked straight ahead with a calm, almost gentle expression.

'No, Your Grace, we are not here to move you,' said Woodville, his voice breaking.

Sir James Fogge broke across him, hoarse and rapid, 'Oh, for God's sake do it!'

'Who are you?'

'Friends,' said Richard, 'come to shrive you. You have nothing to fear. You will surely feel as great a rapture to stand before your Creator as will he to receive you.' And he drew a long, beautiful Italian dagger of silver and gold and held it up as if it were a cross.

The thin, limp mouth dropped. A flash of understanding passed through the vague eyes. Raphael tried to cry, 'Don't!' but no sound came from his throat.

'Yes,' whispered Henry. 'I see, and I forgive you. May Almighty God do the same, when you stand before him on the final day, but first, pray with me. Let us pray for our souls, before you dispatch mine to heaven, for you are more in need of it than I.'

He rose, his stool scraping horribly on the floor as he did so. Perhaps the prayers would have averted his fate. All the men looked sick and shaken now, and Richard was white. As the old King rose, Fogge gave an animal cry, and lunged at him.

He missed; Henry lurched forward in acute terror. Stumbling, he fell over the corner of the table. Fogge grabbed his hair as he went down, so that Henry finished up on his knees, head back, mouth gaping, thin chest rising and falling. Then Woodville grabbed his wrists and held them behind him, making him gasp. His chin wobbled as prayers spilled from his lips.

'A discreet wound,' said Richard, 'that will not be noticed when he lies in state.'

It was Richard himself who knelt in front of Henry, as if to pray with him, then with one minimal gesture, as if it took no effort at all, he slipped the long Italian dagger under Henry's breastbone and up to the very hilt in his heart.

Blood gushed after the blade as Richard withdrew it, a red river flowing over his hands. Henry stared up as if in surprise. With his lips still moving he twitched, turned grey and was dead in seconds.

*   *   *

'What's wrong, man?'

Raphael struggled out of a sleep that held him in a quagmire, black and treacly. He couldn't understand how he'd come to be in bed, or asleep; the walls of the chamber moved like spectral curtains.

'Iesu's blood, you look deathly,' said Francis. 'You were writhing like a beetle on its back. Wake up, Raphael, tell me what the matter is.'

'Terrible,' he whispered.

'Has this happened to him before?' Francis said, and Raphael realized Will Shaw was there too, looking blearily over Francis's shoulder.

'Not as far I've ever noticed, but I sleep like the dead, anyway,' said Will. 'What's up, Raffel, a bad dream?'

A dream, Raphael thought. 'No, no, it was real, I was there . . .'

Even as the denial came out, reality shifted, and he perceived the scene as a separate entity, real yet unreal, like a play. Too vivid for a dream . . . but what else could explain it? Vaguely, as if it happened a year ago, he could remember falling drunkenly into his bed, and the scene itself had had no context. Yet it was so powerful he couldn't shake himself free.

'Where?' said Will. 'You've not moved from that mattress, unless you walked in your sleep.'

'It was terrible – so real – I dreamed they murdered poor Harry in the Tower.'

Francis Lovell frowned. All mirth fled his face. 'Who murdered him?'

Raphael named them.

Francis was silent for long moments, lacing and unlacing his fingers. Eventually he said in a cramped tone, 'Poor Henry, may the Lamb acquit him, did die last night. I've heard it myself, only this hour past.' Raphael realized that dawn was flushing the window, and that Francis was dressed. He added, 'But he died of sickness; of melancholy.'

'But I saw—'

Lovell was shaking his head. He looked so aghast that Raphael feared he'd lost his friendship, almost before it had begun. 'Never speak those names again in connection with murder. It didn't happen. You had a nightmare.'

'Were you there?' Raphael spoke sharply, sitting up.

Another long silence. Francis swallowed, the muscles around his mouth bunching. 'No.' Then quickly, 'It was a nightmare, Raphael! *Your* dream, not reality. Some foggy humour in the air must have afflicted your mind.'

Raphael could feel the nauseous headache of too much drink. He was heavy with sleep, dazed by the apparent reality of what he'd seen, not only sights but smells too. The fall of light on Henry's upper lip as he prayed, the feel of rushes under Raphael's feet – he couldn't shake it off. And yet, the clues were there. The clothes they wore and the way they spoke had been subtly wrong, in the way of dreams. And the very fact that Raphael had been there, an invisible witness to whom no one spoke, proved it could not have been real.

'They say that foggy spirits gather around the dying, and enter the thoughts of sleepers,' Raphael murmured. 'Yet it was so vivid, Francis! Are you sure?'

Lovell's mouth was thin with annoyance. 'How the devil could you even imagine that our Dickon would murder a king, a deposed king, in cold blood? He'd never do such a thing. Others of Edward's hangers-on might contemplate such an unchivalrous, bloody deed, but not Richard!'

'No,' said Raphael, ashamed of himself and trying to blink away the image that repeated itself persistently behind his eyes. 'No, he wouldn't.'

Will put his big fists on his hips. 'I warned you to keep off the hippocras. I tell you, Lord Lovell, one pint of ale and he falls over. I never could toughen him up.'

'Warned me?' Raphael gasped. 'You were the one pouring it down my throat!'

'For our Lady's sake,' Lovell said softly, 'I've seen some

bad mornings after a night before, but this caps it all. Take more water with it next time, eh?'

'It wasn't the drink,' he said, sitting up, trying to pull himself out of the vision's sticky webs. Pain lurched about like a cannon-ball in the centre of his skull. He groaned.

'Whatever it was, it's over,' Francis said gently. 'Put it out of your mind. Don't speak of this to anyone else, whatever you do, or you'll set them thinking you're possessed. My lips are sealed.'

The Palace of Westminster was the antithesis of the Tower. An edifice of glowing creamy stone, patinated with hints of other hues: green, gold, ruby, specks of fool's gold. The buttresses were surmounted by leaping animals: pard, gryphon, bear, graylix. The planes of its roofs were tiled as if with butterfly scales, a dozen subtle tints of ruby and rose, cream, lilac, amethyst, leaf-green, the overall effect a glimmering rainbow. Gilded suns encircling silver roses studded the walls. Workmen were on scaffolding, painstakingly dusting silver leaf onto the mouldings.

Here Raphael had his first taste of life at court, luscious as cream but tainted with rancidity as Lovell had warned. Even so, it was unutterably exciting to be there, in a vast hall of polished pale-gold marble, looking out at trestle upon trestle of fabulously garbed lords and ladies, bishops, knights and courtiers.

It was hard to imagine that, only days ago, many of them had reeled bloody and fatigued from the battlefield of Tewkesbury. The air bristled with a near-hysterical joy.

The thin golden ache of trumpets announced the entrance of the King and Queen. Edward was magnificent in golden velvet slashed with blue. Over it, he wore a cloak of azure cloth of gold, sewn with silver suns, lined with white damask and edged with a wondrous golden-ochre fur, tipped with black. His slippers were fashioned from the iridescent skin of the horned toad.

Queen Elizabeth was like an empress gliding beside him,

her hand balanced imperiously on his. She threatened to eclipse him. From her head-dress, towering yet gossamer light, swathes of silver tissue cascaded down her back, a tantalizing echo of her hair. She was in a leaf-green shimmering silky velvet scattered with pearls. The skirts were gathered back to frame a central panel, a window into a courtly myth. Salukis chased a hart across a field of green strewn with heraldic lilies. Raphael gaped at the illusion. It was long minutes of wonder before he saw, by the shift of light, that the picture was embroidered from thousands of tiny beads, each bead a precious stone.

Her face was flawless, with long green eyes. As her cool gaze slid over the scene, the court went down in a rippling motion of obeisance like swathes of cut flowers. The perfect eyes narrowed with pleasure.

With loud laughter and many embraces, King Edward greeted a mass of finely dressed men and women, many of them as fair as the Queen and very nearly as beautiful.

'Her brothers and sisters,' Francis Lovell was whispering in Raphael's ear. 'Anthony you've seen. That's Edward Woodville, and the Bishop there is Lionel. I always mix up the women, there are so many of them. Those two young bucks are her sons, Thomas and Richard Grey, from her first marriage. Edward adores the whole clan, so no one dares say anything against them.'

'Edward loves everyone, apparently.' said Raphael.

'And often people he really shouldn't.' Lovell, taking a drink from a large goblet of Roman glass, raised an eyebrow at him.

'I shouldn't like to make enemies of them.'

'Unfortunately, not everyone's as wise as you.'

Raphael followed his gaze to the Duke of Clarence, who was standing to one side of Edward's dais and talking loudly to Gloucester, William Hastings and a handful of others. Clarence was as fabulously dressed as the King, in white and gold, blatant in his efforts to outshine the Woodvilles. He looked edgy and full of bluster.

'Clarence loathes the Woodvilles and hasn't got the wit to conceal it,' Francis whispered, carefully positioning the goblet to conceal his lips. 'He was nearly as furious as Warwick when he found out Edward had married Dame Grey. Richard has the sense to keep quiet, but Clarence never has, then or now. The feeling is mutual. They say the Queen tried to persuade Edward to execute him.'

'For siding with Warwick?' said Raphel.

'Quite. For plotting to dethrone her husband, not to mention the part he played in killing her father Sir Richard and her brother John during that episode.'

'Then she has a point. I'm amazed Edward's so forgiving.'

'Not as amazed as she, but that's Edward. He loves his brothers. He knows Clarence is an idiot, and forgives him, but the Queen and her family never will.'

Servants were hurrying among the tables. Dish after spectacular dish was carried in to dazzle the gathering. Banners dripped from the high, gilded ceiling. Musicians played. Psalteries, reed pipes, shawns, drums and sweet human voices floated faintly over the roar of the gathering.

There was so much to look at that Raphael forgot to eat. The men wore slim-fitting trousers of fabric matching their doublets, laced all down the outer side to make the legs look long and lean, the effect completed by soft boots with long, pointed toes. The doublets were stiff with boning, the shoulders sculpted into swept-up shapes over full, slashed sleeves, fabric falling from the waist into curved points over the thighs, like bats' wings. The dresses of the women had the same sculptural shoulders, long sleeves drooping almost to the floor, boned and laced waists that gave an exquisite shape. Their full skirts shimmered, inset with panels of beaded heraldry or with mythic scenes; the Queen herself had started this fashion, it was said. Their hennins were delicate cages draped with the finest voile, through which the full glory of their hair could be seen.

Jewel colours were in abundance, encrusted with gold or misted with silver, and much black, popular because it was the most expensive and difficult dye of all.

Raphael observed all this through a veil of wonder. He'd imagined the splendours of court a hundred times. The reality was infinitely more colourful, rich, noisy and wasteful than he'd ever dreamed.

Suddenly he recalled the violence that had bought about this celebration. The truth of it was stark and made the scene bristle with garish sharpness. Everything he witnessed was tainted by the ghastly dream. He'd seen these laughing, triumphant folk murdering a confused old man. He suspected they all knew, were all in on the conspiracy. He could observe nothing in innocent delight. He hardly dared touch his wine, lest there was some worse horror waiting to reveal itself to him.

He had looked about for Katherine but had not found her. Although Clarence was at court, his wife Isabel and her ladies were not. Kate was the one person who might have made sense of his vision.

'Come, cheer up,' said Lovell, leaning over to fill his goblet with burgundy. 'Who put you on a platter and stuffed you with chestnuts?'

'What?'

Francis indicated the huge, staring fish that had been placed before them. 'You look as joyful as that pike. More bad dreams?'

'No.' He gave a smile. 'I was thinking about ... the battles, the executions.'

'For Creator's sake, put that out of your mind. What d'you think feasting is for? If a few heads cut off means peace, it's worth it.'

'I feel out of place.'

'Nonsense. You're here as a faithful knight of Gloucester, at his pleasure. That makes you more fit to be here than half the folk in this place.'

'Oh? Which half?'

'You're a fast learner.' Lovell winked. 'What better excuse for gossip?'

Francis schooled him well. By the time the hall was readied for dancing, he knew the main players. The Queen's relatives were a court in themselves, a shining halo around her, plying the King with flattery, quips and backslaps. King Edward loved it, gorging happily on their adoration. Raphael watched the Queen's brothers who rode high in Edward's favour: Anthony Woodville a powerful presence of silver-fair energy; Edward Woodville a darker, sterner creature with narrow eyes. The two strutting young stags, the Queen's sons by her first marriage, Thomas Grey, Marquis of Dorset, and his younger brother Richard Grey, were all arrogance and bravado. It might have impressed some, but Raphael could understand why Richard wanted nothing to do with their circle.

As various courtiers paid their respects to the King and Queen, Raphael noticed their expansive smiles, the curtseys and bows and hand-kissing as they greeted one another, the mutual flattery and assurances of love, then how they fell into their own little cliques, looking about them with slitted eyes like daggers.

He learned the faces of the Stanley brothers, Thomas and William, with their neat beards and watchful eyes. They sat in a little enclave with a tiny, rigidly dignified woman who was dressed as austerely as an abbess. Francis told him this was Lady Margaret Beaufort.

'And yes, she always looks that miserable,' Lovell whispered. 'They say that all she thinks of is her son, Henry Tudor, gone into exile with his uncle, Jasper, who fled to France to avoid Edward's wrath. Jasper was about to fight for Marguerite, until Tewkesbury put paid to her.'

'And who is he, the Bishop with them?' Raphael asked.

'Morton,' said Lovell, as if he'd tasted vinegar. 'He transfers his loyalty from one king to the next with the ease of a snake upon soap.'

Most of the bishops there were dressed in silver-white

and yellow pomp. Morton was subdued by contrast, in bruise-purple. He was sleek and plump, watching the proceeding from the mild, dark pools of his eyes. Beside him was a gaunt, shorn-headed man whose blue-veined skull shone.

Raphael laughed. 'And the one next to him, who looks like a half-starved monk?'

Francis shrugged. 'Just an assistant, I think. I can't recall.'

The Duke of Gloucester was on the dais at the King's table with his brother George of Clarence, the forgiven traitor. Raphael watched them. Clarence, as if trying to ape the elegance of Edward, had upholstered himself with too much fur and gold damask. Sweating, throwing off layers, he now looked dishevelled and wine-stained.

Richard was his self-contained opposite. He looked isolated, Raphael thought. Against the florid splendour of the Woodvilles he stood out in the sombre colours he wore: violet and dark blue. Perhaps even his dress looked like a snub to them, a silent accusation of excess. He joined the conversation in brief, intense bursts; at other times he sat as still as a priest, with eyes only for Edward.

When Edward seized Richard, embraced him and sang the praises of his incredible bravery loud enough for the whole court to hear, the faces of all the Woodvilles – especially that of the Queen – drew tight with resentment.

Afterwards, Richard, somewhat flushed with embarrassment and pleasure, came to sit at the table with Lovell and his other friends.

'How are you faring, Raphael?' Richard asked.

'Dizzy,' Raphael said, and everyone laughed.

'Did you see the Queen's face while Edward was extolling your virtues?' Lovell exclaimed.

'No,' Richard said with a grimace, 'but I could feel my skin burning black and falling off my bones.'

More laughter. Raphael's eye was caught by a heart-stopping flow of bright golden hair. A slender creature was edging around the crush of dancers towards their table.

The golden hair, unveiled, poured over her shoulders to her waist. Mysteriously, she was dressed in man's clothes, maroon velvet patterned with gold lions.

Raphael, staring, said, 'Who on earth is *she*? Why—'

The roar of mirth that erupted almost knocked him off his chair. Lovell actually had tears running from his eyes. He put his arm round Raphael and his head on his shoulder, and leaned there, shaking. When he could speak, he gasped, 'Raphael, *she* is the Duke of Buckingham. He's all of fourteen. Oh God, I have to leave, excuse me.'

Lovell slipped away, still choking, as the slender Duke came to them and threw himself into an empty chair next to Richard.

'Edward must hate me,' he said.

He pushed back the blond hair and Raphael saw it was indeed a boy, albeit with a very pretty, full-lipped face.

'What's wrong, Cousin?' Richard asked, smiling at him. William Hastings, Edward's friend, approached and stood leaning on the two chair backs, which were of ebony carved with snakes. Hastings looked huge in an elaborately puffed and padded gown of sky-blue damask.

'He has still given me no high office,' said Buckingham.

'Lad, you're but a youth!' Hastings said jovially.

'You forget yourself, my lord; the correct address is "Your Grace",' Buckingham retorted. 'I could be sixteen or twenty-six, it would not make the King treat me as I deserve. I'm old enough to know that he has taken advantage of my youth! His dealings with me have been an abomination!'

'What's he done now?' Richard asked gently.

With his face set in a sulk, Buckingham jerked his head at the knot of the Queen's sisters. Raphael saw one of them look across at him. She was large and well-proportioned, blonde like the Queen but more mousy than silver, her eyes dark and stern-looking.

'Ah, Catherine,' said Richard. 'Harry is married to her,' he said, by way of explanation to Raphael.

'Forcibly married, when I was too young to protest, or be heard! I am a duke. I should not have been made to marry a commoner, especially not *that* commoner.'

Raphael looked again at Catherine Woodville. She was a good deal older than Buckingham, and looked as if she would crush him in bed. He tried not to smile at the image. Buckingham's distress was real.

'I agree with you,' Richard said, his expression darkening.

Hastings said, very low, 'It is disgusting how every noble family in the land has had a Woodville thrust upon them. Elizabeth's quite the equal of Marguerite for grasping ambition.'

'I want a divorce,' said Buckingham. 'Either that, or recompense, reward, *some* recognition of who I am!' He thumped the table, then looked pleadingly at Richard and Hastings. 'Will you intercede with Edward for me, gentlemen?'

Richard sighed. 'We'll try, Harry. He does as he likes, though.'

'He'll listen to you,' Buckingham said, and he flung himself out of the chair and strode away, buttercup hair floating behind him.

Shaking their heads, Richard and Hastings went towards the King's table, and were lost in the crowd.

Raphael watched the steady disintegration of the evening from pomp to chaos: Edward, drunk and red-faced with laughter; Clarence drunker, banging his fist on the table in argument. Cloaks were thrown off in the heat. Wolfhounds and salukis ran loose, scoffing the debris of bones and spilled food from the floor. The dancing, stiff and stately at the beginning, grew ragged and hilarious.

Raphael saw, suddenly, a much fatter man in the King's place. Bronze beauty bloated by ceaseless excess. Shocked, he blinked hard and the illusion was gone. Edward was lean and magnificent again.

He had his arm crooked around the neck of William

Hastings. Somehow Raphael doubted they were discussing the Duke of Buckingham's troubles. As they roared with laughter together, Raphael saw the Queen's son, Dorset, looking at them and leaning to whisper something to his uncle Anthony. The uncle, abruptly sober, gave a mysterious smile and tapped a finger to his own cheek. He rose and moved away.

'And you, my dear sir, who might you be?' said a friendly voice. It wasn't loud, but burst upon Raphael so unexpectedly that he started. He looked up in shock to find Anthony Woodville in front of him. He rose to his feet, bowing awkwardly, but Woodville pushed him down and sat beside him.

'I'm Raphael Hart.'

'Duke, lord, knight?'

'The last.'

'And nothing wrong with that. My good father, Creator acquit him, was once a plain knight and none the worse for it.' The face that looked keenly into Raphael's was big and strong-boned, with peridot eyes full of intelligent curiosity. His doublet was silver-grey, pleated and jewelled with tiny flame-coloured garnets. Against the silver, his thick fawn-blond hair had a yellow tint. Jewels sat proud upon his fingers and in his velvet bonnet. Anthony Woodville was immaculate, and exuded a scent of perfumed oil. 'Welcome, then, Raphael Hart, to the court of my noble sister Elizabeth.'

So grand that even her own mother must kneel to her. Lovell's acerbic words sprang into Raphael's mind. He pressed his lips together, trying to forget all the whisperings he'd heard about the Woodvilles.

'Honoured to meet you, my lord.'

'I make a point of welcoming every new face personally.'

'You're most kind.' Raphael was shocked to find this great man talking to him. He'd formed the impression that the Woodvilles were too high-flown to deal with commoners, as if the contact might rub the gilt off them.

'How are you enjoying the service of my lord of Gloucester?'

'I would be with no one else,' he said passionately.

'Ah, loyalty, the most excellent of virtues. The star your master follows to the utmost.'

'That's true.'

'We are all loyal to the King, God keep him. The King!' Anthony Woodville yelled suddenly, and a score of voices joined in, raising vessels in a ragged toast. Raphael hurriedly lifted his own goblet. Anthony laughed. 'I never tire of doing that. So you have been in Gloucester's service – how long?'

'Since Barnet.'

'Ah, then you're the lad who lent him the horse?'

Raphael smiled, flushed with pleasure. So, tales had been told about him. 'Yes. My own lord was killed. But I knew the Duke before that. I met him once as a child, and he remembered me.'

Anthony Woodville looked thoughtful, nodded. 'He is the sort of man one either loves or loathes. I see straight into your kindly, open heart and know that you love him.'

'Yes, my lord, I do.'

'Good, good. What do you think of that, then?' He leaned over, nudging Raphael with his shoulder, and nodding at the royal dais. Edward had his arm round Clarence; was holding forth to the nobles clustered around him. Elizabeth sat rigid, her perfect face white and sour as alum, her pale green gaze fixed on nothing, suddenly finding, and fixing on Anthony. Looking at him, she saw Raphael. He shrivelled. That was a look to strike a man dead. Awkwardly he bowed his head to her, and when he looked up, her attention was elsewhere.

'What, my lord?' Raphael breathed.

There was an edge in Anthony's voice. 'That traitor there, the turncoat Duke of Clarence, clasped to the bosom of the brother he tried to destroy.'

Raphael's mouth went bone-dry. He was being asked his opinion for a reason. 'Well, it's the Almighty's will, isn't it, that we forgive . . . the prodigal . . .'

'And you are a right generous soul to think it, but my sister, you know . . . Don't you agree, it must be hard for her to watch her husband embrace the man who razed the heads off our beloved father and brother?'

'And hard for your lordship, too,' Raphael said uncomfortably.

'He and Warwick were equal in guilt. Clarence drove my sister into sanctuary, her husband and brothers into exile. Treason, treason. Is this how the King rewards treason?'

'It's how he rewards his brother for coming to his senses,' Raphael answered carefully.

'And for neatly dispatching Edouard of Lancaster.'

'The King has a generous soul.'

'Too much so, some might say. It's a reckless virtue, to love everyone. And you, Sir Raphael, say it had been Gloucester who revolted, to whom then would you have lent your loyalty – your master, or your king?'

'That's easy to answer. I shall never in my life have to make that decision, because my lord will never be anything but unswervingly loyal to the King. It must have been a bitter decision for Warwick's men. I'm glad I'll never have to make it.'

He thought he'd answered well, but Anthony raised his eyebrows, gave a conspiratorial smile. 'Ah, too hard to make? That's answered me, then.'

He opened his mouth to deny any disloyalty to the King; horribly aware he was going to tie himself in knots while this clever charming man sat laughing at the sport. Before he could dig himself deeper, a voice interrupted. Richard was there, Francis Lovell at his side.

'My lord,' Richard said coolly. 'I hope you are not subverting my knight.'

Anthony Woodville, Earl Rivers, bowed graciously, with no sign of mockery. His velvet cap was swept down almost to his elegantly pointed toe. 'Your Grace, I always make a point of welcoming new blood to the court. I congratulate you on finding a noble and comely young man to replace those you sadly lost. I've no doubt he'll do you credit.'

Richard blinked, black eyelashes curtaining and framing his wintry gaze. 'It's good of you to sound out my men for me, Anthony, but there's no need, I trust my own judgement.'

Anthony gave a broad, warm grin and clapped Richard on the shoulder. 'Anyone would think you'd something against simple friendliness, gentle brother-in-law.' With a casual flourish he strode away, to be welcomed into the arms of his adoring sisters at the royal dais.

Richard sat down, put his elbows on the trestle and his head in his hands. He sighed. A moment later he sat up straight again. He folded his long hands. He wore a single ring on the middle finger, heavy silver with a large blood-red garnet.

'Raphael, what did he say to you?'

Nervously, Raphael told him. Richard listened, his face tight with silent anger, just as he'd looked when they walked to the Wakefield Tower. But no, that hadn't happened . . . however real it had seemed. He could not, in a thousand years, mention it to Richard himself.

When he'd finished he sat uncomfortably, waiting for the Duke to respond. But he wasn't even looking at Raphael.

Eventually he said under his breath, 'These bloody Woodvilles.'

'My sentiments exactly,' said Lovell.

Richard turned to Francis and said in the softest voice, 'The worst thing is that I almost don't blame Warwick. Never could I condone his treachery, but I can see why he was so inflamed. His proclamation, against the "deceivable and covetous rule and guiding" to which Edward is subject, was the plain truth.'

'Blood of Iesu, man, you're not suggesting you're tempted to rebel as well?'

Lovell was probably the only man who could have got away with saying it. Richard's eyes were two burning-cold stones. Raphael was glad that the look had not fallen on him. Although Richard's eyes stayed frigid, he smiled. 'Very funny, Francis.' He rose, about to walk away. 'Even funnier, addressed to the one subject in the realm who would never speak such treason.'

When he'd gone – a narrow shadow swallowed into the swirling coloured mass of the hall – Raphael felt close to collapsing with anxiety. He put his hand on Lovell's arm for support. 'What will he do to me?'

'What?' Lovell said. 'Lamb's blood, Raph, what's wrong with you? You didn't say anything wrong. He's angry with Woodville, not with you. If you'd said anything out of place, believe me, he'd have told you! Drink this.'

Raphael couldn't form words to explain that it wasn't the exchange with Woodville that suddenly choked him, but the haunting vision of murder. He could barely breathe. All he could see was the knife blade sliding easily and dispassionately under Henry's thin breastbone. Wine was thrust at him. He took a gulp and the room became clear again.

'I'm sorry, Francis. I'm new to this. I feel as if I'm going to drown in it.'

The chamber to which Richard summoned him was luscious with red walls, a frieze of gold-leaf fleur-de-lys and silken drapes hanging heavy on the great bed. Two chairs of molasses-dark oak stood on either side of a small table. Richard bade him sit down and he felt the lick of heat from the fireplace. A page poured claret, and was dismissed. Richard leaned back in his chair, his left side painted luminous red by fire, the right side in velvety shadow. He looked distracted and serious. Raphael was uneasy. He took a sip of his wine and found his hand shaking so much he nearly spilt it.

A line indented Richard's forehead. 'Francis tells me he fears you are unwell.'

'I am perfectly well, Your Grace.'

'Not tempted to gorge yourself on the feast?'

The corner of his lip curved up. Raphael knew he meant the stew of Edward's court. 'No, my lord, then I should be ill for certain.'

'Wise,' said the Duke, then, starkly, 'Beware of my family.'

Images of Henry's murder flashed into his mind. 'Yes?'

'They will probe you to test your colours, to see if you may be persuadable or useful, to see if you might spy upon me for them. You have gone quite white.' He leaned forward. 'What is it, Raphael? You must understand one thing about Francis, he's no tell-tale. I don't know why he thinks you may be troubled, nor why he suggested I speak to you, but I know he did so out of kindness. For him to ask at all, it must be serious.'

'It was only a dream.' The words spilled out, like a child's confession.

Richard sat back, his chin resting on curved fingers. 'What dream?'

He listened without comment, without expression, as Raphael miserably told him everything. When he finished, he sat twisting his sweating fingers together until they ached, waiting for the sky to fall.

'This has been preying on your mind?' Gloucester asked tonelessly.

'It was so real!'

Richard breathed in and out, slowly and heavily. 'Let me tell you what actually happened. When Henry was told of his son's death, he didn't react, they weren't sure he'd even understood. Later, however, he asked for wine, which was not his usual habit. His warders served him, and left him to sleep. In the night they heard a sound, a soft *thump, thump, thump*. Going in to Henry, they found him dashing his head against the stone of his walls. It took two men to stop him. Almost at once he fell insensible. He did not wake again. By morning he was dead, Creator acquit him, and I think it was a mercy for us all, most especially for him.'

Raphael couldn't speak. He was certain now that Richard would dismiss him from service in the same gentle, passionless tone. The lord he loved now thought he was mad, or possessed. Tears squeezed from his eyes but they were for Henry, not for himself. Nothing seemed to matter.

Then Gloucester leaned forward a little and spoke again. This time his voice was entirely different, not much above a whisper but fierce with emotion.

'That is the official version,' he said. 'I cannot say it is untrue. But you are thinking, aren't you, as all men will think, that it's a hellish coincidence that the night Edward returned to the Tower, the night of his victory, was also the night that Henry died? He'll trouble us no more. All evening, Anthony Woodville and others had been whispering in Edward's ear, "Finish him, and he'll trouble us no more." Edward listens to them too often, and if he took little persuasion this time, he can hardly be blamed. It was a vile act, to murder a blameless old man. But what else is there to do with a deposed king?'

'Are you saying that Edward . . .' his words dried up.

'Well, which version seems the most probable to you?'

Raphael could not, dared not answer. At long last Richard sighed, a tired hiss through his teeth. 'I hate the court,' he said.

Raphael looked up in surprise.

'I refused to take part,' Richard went on. 'I don't want to know what happened. However, since I still sup with Edward and love him and keep my mouth closed upon the subject, that makes me as culpable as he is, or is not. I can't condemn you for a poisonous dream, Raphael. What have your thoughts had to feed on here, but poison?'

'Please pardon me, Your Grace. I wouldn't have dreamed such evil of you for the world.' He looked straight into Richard's glass-grey eyes. 'But I couldn't lie to you.'

'And the trouble is that your dream, in itself, was not a

total lie, rather a stark revelation of what is in our hearts. How shall we be judged for killing a saint? We didn't want to damn our immortal souls with his blood, but by the Lamb, we wanted Henry dead. Are you a prophet, dear friend?'

Raphael felt a strange, thrilling shock that Richard called him *friend*.

'No. Just a victim of too much hippocras.'

The Duke's lips shifted into a slight smile. 'Well, don't ever be afraid to tell me what's in your heart. If you have any more dreams, Raphael, I trust you will tell me of them? In fact, I lay an obligation upon you to tell me.'

Chapter Eight 1477: Ankarette

> These three brothers, the king and the two dukes, were possessed of such surpassing talents that, if only they had been able to live without dissension, such a threefold cord could never have been broken without the utmost difficulty.
>
> *Croyland Chronicle*

Katherine came out of the door into the courtyard and leaned in the archway, looking at the rain. Drops skimmed her face, dampening the ends of her hair. She turned her weary face to the sky and let the grey rain fall. The sky was weeping for her.

Perhaps it would be a blessing to enter a nunnery, she thought. A woman could order her own life, and not be brought constantly to childbed, eventually to die there. Her mother had taught her secret ways to avoid pregnancy – the forbidden wisdom of Auset – the little cups of bark or oiled seed husks that could be inserted, the herbs that worked without poisoning. Yet when Kate had offered these to Isabel – by then the mother of a thriving boy and girl – she had been horrified.

'It's unholy magic, contrary to the laws of the Church,' she'd said, frowning in indignation and speaking very low. They had concealed themselves in an alcove behind a thick velvet curtain, although there was no one to overhear. 'I know you're only trying to help, Kate, but how could you think I'd use such things? You are outrageous. I like my children, why should I bar their entry to this life? I'll bear George as many babes as I may; I'll prove myself just as much a woman as that Elizabeth Woodville, who farrows incessantly like a sow!'

Kate had rarely seen her so angry. 'You are not a sow, and it's not a competition.'

'Nevertheless I couldn't. I couldn't.' Yet a shadow passed over Isabel's brow, and Kate felt rueful for having tempted her. 'Let us forget that this talk ever took place.'

Without expression Kate answered, 'I'll not mention it again, Bel. If you wish to farrow like a sow, spawn like a fish or lay eggs like a duck, I am here only to help.'

That set Isabel laughing again. She was never angry for long. Although a mother and a duchess, she still loved to curl up on a window seat with Katherine and whisper and laugh.

Kate remembered her framed against the tall leaded windows with her head tipped back against the glass and her red hair spilling over the dark blue velvet of her gown, weeping for her father the Kingmaker. Even then she hadn't been sad long, hadn't wanted to mourn alone, but had demanded Kate in her arms to hold and bring comfort and, eventually, sad smiles again.

She'd been so full of life, Isabel. It had shaped her beauty. The richly painted corridors of Warwick Castle still echoed to her footsteps. The flying fox-tail of her hair. No more would it lead Kate on into mischief.

The flame of life had burned too bright and fast in her, like fever.

For months, Kate had worked with Ankarette, Isabel's chamber woman, to save her. At the birth, Kate had been the surrogate as always, taking on the burden of Isabel's pain, sweating and crying out with her, never able to take enough of it away. Ankarette was the midwife, watching over them both. Isabel's labour had not been long this time, but the boy had come too fast, tearing something inside her. For all their efforts, they hadn't been able to prevent it. Isabel sank into blood fever. In the last few days, her husband had fretted and paced and raged, as if his anger was all it took to change things.

But all Ankarette's experience, their combined herbal knowledge and Kate's desperate appeals to Auset, Mary and even to Almighty God had been of no avail. Isabel had slipped away, pale and blue and serene, holding Kate's hands. Her child survived her by a few days.

Afterwards, Ankarette held Kate to her vast bosom and crooned to her like a mother. 'Ah, well, this is the gamble of life. I have seen it a hundred times. God protects the noble no better than he protects the common woman, and these Neville girls are not strong.'

'She was my best friend,' was all Kate could say, like a child. Ankarette Twynyho was a well-to-do widow who'd attracted the Queen's favour and served her for a time, then been sent – in a generous gesture on the Queen's part – to attend Isabel. Although not a member of the Motherlodge, she was sensible and motherly and had seen everything in her time. But for all their skill, something had happened to Isabel they couldn't understand or cure.

Now Isabel lay in state, and Katherine had been to view her body: a sleeping princess in a bower of candle-light. Her sister Anne had been there too, like a veiled ghost weeping and praying over her. Kate hadn't spoken to her.

'What good is it?' she said to herself, leaning in the doorway, hugging herself with her hands tucked under her arms. 'Dark Mother, why didn't you let us save her? Auset, if you are really there, why do you let such things happen to your daughters?'

'I'm away, then,' said Ankarette, pushing along the corridor behind her with a large bundle. She wore travelling clothes: a thick wool cloak and a wimple of white cloth. 'There's my lad, come to take me home.'

Peering through the sheets of rain, Kate made out a carriage on the far side of the courtyard, with a drenched horse standing between the shafts, and an equally drenched young man holding its bridle. 'Why don't you wait until this lets up?'

'Oh, it'll stop in its own time. I just want to be away from here.' Ankarette stopped, breathing heavily as she hefted the bundle on her knee. 'Where will you go, dear?'

Katherine started. For the last seven years and more, her home had been where Isabel was, wherever George of Clarence had taken them. Into her mind leaped the words that of course she'd stay here, serving the lady of the household . . . but the lady was gone. She had to keep reminding herself of that. It hadn't become real yet. 'I don't know.'

'Come with me, if you like. We've a nice little manor in Somerset. Unless the Queen sends for me again I'll be glad to retire there, after all this time.'

Kate looked at the rain, and sighed. 'Thanks, Ankarette, but I'll stay here a while. The Duke may need my comfort.'

The widow pulled a face, her head drawn back. 'I'll bet he will. You be careful, girl, or you'll be warming his bed with no thanks for it, and kicked out as soon as he finds some other hapless heiress to marry him.'

Kate exclaimed in disgust. 'I meant spiritual comfort! Gods, good mother, I'd rather marry that drowned horse over there than go to bed with the Duke! What do you take me for?'

'A wise one,' said Ankarette, chuckling. She patted Kate's shoulder, and turned to walk away. A moment later Katherine came to her senses, ran after her, and carried the bundle for her to the carriage.

With the kindly widow gone, Warwick Castle seemed as quiet as a tomb. Everything had changed. Anne had lived with them for a time, but she was long gone, remarried and living in the north. Her marriage to Prince Edouard had been wretched, but brief. Tewkesbury had made her a widow. George of Clarence had made her a widow, in fact, so it was rumoured. Kate thought it interesting that he had slain her husband, then taken custody of her, for

203

it also gave him control of her vast inheritance. He had no legal rights over her, but that didn't stop him. Soon the bitterest of arguments had raged over Anne Neville, a time Kate still remembered, despite all the care she'd taken to distance herself, with stabbing pain.

Richard of Gloucester proved to be Anne's only champion. He had wanted to marry her. An inevitable union, given their rank, but George had been unwilling to let his sister-in-law go. His own wife's half of the Warwick estates were not enough for him, he wanted everything. God forbid his brother should seize half. He had even stooped, ridiculously, to hiding Anne in a friend's house, disguised as a maid. But Richard had found her, the marriage had taken place, and George had been left to sulk and moan about the terrible injustice done to him.

Kate had deliberately kept out of the way. Whenever Richard had come to Clarence's London house, she would make certain to be out, or closet herself away in the furthest chamber. Their arguments were spectacular, she'd heard, but she didn't want to witness them. Above all, she had no desire to see Richard and Anne together. If she didn't see them, she could pretend none of it was happening, and thus, by cunning, she had avoided coming face to face with Richard. He must have known she was there, but she doubted that he was interested. She congratulated herself on avoiding him. It had been troublesome, but better than the excruciating awkwardness of meeting him.

She barely knew him and cared nothing for him. She had never grown close to Anne. It should not have mattered. But when Raphael had written to her, describing this romance in amused and glowing terms, she had sometimes been so enraged that she'd torn the letters up and thrown them in the fire.

Anyway, it was long over. Richard and Anne had gone to live at Middleham Castle in Yorkshire, their childhood home. They had a son called Edward. Raphael had gone with them and still wrote sweetly to Kate, at least once a month. She was bad at answering, had little to say. The fact that Richard was married meant nothing. It maddened her that any reminder of it still felt, without reason, like a poison-dipped blade in her heart.

The Countess, Anne Beauchamp, was gone too. She'd fled into sanctuary after Warwick's death, emerging eventually to live with Anne and Richard at Middleham. Kate hadn't seen her for years. The heart of the household was gone, its lifeblood drained away in fog and rain.

Now Ankarette was gone as well, Kate missed her. She wondered if she would serve Queen Elizabeth again. Impudently, she had once asked, 'What is the Queen really like?'

'Elizabeth,' Ankarette had given a wry chuckle, 'is not as terrifying as many think. A proud woman, ruthless, but frightened sometimes. She's achieved the highest station, and therefore has a great deal to lose. I believe that's why she makes a show of arrogance, to hide the fear. It's in her interests to keep people a little afraid of her.'

'My mother has said the same to me,' said Kate. '"We must keep them afraid, but not so afraid that they destroy us."'

'I shouldn't like to get on the wrong side of her, I must confess.'

'Is it true she once had a man executed for insulting her?'

Ankarette's kind face had clouded. 'Lord Desmond. The charge was one of treachery. The worst was that they slew his two little boys, too, who never hurt a soul.'

'Was that the Queen's fault or a misunderstanding?'

'You ask too many questions.'

'Our tradition doesn't see the world in plain terms of good and evil,' Kate had answered primly.

'I was lucky that she liked me, and so seemed quite likeable to me in turn,' Ankarette said. 'However, I must admit that I wasn't sorry when she sent me to the Duchess Isabel. Elizabeth made for hard work.'

Contrary to Ankarette's warnings, after Isabel's funeral Kate barely saw George of Clarence. He was in and out of the castle, bustling, conferring with his men-at-arms. The few times she glimpsed him, he looked crimson-faced, preoccupied, perhaps drunk. He barely spared her a glance. When he did, something venomous spat from his eyes. She was glad he kept out of her way.

Kate spent her time in the nursery with Isabel's little son and daughter and their nurses, or writing letters to her mother. There was tension among the staff. Never the happiest of households, George's; his servants were wary of his temper and capricious demands. Kate looked sadly on them. She'd decided long ago to stand up to him, and he seemed to respect her for it.

Sometimes she would start up from a reverie, and think she was late attending Isabel – only to remember, with falling heart, that there was no one waiting.

Winter was miserable. She decided, at last, that when the weather cleared she might as well go back to her mother. The thought startled her. It had been too easy to avoid visits and awkward conversations with Eleanor, difficult meetings with the woman, Jenny. The rosy fledgling in Jenny's charge was not Kate's and yet he was, but no one must know. Although she wanted to see him it was easier not to. The pleasure was too painful. Kate had learned to be ice-cold, to cut herself off from all thoughts of him, but sometimes it hit her like a searing flame from toes to crown. Could she bear to go back, to see him growing, his father's face echoed beautifully in his as a constant reminder? She drew a breath. Perhaps she should. From the moment of his birth he'd been a reward, not a punishment. She'd been so lucky. She couldn't possess him, but that he was alive and healthy was surely good fortune enough.

She began to pack her belongings, then sat down on her window seat, with watery nets of sunlight dropping over her, to write and let Eleanor know.

It was then she heard a commotion below her window:

dozens of sets of hooves on stone, men's loud voices, the clatter of armour, saddlery, spears. She jumped. For a horrible moment she thought the castle was being invaded; nothing was beyond possibility. Looking out, she saw a troop of some eighty men in the Duke of Clarence's livery in the bailey. She was relieved until she saw in their midst a woman in a linen head-dress, the unmistakable, ample form of Ankarette Twynyho, mounted on a bay cob, and with – dearest Dark Mother – with *ropes* around her wrists.

As Katherine stared, unbelieving, she saw the armed men roughly dragging the widow from her horse. Ankarette cried out, stumbled to her knees on the courtyard stones and was jerked to her feet again. She stood shaking visibly as George stepped out of the castle and strolled in his yellow and gold finery towards her.

He extended his hand and slapped Ankarette across the cheek. Then he spat into her face. Kate screamed.

She ran for the door of her chamber, down the spiral stairs to the outside, only to crash hard into the breastplate of one of Clarence's bodyguards. The man seemed huge in the darkness of the stairwell. She fought him as he bundled her back up the steps.

'Take your hands off me! You'll be sorry you man-handled me – what's happening? Let me past!'

'My lady, I'm sorry,' the man said hoarsely. As they came back into the light of the chamber she saw his face was flour-grey and haggard. He put his big hands up to ward her off; a gesture of apology. 'The Duke has told me to detain you in your private chamber and not let you outside. Pardon me, I beg you. It's the Duke's command. I daren't disobey. He's mad with grief over his wife.'

'Is he?' Kate hissed. 'He cared precious little for her while she lived! What are they doing with poor Ankarette out there?'

His mouth opened helplessly. 'They . . .'

'Well, come on!'

'The Widow Twynyho is accused of poisoning the Duchess and of doing away with her and her babe by black magic.' His voice cracked like old wood.

'*What?*'

To Kate it seemed as if the whole castle was shaken by cannon fire. It began to spin around her. She fought for breath. Her head was like thistledown, floating. She ran to the window again. The bailey was empty.

'Where have they taken her?'

He cleared his throat. 'Into the town to be tried by jury. If she's found guilty, she'll be hanged for witchcraft.'

'That's illegal,' she whispered, when she could speak at all. 'That's against the common law, the King's law. They can't execute us for—'

'I meant for poisoning, for murder. I don't know!' the man said, helpless.

'But – but I must go and testify for her. I know she did Isabel no harm! We did everything to save her and the child! We—'

We.

'I'm sure you did, my lady.' The man was crying.

'Please let me out.'

'I can't. Don't make me stop you bodily, it would be wrong on both of us and there are other men on the stairs and the doors.'

His tears made Katherine cry with him. 'We're all grieving for Isabel,' she said. 'Is George so grief-stricken that he must find someone to blame, however innocent, however faithful to the Duchess?'

'I couldn't say, my lady. Please.'

She sat down and put her face on her hands. Great Lady Auset, punish those who do this. Punish them with all the fires of the hell that they believe in!

Later, a page crept in and brought her supper. She sipped at the claret, but could not touch the food. One of the children's nursemaids, a dark girl called Ursula, came to sit with her, to save her being left alone all night with Clarence's henchmen, she presumed. Eventually she curled up on the bed and slept.

She woke, drained and fragile, to the face of George's clerk bending over her. It was night and felt very late or early, close to dawn.

'My lady?' he said delicately. 'My lady, His Grace wishes to speak with you.'

'Wait.' She rose dizzily from her stupor.

'His Grace will not wait.' The clerk was pale, his plump hands trembling.

'Wait,' she said sharply, 'at least for me visit the garde-robe and to order my hair!'

He fell back, blustering with embarrassment. 'Of course, of course.'

'Sir . . .' she rose with stiff dignity and stood looking at him, her mouth sour. 'Tell me plainly, did they hang the Widow Twynyho?'

'Yes,' he whispered.

'Thank you.'

In the latrine, she coughed a thin stream of bile into the darkness and thought of throwing herself after it, down the long stinking throat of stone. Instead, she calmly passed water, straightened her skirts, came back into the chamber and gathered up her dishevelled hair beneath a hennin.

George of Clarence was waiting for her in the presence chamber. He sat in his huge chair of carved oak that was almost a throne, one long leg stretched out, one elbow lolling over the arm of the chair. Any beauty in his face was extinguished by the flush of malice. His curly fair hair hung flat with sweat. His eyes were glittering.

In all her life, Kate had never known such fear. She stood before him like a willow wand, stripped white. He only had to lift a finger and his men would come and take her, as they'd taken Ankarette; reluctant, trembling, apologizing, perhaps, but implacable because they feared the Duke more than they pitied her.

She thought of scaring him, as her mother had once

scared the lowland marauders, by revealing the crowned serpent that hung between her breasts – but that would be to admit her guilt – what guilt? Complicity – in what?

'Anne's written to me,' he said in a slurred voice.

'What? My lord—?'

He spoke again, slow and careful, a drunk trying to sound sober. And he was drunk, she saw, nothing new, except that he was terrifyingly lucid with it. 'My sister-in-law Anne, Duchess of Gloucester, has written a letter to me. Now that Isabel is gone from us, she has asked for you at Middleham. She desires your services as lady-in-waiting, Lady Katherine.'

It was the last thing she'd expected him to say. Her voice emerged a faint dry husk. 'Her Grace honours me.'

'Why then do you stare at me as if you've seen a basilisk?' He lurched up in his chair, making her start. She saw the glimmer of his tears like liquid glass; madness trembling on a razor-edge of grief.

She dropped her gaze and stared at the hem of blue velvet and fur, the long toes of her slippers embroidered with tiny lilies.

'Come closer,' he said, and she obeyed, shuddering as the stale alcohol smell of him reached her. 'Look at me, you silly child. Look upon the King of Burgundy!'

She looked up, and he was laughing, teeth stained wine-black against his crimson skin. She thought then that he had lost his mind utterly. He was suffering from delusions. The King of Burgundy, what in heaven was he talking about? But the sight of his laughter made her abruptly and incandescently furious.

'You knew she was innocent!' Kate cried. 'She never hurt a soul in her life! You should be damned to hell for what you did!'

The smile died.

She heard the gasps of his henchmen from the edges of the room. Then a thick silence. She was sobbing without sound, imagining that if she made no noise she might vanish. Waiting for the hard hands to grip and drag her out, wondering what Ankarette had felt when she saw the gallows waiting.

He said softly to his men-at-arms, 'Get out.'

Now she was alone with him. Her mouth was sawdust.

'Do you not think I would have made a good king, Lady Katherine?' he asked.

'I – I couldn't say, sir.'

'Edward and I were born the wrong way round, that's all. It should have been me. I have been a faithful husband, a good Christian knight. *I* would not have surrounded myself with whores, witches and arse-licking nobodies. All I did was for England's good! And what reward was I given? Not even my good father-in-law's estates, Creator acquit him, but Dickon has to wrest half of them from me. Even you, gentle lady, would send me to hell on top of it.'

'Perhaps you should go to your bed, sir, and rest,' she said. 'You have had a very full day. I am sure things will seem better for you in the morning.' For *you*, she added silently. Not for your victims.

'Even the venom of your tongue is passing sweet,' he said. 'I asked the Widow Twynyho that question. "Shall I not make a splendid king of England?"'

'And what – what did she reply?'

'"No,"' Clarence said viciously. '"Never," she said. "It is not your destiny," she said. And thus I knew Ankarette was a witch.'

'How?'

'Because she had prophesied against me! And then I knew, I knew what had befallen poor Isabel! The witch murdered her. Gods, d'you think that if I had not slain her, she would not have come back and poisoned my other son and daughter?'

He really believed it, she saw, or had convinced himself of it, at least for as long as the rawness of passion lasted. And after that, she thought, he will still find some way to justify it to himself. She tried to rub the sweat from her palms, but more came. Does he know what I am? He must know what I did for Edward during the battle of Barnet, unless he's forgotten, or wasn't told. Taken Ankarette for a witch, but not me? Kate didn't know whether he was foolish, or simply unobservant, too concerned with his own affairs and opinions to see what was actually around him.

'She never will now,' Kate said softly. 'She had no reason . . .'

'No reason but the money, the reward, the pure delight in evil,' he said.

'Reward?'

'Who d'you think set her on? Where did she come from?'

Kate paused, lips forming a soundless O. 'The Queen.'

'Yes, yes, you see it now, eh? Elizabeth Woodville sent her waiting woman to murder my wife and children. This is all her doing, her vengeance, the damned Woodville witch, she's conspired to destroy me from the beginning. No more. I have the evidence against her now.'

Kate was incredulous. If he presented this story of conspiracy to Edward, the King would laugh in his face. She studied Clarence and still did not know if he was insane or demonically cunning.

He said, 'Well, she and you have your wish, lady. I am in hell.'

'Then we both are.'

'Do you think I did not love my wife?'

She stepped closer, fervent. 'We all did! She was not poisoned. Even the Queen would not visit such malice upon you. Bel was ill, very ill. Bearing the child weakened her. It's tragic, but that is all.'

She expected raging denial. Instead, to her horror, Clarence snaked forward and put his arms around her. They encircled her hips, and his heavy head was pillowed on her abdomen. He was shuddering with sobs. Kate was locked there, mortified, while he soaked her with his open-mouthed grief.

She thought she might be held there for the rest of time, in some ghastly penance for Isabel's death. At last, at last he let his arms slide away. Slumping back in his throne, he sat back, face empty, staring at a void she couldn't imagine. She slipped carefully away from him and found a tapestried footstool to sit on before he grabbed her again.

'Can you prophesy, Kate?'

A chill rushed over her. 'No, my lord.'

'Strange, when you worked so close with the widow, that her ways did not rub off on you. Or did yours rub off on her? Did you conspire with her, listening to her whispering innuendos? Did she confess that my enemies paid her to destroy my dynasty? I thought you an innocent, so fair, so beloved of my wife . . . but I don't know, I don't know. I have heard that your kind are to witches as cardinals are to simple monks.'

So he did know. He was playing a cruel game, batting her all around the room like a cat with its prey. George was unpredictable, running with whatever caprice seized him. She couldn't tell if his rage had burned out, or would flare again at a wrong word.

She took a deep breath, told herself, I must be prepared to die with dignity, as I'm sure dear Ankarette did, then I can speak without fear.

'Your Grace, are you threatening me that if I do not give you a prophecy that pleases you, you'll have me hanged?'

He moistened his lips and gazed at her from heavy-lidded eyes. 'I could do what I damned well please with you, Katy Lytton.'

'My mother told me there is no such thing as pre-ordination, only splits in the path according to what choices you make. How should I predict what choices you will make? Perhaps if you repent and become a good man, you will become King of Burgundy, France, England and the whole world.'

'How dare you mock me?' he gasped. 'I shall rule

Burgundy! Margaret, my sister, has offered me the hand in marriage of her step-daughter Marie. And Marie is—?'

'The Duchess of Burgundy,' said Kate.

'And Burgundy has a great army.' Clarence sat back, his large hands clawing at the arms of his chair. 'I'll become its duke. I can make myself its king, and from there—'

'You never give up, do you?' she cried. 'And Isabel barely cold.'

'There's a horse,' he said savagely, huge glassy tears spilling suddenly down his face. 'There's a horse made ready for you in the courtyard, my best grey palfrey, with eight of my men for escort and a girl called Ursula to attend you.'

'I know Ursula,' Kate said faintly.

'Never forget, I could have hanged you for conspiracy with the widow. Instead I send you to my sister-in-law, that Dickon may have as much joy of you as I have had.'

Ice-cold, Katherine started up from her stool. She wanted to run from the chamber, but held back. She walked steadily to the Duke, stopping for half a second to touch his hand. It was an impulse, part caress of sympathy and part pinch of hatred. She held the warm thick fold of his palm between her thumb and forefinger, gripped it briefly, swallowing sourness as she realized that his incontinent grief had caused Ankarette's unfair death, and worse, that his twisted mind had turned Isabel's death to political advantage without missing a beat. She hurried on her way, head averted, unable to look at him.

Afterwards, she wondered if he had spared her because he was afraid of her.

She broke her journey to visit her mother, arriving in Lytton Dale on a bright, overcast winter afternoon. The moors looked high, frost-coated. In the valley snow had fallen lightly, turning the day softly luminous.

Eleanor looked no older. Serene and proud, she stood in the doorway to greet her daughter. Under the eyes of

Clarence's dour men-at-arms, they embraced and held each other warmly. Then, resting her head against her mother's shoulder, Kate began to spill out her tale. She was still talking as her mother led her up to the solar, sat her down and gave her elderberry wine to drink. She didn't raise her head or pause until she had finished.

'How long will you stay?' Eleanor asked gently.

'Only one night. I'd not want Clarence's lads to have their noses in your trough longer than that.'

Eleanor smiled. 'That doesn't matter. It would do you good to rest in a friendly place for a while. Oh, Goddess, poor Kate . . .'

'Poor Bel, and poor Ankarette,' Kate said briskly. She wanted no sympathy, no comments on her tale, and Eleanor was too canny to offer them. She looked up, glad to see light still strong in the windows. 'Is there anything to eat? All this travelling has made me so famished I could swallow two deer and a roasted porcupine.'

Later, she slipped away from the house and, wrapped in wool and furs, ran headlong into the snow-clotted folds of the demesne. What sweet relief to be alone. The land was as beautiful as ever. Nothing had changed. Her mother still exercised her gentle guardianship, ever busy and watchful, holding the demesne like a tiny kingdom. Katherine trudged across folded sheep meadows, down between the limestone gorges, until she came to the wide shallow river Melandra. Ice crusted its margins, but the water still ran strongly. Its bubbling whisper was the same, the unending tale of the earth's heart. She walked along the banks until she came to Old Mag Heads, where two tributaries gushed over waterfalls and joined to form the main river. The hill that reared behind them was winter-bleak. There she crossed the stone bridges over the falls, and went on her way up to Briganta's Cave, the sacred Cauldron Hollow.

She had visited the cavern in all its moods. Today the weather was icy and brooding. Hag weather. A chill breeze chased the clouds and blew cold, thrilling breath into Kate's lungs. She passed under the great curved arch and into the chill of the cave.

She'd had nightmares of seeing this sacred place as Edith had described her own Hollow: cordoned by pompous priests and soldiers and desecrated; elementals affrighted so they fled, leaving the place grey and lifeless.

Anyway, not yet.

Kneeling beside the spring, she sipped the icy water. The clear blood of mother earth was given bountifully, not in rationed sips by a priest.

'Auset, I invoke thee,' she said under her breath. 'Take Isabel and Ankarette to your breast, for they were your daughters. Show me a way as thorny and narrow as you like, only give me a little guidance upon it now and then.'

The murmur of water roared in her head. She closed her eyes and felt the creatures of the hidden world stirring behind the hair-thin veil. The ground beneath her knees became the pulsing hide of a snake. She could feel the swell of its muscles. In her mind's eye hung a dark face, half woman and half serpent, with a long scaled nose and eyes like sunlight on water, commanding, challenging.

'Here you are,' said a voice, very soft.

Kate opened her eyes and saw Eleanor picking her way into the cavern. She was dressed in grey and silver, the threadbare hem of her skirt brushing the limestone. The world settled, but the hush of power remained. Her mother knew better than to disturb it.

Kate asked, 'Are we still safe . . . with Edward?'

'Oh, he is as good a protector as we can hope for,' her mother said, kneeling beside her. 'He understands. He promised me he's forbidden his bishops to interfere with our traditions. But it's not his greatest priority. If ever they're let off the leash . . . if ever the Lancastrians get in the ascendant again . . .'

'Goddess and God protect King Edward, then,' said Kate.

'Amen,' said Eleanor, and laughed. 'Kate, I've something

to tell you. The Motherlodge have named me Dame Eylott's successor.'

Kate hugged her. 'That's wonderful, but hardly unexpected.'

'My thanks for your faith, love, but to be *Mater Superior* is a great responsibility. And it's sad to know that Dame Eylott is unwell and not immortal.'

'Yes, but since we can't change that, I'm glad they've chosen you. It's right. And something to be happy about, after all this trouble.'

Eleanor nodded, smiling agreement. 'Yes, love, it is.'

'And you have had no more trouble from Lord Stanley?'

Eleanor sighed. 'Kate . . . Thomas Stanley is not such an ogre. He has a gentler side that isn't deaf to reason.' She fell silent and bit her lower lip, turning it pink.

'What exactly do you mean?' Kate said, frowning.

'No one is utterly bad, Kate. I grew, if not fond, at least to find him pleasant.'

Kate sat upright with a cry. 'What? When did this happen?'

'Years ago.' She stroked her daughter's hair. 'He visited me a time or two. Since he found another match for his son – a Woodville, naturally, a niece of the Queen's in whose right he became Lord Strange – there were no hard feelings. We had many interesting talks and we reached an understanding.'

'Are you saying . . . ? No, don't tell me any more.'

Eleanor was laughing. 'Kate, you've been far too long in the outer world! Indignation doesn't suit you. I'm saying that things changed between us; he realized he'd been a brute and decided to be a gentleman instead, and let us be.'

'In that case, why didn't you just marry him?'

Eleanor's smile expressed irony. 'If he'd fallen in love with me, he still wouldn't have let his heart rule his head. Only an heiress on a grand scale such as Margaret Beaufort could interest Thomas Stanley, which is my good fortune since I would not want him as a husband. Too cunning by far.'

Kate found a pebble and sat rolling it in her palm. 'You probably have dozens of lovers that I don't know about.'

Eleanor only smiled sweetly.

Kate added, 'You have a secret life. Are mothers allowed to do that?'

'The sisters of Auset are. Is there anything you'd like me to do about what you told me – about the Duke of Clarence?'

'No, no!' Kate threw the pebble down. 'I didn't come crying to you, expecting you to make it better! Tell tales to King Edward? Who am I, a glorified abigail, to make a complaint? And have George find out, and come after me? No, Edward will find out soon enough, and from more consequential voices than mine.'

'Well, that's a wise answer.'

'Still, I'd like to ask you about Anne Beauchamp.'

'What about her?'

'How could she reach such high degree in the Mother-lodge yet teach nothing to her daughters?'

Eleanor sighed through her nose. After a pause she answered, 'Because of her husband. Because of his position, close to the royal court and the Church. He forbade it. Whatever his wife did in secret, he turned a blind eye, but he would not have his daughters taught the old ways. That might have brought him into disrepute, and into conflict with the Church, not to mention making them unmarriageable.'

'Unmarriageable!'

'In the eyes of the princes or dukes he wished them to marry.'

'And anyone would do, so long as he was a prince.' Kate spat. 'If you'd been in her position, you would have disobeyed your husband and taught your daughters behind his back. I know it.'

'I would not have married the Earl of Warwick in the first place,' said Eleanor.

'However, he is dead now.'

'And his daughters have Christian husbands.'

Kate was seething, years of frustration erupting. Eleanor only laughed sadly. 'This is the way of the world,' she said. 'I have raged against it like you, but raging only drains our energy from more important things.'

'Then I would like to change the world! If I could have made Isabel see that two fine children were enough, and she need not go on bearing more until it killed her – if her *mother* had taught her that! – she might have lived yet. Wasn't that important?'

Eleanor's mouth was pale and tight against the hopelessness of Kate's anger. 'The best we can hope for is to find a good man who believes as we do. They exist, but are as rare as a sleek silver pard among a pack of graylix. Failing that, at least a husband who'll leave us to our own devices.'

'Would my life be easier, then, if I surrendered myself to the Church and married a noble like George of Clarence? I think not. It would be infinitely worse!'

'Be glad of what you are,' her mother said passionately. 'I am. There are those who would like to crush us for being different. But the last thing I'd want is for you to give in! Someone must tend the serpent flame, or . . .'

Kate nodded. 'I wonder what will become of me.'

'Come, let's return to the house and warm up. I am frozen. Martha is waiting, and certain others who would like to see you before you leave.'

Kate asked quickly, without tone, 'How is the little bird?'

'The little bird is thriving.' Rising, Eleanor added, 'You know, you needn't go to Middleham. You can stay here.'

Kate paused, chewing her lip. 'No, I'll go. A duchess has summoned me; I cannot refuse.' Dropping her sour tone, she laughed. 'I won't be friendless. That girl Clarence sent with me, Ursula, is sweet. And Nan has asked to come too. I should look quite impressive, arriving with two attendants.'

'And Raphael is there.'

She grinned. 'Yes, Raphael, but he's not the reason. Mama, of course I'll serve Anne if she wants me. I must go out and battle in the world, not hide behind your skirts. You wouldn't expect less of me, would you?'

'Hardly. You are my daughter.'

Katherine had never been further north than York before. She expected high wild country, and the castle to be a bleak pile set on a windswept escarpment, the bleakness a perfect setting for its warrior ruler, Richard of Gloucester. He had won a fearsome reputation against the Scots since she had last seen him.

The Yorkshire Dales, however, were green. Drenched in endless rain, with massive outcrops of limestone overhanging the spindly, muddy track on which they rode, but as lovely as the land she was used to. The people they met on their way were close-mouthed, and glanced at Clarence's livery with suspicion; but they looked with warm empathy at her when they heard her Derbyshire accent, and were told where she was going.

As they reached Middleham the clouds split and brilliant sunlight spilled through. There was a village like a little ochre patchwork, and just above it, almost part of it, the castle. No grim fortress, but a modest square structure, elegant, warm, golden-grey. Meadows spread around it, beaded with the deeper green of forests and, in the distance, the shoulder of the fells, blue and remote. Nan and Ursula exclaimed in pleasure.

Katherine saw a bird of prey wheeling above the castle and its estates. She watched until it dropped out of sight. Her party rode between the straw-coloured cots of the village, with dozens of children and adults collecting along the path to watch and gossip, up to the curtain wall of the castle, across the wooden bridge, through the open gate and into the castle courtyard.

Kate looked up at the tall oblong of the keep in front of her. A flight of stairs led up to it. Above, there was a covered bridge that led back to the outer ward of the castle. On the towers fluttered the banner of Gloucester, the white boar against blue and red. The sight made her shiver. The castle looked approachable and graceful, but it was still majestic enough to intimidate her. Its walls were the blank walls of her future. Someone came for her horse and she dismounted and gave the palfrey over without taking her eyes off the keep.

'Kate?' said a familiar voice.

She turned and he was there, a huge black gyrfalcon on his wrist, a dazzling smile lighting his face. Raphael. Joy leaped into her heart, the first joy she'd felt in months.

'Kate, at last, thank all the gods,' he cried, starting forward, then stopping as the falcon, disgruntled, unfolded and shook her vast wings. 'What took you so long?'

My tutor sat enthroned in his office, in a glare of slanted sunlight that illumined every floating dust particle. He was behind a desk the colour of molasses and his grey hair was primped with hair cream (or grease – I gave him the benefit of the doubt) and too long over the collar. He wore a flowery waistcoat, glasses on the end of his nose, an impatient air.

'I know it's not part of my course work,' I said. 'It's only . . . an interest. A hobby.'

'I don't have to point out,' he cleared his throat, 'that hobbies are to be kept separate from studies and not to be allowed to impinge upon them. Your last essay was just about adequate. I know you're capable of better. If you want a pastime, why not try joining the choral society, or drink yourself silly like the other students?'

'Just one question.' I began to spread books on the table. 'I'm sorry to bother you, but you're the only person I know who's actually qualified to answer.'

'Oh, flattery, is it?' He pounced on the books, began to glance at them and toss them aside with sighing disdain.

'What is it?' I said, annoyed but trying not to show it. 'I haven't even asked the question yet.'

'Then do so. I haven't got all day.'

'The image of Richard the Third that everyone thinks they know is of a hunchback who murdered his nephews,' I began, stomach sinking. 'I've read book after book that refutes it. There's no proof he killed them. He had no reason to, since they'd been declared illegitimate. They were no danger to him. Some historians go to great lengths to show that the Duke of Buckingham actually had a stronger motive, and the opportunity—'

'Aargh!' My tutor flicked his hands in the air, letting them land like two naked rats on the books. 'Don't go this way. Don't bother with the apologists. Amateurs, half of 'em.'

'That doesn't mean they're wrong or less well-informed,' I said. 'Mightn't it make them more open-minded?'

'It might. It might also mean they're on some misguided crusade to prove a guilty man innocent. What is it with this blasted king?'

'It's medieval history, sir.'

He folded one leg over the other, looked at his pocket watch. 'Only if you treat it as impartially as you would any other period; as indifferently as you clearly treat the twelfth century. How many lectures have you missed?'

'Only two.' I felt myself flushing. 'I will catch up. I just wanted to know what you think about this, then I won't mention it again.'

'I'm glad to hear it. The benefit of my wisdom is this. Don't get emotionally involved. Deciding what you want the truth to be, then bending the facts to fit, is not the way to study history. Stick to facts, my dear. Bone-dry facts.'

'But isn't caring about something what makes you delve deeper and deeper into it? Isn't that what sparks real research?'

'Well.' He pulled a face, as if he'd tasted something foul. 'That depends whether you want to tell yourself a comforting story or get at the truth. It may involve accepting that there is no concrete truth that can ever be discovered. Just a balance of probabilities.'

I persisted. 'So what do *you* think is probable?'

'Of course the Princes were still a danger to him!' He spoke fervently, for a man who'd told me not to be emotional. 'No one believed the illegitimacy story, least of all Richard himself. No one could have gained access to his nephews without him knowing. Ultimate responsibility for them lay with him. *Ergo*, of course he did it.'

'Ha,' I said, triumphant, 'so you do have an opinion after all.'

And I saw the merest, reluctant twinkle in his eye.

'Guilty as hell.'

Chapter Nine 1477: Anne

ANNE
> Thou wast the cause and most accursed effect.

RICHARD
> Your beauty was the cause of that effect –
> Your beauty, that did haunt me in my sleep
> To undertake the death of all the world,
> So I might live one hour in your sweet bosom.

Richard III Act I scene 2

Katherine hardly noticed that a groom took her horse, while a pair of spindle-legged pages relieved her of her small bundle of belongings. She was looking at the mass of people collected in the bailey and on the great covered staircase that led to the upper storey of the keep: peasants, merchants, officials. The courtyard was busy with their murmuring voices, shifting colours. There were horses everywhere, ripening the air with a warm familiar scent of sweat, manure and oiled leather.

'All these folk!' she said. 'Why are they here?'

'To see the Duke,' Raphael answered, smoothing the feathers of the black gyrfalcon. Kate reached out to stroke the bird's breast with a curled finger. She tolerated Kate's touch, head raised imperiously, her eyes blind behind the hood.

'You mean he gives audience to . . . anyone?'

Raphael smiled, eyebrows tilted at her question. He looked sun-browned and happy, and he'd begun to pick up the Yorkshire accent. 'Well, of course. He is their lord.

He considers their petitions, sorts out their disputes with their neighbours, dispenses justice, generally to everyone's satisfaction.'

'I don't remember Clarence doing that,' she said under her breath. 'I remember him doing many things, but not that.'

'Richard is nothing like his brother,' Raphael said vehemently. 'Whatever you think you've learned of the behaviour of dukes from Clarence, prepare to unlearn it. Richard listens to his subjects. You only have to see how many go away content, saying what a good and fair lord he is.'

'What about the ones who don't?'

'They're only the ones who tried to get away with some crime or injustice, and were found out. They say Richard sees straight through people, and it's not a pleasant experience.'

Ice threaded through her. She thought of the last time she'd seen him, in the market-place at Tewkesbury, the cloaked executioner. 'No, I should imagine it isn't.' She looked up at the high walls of silvery stone all around her. She saw Nan and Ursula hesitating, wanting to follow the pages, but looking back anxiously at her. 'Shouldn't I tell someone I've arrived? The chamberlain, or the steward?'

'I'll look after you,' Raphael said. 'Come with me Kate, while I see to the falcons; then I'll show you around. The Duchess will be in the nursery, no one will miss you for an hour or two.' His sweet smile disarmed her. It was a relief to be greeted by a friend. The sooner Clarence's men were gone back to their master, the better. She waved her companions on their way and they went, Ursula frowning, Nan – who knew her – with a good-natured shrug.

In the falconry, next to the stables, Raphael settled the gyrfalcon on her perch and showed Kate his charges with affection and pride. Firehawks like burning coal with red flashes in their tails. Tiercels, small and elegant. Kestrels, sparrowhawks, a type of small eagle called a red griffin that was as glossy-brown as a chestnut. Their housing was immaculate: the walls painted dusky white, the floor clean and strewn with sweet straw. The raptors perched sleek and content in their niches.

'This is Richard's favourite,' Raphael said, caressing the gyrfalcon he'd been flying. 'And this one . . .' he indicated a dainty snow-white merlin, 'is Lady Anne's.'

The mention of Anne Neville's name still sent an undefined pang through Kate. She had once pitied Anne, forced to marry Prince Edouard, then widowed, and kept in ignorance of the path of Auset. But now she was Richard's wife, and Kate only a long-forgotten lover.

Still, it's better this way, she thought. It can't be an easy marriage. I never wish to be subject to a husband.

'If you'd like a hawk of your own, I'll find you one, a beauty,' Raphael was saying.

'You're so kind.' She touched his arm. He looked at her with glowing eyes, it was all she could do not to kiss him, but she held back and the moment passed. Both awkward, they distracted themselves by admiring Lady Anne's merlin.

'No graylix?' Kate asked, her fingers exploring the soft springiness of the wing feathers.

'We don't keep them here.' His voice was low, sad. 'Richard said they remind him too much of Marguerite, who used to keep great packs of them. Tyrant went into the menagerie at the Tower. At least he's well cared for there.'

'Despite mistaking his keeper for his supper every day?'

His mouth twisted at the corner. 'No one thinks the pard is ignoble, for being dangerous. I miss him.'

'You're so sweet-natured, Raphael, to love such an unlovable beast. And talking of that, how do you find the Duke?'

'Why do you speak so unkindly of him?' Raphael was indignant.

'A jest. It's only that the last time he spoke to me, he was less than courteous. I'm being unforgiving, I'm sorry. I'm sure he's an excellent master.'

'He is,' Raphael answered. 'As I knew he would be, from the first time I saw him. It only happens once in a lifetime, I think, that you cross paths with someone so out of the ordinary that you have no choice but to follow them.'

'Just like Christ, then,' she said mischievously.

'He's not that.' Raphael looked sideways at her, serious. 'You can't hold a position like his without making hard decisions. Whatever he does, he never acts without a logical reason. He inspires loyalty. He's as loyal to his friends as we are to him, and Creator knows, he doesn't want flatterers around him. I've sometimes said things to him that would have got me thrown in the Tower if I'd said them to the King. He's the centre of everything in the north, as Edward is in London. I'm meant to be here, that's all I know.'

'I'm glad you're happy.'

'Richard likes everyone to be happy. He's a gentle lord, Kate, you've nothing to worry about there. We're all expected to attend chapel, by the way.' Raphael said it almost nervously.

Her lips thinned, but she quickly smoothed her expression, hoping he hadn't noticed. Her own beliefs did not deny the Church, it was they who denied hers. Still, she was used to kneeling in churches and focusing upon Mary who – although it could be viewed as heresy – was the Blue Mother, a face of her Goddess. In Isabel's service, she'd grown adept at avoiding the attentions of priests. Here, perhaps, she wouldn't be so fortunate. 'Then I'll attend chapel,' she said. 'So, the Duke is only fearsome to his enemies?'

Raphael nodded. 'He's got more energy than anyone I've ever known. He's off to the borders fighting the Scots, down to London to attend Parliament, and in York almost every week. He never rests.'

'And he's away often.' She felt an obscure relief. Thank Auset he wouldn't always be there, a disturbing dark angel constantly haunting her; a dark presence, somewhere in the castle, walking through her dreams.

'Which means I am, too. It's lucky I can trust the falcons to Will Shaw's care.'

'Oh, Raphael, I arrive only for you to tell me you're hardly going to be here?'

He looked gravely at her. 'You sound as if you really mind.'

'Of course I do.'

In the half-light he had the same dark-angel look as she remembered in Richard, a quality that mysteriously dissolved all her common sense. Raphael was different, though, kind, transparent, an equal. He stared unhappily at her.

'I don't always go with him,' he said. 'And we always come back. This is his home. I know Lady Anne hates him to be away for too long.'

She put her head on one side. 'And are you married?' she asked, trying not to mind what the answer was.

Someone coughed, very loudly. The noise rang off the walls, making her jump.

'Our Raffel, married? You must be joking! Plenty of maids in the village queuing up on the off-chance, though. He could've married fifteen times over in this past year. Too picky.'

'Will, for Christ's sake!'

A broad man in linen and leather came strolling towards them. He had curly hair and a round grinning face. Raphael had turned scarlet.

'This is Katherine, daughter of Lady Lytton. My lady, this is a rogue by the name of Will Shaw. Will, if you dare say anything coarse, I'll kick you from here to the Scottish border.'

Shaw feigned indignation, dropped to one knee and pressed damp lips to the back of Kate's hand. She sensed no harm in him, mischief and a dash of lechery, but nothing worse.

'We've met before,' she said. 'In the friary, after Barnet.'

'And it was an honour I recall vividly. My lady, I am

your servant. Raphael is the rogue, to speak such slander of me.'

'I'm sure he spoke in affection, as you did of him.'

'You're as gracious as the Duchess.' He rose, bowed deeply. 'He speaks about you all the time.'

'All the time?'

As she and Raphael looked at each other, she felt her face blush as bright as his. With a grin that managed to be both insinuating and harmless, Will Shaw edged past them. 'I'll be about my tasks, then, my lady and my lord; don't let me interrupt you.'

'Come on,' Raphael said. He took her hand, and they hurried out into bright daylight, laughing. 'I've more to show you. Don't mind Will, he's an idiot but as loyal as they come.'

On the high tower on the south-east corner of the keep, they stood leaning out over the battlements with the glassy-cold wind blowing hard. White boar banners fluttered above their heads, all the green glory of the dale spread below them. The distant fells were an intense blue, like dusk. Cloud and sunlight flowed over them in shining tatters. Kate tried to keep her wild hair under her head-dress and failed. She laughed in exhilaration. The horror of Clarence was gone, blown away on the clean Wensleydale breeze.

'The great hall is within the keep, we'll dine there later. The Duke and Duchess always eat with the household. Next to it the great chamber where the Duke receives his petitioners, and his inner chamber. Kitchens and cellars beneath.' He gestured down at the high, pointed roof of a construction projecting from the main body of the keep. 'There below us is the chapel. The priests and their clerks live in the chambers underneath it.'

'Good, now I know the place to avoid.'

He shook his head. 'Don't say such things to anyone but me.' His hand described three sides of the four walls that framed the bailey. 'There's a range of living chambers along each wall. Almost every one has its own latrine, piped water and a fireplace, and is very finely furnished. It's outrageously comfortable here. I hope you can bear the luxury.'

'I lived at Warwick, I'm sure I'll bear it.'

He indicated a high, covered bridge that led from the keep to the outer walls. 'The hautpace there leads to the Duchess's chambers beside the round tower. On the other side of the tower is the nursery. Her ladies live in those chambers.'

'And where is your chamber, sir?' she asked, winking.

He pulled a face, and pointed out across the high wooden roofs of the keep. 'Far over on the other side, above the stables, near the auditor's chamber. I share with other knights, who aren't always the best of sleeping companions.'

'Still, better than bedding down in the cellars with the servants,' she said sardonically.

'I'm not so sure.' He was smiling. 'Do you think you can be happy here?'

'I hope so.'

'You belong here, Katherine. This was meant to be.'

They were close, shoulders almost touching; again she thought he might kiss her, but it was too soon. Instead she put back her head, welcoming the vibrant wind. There was a vast elemental moving within it, a near-invisible, shining, massive presence like a sheet of liquid glass. She dipped her head in greeting and respect. And then she saw, down in a meadow clearing between emerald clusters of trees, four priests at work.

She stiffened. It was plain what they were doing, she'd seen it many times. The priests formed the corners of a square. She couldn't see the objects they held but guessed that one would be holding a cross, one a Bible, one holy water and the last a bell. They were chanting, praying. Their faces were turned angrily to the sky and their voices drifted up in faint fragments, hard and fervent.

They were trying to exorcise the wind spirit. To bind it,

to send it back to the netherworld from which it had come. The elemental would retreat from their angry energy and they would think that they'd triumphed.

'Don't they ever give up?' Raphael said benignly.

Kate held back her pointless rage. She breathed crystalline air and let it go in a long sigh. 'They're fools, Raph. They try to pin down the powers of the earth, cage them with crosses and incantations, dissolve them with holy water. They might as well try to pin down the wind! They're so afraid, yet they don't even know what it is they're afraid of. They may succeed for a little time, but the power will break loose eventually.'

He was looking seriously at her, frowning.

She said, 'Are you sure they haven't been whispering the fear of devils, sorcery and witches into your ear? Are you seeing me differently?'

'No, no.'

'I'm still the same.'

'I know. It's not that. Kate, I . . . When I was in London . . . It was the night King Henry died . . .'

She waited for him to go on. The breeze blew steadily between them. She said at last, 'What?'

'Nothing.' He was turning away. 'We should go down now. You must be hungry and tired. I'll find someone to take you to the Duchess.'

As they emerged from the staircase into the great hall, a child came running towards them. He nearly ran straight into Kate's skirts, stopped in his tracks and gawped at her with all a child's unselfconscious bewilderment. He was tiny, with a dense silky mass of raven hair, dark grey eyes and a serious expression on a sweetly beautiful face. He was the image of Richard. The image.

Kate stared back, matching his childlike confusion. The chamber whirled and she was in another place not understanding how this could be. As his nurse came hurrying to recapture him, Kate went on staring. By the time she came to her senses the child was gone, carried away by the

232

gently scolding nurse. She thought, Richard has a son. He's married and he has a son . . .

She'd known, but it hadn't seemed real until she came here and saw with her own eyes. Something intense and painful moved through her, without shape, like the glassy elemental of the sky.

'Katherine?' came Raphael's concerned voice. 'What's wrong?'

'Nothing. Why?'

'You look as if you're going to faint. That was a little boy, not a ghost.' He spoke lightly, but sounded worried. She did her best to compose herself.

'He gave me a start, that's all. Richard's boy?'

'Edward. Lovely-looking child, isn't he?'

'Beautiful,' said Katherine.

'Such a good-mannered little scrap, too, a credit to his parents . . . Are you sure you're well?'

'Perfectly.' She smiled, despite the sharp pressure in her eyes. 'I've had a long journey, that's all. I'm starving.'

'You attended my sister when she died.'

'Yes, Your Grace.'

Anne's face was long and square-chinned, like her father's, her skin clear and bloodless but for the amber stain of her lips. Her hair, a pale russet, floated down past her hips. She wasn't beautiful, but had an astonishing quality of serenity, a preternatural calmness and stillness that made her seem partly of another world. She was the opposite of Isabel – the inferno of affection and mischief. Her serenity must make her invisible to some, to others, incandescent like a saint.

'She was exceedingly fond of you.'

'And I of her.' Kate found herself wanting to cry. She bit her lip. A tear escaped down her cheek. Anne must have noticed, but only watched her. She'd shown little emotion at being forced to marry Edouard of Lancaster, less, after his death. Only this same, piercing calmness.

'You must have given her great comfort.'

'I tried. I wish I could have given her healing, but . . .'

'It's all right, Kate. We're puppets. All that happens to us is God's will; accept this and the torment stops. It's how I got through my time in the household of Marguerite and Prince Edouard, though I can't say I didn't thank God when it ended.'

Kate rubbed the tear away. She wondered if the torment included being married to Richard of Gloucester. She couldn't imagine him being a loving husband, only cool, businesslike and distant. Perhaps that was what Anne preferred.

'I was afraid for you,' said the Duchess, 'left with my brother-in-law of Clarence.'

'I was afraid for myself, sometimes, madam.'

Anne's mouth flattened with regret. 'George was always given to excesses. You're safe with us, Kate. There's always a home for you here.'

'Thank you,' she answered, so grateful for Anne's cool kindness that she almost gave in to tears again. She burned with shame that she could think anything ungenerous about Richard and Anne. Yet part of her stood aloof, thinking, I am not some peasant girl to be grateful for charity, I am a sister of Auset, I come and go as I please . . . knowing, in truth, that her freedom was illusory. There were only two places she could be safe: here, or with her mother.

Anne's chamber was simple, the walls hung with ivory silk and a handful of religious paintings in the Byzantine style that gleamed gold in the firelight. There was a beautiful eastern rug on the floor, cream and gold and blue. All the furnishings were covered in thick oyster-coloured silk. Anne indicated a settle near her own chair.

'Please sit down. It's such a pleasure to see you again, Katherine. Will you call me Anne? You always called Bel by her first name, and you're older than me, and wiser, I'm sure. I'll never forget how you helped her when we were stranded outside Calais.'

'Madam. Anne. I can't work miracles, I couldn't save her baby. In the end I couldn't save her.'

Anne didn't respond. Perhaps she didn't want to be told that. After a pause she said, 'You know how I came to marry Richard? I didn't see much of you while it was going on.'

The pang came again, like a dull knife. 'I must confess, I tried to keep out of the way. George was using every person he could lay hands on as a weapon in his struggle and I didn't want to be dragged in. I know he was foaming at the mouth over it.'

At that, she smiled. 'I think Bel and George loved each other in their own way, which was just as well, since she had no choice. My father wanted a daughter upon the throne of England: Bel with George or me with Lancaster, he didn't care how it was achieved. George in turn saw his chance to get hold of all the Warwick estates, all my mother's lands, all *my* lands. As long as he kept me close, I was no danger to him and in no position to claim my birthright. I didn't want much, Kate – only this castle, my home – but even that was too much for George.

'Richard was the only one who could help me. When George found out we meant to marry he did everything in his power to prevent it: he argued in court, in Parliament, he raged at the King. He even stuffed me into the house of his friend where I was kept a virtual prisoner, forced to pretend I was a servant. So ludicrous, I can't believe it happened.'

'We didn't know where you were,' said Kate, uneasily. 'George made all manner of excuses to Isabel, and told me nothing at all, of course.'

'My brother-in-law is cunning, but not the brightest of men. Richard was bound to prevail. He married me, and made sure I received everything to which I was entitled.'

She spoke glowingly, as if her husband had achieved something heroic.

'And by marrying you, Richard helped himself to a

235

massive share of the Warwick estates,' Kate said evenly, 'which I thought still belonged to your good mother the Countess.'

'Lamb's blood, Kate, are you such a cynic? Edward himself wouldn't let my mother keep control of her inheritance, not after my father's behaviour. At least this way we have saved half. Richard did it to help me, out of affection for me. Any reward he's received for himself, well, he deserves it. What's mine is his. Creator knows, I can't take my lands to the afterlife with me and I know he cherishes them. Ask anyone, from the highest to the lowest, he's a better ruler in the north than Edward is in the south.'

'So everyone's said, from the moment I arrived.'

'You know my mother had to flee into sanctuary when my father was killed at Barnet? Richard got her out, and brought her home to live with us.'

'Is she well?' Kate felt apprehension clamping her shoulders. She wasn't sure she wanted to see Anne Beauchamp; she who had tried to live completely in two worlds at the same time and had thus betrayed both. Betrayed her own daughters, in Kate's eyes.

'Yes, though she lives very quietly here, and keeps much to her own chambers.'

'Does she not . . . go out?'

'Where would she wish to go? She claims she's too old for pilgrimages.'

'Anne!' Kate said, exasperated. She was on the edge of impertinence, and made an effort to draw back. 'Your Grace. She might go to York, to visit her – her sisterhood. She might be needed as a midwife, healer, or priestess. To pass the dead into the arms of the Dark Mother. All the things that the daughters of Auset are duty bound to do for those who ask. Services that may also cause me to beg leave of you. If my Motherlodge has need and sends for me, I must go.'

A subtle change came over Anne's face. Still smooth and

tranquil, there was shock etched around her eyes, as if a page had said an obscene word in front of her.

Kate added, 'I cannot believe that you and Isabel were unaware of your mother's allegiance. I'm certain Bel knew.'

Anne drew in then released a breath. She picked at a loose thread of embroidery on her dress, not looking at Kate. Finally she said, 'We knew, naturally, but it's all at an end now.'

'How?'

'Whatever business my mother had with – with anything other than the holy Church is finished. She's renounced those days, they are over, forgotten and forgiven.'

'That's what she's told you?'

'It's the truth. Do you doubt my word, or hers?'

'No, no. If you say it's so . . .' Kate thought she was speaking reasonably but her face betrayed her; her blue-fire eyes glared into Anne's soft brown ones in challenge.

Anne shifted a little, uneasy in her quiet, sad way. 'Katherine, I can't let you go out from this castle in the service of a form of . . . I don't want to give it a stronger name than heresy, though I could. You must put all that behind you now. It's in your past. Here we live a devoted spiritual life. You'll find all the contentment you need in the chapel, and work enough within the household.' She spoke sweetly, as if questing for Kate's agreement, but there was steel behind her eyes.

'Madam, are you telling me I may not go?'

'I'd rather you saw the wisdom of it for yourself. We're Christians here. Really, it's best you fall in with our ways, and leave behind . . . what you were. You'd be happier, and—'

'Not go to hell?' Kate said, lifting her eyebrows.

Anne opened her hands, palms upwards. 'Well, yes, Kate, truly. I know you're a good person. I want you to follow the right path, not for us to argue.'

'Did Ri— did His Grace your husband ask you to say this?'

'No. However, we are in agreement about it.'

Katherine released a breath through her teeth. Richard and Anne stood like a wall of piety in front of her. This was always going to be the way of it. She couldn't win. Insist on her freedom, and there would be more gentle, reasonable argument, and the priest called, and perhaps the Duke himself – the last person she wanted to argue with – and the pressure would go on and on until she walked out or gave in. That was her choice, then: flee back to Eleanor, or stay here, compromised.

'May I still visit my mother in Derbyshire?'

'Of course. You may go out for any reason you like, but if you go for the reasons I've mentioned, I can't condone it. That's all. This isn't a prison.'

'I only wish to discharge my duty of love to my mother. Of other matters, I'll not speak again.'

Anne's frown smoothed into relief. 'Thank you, Kate.'

So it's all swept under the Byzantine rug, and peace can reign, Kate thought. I should be glad they don't want to drag me out and hang me, like poor Ankarette. But I'll stay, because Anne is my last link to Isabel, as I am hers. Because Raphael is here, and because going back to my mother would mean admitting defeat.

'You'll be comfortable here,' Anne went on. 'I'm an easy mistress. All I require of you is company, perhaps to read to each other, as we used to? The smallest of tasks. Sometimes to supervise my household if I am ill. I have others to help with my dress and toilet, and nurses aplenty for Edward. Still, you might care to play with my son, if it pleases you. He's a sweet boy, and a quick learner.' She looked wistful. 'I must make the best of him, before he's gone.'

'Gone?' A nebulous fear rolled like smoke down Kate's spine.

'In wardship, to another castle. I wish I had a daughter,

238

then I might keep her.' Anne's face was drawn, luminous, sightless, like that of a plaster mourner at the foot of the cross. Then she came back from the lost place, and smiled. 'Your chamber, Kate, is it to your liking?'

The chamber was very much to her liking. It was in the round tower on the south-west corner of the castle, close to the Duchess's apartments and reached by spiral stairs. She was to share it with Nan, Ursula and another of Anne's ladies, Mary Bagott, a sanguine-natured but dull and pious woman, nearly as wide as she was tall.

The chamber was also round and roomy, with a view over the gorgeous dale. The walls were painted a soft green and hung with long narrow tapestries each portraying an elongated saint picked out in beads and gold thread. The bed was luxurious, with a big soft mattress, feather pillows and lush hangings of green and russet. Kate and Mary shared the bed, with Nan and Ursula on pallets at its foot. The two girls – Kate thought of Nan as a girl, with her simple, childlike nature, though she was older than Kate – had formed a firm alliance and taken a mutual dislike to Dame Bagott.

Kate slept as if dead the first night. The next night, however, she was restless, uncomfortably aware of Mary's hot bulk and her snoring a few inches away, and glad the bed was no smaller. She could hear Nan and Ursula whispering. Although she was pleased they'd made friends, the sound was annoying. Ursula was a good girl but sharp and cunning; Nan easily led. Kate was their mistress, and they resented Mary's presence and being expected to run about at her beck and call. Friction was brewing, but Kate wanted none of it. She'd always extricated herself from such stews of rivalry.

She had seen the Duke of Gloucester only twice since she'd arrived, and only at a distance. He'd been at the top table in the great hall at dinner, while she was seated further down with Anne's ladies. He'd looked magnificent, immaculate in rich dark robes of black and blood-red, his hair like polished jet under a soft velvet cap. A duke in full command of his domain, with none of Edward's noisy flamboyance, just a restrained, graceful confidence.

It had given Kate a strange feeling to see him. She felt an odd antipathy towards Richard, almost a form of jealousy to find him so wealthy and powerful. How unspeakably difficult it was to see Anne at his side, as if it were the most natural thing in the world. Kate gazed at him constantly, yet he never gave any sign he'd seen her. If he had, she would have looked away.

She was growing annoyed with herself. She didn't love him, couldn't like him. All she felt was the impersonal respect she was bound to give her lord. There had been lust, once, yes, but that was long ago, when they had both been young and impulsive. What was it that stabbed her, then? Wounded pride? The fancy that, even though she had only used him, he should have fallen violently in love with her and never looked at another? Ridiculous. Even if that had happened, he would still have had to marry an heiress. That was the way of nobles.

Kate turned, sighing, in bed. The girls had stopped whispering and she could hear the slow breathing of sleep. The room was too close. She would have to go out into the cold air to clear her head.

She kept the secret, like a little jewel she'd stolen, a white boar of pearl. She half smiled as she placed her feet on the cold floor. Once, long ago, she had seduced him, and Anne didn't know. Nor did Raphael. Would he mind? She had a feeling that even if he knew, he wouldn't think any the worse of her. He was kind and tolerant, not judgemental. He didn't give the impression that he expected women to be more virtuous than men. Still. There was no reason for anyone, ever, to know. Such knowledge would only hurt them and humiliate her. To be seen in the same light as King Edward's cast-off conquests – great Goddess, the idea was disgusting beyond contemplation. No, a secret it would remain. She had more to do than be merely a wench, a womb, a commodity.

More than ever, she wished that Auset had sent her a passing shepherd, someone she need never have seen again. That would have made it easier for the whole episode to be thrown down the black-throated garderobe of the past.

Alone on the roof of the round tower, she leaned shivering against the battlements, with the night blue-black around her. The stars looked like a snowstorm. She was thinking of the child, couldn't get him out of her mind.

Someone moved behind her. She heard a soft footfall, a man gently clearing his throat, and thought it was a guard. Then he moved beside her, even before she could turn round, and it was Richard. His pale hands were folded on the battlements, the rest of him was dark. His hair, uncovered, was full and a bit dishevelled on the shoulders of his mantle, black against the sky.

Her mouth turned dry. Automatically she dipped her knee and croaked, 'Your Grace.'

He didn't appear to notice her obeisance, he was looking at the stars ribboning above them. He said, 'I've been wondering all day how I might speak to you alone.'

'Here I am.' Feeling startled and self-conscious, she pulled her cloak tight around her throat. Her hair blew loose. 'I couldn't sleep.'

'Nor could I. I sleep abominably sometimes and haunt the battlements at all hours of the night. The guards are used to me.'

'They might have to get used to me as well,' she said, then felt her face turn to flame. Somehow she had turned him into a distant icon. She couldn't believe he was standing talking to her, and with the quiet candidness she remembered, as if they knew each other inside out. The night helped.

'Well, I surely hope you'll feel at ease here. I know Anne wishes it.'

So he pushed his wife's name straight into the conversation, a line in the sand. After the dull knife came relief; everything was clear. She would be businesslike. The last thing she wanted was for him to think that she had lingering feelings for him.

'You're very good, then, to let her summon me,' she said. 'You can't have wanted me here.'

She looked at him and smiled. His face stayed in profile and the one eye she could see was an arc of frost. 'I wouldn't say that. Anne needs someone strong. We agreed everything else was forgotten, didn't we, my lady?'

Kate gave a minimal nod. 'She doesn't know, does she?'

Richard looked down at his folded hands. 'Katherine, you were not my only indiscretion. Anne knows I've not been perfect. I have two bastard children – born before we were married – and she's as kind as a mother to them when they visit me. But she doesn't want the names or faces of my past lapses paraded before her. So of course I haven't told her, and I trust you won't.'

Kate was struck dumb for a minute or so. Other indiscretions, other children. She glared at the star-washed side of his face and wished her gaze were flame to consume him where he stood. *Iesu's blood, I am jealous enough to kill him! What is the matter with me?* She swallowed the feeling, as her mother had trained her, until she almost choked on it.

'Of course I wouldn't tell her, she'd think I'd gone mad.'

He turned and looked at her, frowning. 'Mad, why?'

She gave a thin smile. 'Because she'd assume I was making it up, and why would I say such a thing, and get myself dismissed, unless I was mad?'

'Yes,' he murmured. 'Anyway, she knows I am faithful. I have never broken my marriage vows. We're content.'

'Is that all, then?' Kate said coolly. 'You wanted to ask me to keep my mouth shut, which you should have known I would do without being asked?'

She made to walk away towards the little oak door to the stairwell. He put his hand out and gently stopped her. His hand on her arm was pleasantly warm, but stayed there only a second. 'No. You brought the subject up, not me, and I answered you honestly. No, I wanted to . . . Last time we met, I offended you. I'm trying to apologize. Not to give an excuse, only a reason: that I was tired and distraught. I wasn't railing at you, only at forces that seemed to be doing their damndest to destroy Edward and still are. I upset you. I'm sorry.'

'All that upset me is that you don't know what you are railing against.'

'I don't understand anything south of the Trent,' he said darkly. 'Here, things are simple. I carry out the law with fairness and, I hope, good sense, and I ensure that all my subjects can feed and clothe themselves. What more is there? But no, in the south there are half a dozen factions trying to eat each other up with jealousy, hatred and sorcery. God, I'm glad to be out of it.'

He stood, a narrow shadow against the curved wall, and her body – independent of the cool decisions of her mind – tingled with a magnetic urge to put her arms round him. Resisting the impulse was painful.

'So am I,' she said.

'Yes, Kate, I'm sorry.' His hand came out of the darkness and found hers, pressing it to the stone. His voice was husky. 'That you endured such misery at the hands of my brother – tenfold what he caused Anne, for he wasn't so crazed then – I can't tell you how ashamed I am. But I must know what happened. This is why I wanted to speak with you alone. It's desperately important. I've heard some of it, so outlandish it surpasses belief. Would you tell me what really happened?'

He asked with such desperation that she couldn't refuse.

All her ignoble anger vanished. As frank and fearless as she would have been with Raphael, she told him everything.

'Oh God,' he said at the end, and put his head in his hands. '*Did* this Widow Twynyho intend harm to Isabel?'

'No, of course she didn't.'

'Was she a witch?'

Kate shrugged. 'That would depend on what you mean. She was a good midwife, a wise woman skilled with herbs, enough to get her accused by the malicious, but not a thread of harm in her. Even if Queen Elizabeth had wanted to kill Isabel, Ankarette would not have agreed to it in a thousand years. George went out of his mind when Bel died. He knew full well that Ankarette was innocent. He saw a chance to attack the Queen, and perhaps in his twisted way he convinced himself of her guilt. In truth, I believe he wanted to silence Ankarette, because he'd asked her to prophesy and work influence that would help him become king. It was all quite convenient for him, but a woman died.'

'Oh, God, George—'

'He asked me to prophesy too, with threats and insinuations. He knew how I'd helped Edward.'

Richard was glowering at her. 'What did you say?'

'I refused. I don't know how I escaped with my life, except that Anne had sent for me. It would have looked a little suspicious if I had died too. And I think he was afraid of me, as he wasn't of Ankarette.'

'You do have a look of the Medusa, when you are angry.'

'You flatter me, sir,' she said through her teeth.

He gave a dry smile, eyelids lowered so he didn't meet her gaze. 'It's as well you had some defence against him, when you're so . . . He's not much better than Edward in that way. He didn't try to force himself upon you, did he?'

'No, I'm quite unspoiled,' she said thinly. 'He didn't want a serpent in his bed and I didn't want a drunken oaf in mine.'

'Katherine, he is still my brother.'

'And he's still a drunken oaf!' she said. 'Excuse me, but it's the truth. No, he was more concerned with marrying Marie of Burgundy.'

'Oh, saints help us! Edward will never allow that! Never. Iesu's blood, what the hell is George playing at this time?'

'He has the idea that becoming Duke of Burgundy will be a springboard from which to become king – of anywhere, I think, as long as he *is* a king.'

'Christ.'

Kate saw that Richard was in anguish, but all she could do was to stand there, feeling immensely sad and helpless. 'I'm sorry to bring you such an array of bad news,' she said. 'I wish I could say I exaggerated, but I can't.'

'Thank you for being honest,' he murmured. Cautiously, she let her hand creep onto his. He didn't withdraw, but caught her fingers and held them tight. 'And I wish I could say I don't believe you, but I do. George has been troublesome and intemperate for years. He's learned nothing from his mistakes. I feel bitterly ashamed of him for threatening you, when all you've done is help him. It's unforgivable.'

'It's not your fault.' She moved closer. Their arms touched to the elbow.

'Isn't it? I feel I should have done something.'

'I'm glad to know that you wouldn't wish to see me hang,' she said quietly. 'I know you don't approve of me, but I've never wished you harm. Please believe me. I served Edward. I'm here to serve you. I haven't fallen off the holy path but come to you along a different path, one much older.'

'I don't know what you are, Kate, but I also never wished harm to you. If I was unchivalrous, out of youth or misunderstanding, I regret it. Can you ever forgive me?'

'Since you ask so graciously.' She wasn't sure how it happened but they turned naturally towards each other and she found herself suddenly locked in a hard embrace,

245

his cheek resting on her hair. Stunned, she let her arms creep around his back, felt his body through his mantle as lean and tantalizing as she remembered it. They stood and held each other as if their lives depended on it. She had no idea what it meant. It felt dream-like, desperate and utterly confusing.

He spoke into her hair, muffled. 'Kate, that time I met you ... I was with Edward in Norfolk. When I left, I returned there. Yet your demesne is in Derbyshire, is it not? More than a hundred miles away. How is that possible?'

'You came through the hidden world,' she whispered. 'The hidden world can be anywhere and everywhere.'

'That does nothing to reassure me ... but it would explain more than you know.' His arms drew tighter. 'It frightened me half to death. Nothing in this life has ever unmanned me as that did.'

'I didn't lure you there. You stepped into it yourself. You came to me of your own free will.'

'Then God help me.'

'I'd like to think you remember pleasure as well as fear,' she said. 'I do.'

She felt him breathe in and out. He whispered very softly in her ear, 'Morgana.'

Nothing else. He kissed her lightly, three times, on her temple, cheek and mouth; then the moment was over. They let each other go and stood guiltily apart. She had no idea why he'd hugged her, but it left her heartbeat shaking her whole body. They stood looking at the night, breathing hard and trying to pretend nothing had happened.

He broke the silence. 'We should go back.'

'What will you do? About Clarence, I mean?'

Richard exhaled. It sounded like relief at returning to safe ground. 'Being obnoxious is one thing, undermining Edward's authority and taking the law into his own hands is a darker matter entirely. George is living in a dream. He seems to think he can get away with anything, that

Edward is too soft to retaliate, but even Edward's patience will have worn to nothing by now. I might be able to talk sense into them both, if no one else can. I shall have to go to London.'

'When?'

'Whenever I go, it always seems too soon.'

'Raphael says you hate it there.'

'Does he? Does Raphael confide much in you, then?' His tone was light, but just probing enough to make her uncomfortable.

'He extols you as a dutiful lord, except that those duties take you away from home too often.'

'He speaks the truth. However, I think it's just as well, don't you?' She heard painful amusement in his voice. 'Go back to your chamber, dear Kate. I'll go after, so no one sees us together. And thank you.'

She fled, looking back once to see him standing against the sky, a silhouette cut in the graceful form of a knight. She only had to step away from him and he was a stranger again, an image of perfect self-control, so remote it seemed impossible that she had ever touched him.

Chapter Ten 1477–8: George

CLARENCE
  I passed, methought, the melancholy flood
  With that sour ferryman which poets write of,
  Unto the kingdom of perpetual night,
  The first that there did greet my stranger soul
  Was my great father-in-law, renowned Warwick
  Who spake aloud, 'What scourge for perjury
  Can this dark monarchy afford false Clarence?'
  And so he vanished. Then came wandering by
  A shadow like an angel, with bright hair
  Dabbled with blood, and he shrieked out aloud,
  'Clarence is come – false, fleeting, perjured Clarence
  That stabbed me in the field by Tewkesbury.
  Seize on him, furies, take him unto torment!'

Richard III Act I scene 4

Kate went cautiously into a chamber that was as plain as a nun's cell. The firegrate was dead, the gloom sparsely lit by three tapers. Anne Beauchamp was sitting in a chair in the centre of the room, as if stranded in the middle of nowhere. Only the vaguest pool of light fell on the book she was reading.

She looked old. She was dressed in black damask that had turned charcoal with wear. The fabric hung loose on her once-statuesque frame.

Kate had been ready for a fierce argument. She'd expected to interrogate the tall, proud woman who'd once so intimidated her. Instead she saw no adversary, only a frail creature wrapped in cobwebs.

'My lady?' she said. She spoke softly, but the Dowager

Countess of Warwick started, nearly dropping her book. It was a book of hours – prayers framed by bright illumination. 'It's me, Katherine Lytton.'

'Oh, Kate.' The voice was light, surprised.

'Madam, how are you?'

'Never mind me, how are you?' A long bony hand came questing towards her. Kate took it, feeling the flesh cold and loose against her lips. 'How sweet to see you.' The hands cupped her face. In Anne Beauchamp's eyes there was still a spark of the iron spirit Kate remembered. 'You look well, and your eye is as bold as ever. Has your taste for wickedness diminished in any degree?'

'Madam!' Kate took the hands away and held them, kneeling beside her. 'One act of foolishness in my youth and I'm branded for all time! It's past . . . Oh, you haven't told anyone here, have you?'

'As dumb as stone am I, my dear. Since he is my son-in-law, I'd not want my daughter hurt by rumours.'

'Oh.'

'As you say, it's past.'

'It's cold in here,' said Kate. 'I'll send for servants, have them make you a fire. Where are they all?'

The Countess was shaking her head. 'No, no, I sent them away; they disturb my peace.'

'Shall I make up the fire for you, then?'

'No.' A hint of her old sternness. Then her voice was mild again. 'I don't feel the cold. They say the dead don't feel it.'

Her words disturbed Kate. 'Madam, have you seen my mother lately?'

'Not for some years.'

'Did you know that she has been chosen to succeed Dame Eylott?'

'Oh, I'm glad for her. She deserves it. But no, I didn't know. After my husband Warwick died I went into sanctuary, in fear of Edward's vengeance upon me. He exacted it, anyway, without much heed to the law.'

'So you have not had any contact with the Motherlodge of late?'

The Countess did not answer for a time. Her drooping mouth worked and her eyes looked watery, as if blinded by the sun. 'Ashes. No, I'm done with all that. Done, as if it never happened.'

That relit Kate's anger. She let go of the chill hands. 'Done with it, my lady? But the Dark Mother was your strength! Once we give ourselves to Auset, there is no turning back. You can't renounce her!'

'But I have.' The Countess smoothed her prayer book.

'Why? I suppose they persuaded you back to the Church in sanctuary. Did they fill your ears with lies about devil-worship and redemption?'

'Hush, Kate, such passion. I don't see it as redemption, rather as peace.'

'Yes, I've already found it's more peaceful simply to give in to them. But they can't control our inmost thoughts and beliefs! They think they can change us but they can't!'

'Kate, don't, I'm so tired.'

'You were never fully committed, were you? You tried to live two lives at once, and ended up surrendering to the outer world. You didn't even pass your wisdom on to your daughters, from fear of what people might think. Now Anne's only strength is in living like a saint, and Isabel was killed by it!'

Anne Beauchamp stared down at her, her lined, power-ful face as fearsome as it had ever been. 'Killed?'

'She thought it against the Church's teaching to use . . . certain methods to preserve her health.'

She expected an explosion, but none came. The Dowa-ger's voice was stiff and fragile. 'You're right. I tried to live in both worlds and the struggle tore me apart. What good was the sisterhood to me, while I was battling to keep my lands? I'm tired, Kate. I lost everything. Edward took all that was legally mine and carved it up between my two sons-in-law. Like wolves they were with my daughters and my estates. Petitmorts upon my corpse.'

Katherine gazed at the pain in her face, an utter weariness of spirit, as if her soul were a broken web behind her eyes. She had to force herself not to look away.

'Anne loves you. She can't want you to live in such austerity.'

'She has ceased arguing with me, which is a mercy. The quiet darkness and the chill suit me well, since I am dead.'

'Dead?' Kate laughed uneasily. Gently she pinched the Countess's wrist between her thumb and fingers. 'Good mother, if you can feel this, and argue with me, you are far from dead.'

The widow gave a ghastly smile, showing yellow teeth. 'If you think I've lost my mind, holy Mary, I wish I had! Edward wrested my estates from me, and generously rewarded George and Richard with them, by declaring me legally dead.'

Kate was silent, lips parted. The tide of outrage that washed through her brought her mother's voice, '*There is no use raging against the injustice of the world.*'

'There is a use,' she whispered.

'What do you say, dear?' the Countess asked, leaning down.

Kate looked up into her face. 'Do you hate Richard for it?'

'No, St Akelda bless him, I don't hate him. He won back my daughter's birthright, and brought me home – a widow grateful for charity. He can be extremely kind, but then he can afford such largesse. There was nothing in him as a boy to suggest . . . but no, I should have seen it. The youngest, he was bound to compete the most fiercely to prove himself to his brothers. It's that which has made him capable of such intense ruthlessness.'

Kate noted the judgement, and stored it away. 'I suppose he needs to be ruthless.'

'That's the way of the outer world. He had the supreme teacher: my husband Warwick.'

The Countess lowered her chin and seemed to be dozing, but after a few moments she opened her eyes again. 'Katherine, would you come often, and read with me?'

Kate's rage against Anne Beauchamp was spent. She'd said what she had to say, and the words had fallen like blunt arrows against a wild boar's hide; and it didn't matter. She couldn't be angry with the Countess for not being the sisterhood's Queen Marguerite. Even the strongest warrior might withdraw from the field, wounded. She kissed the tremulous hand.

'Aye, and bring you firewood, candles and cushions, and force you to a little luxury whether you like it or not.'

'Can you get away?' Raphael asked. It was the first warm day of spring and he and Kate had bumped into each other by the wall of the bakery. His jade eyes held a passionate light of pleasure at seeing her. 'I'm not wanted until this afternoon. I could get your horse and mine saddled and—'

'I'll slip into the kitchens and beg some demain bread and claret from the cook,' Kate finished, with a delighted grin of conspiracy. The day's thrilling warmth infected her. It was the first time she'd felt light-hearted for months. 'Auset grant that the Duchess doesn't send for me before we make our escape.'

They rode to Aysgarth Falls, where the river tumbled in slides of dark glass and white foam over the stepped rocks. On the far side curved a wall of trees; on the near bank a meadow sloped up from the river's edge, with thick bushes to hide them, and not another soul within sight. Capricious sunlight slid over the landscape. The day was perfect.

Her grey mare and Raphael's big brown cob grazed while she and Raphael sat on the river-bank amid a tumble of smooth stone and damp grass. He put his arm around her but seemed shy of doing more. She felt so at ease with him that they could have been sister and brother. They ate bread together, drank from the same cup.

'Well, are you happy at Middleham?' he asked.

'Yes. I didn't think I would be, but I am.'

'I knew better than you, then,' he said. His eyes crinkled with tenderness and the sun lit fires in his hair. He was as clear and warm-hearted as Richard was closed and complex. He didn't know that Richard had whispered to her and hugged her in the dark . . . but Richard had withdrawn again and had barely spoken to her since, beyond the most formal, polite public greetings. There was nothing to tell. They'd made their peace, gone their separate ways. There never had been anything between them, Kate knew now, but the briefest of surreptitious exchanges that meant little. She suspected that Richard saw her as a temptress who had caused him nothing but feelings of guilt. If that were the case, she couldn't tolerate being seen in such a narrow light. Neither of them had any choice but to continue as if nothing had ever happened.

Richard lived in another world, but Raphael was here, kind and tender.

They kissed. It was inevitable, sweetly warm and startling. Breaking apart, they sat looking at each other, pleased and breathless. Raphael's hands were on her shoulders, hers clutching his forearms.

'Oh, gods, I think we'd better stop that,' he said.

'While we still can?'

'Yes. Yes.' He jumped to his feet, helped her up and slipped his arms around her waist. His body was deliciously hard, like Richard's, from battle training. 'Kate, I've thought about you all the time we've been apart. I love you. I wouldn't dishonour you for anything.'

'What an honourable knight you are,' she said with her head against his shoulder. She felt hot and disappointed, thinking of the anguished balance between temptation and danger. She wondered if he would be shocked to know how quickly she desired him, when a gentlewoman was supposed to be aloof, virtuous and worth the winning. In the outer world, at least.

If he knew the mischief she had in her, would he turn from her in disillusionment, as Richard once had? 'I love you too, Raphael.'

He looked so happy she thought he was going to weep. 'Let's walk for a while, shall we?' he said, awkwardly taking her hand. 'I was thinking about Edward's Queen, who is so beautiful it takes your breath away.'

'Oh, and there was I thinking I was your fancy!'

'Let me finish,' he said, laughing. 'Real beauty is compassion in someone's face. The Queen lacks that, but you have it. It makes you a thousand times more beautiful than her. You have a kind spirit, and it shows.'

'I may be kind, but I'm not weak. I can be a graylix, to those who deserve it.'

'I know how to handle graylix,' Raphael said, and winked.

The stream raced past them on their left, filling the air with its vitality. She felt poised on an edge, light-headed with the ache of wanting him but having to hold back.

'Now I must begin to torment myself,' she said.

'How?'

'By asking if you have encountered many obliging wenches on your adventures?'

'Oh, God, Kate,' he said. 'A few. It was usually Will Shaw's fault, or mine for having no head for drink, and they left me nothing but disappointment that they weren't you.'

'That was well said. Let's sweep the confessions out of the way quickly, and forget them. You know I'm no innocent, don't you? My mother took me about the village with her from childhood; I was spared nothing. I'm a healer, midwife and surrogate. There's nothing I haven't seen. I even know what childbirth feels like.'

'That's one thing . . . but have I anyone to be jealous of?'

Kate hesitated. She wanted to tell him the truth, but it was too soon, they didn't know each other well enough. Raphael adored Richard. It would only hurt him to mention the Duke's name, or worse, to give a false impression that she was suffering some form of unrequited love. 'No, no one.'

'No one, ever?'

'I'm not a virgin,' she said quickly.

'Oh. Well, few maids are, these days, but most aren't so blunt about it.' He gave a rueful smile.

'It was someone, once, long ago, when I was young and silly. We didn't love each other; we barely met. It was a foolish mistake. Don't let's talk of the past. We've no reason to be jealous, either of us, have we?'

'No.' He picked her up and whirled her round until they were both staggering with dizziness and laughter.

They walked upriver, hand in hand, reluctant to go back. The castle would mean separation, duty, decorum. Half a mile on, they reached a curve where stepping stones made a precarious road to the other side of the water. It led nowhere but to a niche eroded into the high bank of earth and stone, clasped by tree roots.

'I suppose we should turn back, before some rogue steals our horses,' said Kate.

'There are far fewer rogues about, since Richard became lord,' said Raphael. He placed a kiss on her neck, but the niche seized all her attention. It was too shallow to be called a cave, more a shrine, filled with tumbled rocks and a silver cross thrust into the threshold and leaning at an angle, its dagger-points held out like warding arms.

'Oh, no,' Katherine breathed.

Before Raphael could stop her she'd taken off her shoes and, holding her skirts up around her knees, was treading her way across the river. The stones were like glass, the gaps between them so wide she must jump, slipping and swaying. The river surged beneath her.

'Kate!' he cried. She ignored him but heard him coming after her, cursing once or twice under his breath.

Reaching the far side she leapt lightly onto the dry floor of the cavern. Splinters of limestone were strewn about, as if someone had attacked the altar with a mallet. There were big chunks of black rock, too: the remains of the Goddess's statue, smashed.

'Bastards.' She grated out the word so hard that it made her throat sore. Seizing the pointed cross that had been placed to ward the entrance, she flung it as hard as she could downriver. The swing of her arm nearly knocked Raphael over.

'Bastards!'

'What on earth are you doing?'

She dropped to her knees, scooping the black chunks of rock into a single stack. 'I'm sorry. Great Mother, I'm so sorry.'

'Kate?'

'Help me find all the pieces. We can put her back together. Iesu's blood, this makes me so angry. They think, with their prayers and bit of metal, they can destroy us.'

Raphael knelt beside her and helped. 'Was this a . . .'

'A Hollow, yes.' Calmer now, she became still, scenting the air, feeling the sulky echoes of elementals all around her. The swift spirits of the river emerged subtly from the bubbling ripples of water to chill the air. She sensed those of the earth rising beneath her feet, clawing their way upwards, blind and gnomelike. Cracks in the rock became vague, craggy faces. 'It still is, or could be.'

She got three pieces of the statue together, the belly, chest and head resting one on the other. It would take mortar to reattach the arms and legs. Perhaps it didn't matter. As she set the bulbous, primitive figure on the chipped boulder that had been the altar, it still had presence. She had no candles, no incense, no offerings. Tears ran down her face and she wiped the moisture away and smeared it on the statue instead: an offering of herself.

'Great Mother, let me heal what they have desecrated,' she murmured.

The hidden world was glimmering blue around her. Raphael caught his breath and grabbed her arm so hard it hurt. Auset's answer came all around her in a soft, booming whisper, making her laugh and weep.

'I can hear something.' He sounded awestruck. 'A voice. What is it saying?'

Kate gave a quick, wondering laugh. 'You hear it?'

'Yes.'

'It's the voice of the earth. What the priests don't understand is that they can't destroy the sacred places. Chanting prayers, breaking statues and planting symbols changes nothing. It affrights the spirits, warns good folk away and masks the doorway, but they can't seal it. For all their efforts, they can't seal the door!'

They were kneeling face to face. Raphael was gazing at her, his face flushed with awe. She reached for him, sliding one hand beneath his shirt to caress his bare chest. The skin was fine and hairless and she felt the strong beating of his heart. He gasped.

'I am a priestess and your lover,' she said. 'Raphael, you are born to this as I am. Give yourself to the Hidden One, Auset, Mother of All; give yourself, in perfect love and perfect trust.'

'Yes,' he breathed.

'Help me drive out all the cold lies. Help me bring back her energy to this place, her vitality, her presence.'

He held her face. 'How?'

She could feel his tension and the growing heat of his body, the lightest dew of sweat forming on his skin. Warmth swelled and ached between her thighs. Unseen power trembled in the air.

'With the most precious thing we have to offer her,' Kate answered. 'Our ecstasy.'

Months later, Raphael still thought about that afternoon.

Whenever he was separated from Kate, by distance or by propriety, he remembered and smiled. London, wet and wintry, was a stew of bodies and overripe colours, of stench, gossip, perfume and intrigue. Yet to escape it, he had only to close his eyes and the thin cold light flamed orange, casting long shadows from his feet and Kate's as they had walked home, twining frequently around each other in the languid afterglow.

The world had seemed hallucinatory. As reluctantly as schoolboys dragging to school they had walked back towards their horses, knowing they wouldn't reach the castle before dusk and that there would be questions and teasing, but not caring. Kate still looked proud and untouched, as if an ice rose would emerge as perfect from her mouth as it went in. Raphael smiled. He knew the truth. He'd promised not to dishonour her, only to discover a short time later how unnecessary the promise was. Kate was not a woman who could be dishonoured. She was a priestess, a lioness.

Each time he was away from Middleham as part of the Duke of Gloucester's entourage, he missed her. Anne suffered frail health and often preferred to stay at Middleham than be separated from her son, Edward, so her ladies stayed at home with her. Even if the Duchess did accompany her husband, it was usually impossible for Raphael and Kate to meet alone. Yet it made their snatched encounters – and the memories – more poignant. He felt almost guilty for being so happy these past few months, when Richard had had such troubles.

George, Duke of Clarence was in the Tower, sentenced to death for high treason.

King Edward had reacted to Clarence's plan to marry Marie of Burgundy with a counter-intention, that Anthony Woodville should marry her instead. The marriage hadn't taken place but the intention, reportedly, had propelled Clarence into a spiral of rage and ever more extravagantly provocative behaviour. At Edward's command, two of his servants had been arrested, tortured and executed for alleged conspiracy against the King, but Clarence had ignored the dire warning. Instead, he had burst in upon a Council meeting and pleaded his servants' innocence, thus undermining the King's justice and assuring his own arrest.

From all accounts, his imprisonment had shaken him. He had never expected King Edward to arrest him, let alone to find him guilty. He'd been arrogant at first, assuming his incarceration would be short, convinced he'd done nothing wrong and that Edward would soon perceive his genuine sense of injustice. He was wrong. Edward's patience had expired.

Even after what Kate had told him about Clarence, Raphael was surprised to hear the list of accusations against him. Forgiven for his treachery with Warwick, showered with gifts of land and titles, nothing had satisfied him. He was accused of stirring rebellion, of perverting the law, of slanders against the King and Queen, of impugning the King's justice. None of the charges seemed enough to earn him the death penalty, especially not for a man of his rank, the King's own brother.

Edward, though, had changed. He was growing coarse, lazy, addicted to self-indulgence and to the flattery of the Woodvilles and his other drinking companions. Only Richard's black-diamond presence seemed to snap him back to a semblance of his old self. Richard was in agreement with Edward that their brother needed a sharp lesson, but he wanted George punished, frightened back to his senses, not killed.

George of Clarence had become a desperate embarrassment.

Richard had brought his most trusted men-at-arms with him. Raphael had learned that he didn't trust many. There was Francis Lovell, Raphael's good friend; Richard Ratcliffe, red-haired, outspoken, and devoted to Richard; James Tyrell, who was taciturn but energetic and utterly dependable; Robert Percy, a cheerful, helpful soul. They stayed in

Richard's house, Crosby Place, a handsome building with the look of a cathedral. From there Richard went daily to court and Parliament, trying to resolve the matter.

Winter fell cold and wet across the city, choking the streets with snow and then with filthy meltwater. The Isis surged brown and angry between her banks. Raphael was resigned to the season's daily discomforts: from frostbitten fingers, leaking boots, damp clothes to the stifling heat of Edward's palace. Returning to the stately, echoing silence of Crosby Place was always a relief.

Like his master, he was morose and restless to go north again. He wrote to Kate daily, wondering if the letters would ever reach her along the bogged roads. Today, Richard had gone to the palace with only Ratcliffe at his side, leaving Raphael and the others behind.

'Wake up,' said a crisp voice. 'The Duke is home.'

Visions of Kate in the sunset vanished. Instead Raphael was looking at dark red walls, a vaulted ceiling, twisted pillars of blue and gold and Francis Lovell, facing him across the great hall's table of dark oak. Raphael jumped to his feet, hurried to take Richard's cloak and to summon pages who were waiting to bring him wine and fur-lined slippers to replace his damp boots. Richard brought the scent of winter in with him.

He pulled out a chair and sat at the table, looking grim and colourless. His companions took seats around him.

'The Woodvilles have spies in the Tower,' he said, folding his hands on the tabletop. 'They report to the Queen the venom that George spills daily against her and the King. His confinement has taught him nothing, only made him resent Edward more violently than ever. I never thought I'd feel sorry for George, but I do.'

'Sorry for him?' said Lovell.

'The Queen insists that he shall be properly punished for his insults and damage to her reputation. The Queen's reputation!' Richard's laugh was hollow. 'It's she and her brothers and sons who have persuaded Edward to put him to death.'

After a long and awkward silence, Lovell spoke. 'Are you sure he needed much persuasion?'

Richard didn't answer. Firelight carved shadows into his face.

'He has committed treason,' Lovell added. 'He was aiming at the throne.'

'In the most blatant, bungling way possible,' said Richard. 'How can such a reasonably intelligent man act like such a fool? I've spent half my life being furious with him or despairing of him. He has cried from the rooftops what most only dare think of the Woodvilles in secret. For being ambitious and jealous but lacking any common sense; for this he deserves the Tower, or to be stripped of all his land and titles. But to die? He is still our brother.'

As he was speaking, another man came into the doorway, breathing hard. He threw his heavy cloak at a servant and came striding into the hall, rain flying from his yellow hair. Raphael recognized him. The Duke of Buckingham would no longer be mistaken for a female, but he had the same glorious hair and the look of a finely dressed angelic messenger.

'Richard, I agree with you,' he said, throwing himself into a chair next to the Duke without waiting for an invitation. 'I've been trying to catch up with you all the way from Westminster. I hadn't the sense to keep secret the fact that I despise the Woodville mare they made me marry. I had the excuse of youth, but still, Elizabeth cannot forgive me for loathing her sister and saying so.'

'You still managed to get her with child,' said Francis, and Raphael saw Richard smile involuntarily. 'A fair daughter, I heard.'

Buckingham recoiled in plain revulsion. 'Entirely at her instigation, not mine. One could endure it by closing one's eyes and pretending ... The point is that the Queen hates me, as she hates Clarence. That's why I've never received my rightful position at court. The Woodvilles are too powerful.'

'So, Harry, you've chased me across London to state the obvious?' Gloucester said. He tilted his head to look at Buckingham, not unkindly.

The young Duke paled a little, twisting his beringed hands together. 'You can see how obscenely powerful it will make them, if they are perceived to have brought about the execution of the King's own brother.'

'Perception is everything,' Richard said, his head lowered. 'I have tried to make Edward see this. He's intransigent . . . but he has hesitated for days since the sentence was pronounced. I've not entirely given up hope.'

'If you cannot persuade him, no one can,' Buckingham said quietly.

'I'm touched by your support, since you were the one who pronounced the sentence upon him in Parliament.'

'Only to save you from having to do so.' Buckingham touched Richard's arm. 'You know that.'

'Yes, and I'm grateful to you for taking that burden from me. But no one should have had to do it.'

'I wish to make it clear that, despite the duty enforced upon me, I can't support the King in this,' said Buckingham. 'I support you.'

'And I'm grateful, Harry.' The Duke of Gloucester looked up. His eyes were narrow, fierce. 'I can't let the Woodvilles win. They'll execute one brother, only to make an enemy of the other. Now I know they certainly would not stop short of killing me if the opportunity arose.'

'They're going to say that you benefited from Clarence's fall.'

'I suppose they will. He's forfeited his right to his estates and titles, and I know that Edward will give a proportion of them to me. But I repeat; I wanted him to desist, not to die, if only for our mother's sake. I might still . . .'

'Richard,' Buckingham said, closing his eyes in pain. 'I came to tell you that Parliament is going to press the King to carry out the sentence. I heard it whispered, minutes after you'd left. They mean to have Clarence executed within two days.'

Richard had returned to the Palace of Westminster to plead one last time for George's life. It could be a long night, he'd said, looking exhausted before it even began. He'd taken Ratcliffe, Tyrell and only a few other men with him, leaving the rest at home, including Francis Lovell and Raphael. There was nothing for them to do but drink and play disconsolate games of dice. Something malevolent was creeping through the streets, Raphael could sense it. Dark shapes flapped overhead, like gigantic bats, paper thin, but when he looked out of the windows, there was nothing there.

He was too sensitive to the atmosphere. It seized him and made him wretched. He dreaded sleep. He knew that something hideous was waiting for him within the feathery breast of oblivion. Deep into the night he tried his hardest to stay awake over dice and other games, but the men were beginning to drift to their beds or fall asleep where they sat. Tiredness dragged at his eyes. The dreadful presence waited for him and there was no way to avoid it. It was like time itself. A man couldn't go around it, only through it. Better to get it over with.

The fire burned low, painting the room with a sweating dull gold aura. Resigned, Raphael had a last drink of claret, and took himself to the chamber he shared with Francis Lovell, lay down and closed his eyes.

He was walking through thick fog near the Tower. The grey curtains rolled back and revealed to him three figures, standing under the ancient mottled flank of a wall. Dark vapours whirled about them and strange shadows spread from their feet. Two of the men were indistinct: ruffians, they appeared, with drab clothes and narrow crafty eyes. The third was Richard.

He looked as Raphael had never seen him before, his shoulders bent as he whispered with the two men, and a terrible look on his face: a grin that had no mirth, only a chilling, cynical look of hell in it.

'Sirs, be sudden in the execution,' he said. 'Withal obdurate, do not hear him plead, for Clarence is well spoken, and perhaps may move your hearts to pity if you mark him.'

The first man tutted. 'My lord, we will not stand to prate; talkers are no good doers. Be assured, we go to use our hands and not our tongues.'

'Your eyes drop millstones when fools' eyes fall tears,' Richard answered. 'I like you, lads; about your business straight.'

Raphael was moving through the interior of the Tower, icy with terror. The dun material of his sleeve looked odd and there was a knife in his hand. He sat in the mind of one of the murderers, seeing through his eyes, and before him swam a scene of nauseous horror. A cell, a bed tangled and rucked like a stormy sea and, starting up in it, the Duke of Clarence.

He, too, looked wrong. He was older than Raphael remembered, and his face was gouged with misery and fear. From his mouth fell an endless string of words, each dull and painful as a tolling bell, describing some grim nightmare of treachery and drowning, on and on, until Raphael would have stabbed him just to silence him. The scene was a corner of purgatory. It soaked each fibre of him with the thick yellow bile of dread, then pulled those fibres apart with soft fingers. Something evil dwelled here. Surely Clarence, even treacherous Clarence had not deserved this.

Raphael looked at the man beside him and saw his face gaunt with fear.

'What? Art thou afraid?' said Raphael through the first murderer's mouth.

'Not to kill him, having a warrant,' said the second, 'but

to be damned for killing him, from the which no warrant can defend me.'

'I thought thou hadst been resolute.'

'So I am – to let him live.'

'I'll back to the Duke of Gloucester and tell him so.'

'Nay, I pray thee, stay a little . . .'

Raphael clutched the hilt of his dagger. His breath was thick between his teeth. 'Remember our reward, when the deed's done.'

'Zounds, he dies!' cried the man. 'I had forgot the reward.'

'Where's thy conscience now?'

'O, in the Duke of Gloucester's purse.'

Clarence was sleeping again as they crept towards him across the cold little space of the cell, but as they reached him he woke, befuddled as a child. In panic, Raphael's companion hissed, 'Strike!' but now it was Raphael who was paralysed.

'No, we'll reason with him.'

'In God's name, what are thou?' Clarence cried.

'A man, as you are,' Raphael said. The power of life and death felt horribly intoxicating.

'But not, as I am, royal.'

'Nor you as we are, loyal,' said the second man.

'Thy voice is thunder, but thy looks are humble.'

'My voice is now the King's, my looks my own,' came the words from Raphael's mouth.

'How darkly and how deadly dost thou speak! Your eyes do menace me. Why look you pale? Who sent you hither? Wherefore do you come?' They tried to answer, stammering. 'To murder me?' Clarence said. 'You scarcely have the hearts to tell me so, and therefore cannot have the hearts to do it. Wherein, my friends, have I offended you?'

He was dignified, but pitiful.

'Offended us you have not, but the King.'

'I shall be reconciled to him again.'

'Never, my lord,' said Raphael's companion. 'Therefore prepare to die.'

Clarence pleaded, as eloquent as Gloucester had warned he would be, and Raphael was crushed in the spiked closet of the nightmare, feeling it would never end.

'If you do love my brother, hate not me. I am his brother, and I love him well. If you are hired for meed, go back again, and I will send you to my brother Gloucester, who shall reward you better for my life than Edward will for tidings of my death.'

'You are deceived. Your brother Gloucester hates you.'

'Oh no, he loves me and he holds me dear! Go you to him from me.'

'Aye, so we will,' Raphael murmured, relishing the irony.

'Tell him, when that our princely father York blessed his three sons with his victorious arm and charged us from the soul to love each other, he little thought of this divided friendship; bid Gloucester think of this, and he will weep.'

'Ay, millstones, as he lessoned us to weep.'

'O, do not slander him, for he is kind.' Tears flowed now down Clarence's ravaged face. And while he was pleading with the second murderer, it was Raphael who struck, in sudden hot anger, wanting to end it, stabbing, stabbing, and blood running everywhere, hot and bright as wine, his head pounding, the whole scene throbbing to a painful heartbeat as he dragged the weight, the weeping, gasping, dying weight of Clarence across the floor of the cell.

'If all this will not do,' he rasped, 'I'll drown him in the malmsey-butt within.'

'A bloody deed, and desperately dispatched!' His companion's voice came spiralling after him, a ghost-wail. 'How fain, like Pilate, would I wash my hands of this most grievous murder!'

Raphael woke in choking horror, then came a sense of

exhilaration, as if an eagle were trying to burst out of his chest. Holy Mary, it had been more than real, but he knew at once that he'd dreamed it. That awareness helped him to control himself, and not cry out. He didn't want them rushing around him thinking he was possessed, sick or mad.

'Oh, Creator,' he breathed, his palm sliding over his forehead on a soap of sweat. 'Oh Iesu, Lamb of God, Dark Mother, help me.'

What had he done to deserve such visions? All along he'd known it wasn't real, yet he could do nothing to escape. As vivid as reality, yes, but a puppeteer had moved him through the motions. That was it. It was as if it were truly happening, yet false, like a masquerade. Theatre.

'I saw something real,' he whispered into the dark, 'but not about the Richard I know. Why, why do I keep dreaming he's up to his neck in blood, when I love him like a brother? How in heaven's name can I dream up such villainy about him? I can't live with myself . . .'

Someone prodded him. 'You're talking in your sleep,' said Francis Lovell. 'Wake up! If you go off in the screaming horrors again, I'll throw you in the river!'

'Oh, Iesu,' Raphael gasped, sitting up in a tangle of bedding.

'It's London gives you nightmares,' Francis said, sitting on the end of his bed and pulling narrow trousers onto his long, pale legs. 'It's the bad vapours off the Isis, it affects some like that. What was it this time?'

'I dreamed two murderers had stabbed the Duke of Clarence, and finished him off in a vat of malmsey wine. I was the one who did it. Richard was going to pay me for it.'

Lovell tipped back his head and laughed. 'Saints above, I'm glad I don't have your imagination! Who was the other murderer? Me?' Abruptly he sobered, remembering there was nothing to laugh at. 'Christ, Raphael, are you going to tell him about it?'

Raphael hung his head. 'I promised him that I would always tell him my visions. But this . . .'

'Mm. To tell him you dreamed he'd paid murderers when the opposite is true.'

'He'd be furious,' Raphael said, wretched. 'Outraged. How could he not be? It's not what I think of him. How can I explain where it came from? I don't understand it myself. I'll have to break the promise. I can't tell him. Not this.'

Francis rested a hand on his shoulder. 'I think you're right, friend. At least that's one dream we know won't come true. Richard's spent all night with Edward, pleading for their brother's miserable life.'

'Gods, and all I can do is weave these vile dreams.'

'I hear something.' Frowning, Francis rose, pulling on a shirt of freshly laundered ecru. He went to the door and opened it. Lamplight spilled in, shining bronze along the passageway, and from the hall there came the murmur of men's voices.

Lovell turned to Raphael, his face grave. 'Get dressed quickly. He's back.'

The Duke of Gloucester was in his chamber, which had battle scenes woven in vivid colours hanging upon the walls, with Ratcliffe and Tyrell. He had been weeping. As Raphael entered with Lovell and Percy, he made no attempt to hide the fact, only acknowledged them with a look that said everything. He wouldn't have let anyone but his closest circle see him so drawn and red-eyed; his trust was heart-turning. Raphael felt dizzy with shame. He was part of the trusted clique, yet had been betraying Richard all night with ghastly melodramas.

Richard sat with his elbows on the table as they gathered around him.

'Well, that's it,' he said, indistinct. He rubbed his hands over his face and sat back. 'I was too late. Edward drank himself into a rage, and couldn't be dissuaded. He said that

I had gone too far along this road with him to pull back now, and that George had broken all fraternal ties with us, and nothing short of death would still his quarrelsome nature. And I was too late. The only plea Edward heard was my mother's, that George should be executed in private, by a method of his own choice. All the time I was entreating for his life, George was dying. A last indulgence in malmsey wine. Then, once he was in a stupor, drowned in it.' The spectre of a smile touched his lips, ghastly. 'Typical of him. So, the Woodvilles won. George is dead. Edward thinks he can live with himself! In time his regret shall turn as bitter as wormwood. And I don't care if I never set foot in his cursed, hell-possessed court again.'

Visions inside dreams inside visions. When Raphael had the nightmare about the murder of Clarence, it shocked me to the core. He had lived through a scene in Shakespeare's play. How was that possible? It was in a different time, even a different world. He couldn't possibly have known.

Had I fed it to him? I was sure I hadn't. I don't know it by heart, I hadn't even been thinking of it. No, Raphael had some connection to my world that I couldn't comprehend, and it was nothing to do with me. I was merely a spectator.

It made me think of the other vision he'd seen: the murder of Henry VI. I remembered how Richard had seemed to deny it, then seemed to admit it, leaving it all as mysterious as ever. Poor Raphael was not only living through reality, but seeing how reality would ultimately be distorted and blackened.

He was seeing the legend in formation. Shakespeare's glorious and terrible creation. The poison pens of historians, Carmeliano and Rous, who saw no problem in praising Richard while he was alive and reviling him when he was dead, of André who used the images of evil Richard and angelic Tudor to illustrate the concept of divine justice; and the masters, Polydore Vergil and Thomas More, who, in order to write their morality tales, would dissect him with such skill and sophistication that his reputation, despite the efforts of later writers, would never recover.

I needed to calm down a bit. I went to our café for

a cup of herb tea, but Fin wasn't there just when I really needed to talk to her. Instead I sat scratching on a notepad, trying to think.

So frustrating. I couldn't reach Raphael to explain. That is, I could have told him *what* he was seeing, if not why. Yes, he seemed to look at me sometimes, but in my daydream narrative, no matter how hard I tried, I could never make him hear me, any more than I could make the actors in a film hear me.

Richard himself, meanwhile, was giving me no answers at all.

What did it mean, a phantom lover who came to me in the darkness, folded me in raven's wings and velvet, and would reveal nothing?

So there he was.

Shakespeare's 'bottled spider', an 'elvish-marked, abortive, rooting hog', evil for the sheer glee of being evil.

Or a cynical opportunist.

Or a paranoid man, who destroyed his rivals from an unfounded fear of what they *might* do.

Or an upright, genuine man, forced to defend himself against scheming enemies.

Wickedly intelligent. Rashly impulsive but not that bright.

A good king, who took the throne to save the country, and was vilely betrayed for his pains.

A paradox.

Through Kate and Raphael, I was delving for some connection to the truth. I rarely had actual dreams about them; if I did, they were just dreams, surreal and transparent. No, the waking visions I enjoyed were different: solid, even verifiable. I could go to my books and check facts. Except . . .

There was so much I couldn't place. The degree of technology seemed slightly too far advanced, their exotic architecture and spectacular attempts at plumbing. And at the other end of the scale, a belief in magic

271

and in some kind of hidden world, the land of Faerie, is universal, but in Kate's world it lay beneath a very thin skin indeed.

There was no mention of a Dr Fautherer. The nearest equivalent I could find was Reynold Bray, Margaret Beaufort's steward and carrier of secret letters, who'd schemed so hard for Richard's downfall.

No trace of the Motherlodge. It seemed to be a remnant of Isis worship brought to Britain with the Romans or their Egyptian servants, fused with timeless Celtic and native beliefs. Was it possible that such a religion had survived, but been expunged from our records, as kept by men? Or just an anomaly of my daydreams?

Raphael and Kate drew me on a fascinating journey, following history so closely, yet so oddly skewed. I felt privileged and scared to death.

In the real world, I'd travelled quite a bit, too. There were several sites to visit: castles where Richard had lived; places where he had stayed; a sad and mysterious tomb in Kent where a natural son of his was said to be buried, with a heart-rending story attached. None haunted me as Bosworth did. The bleak peace of the battlefield always induced in me the strongest, most detailed narratives.

I had to go there again. I rose and began to gather my books. I might see Raphael . . .

And suddenly, I understood. I froze and gave a gasp that made the students at the next table look at me. I couldn't contact him to explain, because he must learn the truth for himself.

Chapter Eleven 1478–83: Edward

RICHARD
And, if I fail not in my deep intent,
Clarence hath not another day to live;
Which done, God take King Edward to His mercy,
And leave the world for me to bustle in!

Richard III Act I scene 1

Richard proved himself an energetic and efficient king.

Charles Ross, *Richard III*

The little church lay on the coast of France, the heart of a village that was poised on a crag and buffeted by sea storms. Inside, the walls were stained yellow with candlelight. The air itself shimmered thickly with the smoky golden glow. Dr Fautherer had lit the many fat candles in their brass sconces and placed holy water and wine and the sacred mantle upon the altar. Now he raised the lamb. It jerked and bleated in his grasp, flicking its ears.

Gathered around the altar were the remnants of the House of Lancaster: Jasper Tudor and his nephew Henry, both in exile, the latter a thin young man with a gaunt face and wary eyes. Then the visitors: Henry's doting mother Margaret and her friend, Bishop Morton. Lady Margaret's latest husband, Thomas Stanley, was also present, standing apart and mouthing the amens. He looked stiff and uneasy, Fautherer noted. Morton, by contrast, was serene and confident, his plump face beneficient.

The crossing had not been easy, but Margaret Beaufort

had stood pike-straight at the rail of the fishing vessel and not shown a glimmer of discomfort; such was her strength of will. She had been desperate to see her only son, but had never shown that desperation, only this tight, steel-hard determination.

The Lancastrian exiles had greeted her warmly, bringing a smile to her tight face. Now they filled the front four rows of pews, watching the ceremony that might at last bring them slender hope.

'We praise Almighty God for the scything down of Clarence,' said Bishop Morton. 'One more sinful soul gathered in, one more scion of York destroyed. This is the judgement of God. The House of York is divided against itself and will destroy itself.'

'Amen,' murmured Fautherer, the congregation echoing him. The lamb's bleats were shrill, plaintive. Its warm fleecy body was housed in a little coat sewn with white roses.

'The last precious blood of Lancaster resides in my son, Henry Tudor,' said Margaret Beaufort. 'May Almighty God preserve him, bless him, elevate him to his rightful station.'

'Amen.' Jasper Tudor's voice boomed out strongly.

The mantle that lay upon the altar was embroidered, like the lamb's coat, with roses, but these were the red blooms of Lancaster. Beside it lay a crown of gold filigree.

Morton signalled with a thick finger. Humbly, Fautherer laid the lamb upon the altar and slit its throat. Blood flowed. Wisps of shocked breath came from the onlookers.

'Thus let the House of York die,' intoned the Bishop. 'O Lord Creator, accept this sacrifice of innocent blood to nurture the field of the red rose. May all the sins of York flow out and be expiated in the redemptive light of Lancaster. Accept this thy son, Henry Tudor, King of England and of France.'

'Thy will be done,' said Lady Beaufort, and the echoes rippled after her.

Some of the lamb's blood had flowed onto the mantle,

staining the precise red roses with a chaotic splash of scarlet. Fautherer nodded; it was a good omen.

'This cloak, the kingdom of England,' said Morton.

Jasper and Lady Margaret lifted the mantle and placed it on Henry Tudor's narrow shoulders. Bishop Morton anointed him with lamb's blood and set the crown upon his head.

'This crown, the crown of England. As in this sacred space, so in the outer world. Thy will be done.'

'Amen,' came the answering voices, strong with hope.

Henry, who had looked weighed down by the mantle, put his shoulders back. His chin came up and the wariness in his eyes cleared. He looked, at last, resolute.

As the hymn of thanks began – the hymn that, Fautherer knew, would one day be sung at Henry's coronation – he saw Lady Margaret touch Morton's arm and heard her whisper, 'I must thank you for your steadfast friendship, and Dr Fautherer for conveying my messages in these difficult times. One would think he was everywhere, like smoke. And my thanks to both of you for keeping my secrets.'

'Anything, madam, if it means restoring the rightful house to the throne,' Morton answered warmly. 'And our faith to its true centre of authority.'

Lady Margaret was silent for a moment. Fautherer saw her husband looking at her; his face with its neat beard impassive, the eyes shrewd, sly and measuring. Fautherer recognized a kindred spirit. He said nothing; his function was only to serve.

'However . . . this seems a little uncomfortably akin to sorcery,' Margaret Beaufort said at last.

Morton inclined his head, acknowledging and dismissing her concern in a single gesture. 'Madam, to activate the will of God is not sorcery,' he said. 'Heathen devil-worshippers cling to the house of York like blackfly to a white rose. *Their* practises are sorcery. Ours are holy rite.'

In the body of the church, the Lancastrians in exile were

dropping to their knees and crying out as one, 'God save King Henry!'

Katherine was on the stairs to the keep, watching. Down in the bailey was the bustle of the Duke's party arriving home: men-at-arms, coursers and sumpter-horses, castle servants rushing to welcome and tend them. A few minutes later, with a retinue streaming after him, Richard passed Katherine on the stairs. In his sombre glory of velvet and fur and long leather boots, he passed so close she caught the scent of rain rising off his clothes, but he spared her not a glance.

When he had gone, Kate ran down into the bailey and stood looking for Raphael. Someone touched her elbow, she turned, and he was there.

They stood face to face, smiling. He looked older, with more presence about him, as if the journey had hardened him. He was every inch the nobleman to match Francis Lovell or Richard's other close servants; his garments were of sombre hues worked with gold.

'Look at you,' said Kate. She fingered the fur and quilted velvet of his doublet, his soft cap that had a silver fox-cub tail depending from a jewel in the form of a white rose. 'I don't recognize you. Did these clothes come from London? You look a true nobleman. You must have been magnificent at court.'

'That is the idea,' Raphael said. He glanced down at himself, half-embarrassed. 'Richard can't have his retinue looking less impressive than another duke's. He's paid for all our finery out of his own purse, in fact.'

'How generous,' said Kate. 'How was London?'

He pulled a face. 'Overripe, cruel and stinking. Creator, I'm glad to be back. We all are.'

'Is it true about the Duke of Clarence?'

'Shh.' He glanced around. 'Richard was distraught. He doesn't want to overhear people gossiping about it.'

'Believe me, it is not gossip,' Kate said thinly.

'Can you meet me by the bakery in ten minutes?' he said. 'I'll change into something you recognize me in. I've so much to tell you.'

'So Clarence is dead?' Kate asked. They had ridden out to their secret place, Aysgarth. The day was wet and chill; the trees were leafless, the river high and fast.

'Yes,' Raphael said. 'At least they spared him a public execution. It's said that he asked to be drowned in a cask of wine.'

'And some say it would have been faster had he not got out twice to visit the privy.'

'Kate!' Despite himself, he laughed.

'Well, you look so miserable. He must have died happy, since he was in his natural element. I can't say I'm sorry, after the things he did. It seems strange, though, that he isn't there any more, and his poor children have no mother or father. He spent years inviting trouble as if he was hell-bent on seeing how far he could go. Still, to be executed by your own brothers – dreadful.'

'Richard had no part of it. He tried to stop it.'

'Did he?'

Raphael was quiet, remembering Richard in the fireglow, his face ashen, tears dried to salt, telling them, 'I am not guiltless. I played my part in bringing him to justice over these past months. I wanted him tamed! To learn his lesson, to be scared back to common sense. Not killed. But still, I acted in cold anger and this is the result. Edward wanted blood, and I, having gone so far with him, could not draw him back from the brink. Who made him thirst for his own brother's blood?' The Duke's voice had been soft, like the scrape of a barber's blade. 'Voices pouring honeyed venom into his ears. The Queen and her family. They despised George and bore him a grudge heavy enough to sink England in the sea. They could never accept Edward's forgiveness of him, nor the favours he showered upon him. God knows, George had done as much to hurt me.

There was no love lost between us, but I had better things to do with my energy than waste it on grudges. But not the Woodvilles. They breed grudges, and feed and groom them like fattened livestock.

'All Edward could say to me was, "It's for the best." He looked like a fat bishop, red-faced and dissolute. I looked back at him and could say nothing at all. All my pleading had been the bleating of a schoolboy who knows himself to be as guilty as the Devil.'

He had tipped back his head and sighed, then looked at Raphael, Francis and the others. Something had changed in his eyes; a gleam of wariness turned hard and bright with cynicism. 'If not for the Woodvilles, Warwick and Clarence would not have betrayed Edward in the first place. If not for the Woodvilles, they would both still be alive.'

Raphael closed his eyes in pain, recalling Richard's grief. He had the physical memory of murdering the Duke of Clarence. For all he told himself it had been only a nightmare, the memory felt real.

Later, as they'd ridden back to Yorkshire, Richard had spoken again. It was in the twilight, with the wild sky silver and black behind him. 'I have one thing left, and that is the fact that Edward trusts me. Loyalty binds me to him, no matter what he does. That's the one truth that never changes, and he knows it.' His voice fell in with the rhythm of the horses' hooves as they rode, and it was compelling, like low music. 'The Queen is a jealous mistress. She and her kin hate me for any favour Edward shows to me, or to William Hastings, or anyone not of their blood. It's unfortunate for them that they can find no pretext to destroy me. Yet.'

Raphael had said, 'Perhaps they feel insecure on their perch, to cling to it so viciously.'

Richard had smiled at that. 'That's a fair point. They could suck the King's blood for a thousand years and it would not make their own more noble. That makes them furious with envy and malice. At least I know the worst

278

now. Given the chance, they'll stop at nothing to destroy me as they destroyed George.'

'Not while you have stout friends around you, Dick,' Lovell had answered. And they'd ridden hard into the night, as if riding towards the edge of the world.

Raphael related all this to Kate. The only thing he didn't tell her was his dream. They walked slowly, arms around each other under their cloaks. She felt beautifully slim and warm, her hair falling enticingly around her like water in shadow.

'Tell me about the court,' she said.

'It was vile,' he said. 'Luxury, marble floors, gilding, gorgeous clothes and jewels such as you've never seen.'

'It sounds like purgatory.'

'Let me finish! It's the people. They're like painted dolls. There's something depraved about it: so much excess, and all the jealousy and fawning.'

'Is Queen Elizabeth still beautiful?'

Raphael gave a sneering laugh. 'It's hard to tell, under the layers of silver and veils and jewels. But yes, she's still beautiful. She has a perfect little oval face and long narrow eyes the colour of peridots. You would never know how many children she's had, her waist's as thin as a willow. She walks about like a faerie queen. You'd never dare address her because she looks as if she'd turn you into stone. She's always whispering with her brother Anthony. He dresses even more gorgeously than she does. He goes about stroking his chin and smiling and being friendly with everyone, which is as sinister as the Queen's iciness. But he's very charming. They say he's read every book ever written.'

'You sound as if you hate them.'

'I don't hate them, but I want nothing to do with them. The Queen's younger son, Richard Grey, is a typical courtier, full of himself but with no character that I could discern. There's only one I took a real dislike to and that was her oldest son Thomas, Marquis of Dorset.'

'Why?'

'He has that special arrogance of a person who fears they are nobody, and has to spend every moment proving they are somebody. The man's an ass.'

Kate was amused. 'I would like to meet them and make up my own mind, but . . .'

'But?'

She turned and pressed close against him. 'I've more important things to do.' Opening her lips, she received him with a kiss so deep and passionate that it was all he could do not to push her down on the wet grass. He tried to hold her away.

'Love, we can't—'

'Why not?'

'It's cold and wet.'

'The shrine will be dry,' she said, pulling him towards the path of stepping stones. They looked glossy and perilous in the high water. 'I haven't seen you for weeks.'

Kate was right. Beneath the overhanging bank the Hollow was dry and if not warm, at least sheltered enough for their purpose. As Raphael lay twined against her sweet body, satiated at last, he felt unguarded, and wanted to confess his hideous dreams. If anyone could illuminate their meaning, it was her.

'I've always been happy at Middleham,' he said. 'I didn't think it was possible to be any happier.'

'And look at me, who thought she never wanted a man!' She twined around him languidly. The Goddess of broken black stone watched benignly over them. Outside their refuge, rain began to fall.

'Oh, Raph, look,' Kate said suddenly. 'Someone's brought her an offering!' He looked and saw that a posy of primrose and crocus had been placed before the black figure. Kate turned her eyes back to him, bright sapphires. 'We've done some good, then. But we must be vigilant. Unless we tend the sacred places, they'll be like ruined gardens, gone back to the wild. Their power will be lost to us, changed, hostile and out of our reach. We must tend the serpent power or we will lose it. There'll be no fire to warm the land's heart. It's already happening. Will you help me?'

Torn flashes of memory. Priests and knights in white armour. His mother falling, his brother dying. He was afraid. He knew it was against the Duke of Gloucester's own beliefs, but he couldn't refuse her. 'Yes. You're the wise one.' He sat up and rearranged their clothing, wrapping her cloak tenderly around her. 'Katherine . . . Do you know how it feels to be utterly loyal to someone and yet to have unbidden thoughts of disloyalty?'

She smiled impishly. 'Have you got designs on the village maids again?'

'I don't mean my loyalty to you. I meant . . . to the Duke.'

She looked shocked. 'Well, I've sometimes been angry with my mother, but I've still loved her.'

'This isn't anger. I don't know what it is.'

'What on earth are you talking about?'

He wanted to tell her. The dreams felt like tar, wouldn't come out of him. It seemed unfair to inflict his vile imaginings on her. Eventually he asked, 'What do you think of him?'

'Richard?' Her voice was mild, but he felt her shiver a little. 'I'm not sure. He makes me afraid, sometimes. Oh, not as Clarence did, not afraid for my life. It's less clear than that. Unease.'

'Why?'

She hesitated. 'I don't know. He can be cold. It's so hard to know what he's thinking.'

'He's not cold, Kate,' Raphael said with feeling. 'I've seen him like stone to the Woodvilles, but not to his friends.'

'Like stone to those he considers outside the Church, also. I know full well he doesn't approve of me. I think he avoids me because of it.'

'Are you sure? He's always courteous to women, Kate.

Not like King Edward, who'd put his hand up your skirt before he even looked at your face.'

Kate laughed. 'I've met Edward. He was charming.'

'So they all say. What's Richard done to upset you, then?'

She shifted, not looking at him. He sensed that neither of them was being honest, and it unsettled him. 'What's he done to make you feel disloyal?' she countered.

'Nothing. Truly, nothing. It isn't him, it's some idiotic fancy of my own, born out of the foul humours of the court. I'm not breathing that poison any more. He's had so much pain in his life, you can't expect him to be light-hearted.'

'The same pain as Edward. From what you've said, it hasn't stopped him making the most of life.'

'Richard takes his duties more seriously,' said Raphael. 'If you ask me, he's disillusioned with the King. Not that he'd admit it. But I don't believe he's felt the same about Edward since he made that disgraceful treaty with the French. He went to make war on them, but ended up accepting a shameful bribe from them to take his army away. I've never seen Richard so angry. And he hates the behaviour at court: Edward seducing every woman he can lay hands on, then passing them on to his friends. Hastings and Dorset have almost come to blows over some of them. It's quite funny to watch, really. Or it would be in an alehouse, but not in the royal court.'

'Richard doesn't find it amusing, obviously,' said Kate.

'He loathes it. He thinks that the Woodvilles delight in encouraging Edward's depravity, and Lord Hastings, who should know better, is colluding with them.'

'You seem to know Richard much better than I do,' she said thoughtfully.

'Well, I would hope so,' Raphael said, surprised. 'I hardly know Lady Anne, and wouldn't expect to, either.'

'Don't you find it odd that he's so straight-laced?'

He shrugged. 'No. I find it reassuring. You know where you are with him.'

Her eyes widened briefly, a sceptical look that he couldn't interpret. Then she kissed him. 'I don't know why we're talking about our master. He's not going to stop us being merry.' Kate grinned. 'Richard may object to my beliefs, but as long as I keep them to myself, he has nothing to complain about. I do my duty and spend as much time kneeling on a cold chapel floor as everyone else. I'll never leave the Motherlodge. It seems a strange objection, since it's not the sisters of Auset that make war or chop people's heads off. Whatever do they fear from us?'

'That you are secretive, and not subject to the Church,' said Raphael. 'If you rode into battle and cut heads off, they would understand you.'

'Ah.'

'We had better go back,' he said, looking at the rain. 'Kate, I wish we needn't be separated at night, and have to meet in secret like this.'

She made no response, only stood up and said, 'Let's go back.'

Anne lay with her head on Katherine's lap, pale and drained by her monthly pains. She stared, dry-eyed, across the room, where Mary Bagott sat plucking tunelessly at a small harp. Nan sat at Mary's feet, sewing. Kate stroked the long, fine russet hair and at last Anne admitted what was wrong.

'We had been married for five years before Edward arrived. I miscarried once before him, and twice after, and since then, nothing. He should have had brothers and sisters; it's not fair on him. One little boy, to carry all our hopes, and children are so frail. We are all so frail.'

Katherine went on stroking her hair, keeping her own thoughts dark and close. She had noticed that whenever Richard came home, from York or London or campaigns in Scotland, Anne looked drawn and anxious. Kate had jumped to the wrong conclusion at first. Now it was plain why Anne looked worried, not because she was unhappy with her husband, but with the renewed strain of wondering if, this time, there would be a child.

The knowledge still sent a little strand of sourness through Kate. Though she couldn't admit it to herself, believing the marriage to be unhappy had appeased her jealousy. She had never seen any sign of passion between them – only courteous friendliness – but that might be simple decorum. They shared a bed.

Kate accepted the way of things, and loved Raphael. However, the strand of pain, a mere habit now, sometimes pulled at her without warning.

She and Anne had grown closer. They had little in common, but the connection between them was Isabel, like a strand of red silk, of fox-red hair, alight and burning, a shrivelling wisp. This fragile fire bonded them together. Anne was not like her sister; she was self-contained, rarely inviting touches or hugs. For the Duchess to lie in Katherine's lap like this was unprecedented.

'Kate,' she whispered, so faintly the others would not hear, 'is there something you could give me?'

'Only good food, my lady, and instructions not to ruin your life worrying about it.'

'I can't help it. I feel like a dried-up stream.'

'Is it you who is so concerned, or your husband?'

'It's all me.'

'Are you sure? Or does he blame you?'

'No, Kate, he doesn't blame me. He says that it doesn't matter at all, and we are blessed to have Edward, and if others came it would be a gift, but if they don't, it's the will of our Creator.'

'Perhaps you should listen to your husband,' Kate said evenly.

'I should, but it would so please him . . . I don't want Edward to grow up alone. He needs a brother, a sister. I'd do anything. Kate . . .'

The word was loaded with despair. Kate leaned down, kissed the high forehead where a vein showed blue through the fragile skin. 'What would you have me do? I can take you to the shrine of the Dark Mother and have you kneel before her, our black Madonna, and open your soul to her. She may grant your wish, but beware; her gifts come with lashing serpent twists in the tail.'

Anne drew herself out of Kate's lap and sat up, looking shaken. 'Why do you say this?'

'How far would you go? What is your price?'

'Katherine, you look like an angel and talk like a demon.' Anne's hand crept onto hers. 'Shrine . . . what shrine?'

'I could take you there. You could offer your devotion in return for your wish; but if you say to her, "Send me a child", she may send one that kills you as it is born, or grows up to destroy his own family, or someone else's child. Something may happen, but not the thing you intended.'

Anne's eyes were wide-open, dark as blood. 'Such power isn't holy. I've begged you to turn away from it.'

'And you know I can't. Yet you are still sitting there, wondering if it might work for you.'

'Sell my soul, for another babe?'

'Your soul is your own, and there are no guarantees. And there's the reason I can't help you, you've put your finger upon it. You believe it to be Devil-worship. If you took that path, you'd never have peace again. You'd be constantly at confession or doing penance. You'd even be worried that the babe itself, if there was one, came from the Devil.'

Anne put her hands to her face. When she took them down again, she looked ghostly but calm. 'Yes, you're right. I don't accuse you of worshipping devils, Kate, but I do fear for your soul, and I can't do it. No. There are prices too high to pay. I'll pray to St Akelda, and leave myself in God's hands.'

'Or appeal to Auset and leave yourself in mother nature's hands,' Kate said gently. 'There's little difference, except that one of the terms comes defensibly arrayed with raging priests, original sin and hellfire.'

Anne's amber mouth formed a half smile. 'I know what you're doing, Lady Katherine: playing Devil's advocate. I've been tempted, and I've passed the test. You've shone a clear light for me. Bless you for it.'

'You're welcome,' Kate said, taken aback. 'But what have you decided?'

'That I should rest in God's hands, and stop fretting.' She rose, cool as rose-water.

'Are you going to the chapel?' Kate asked. She would have gone with her, although she didn't relish the idea of kneeling on cold stones for an hour.

'No,' said the Duchess. 'I'm going to the nursery, to play with my dear only son.'

The years passed, and no children came for Anne; none for Kate, either, since she used the skills developed by the Motherlodge to prevent conception and the ensuing scandal. It saddened her that while she fed strengthening concoctions to Anne to help her conceive, she was taking others for the opposite purpose. Her own remedies worked, Anne's did not.

Young Edward of Middleham was growing into a handsome, serious boy. Although Anne and Richard doted upon him, he remained wonderfully unspoiled. Kate wondered long and hard about what kind of childhood it was that caused ruination. They had called George of Clarence 'spoiled', and she wondered who had spoiled him; because Richard was his opposite. Spare, dark, honourable, and ridiculously self-controlled.

Whatever frail ice-bridge had once existed between Richard and Kate had long ago melted to nothing. His eyes upon her were frost. He showed her the reserved courtesy that any duke should show his wife's lady-in-waiting. In return she gave him the correct deference. All was as it should be.

She'd told Raphael she was afraid of him, but Kate did not fear Richard exactly. It was something he carried with him, like a great winged shadow, that both repelled and drew her. Every time she saw him, she still experienced a little jolt, as if she'd never seen him before. The darkness of his hair and eyes, the graceful energy of him, his very presence, which seemed to make the world grow still and gather around him. She was not the only one who'd noticed this quality. People reacted strongly to him, not only to his wealth and rank, but to something intangible.

Sometimes, when she knew full well he was away, she would see him in the distance on the battlements, or sense him behind her, only to turn and find no one there.

Raphael had asked her a dozen times to marry him. She kept putting him off with light remarks, laughter and kisses. *Yes, but not yet. I like being as we are. You're always away in your lord's service. Anne needs me. We will, but not yet, not yet.*

He was patient, but his face grew a little graver each time. 'You know that Richard would give us a grant of land, don't you?' he said once. 'Our own manor.'

'What time have I to run a manor?' she answered. 'The Duchess relies on me too much, and the Duke on you. Later, when the time is right.'

The truth was that Kate enjoyed being a lover, rather than a wife. She liked both the subterfuge and the freedom. She feared that if she married Raphael he might change, grow bored and possessive, as husbands sometimes did, and turn elsewhere for pleasure.

Yet each time she came close to having to make the decision, something intervened to give her a reprieve. This time it was the news that Kate had dreaded: Dame Eylott, high priestess of the Motherlodge, was dead. Kate wept, remembering the sweet heart-shaped face and all the care the Dame had given her at the hardest time of her life. It also meant that Eleanor's time had come at last. She was to be invested as *Mater Superior* of the Motherlodge of Auset.

Kate went to York to attend her. Eleanor looked beautiful, her coppery hair long and loose on her shoulders. She wore a robe of dark-blue silk, thickly embroidered with fruit and flowers, and over it a black mantle edged with gold. The cellar temple glowed in the flickering light of cressets. Wreathes of incense layered the air, peppery and fragrant. So many women packed into the small space – men as well – that it was hard to breathe.

Kate and Martha acted as her mother's handmaidens, washing her hands and feet; Bridget Marl conducted the ceremony, calling down the elements and the presence of the Goddess and anointing Eleanor with oil. On her hair they placed a coronet in the shape of a serpent, its raised head crowned with a sphere of opal for the moon.

When the traditional salutation was murmured, '*All hail, Queen of the Underworld,*' the hairs prickled on the back of Kate's neck. She wept. Her mother was transformed, a goddess.

As they came out of the cellar temple and crossed the courtyard – the same courtyard in which Kate had first met Raphael – Eleanor took her hand.

'Do you feel different?' Kate asked.

'I feel as if I'm going to sneeze,' said Eleanor, and did. 'They overdid the incense somewhat.'

'Well?'

'I feel a huge sense of responsibility. To preserve the lodge and protect our followers . . . the task can only grow harder.'

'But nothing is impossible to the Queen of the hidden world.'

'As Queen I'm there to serve, not to rule, like the King in the outer world. Anyone who thinks they can rule the hidden world is an enormous fool. Yes, I feel changed, Kate, but I'm still myself.'

They stepped into the street, with dozens of followers arrayed in midnight blue, bearing flowers and black banners powdered with moons and stars. Kate smiled at the dark-haired boy who carried Eleanor's train. Even Friar Bungay and Father Dunstan wore blue robes to show their support. It was a tradition, that on the inauguration of a new *Mater* they paraded to a tavern, the Yellow Pard, there to partake of a celebratory feast. It was one of the few times the Motherlodge showed a public face. Citizens gathered to watch them pass. Some cheered and threw flowers in their path.

Kate laughed, and her mother said, 'What is it?'

'We are so disapproved of, but look how many people are grateful for us. What I am can't be acknowledged at the castle. If they only knew how many women come to me in secret for advice or help. Men, too. It amuses me.'

'Such is the paradox of our existence,' said Eleanor, squeezing her hand.

As they rounded a bend in the street, with the creamy-grey walls of the houses rising on either side, they found the way blocked by a wall of men. Friars, priests, a handful of angry laymen who looked like no merchants of York Kate had ever seen. In their centre was a tall bishop, resplendent in yellow vestments and a dark purple cloak with stiff, square shoulders. He planted his crook on the pavement and raised a hand to halt the procession.

Eleanor marched on until she was nose to nose with him. Then the parade came to a ragged stop, those behind them treading on each other's heels.

Kate recognized him. It was the Archbishop of York, Thomas Rotherham. His heavy red face was angry, even a little nervous.

'Madam, your procession is an abomination and an insult to the Almighty.' His voice shook slightly, but was gravelly with authority. Kate wondered if he had been pressured into this confrontation by others. 'Take down your banners and disperse.'

Eleanor glared at him, speechless. Rallying, she said, 'We will not, Your Grace. Our procession is a lawful tradition. Please stand aside.'

'You shall disperse, for we shall not move until you do so.'

'We could all be standing here for quite some time, then,' she answered politely.

'Please understand our message,' said the Archbishop. 'Your temple is an affront to the Holy Church. It may be accepted by temporal laws, but not by God's. Be warned. We shall not tolerate it. Your days are numbered.'

'At whose behest do you threaten us?' Eleanor spoke mildly, but Kate – who knew her – saw the glitter of danger in her eyes.

'We are harming no one,' said Bridget Marl beside her. 'We help many. Only ask these good folk around us.'

'Seducing good folk away from God is the worst harm you could do. Take down your banners.'

'Put plainly, Your Grace: no.'

They stood off for a moment or two. The Archbishop looked furious and embarrassed. Suddenly one of his followers, a monk, rushed at a girl who stood just behind and to one side of Eleanor. He seized the pole of her banner and tried to wrest it from her. She struggled, crying out, but the banner came down, falling across those who were standing nearest. Fabric fell across Kate's head and she angrily pushed it off, swung round and grabbed the monk's arm.

'How dare you—'

Turning, he shoved her over. She hit the cobblestones, more indignant than hurt. All around her were cries, chaos. She heard Bungay's voice, yelling, 'What? You'd attack innocent women, Your Grace?'

'There are men among you,' a priest yelled at him, 'who should know better! Like you, devil's arse-licker!'

Eleanor leaned down to help Kate up. They were caught in a nascent riot; the priestly mob surging forward, the followers of Auset stung to retaliation and striking at them with the banners they were trying to pull down. The street boiled. Rotherham was jostled against Eleanor and his mitre was knocked off.

'Oh – I didn't mean this to happen,' he said.

Dame Marl raised her arms and yelled, 'Stop!' but she might as well have yelled at the tide. She was trying to shepherd Eleanor, Kate and Martha to the side of the street when they heard, above the noise, horses' hooves clattering towards them from the direction of Micklegate Bar.

The crowd spilt raggedly in two. The fighting died. Into their midst rode the Duke of Gloucester on a big bay courser. There was another nobleman with him, mounted on a grey. It was the Earl of Northumberland, Henry Percy, a thin pale-haired man with a beak of a nose, who always put Kate in mind of a heron. With them came their liveried retinues, a good forty mounted men wearing Gloucester's white boar or the white crescent of the Earl.

Richard, stony-faced, rode his horse at a brisk walk straight towards the Archbishop. He drew to a halt with one gloved hand on the reins.

'Your Grace,' Richard greeted him. 'What's happening?'

'Yes, what the Devil is this?' said the Earl. 'A riot?'

Stammering and redder than ever, Rotherham began to explain. 'We felt duty-bound in good Christian conscience to make a stand against the continued presence of these heathen temples in our towns. These witches mean to parade blatantly among us. It cannot be tolerated.'

Kate bit her lip and stared at the ground. She knew that Richard would agree with the Archbishop. His position alone would not allow him to do anything else. Beside her Eleanor waited, silent.

'Let them pass,' said Richard.

'What?' Rotherham said, rude with disbelief.

'Remove yourselves from the street and let the sisters pass unmolested. Some may not like it, but they have the right.'

'But my lord . . .'

'Do it, or you will answer to me. I take disturbances of the peace very seriously; and you, Archbishop, should know better than to encourage such a disgraceful exhibition. I do not believe that your protestors are even citizens of York, are they?'

Rotherham fell back, chastened. Gloucester signalled, and his men moved forward to chivvy the demonstrators out of the way and make a clear passage for the sisterhood. A loud cheer rose from the onlookers, for the Duke or for Eleanor, Kate wasn't sure. Both, perhaps.

The Earl of Northumberland was having difficulty controlling his horse. 'You astound me, my lord,' he said, out of breath. 'It's not what I would have done, but your command of these people is impressive. I can't bear mobs.'

Kate looked up, and found Richard looking straight at her. His face was serious, his eyebrows raised. She looked back boldly, not caring what he thought. Then he gave her a faint smile, a rueful look, more tolerant than she'd expected. Normally the look would have made her bristle but now, for some reason, she felt grateful.

'Go in peace, good mother,' he said to Eleanor. 'The Earl and I will ride before you, to ensure you encounter no further difficulty.'

'Thank you, Your Grace,' Eleanor said with dignity.

The sisterhood of Auset passed on their way to the Yellow Pard, preceded by the two greatest lords of the north: Gloucester and Northumberland.

Anne was ill. For three weeks Katherine had worked day and night, making concoctions of herbs, flowers and roots to ease her fever and cough. She'd driven out the physician, who she suspected might actually have killed Anne with his potions of mercury and powdered amber. She attended Anne constantly, delegating tasks to her other ladies, sending the cooks scurrying to prepare dishes to tempt her, coaxing her every mouthful. At night she slept on a bed beside Anne's, waking every half hour to monitor her condition.

Then, as the fever subsided and the danger passed, she

sat reading to her from Mallory, Christine de Pisan and the new printed books that came up from London.

Richard had been away, touring his other castles in the north. He didn't know Anne had fallen ill. Kate was determined that she should be better by the time he came home. Life had fallen into a gentle rhythm over the years, and now Kate could not imagine living anywhere but at Middleham. It had been a struggle of will power, but at last she could enjoy the presence of Anne and Richard's son without being constantly, painfully reminded of another child she rarely saw. Eleanor wrote often, and she had pleasing if strange news. Attacks upon sacred Hollows, at least in Richard's domain, had ceased.

Kate had travelled twice to court with Anne, accompanied by Nan and Ursula, and had found it at once fascinating and loathsome, as Raphael had described, an indigestible mixture of smothering etiquette and debauchery. Nan had been overwhelmed; Ursula had loved it. The last time, in the January just past, King Edward had bestowed even greater powers upon Richard, effectively making him king of the north, and of any part of Scotland he could conquer. Relations between the two brothers had appeared warm.

Kate, though, had hardly recognized the King as the handsome young man who had once tried to seduce her. He was almost a caricature of his loud, generous self and grossly bloated. A pretty blonde woman – his famous mistress, Elizabeth Shore, who was known as Eliza – had sat on his fleshy knee in full view of the Queen. And the more ferociously arctic Queen Elizabeth had become, the softer, sweeter and more full of laughter Eliza had appeared in contrast.

'Kate,' said Anne, interrupting her thoughts. 'Kate?'

Starting, she saw the Duchess trying to get out of bed. 'Madam, what are you doing?'

'Help me to my chair, I'll sit up for a little while. Richard is coming home today. I don't want him to discover his wife a bedridden invalid.'

Still the habitual little pang at the mention of his name. Kate supported Anne's thin frame to her favourite chair. She seemed so delicate and still so young, a child-saint.

As Kate set her down, Anne said, 'Richard has emulated all the best of my father and created a kingdom of his own. I've never seen him happier. I think from now on our lives will become as they should be, and we can leave all sorrow and conflict behind us. A peaceful kingdom for our son to inherit.'

'I hope so,' Kate said with feeling. As she made to move, meaning to fetch a coverlet to put over the Duchess's knees, Anne caught her hand. There was a glint in her eye.

'Katherine, dear, isn't it time that you and a certain Sir Raphael were married?'

Kate nearly choked. 'My lady?'

'It's an open secret that you dote upon each other. Six years is a long courtship. He's had no reason to hesitate so long to ask leave; Richard will grant it gladly. I'm not suggesting that anything improper has occurred between you, but you'd do well to avoid even the risk of causing a scandal.' She spoke teasingly.

'Yes,' Kate muttered.

'Why do you look so astonished?' Anne gave a gentle smile. 'Do you want me to speak to Raphael myself, or the priest to do it?'

'No! No, madam, it's all right. He's asked me a dozen times; it won't be a shock to him. In fact he might swoon when I say yes.' Kate took a deep breath. Anne was right. She loved Raphael; she'd only delayed out of fear of change, the faint ghost of the past. 'Yes, dear Anne, you're right. Thank you.'

'A spring wedding will be beautiful. Write to your mother. All the village will come, and crown you with flowers.'

It was panic that stopped Kate sleeping that night, panic

that drove her upstairs onto the roof of the round tower. The April night was thick with cloud and wind, winter still clawing at the hem of spring.

She'd agreed to marriage. It had seemed a good idea when she'd said it, but now she was terrified. She clutched her cloak around her throat. She'd spoken to no one of it yet, not to Nan or Ursula who were her confidants, not even to Raphael himself. She loved him, but to give up freedom, give up all other possibility . . .

Richard was on the battlements. When she saw his unmistakable silhouette some distance away on the western wall, her heart sank. He was talking to a guard, both men leaning on the parapet. Then the guard went on his way and he was alone.

The temptation to walk softly to his side and surprise him was overwhelming, but the counter-pull proved stronger. There was no point. There was nothing between them and never could be. She couldn't stand his polite self-restraint, nor the emptiness of disappointment that would follow . . . even though she had no clear idea of what she wanted of him. A *frisson* of clandestine excitement that Raphael could not give her? Kate cursed herself, dismissing the urge as pitiful. When she looked again, Richard had gone.

A few minutes later, growing cold, she began to descend the spiral stairs, feeling her way in the dark. Just as she reached the landing that led back to the chambers, she collided with someone coming up from below. Both recoiled, apologizing. Richard's hand was on her elbow, steadying her.

'We should carry lanterns, not creep about in the dark,' he said. She heard a smile in his voice.

'Then how could we creep about successfully?' said Kate. 'My apologies, Your Grace.'

'And mine. I didn't mean to alarm you, my lady.'

'No harm done.'

'Sleepless, like me?'

'Yes.' Kate sighed. 'I was going back to bed, but only to listen to Dame Bagott snoring.'

'Ah.' A soft laugh under his breath. Then he said suddenly, 'Come with me.'

'Oh?' Kate took a step towards him, puzzled.

'Yes, come on. I've something to show you.'

She followed him down. It was strange, but now he was there, all her over-magnified spectral images of him vanished. He wasn't cold, wasn't threatening, was just a man she found easy company and charming . . . and still painfully attractive, in the most dangerous way.

He led her down into the bailey and towards the stables, with the walls of the western range on their left and the tall keep on their right. She pulled her cloak hood over her head. The guards might see them. A man and a woman alone in the night could never be viewed as innocent. The mere fact that they were together made them as guilty as sin.

As they walked, he said, 'From all reports, it seems I must thank you for saving Anne's life.'

'That's putting it a bit strong,' she said. 'I stopped the physician killing her, possibly. The rest was common sense, to ease her fever and make sure she ate the right things.'

'All the same, without you . . .' She could barely see him in the darkness. His voice came, velvety, out of nowhere.

'And yet you're not at her side?' Kate glanced up at the slaty sweep of the sky. Night lights glimmered in some windows, others were dark. She imagined the hundreds of people in the castle breathing steadily in sleep.

'She needs her rest. Despite riding all day I'm still wide awake, which is nothing new. I went to look at my son, who was soundly dreaming and didn't know I was there. All that's left is to haunt the battlements.'

'Which you do so well,' said Kate.

'And you?'

'Oh, just . . . a decision that's unutterably hard to make, even harder to unmake.'

'Can I help?'

She laughed. 'Thank you, my lord, but I doubt it. Still, it's kind of you to take an interest.'

'It's what noblemen are bound to do,' he said drily. 'Our duty.'

'Was it part of your duty to protect my mother in York that day?' A faint luminance drew a pearly outline along his straight nose and high cheekbone. 'I should have thanked you for that, but never had the chance, somehow.'

'No need to thank me. I was upholding the law. And I don't especially like Rotherham, I must admit.'

'Oh? Are you supposed to say that?'

He laughed quietly. 'Only in private.'

'Thank you, anyway.'

He was keeping a careful distance from her and yet, to her own dismay, she felt a familiar magnetic pull towards him. She wanted to touch him, as she would have touched a mantle of sable fur, or a handsome black gyrfalcon. All her careful avoidance of him had made no difference. She had to remind herself that the feeling was an illusion. They had nothing in common; she didn't know him.

At the stable, he opened an arched side door and let her through. A stable boy, sleeping on a pile of straw just inside, didn't stir. Richard took the lantern that burned beside him and lit their way along the cobbled row of stalls. Bay and grey heads turned to watch them pass. The scent of horses was thick, ripe and comforting.

'Do you have a horse, Kate?' he asked.

'No,' she said. 'I make free with yours. Do you mind?'

'Of course not,' he said, smiling.

'I used to have a little grey mare, Mab. She died last year. She was eighteen years old.'

Her throat went tight, unexpectedly.

'I remember your little grey mare.' He sounded wistful. The pang spread from her throat and rippled downwards.

'Yes, I should hope you do.'

'She was a beauty. You must miss her.'

Reaching a stall, he slid back the bolt and let her through, following and closing the half-door behind them. Inside was the most beautiful horse Kate had ever seen: a flashy dapple-grey mare with jet-black mane and tail, an arched neck and a long head with huge, liquid black eyes. Her mane flowed right down over her shoulder like a woman's unbraided hair.

Kate put her hands to her mouth. 'Oh, Mother of God, she is *exquisite*.'

'She was sent to me from Spain a few weeks ago,' Richard said, scratching the mare's neck. 'She's as sweet-tempered as a dove. She's yours.'

'What? Why?'

'For your devotion to Anne. Tomorrow my steward is going to present her to you officially. Try to seem surprised.'

Kate could only stare, tears overflowing. 'More surprised than this?' The mare extended an enquiring nose, nuzzling at Kate's palm. 'Impossible. I'll cry at her beauty. That won't be hard.'

Richard said softly, 'I'm glad you like her. Oh, Kate, I didn't expect tears.'

'Anne should have her, not me.'

'Anne has many fine horses already. This one is yours.'

'I don't know what to say.' Now she was fighting tears in earnest, and it was not only the mare, but the thought of Raphael, and Richard's unbearable closeness.

'Don't cry.' He reached out and brushed the moisture from her cheekbone. 'What is it?'

She looked up fiercely. 'Did you know that I'm to be married?'

'Yes. I heard. Raphael is the most fortunate and blessed of men.'

'Great Goddess, news travels fast. I haven't even spoken to him about it yet.'

'Anne told me.'

'I see,' said Kate, and stood mute.

After a time, she heard him breathe in and out. 'Kate, you do wish it, don't you?'

'What's the meaning of this gift?' she demanded, almost before he'd finished the question. 'It's the sort of thing a – a nobleman would give to his mistress. Don't think I'm ungrateful. I just don't understand.'

He stood back, resting against the mare's placid shoulder. He combed his fingers through his hair, leaving it dishevelled. 'It seemed fitting, for your care of my wife.'

'Then you could have left the giving to your steward.'

'Yes. I don't know what I intended. This was ill-considered.'

Panic was rising in her chest. She felt close to spilling out something idiotic that would ensure he never came near her, never looked on her with a drop of respect again. 'No. It was sweet and gracious. But why consider it at all?'

'Foolishly I never thought I'd hear that you were to be married. I imagined you always a maiden, as the first time we met.'

'I had no idea you imagined anything, or even cared.'

'Bewitchments can be resisted, but they don't fade away.'

'I never bewitched you,' she said angrily. 'What do you want?'

He was so close to her that she felt his body warmth prickling on her skin. Angry as she was, it only drew her closer. They touched. His hands slid lightly over her hair. 'I could wish we had more memories, before we were both bound to other duties.'

'This isn't fair,' she said, trembling. 'You ran from me. It was your choice.'

'Kate . . .' He held her away from him, his hands tense on her arms. 'If I was Edward, this wouldn't afflict my conscience for a second. But I'm not him. I can't betray my wife. I can't take a woman betrothed to another man, one of my own knights. Not in a thousand years could I do that.'

'She's a goodbye gift, then,' said Kate, crying. 'A wedding present.'

'I suppose so.' He lowered his head to touch hers. For as long as his hands stayed on her, she clung to him to keep him there. She knew that as soon as he let go, they would never touch each other again. 'Don't cry, Kate, sweet Morgana.'

Kate said thinly, 'It's as Elizabeth Woodville said to King Edward, as the story runs: "I am not good enough to be your wife, but I am too good to be your mistress."'

'Raphael will make you happy. If not, he'll answer to me.'

What else he might have said to her, she never knew. There were sounds outside, the creaking of gates, rumble of galloping hooves, men shouting. The beautiful Spanish mare put up her head and whickered. Richard looked over his shoulder in concern, gave Kate the briefest kiss on the cheek, and was gone.

Taking the lantern, she followed him towards the gate-house.

A horseman was riding hard through the rain, cloak flapping, his horse soaped with sweat. He had raced through Middleham village and come clattering across the bridge into the castle courtyard. There, he flung himself out of the saddle and onto the first guard he saw, not even realizing that Richard himself was in earshot.

'From William, Lord Hastings,' he panted. His face was candle-white and drenched with rain. 'Take me to the Duke at once. King Edward is dead.'

Chapter Twelve 1483: Anthony

QUEEN ELIZABETH
  Ah, he is young; and his minority
  Is put unto the trust of Richard Gloucester
  A man that loves not me, nor none of you.

Richard III Act I scene 3

Night. A road unrolling into the darkness, on and on. A tunnel of trees, the hard glint of lantern light on stones. Red flashes spitting from the horses' hooves, and within the forest the steady green eyes of its unhuman denizens.

The party rode hard, silent with exhaustion. Raphael was beyond tiredness. He rode up at the front with the handful of northern lords who accompanied the Duke of Gloucester: Lovell, Ratcliffe, Rob Percy and Lord Scrope. Behind them came a great comet-tail of horsemen: three hundred gentlemen of the north and their servants, all in mourning black. They had been riding so long that Raphael's whole existence was narrowed down to the long, swallowing throat of road and trees, the rumbling roar of a thousand hooves. The men around him seemed spectral. He felt alone.

Richard, leading them, was grave and businesslike. The news of King Edward's death had stunned everyone. It was so unexpected. No one knew how Richard had reacted when the messenger from London first came, Raphael hadn't seen him weep, but he'd caught glimpses of a livid fire in his face that looked to be consuming him from the inside. Within the hour Richard had gathered his friends to him and told them to make ready to ride south.

'The news of the King's death reached me days later than it should have done,' he'd told them. 'No one at court thought to inform me, no one but Edward's good friend, William Hastings. He sent an urgent message the moment he realized the Queen had neglected to do so. She and her family have deliberately withheld the news from me, in plain defiance of Edward's last wishes.'

Hastings' letter had been full of outrage and warnings. Dying, Edward had named Richard as Protector of the Realm and guardian of the new King until the boy reached the age of majority. Although Anthony Woodville, Earl Rivers, had been the young Edward's guardian all these years, it was traditional for the late King's brother to act as regent in such a case. And Edward, Raphael thought, must have felt the only person in the world he could truly trust was his own brother.

According to the indignant Hastings, the Woodvilles intended to exclude Gloucester from his rightful position. The naming of him as Protector had made them panic and they were scrabbling to hold on to their power. If they lost the young King to the Duke of Gloucester, they lost everything. So they had plotted to delay him, intending to keep him in the dark while they rushed the boy from Ludlow to London and got the crown on his head as quickly as possible. Thereafter, their position would be unassailable. Richard must come to London at once, Hastings insisted, to avenge the insult done him by these jealous upstarts. The only sure way would be to intercept the young King and take him under his own protection and authority before they reached the capital.

Raphael remembered the rivalries of the court with unease. The Woodvilles were seen as glittering nobodies who had stuffed themselves into positions of power and privilege. The old nobility, on whose behalf Lord Hastings spoke, loathed them. But they had all been loyal to King Edward. He alone had bound them together. Now he was gone, like a jewel hacked from the centre of a tapestry, the fabric was fraying. The Woodvilles had been safe while Edward was alive and bestowing his favours upon them. They would remain safe only if they kept control of the new King, their kinsman and puppet. It seemed they would do anything, fair or foul, to prevent Richard of Gloucester becoming Protector.

They had even proposed to bring the boy from Ludlow with a great army to prevent Gloucester seizing him. Only Lord Hastings' counter-threats had stopped the scheme. Now the young King was being conveyed south by his uncle Earl Rivers and his half-brother Richard Grey and a more suitable escort of two thousand men.

There had been more letters waiting for Richard at York, where his supporters had gathered, and at Nottingham. A messenger came from the Duke of Buckingham, offering his support. He would meet Richard at Northampton.

And Richard had sent letters of his own: gentle letters to console the Queen and promise his fealty to her son, and others to the Council, cordially reminding them to honour his late brother's wishes. He had written also to the new King himself, asking that they join him en route and so make his entry into London the more magnificent.

Further south, they had met Earl Rivers' messengers on the road. The Earl courteously acquiesced to Richard's suggestion. He would wait for him at Northampton.

That made Raphael wonder if Rivers feared Richard after all and if Lord Hastings was in a lather over nothing, or if his cordiality was all part of the game, whose sinister layers no one fully understood.

Raphael almost wished he could have stayed at Middleham. He hadn't wanted to leave Kate. A few hours before Hastings' messenger had arrived, the priest had approached him smiling, said that the Duchess had spoken to him, and he would wish to see Raphael and Kate on the morrow to discuss their betrothal. Raphael had been elated to realize that Kate had changed her mind at last. However, he hadn't been able to find her, and then Richard had whisked him away. Service to a lord always came before love. It was unquestioned.

The road curved into a flatter landscape. Raphael found himself looking at a wide, barren plain, lit with a dusting of yellowish light. On the plain walked a solitary, lean figure with the soft-moving grace of a prince, dark hair blowing back over his shoulders. The head was slightly bent, as if with the weight of thoughts or memories. It was Richard. The sight of him utterly alone, delineated by that faint, ancient light, filled Raphael with terror and an ineffable sense of mystery.

'He will destroy the House of York, you know.' The voice in his ear made him start. Raphael glanced round and saw a cadaverous face, a robe of priestly purple flowing away into the darkness. He'd seen the face before – Dr Fautherer.

'He *is* the House of York,' Raphael answered.

On the plain, Richard turned and lifted his head and looked straight at Raphael. The eyes glimmered, sorrowful, demanding, untouchably distant. Raphael cried out.

He jerked in the saddle and woke himself up. There was no plain, and Richard was only a vague shape on horseback ahead of him. Certainly there was no strange clergyman at his shoulder, only Francis Lovell. He shivered to realize that a vision had seized him out of nowhere. There'd been no violence, this time, but the mystery of it wormed deep inside him and stayed there, eerily.

'Northampton,' said Lovell.

A town appeared out of the darkness, aglow with hundreds of small lights. A thin sharp drizzle began. Raphael could hear the men behind him grumbling, though it was more with relief than complaint. They could rest soon.

There were three great inns in the main street, grey and ghostly through the rain-drenched night. Lamps swung in the wind, catching blonde glints on the thatch. There were men and horses all over the pooled reflective surface of the road: a welcoming party. Ostlers were running about to take charge of the horses, townspeople gathering to watch the spectacle.

Raphael recognized the figure at the centre. Earl Rivers, a handsome, imposing man in silk and velvet finery, quilted and worked with silver thread, a cap and a cloak of fur, all in the black of mourning. He stood in a silver halo from the lanterns held by his servants. Raphael had the impression that even the rain would not dare land on him. The whole tableau glittered; even the activity seemed muffled, as if an intense hush lay over everything like a held breath.

'So, our friend is already here,' said Richard.

'To check how many men we have,' Ratcliffe said shortly.

'And to soothe our suspicions of him,' Lovell added.

'Then let's soothe his, in return.'

Richard dismounted and went forward. He was dressed in plain black cloth, which, like soot, gave back no light at all. The only jewels about him were jet. Rivers resembled a padded couch next to Richard, who looked slender and dangerous, a sword blade.

The Earl and the Duke greeted each other with clasped hands, and then an embrace, as friendly as could be. Raphael stood watching in amazement. Their diplomatic play acting was so convincing he wondered if it was not entirely feigned, after all.

'Your Grace, my Lord Protector, most beloved brother-in-law,' said Rivers. 'May I offer my deepest condolences on this grievous loss of your dear brother the King. Creator rest his soul.'

'Amen. And my equally heartfelt condolences to you.' Richard sounded hoarse. 'It is a most grievous loss to us all. One the kingdom can barely support.'

'And which has made necessary our tedious journeys. You must be tired, sir, and heartsore. These inns are ready and eager to accommodate us; everything is arranged.'

'You're very kind,' Richard answered quietly. 'Will you take supper with us?'

'Gladly. Come, we'll dine together and console each other. We've much to talk about.' Warm, hearty, elegantly mannered, the Earl was not to be resisted. Raphael suspected that Richard hadn't expected him to be so friendly, but his only response was to look round at his supporters, one eyebrow lifted in an otherwise expressionless face.

'Indeed we have.' Richard looked calmly around. 'And we have a new king to comfort us . . . but where is he? Abed?'

'Yes, yes, I should hope he is,' said the Earl.

'I should like to see him, and pay my respects.'

'Naturally, my Lord Protector, but in the morning, if it please you.'

'Why not now? He's twelve, not an infant.'

'Because, my lord, I think you would not want to ride another distance tonight.' Woodville put a too-familiar hand on Richard's arm. 'The King lodges tonight at Stony Stratford, in the care of his brother Lord Grey and other faithful servants.'

Richard's silence could have cut bone. Raphael looked sideways and saw the frozen expressions of the other men. Earl Rivers should have waited for Richard with the King, acceding to the Protector's authority. It was an appalling presumption and a discourtesy for him not to have done so.

Mildly, Richard said, 'Why isn't he here?'

'It was of necessity, since the inns here are all full and I was concerned to secure him lodgings properly fitted to his station. I took him there myself and came back to meet you.'

Richard showed no anger. He smiled. 'Then you have had a tiring day,' he said lightly. 'Allow me to ensure that all my men and horses are properly accommodated, then we'll dine.'

The landlady was a sister of Auset. Raphael saw that at once, though no one else appeared to notice or care.

Perhaps they didn't see the subtle signs: her demeanour of watchful, quiet confidence, the way her indigo gown swathed her well-rounded body, cut closer than the usual fashion. The steady clarity of her gaze was something he recognized from Kate, and from other sisters he'd met. Perhaps his own mother had possessed it; he couldn't remember. As she held up her lamp to welcome the travellers inside, her eyes caught Raphael's. She smiled.

The dining hall was a fine little room, long and narrow with heavy beams and a good fireplace. Its stone flags were immaculate and the walls were hung with ivory damask. A long table ran almost its whole length, leaving room for the servants to pass round it. A spider's web of lace lay over a pure white cloth, and there was silver plate and candles in holders of coloured glass that scattered rainbows of ruby, violet and green across the table. Richard and Anthony Woodville sat opposite each other with the other lords – all Richard's – ranged informally on both sides. The atmosphere was subdued but friendly enough.

Woodville fussed charmingly over the food, telling the landlady it was perfect, but would be even better if she would only encourage her cook to use *this* French technique, or a pinch of *that* spice. He spoke teasingly, with a flirtatious gleam in his eye, so that she could only smile in return, but Raphael suspected she would have liked to punch him square in the face.

Richard sat patiently through this pantomime with a slight smile on his lips and eyes of brilliant ice. Earl Rivers' presence filled the room, marvellous as a groomed lion. He was a true knight, accomplished in many arts, and liked the world to know it. Raphael could see why he was so popular at court. While he scattered light and energy wantonly, Richard was the still, dark core of something occult. He did nothing to draw attention to himself, but drew it irresistibly, nonetheless.

When game pies and poultry had been brought, and the

inn servants had withdrawn, Anthony Woodville described the death of King Edward.

'As you know, he had grown corpulent over the years, which must have weakened his health. He got a chill after a fishing trip and took to his bed. The malady seized upon his lungs. He was fully expected to recover; it was to our great shock and grief that he suffered a relapse and deteriorated so suddenly that his physicians were helpless.'

'I wish you had sent for me as soon as he fell ill,' Richard spoke sadly, with no hint of rancour.

'We didn't expect him to die. He seemed to be recovering. Perhaps we missed the signs, or perhaps he was putting on a show to ease our concerns, so great was his heart. His relapse took us all by surprise. There is a new school of thought among the Florentine physicians that long inactivity thickens the blood and congests the organs; I suspect it was such a complication that took Edward from us.'

'You're as well-versed in medicine as in everything else, my lord,' said Richard.

'He knew he was dying.' Rivers shook his silver-blond head. 'Whether it would have been easier if he hadn't known, I can't say; but at least, knowing, he was able to make his peace with God. And also to make peace between all of us who had quarrelled. Lamb's blood, he even made Hastings and Dorset shake hands and kiss! He did much good upon his death bed.'

'And upon his death bed, I gather, he named me Protector.' Richard sipped from a glass of claret, his diamond eyes on the Earl.

'Indeed, so he did, and I am most grateful of the chance to clarify the matter to everyone's satisfaction.' Woodville wiped his mouth with a napkin and folded his hands on the table. Raphael noticed how soft they were, the nails polished like pearl.

He was starting to speak again when the door opened.

Everyone looked up. On the threshold was a framed apparition: a slender young man with long hair like a stream of white fire in the lamplight. He wore blue, and over it a black cloak lined with blonde fur and black gloves with heavy gold rings on the fingers. If he had sprouted wings, or produced a fiery sword, Raphael would not have been surprised.

The Duke of Buckingham stood there for a few moments, as if aware of the effect he was having. Then he came striding into the room, fell to one knee beside Richard and kissed his hand. Mouths fell open. It was an unusual greeting between two dukes.

'My Lord Protector.'

'Harry, it's a pleasure to see you,' said Richard as the young man rose. One of the inn servants, a boy, came running to take the heavy cloak. 'You're not too late for supper; we're still in the middle of it. Francis, move up. Earl Rivers here was just instructing me on my role as Protector of the Realm.'

'Was he?' The sarcasm in Harry Stafford's voice reminded Raphael of why some people didn't like him. 'Don't let me interrupt, my gracious lord.'

Anthony Woodville was looking at the newcomer with plain dislike. He masked it quickly, found a clean glass and filled it with blood-red claret for the young Duke.

'As I was about to say, there's no one better fitted than His Grace of Gloucester to protect the young King, and such was Edward's wish,' Rivers said smoothly. 'The role of Protector has been much discussed in Parliament and its precedents are clear. It is not, and never has been, a role that continues until the King's majority.'

Richard put in softly, 'It's strange you mention that, because I don't recall any discussion of the length of the Protectorate. I understood from Lord Hastings that Edward intended me to govern on his son's behalf. I can't see Edward wishing me to abandon his heir before he is sixteen at the very earliest.'

'No one would wish you to abandon him, not in an informal, familial capacity. However, the Council is agreed that the Lord Protector's role is to safeguard the King until his coronation. No further.'

'I see.'

'You will appreciate the, ah, unfortunate precedents that make the Council unwilling to appoint a single man as regent. Government shall be carried on by many persons, of whom you, naturally, shall be accounted chief. The Council has elected you its leader, bestowing upon you authority and a voice in government as befits your high estate.'

'And this is all decided?'

'All agreed.'

The two men looked at each other; Rivers powerfully insistent, Richard expressionless. Buckingham watched, gnawing delicately at a chicken thigh. Compared to the younger Duke, Anthony Woodville looked heavy, ageing. His fair hair seemed merely grey. He was the one who appeared to hold all the power, Raphael thought. Buckingham was a willow sapling beside him. But there was energy in the angelic Duke, like an unused, coiled-up sting.

'I shall accede to the will of the Council,' Richard said at last. 'My only wish is to serve the good of the new King and his kingdom.'

'Then there is no misunderstanding between us,' said Woodville, grave. 'We both serve the King.'

Richard raised his glass. 'God keep the new King, Edward the Fifth.'

'God save the King!' came the loud response.

The talk went on for some time, mostly of pleasant, inconsequential matters. Fresh courses and new wines were brought, scavenged dishes taken away, until most of the company were replete and half asleep. Eventually, Anthony Woodville took his leave and went to his own inn, bidding them all a gracious good night. Most of Richard's men went shortly afterwards, even Francis, who was visibly fighting sleep.

Only Ratcliffe, Buckingham and Raphael remained with Richard in the dimly flickering jewelled light. Raphael was sober. None of the others looked sleepy or even slightly drunk.

He noticed Harry Stafford gazing at him sideways from languid green eyes. Richard noticed too. 'Harry, that's Sir Raphael Hart you're staring at. You can speak freely in front of him.'

'Of course. I have seen you a time or two, Sir Raphael. Pardon me, it took me a while to recollect.'

Raphael coloured. The Duke's attention made him uncomfortable. His words were mild but his tone acerbic. His disdainful manner and vanity couldn't be the only things that made him unpopular at court. Ratcliffe poured more claret. Richard breathed in and out, tapping his fingers together. There was a silence, laced with grim amusement. Then Buckingham spoke.

'Who does he think he's fooling?'

'A neat move, lodging my nephew out of my reach, not to mention fourteen miles closer to London,' said Richard. 'If my brother's health was ruined, it was with the encouragement of his companions in vice: Anthony Woodville, Richard Grey and Dorset not least of them.'

'He grows fleshy himself, though he'd die before he admitted it,' said Buckingham.

'They're the ones who ruined Edward, the Queen's wretched brothers and accursed sons,' Richard said quietly. His face was drawn. The rims of his eyes ran with light.

'And he's spent all night trying to put you in your place,' Ratcliffe said passionately. 'A short-term, limited role on the Council. A bloody insult!'

'That's only Rivers scrabbling to cover his tracks,' Richard said coolly. 'If Hastings hadn't alerted me, I'd not even have been granted that small concession.'

Buckingham gripped Richard's forearm, trembling as if he'd explode with the need to speak.

'Richard, you comprehend only a fraction of what's

311

occurred! Why do you think I'm here? *Someone* had to tell you, and if I'm the only one who cares, who owes you this out of our deep friendship . . .'

Gloucester frowned. 'Say on.'

'The Council divided into three factions. The largest is the Queen's, supported by Rotherham and most of the bishops.'

'Rotherham,' Richard murmured.

'The second party is led by Hastings with Thomas Stanley's support. The old nobility who oppose the Queen. Then there's a third party, including Bishop Russell and the Archbishop of Canterbury, who won't commit themselves either way. They argued for days. But they're frightened of the Queen, and therefore the Woodville faction tends to get much of its own way. Some argued that Edward meant you to have sovereign power, but, as you'd imagine, the Woodvilles were frantic to prevent that. They fear your revenge for Clarence.'

'Well, I haven't forgotten. Guilty consciences at play.'

'The outcome is that the Queen manipulated the Council into overthrowing your late brother's wishes. The Woodvilles want no protectorship. They want the King crowned immediately, and a regency council headed by the Queen, or Dorset or Rivers, set up to rule in your stead. They've been plotting to seize power and cut you out entirely. Her brother Edward Woodville has taken to sea in command of the royal fleet—'

'He's done what?'

'And her son Dorset's taken possession of the Tower and seized the royal treasure. He's divided it between himself, his mother and Edward Woodville.'

Richard ran his hands over his hair. He closed his eyes. 'Of course, I should have expected it. But I had not credited them with this depth of iniquity.'

'Their iniquities are endless. I've had spies in London, spies at Ludlow—'

'Gods, I must be some kind of holy innocent, not to place

spies everywhere.' Now his expression was hard, his eyes slits of shadow.

'The Woodvilles are plotting to destroy you. Not only you, but all the old nobility that threaten them – but most especially, you.'

Richard turned to Buckingham and gave him a thin smile. 'This is absolutely no surprise to me, Harry. I should have expected no less of them.'

'No, no, not just to cut you out of events. They mean to kill you.'

The Duke looked sceptical. 'Actually to murder me?'

'Yes. All this conviviality and cooperation tonight was to lull your suspicions!'

'Clearly. But murder? Are you sure?'

'Utterly positive.'

Richard smiled. 'Then I must have terrified them even more consummately than I realized. It's almost pleasing.'

'Of course you terrify them. You're the most powerful man in the kingdom, now that Edward is gone. And when you say the Woodvilles as good as killed him, you are nearer to the truth than you know.' Buckingham spoke dramatically. 'Rumours have been whispered that they poisoned him.'

'Poisoned?' Richard turned on him, his eyes dangerous. 'What the devil would they have to gain from that? They'd not kill their source of power!'

Buckingham shrugged, his flaxen hair spilling over his shoulders. 'Unless they felt that they'd sucked the nanny goat dry. He was standing in their way, can't you see it? They'd got all they could from him. He'd persisted in favouring people they despised, such as Hastings and especially you. When Edward made you, to all intents and purposes, sovereign of the north, it was the last straw. They believed Edward had thrown you a sop, to keep you out of his hair, to stop you becoming another Clarence.'

'They thought that?'

'They're miserably jealous of you.'

The dangerous eyes widened. 'Probably, but you won't inflame me with opinions, Harry. Stick to the facts.'

Buckingham bridled, sucking in his cheeks. 'The fact is that, whatever the cause of his death, Edward left a great chasm of power and the Queen's clan are poised to grab it. The boy is all his mother's by temperament and his uncle's by upbringing, wholly Woodville and completely in their thrall. Through him, they will rule the kingdom, as they never quite managed to rule through his father.' Curling his long soft hands into fists, Buckingham struck the table. 'Remember how they dealt with George of Clarence! I can't stand by and see you so insulted! By Iesu's blood, how I loathe that tribe! I'd do anything and give everything to aid you in crushing them!'

Ratcliffe said bluntly, 'Forceful words, my lord, but why are you helping us? You're a Lancastrian, born and bred. And furthermore, you're married to a Woodville.'

At that, Buckingham turned scarlet, like a clear glass filling up with wine. His water-nymph eyes flashed vitriol. 'Yes, Lancastrian, and that is why Anthony Woodville approached me for help, which is how I divined so much of his evil schemes.' There were breaths of surprise. 'As for my Woodville wife, what better cause could I have to hate them than for foisting that common mare upon me? For God's sake, I'm the foremost peer in the land after our noble lord of Gloucester! Never have I been given the recognition that's my birthright. None of us can go on enduring these insults. York, Lancaster, it doesn't matter! We are all of the old nobility, and as such we stand or fall together! I'm yours to command.'

'Calm yourself, Harry,' said Richard. His fingers were curled around the stem of his glass, his face as grave as an effigy within the shadow of his hair. 'I believe you. The Woodvilles have done us all much wrong. This time they will be stopped, and they will be sorry. I'm convinced of your fealty.'

'To the death,' said Buckingham. He clasped Richard's

314

hand, leaned in close to him and stayed there so long Raphael thought he was going to break down and weep.

'It's plain what must be done,' Richard said, gently detaching himself. 'We must take Earl Rivers by surprise. No doubt he means to delay us in the morning while his supporters spirit Edward to London.'

He rose and went to lean against the fireplace, looking down into the embers. Raphael heard a merciless edge in his voice. Whenever he was hard-pressed, this unnerving strength rose inside him, an adamantine blade that turned everything aside. 'We arrest Rivers, ride to Stony Stratford and take the new King into our protection. We must act swiftly and firmly. No bloodshed. The last thing I want is the boy distressed. The more decisively we act, the cleaner and less violent it will be. Are we all agreed?'

They all murmured assent. Buckingham sighed between his teeth. He was staring hungrily at Richard.

'What a shame that we are saddled with this child-king,' Buckingham said. 'The minority of a king never brings aught but disaster. What we need is a grown man, a man of strength and wisdom upon the throne . . . someone like you, Richard.'

Richard raised his head. The two men looked steadily at each other, as if no one else was in the room. Eventually Richard broke the stare and said evenly, 'Be careful, Harry. You are very close to speaking treason.'

Raphael couldn't sleep. He dreaded a dream-vision. The room around him felt real and ordinary enough. Yet something had disturbed him. He saw a little grey elemental crawl across the floor, like a tiny flattened human figure made of smoke. It vanished under the door.

Raphael started up in bed. Such spectres held no harm, so he'd heard, but they were echoes, an essence of something real that might be present nearby. He got up softly, thinking that he'd go to the kitchen and beg some milk to help him sleep. He'd been given a little room on his own, hardly more than a cupboard. He wished he were sharing with Francis so that they could talk about the evening's events.

Where the corridor bent sharply onto the stairs, he met the landlady. She was a substantial shadow, making him jump. While he was backing away, muttering apologies, she put her finger to her lips. Her eyes were bright moons in the gloom.

'Sir, please aid me. There's an intruder in my house.'

'Intruder? Lady, are you sure?'

She whispered, 'I know the difference between my guests and servants and a shadow that creeps around on slippered feet with a dagger in his hand. I don't think he was aware I saw him.'

'And the little grey . . . ?' He flattened his hand to indicate the elemental he'd seen. Others might have looked blankly at him, but she knew what he meant. Her eyes widened, and she nodded.

'That's what warned me of the intruder.'

'Where did he go?'

She indicated a corridor that bent off to her right. Down there were the rooms assigned to the Duke of Gloucester. 'Is the Duke in bed?' Raphael whispered.

The landlady shook her head. 'Still downstairs, with the other lord.'

'Stay back. Don't fear.'

Easy to say when his own heart was jumping. Barefoot and unarmed, he began to creep along the narrow, crooked passageway. The oak walls and floor were dark and treacly, glistening with a faint wash of moonlight through a leaded window. He should have gone back for his sword, should have woken Francis, but there might not have been time and now it was too late.

Raphael entered Richard's chamber and knew, at once, that the soft-footed assassin was hiding there. The door stood ajar. He could hear faint breathing as he held his own breath but couldn't tell where it came from: behind the door, concealed in the curtains on the far side, or within the bed hangings. The room seemed all folds of smothering velvet.

Raphael pushed back the door until it touched the wall. It creaked upon its hinges. Now the assassin knew he was there.

'Reveal yourself,' he said, as commandingly as he could. He wished he had Tyrant to unleash. 'We know you're there. Give yourself up!'

There was a long, soundless pause.

Suddenly the figure came roaring out of the darkness. Raphael caught him in the doorway, taking the full weight of him in his flight, and found himself grappling madly. He wrested a knife out of the intruder's hand. A blow landed on his hip. It had been aimed at his groin and had missed, but was still enough to knock him off balance. The intruder fought past him and into the corridor.

He turned to see the landlady trip the man. As the assassin sprawled over her outstretched leg, she began to yell in a startlingly loud, commanding voice. Doors were opening, footsteps shaking the stairs and floorboards. Raphael leapt to her aid and between them they got the man flat on the floor with his arms twisted up behind his back, wrists and ankles bound with the landlady's torn veil. By then he was spluttering with fear, crying, 'Get her off me! Get the witch off me!'

He was a skinny man, with a thin, not very bright face. Not so terrifying, out of the shadows. Raphael had seen him earlier among Anthony Woodville's entourage.

'Whoever sent this worm into my house is going to be sorry,' said the landlady. Her handsome face shone with rage and relief. The man gave a choked whimper. 'What shall we do with him?'

Raphael visualized the candles burning low in the dining hall, the astonished faces of Richard, Buckingham and Ratcliffe as the door flew open and framed the proof of Anthony Woodville's schemes.

'Take him before the man he was planning to kill,' he said grimly.

In the silvery dewy dawn, Anthony Woodville woke to find his inn surrounded by men wearing the livery of the white boar and the Stafford knot. Raphael pictured him putting his immaculately groomed head in his hands, and felt sorry for him. His game was over.

Buckingham had been almost gleeful at the assassin's arrest. Ratcliffe and Lovell were outraged, Richard grim. Now Earl Rivers and his accomplices were away not merely to imprisonment, attainder or exile; they were away to their deaths. Pontefract Castle, vaunting on the green stepped layers of its hill, was waiting for them.

Daybreak had barely whitened the sky when they reached Stony Stratford. Raphael suspected that Richard had not slept at all the previous night. He looked tired now, the skin around his eyes tinged with violet. When they found the King and his escort already mounted and poised to leave – confirming that Earl Rivers had never meant Gloucester's party to catch up with him – Richard laughed bitterly.

'We were right about them,' said Buckingham.

'And strangely,' Richard murmured, 'they were also right about us.'

Unaware that his uncle Anthony had been arrested, twelve-year-old Edward waved and called out in plain delight. His half-brother, Richard Grey, looked on with adult suspicion. Gloucester dismounted, directed his companions to do the same. Following his lead they all went down on bended knees and made obeisance to the new King.

Edward was a milk-white child, like a plant grown in a cave. A long colourless stalk of a youth with blanched hair, veins showing blue through the pearly skin, and narrow blue eyes. He smiled with pale, tired joy at their endearments and condolences.

Then he asked, 'Where is my uncle Rivers?'

Still on one knee, Richard took his hand and said gently, 'Your Grace, you must know that your beloved father, Creator rest him, wished the best and safest guardianship for your royal person. He willed me be your Protector. None other.'

Edward began to look distressed. He shook his head, pulling his hand away. 'That's not true. Pardon me, my lord of Gloucester, but I don't know you. I want my uncle.'

Richard rose. 'Alas, you have been deceived, sire. These men whom you have called uncle, friend and brother sought to manipulate and abuse your power for their own ends. Your father feared this, and that's why he sent me. Just in time, it seems. These men have committed treason. They will be taken away, and we shall bear you safely to London and your coronation. Be of good cheer, dear nephew. You're safe now.'

Edward stood wordless and shaking as his companions – his half-brother and other men he'd known all his life – were arrested by Buckingham's guards. They accepted their arrest with dignity, faces etched with bitter resignation. They didn't look like bewildered innocents, Raphael thought, but like criminals caught in the act.

Suddenly the boy broke his silence, drawing himself up in a burst of haughty rage.

'I need no Protector. I am almost a man. In any case I am the King and I command you to bring me my uncle!'

'Your Grace, I am your uncle.' Richard spoke with gentle warmth, but his tone could not be disobeyed.

'I command you to release my guardians,' Edward said less confidently. His voice was folding towards tears.

Richard put his hand on Edward's shoulder. He looked down into his eyes. Somehow, his own calm certainty seemed to disarm the boy. 'Sire, I cannot carry out a command that would harm you. Didn't your noble father always act in your best interests?'

'Yes. Yes.'

'Then we both must do as the King your father willed.'

'I see what you mean,' said Fin. 'It has got quite an atmosphere.'

I'd brought her to the battlefield with me. I appreciated her company. I'd rather be alone than with a companion who was bored, or making inane remarks the whole time, but Fin entered into the spirit of things.

The day was grey, slightly wild, with transient sunshine winging across the hills. We watched a small group of people placing white roses around the stone that marked the place where Richard fell. Two grey-haired women and a man and a younger couple in matching green rambling jackets. As we drew near, I saw that they all wore Richard's white boar badge in their lapels. They stood with their heads bowed, hands folded, as if visiting a grave.

Fin and I stood near them, respectfully silent, although she did shoot me a quick look of incredulity which fortunately they didn't see.

'Afternoon,' said the older man, when their meditation was over. The wind blew his white hair about.

'It's nice to see young people taking an interest,' said one of the women, his wife, it appeared. They were chatty, friendly. 'Don't believe everything you read about King Richard the Third. He was royally framed by the Tudors, you know.'

I nodded, smiling. 'Best king we ever had,' I said, borrowing the sentiment from Fin's Yorkshire friend. It made the group beam. We talked for a while, and their knowledge left me breathless. I suspected they knew more about the subject than I ever would.

'What people don't understand about him,' said the second, older lady, 'is that Richard was a very religious man. If they knew that, they'd realize that he couldn't possibly have murdered his nephews. No one that devout could possibly commit such a crime.'

'Torquemada?' said Fin.

I started to laugh and struggled to swallow it because I sympathized with these earnest people and didn't want them to think I was taking the piss. They bridled. That was different, quite, quite different.

Then Fin said something that amazed me.

'Do you know the legend of the Lame King?'

They admitted that no, they didn't. The white-haired man said, 'There's no evidence that Richard was lame or deformed in any way. Even those who said he had one shoulder higher than the other couldn't agree which shoulder it was.'

'No,' said Fin, 'but he's always been portrayed as crook-backed and lame.'

They agreed that this was so.

'And Richard's deformities were exaggerated or invented as a metaphor for his supposed wickedness, weren't they? In early times, the king's power was believed to be divinely bestowed. If the king were fit and healthy, the land would flourish. If he were ill or disfigured, the land would sicken. If that happened, he must die. Folklore is full of lame kings: Richard is one of many. In pagan times, according to certain scholars, the Sacred King was sacrificed at the end of a fixed period so that his blood would bring the land back to life. And just before he was sacrificed, he would be ritually maimed. Perhaps it was to do with making the king physically imperfect so he could be killed, drawing the attention of sinister powers towards him and away from the community.

The lamed Sacred King becomes the scapegoat, taking upon himself all the ills of the land, and when he's slain, he takes the ills with him, and the land is healed.'

The group stood hushed as she finished. The old man's eyes were watery.

'So you're saying that Richard had to die?' he said.

'In a symbolic sense,' said Fin. 'Yes, I suppose I am.'

'And it wasn't for nothing.' The members of the little group looked at one another, sober and thoughtful. It was an astonishing moment. 'That helps, that does. That helps.'

Chapter Thirteen 1483: Eliza

[Archbishop Rotherham took the Great Seal to the Queen] . . . about whom he found much heaviness and rumble, haste and business, carriage and conveyance of her stuff into sanctuary: chests, coffers, packs, fardels, trusses, all on men's backs, some breaking down the walls to bring in the next way. The Queen sat alone, a-low on the rushes, all desolate and dismayed, whom the Archbishop comforted in the best manner he could, showing her he trusted the matter was nothing so sore as she took it for.

Sir Thomas More

Kate had forgotten the bustle of London, how beautiful it could look in the early morning swathed in vaporous fogs, how ugly it could feel in atmosphere. The streets purred with gossip. The Duchess of Gloucester's party, resplendent with the white boar and Anne's own Neville arms, caused a stir as it passed along the streets. They were stared at, bowed to and cheered. The cheering startled Kate. She had to chide Nan and Ursula for waving back.

They arrived at Crosby Place: high cathedral walls outside, inside all bronze and gold leaf, black stone and blood-red walls embellished with golden motifs. The great hall had the most magnificent ceiling she'd ever seen.

Katherine liked the warmth and drama of the house, but Anne wasn't happy to be here. She was torn. She'd wanted to stay in the north with her son, but Richard had sent for her because naturally he wanted her to be present at the coronation. Anne rarely complained, but Kate could read her subtle humours and tried keep her in good cheer.

For herself, she was glad to be in the heart of things, to be with Richard and Raphael, for once, instead of always left behind.

After nightfall, when Anne and her attendants were asleep, Kate slipped quietly out of their apartments and found a gallery with a row of tall windows. Richard had separate chambers and had not, as far as she knew, joined his wife. Not that it was her concern. At Middleham, Anne's ladies had usually withdrawn from her bedchamber at night before her husband came there. In any case, Kate had become adept at turning a blind eye.

The view was spectral: hundreds of roofs washed in star-light, some steep and austere, others tiled and shimmering like butterfly wings. No two were alike. A forest of gilded church towers; the *shush* of spiral mechanisms channelling water to the houses of the rich . . . the scene was timeless.

A finger touched her elbow. There was warm breath on her ear. 'Kate.'

She turned and Raphael was there, grinning.

They hugged, kissed, laughed. Caressing each other with intimate hands they laughed again, soft as thieves.

'You're here,' he said. 'I was so glad when Richard told us he was sending for you. For the Duchess, I mean, but I knew she wouldn't come without you. I seem to have been waiting for you forever.'

'Tell me everything, everything,' said Kate. They stood with their arms around each other for warmth, no sound around them but the soft throb of water and the other-worldly, cathedral hush of the night.

'Iesu, where do I start? You must have heard some of it. How Richard took the King out of the clutches of the Woodvilles.'

'We've heard stories and rumours, but no clear details. I don't know what the Duke may have written in his letters to the Duchess. We're only women, after all, the last to know.'

He ignored her sardonic tone. His mood was volatile,

flickering from grim concern to an excitement so vivid he shone with it. 'I'm more than glad you are a woman, beautiful Kate, I can assure you,' he smiled, stroking the curve of her hip through her dress.

'Never mind that. Tell me.'

He told her about the Woodville plot to exclude Richard from power, the discovery of the would-be assassin, the arrest of Earl Rivers. His tone was low and matter of fact, with no bravado in describing his own actions. His lack of boastfulness was a quality Kate had always found endearing. 'We entered London in state. It was like wading through a cheering, shouting sea. Richard looked magnificent, even in plain black mourning. He and Buckingham rode on either side of the King and they were glorious, like night and day.'

'And the little King?' Kate asked. 'You seem to forget the most important person.'

'Edward was in blue. I was so proud to be riding with them, but I remembered how overwhelmed I was the first time I entered London. It made me feel sorry for the King. It must all have been startling for him. He was as stiff as a reed on his horse, his face like milk and his eyes darting about everywhere.'

Kate put in, 'Yet he must have been to London before?'

'Of course, but . . . I can't put my finger on it. He seems afraid of Richard.'

'Well . . . Richard can be . . .'

'What?' he said.

'Intimidating. He has a very strong presence but you often can't tell what he's thinking; he's like a bird of prey.'

'That's unfair.' Raphael frowned, touchy at perceived criticism. 'You don't know him.'

'I'm only suggesting that it might be unnerving to a boy who's only met him a handful of times in his entire life. And Richard had just taken all his familiar companions away from him.'

'I think there's more to it than that. I think that Rivers

and Grey between them have poisoned Edward against Richard. God knows what they'd said about him, but Edward will have drunk it all in as gospel. He seems intelligent enough, but there's no worldly wisdom about him at all.'

'Oh dear,' Kate said under her breath.

'What are you thinking?'

'About the Motherlodge. About Anne Beauchamp and my mother arguing over who should be king, the divine heir by birth or the best man for the job – as if they had the faintest influence over it! But a young boy . . .'

'That's what Buckingham said. A child-king is always a disaster. His guardians fight among themselves and it deteriorates into years of warfare. Young Edward barely knew his father. They're saying he's a pure Woodville, which pleases no one except the Woodvilles themselves. I suppose it's no wonder he's nervous of Richard. And Richard sent criers ahead to inform the city of their treachery, which can't have made him any happier. He was looking brighter by the end of the parade, though. A great escort from the Lord Mayor, hundreds of mounted men in scarlet and violet and bishops bowing to him, all those people thronging in the streets to welcome him. It made me wonder, though, if they wouldn't cheer an ape if we'd dressed it up in blue velvet and told them it was the King.'

'Raphael!'

'Unworthy thought, I know. It just seems a shame King Edward couldn't have lived another four years, and brought up his heir in a different circle.'

'What else?

'Well, Richard's coup was effective. It's thrown the Woodvilles into complete disarray. The Queen's fled into Westminster Sanctuary with her son Dorset, and she's taken her daughters, her youngest son Richard of York, and all the royal treasure she could stuff in there with her. Her brother Edward had already put to sea in command of the navy.'

'They're so afraid of Richard?'

Raphael grimaced. 'If they are, they've brought it all upon themselves. They've only made things worse by panicking. Richard was quite angry. As he pointed out, he's about to crown the Queen's son, so what's she got to be frightened of, unless it's her own guilty conscience? Buckingham was almost leaping out of his skin with glee.'

'I seem to have missed a lot.'

'I wouldn't have wanted you here in all that disturbance. The Isis was choked with boats full of Gloucester's men, stopping anyone from entering or leaving sanctuary. There were lords and citizens in full armour in the streets as if battle was imminent. It's not been pleasant, Kate. The city's mad with rumours.'

'Saying what?'

He didn't answer. 'Richard's been trying to persuade Elizabeth to come out of sanctuary, but she won't listen to reason. She can't be that afraid. She's just trying to embarrass Richard, making a great show of being terrified. It's a reproach to him.'

Kate went suddenly cold, thinking how different this account would be if Raphael and the sister of Auset had not discovered the assassin. Richard might have gone to bed unknowing and been murdered there, then the great clan of Woodvilles would have claimed total victory over England and commenced lapping up its riches. Anne, widowed, would have been given the chance of marrying one of them or entering a nunnery, either way adding the prestigious Neville lands to their collection. Most likely, there would have been yet another civil war for control of the King. Life would have continued but as if the sun had been extinguished. Not a bright angelic sun, rather one that was dark, shadowy, strange, warm, blood-red as a furnace, the heart of everything; gone.

She stood with her lips frozen open until Raphael said, 'Are you listening?'

'I'm sorry. I was imagining if Richard had died.'

'Well, he didn't. I was saying that we took the King to the Bishop's palace, then we lodged at Baynard's Castle. I've never liked the place: a huge echoing space that seems all dark blue and silver, and always freezing cold. Richard's mother Cecily lives there. She's still beautiful, with snow-white hair.'

'Did you see her?'

'Once or twice. Everyone's afraid of her. She stalks about like a severe old abbess.'

Katherine wondered if Cecily Neville was still tormented by past hurts, the loss of her husband and three of her sons, or if she had subsumed it all with rigid willpower. A pity she didn't give that strength to Auset, Kate thought. Kate had the idea that devotions to God floated up into the ether, and were lost, while those to the Serpent Mother went deep into the earth, feeding her strength.

'Anyway, I'm glad we've moved here,' Raphael went on. 'And the King's been lodged in the Tower. Buckingham suggested it.'

'A more suitable palace for the monarch,' said Kate. She couldn't let Raphael think she knew nothing of London. She felt mildly envious that he was privy to all these activities – if not actually in meetings, then in a position to hear all about it immediately afterwards. The world of men, she thought with a sneer. The priestesses of Auset should be appointed to government in equal numbers to bishops, then there would be a true balance. And graylix might fly.

'Exactly. They say the royal apartments in the Tower are wonderfully sumptuous. The walls are painted with gilded angels, and even the floor tiles are decorated with silver pards and white harts.'

'Is Richard officially Protector now?' Kate asked.

'Yes, Protector of the Realm, but only until Edward is crowned. He's been given sovereign power, just as if he were a king. The Council were as glad as anything to do that. However, he's trying to have his role extended until the King is sixteen; it will be disastrous if he fails. But some dissident voices have sprung up, complaining it will make him too powerful.' Raphael sounded disgusted. 'Too many Woodville sympathizers.'

'Who supports him?'

'The Duke of Buckingham, of course, Lord Hastings and John Howard; all the old nobles who hate the Woodvilles. And he means to . . .' His voice fell.

'What?'

He finished in a whisper, 'To have Earl Rivers, Grey and their supporters executed.'

She was shocked. 'For plotting against him?'

'And because, if he lets them live, Edward will release them from prison the moment he takes the throne and restore them to power. They have to die, or Richard will never be safe.'

'I see.' Kate's mouth was dry, but she accepted Raphael's explanation. It was what nobles had always done, all through her life – executed their enemies. Shown mercy, such traitors only savaged the hand that blessed them. 'And Buckingham?'

'I'm not sure I like him. He's strange. Still, I've never seen anyone so utterly devoted as he is to Richard. He can't do enough for him.' Raphael turned, a conspiratorial smile on his face. 'Buckingham loathes the Woodvilles. Imagine his delight at getting his revenge. He was deprived of an inheritance by the late King, which he trusts Richard will restore to him.'

'So he has an ulterior motive.'

Raphael opened his hands, palms outwards. 'Of course. But, Kate, who doesn't? Richard has no choice but to play upon people's ambition to find support. It's the nature of the game.'

Kate paused, flexing her fingers on the window frame. 'So Richard is presently the most powerful man in the country.'

'Yes.'

'He might not wish to give that up.'

His hands, which had crept around her waist again, loosened. 'I could hardly blame him, could you?'

'No,' she said under her breath, thoughtful, 'but I don't see how it's possible.'

'What are you implying?'

'Raphael, I know something's happening. You're so on edge and exhilarated, as if you've seen a holy vision. I've been in the streets of London; I've passed through the kitchens and the servants' chambers and I've overheard the whispers of the household. The constant rumour is that Richard has no intention of crowning his nephew. They're saying that he means to take the crown for himself.'

His face lengthened. His green eyes were more wary than surprised.

'Well? You're with him every day. Is it true?'

'No,' he said. 'It's not true. He's here to carry out his brother's will, not to take a throne that isn't his. But I'll tell you this, Kate; I wish he would.'

'Treason,' she mouthed. They stood in silence in the deserted length of the gallery. They held each other close, but had managed to shock themselves out of all amorous intent.

'Well, would you?' he said into her ear. 'Knowing yourself a mature, experienced leader, give up your power to a sullen youth whose family hates you? I tell you, he'd be a better king than this realm deserves.'

Something howled past the window, rattling the frame and making them both reel back in fright. A grey, winged rag with a grinning mouth and sly malevolent eyes. The face looked briefly, horribly familiar. There, then gone in a flash.

'Christ Iesu, what the devil was that?' Raphael exclaimed.

'The wind,' said Kate. 'A waft of smoke. An elemental. Nothing.'

The Duchess of Gloucester was not a demanding mistress.

330

Kate had heard alarming stories of some great ladies – Elizabeth Woodville and her mother, Jacquetta of Bedford, among them – who never let their ladies-in-waiting out of their sight but must have constant attention. If they could not sleep, their attendants couldn't sleep either, but must be on hand to cosset their disagreeable humours. Fortunately, Anne was not one of those. If anything, she asked too little. It was always easy for Kate to get away on her own business.

Often, she had slipped away at night to lie with Raphael. This time, though, she was making her way in daylight to the London Motherlodge of Auset. She'd been here before, when George of Clarence had brought his household to London, on the rare occasions she could escape.

The temple was in a cellar beneath a great stone warehouse in an alley that led down to the docks; an insalubrious area of cranes and warehouses. Ships creaked, heavy with cargo; their masts a sinister, leafless forest. Katherine hesitated at the head of the stairs, then caught her breath and started down. It was dank and smelled strongly of the river. The walls were glistening black, shining from the light of many tapers.

At the bottom of the stairs was a circular chamber, the roof vault supported by thick columns. A stone basin stood in the centre, some five feet in diameter, filled with brine. Katherine went closer. In the water swam a black sea-snake, round and round, like a huge bracelet scaled with jet; the serpent eating its own tail. Carefully pricking herself on a thorn, she threw her offering of a white rose and a drop of blood onto the water.

Another woman was on her way down the stairs. Her small body was concealed in a nun's habit, but as she reached the temple she impatiently pulled the cloth from her head and shook out a cloud of golden hair. Her sweet, heart-shaped face looked familiar. Passing Kate, she said warmly, 'Good day, sister.'

'Good day,' Kate answered, watching the woman as she

went into one of several recesses on the far side. Candles glimmered there and voices floated out. They were private places, like chapels, where sisters were free to petition their goddesses for whatever purpose they wished. Suddenly Kate realized who the woman was – or had been. It was Elizabeth Shore, no less: King Edward's celebrated mistress. Now, according to rumour, the mistress of both William Hastings and the Queen's son the Marquis of Dorset. Kate raised her eyebrows. She'd had no idea of Eliza Shore's secret affiliation. She wondered if Edward himself had known.

'Katherine,' said a velvety voice she knew.

Into the light came Bridget Marl, Dame Eylott's good friend, neat and handsome like a nun. 'Sweet daughter, it's been so long since we last met.'

'Yes, and I *have* grown,' Katherine said, laughing. The two women embraced. 'Mother Marl, you look no older.'

'Such is Auset's blessing, which the ignorant call witchcraft,' Bridget said with a wink. 'How is your mother, our beloved *Mater Superior*?'

'Very well, when last she wrote to me,' said Katherine.

'I am glad to see you, daughter. What brings you here?'

The priestess's bluntness was usual. Kate hadn't been here for years, yet it felt natural to drop into the familiar old patterns of straight speech. There was no dance of formality to negotiate.

'I'm living in London for a while.' She tilted her head to indicate the direction that Eliza Shore had taken. 'I had no idea that *she* . . .' In the recess, Kate could just see a flicker of red light outlining a kneeling figure, a curve of blonde hair, pale hands cupped as if in prayer.

Mother Marl put her finger to her own lips. 'Discretion, if you please. You'd be surprised at who comes here, where there is no identity, no rank. She has been of the sisterhood for years.' The elder women gave a lop-sided smile. 'In the hidden world, no one condemns her for being . . . profligate with her affections.'

332

'Nor do they in the outer world, much,' said Kate. 'What it is to be popular!'

'Never mind her. What of you?'

'I'm one of the Duchess of Gloucester's waiting women. In the household of—'

'Ah, the Lord Protector. Yes, I see.'

'Mother, do you think . . . You must have heard the rumours that . . .'

'Dear, I probably spend more time in the tavern round the corner than I do here. Of course I've heard the gossip that perhaps, who knows, the Protector *might* be aiming at the throne. It's rampant.'

They were whispering very low, but still the words seemed to lash the chamber walls. Kate involuntarily raised her hands as if to still the echo.

'Should he?' she asked helplessly.

'What a thing to ask! Do I sense loyalties in conflict?'

'I talked about it to my lover, who serves Richard of Gloucester. A child-king is too dangerous. I half wish Edward's precious sons didn't exist; then Richard would be king without argument. I know he would be strong and fair, a better king than his brother, but . . .'

The priestess's face became grave. She pointed at the serpent in the basin. The creature's behaviour indicated the Serpent Mother's mood. 'The dance of the serpent does not bode well. The Church is jealous of its power and they're constantly pressing for more control, more rights of interference. Their grip will increase until they are persecuting us openly.'

'Under Woodville rule?' Kate asked, surprised. 'All they're interested in is wealth, status and luxurious living; they're hardly the Church's dearest allies.'

Bridget laughed heartily, clutching her thighs. 'Gods, Kate, you've a lot to learn. When has the Church shown itself uninterested in wealth, status and luxury? They can't maintain it without keeping a stranglehold upon every soul in the kingdom. Anthony Woodville himself is a deeply pious man, I've heard. His brother's a bishop. We're the fleas in their hair shirts.'

'Still, I don't think Edward the Fifth is any greater threat to us than Edward the Fourth was, Auset rest him. His family don't think we're important enough to care about.'

'It would depend what bishops are allied to them. If they're weak or uncommitted – whether to protecting us or to destroying us – the single-minded will make a path of them, trampling them down like barley.'

'Either way, we can't win,' Kate said flatly.

'You have it, madam. What of your Protector, then?'

'He's not "mine",' she said with a sigh. 'I'm not sure. It's all a paradox. My heart says he would make a good king. However, my head reminds me that he is staunchly committed to his religion, and that means he might prove extremely dangerous to us, as Edward the Fourth never was, and even as Henry the Sixth never was.'

Mother Marl pursed her lips. She trailed her fingertip on the water and the serpent followed it round and round, jaws gaping, round eyes bulging above the surface. A needle-fang caught. Bridget jerked her hand away with a curse. A strand of blood ribboned the water.

'There, she has a little gift from me.' She sucked the wounded finger. 'Perhaps she'll give a word of advice in return.'

'Good mother, I know you're speaking the truth. I've felt it myself. Our wisdom will be rejected and called witchcraft. No one will benefit from this; but they'll do it anyway. I've already seen too many Hollows desecrated. Without our devotion, the Dark Mother will go deep into the earth and our descendents will be scraping about on barren land, not even knowing what they've wasted!'

'Don't get angry, sweet,' said Bridget.

'But if we don't get angry, how shall we survive?'

'We'll fight it with all our strength; but I won't offer you false comfort. I don't think the identity of the king matters.

334

Any king will bow to the pressure of the Church, and the pressure is growing. They will close the loophole by which we are allowed to exist. It will happen anyway; but a pious king – perhaps Richard – would make the process a lot faster and more brutal, for certain.'

'What should I do?' Kate groaned. 'What an idiotic question. There's nothing I can do; I have no influence.'

'And there are altogether too many others in the stew already,' said Mother Marl, patting her shoulder. 'Come, take a little wine with me.'

She strode off towards her private chamber on the far side of the cellar. Following slowly, Kate had a clear view of Eliza Shore at her work. She was bathed in candlelight that shone though a red glass holder. Her eyes were closed, her lips moved slowly and she coiled between her hands the snake-like form of a large elemental. It had a distinct look, smoky and translucent, the sort that was found clustering about the sick and feeding on their strength. Kate had never seen one so large, certainly never managed to catch one between her hands; still less wanted to. Yet Eliza handled the creature with sensuous dexterity, as if it were a necklace of gold and diamonds sliding through her hands and around her wrists. The sight was so strange that Kate, forgetting Motherlodge etiquette, stopped and stared.

Eliza Shore opened her eyes. They were brown, friendly and innocent. As she stood up, the smoke-entity slithered over her shoulder and vanished.

'What is it, sister?' she asked.

'To command such an elemental is a remarkable talent,' Kate said softly.

'To be able to see them is remarkable, too.' She spoke with trusting intimacy, the uptilt of her chin so charming that Kate could see why men fought like tomcats over her.

'It surprises me when people can't,' said Kate. 'Priests throwing holy water in the wrong places . . .'

Mistress Shore laughed. 'While the sprites pull faces behind their backs.'

'Still, it's not safe to play with them as you were doing. Not ones of that kind. They can't be tamed.'

'Sweet sister, I was not playing,' Eliza said in the same mild tone.

Kate folded her arms. She felt like a schoolmaster scolding a child, but it had to be said. 'Then I don't have to remind you that any working that's liable to cause harm is forbidden in the outer world and discouraged by the Motherlodge itself.'

The beautiful golden head dipped appeasingly. She placed both hands on Kate's forearm. 'I know; but I trust you to tell no one, dear sister. I don't have to remind you, either, that everything that takes place in the Motherlodge is secret, secret as the grave. Forgive me for enjoying my little flirtation with danger. Let's both keep our counsel.'

She kissed the startled Kate on the cheek, brushed past her, and was gone.

Kate emerged from the temple feeling depressed. She went down to the docks, leaned on a wall and stood listening to the lap of the water. There lay the treacly obsidian waters of the Isis, reflecting ghost-shapes. Barges slid past, some carrying magnates or bishops under cloth-of-gold canopies from one palace to another. She doubted they were even aware of the river's essential soul. It was a powerful entity, a serpent deity in its own right, a vast liquid body shaped by its banks. Oozing on its slow way to the sea but never ending: immortal. She uttered a wordless invocation to the dark green Serpent Mother of the river to rise and lend her energy to the aid of her children.

William Catesby sat at the table, his thin white fingertips resting together on the polished cherry wood. His straight grey hair gleamed silver in the firelight; his narrow but handsome face was the colour of ash.

'There is no possibility,' he said, 'that William Lord Hastings will consider supporting any bid on your part to become king. His support for you extends only to your

336

protectorship, insofar as it has thwarted the Woodvilles, and that only until the coronation. His loyalty lies with Edward the Fifth. Although I presented the possibility as subtly as I might – as a general rumour, not a concrete suggestion – his response was . . . terrible.'

Richard was on his feet, slowly pacing the width of the room in front of the fireplace. They were in a private chamber in Crosby Place, a warm and gleaming room with rich red walls and a motif of harts and leopards. His supporters – Richard Ratcliffe, Francis Lovell, John Howard, James Tyrell, Raphael and a handful of others – were grouped around the table, watching him.

'Terrible?' Richard said. He approached and leaned on the back of Raphael's chair, staring at Catesby. 'In what way? In the sense that once he's finished blustering, he might be persuaded?'

'I'm afraid not, my lord,' Catesby answered evenly. 'He turned a deeper crimson than these walls. He used words I dare not repeat. I know him – better than you, if I dare say so – and I know him to be not only secure in his convictions, but stubbornly immoveable in them.'

'I see,' said Richard. 'He seems to have spoken openly to you.'

'He spoke very openly. He still trusts me.' Catesby blinked. 'He's something of an innocent in that way. He expects everyone to be as transparent and straightforward as himself. His loyalty to young Edward will not be shaken.'

'Well, that's most commendable,' said Richard. No one spoke. His expression darkened. 'Now I know the position, I shall have to decide what to do. After all the love he showed me when we first arrived! Now the truth becomes apparent. He used me to oust the Woodvilles, and now wishes I would conveniently disappear . . . but I won't.'

'He'll soon know it,' said Ratcliffe.

Richard went to the fire and leaned on the mantle. 'I used to like Hastings . . . but I believe I've seen him reeling drunk more times even than I've seen my brother in that state. He encouraged my brother's ruin fully as enthusiastically as Rivers and Dorset. He didn't scruple to wait for Edward's corpse to cool before he rushed Mistress Shore into his bed . . . and she's still sharing her favours with Dorset, and who knows how many others. To say it corrodes respect is an understatement.'

'William Hastings will make a dangerous enemy, my lord,' said Catesby.

The atmosphere in the chamber was close, bathed in fiery light. Raphael had begun to feel oppressed by these endless secret meetings, his vision clouded by the body-heat and breath of men who sat closeted together hour on hour, filling the space with emanations that took on their own life and atmosphere, becoming elementals, essences, entities like tiny fire-demons, twisting like corkscrews, groaning. He wondered if anyone else saw them, or if he was unique in being cursed to see glimpses of the hidden world all the time.

'And is busily plotting the same,' Lovell put in.

'Outrageous,' said John Howard, Duke of Norfolk. Raphael liked him; he was a solid, straightforward man who doted upon Richard like a grandfather.

Catesby, a dry-voiced lawyer, had been part of Richard's circle only a short time. He'd been Hastings' confidant, but had switched allegiance to Richard almost from the moment they'd met. Raphael had seen it happen, and had smiled. Richard had an extreme effect upon people: he drew them irresistibly, or he repelled them. While Hastings assumed the lawyer was spying upon Richard for him, it was actually the other way round.

'The councillors are apprehensive,' Catesby continued. 'They perceive my lords Buckingham and Norfolk as too influential. They are alarmed by the abrupt downfall of the Woodvilles. They have suspected your intentions from the beginning; my sounding out of Hastings will no doubt have confirmed them, and thrown them into panic.'

Richard laughed. 'Panicking at their own imaginations or consciences. What have I done all this time, but made arrangements for Edward's coronation? And I'd crown him gladly; but where are their assurances of *my* fair treatment in the future? I know that Parliament won't agree to extend my protectorship beyond the coronation. Edward Woodville has fled to France, the Queen sits stubbornly in sanctuary, and Hastings is plotting against me.' The only colour in his face was from the firelight as he looked down into the flames. It seemed to reveal starkly all the subtle workings of his soul that were usually concealed. 'I would suggest they are narrowing my choices; that this situation leaves me no choice at all.'

Catesby cleared his throat. 'I have more to report, Your Grace.'

'Yes,' said Richard, pacing again. 'I'm sorry, William, continue.'

'I understand Lord Hastings' circle of those antipathetic to you has increased. In addition to the Bishops Rotherham and Morton, Thomas Stanley was privy to their last meeting.'

'Stanley!' Howard exclaimed. 'Ye gods, it must be serious for him to come down on one side or the other.'

Lovell asked, 'Did Morton have that bony clerk with him, Fautherer?' Catesby nodded. 'Then I swear there are two of him, for every time I see Margaret Beaufort, he is with her, too.'

'It grows worse,' Catesby went on. 'They discussed arresting you. Lord Hastings is so worried that he is even willing to join forces with the Queen, whom he loathes, to thwart your supposed designs on the throne.'

Richard looked up. His eyes were like stone. 'Have you proof? If he had gone into sanctuary to see her, I would have been told.'

'He sends Mistress Shore as a go-between. She goes in and out of sanctuary dressed as a nun. No doubt it enables her to see much of the Marquis of Dorset.'

Raphael said, 'I would have thought the Queen hated Eliza Shore.'

'Not necessarily,' said Francis, shaking his head. 'The Queen knew what Edward was like and tolerated it. From what I understand, since she couldn't persuade him to give up his favourite harlot, she decided to befriend her instead. Elizabeth cannot bear not to be in control of everyone. And they've shared a common grief, of course.'

'In any case,' said Raphael, 'what would she care, as long as Mistress Shore is a useful messenger? I suppose the Queen and Dorset have thoroughly groomed her to persuade Hastings to their side.'

'Gods, and you're right, Raphael,' Richard said near his ear, making him jump. He looked icily furious. 'Catesby, I must thank you for this.'

'I'm sorry to bring such displeasing news. Slay the messenger if you must, but it was essential you be told.'

'I'm angry, William, but not with you, or any of my friends in this room. And I'll show my gratitude for this, believe me.'

'I have a further report,' Catesby said quietly, looking down at his steepled hands. 'Something I learned just before I departed my house this evening. I have it on authority that Hastings and Bishop Morton went to the young King and expressed their concerns about you.'

'He did what?' Richard loomed over the table, white and dangerous.

'And the young King replied, instructing them to do everything within their power to remove you as Protector.'

Ratcliffe shot to his feet, all florid outrage, and stood there breathing hard, speechless. John Howard said, 'Christ!' Then there was heavy silence, filled, in Raphael's eyes, with a mad dance of fire-demons. The air was hot with foreboding.

The door opened and a servant announced the Duke of Buckingham. No one responded. The Duke appeared, making his usual impressive entrance in a swirl of blue, red and gold, like some mythical prince. Still no one acknowledged him. He frowned.

'Have I arrived at an inconvenient moment, my lords?'

Richard finally spoke, addressing Catesby. 'Good. Now I know precisely where I stand.' He patted Ratcliffe on the shoulder. 'Sit down, Dick. Harry, welcome. Pardon our bad manners. You've arrived at the best moment possible.'

Confident again, Buckingham strode in and kissed Richard on both cheeks. 'I've found him.'

'Who?'

'The man who has the proof. Bishop Stillington.'

'Gods, Harry, are you sure?'

'He's here. May I bring him in?'

Raphael, confounded by this exchange, watched as the prelate was ushered into the room by Buckingham. Stillington was a tall, stooped man with a mournful face and a nervous manner. His snow-white robes hung loosely on him. There was no sign of arrogance or excessive piety about him; he looked very human.

There was a pause while obeisance was paid to the Bishop, and servants moved quickly to rearrange chairs and place refreshments on the long oak table. Once they'd gone, Buckingham impatiently shut the door behind them.

'What news? What have I missed? You all look ready to do murder.'

'Yours first,' Richard said coolly.

Buckingham had the air of a hunter bringing home a trophy kill. 'Do they know?'

Richard exchanged a meaningful glance with Francis Lovell. 'Only Francis.'

'Well, listen to what Bishop Stillington has to say.'

The Bishop interrupted. 'Er, my lord Duke, in private, if it please you.'

'This is private,' Richard answered. 'There is nothing I would not have said in front of my friends. Be seated, please.' Raphael jumped up and held chairs for Buckingham

341

and Stillington. Richard sat down next to Buckingham, opposite the Bishop.

'What is it?' asked John Howard.

'Something Edward once told me,' said Richard. 'It was a long, long time ago, before he married Elizabeth Woodville. I was nine or ten at the time and he was in his cups, of a mind to instruct me in the ways of women. He spoke of one noblewoman so virtuous and unpersuadable that in order to seduce her, he had to go through a form of marriage with her. He roared with laughter as he told me this. It was an example of the lengths of deception he was prepared to go to, to illustrate that no obstacle in this world would ever prevent him getting what he wanted.' Richard looked pale as he spoke. 'Doubtless I laughed with him at the time, and admired him for it. It was only in later years that his behaviour struck me as repulsive. I wondered, what noblewoman? What marriage? Did it truly take place, and if so, would it not have made his marriage to Elizabeth Woodville invalid?'

Stillington's lower lip shook, shiny pink. 'That is it, my lord. The marriage *was* invalid. Edward married Elizabeth bigamously. The ceremony, which was in any case rushed and secret, was unlawful. He was already joined to another woman. I know, because I was the one who – who joined them.'

Buckingham sat forward triumphantly. The rest were stunned. Gloucester was rigid, eyes narrow. 'What woman?'

'Lady Eleanor Butler,' Stillington said unhappily. Lovell and the others gasped. 'Perhaps King Edward – let us give him the benefit of the doubt – had true intentions towards her at the time. Certainly she would allow no sin to take place; and so he was formally betrothed to her, by myself, which ceremony, followed by, er, by consummation, as you know, is as binding as marriage and he was therefore not free to—'

'Yes, you make the point very clearly.'

'True intentions?' Buckingham exclaimed. 'I think not. He cast her in a nunnery when he'd finished with her!'

John Howard put in, 'Lady Eleanor Butler died some years ago, did she not?'

'She was, er, very much alive, my lord, when he made this dishonest marriage to Dame Grey,' said Stillington.

'Yes, but after her death,' said Howard, 'all he had to do then was to remake his vows to Elizabeth and their union would have been legal. Why did he not?'

'How could he?' Richard said. 'To do so would have been hideously embarrassing, especially to the Queen. Perhaps she didn't even know. He would have had to admit wrongdoing, bigamy, go through another ceremony and have his children declared legitimate by Parliament. Much easier just to let the matter lie and hope no one ever found out.'

'Still, better to endure some embarrassment than to leave your sons illegitimate and disinherited,' said Lovell.

Richard put his head in his hands. 'Oh, gods, Edward!'

'I thought this news would please you,' said Buckingham, crestfallen. 'I thought it was what you hoped for!'

Gloucester raised his head, struck the table with an open hand. Stillington jumped. 'Please me? To hear that my brother's married life was a sham, all his children bastards, and that we have suffered the depredations of the Woodvilles for nothing? It doesn't please me. It doesn't surprise me. It makes me despair to be part of my own family.'

'The only worthy part,' Buckingham said under his breath.

'However.' Richard exhaled. 'However, it's done. I asked for the truth and I can't claim to be amazed at it.' He leaned towards the Bishop. 'Your Grace, would you swear the truth of what you've told me in public?'

'I would, my lord.'

'Or would you swallow the secret and take it to the grave?'

Stillington's lip quivered. 'Whatever you command, Lord Protector, I shall do.'

'Good. Do as I command, and you'll find me most grateful. For now, say nothing, and await my word.'

After Buckingham had shown Bishop Stillington out and returned, Richard sat with his elbows on the table, hands clasped. His forefingers tapped silently together, over and again; otherwise he was motionless.

'We don't have to tell anyone of this. I can silence Stillington. We can purge our memories, seal our lips, make masks of our faces. We can go forth and put young Edward on the throne, all as it should be, while I do what little I can to curb the excesses of his family. But.' Tap. 'But.' Tap.

He drew a breath and went on very softly, 'In four years' time Edward will reach his majority. Witness he has already asked Hastings to destroy me. Shall he not take his revenge on me, for removing his uncle and half-brother and all his beloved servants? What I did was necessary, but he will never understand that and certainly never forgive it. He's a clever boy, calculating and vengeful like his mother. There will be factions, wars. If they are not making war upon me within the year, it will be a miracle. They'll find some excuse to take my kingdom of the north from me.'

'Gods, no!' Francis Lovell cried in disgust.

'If I end up as George did, I'll not marvel at it. If I were unmarried, it would matter less to me. I'd as soon go into exile, and sell myself as a mercenary to fight the Turks. I'm not alone, however. I have my wife and my son to consider. Must I stand by and see my son lose his inheritance, birthright, future, everything that should be his?'

Richard paused, his voice darkening. 'Do you know how many times Edward asked Parliament to grant him money for war? Then there *was* no war, but the Queen's family grew a little richer.

'Cursed is the day that Edward my brother feigned marriage to Elizabeth Woodville.' He looked at each of them in turn. His eyes were red-rimmed. 'Should I exert myself to put her bastard upon the throne, at my own son's expense? I will die before I see a Woodville government of this realm.'

Buckingham placed his hand on Richard's forearm, warm, too familiar. He kneaded Richard's flesh like a lover. 'We all know you must take the throne. This is your means to do it. Your legitimate, legal means. The boys are bastards.' His green eyes shone with preternatural light, elf-like.

'I know. And I expected to feel glad, but . . .' Richard rose from his seat and stood in front of the fire, inky against the flaming glow. 'I could still pull back,' he said. 'It's not too late. At this moment I am the most powerful man in the kingdom. Do you think I wish to give that up on the twenty-second of June at Edward's coronation?'

'No, and nor should you,' said John Howard.

'But if I go on, you must all come with me. One more step and we'll turn all their nervous rumours into truth and there'll be no going back. Don't think for a moment this will be easy. Start, and we must go on to the bloody end.'

Buckingham was the first to move. He went to Richard and fell to his knees, his hair spreading over his shoulders in a sun-coloured veil. His fervency was strangely disturbing. Catesby was next, then Raphael with Lovell beside him, then Howard, Ratcliffe, Tyrell amd all the others swearing loyalty. Raphael's heart was pounding furiously. This was terrifying, and he could hear Kate talking of branches in the path, but this was the only path he could see, richly glistening with rubies.

Richard looked down at them with tears in his eyes.

'You are the King, Richard,' said Buckingham. 'The rightful King.'

Anne was asleep, the lights burning low in her chambers. Her women were abed, or undressing, all but Katherine. If anything was said about her comings and goings, she knew how to silence the gossipers with a basilisk stare; but she was always as discreet as possible. She was slipping out of the door to meet Raphael, only to find her way blocked by a dark figure in the corridor outside.

She started. It was Richard, alone and so quiet she hadn't known he was there.

Recovering, she made a minimal curtsey out of habit. A safeguard, to renew the wall of distance between them. She went to open the door to the Duchess's apartments wider so he could go through, but he didn't move.

'How is Anne?' he asked.

'Tired out,' Katherine answered. 'Asleep.'

'Then I won't disturb her.' Katherine pulled the door to and stood waiting for him to go. He didn't move. He asked softly, 'How does she seem to you?'

'She's anxious, and not very happy,' Katherine replied frankly. 'She misses her little boy. And I believe she's troubled by rumours that she may rather unexpectedly become queen.'

Richard's eyes narrowed, glittering. The stone-grey light that poured from them reminded Katherine of why people were sometimes so afraid of him. He had a way of freezing, as if he'd turned to a demon-winged statue. She'd said many impertinent things to him in her time, but now she feared she'd finally overstepped the mark.

He breathed out softly. 'Anne isn't one to let idle rumours trouble her.'

'I know, which makes her concern all the more telling. Is the gossip idle? There's only one man who can answer that, but I imagine I'd as soon get blood out of a rock as I would get the truth from you.'

Richard looked at her. He didn't seem the same man who had given her the Spanish mare; he was guarded and preoccupied, not himself, unless it was a self she had never seen before. Then he gave a dry smile. Moving closer to her, he said very quietly, 'Does it surprise you that I have thought about it?'

'No.' Her skin prickled from his closeness. 'I wouldn't blame you at all.'

'Is not blaming me the same as supporting me?'

She felt her blood rising and heat flashing over her body. 'Are you admitting that you aim to—'

He took her arm and drew her under the edge of an arras. Behind it was a little alcove, a doorway onto a roof. Moonlight came under the door, a bar of silver.

'There is really no other answer, Kate.' His face, not quite hidden in shadow, looked sad, gaunt and chillingly determined. 'I wish my brother hadn't died, so we could have stayed in the north. However, he is gone, and his death has thrown us into chaos. A child-king always brings factions and bloodshed. I'm the only one who can stop it. To end this uncertainty and shape the world as I want it? Of course I shall aim for that.'

Her heat turned to shivers. He had just confessed to her what he had been denying in public. The darkness around him seemed to be moving, like a heat haze. At last she managed to ask, 'What will you do?'

'Whatever I must.'

'Legally? I don't see what can be done to remove Edward—'

His expression silenced her. 'Fear must help me where the law won't. I desire a strong and stable kingdom, Kate, not another thirty years of warfare. *I have no choice.*'

Determination shone out of him like fireglow from the heart of coals.

'It sounds unbelievably dangerous. If you fail, you're inviting assassination, attainder, execution—'

'I know.' He looked steadily at her. Again, she had the disturbing impression that there was a haziness around him, rearing over his left shoulder. 'It's kind of you to worry about me, but you mustn't. Nothing was ever gained without risk. I seem to have a taste for it.'

'You should be telling your wife this, not me.'

He leaned against the wall and closed his eyes for a

moment, as if in pain. 'Anne is exhausted. When she's stronger, when there is firm news, I'll talk to her then. Now . . . this would only add to her well of troubles.'

Kate arched her eyebrows. 'Whereas I am a bottomless well?'

He placed his hand on the velvet of her sleeve, touching only the material, not pressing her skin. 'Yes, you are, and that is a pure compliment. I know that any secret I ever share with you vanishes as if into a locked vault.'

That's truer than you know, she thought. 'I'm no gossip, my lord.'

'Well, I've told you now,' he said, so low she could barely hear him. 'What are you thinking?'

'Why do you care what I think?' she whispered back. 'I have no political power.'

'No. But you always speak frankly to me. And if you're going to give me Medusa stares and disapproving looks for the rest of time, I'd like to be forewarned.'

Katherine nearly laughed and bit her lip to stop herself. How eerie, to be whispering to him in the dark, to be alone with him in the very heart of the plot, enfolded in dark radiance as if they were under the bedclothes together. His hand on her sleeve felt like adultery.

'I think,' she said slowly, 'that England should have the best king possible. The best appointed. That is the philosophy of the Motherlodge.'

'Diplomatic Kate. Would *you* be glad?'

'Yes.' Her whisper coiled around them, a hissing snake. 'Yes, I would. I'd have you a thousand times rather than that reed of a Woodville child. You have nothing to prove. Wouldn't you rule the whole kingdom as fairly as you ruled the north? Who could not prefer you? And no, because it will bring you danger and Anne unhappiness. But mostly, yes. I suppose I've spoken treason, but you wanted the truth.'

'And it sounded fervent.'

'Did you doubt my loyalty?'

348

He studied her for a time, his eyes changing like water: gentle, shrewd, thoughtful, calculating. 'No, but you're no flatterer saying one thing to my face and another behind my back. You see more clearly than most. I value that.'

'I'm here for the comfort of your wife,' said Kate. 'She may wish this wasn't happening but she will support you wholeheartedly, whatever you do. And so will I.'

Richard nodded gravely. 'To crown a king I trusted, then return to my life in the north . . . that would have been my desire, but it can't happen. It never could. And I've gone too far along the road to turn back.'

Then he lowered his head, breathing out as if all the strength had gone from him. There were bruises beneath his eyes.

'I think you should go to bed and not haunt the roof all night,' she said. 'You don't look well.'

'To tell you the truth, Kate, I have not felt well these past few days. I can't eat, can't sleep, there is a strange numbness in my right arm.'

'Is there anything I can . . .'

'It will pass.'

She had trailed off because the fog that hung about him suddenly resolved into clear focus. A thick-bodied, gossamer eel was coiled about his chest and neck, squeezing. It looked like the elemental that Kate had seen Eliza Shore summoning in the Motherlodge. Its shapeless head hung over Richard's shoulder, regarding her from languid half-moon eyes.

'Oh, *shit*,' she whispered.

He looked quizzically at her. 'I'm sure you have a good reason for swearing at me. May I know it?'

'You have a . . . someone has . . .'

'What?'

'You feel as if something is feeding upon your strength, don't you?'

'Yes. How did you know?'

'Because there is an elemental attached to you, the

sort that usually lingers near the sick. A body made of many elementals, rather. It will not have attached itself of its own volition, only if someone shaped it and coaxed it to attack you. Someone who knew what they were doing.'

Richard was staring at her as if she'd told him there was a deadly scorpion upon his neck. 'A sorcerer?'

She nodded miserably. She couldn't mention Eliza Shore's name. It was part of her oath to Auset, never to betray a sister.

'Can you . . . ?'

'I'll try,' she said. Her skin crawling, she reached towards him, her hands travelling over his chest, into the body of the elemental. It was like thin air; she couldn't grasp it. Then she felt her skin tingling. Grey coils went around her arms. They were both caught and she was suddenly terrified. If she recoiled, it would split in two and they'd both be infected.

Forcing herself to breathe, she whispered to the elemental, coaxing it as Eliza had, as if enticing a shy wild animal. Gradually it began to slither onto her. She turned cold. Thousands of tiny fangs nibbled at her skin. Weariness crept over her and she could have fallen down and slept where she stood, not caring if she never ate, drank or saw the sun again.

She made herself think of sunlight, imagined light shining out of her own heart, her whole being like a rosy apple, all health and vitality. The entity recoiled, detaching itself from her body and sliding down her arms. Once it reached her wrists she flung it away and saw it dissipate into a thousand wisps that vanished under the moonlit bar beneath the door.

'It's gone.' She sighed, shuddering. Turning, she looked into Richard's grave, incredulous face. 'Whoever conjured it wanted to harm you. I doubt it would have killed you, just made you feel too deadly to do anything.'

'I wouldn't believe it, were it not for the fact that I

felt you take it from me. I felt it leave!' He touched his collarbone where it had lain and began to rub his shoulder. 'Gods, the feeling is returning and tingles like fire. Some enemy sent a demon to afflict me! Will it come back?'

'No. And it wasn't a demon. These beings are stupider than a horned toad and they have no more malice in them than a flea that sucks your blood.'

'But to think I had no idea it was there . . .' He crossed himself. She smiled sourly.

'Then it's a good job I did.'

'Yes. Forgive me, I don't know what to say. Except my heartfelt thanks.' The back of his hand rested briefly against hers.

'You'll be able to rest and eat now,' she said briskly. 'In my capacity as healer, I suggest you go and do so.'

He stirred and held back the corner of the arras for her. 'You were on your way somewhere,' he said. He sounded vague with shock. She could only wonder at what was in his mind. 'May I walk with you?'

Kate hurriedly shook her head. She couldn't tell him she was on her way to Raphael. Her lover would have to endure the night without her. 'No, it was only that I thought I heard something outside the door. Good night, Your Grace.'

'Good night, my lady.' He turned, and she watched his narrow form moving away until it melted into the blackness.

A butcher's block, stained crimson, oozed blood on the sloping green beneath the walls of the Tower. It was all that remained to mark Lord Hastings' demise.

Now it was over, Raphael felt drained. He saw the same blankness on the faces of the other men who'd arrested and executed William Hastings. There had been a soaring exhilaration in it – seizing a lord out of a council meeting, manhandling him down the stairs and into the

351

dusty summer air, forcing him down upon the block and the axe falling, Buckingham supervising like some deathly seraph – a horrific thrill that soon congealed. In the aftermath, a handful of them sat in a guardhouse that looked out upon the green, trying to numb the shock with ale.

The door was open and Raphael and Francis Lovell were sitting side by side on the step.

'Hastings was a conspirator and a traitor,' Lovell said very softly to Raphael, 'but people are going to ask why he didn't get a proper trial.'

'Should he have done?' Raphael asked. 'The end would have been the same. He doomed himself.'

Lovell's face, usually cheerful, was grave. 'Richard couldn't afford to wait, or risk him being acquitted. The same with him sending Ratcliffe north to order the execution of Rivers and Grey, even though the Council refused to agree to it. He has to strike fast and hard, or he won't survive. But it's dreadful work. I fear it will do great damage to his reputation. He might salvage it, if he acts quickly. He's walking on the edge of a bloody sword, Raph, but there's no other way.'

'And we promised him we'd walk all the way with him,' Raphael said. Their eyes caught and held for a moment, confirming the pact. Francis gave his forearm a quick, steadying touch.

A traitor, Raphael thought. He felt a mixture of sorrow and contempt for Hastings; his naivety, his disbelief at being found out, a stumbling confession of guilt and insistence that he'd meant no harm. Horror as it dawned upon him that the Lord Protector, a man he'd considered a friend, was not inviting a debate, but dispatching him to immediate death.

Richard had trapped the conspirators. He'd summoned them to the White Tower, ostensibly to discuss the coronation: Hastings, Bishop Morton with Dr Fautherer at his side, Archbishop Rotherham, Thomas Stanley and their various assistants. A charming and affable Duke of Gloucester had greeted them, lulling their suspicions. Then Richard had left to ensure that his men-at-arms were quietly positioned outside the doors. None of them knew he planned anything beyond the traitors' arrest, not even Buckingham. Raphael suspected the execution had not been planned at all.

'I called you here to discuss political matters,' he had said on his return. 'However, it seems we must discuss the cousin of politics instead. Conspiracy.'

And with those words, the convivial mask was peeled back to reveal an inferno of terrifyingly controlled fury. Richard presented the accusation that they had conspired with the Queen to destroy him. Even the smooth face of Morton turned to wax. The Bishop realized, faster than the others, the peril they were in.

'Have I fought at my brother's side all my life for this? To place a clan of gluttonous, drunken wastrels in charge of the kingdom? To see another thirty years of strife over them? I fought beside Edward but you' – glaring at Hastings – 'you drank with him and ruined him. You, Rivers and the Queen's depraved sons. The Queen and Mistress Shore have practised sorcery upon me, and you colluded, in the hopes that I would wither to a shadow and vanish. But I am still here. There's no evil act you've committed that I have not discovered.'

Raphael had never seen anything as pitiful as Hastings sickly, astonished face. He'd thought he could manipulate events as if it were some idle game of chess, with no one hurt. When Richard leaned over him, one finger pointed dagger-like at his heart, he physically shrank.

'There is no worse traitor, my lord, than a friend. Who slid the nectar of poison into your ears?' The room was silent. Incredible to see all those powerful, voluble men in thrall to Gloucester's presence. Indicating Morton, 'Cosy, the image of you whispering with this bishop, this lover of Lancaster.'

'Richard, I never betrayed you,' Hastings gasped. Perhaps he'd seen Richard's ruthlessness. His fear was sudden and absolute.

'No, far worse. You betrayed England. Now let all traitors see what they shall receive for their treason!'

At that shout, the doors to the chamber burst open. Dozens of armed men surged in. There was a scuffle. Raphael remembered the sound of Thomas Stanley yelling indignantly. Even Morton had uttered moans as two armed men seized him, sweat drizzling down his face. Raphael himself had been directed to seize Fautherer. The Doctor of Divinity had remained passive and expressionless in Raphael's hands, and his limbs had felt like those of a skeleton through his robe. Even now, Raphael couldn't shake off the remembered feel of bones through cloth.

Hastings went quietly at first, limp as putty in their hands. It was only when they got him outside and he saw the wooden block – hurriedly dragged into place at Richard's order – that he had begun to fight then, when a priest was brought, to weep.

Richard had been like iron, implacable. Raphael thought he would execute them all, even the bishops, and from their faces they were sure of it too. Instead, he had brusquely ordered them to be imprisoned. It was over.

'Their faces as they were taken away,' said Raphael. 'The bishops and Lord Stanley, I mean. I never thought I'd see such powerful men reduced to the state of frightened children.'

'Quite pleasing, to see Richard knock them off their perch,' said Lovell. 'Hastings knew the risk he was taking, and he was jealous of Buckingham. Richard was never sure of him.'

'He's sure now,' Raphael said drily, and Francis grinned. 'He doesn't waste any time, does he?'

'Don't look so worried. Just learn a lesson: don't get on the wrong side of him.'

Raphael frowned. 'His anger in the meeting . . . that

wasn't a performance. He was genuinely, passionately furious.'

'And afterwards, as white and shaken as Hastings. He's strong, Raph, but he's not made of stone.'

'What will happen next?'

Francis shrugged. 'As far as everyone knows, the coronation of Edward the Fifth is still due to take place. If only he can persuade the Queen to let Richard of York out of sanctuary to attend his brother's coronation, otherwise York will be a focus for rebellion, and that's the last thing Richard needs.'

'The Queen must let the boy go,' Raphael said suddenly. 'There will have to be sermons, public declarations that Edward and Richard of York are bastards, barred from the throne. The citizens will have no choice but to ask Richard to take the throne instead. Most will be relieved. As for any that oppose him – after today, they won't dare say a word. Richard will be king.'

'What?' Lovell exclaimed. 'Where did all that come from? Are you a seer?'

'I don't know,' Raphael said, startled. 'I can see it, as if it's all happened before.'

Katherine lay awake long after Raphael had fallen asleep beside her. He'd described the day's events in details so vivid she could see, touch and taste them. She shouldn't have been shocked by Richard's actions; she'd known for years that he could be ruthless, and what else could be expected? His own father and brother had had their heads sheared off and stuck on spikes for the world to gape at. What other way did he know? It wasn't so much the beheading that shocked her, as the fact that Richard had all but told her, in advance, that he was preparing to do it.

Did he say that? she thought, struggling to remember. Or am I reading too much into his words, an intention that wasn't there at the time?

How did he know about Eliza Shore?

I didn't tell him, she thought in frustration. I didn't even tell Raphael, so he can't have passed it on. How did he find out? Will Mistress Shore assume I betrayed her, and complain to the Motherlodge? What if Richard finds out I knew and didn't tell him?

Kate tried to calm herself.

She imagined Hastings, smugly plotting, savagely awoken. She murmured into the darkness, 'If only he'd executed that oily Bishop Morton alongside him, and that miserable red-faced Rotherham. Not the done thing to execute priests indeed!'

A cry startled her, making her heart race with infectious fear.

Raphael had woken, and was sitting up, trembling. As she reached for him, she felt cold sweat on his skin. Her touch made him jump. He turned and glared at her, eyes mad, as if he didn't know who she was.

Alarmed, she fumbled for the low-burning lamp and turned up the wick. His face was streaked with sweat. His chest glistened, rising and falling like a panting hound's.

'Raph, sweetheart, what's wrong?' she said.

No answer. His expression contorted suddenly with despair, or disgust. He turned his head away.

'Raphael!' She spoke sharply, gripping his arm. 'Wake up! It's all right. What was it, a nightmare about the execution? It's all right, it's over. Raph? Tell me about it. Then it will go away.'

After long moments, his face cleared and he lay down again. He stared up at the ceiling, both hands on his forehead.

'No,' he said at last. 'It wasn't the execution.'

'What, then?'

'It was about a man writing a book.'

She didn't mean to laugh; it was an expression of surprise. 'Writing? How was that so horrifying as to make you wake up in a sweat?'

'Don't laugh at me!' he said savagely.

'I'm not laughing. Tell me.'

He groaned. 'It hasn't happened for a long time. I hoped it was over. I saw a – a clergyman of some kind, walking up and down in a long galleried room with a row of high windows. It was very clear. Dusty light coming in and shining on dark wood and gold. He was describing what happened today, dictating it to a clerk. That's all. The scene was bland, yet it filled me with this ... this ineffable dread, a feeling that I was going to be trapped forever in that room with the man droning on and on. He was describing what happened at the Tower meeting, but he kept stopping, backtracking to embroider what he'd already said, to make it more and more dramatic, and to show Richard in the worst possible light. He had Richard accusing all and sundry of witchcraft, of withering his arm and deforming his body, things like that. And each time he described something new, it was as if I could see it, and I would be stuck there forever, seeing the same thing over and over again, and our good master a little more deformed and wicked each time, until he was a monster. It was hideous. That's why I cried out.'

'Oh, love,' Katherine whispered. She didn't know what else to say. She pressed close to comfort him, but his body stayed rigid and resistant to her touch.

Raphael asked softly, 'Is this wrong?'

Kate grinned. 'What? That we're lying together and still aren't married? That makes us no worse than half of London and no better than most of the court.'

'No,' he said, kissing her head. 'I mean Richard taking the throne.'

She rose on one elbow to look at him. 'Why? Are you having doubts?'

'I don't know. I love him, but the dreams . . .'

'Your dreams seem to me an expression of your own fears, and those fears must come from too close an adherence to the outer world.'

He frowned at her. 'What do you mean?'

'The outer world is black and white and goes in a straight line. It says that really, Edward the Fourth's son should follow him, no matter what. But the hidden world goes in spirals and tangents. There is no King Arthur coming to save us, love. We must make do with the best king available to us at the time. That isn't always the rightful king, but it must be the best appointed king.'

'Strange,' he said, curling strands of her hair around his finger. 'You never say what I expect you to, Kate, but it's always right.'

The coronation was magnificent, the most glorious England had ever seen.

As she moved into the cathedral, part of the procession holding Anne's train, Kate could hardly believe it was real, still less that she was part of it. Later she would write to her mother, telling her everything: the sparkle of jewels, the froth of lace and tissue; the seas of knights, lords and ladies; the floods of cardinals and archbishops. Everything shone, painted with light. Gold and crimson, lush ermines, violet and lapis, emerald and sapphire; the colours blurred and shimmered in her sight. Her heart lifted with awe. Richard was King.

The King of England was once my lover, she thought, faint with the wonder of it. Now I hold the train of his wife, his Queen, and I love her, and I would not have anything different, but . . .

One of the other train-bearers caught her eye. It was Margaret Beaufort, the noble and immensely rich widow who had married Thomas Stanley. Kate barely knew her except by sight. They had nothing in common. Lady Margaret was of different rank, age, disposition, religion, everything. She was tiny, narrow-faced and intimidating. (How Thomas Stanley could have preferred her to Eleanor was beyond comprehension; the allure of her estates must have been overwhelming.) Kate desired no contact with her, but they were yoked together on either side of the train and she was examining Kate from beady, perceptive eyes. The look was one of haughty judgement and contempt, as if she'd caught Kate dancing naked under the moon. It said, *I have your measure, witch.*

Kate looked away, burning. The voices of the choir were like crystal, rising into the lofty vaults above them, lost in the ether yet constantly renewed. Like flock upon flock of birds spun from golden glass, the voices soared. Katherine saw Richard with his eyes closed, caught up in the music. Anne was solemn and dignified, but her face showed strain. She found a frail smile for Kate and her other women.

Kate witnessed the King and Queen stripped to the waist and anointed with holy oil, their heads tipped back, their hair falling on their shoulders – Anne's fine red-gold, Richard's sable – as they made their sacred vows. Then clothed again in finery.

So Anne's father, Warwick the Kingmaker, had got what he wanted after all. A royal crown upon his daughter's head. They sat together at last upon the throne of England: King Richard III and Anne, his Queen.

Kate wondered what Edward and his little brother were thinking in their Tower apartments. Were they sad, or bitter, or playing some game, oblivious to what was happening? Even relieved. The danger was over: the Woodvilles broken; the House of York restored; Richard safe, his family and his supporters safe; there would be no more war. From where he stood in the ranks of knights, Raphael caught her eye, and they both smiled.

Katherine looked up at Richard, glorious in velvet and furs upon his throne. He was gazing straight over her head, oblivious to her, so she could stare at him unabashed. He was the centre of the world, darkly shining, enigmatic, compelling. Perhaps she was only seeing an image of her most extreme desire, not reality. Yet for a moment she came close to hating the pale, resigned woman at his side. No, not hating Anne, never that. Only wishing her to vanish.

The King of England was once my lover, she thought, and wept.

Chapter Fourteen 1483: Robin

He contents the people where he goes best that ever did prince; for many a poor man that hath suffered wrong many days have been relieved and helped by him and his commands in his progress. And in many great cities and towns were great sums of money given him which he hath refused. On my truth, I never liked the conditions of any prince so well as his. God hath sent him to us for the weal of us all.

Dr Thomas Langton, letter of 1483

The Duke of Buckingham paused in an antechamber to the King's apartments to admire his appearance in a mirror. The reflection pleased him. His face was a perfect oval, as beautiful as a boy's. His cheeks had been shaved to glassy smoothness, eyebrows plucked into arches that the ex-Queen Elizabeth would have envied. His hair lay groomed to golden perfection over his shoulders. He thought of it as a Lancastrian look: an ethereal shape gifted by God, the outwards sign of their moral superiority over the earthly Yorkists.

Still, he was a Yorkist now. His magnificent clothes of sapphire coloured velvet, all his new servants, his countless lands and titles, he owed to the Yorkist King he'd helped to create. The costly chain he wore was set with white roses, not red.

'Kingmaker,' he mouthed to his reflection. Raising one eyebrow, he gave himself a long, satisfied look.

Buckingham had hated the late King. Edward had given him nothing, no preferment, not even his legal rights to the inheritances that had been stolen from him. He had pushed him out of office and out of court, only using him when it suited him. Edward had made no secret of his dislike for him, and Buckingham's resentment had grown extravagant. How he had loathed that gigantic, coarse-living idiot.

Richard was his opposite. Richard was spare and dark, thoughtful and discreet. He was strong-willed, and yet amenable to good ideas and common-sense suggestions. He was the very centre of the world. In him, Buckingham had found the twin half of his soul.

He'd joined Richard in his own dukedom of Gloucester. The King was some way into his royal progress, which would take him on a serpentine route throughout the realm. At Reading and at Oxford he had bestowed generous honours on his supporters, and shown kindness to the widows of the traitors he had executed. He wanted it to be seen that his quarrel was only with the men themselves, not with their families.

Henry Buckingham moved towards the doors that lead into the King's private chamber. He'd imbibed several glasses of wine, but was not so drunk that anyone would notice. Attendants announced him, ushered him in and retired. Richard was alone. Even the ever-present Lovell, Hart and Tyrell were absent. Buckingham liked none of them.

Richard was dressed in crimson, the doublet cut close to his slim form, with long pointed sleeves lined with green silk. The colour was dramatic, and suited the darkness of his hair and brows. He might not have the height or flamboyance of his brothers, but he knew the importance of presenting himself as a king. Appearances were everything. Yet there was a quality about him, deeper than the trappings of monarchy could bestow. It was a presence, a strength and a vigour of spirit that shone out of him; and something of a wounded quality, too, that made him wary of his peers, yet tender towards the downtrodden.

He is more than a king, Buckingham thought. He is . . .

blasphemous to think it, but he is like a quiet god. And if he is a god, then I am his archangel, ever at his side and armed with swords of flame. Ha.

The image pleased him. Dark and light. Together, they made a whole.

'Harry, welcome.' Richard was rising from his seat, smiling. The Duke knelt and kissed his hand; the gesture transmitted a current of joy between them. *Together we overcame our enemies.*

'Your wife has not yet joined you upon your progress? I trust Her Grace is well?' Buckingham spoke disingenuously. He knew perfectly well she wasn't there, and was indifferent.

'She remained in London to rest for a few days. She'll join us later. By the way, I've a present for you.' The King turned and took an object from a sideboard, holding it out across his palms. It was a sword in a scabbard. 'It belonged to my father-in-law.'

He meant the Earl of Warwick, who had been so loved and so hated. Harry breathed out in awe. How uncannily appropriate this was, as if he and Richard had been sharing the same thoughts. It was a gorgeous object, the scabbard as hard as polished wood and set with rubies, the hilt of black bronze sporting a ruby the size of a walnut.

'Have you not given me enough?' Buckingham received the sword with grace. He drew the blade – only an inch or two – and the steel was as lovely as silver. 'You can't part with this.'

'A gift lightly parted with is not much of a gift. Here, I'll place it on a table for you to take when you leave.'

'Thank you,' Harry said softly, and kissed Richard's cheek. The present was astonishing, and made him feel oddly restless. There was something ominous in it, reminding him that no gift of Richard's ever seemed quite enough to content him. I'm like the graylix, Harry thought, disturbed. The more I eat, the hungrier I feel.

'Sit down.' Richard waved him to a chair and leaned

over the table that stood between them to pour claret into goblets of purple Roman glass. 'It's good to see you.'

'I hear that the royal progress is going wonderfully well.'

Warmth suffused Richard's face. 'Yes. To my surprise.'

'Why are you surprised?'

'I'm not the king they were expecting.'

'A better one by far,' Buckingham said fervently. Their glasses chimed. He drank deeply. 'Don't be surprised, Richard. Your reputation is known, your appearance and retinue as magnificent as befits your station. People are much taken with your generosity and charm.'

'Harry, please. I don't want to see my last meal again.'

'I'm stating facts. You're a grown man, not an untried child. The acclaim with which they greet you is a simple measure of their relief and trust. They love you.'

Richard sat forward, resting his elbows on his knees, twisting the stem of the goblet between his fingers. 'Apparently. Which is gratifying. Some, but not everyone.'

'They're not worth your attention.'

'A plot to release my nephews from the Tower, thwarted. Another plot discovered, hatched by Elizabeth Woodville to spirit her daughters abroad, so that if anything befell the boys, she might marry the eldest to some foreign prince who'd be happy to aid her in claiming the throne. Certain factions will not desist until they are in the grave. I have to give this a little attention, at least.'

'None of her children has any claim! Bastards, all!'

Richard sighed. 'The trouble is, few believe it, especially in London. They think that the story of Edward's first betrothal was concocted. My enemies were bound to say I invented it. Or, knowing Edward, they might well believe it, but still think it would have been good manners for me to ignore it.'

'How are the former conspirators behaving themselves?'

'Fangs drawn. I pardoned them quickly to reassure the rest of the nobility that the danger was past. Rotherham is contrite and doing his duty assiduously. Thomas Stanley made his peace with me – swore it had all been a misunderstanding and he'd be the most dutiful of subjects from now on.'

Buckingham gave a sharp grin. 'It must have been quite pleasant to see a sheen of fear on his pompous face.'

'It was,' Richard said softly.

'Do you trust him?'

'Not as far as I could throw him in full armour. But he values his survival. For as long as he's frightened of me, he'll make a good workhorse.'

'Wise Richard.'

He grinned, mouth twisted up at one corner. 'I'm not sure I've done anything wise in my life. Only expedient. How is our friend the Bishop?'

He was referring to Morton, who had been placed in Buckingham's custody in the Duke's chief castle in Wales. Harry shrugged. 'A docile prisoner. Guest, I should say. He thinks of himself as my guest and I treat him as one. It's more civilized that way.'

'Contrite?'

'I doubt it.'

'No. That's why I gave him to you. He's not one to be cowed into submission and he'd give up breathing before he gave up plotting. It's best he's out of harm's way.'

Buckingham looked at his master and felt the same pang again, stronger now. Desire, envy. Richard was as elegant as a panther, with just that edge of self-deprecation that made him irresistible.

Harry thought of all his own achievements: he'd spoken eloquently on Richard's behalf; persuaded Parliament to accept his claim; presented their petition to Richard that he take the crown; presided over the coronation. Richard had showered him with rewards. He, Buckingham, had risen from nowhere to become the most powerful man in the kingdom. And yet . . .

Nothing was ever enough. The moment he'd seen Richard

crowned and anointed, something coldly acidic had begun to gnaw at his heart. A strange series of gauzy imaginings had passed through his mind. He saw himself at Richard's side in place of Anne, both of them with their heads thrown back as the holy oil sheened their chests. Their sable and blond hair streaming, set on fire by light that dropped through high cathedral windows . . .

He wanted to be Richard's equal, to rule with him, to press close to him, to pass inside him and through him . . . *to be him*. Impossible. There could be only one king.

'You're frowning,' Richard said after a few seconds. 'Is something wrong?'

Buckingham's hand shook. He took another gulp of wine. He'd had enough now to make him pleasantly dizzy and unguarded. 'One or two unfinished matters.'

'Have I left anything out? Neglected some estate, title or office that you wanted?'

Harry drew closer, poised on the edge of his chair. 'You have given me more than I asked for or deserved. Never think that I am ungrateful. No, I was only musing . . . Do you love your wife?'

Richard looked sideways at him. 'What a strange question. Yes, I do.'

'Come on, I know there's no passion between you.'

'She has often been ill.' The words fell coldly.

'I wish to God mine had. Creator knows, you were lucky to choose your own wife and not have some great Woodville heifer thrust upon you, some lumbering milk-maid with a better moustache than her father.'

The King laughed out loud. 'That's a frightening image, Harry.'

Buckingham turned hot. 'It was not meant to be funny.'

'Catherine's not so bad. She's nearly as fair as her sister.'

'And nearly as much a bitch, but without the charm!'

'Calm down.' Richard spoke kindly, still laughing. His

very kindness made Harry more furious. 'You were one more victim of the Woodvilles' greed, but it's over now – you've got your revenge. Do you want a divorce? You might have grounds for annulment, but only the Pope could sanction it. If you have a new wife in mind . . .'

Harry shook his head impatiently, took control of himself. 'No, no. I would prefer no wife at all, but I wouldn't cause such pain to my children. They see something to love in her even if I can't. I have a daughter. You have a son. We spoke some time ago and agreed that it would be a fair idea if they were to be married.'

And then one day I would be father to the Queen, just as Warwick was, though he never knew it. And like Warwick, it's the closest I will ever get.

Looking up, he saw the withdrawn light in Richard's eyes and his heart tumbled in disbelief.

'Well,' said Richard, and paused. 'Nothing was agreed. You mentioned it and I may have said it was a fair idea and said I would consider it, that's all. Harry, dear friend, I understand, and if I had a second son, I'd give him to your daughter gladly. But Edward is Prince of Wales. I'll almost certainly have to make a foreign marriage for him. It's politics, that's all. You appreciate that.'

Buckingham expected to feel rage and instead felt an odd hollowness, hope falling away. 'I believe this is the first time you have refused me anything.'

'Then forgive me for refusing you in just this one thing.' The steel eyes regarded him with measured warmth. 'It's only politics. I've tried to express how much I value your support in words, in rewards; nothing is adequate. So the greater part of my gratitude to you goes unspoken, but never doubt that it's there.'

Harry leaned back in his seat. His thoughts were awhirl.
'Well, the truth is . . .'
'What?'
Even half-drunk, Buckingham realized he was about to say too much. *The truth is that I don't care for my*

367

daughter's status, except in as far as it enhances mine. I want it for myself, not for her.

Amid an ocean of reward, the single refusal of favour had made him feel desperately insecure. He must claw back what he'd lost, bind Richard eternally to himself with chains and blood. The facts sobered him. *All the power I have is through Richard alone, and I must remain the archangel at his right hand, or lose everything.*

'The truth is I'm not concerned for myself,' Harry said. 'I'm more concerned about these plots you mention.' His voice fell. 'The Princes . . .'

'What of them?'

'As long as the Princes, the *ex*-Princes, live, the Woodvilles will never stop plotting rebellion.'

Richard didn't know it, but Harry was parroting the words of Bishop Morton. Buckingham and Morton had spent several evenings sitting on either side of the fireplace, as he and Richard were doing now; and although Harry had been reluctant at first to spend time conversing with the enemy, he'd gradually found the older man's company seductive. There was something compelling in Morton's smooth, plump, clever face. He was worldly and funny; but there were hidden streams inside him. Harry found him fascinating to talk to. It was a game, to guess what was going on in Morton's mind, what he would say next.

In the course of a late-night conversation, the Bishop had uttered the last thing Harry would have expected. It was a confidence, spoken in his low, melodic voice, not a remark for public consumption, but the plain truth. 'You know that as long as Prince Edward and his brother live, the Woodvilles will never cease plotting to place him on the throne. No wise king would let them live. And if Richard falls, so will you.'

'They are a problem,' Richard said.

'Which will only grow worse as they grow older.'

'I could certainly wish them not to exist.' Richard stared into the fire. 'But since they do, there's nothing to be done but to keep them close and powerless.'

'Nothing to be done?'

Harry leaned forward and placed his hand on Richard's knee. Richard gazed at him. Dark understanding passed between them.

'I cannot arrange their murder, if that's what you mean. They are children.'

Harry gave a soft sneer. 'They are almost men. If Edward considers himself old enough to be crowned, then he's old enough to swallow the fate of all deposed kings.'

'Choose your words carefully, my friend.' Perhaps Richard's smile was meant to soften his words, but it only made him look more menacing. 'You seem to be suggesting that I deposed him, rather than being offered the throne by right.'

'No, no.' Buckingham sat back, flustered. 'My words were badly chosen. I am only thinking of your security, your well-being.'

'I am not sure their deaths would aid my security. I must think of something to do with them that will not have their supporters forever rallying armies against me and soaking the land with blood for another thirty years.'

In a quick movement Harry was kneeling in front of the King, hands clasping his arm, urging and desperate. 'Kill them. It's the only way. If we are to go on ruling . . .'

His breath dried his throat. Richard sat so still under his hands that he might have been dead. Eventually he tilted his head to look down at Buckingham. His eyes glittered under the thick soft lashes. His lips were parted.

'Take your hands from me.'

Harry obeyed. He jerked back as if stricken by a bolt of leaden lightning. The King's face and demeanour were like granite. He slumped on his knees, shocked to numbness and unable to shape a single clear thought.

'We? Did you say *we*?'

'A slip of the tongue.'

'Really. Do not tell me what to do, Harry. I have no feelings for them. They are only a reminder of all the harm my brother's passion for a Lancastrian wrought upon this family, but I cannot kill them.'

'Alive, they're too dangerous.'

'And dead, they're a source of opprobrium, fuel to the fire of any chancer, such as that posturing idiot Tudor, who thinks he can lay claim to this throne. But the throne is fully tenanted.'

'I know.' Buckingham hung his head. All his eloquence and composure had deserted him. He burned with confusion and Richard had done this to him, Richard alone.

'For God's sake, get up. Are you drunk?' the King said mildly, and he obeyed. Richard uttered a soul-deep sigh. The only colour in his face was from the fire. 'Harry, both boys are ill. I dare let no one see them. They're kept in the finest apartments, with the best doctor in London to attend them, but I don't know what will happen. Half of me wishes they would die, but the better half of me dreads it. If they do, I know I'll never sleep a quiet night again.'

'Oh, God,' whispered Buckingham. Richard looked so haggard that he felt sick. 'But my dear lord; they would be better gone.'

'And so, my lord, would you. Never speak to me of this again.'

At that moment, Buckingham's confusion resolved into clarity. Love and hate were a breath apart. The image of Richard shifted even as he regarded it: a dear friend, a figure of power, an object of desire. Object of envy. Obstacle. This was the closest Buckingham was ever going to come to him. He could not love him physically, nor cling so close they became one fused being, a god-king. Richard was always going to be there, but separate, standing between him and fulfilment: a wall.

That was all Richard was now. He saw it clearly. A maddening, untouchable basalt wall. Buckingham wished he truly were an archangel, with eyes of flame to burn the King he'd created to ash.

Richard was oblivious. For that, Harry hated him more.

The King tapped his fingers to his lips, hands in the prayer position. When he looked up at last, his face was calm but his eyes were bleak and formal. 'Harry, we must still work together. This has been an unfortunate misunderstanding. We'll forget this conversation ever took place, and no more shall be said.'

'As you wish.' Buckingham bowed, equally formal. 'If I spoke out of turn, pardon me.'

'Don't let me keep you from your lodgings. I'm tired. I'll write to you at Breccon.'

'Yes, sire.'

'Don't forget the sword.'

'Of course.' Buckingham swallowed. It gave him a sour feeling to receive the beautiful weapon, but he took it anyway. Their hands brushed. 'Thank you.'

'Don't let's be at odds,' Richard added gently. 'I have need of you.'

If only you did, Buckingham thought, as he slipped away to be alone with his misery. If only you did.

Each time Katherine visited her mother, the landscape of Lytton Dale still amazed her. Escarpments swept up to the sky, rugged but softened by dappled light, in ever-changing shades of green. Limestone crags stood scoured bare. She saw the familiar peak of Bride Cloud, the sloping sheep meadows and, below, the winding wooded griffes of home. She saw the steam of the falls at Old Mag Heads rising through the trees. All so poignantly familiar and yet strange, for it was so long since she'd been home.

Trapped in London until Anne was ready to leave, Kate had been desperate to join the King's procession. She envied Raphael, always in the thick of affairs. By the time the day came for them to join the King at last, Kate had felt like a graylix unleashed from the chain.

The reception that the King and Queen received had amazed her. It grew more ecstatic the further north they went where Richard was known and loved. Sometimes the intensity of the greeting, as they entered each town in turn, brought Kate to tears. It was hard to reconcile this with the swirling treachery of London.

As they travelled towards York, Kate felt an itch of obligation and longing. She'd asked leave of Anne to visit her mother and ridden here with Ursula and Nan and a handful of men in royal livery, to startle Eleanor with their finery. The tireless Spanish mare Richard had given her had carried her all the way. The whole village had turned out to see them arrive.

'It's such a shock,' Eleanor said later, when they were alone in the solar. 'Richard of Gloucester taking the throne, I mean. Such a great change.'

Katherine knew her mother had had a certain fondness for King Edward. She'd been deeply upset by his death. 'For the better?'

'I don't know, dear. I don't know him. I know he is well-loved in the north, and adored in York. I'll not forget the way he protected us on the day of the ceremony. All I can say is that I am heartily glad it's not his brother George.'

Kate said thoughtfully, 'It's as if everything was leading to this.'

'Will he come here on his royal progress?' asked Eleanor; naively, Kate thought, which was unlike her.

'I don't think so.' Kate laughed. 'He can't call at every tiny manor! You are talking of the King.'

'I've dealt with kings before,' Eleanor retorted.

'Yes, I know, but of course he won't come here. He and the Duchess – sorry, I mean the Queen – they can't wait to reach Middleham to see their son.'

Eleanor looked steadily at her, and Kate realized her question had not been naive at all. 'That is why I wondered if he might come here. Not to honour me.'

Kate said nothing. She pressed her lips together. Her throat hurt unexpectedly.

'You still haven't told him?' asked her mother.

'No. I decided I never would. You know that.'

'Not even now?'

'Now would be the worst time of all! It would look as if I expected money, reward from him, compensation, advantage. I couldn't. The humiliation of being paid off! It would be an insult to my dignity!'

Eleanor was nodding. Her face bore the hint of a solemn smile. 'A determined woman with a cool head.'

'In some ways, I am your daughter. In others, I'm a rag-bag of confusion.'

A floorboard creaked. A boy stood in the doorway, awkwardly twisting a cap between his hands; a slim lad in rough linens, a battered leather jerkin and long boots, with the smell of horses rising from him. Kate started. Her mouth dropped in amazement at how tall he'd grown.

'My lady,' he said, bowing to Eleanor and Kate in turn. 'My lady. You sent for me?'

He was soft-spoken, with a long, pale, gentle face and thick dark hair to his shoulders. Thirteen years old now. He was the image of his father; no one who saw them both would have a moment's doubt. Every time Katherine saw him – too rarely – the resemblance took her breath away.

Eleanor said, 'Yes, Robin, Lady Katherine is here. Come, sit down and talk with us.'

Hesitant, the boy went to them and perched on a foot-stool. Katherine never knew what to say to him. It had been easy, when he was a small child, to dandle him on her knee for a few minutes, then hand him back to the woman he called mama; when he was older, to play games, to read with him or talk of animals, fishing, hunting, trivial things. Now, though, he was too old to be treated as a child, too young to be called a man.

There was no surliness in him, despite his age. He regarded her, as he had from the beginning, with cheerful, intelligent eyes. He loved horses, but he also loved books. He'd received all the good care and affection that Eleanor had lavished on a dozen natural children, and had grown up good-natured and bright: a son of Auset. Eleanor was training him to assist her steward, one day to take over the management of her estate. For all his scuffed clothes, he was a young gentleman. Katherine felt the usual guilt and sorrow sweeping over her more strongly than ever this time.

'How are you?' she managed at last.

'Very well, my lady,' he answered, cheeks flushing. He loved seeing her; that was always heartbreakingly plain.

On an impulse, she took his hands and folded them between her palms. 'What have you been doing?' She could hear the tremor in her own voice.

'I've got a hawk,' he said excitedly. 'My own firehawk. I call her Kit.'

Oh, Goddess, I am going to cry, Kate thought. She had never allowed herself to grow too close to him. The wave passed and she said, 'Will you show me?'

'With pleasure, Lady Katherine!' he said, jumping up and taking her hand, like a nobleman taking his lady to a royal banquet. Eleanor watched them go. Kate glanced back to see her smiling ruefully.

Outside, the day was beautiful, the sun a gold haze through floating pollen. The red house basked in utter peace. She heard the old familiar sounds of home: hens clucking, the occasional snort of a horse, the voices of men and women working the fields, the constant bleating of sheep. She smelled the scent of baked grass. She thought of her adored mare, Mab, long dead, but Kate felt she only had to look over the stable door and she would be there.

'You're always away for such a long time, my lady,' said the lad as they walked the length of the house towards the stables. 'I hardly know you when you come back.'

'I know. I'm sorry, Robin. You know why, don't you? I'm lady-in-waiting to the Duchess of Gloucester, who is now the Queen.'

'And you can't often leave such an important person,' he said seriously.

374

'Not often, no,' she said. 'I'm glad you understand. But I come as often as I can.'

'Kate,' he said, turning to her and shielding his eyes from the sun. She always told him to call her that, but it always took him a while to do so. 'May I ask you a question?'

'You may, my lord.'

'Are you my mother?'

She stopped in her tracks. The question was so blunt, so casually asked. Her answer came out like a reflex from a blow to the stomach. 'Yes.'

'I thought so.' His eyes and nose were screwed up against the bright light.

'Who told you?'

'No one. I knew, that's all. Why would you pay so much attention to me, but not to the other boys around the place? And I worked out that Jenny wasn't.'

Jenny was a young woman Eleanor had brought from York to pretend the babe was hers in return for a comfortable position in her household.

'How?' Kate, stunned, could only utter monosyllables.

He shrugged. 'I just knew. Not when I was little, but by the time I was seven. She's so different to me: looks different, has different ideas, everything. So I asked her one day if she was my mother. She went red and hesitated a lot but in the end she said no, she was my adopted mother because my real mother had had to go away. I asked her straight out, like I asked you. She wouldn't say if you were my mother. I thought about it for a long time, but it wasn't that hard to work out.'

'Well, aren't you clever!' Katherine growled, laughing at the same time.

He grinned back, not hurt but pleased with himself. 'Then it occurred to me I ought to make sure. I thought you might lie about it, but I'm glad you didn't.'

They stood looking at each other. Again her mouth ached with tears.

'Don't cry,' he said. 'Why do women cry so much? I'm quite glad to have you as my mother, actually.'

'Well, thank you, kind sir. And I'm glad to have you as my dear son.'

Kate saw no need to tell him she was sorry. Among the nobility it was common for sons to be cared for by nurses and taken from home early, while the mother was a distant figure owed respect. It was also usual for a woman who had a child out of wedlock to hide the fact and leave the infant with others. Robin knew that. Eleanor had not shielded him from real life, only from one crucial fact.

His real name was Richard, but he had been nicknamed Robin for his round, perky charm as a baby.

'I wish someone had told me before,' he said. 'Why didn't you?'

'Because I wasn't married to your father. I was in disgrace.'

'Oh. Are you married to him now?'

'No, dear.'

'Are you still in disgrace?'

She laughed. 'I might be, but only in the outer world. In the hidden world, it doesn't matter. I know Eleanor has taught you that. Unfortunately, the outer world is the one that holds sway.'

'It's all right.' he said quickly. His eagerness to reassure her was touching. 'I wanted to know the truth, that's all.'

'And I . . . I'm glad you know.'

'That's all right then. Come and look at Kit.'

He brought the firehawk out to her, poised on his gauntlet. As they stood in the stable yard, admiring the raptor and stroking her small fierce head, Kate said gently, 'Robin, you won't tell anyone what you know, will you?'

He looked at her, his steel-blue eyes serious. 'I'm not ashamed about it.'

'I know, but everyone believes you are Jenny's child. It wouldn't be good for people to know the truth. Perhaps there are a few who suspect, but as long as the official story stands that you're Jenny's, they can go along with it and save causing themselves or us any embarrassment.'

Robin frowned. His mouth was sad. 'I can keep a secret. It doesn't seem fair on us, though. What's wrong with you having a son? We're as good as anyone. What have we done wrong?'

'I know. It's utterly mad. But we really can't tell anyone yet.'

'Will we ever be able to?'

'One day. We're not the only people this has ever happened to – it's just that in the outer world, the mother always gets the blame.'

'Turn the world inside out, I would,' Robin said under his breath. 'Wouldn't you, Kit?'

'She is magnificent, isn't she? Would you show me how she flies?'

Kate watched him, so thrilled by his hawk wheeling above the crags and folds of the demesne. She wanted to be proud of him, but couldn't let herself. She had done nothing to shape him into this straight-limbed, sweet-natured boy. He could so easily have been bitter and hated her. His good character was just the whim of fate.

They walked back to the house together in silence, the firehawk proud on his arm. Presently he asked lightly, 'Who is my father?'

She groaned. 'I can't tell you that. The time isn't right. I will tell you, eventually, I promise; just not yet.'

He considered this. He was a child who considered deeply but without malice, she observed. 'All right, I'll wait, on the condition that I may ask three questions about him.'

'You are very pert,' Kate gasped, amused. 'Go on, then. I don't promise to answer, but you may ask.'

'Was he a great knight?'

'Very great.'

'Is he still alive?'

'Yes.' She awaited, in apprehension, the last question.

'What would my surname have been, if you'd married him?'

'You cheeky—' She exhaled, and stroked his hair, one brief gesture of affection. 'Our secret?'

'I promise, on Kit's life.'

'Your surname would have been the best.' And she whispered it into his ear.

Leaving the boy to tend his hawk, she returned to her mother. Eleanor was in the solar, poring over a huge book of household accounts. The light in the room was all amber and dusty red, flaring in a pure white line around her mother who sat there elegant in russet, her feet resting on a tapestry footstool.

'He knows,' Kate said helplessly.

Eleanor looked up. 'I didn't tell him.' She beckoned Kate to sit beside her on the settle.

'He worked it out for himself, little devil.'

'I must say I'm not surprised. Was he upset?'

'He didn't seem to be. He's a wonderfully clever boy,' Kate said, and stared at her hands. 'He's probably realized who his father is by now.'

'No wavering, now, and no regrets,' Eleanor said, calm and firm. 'We did what was best; we could have done nothing else. We shall have to decide what to do for his future; whether it is best for him to leave here, after all, though the Goddess knows, I should miss him sorely. We don't have to decide now, but soon.'

'Yes.' Kate sighed. 'So much to decide.'

'Have you told your young man about him?'

'Raphael? No. I suppose I should have done, but I couldn't. I think he would have accepted it, but . . . the words wouldn't come out, and now I've left it too late. Mama, I have never told anyone. A dishonoured woman is not who I am in the outer world, I can't break my own image into pieces. And Raphael would want to know who the father was, which would make it a thousand times worse. Gods, how could I ever tell him *that*?'

'Well, it is your prerogative, but it might be a shock to him, if he ever finds out.'

'He doesn't own me,' Kate answered. 'There's no reason for him to find out.'

Carefully, Eleanor asked, 'Are you going to be married?'

'I suppose we will.' Her mouth dimpled. 'Let me put it this way: we really *should* have been married six years ago. We meant to do so this spring, but King Edward's death and everything else got in the way. Now there never seems time. We are always at the beck and call of our master and mistress. Our lives are theirs, not our own.'

Eleanor gave her a probing, serious stare. 'It takes but a few minutes to marry.'

'And a lifetime to wish you hadn't,' Kate muttered.

'I'm not bullying you into conforming with the outer world, but we must be practical. This is important, because it pertains to the future of Lytton Dale. If you marry Raphael, he will be our lord, and your children will inherit. If not, young Robin may be able to inherit, but only if the truth of his parentage is made official, and if special provision can be made by the King. But you refuse to tell the King. All in all, it could be a tangle. And what if you had another natural child?'

'Mama, I won't. I am very practised with herbs, charms and the phases of the moon. Other women come to me for instruction all the time.'

'Is Raphael a good man? A true son of his mother? A man who can be part of us, part of the hidden world, who would strengthen us and not undermine us?'

'Yes, Mama. All those things.'

'Then would you explain to your obtuse old mother why you are plainly putting off marriage to him?'

'I don't know!' Kate cried. She leaped up and paced around the solar. 'I love him dearly, but the idea of being his wife – of losing my freedom – it makes me panic. I would feel like a trapped bird, trying to beat its way out of a cage. We like being lovers and friends – but marriage? I don't know. It seems so absolute, like the clang of a prison door. An end to any other possibility. It scares me. I don't know.'

Eleanor rose, went to the door and glanced out – to make sure no one was nearby listening, Kate realized, turning warm – then closed it.

'I doubt it would be that dreadful. It would quickly feel quite safe and ordinary. What does he say? Has he pushed you on the matter?'

'Sometimes, but not of late. I think he's realized I always change the subject. And, as I said, we've been too busy to think of it. We're happy as we are.'

'You know it's rare for women of our station to have the luxury of falling in love and choosing our husbands. Many might wonder why you're hesitating. "An end to any other possibility." Whatever do you mean?'

Kate went to her mother and clasped both her hands. It was hard to catch her breath properly. 'Mama, is it possible to love two men at the same time? Each in an entirely different way?'

'This second man would not be your dear late father or some kindly uncle, then?' Eleanor said drily. 'Raphael has a rival?'

'No. He's married, he cares nothing for me, but . . . I can't stop thinking about him. He haunts me. I don't know that I even love him. I don't know what to call it.'

'Infatuation?'

Kate shook her head vehemently. 'Gods, no, it's far beyond that. I can't describe it. It's like being ensorcelled. Very slowly bewitched and chained in velvet, so soft you don't even know it's happened until it's too late. It's terrible, yet I don't want it to stop. I cannot marry Raphael while I feel like this about another man.'

It took a lot to shock Eleanor, but she looked astonished. She held her breath for so long Kate thought she'd turned to wax. 'Well,' she said, and laughed. 'Actually, many women have married while they felt like that about another man. You are fortunate indeed to have a choice. Who is he?'

Kate pressed her hands to her face. 'Oh, gods,' she murmured at last. 'Don't make me tell you. It's Robin's father.'

'Oh, Kate!' Eleanor's cry made her jump. 'After your protestations that he meant nothing, that he might as well have been a passing shepherd? After you have served his wife all these years?'

'There's no need to examine every detail of my humiliation,' Kate snarled.

'How has this happened?'

'I don't know. Being too close to him all this time, I suppose. Or else I was lying, when I said the first time I met him had no effect upon me. Yes, I was lying through my teeth, especially to myself.'

'Has anything else . . . occurred between you?'

'No, of course not. We agreed we would be as strangers and forget the folly of our extreme youth. And he is renowned for his faithfulness to his wife. And I love Raphael.'

'Oh, Kate,' she said again. 'He's the King.'

'I had noticed.' Katherine drew herself up. 'But he . . . he confides in me sometimes. You know the beautiful mare I rode here? He gave her to me.'

Eleanor looked scandalized. 'Did he? Why?'

'Supposedly for nursing Anne through an illness.'

'Which is only your normal duty.'

'I know. I don't know what he was thinking.'

'You should have refused the gift.'

'How could I?'

'Because he's no business to be toying with your feelings in that way! This is impossible.'

'I'm fully aware of that.'

'Let's see. Could your feelings stem from awe of his position? Kings, saints and lords do tend to attract excessive

381

devotion. Added to that, you can't have him. When you could, you didn't care; now you can't, you're obsessed.'

Kate gripped her own elbows, fingering the hard angle of them through her sleeves. 'You may well be right. Next time the fever comes over me, I'll think of what you've said. Yes, he is unobtainable, and always was, apart from a few impetuous minutes; and so am I. I wouldn't want to be his mistress. I just like the thrill of his presence, and having this secret. I can't help it, or reason it away. I don't even want to give it up. But that's why I can't marry Raphael.'

'Does Raphael know?'

'Of course not! I could never tell him. Imagine how hurt and betrayed he'd feel.'

'There is an answer.'

'Yes?'

'For you and Raphael to leave the King's service.'

Kate stood silent. At last she gave a hard shake of her head. 'Raphael would never leave him, not if archangels came down from heaven with a divine command. And I can't leave Anne.'

Eleanor's eyebrows twitched. 'From what you've said, you should be violently jealous of her.'

'I have been, but it's separate. I've grown to love her as much as I loved her sister.'

Her mother pressed the back of her fingers to Kate's cheek. 'I can't berate you for having altogether too much love in you. Better too much than too little, especially in a priestess of Auset.'

'This concern is only a corner of my life. It doesn't rule me.'

'But it's preventing you from marrying. You *could* leave, if you wanted.'

'Obviously, then, I don't want to. I like tormenting myself.'

'Then I give up, Kate! Do as you will; but be on your guard. I know how easily passion can turn to hate. I hear

382

the King has enemies enough without you turning against him also.'

'I won't do that. The best appointed, yes?'

'So it is felt by the York sisterhood.'

'I was at the London Motherlodge. Bridget Marl said the same to me. So I try to love him purely as my king and do all in my power to aid him.'

'Wise Kate.'

'By the way, you're not obtuse, Mama, or even so old.'

Eleanor's eyes glinted. 'Thank you. Just as well, in the *Mater Superior*. Your son's future is important, but so is yours. I need you out in the world, and your position is ideal. You mustn't be turned aside by sentiment, nor by distractions in the shape of men. Marry, or not, as you will, but don't be turned aside. Kate, I want you to follow me as *Mater Superior*. All the sisters are in agreement. You are as much heir to the hidden world as the Plantagenets are to the outer.'

Buckingham sat at his own fireside in Brecknock Castle, huddled around a bowl of mulled ale. Every bone ached from a long and furious ride. Bishop Morton paced slowly – glided, rather – about the large, shadowy, firelit room.

'He expressed a wish that the Princes should die,' said Buckingham. 'I was shocked. I wept, I trembled, I tried to dissuade him; he was like stone.'

Morton stroked his chin as he paced. He looked thoughtful and compassionate; impossible to tell what he was really thinking. 'Let your conscience be clear; you did what you could. Not your fault that he was deaf to your tender entreaties.'

'I did my best.'

'And this has plainly distressed you,' Morton said gently.

'Creator knows what price I'll pay for it.'

'You are afraid of him?'

'Of course I'm bloody afraid!' Buckingham exclaimed.

'Look how he dealt with Hastings, with Anthony Woodville!'

A low muttering came from Morton.

Harry said, 'What are you doing?'

'Praying for you.'

Fear turned into a flood of terror. The story he told Morton might have been skewed, but the result was the same: he and Richard no longer trusted each other. 'Thank you, Your Grace, but there's no need.'

'Alas,' said Morton. His hand, plump and warm, passed over Harry's silken hair. 'His actions towards the Princes have already made him unpopular. If they die there will be a turning of the tide against him such as this kingdom has never seen. And if he falls, Harry, you fall with him.'

Buckingham sat shivering. Morton was right. 'A rebellion? They won't dare.'

The Bishop leaned down and whispered in his ear, making him start. 'It's already begun. A strange alliance of Woodvilles and Lancastrians, in truth, but it only serves to show that the whole world will unite against him. And you, his prime henchman.'

'What shall I do?'

'Distance yourself from him. Do so immediately and decisively. Make it clear you are his henchman no longer. If he falls, you need to be on the winners' side, not the loser's.'

'Oh, God,' Buckingham moaned. 'Richard, Richard . . .'

'Don't lament, my lord. He's betrayed you. He's not the man you thought he was. He's impulsive, ambitious, violent – a Yorkist, through and through. And you, I know, are at heart a Lancastrian still. Look at your angelic hair, your fine lineaments, your noble blood. Your own claim to the throne is the equal of his, is it not? A case could certainly be made.'

My claim to the throne, Harry thought, electrified.

'Think what fate will befall you if Richard remains on the throne. Think of poor Hastings who counted Richard a friend. Don't hesitate until the same happens to you.

Seize the initiative. Ride the flood that will sweep him away.'

'Yes, but, my claim. My claim! You speak as if the Princes were already dead.'

'King Henry the Seventh. Good King Harry.' Morton gave his closed-mouth laugh. 'The crown would look very fair upon your golden head. The portraits will be striking.'

'This is all very well,' Buckingham said, rising to his feet to escape the stroking hands, 'but what of your friendship with Margaret Beaufort, and your known support for her son, Tudor? A rebellion must have a figurehead. No one will accept me in that role!'

'It will be Henry Tudor, of course, but he's weak. Let him lead. Support him. Later, you will be the real power. And in time, the only power. Will you help us?'

Buckingham felt caught up a wild fever. He knew he'd never get what he wanted from Richard. Richard would be cast down. Harry Stafford, Duke of Buckingham, could rise in his place. Tudor was an irrelevance, a straw man who'd be washed away in the autumn rain.

'Yes,' he breathed. 'Yes. God forgive me for loving that Yorkist devil who led me astray. Let me be loyal to my Lancastrian blood.'

'That is my true, good son,' Morton said, and embraced him. 'I will trust you now with some information. It's up to you how you use it: to help the Yorkist hog who's about to fall to the hounds, or to help God's chosen, the rising House of Lancaster.'

Raphael had expected to be in York, amid the festivities to celebrate King Richard's arrival. Instead he found himself on the road with Sir James Tyrell, riding back towards London.

Tyrell was a taciturn man, a good head taller than him and of menacing aspect. Raphael had been uncertain of him once, but now knew Tyrell well enough to feel easy with him. Behind his facade was a plain, honest nature, something the King had recognized at once, although it had taken others weeks to discover it.

Richard had dispatched them to the capital to procure fine materials from the royal wardrobe with which to make robes for his son. Edward of Middleham was to be invested as Prince of Wales. No fabric fine enough could be found in York, it seemed. Raphael could have done without the exhausting journey, but for King Richard, he would climb mountains.

Dreams came to him on the road. For once, they were not distressing. They were all of York, as if he were still there. The delight of its citizens at the arrival of their King and Queen had been wild beyond imagining. Raphael had wept to see them crowded all along the roads and on the walls; the banners, the flowers, the roar of joy that had slammed physically into him. Those images crowded his mind as he slept. The King and Queen and their young son, riding beloved, among their own people, at home and adored and, for once, truly happy.

He and Tyrell had barely arrived in London when a messenger came to them. They were in the royal stables, pulling off their gloves and stretching to ease their aching limbs, thinking fondly of hot baths and a tavern supper, when a man arrived, whey-faced and as nervous as a spy. Robert Brackenbury requested them to come with all speed to the Tower of London.

In the stark light of a lamp that depended from the doorway to the Garden Tower, Brackenbury waited for them. He was a formidable man, but now looked ashen and terrified.

'Sir James, Sir Raphael. I heard you were due on an errand from the King and I didn't know who else to send for. There's no one else I trust. Since you are so close to the King, you're the only ones I dare— You must come with me.'

Within, lamps made chill pools of light. The ascent of the stairs took an age. A climb into a grey tunnel that pressed down with a terrible, groaning weight of stone and age. The others did not speak. Raphael was shaking so violently – from cold or fear – it was all he could do to lift one foot after the other.

This was so like one of his dreams, he could not tell if he were awake or asleep – that was the food of his terror, and the source was the terrible silence that lay above.

It was a pleasantly appointed chamber to which Brackenbury led them. A fair size, with the stone walls hung with tapestries and a huge bed with thick curtains to keep out the cold. Candle flames painted the walls with nervous light. The room smelled of thin sour sweat, of the musty reek of urine, of pus and of sickness. The air was clotted with turbid elementals.

In the bed lay two boys. The elder was dead, his face ghostly blue against the pillow. There was a terrible swelling about his lower jaw and bruises around his eyes. The eyes were half-open and held a look of immense sadness and resignation. The younger boy was still breathing. Each breath came with a shallow, wheezing effort. The bloom of a rash was turning black beneath his skin. His forehead held a frown of intense concentration, but when Raphael touched his wrist, he didn't react. He was deeply unconscious.

Two male servants, the boys' attendants, stood looking on in complete helplessness.

'Where's the doctor?' Tyrell asked. 'Where's the priest?'

'The chaplain was so distressed he wouldn't stay,' whispered Brackenbury. 'What in heaven's name am I to do?'

The younger boy gave up his spirit as they watched. Raphael saw the tiny spectral lights of other elementals gathering, like flecks of dandelion down, attracted by the escape of his soul.

The men crossed themselves. No one spoke. The only sound was a sobbing gasp from Brackenbury. Raphael looked round at their faces and saw that they were not only grief-stricken, but mortally terrified.

After a long time, Brackenbury spoke. 'They're dead. Creator have mercy on their souls. God have mercy on us!'

'How,' Raphael attempted, 'how did this happen?'

Brakenbury spoke in a creaky whisper, as if frightened he would be overheard. 'The elder, Edward, was ill before he came here, with a great abscess in his jaw. The physician bled him, did everything he could, but it only made him worse. A few days since, he succumbed to a great fever and grew weaker and weaker until he faded. His brother had been ill with stomach pains before he was let out of sanctuary. He seemed better at first, but the disease came back and got hold very quickly. I believe they took a fever on top of the afflictions they already had and both were too weak to fight it.'

'Are you sure?' Tyrell said suddenly.

Brackenbury flinched. 'I was here with them every day, I or their attendants.'

'What about visitors?'

'No one came but priests and Dr Argentine.'

'Where's the physician now?' Raphael asked.

'Fled, days ago. He claimed the King had withdrawn him, but I don't believe it. I think he saw the boys were going to die, and fled out of fear.'

'And where's this damned chaplain?' Tyrell asked.

'I've sent for him again. Until he comes, gentleman, will you pray with me? There's no more we can do.' Brackenbury broke down in tears.

Between them they mumbled prayers over the bodies. The two faces on the pillows looked pitiful. Raphael stood dry-eyed and shuddering in this chamber of quiet horrors, knowing the image would haunt him for the rest of his life. He still wasn't sure if this was a vision; he'd had others that seemed as real. At any moment he'd wake up in an inn, still miles from London. But he didn't. The scene went on and on, with no awakening.

At last they crossed the boys' hands on their chests

with the symbol of the Lamb pressed into them, pulled the covers over their faces, and drew the curtains around the bed. Tyrell took charge.

'We must keep this between ourselves,' he said at last. 'It's not up to any of us what we may or may not say about this. Only one man can decide, and that's the King himself. Until he knows, we must all keep silent. Every man in this chamber must swear himself to secrecy in God's name, on pain of damnation if he break his oath.'

All swore.

'Who can bear to break this news to King Richard?' Brackenbury said desperately. 'They were in my care!'

'Someone must,' said Tyrell. 'We're away back to York tomorrow, as soon as we've finished our business at the royal wardobe, Raphael and me. We'll tell him.'

'Is it possible,' I asked, 'that there's a whole layer of history that's been lost, not recorded anywhere?'

'What layer?' said my tutor, glaring at me over his glasses.

'Well, for example, that some form of pagan practise survived into the fifteenth century? I don't mean remnants of folk tradition, but an official, organized temple?'

'Good God, what the devil have you been reading now?'

'Not reading,' I said. 'At least, I'm not sure. I feel as if I must have read it somewhere, but in a book or manuscript I can't find, and that no one else can recall either.' I honestly didn't know how to explain myself to him. There was no way to phrase it that would not bring the full weight of his mockery upon my head.

'Then you probably dreamt it, rather than read it.' He doodled with a ballpoint pen on a pad.

'Not dreamt. It's like a memory. I keep recalling things I'm sure I've learned, but when I go to look them up, I can find no reference to them. It's as if I'm absorbing a history that might have taken place if things in our world had taken a very slightly different path. For example, if Isis worship had survived in Britain . . .'

I cannot describe my tutor's expression as I tried to explain. It was worth broaching the subject, just to see his face. He looked as if he was about to ask if I had 'women's problems' and propose an immediate visit to the campus doctor.

Finally he leaned forward, clasping his hands on the

390

desk. 'Are you sure you're on the right course? Might I suggest a transfer to theoretical physics?'

I gave him the puzzled look he was expecting.

'If it's alternative universes you want, they've got a million of 'em.'

And that was all. He didn't, after all, try to talk me out of my mad ideas. I was starting to like him. Even though I'd tried to talk around it, he seemed to know what I was getting at. *He knew*. I suspect the leathery layers of cynicism are too thick to be chipped away; but at least I'm not afraid of him any more.

It was a probably a mistake to broach it. What could the poor man say? But the story of Kate and Raphael was so vivid, so pressing, that I had to share it with someone. That night, curled up on Fin's sofa with several glasses of red wine inside me, I finally told her everything.

There was some lifting of eyebrows to begin with, but soon she was listening intently, interrupting only to ask pertinent questions. We talked and talked that night.

'You must think I'm utterly insane,' I said at last.

'It's a bit off the wall, like a past-life experience,' she said. 'But the way you tell it is very nearly completely rational.'

I grimaced. 'Thanks.'

'And this is why you said to me, "It's happening now"?'

'Yes. Because it is. To Raphael, and to me. Not in real time, obviously, because his story has gone on for years and I'm experiencing it over a few weeks. But the feeling is unshakeable that in his world, it's happening to Raphael *now*. And to Kate, and to Richard.'

'Wow,' said Fin. 'I'm almost envious.'

'Don't be. I'm scared.'

I drank more wine. She refilled my glass. 'Why?'

'Because I know how the story ends. Richard tries to save the day by making a last, bold charge against

391

Henry Tudor. Men who should have fought with him turn against him and he's cut down and slaughtered, and almost all of his own men are killed with him.' I was shaking.

'And there's no point in me repeating that this was five hundred—'

'No. It's taking place *here*.' I raised my hand in front of my face, touching my nose. 'In a world just a breath away from ours, but which we can never touch. I feel so helpless, thinking there must be something I can do to change things, but knowing I can't.'

'You and Raphael can touch it with your minds, in some way. You said he was having visions of the way Richard will be remembered in our world?'

'I can't be sure of that. I suppose there will be hostile historians and a Shakespeare in his reality too. But yes, I always felt he was picking up fragments from our past, rather than from his own future. The thing is . . .'

'Yes?'

'None of Raphael's visions has ever gone beyond the history of the Richard that I know. The same iron wall slams down.'

Fin leaned forward, frowning, chin resting on her fingers. 'Don't take this wrong, but couldn't that be proof that it's your own imagination generating this?'

'It could be, but . . .' I told her about the exchange with my tutor. 'According to theoretical physics, no less, it could just as feasibly be real.'

'Well, don't be scared, Gus. I'll be here.' She gave me a reassuring pat on the shoulder. As she did so, we both jumped. Something passed through the room, a winged, grey malevolent rag of a thing. I caught the briefest glimpse of its cold, grinning skull.

Fautherer.

Chapter Fifteen 1483–4: Harry

Tell your King Richard that I made him King of a nation
of perjurers and he must not blame me if I was no better
than my fellow subjects. Tell him it is a rotten carcase
he has to rule.

Patrick Carleton, *Under the Hog*

Here all is well and truly determined, for to resist the
malice of him that had best cause to be true, the Duke
of Buckingham, the most untrue creature living.

King Richard III, letter to Bishop Russell

Along the length of the Isis went Dr Fautherer, a death-like
figure luminous in the greenish mists, the ferryman upon
the Styx. From palace to palace he slid silently in his
barge, whispering softly to nobles and courtiers. He passed
from cathedrals to taverns to monasteries, from one secret
meeting to another, spreading rumours like tar.

Dr Fautherer was industrious. Scurrying as surely as
a mole through its secret burrows, he carried messages
between Elizabeth Woodville and her son the Marquis
of Dorset, to Buckingham and Bishop Morton and thence
to Margaret Beaufort. He transmitted their letters and
passionate wishes to Lady Margaret's son, Henry Tudor,
the self-styled Earl of Richmond, exiled in Brittany. *The
time is right. Come home. All God-fearing men are ready to rise
with you and unseat the Hog.*

Discontent stirred, whirling its way in cloudy streams

throughout the kingdom. Rumours rose like the stink of the Isis, like fog creeping up the walls of the Tower. The Princes had vanished. They were dead, murdered by their own uncle.

Dr Fautherer looked upon the web he had woven, and was pleased.

'I can say nothing.' Richard sat immobile. He was a statue of limestone, draped in crimson and black. 'I can say nothing at all.'

They were in York, in an upstairs chamber of the Mayor's house. It was a close, dark room heavily panelled with cherry wood and hung with banners of royal blue. Apart from Tyrell and Raphael, only Ratcliffe and Lovell were there.

'Still, you must do something to—' Lovell began.

'What could I say? What announcement could possibly be made?' Richard's voice was low and distant. The room was too hot. 'If I announce that my nephews were taken by natural causes, none will believe me. They are all too willing to believe the worst.'

His face, shadowed by raven-feather hair, looked hollow and haunted. Tyrell had broken the news in his usual plain-spoken way; the only way it could be told. Richard's reaction had been silence. No words, no anger, only the deathly shock that now lay on them all.

Francis Lovell had wept, and had turned away to hide his tears from the King.

'These rumours began long ago, while the boys were still alive,' Richard went on. 'I could have produced them then. I chose not to, because to do so would have been to lend credence to the rumour-mongers.'

'You can't react to every spiteful tale,' said Ratcliffe. 'It's beneath a king's dignity.'

'I ignored the rumours, and they grew wilder. It seems to me that I'm damned, whatever I do. But who now knows that the boys are dead? No one except we few in this room, and their attendants who were sworn to secrecy. Yet the rumours continue to spread like the plague.' He sat back, fingertips pressing into the table edge. His face was immobile, while his eyes were flooded with the restless light of the fire. 'I cannot answer them. If I were to say, alas, my brother's sons have died of fever, I would still be blamed and called a liar as well as a murderer. And who's to say they are so wrong?'

'What?' said Lovell. He sounded angry.

Richard folded his hands. His eyelids fell, making dark crescents against his cheeks. His voice was raw.

'I knew the boys were ill. They were in my care. There was always the chance that they might die. I sent them the best physician I could find, for all the good he did. Perhaps sun, fresh air and freedom might have effected a cure, but I could not take the risk of setting them free. And there, the Tower itself consumed them.'

Raphel saw the long fingers compressing, turning bloodless.

'No point in worrying who's to blame,' Ratcliffe said gruffly. 'The lads were ill, as you said. It's over and done.'

'But not forgotten. Never forgotten. I shall be damned for it.'

'Tell the truth, then!' exclaimed Raphael.

'I can't,' Richard said patiently. 'They will not believe me, any more than they wanted to believe the boys were bastards. I killed them. I wished them dead.' He looked up, his eyes liquid fire. 'We should be careful what we wish for, in case it is granted.'

The silence was unbearable. Fire elementals rushed up out of the grate, turned to smoke and clustered around the King, glaring over his shoulders like an army of tiny demons. Raphael had to stifle a cry. He blinked hard, and the elementals vanished.

'There will be no announcement,' Richard said at last. 'I'll write only to Buckingham; he'll keep the news close and secret. It may even please him.' He exhaled. 'At least in silence there is dignity, and perhaps the benefit of the doubt. Raphael, you are frowning at me.'

'Not at you, sire. At those who would refuse to believe your word. I can't believe they'd be so perverse!'

'Can't believe they'd dare to think ill of me? That's touching, but you can't be so innocent.' King Richard turned his gaze on Raphael. The gaze seemed to fall from a high, chill place, not of earth; it took Raphael apart. 'I have often cursed their existence. Alive, they were a focus of unrest. Dead, they are still a focus of unrest. I cannot win. Will their deaths make my reign easier or infinitely harder? I wonder.'

Raphael had a sudden violent sense of disorientation. He felt that this had all happened before. He'd gone through this same wretched scene a dozen times, each time slightly different, but as terrible. The room echoed with phantoms.

'We are all agreed, then?' Richard said, quiet and stern. 'Once we leave this room, we never speak of this again.'

York was a sweet illusion, with its pageants and banners and celebrations. Richard was adored there. He always trod easily in the city, as if a mantle of chains had lifted from him. His young son, Edward of Middleham, shone on the cathedral steps, glorious in robes made from the rich materials that Raphael and James Tyrell had brought from London. He stood bewildered and happy between his proud parents, bearing all their hopes: the new Prince of Wales, about to walk the sun-golden carpet of the future. Not for him the destiny of his cousins, fading to skin and bone in the Tower.

Raphael's heart shrivelled. Not for him that fate – as long as Richard was secure on the throne. Nothing was certain. The wheel of fortune lifted men up and cast them down.

After their visit to York, the Queen returned to Middleham with her son, taking Kate and her other ladies with her. Raphael was lonely then, but relieved. He hadn't been able to tell Kate about the Princes' death. Something had turned dark inside him. It was all he could do to look her in the eyes, let alone tell her the truth.

Richard, meanwhile, continued on his royal progress. True to his word, he did not speak of his nephews again. He was self-controlled, calm, even cheerful, as if nothing had happened. But there was a shadow upon him. Sometimes Raphael could almost physically see it.

In Lincoln, where the breeze blew the tang of the sea across the wide, bleak fens, devastating news arrived. It was everything Richard and his supporters had been dreading. Richard's face blanched with anger – as stark as the stone walls of the inn in which they were lodged – as he received the urgent messages sent by his loyal friend, John Howard, Duke of Norfolk.

Treason. A large number of knights and gentlemen – former servants of Edward IV, disaffected with Richard – had formed an unnatural alliance with the Woodvilles and with the pretender, Henry Tudor. Uprisings were planned across the kingdom.

'Buckingham?' said Richard. It was nearly a whisper. 'The Duke of Buckingham is involved in this?'

The messenger, haggard and nervous, nodded. 'It is so, sire. It was Buckingham himself who wrote the letter to Henry Tudor. They have invited Tudor to invade the kingdom, to deliver it – pardon me, sire, these are not my words – to deliver it from tyranny. To claim the throne, on condition that Tudor takes an oath, as agreed between his mother Lady Beaufort and Elizabeth Woodville, to marry King Edward's eldest daughter—'

'Over my dead body will he marry her,' Richard interrupted. 'But, *Buckingham*?'

'The story goes about, as my lord of Norfolk has gleaned, that when the Duke heard of the deaths of the two Princes, he repented with many salt tears that he had ever supported you.'

'He's a bloody liar!' Richard shouted. His voice rang off

the walls. The messenger jumped. His voice fell again. 'The last time I saw Harry there was no hint . . .' He was lost in thought for a moment. Then he gave an ice-cold grin. 'I gave him a gift . . . Oh God. The Earl of Warwick's sword.'

'This is Morton's doing,' said Ratcliffe.

'More fool me, for taking Harry's honeyed friendship at face value. For imagining he was strong enough to resist Morton's wiles.'

Raphael saw his eyes turn silver with misery. He'd never seen Richard look so alone, and so silently furious and impenetrable.

'Margaret Beaufort, who ingratiated herself with Anne and myself deeply enough to carry my wife's train at our coronation, repays me by entering into a devilish pact with Dame Grey. Beaufort's precious son! A penniless fugitive, a nobody, descendent of two lines of bastards. By what reasoning does he make a claim to the throne of England?'

Lovell looked sideways at Raphael. His face was as grim at the King's. He said, 'No doubt Buckingham is egging him on in the hopes of claiming the throne for himself.'

'Yes. Buckingham,' Richard said acidly. Betrayal was the one thing he could not endure. Raphael saw the thorn go deep into him and burn. 'He who swore the utmost devotion of his entire being to me. Tell me, what is the worth of his loyalty?'

Richard turned away and began to dictate the first of many letters to his secretary, only to seize the letter and finish it himself, in a savage, untidy hand, the pen a tiny dagger spilling black blood.

Katherine helped to peel Anne out of her robes. Underneath, her skin was pale and cold, marked by the indentations of seams. She had lost weight, Kate realized, noticing suddenly how thin she was. Although the chamber was baking in the roar of a stoked fire, Anne was shivering.

'Oh, Kate, it never feels real to wear those garments. Not real at all to be called Queen. I feel like a cookmaid dressed up.'

She smiled. The effect, on a face that was bloodless and smudged with brown shadow around the eyes, was ghastly.

'Your father wouldn't like to hear you say so.' Kate wrapped Anne in a thick fleece-lined mantle and sat her down near the fire.

'My father got what he wanted, a daughter upon the throne, even though it was not as he planned it.' Anne's voice had a bitter edge Kate had never heard before.

'My lady, you're not well.'

'A little fever, that's all. Ah, I would keep Edward at my side forever if I could. My son, Prince of Wales. Why are men so eager to be king, when it brings nothing but care? Must he go through years of trouble, the trouble that Richard endures constantly?'

Kate paused in combing her hair. 'What trouble?'

Anne reached for a letter. She unfolded it and held it flat, so that Kate could read it as Anne related the contents. 'An uprising, by the man we thought his dearest ally: the Duke of Buckingham!'

Kate stared at the letter in disbelief. Rebellions fermenting all over the country, an unbelievable coalition between Buckingham, the Woodvilles and Henry Tudor. Richard wrote in such despair that she could almost hear the black laughter in his tone.

'I never trusted Harry Stafford,' Anne said quietly. 'He came from nowhere, promising Richard the world.'

'I didn't think much of him,' said Kate. 'Too fond of his own looks. Barely spoke a word to me. He was full of himself, and resentful of everything and everyone else. But he did seem devoted to Richard.'

'Richard gave him all he asked for, which was far more than he deserved.'

'Then why's he doing this? Has he gone mad?'

'I doubt it.'

'Are you sure, absolutely sure?'

Anne's long hand opened, indicating the facts scrawled in Richard's rushed, passionate handwriting. 'I think that the moment he saw Richard crowned, he was jealous of him. He thought being Kingmaker would be enough, but when it came to the point, it wasn't. It was the same with my father. Harry has a slight claim to the throne, better than Tudor's, whose ancestors' marriages are in such doubt. However, they're both forgetting that it's already occupied.'

'Then why ally himself with Henry Tudor?' Kate was outraged, couldn't understand why Anne was so calm, then realized from her next words that she was not calm at all.

'Because Harry Buckingham's no better than a whore.' The letter's wax seal snapped in two between Anne's fingers. 'He will lie with anyone he thinks might give him the power he covets. I know our Creator meant us to turn the other cheek, and to accept everything that befalls us as his will, but I admit it: I hate Buckingham, and I'm afraid.'

Kate was suddenly full of shivers. It was plain what she must do, and there was no time to argue. 'My lady, will you give me leave to go to York?'

Anne was silent so long that Kate was sure she would refuse. Eventually she said, 'You are fortunate indeed, being free to come and go as you please. I almost envy you for it.'

York was a city of spectres. Warm, golden October had been swallowed by damp mists. Everything was dark with dew, dripping with the condensed breath of fog elementals, brooding. Kate trod the streets as if walking the bottom of deep gullies, feeling mouse-tiny. High grey walls towered around her. Window slits peered down from crenellated heights, the cathedral floated above the rooftops, yet she felt blessedly invisible. Even the Church could not object to her mission, since it was to aid the King.

Katherine had summoned as many sisters as she could to the York Motherlodge. Any sister of Auset could do this when the need was great enough, but it was the first time Kate had exercised the right herself. The responsibility made her apprehensive. Suddenly she had power, and wasn't sure what to do with it.

Entering the sanctum, she was startled to see how many sisters had come. There were women of every rank: wives of barons and of merchants, their serving women, a great many nuns, women she'd never seen at the lodge before, and whom she would never have suspected of secret affiliation. Remarkable, since she'd told no one why she had wanted them to gather. Pleasure warmed her. As Mother Marl said, she thought, I have much to learn.

Eleanor was there, and greeted Kate warmly. There was already power in the air, even before they'd begun work.

'Since you've called the circle, you are *Mater Superior* for the working,' said Eleanor, kissing her. 'What is it you intend?'

'I'll explain once the circle is cast.' Kate swallowed. Her mouth was dry.

Patiently she attended the women as they threw off their cloaks and shoes and unbound their hair. Here they were all equal. She greeted them one by one, each with a kiss and the blessing of Auset. Then she anointed each one in turn: their feet with the crescent moon, their foreheads with the solar circle.

The women formed a circle three deep with Kate in the centre. She called down the blessing of the Goddess, summoned the elementals of wind and fog, of water and earth, of fire and stone, to weave spheres of protection about the chamber. The women responded eagerly, chanting the summonses; their voices were low and eerie, like those of monks. The atmosphere bristled. Incense billowed around them. Kate lifted her face to the heavens, her hair flowing down her back, feeling her own voice vibrate all through her body, strong and clear. For the first time in her life, she felt like a true priestess.

When the circle was cast, Kate paused, and looked round at their intent faces.

Plain, comely, young, old; all looked radiant.

'Our beloved King Richard, best appointed, and approved of by the sisterhood of Auset, is under threat from many enemies,' she said. 'I have asked you here to summon from the earth the powers of the Serpent Mother, in order to aid Richard and confound his foes. By the love of Auset I adjure you to help me. She is the one who takes apart and restores what is scattered. You are bound into the temple and cannot turn back. Come with me now. Have no fear, rouse the wrath of Auset from the depths!'

She saw the women looking nervously at each other. What they were about to do was strictly forbidden by the outer world. Yet no one quailed. A heavy excitement lay on them, and they were wholly with her.

In the centre of the sanctum stood a large stone bowl of brine, containing the black eel sacred to Auset. Its long thick body almost encircled the bowl. Kate looked down at its hideous upturned face, its gaping jaws filled with rows of razor teeth. Legend told that it had been drawn from the utmost depths of the ocean, as wondrous as the horns of unicorns that sailors brought from far-off lands. It glared back at her and she felt a flame of fear slip through her body.

'I want you now to envisage that which we desire. As you tread the circle and sing to raise the power of Auset, keep the intent in your mind, as if it already *is*. Richard's enemies confounded. The King safe. As we will, so must it be!'

Kate began the chant and the women took it up. They began to move about the circle, a slow stepping dance, bare feet slapping on the flagstones. The chill air grew clammy with their heat. The drumbeat of feet and voices sank them deep into trance. Kate saw the energy coming from them as a scarlet mist, made from millions of tiny flames, each an elemental born of their inner fire.

In the bowl, the eel rose from the bottom and began to circle, faster and faster.

Kate lowered her voice and let them speak on without her. The chant rolled on, unstoppable, like low rhythmic thunder. She raised her hands, holding in the right an athame with a twisted snake for a hilt, and pressed the blade to her left wrist and let her blood dribble into the water.

The serpent thrashed madly. The water boiled. Even through the droning chant, she heard soft gasps.

The first woman she called into the centre, beckoning her with a blood-streaked hand, was Eleanor. Kate let a little of her mother's blood into the bowl, sent her back into the throng and called the next. Each woman came without hesitation, wrist bared.

Faster and faster the water whirled in the bowl. The serpent opened its jaws wide to sift the blood from the brine. Kate focused all her attention upon the water until it became the world. The cauldron was the land, the spiralling vortex of water the sky, the eel the raging power of Auset. She gathered all the throbbing, frantic energy of her sisters into a single spear of intent with her hands and voice, with her mind and soul and whole being, and hurled the blazing spear of Auset's rage into the heart of the earth.

It began gently, ominously. A thread of icy wind lifting off the marshes of Kent, sighing down the flanks of the Welsh mountains, ruffling the grey waves of the Channel. Soldiers looked up and shivered. Clouds began to congest the sky, purple and taut with pressure, like storm-swollen sails. All turned black, and the wind rose.

Gales swept through towns and villages, tearing roofs to tatters, sweeping masses of leaves from the trees like a lethal hail of arrows. Rain dropped relentlessly in iron-heavy curtains. Roads turned to streams, meadows to quagmires. Streams branched and joined into single vast sheets of water. Rivers rose like the mounded backs of turtles, filled the fields, swept bridges away.

In the West Country, rebel soldiers closed their eyes against the savage wind, turned their backs and gave up. In Wales, Harry Buckingham urged his soaked and wretched troops onwards to cross the river Severn before it was too late. Henry Tudor's fleet defied the storms in the Channel, only to be tossed back by the peaks and chasms of a raging sea. The sky drenched their tiny ships with its thundering, supernatural displeasure. And since the Creator favoured their cause, it could only be the Devil who sent this deluge.

In castles, manors and cottages all across the kingdom, people sat close to their hearths, starting at each slamming door or moan of wind. Outside, in the storm, they could hear elementals rioting, demons flapping their leathery wings, all the denizens of the otherworld emerging to claim the night.

The cauldron of blood and water whirled. Boundaries dissolved. Hidden and outer worlds became one. Rising, the Dark Mother unleashed long-suppressed passion: the ice of her breath and the downpour of her tears. In the flickering storm, she danced.

As Buckingham's hopes of crossing the Severn leeched away into the swelling mud-brown plain of water, so his troops melted back into the Welsh hills, disheartened and grumbling. Rain was all it took to dissolve their faint commitment to a lord they'd never loved.

The worst storm in living memory held the land hostage for days, sucked the rebellion into its brown floods and swept it away.

The Duke of Buckingham looked out through a small window at the Forest of Dean. Massed trees were all he could see. Great trunks like pillars, branches still thick with leaves in defiance of autumn gales. Russet and bronze were the trees, still green in places. Leaves lay in wet layers on the grass. He could taste the season in the air: woodsmoke and decay.

His greatest pride, his buttery hair, hung in waxy strings. He was alone, deserted, frightened, hiding in this cottage like a toad beneath a stone. His protector was one of his own tenants. He'd never seen eye to eye with the man but was forced to trust him. He chewed at his lip, bitter with humiliation.

It had seemed a bold and faultless scheme, the purging of all his frustration. Bishop Morton, when Buckingham had finally broken down and confessed his confused feelings towards Richard, could not have been kinder. Harry remembered his shining, smiling face, the gentle shake of his head, the plump hands lifting him up. Absolution, that was what Morton had given him. Then hours of kindly concern, showing him the way to salvation. And – for Harry now hated Richard as violently as he had once loved him – a means to exorcise the demon.

Morton's conviction that Richard was of the Devil's party, while his protégée Henry Tudor was divinely marked for kingship, was a firm, practical blend of religious conviction and worldly ambition. Harry appreciated it, but didn't share it. His main concern was to punish Richard. To do it without losing everything, that was the trick. To do it and *gain* everything.

What a fool he'd been, ever to think it was possible.

He should have realized that no one would support his own claim to the throne, but those silver-tongued ambassadors, Morton and Margaret Beaufort and the skull-faced whispering Fautherer, had promised him mountains if he would only throw himself in with the divine Richmond's cause. How easily they had seduced him.

Buckingham had always been a Lancastrian at heart. He was only returning to his true self, he told himself, to the Lancastrians' silver-gold austere piety and fire, to the cause of a king who would be Henry the Fifth reincarnate:

himself. Anyone could make a mistake, and fall. He'd made an appalling mistake with Richard, but he would atone for it, and be lifted up again. It had felt right.

Until the storm from hell had struck them.

Buckingham sat staring into the forest. His mouth was dust and his right knee would not be still, it bounced under his elbow with a violent tremor. All those he had fought for lately, Richmond, Morton, even the Woodvilles, were gone from his mind like phantoms. All he could think about was Richard.

Such was the great, turning waterwheel of fortune. One moment, hand in glove with a king. The next, a fugitive among peasants.

Buckingham pushed his hands through his unwashed hair.

'Creator, why was I such a fool?!' he said aloud.

A shadow, seen from the corner of his eye, made him start. Richard was in the corner of the room, magnificent in black, like an executioner. He looked tranquil with his hands folded and his dark hair falling about him, an angel of judgement.

The perfect lips moved. 'Why, Harry?'

Buckingham fell to his knees. 'Richard, please. Forgive me. I meant none of it. It was all a misunderstanding. Please. I love you.'

'Too late.'

'No.' He looked up. There was no one there. He was pleading with shadows and cobwebs.

Rushing to the window again, he saw movement between the trees. Soldiers in silver, red and blue. The King's livery. He leapt up in panic but there was no escape: they were all around the cottage.

For the delicious reward of one thousand pounds, his tenant had betrayed him.

Salisbury. A plain under a grey and black sky, the tall solid shapes of stone that had encircled their mystery since times unknown. Here they brought Buckingham to be executed.

He had caught a single glimpse of Richard before they cast him into his prison. From a distance, Harry saw him entering the town amid a grim but victorious retinue. The King was aloof upon a pure white horse, unreachable.

'I must see him.' Buckingham was imperious with his gaolers, confident at first, then when they stood about sneering, he grew angry. 'The King will see me. We were friends. Ask him for the sake of the deep love we bore each other, that he graciously grant me an audience. Tell him – tell him that it was all a misunderstanding, I am no traitor!'

They went away to ask. Buckingham sat in the straw, chewing at loose skin on his thumbnail until it bled. All day they had heaped foul news like ordure upon his head. His estates had been confiscated. Bishop Morton had fled – vanished. His tenant had handed him over to the King for a disgustingly large reward. Tudor had also fled, back to Brittany. The rebellion was an utter failure.

All of this news was nothing against Buckingham's curdled terror at his own fate.

Richard would come; would stand there dark and majestic, lift him up and forgive him. There would be angry words, but he would soften. Buckingham knew he had a gentler nature than most gave him credit for. They would embrace, reconcile . . . and if not . . .

Buckingham felt the hard shape of the hunting knife he had concealed in his sleeve. His mind was a blur of flame. He didn't know what he wanted, except that it must be extreme. Richard must love him; if not, he must die.

A key rattled, and his door swung open. Buckingham shot to his feet. A man came in between the gaolers; not Richard but his coarse, unsmiling henchman, Ratcliffe.

'He won't see you.'

Buckingham fell apart. He pleaded, yelled, abased himself. Ratcliffe was unmoved.

'Tomorrow you die as a traitor,' Ratcliffe said quietly. 'Your fair golden head will fall into the dust, like that of any common rebel. The King has nothing to say to you.'

Buckingham's legs gave way. He fell into the straw, giggling, not caring that Ratcliffe stared down in disgust. 'I won, then. Read the bitter hurt in those words, that he refuses to see me. I cut him to the core.'

Katherine was treading the long corridors of the Palace of Westminster, walking very fast, head up, with all the dignity she could muster. She was wearing her finest gown of dark blue, black and silver, completed by a hennin of indigo tissue scattered with silver stars upon her hair. The King had summoned her.

The gallery was thronged with petitioners, lords and commoners who were there to plead their cases, seeking reward or pardon for their part in the rebellion. She eased her way between them, trying to ignore their stares. There were murmurings as Raphael came through to escort her towards the throne room. He looked wondrous in new, beautifully made court livery. They exchanged a tentative smile.

Richard was still in counsel with other magnates, and kept her waiting until her feet ached and her mouth was parched with thirst. Raphael seemed tense, and hardly said a word. He was preoccupied, very much on the King's official business.

'Do you know why he wants to see me?' she asked.

He looked at her, his eyes hollow and wary. 'That is between him and you, my lady.'

'Raph, are you all right? Anyone would think the King had lost, not won, from your expression.'

A smile ghosted across his face. 'I must talk to you, Kate. But not now.'

The doors to the audience chamber opened suddenly. Between two rows of heralds, like a barquentine upon a fair wind, to Kate's absolute amazement, came striding

Elizabeth Woodville. All in pale green and silver, her gown embroidered from head to foot and with a tall confection of gossamer on her head, she seemed immense. She was an elf-queen. Everyone fell out of her way, Kate included.

In her wake trotted a number of fair daughters. The eldest, Elizabeth of York, known as Bess, gave Kate a glance and a sly, conspiratorial smile.

'Elizabeth Woodville has emerged from sanctuary?' Kate exclaimed. 'I thought – I thought she was part of the conspiracy!'

'Hush!' said Raphael, though she'd barely spoken above a whisper. 'She is pardoned, on condition of her future good behaviour and loyalty. Creator knows, she made things awkward for the King, cowering in hiding as if he was some tyrant threatening her life. It's a relief that he's coaxed her out, at last.'

'How did he manage it?'

'Her conspiracies failed. She has nowhere else to go.'

'Richard must have been very persuasive.'

'She came out in return for public guarantees of her safety, and that of her daughters.'

'And what of her sons?' Kate frowned. Raphael looked away, his face taut, eyes black. 'Raphael? Do you know what . . . ?'

'Don't ask, Kate, and especially don't mention it to him. Go in.'

When Kate entered the chamber, Richard was alone except for a handful of heralds and door attendants.

'Katherine, my lady,' he said. He looked down at her from the throne, like a king of the underworld in layers of crimson, gold thread and ermine. The throne itself resembled some fantastical gateway: a flow of blood-red glass caught between ebony columns that soared and branched like trees of the faerie realm. Against the rich darkness of his hair, his face was shell-pale, with lines inscribed about his eyes and mouth. He looked drawn, fierce, soulless. Kate was uneasy under the expressionless scrutiny.

'You asked for me, Your Grace?'

The King rose from the throne and stepped down from the dais. He lifted a hand to beckon her, a ruby shining red on the third finger. 'In private, if it please you,' he said.

He led her into a small privy chamber behind the throne. Dismissing a servant who was waiting there, he leaned on the table, and stood glaring at her.

'Sire?' The word dried in her mouth.

Eventually he said, 'How dare you?' His voice was very low and vibrated with anger.

Her eyes widened. 'How dare I – what?'

'I know,' he said. 'I know what you did to aid my victory against Buckingham and the other traitors.'

She was shocked. Foreboding pulsed in her chest, light at first, then harder and harder. 'What I did?'

'Sorcery. Unnatural weather stirred by a coven of sorceresses, involving blood sacrifice and who knows what pacts with unholy powers.'

She realized her mouth was open and closed it firmly.

'There were a lot of people there, I understand,' Richard went on. 'Some were too elated by their success to keep their counsel. Rumours always reach my ears eventually. No doubt they were sworn to secrecy; but remember, you can never trust absolutely everyone. Is it true? You don't seem eager to deny it.'

She drew a long breath. 'I suppose I could tell you it's all scurrilous rumour, concocted by some enemy who's jealous of me.'

'Is it?'

'No. I'll tell you the truth, but I will not give you names.'

'I'm not asking for names, Kate,' he said thinly. 'The general truth will suffice.'

'Well, then. Yes, we performed a working to aid you. I rather thought you might be grateful.'

Richard drew himself up. His tone was mild but his face was wintry. 'Did I ask you for any such help?'

'No, sire.'

'You know full well it's against the laws of the Church to practise sorcery. How dare you think to aid me by the use of witchcraft? I am not Edward! I didn't ask for this unholy help!'

She could feel her heart beating through every part of her; throat, arms, feet. 'We prefer the term "influence". I did nothing unholy, sire. The Dark Mother is powerful, but sacred. Not evil. We sought to help you.'

He walked a few paces, turned to glower at her. 'I need no help from sorcery,' he said. 'If my Creator is not on my side, then let me lose! I want no assistance from His Adversary!'

'The Motherlodge worked for you!' she cried. 'We have no dealings with Satan, we don't recognize Satan; he is part of your theology, not ours. Ours is an older faith, as old as the bones of the earth, before your devils were even thought of!'

'I'm not standing here arguing theology with you.' Richard was all ice. She'd seen him like this when he had attainted traitors or presided over executions. She shivered, frightened. 'I asked for no help from your sisterhood. I require no help from your sisterhood. I shall win my battles by the strength of my own arm, if heaven wills it, not with the aid of sorcery. Do you have anything to say for yourself?'

She touched her tongue to her front teeth and tried to remember she was Eleanor's heir, and therefore Richard's equal; but that was a flimsy illusion. No one in the outer world would recognize her as such, least of all the King.

'Sire, we acted to help you. We did so without your command or approval. To be plain, I didn't ask your approval because I knew you wouldn't give it. A little secret influence – that's all I intended. If it offended you, I apologize without reservation. It was entirely my idea; no one is to blame but me. Yes, I'm culpable, but only out of love for you. Nothing devilish or evil was involved. Only

411

the love of Auset, whom you revere in her guise as Mary, whose love gives this land her life.'

'That was perilously close to blasphemy,' he said, very low. 'Can't you get any closer?'

'Without a doubt,' Kate said thinly. 'Are you going to cut off my head?'

'If you were a man, I might be tempted.'

'Or perhaps you will make me parade through the streets of London in my kirtle as a penance.'

Richard exhaled. 'If you are referring to my treatment of Eliza Shore, you are hardly helping your own cause. I know she was a member of your Motherlodge, Kate. You could have told me that yourself, but you chose not to.'

'I had no choice,' she said, shocked. 'We take an oath of secrecy. You, of all people, should know that such an oath is binding. I wanted to tell you, but couldn't.'

'Then your loyalty to your sisters does you credit.'

'How did you find out?'

'It's no mystery, Kate. I had her followed. Since you appear to be entirely undiscriminating about who you let into your Motherlodge, don't be surprised if they are not all trustworthy.' The heat had gone from his voice at last. 'The point is that it was not for her sorcery that I made her do penance. I was punishing her for all she represented. Not only for her actions against me, but for her part in the corruption of Edward and his court. I set out to shame her. A dishonourable action on my part, I know, but I was angry.'

'A lesson not to act in anger?' Kate looked levelly into his eyes.

'You might say so. The crowd adored her. I only punished myself.'

'I take it I'm not to get off so lightly, then.'

'Kate, for God's sake. I'm not proposing to punish you. This is a warning. I appreciate your sentiment, but please understand that my enemies will seize upon anything to discredit me. If they can connect me with witchcraft or devil-worship, they will. I have troubles enough already.'

'I can see that. It saddens me that our Motherlodge is still viewed only in those terms.'

'I can't change that.'

'So this is political?'

'Yes, but also personal. My enemies would love to show any pious virtue of mine as sheer hypocrisy. I cannot be seen to seek the aid of the Motherlodge. I don't seek it.'

'Then please accept my sincere apologies.'

He was standing close to her now. She caught the scent of new-made fabrics warmed by his body, scented with spice of cedar wood. 'Kate, I'm thinking of your safety as well. You are allowed to exist, only for as long as you do not practise . . . influence. If you are caught out, it will be just the excuse the Church needs to put pressure upon Parliament to change the law.'

She said nothing.

'I know you meant well. But this must never happen again. *Never*.'

His demeanour was formal; he considered the matter at an end. Kate, still seething inside, could not look at him.

'You trust me,' she said. 'You have always been able to trust me, and you know it.'

'Yes. Do as I ask, and nothing more will be said.'

'I understand.'

'Thank you.'

'Your Grace,' she said tightly, and curtseyed.

He held open the door for her; a strangely intimate gesture, considering the river of polite distance that flowed between them. The gulf had never seemed wider. As imperious as Elizabeth Woodville before her, Kate raised her chin and strode away.

Nottingham Castle was a great, square, crystal-white structure, seated on a massive plug of rock like a cube, a tide of trees washing round it. The perpetual groan of waterwheels echoed, drawing water step by step into its heights. Beyond, Sherwood Forest rustled with the fresh green of April, rich with game and haunted by pagan gods; Robin and Marian. Long gone, yet still present and watchful.

Released from duty for a few hours, Kate and Raphael raced their horses through the trees, laughing and dodging branches. Birds fluttered squawking out of their path. It felt magical to be out of London and away from the court. Kate breathed sweet, fresh air and felt ecstatic. It would have been easy not to turn back, to urge her swift mare onwards and flee. Away from the King's household, away from service and duty; to be herself again. Tempting.

There had been a time of relative peace following Buckingham's execution, but Richard was never still. He travelled constantly about the kingdom, working tirelessly as if driven to prove he had earned kingship. He was generous to the pardoned rebels; he made hundreds of laws to help the poor; he began to win abiding love, but never enough to make him secure. Two blond ghosts haunted him.

It was there, in the forest, as she and Raphael lay together in a green bower, that he told her at last about the Princes. He trembled as he spoke, his head against her shoulder.

'So Richard did not kill them,' she said at last. 'I never believed he had.'

'But he blames himself. In his own mind, he is guilty.'

'Then that is for his conscience, but in public, the truth should be told.'

'But don't you see, love?' He raised his head and his face was haggard. 'The truth would not make any difference. If people are determined to believe the worst, they will. Rumours take on a life of their own, like elementals. The hardest thing is to watch him tormenting himself over it.'

'He doesn't look tormented to me,' Kate said shortly. She had hardened towards Richard since he'd rejected her help. She understood why he'd done so, respected his point of view, but her devotion to him now was distant and formal. Her heart could not forgive him.

'You don't see him all the time.'

She leaned up on one elbow and stroked his cheek. 'Raph, must you take on all his troubles? You're like a mirror. You can't take his pain away by suffering for him.'

'But I can't help it!' His fervency startled her. 'Kate . . .'

'What is it?' she asked, not very warmly.

Raphael frowned. He seemed upset, hostile.

'I can't help if you won't tell me,' she said, but he only looked away. They seemed to be quarrelling without anything being said. When he didn't reply, she exclaimed, 'Richard is like a shadow between us! He's always there! We're never free of him!'

'He's the King! He's my master. If you don't like it—' He jumped up and stomped towards his horse.

'Raphael.' She sighed, following him.

After a few minutes of riding in silence, Raphael said, 'I'm sorry.'

They exchanged a rueful glance. His face relaxed.

'Race you,' said Kate.

As they approached the castle, Raphael let out a grunt, as if he'd been struck. Kate saw leaves whirling across the vault of the sky. Leaves, although it was not autumn? Birds then, or little smoky elementals, crying distress.

In the courtyard there was a strange, subdued chaos with messengers arriving and leaving, officials rushing about with bleak faces. Kate saw Francis Lovell and flung herself out of the saddle in front of him, almost knocking him down with her mare.

'What's happening? Not another uprising?'

Regaining his balance, Francis turned, taking a moment to focus upon her. His kind face was grey, his eyes red. 'No. It's the King and Queen. Their son is dead.'

Anne was asleep at last. Kate emerged into the chill fresh air and looked up at the sky. The faintest wash of dawn was absorbing the stars. There was no hope of sleep now. All night she and the other ladies-in-waiting had kept vigil with the Queen, holding her through terrible bouts of trembling and hoarse cries that were as much of physical pain as grief; fits that faded at last into glassy-eyed, waxen shock.

The King had not been present. Kate hadn't seen him. Perhaps they couldn't bear each other's grief. She didn't blame them.

The other women also slept now, exhausted. Kate was wide awake. She looked up at the salt-white walls rising all around her, ran her gaze along the battlements to the high, square tower on the north-west corner. A pang of anxiety went through her. She remembered how he had always haunted the battlements at Middleham.

Approaching the tower, she saw a couple of Richard's personal esquires just inside the door. They looked pale and grim. Behind them, light was glimmering through the half-open door of the guard chamber.

'Have you seen the King?' she asked.

One of the men tilted his head at the stone staircase that wound upwards. 'I wouldn't, my lady.'

Ignoring his warning, Kate lifted the hem of her skirt and began to climb. She'd taken three steps when the man followed her, pushing a bundle of fabric at her. 'At least take this to him,' he said.

It was a cloak of black wool, fine and warm with a blue satin lining.

'Thank you, Geoffrey,' she said.

When she emerged onto the top of the tower, there was no one there. The area was a well of darkness within the battlement walls; the sky beyond darkest blue. She heard the perpetual soft roar of the waterwheels.

The wind was very cold. She put her hand to her mouth. For one stabbing moment she was sure he had thrown himself off the tower.

As she stood dissolving in panic, she began to make

out a dark shape. It was hardly visible, black on black: a figure slumped against the wall, back curved and legs bent carelessly under him, forehead resting against the stone blocks. He was motionless, as if he'd been there for hours, or died there.

'Richard?' she said very softly. She went closer. 'Richard?'

She leaned down to touch his shoulder. He jumped violently.

'I'm sorry.'

The face he turned to her was dreadful in the gloom. Bloodless, lined, devoid of a soul. 'Leave,' he said.

She knew then why the guards were afraid to come near him. The voice was hoarse, like rusted steel. He looked possessed. What could anyone do in the face of such bereavement, but flee?

Kate knelt beside him and began to put the cloak around his shoulders. He raised a hand to stop her and his skin was ice.

'Leave me!' he said again.

'No,' she answered. 'Have you been here all night?'

'I want no one to see me.'

'I'm not just anyone,' she said brusquely. She went on arranging the cloak and he let her, sitting up so she could wrap it around him properly. Then he leaned back against the wall, and rested limp arms on his knees. Every movement was stiff with pain.

'How is Anne?' he asked tonelessly.

'Asleep, at last.'

He exhaled. 'I don't think we can endure each other at present.'

'I understand.'

'It seems your mother was right.'

'Eleanor? What . . . ?'

'When I was a frightened child, lost in the hidden world. She said my future was all darkness, and she was right.'

'No. She was only saying that we have a choice of

417

paths—' Kate stopped, knowing she'd said the wrong thing, not wanting to make it worse.

'Apparently I've chosen badly. I've tried to take the path of light but I am always pulled back into the darkness. How vain are the hopes of kings. I can see that I need to be taught this lesson, but why my son? Why Anne? How have they offended the Almighty?'

He began to shiver. Kate put her arms around him. Richard didn't push her away but turned towards her, one hand grasping her upper arm so hard it hurt. With his head in the crook of her shoulder, he wept. She stroked his tangled hair. She pulled the corner of the cloak around herself and they sat under it together, sobbing.

'Everything I fought for is ash,' he said, a long time later. 'Without him, there's no meaning to any of it.'

'That's not true.' There was a lot she longed to say, but it stayed inside her. Nothing could comfort him today. To utter platitudes, to say, 'You will have other children,' would be an insult worse than poison.

She said, 'He had the happiest life. Was any child ever better loved than your son? You gave him a happier life than you ever had yourself, I think.'

Richard drew back and looked at her. In the growing dawn his eyes were heavy and red-rimmed, but he seemed calmer. 'That's true enough. God, yes, Kate, that is true.'

'Won't you come down to the guardhouse now and get warm?'

He looked up at the sky. 'Another morning. No morning will ever have my son in it again. Still, I must go down, wash my face, and present a dignified front to the world.'

'They won't expect you to do anything today, surely.'

'Unfortunately, I'm still the King. Affairs won't wait, not even for this.'

They got to their feet. He was unsteady, and she had to help him. In silence they went down the stairs and entered the guard chamber. The esquires, now sitting bleary-eyed in front of the fire, leaped to attention, looking startled.

'Is there anything to drink?' said Kate.

'Only ale, my lady. It's Burton ale, though, the best.'

'Is there something in which to heat it on the fire? His Grace is cold. It will help to restore him. No fuss, just leave him in peace for a few minutes.'

Behind the King's back, his esquire, Geoffrey, raised wondering eyebrows at her, as if to suggest she had worked a miracle.

The men hurried to do her bidding. Soon she and Richard were seated alone at the solid table, with leather flagons warming their hands. Firelight flickered over the beige stone of the walls. The door stood ajar and she could hear the men's voices outside.

He sat with his head in his hands. She didn't know what to say.

'Do you wish me to leave now?' she asked.

'No.' He raised his head to look at her. 'Stay a while, if you don't mind.'

'I'm glad to.'

'Even after I spoke so harshly to you, you are still so kind.'

'You weren't harsh, and I'm not being kind.'

Their eyes caught for a moment. A glint of sad amusement, then Richard looked down again. 'I couldn't weep in front of Anne.' He watched the steam curling from the ale. 'I don't think she could, either. The sound she made was like a *bain sidhe* howling, and she tore at her hair . . . I couldn't bear to witness it. We were like two animals beating ourselves against the bars of cages with nothing to say to each other. She will never get over this. Neither of us will. How can we look each other in the eye? What is there to say? We can't comfort each other.'

'You will, when the pain is less raw . . .'

'I can't imagine such a day. Kate, we both know there will be no more children. She was hardly strong enough to bear Edward.'

'And she's wretched about it. That's the worst of it. Not

only his death, but that he was the only one. She feels she's let you down.'

He was shaking his head. 'I never wanted her to think that! It's not her fault. But I can't stop her tormenting herself over it.'

'Because she knows how much it matters to you. And you can't convince her otherwise, even if you deny it to your last breath. However much she calls it God's will.'

'It's hard to accept God's will, when he is this cruel,' Richard said thinly. 'He has seen fit to take away my heir. I could almost hate him.' His gaze slipped to the door. 'I wonder what they are saying about me out there?'

'Nothing but kindness and sympathy! There isn't a soul in the castle who hasn't wept for you.'

'Ah, it's a wretched state of affairs when I even mistrust my own servants. I spoke unfairly; blame it on tiredness. But there are those who will be rejoicing to hear that my son is dead. They think I deserve it.'

'No,' Kate said, frowning.

'Believe me. My position would be worse if I laboured under any illusion. There are many in this kingdom who have no love to spare for me and are ecstatic to see the end of my dynasty. A ship heading for the rocks; that pleases them.'

'Richard.' Not caring if her touch was improper, or unwelcome, she reached out and laid her hand along his cheek, turning his face towards her. 'You are more loved than you'll ever know.'

He put his hand over hers, keeping it there. There was no trace of a smile in his expression. His grey irises were all splinters of glass. But there was a glimmer of gratitude, enough to warm her.

'Is the King here?'

The voice from outside was Francis Lovell's.

Kate jumped guiltily and put her hands in her lap. Richard sat away from her without haste just as Lovell came in, with Raphael close behind him.

'Thank God, Dickon!' Lovell exclaimed, opening his hands wide. 'We've almost turned the castle upside down looking for you.'

They looked surprised to see her there, but said nothing. Her presence must look strange, but she didn't care. Raphael glanced at her in veiled puzzlement, but Kate felt no inclination to justify herself. The circumstances were exceptional. She had nothing to hide.

'Thanks for your concern, but you shouldn't have troubled.' Richard's voice was rough with tiredness.

'Are you . . . Is there anything we can do, anything you need?'

'The one thing I need, even God can't deliver back to me.'

Both men dropped their gazes and crossed themselves. 'Yes,' said Lovell. 'I'm sorry. Will you breakfast with us? You must eat, or at least try.'

'I'll come, gentlemen,' said Richard, standing up. Francis and Raphael looked relieved, if taken aback. 'There's a great deal to do this morning. Wait for me outside with Geoffrey and Marmaduke, will you?'

They did as he asked. Kate rose decorously, trying to restore the usual polite distance between them. 'I'll return to the Queen, sire.'

'Thank you. If she's awake, tell her I'll come to her within the hour; if not, I'll be there when she wakes.' His storm-washed eyes were gentle upon her. He kissed her hand; his fingers pressing her palm still felt cold. 'This is the end of everything,' he said bleakly.

'No.' She shook her head in denial of what was plain: his greyness, his deathly stumbling emptiness, a light in his soul extinguished forever.

'It is, yet by some ghastly miracle I'm still on my feet. And there is some hope that Anne and I may speak to each other again. Thank you, Kate. I won't forget this.'

Chapter Sixteen 1485: Anne

This only son of his, in whom all the hopes of the royal
succession, fortified with so many oaths, were centred,
was seized with an illness of but short duration and died
at Middleham Castle in the year of our Lord, 1484 . . .
You might have seen his father and mother in a state
almost bordering upon madness, by reason of their
sudden grief.

Croyland Chronicle

'His son is dead. All his hopes for the future lost. No son,
no heir. How tragic.'

Henry Tudor's face was gaunt, intense. He murmured
the words without emotion, but the altar light burnished
his skin with a joyful glow. He raised narrow eyes to Bishop
Morton. He looked, Dr Fautherer observed, cautiously
hopeful, resolute and afraid. Hope always alarmed him,
it meant he would have to act. A terrible thing, ambition
without courage.

'How tragic,' Morton echoed. 'How weakening to his
spirit.'

The chapel was small and high, with stained-glass windows reaching up into the vault. The harlequin light
seeping through them did not reach the body of the
chapel, which remained a well of dim candlelight and
darkness. Bishop Morton stood with his hands folded over
his belly, his broad face content and bearing the hint of a
smile. Richmond was on his knees, as usual. So like his
mother.

'I shall pray for his soul,' said Henry.

Fautherer stood to one side, attendant upon them. He felt quietly pleased with the service he'd done them, the fulfilment of his role: message-bearer between England and Henry's court-in-waiting in Brittany; spy; weaver of webs.

'How vain are the thoughts of a man who desires to establish his interests without the aid of God,' said Morton.

'It is a sign from the Almighty,' Henry Tudor agreed sombrely. 'Even Richard must realize it, writhing in the small hell he's created for himself. He knows now that his days are numbered.'

Tudor placed his long bony hands together and raised his eyes to the lofty windows. His hair hung like dry straw over his shoulders. He looked, Fautherer thought, like a starved saint about to be transubstantiated. There was light around him, a yellowish halo.

'He's almost completely alone now,' said Morton. 'He was too lenient with the rebels he should have punished, too cruel to those whose help he should have courted. He shows too much favour to his northern friends, planting them in the south to the great disgruntlement of the people there. Sire, there are a great many discontented gentlemen of the south ready to rise and follow your red-dragon banner. Furthermore, all the nobles and knights Richard had swear fealty to his son, are now left with no clear path. Old Dick's wife will produce no more children. His dynasty has failed. They will be wondering at the wisdom of supporting such blighted stock, when they could turn to a fresh young sapling: Henry of Richmond.'

'New hope. A new beginning,' said Henry. 'I pray that I shall be the one favoured by God to provide that.'

'It was only by a mixture of sheer luck and devilry that the Hog prevailed against Buckingham,' Morton went on. 'The tides were against us then, but they are turning in our favour. The next time we land . . .'

Tudor looked sideways at the Bishop, a white circle flaring around his irises. Dread. Fautherer doubted that the Earl realized how clearly his inner feelings showed.

'The next time we land,' said Morton, placing a hand on Henry's shoulder, 'we shall prevail. It's our Creator's clear will.'

The Bishop always knew how to steady Tudor. A reminder of his divine destiny usually stiffened his spine. 'Then they'll all cry forgiveness for mocking my sound Lancastrian birthright.'

'Nothing now stands in your way.' Morton looked aside and met Dr Fautherer's gaze.

'And the poison,' said Fautherer, 'the poison of rumour does old Dick more harm even than the deaths of the Princes themselves.'

Morton crossed himself; Tudor and Fautherer quickly did the same. 'Appalling loss,' said Morton, 'but what's done is done. Thank God you are here to fill the breach. The tragedy that lays the way clear for you is the same as will destroy the usurper.'

Fautherer turned away so they would not see his grin. Their self-conscious hypocrisy was delicious. If Edward IV's sons had lived, Henry Tudor could not, in a thousand years, have hoped to come near the throne.

Tudor finished his prayer and rose, stiff from kneeling so long. 'Dr Fautherer, how is my mother?' he asked.

The doctor thought of Margaret Beaufort's tight, pleased little face as he had whispered the news of King Edward's sons, an obstacle removed. Richard's own boy was less important; his death was a moral victory rather than a political one. Tudor would have destroyed him anyway, once he took power. He could not afford to let any member of the house of York live. To Lady Beaufort, Richard's grief was only one less problem for her own son.

'Your mother is well, and as industrious as ever on your behalf.'

The warmth in Tudor's eyes was the closest he ever came to smiling. 'She is a wonder.'

'As I said, old Dick was too lenient with the conspirators,' said Morton. 'Giving her over to the care of her husband, Lord Stanley, as if that would contain her!'

'And Lord Stanley? Still loyal to the usurper?'

'To all appearances,' said Morton. 'He can't afford to appear otherwise – yet. But your mother works upon him in secret. He plays a close game and cannot show his hand until the very last moment, but he will support you.'

'He will, or bear the consequences,' said Henry. He revealed, suddenly, a high, cold authority, seeming to look down upon them from beneath heavy lids. The demeanour of a king, thought Fautherer. He will need it.

Henry spoke again, his voice snapping with anger. 'I am a patient man, but God knows, the waiting is hard.'

If only you had a tenth of the patience of your mother, Fautherer said to himself.

'All will come to pass in God's good time,' Morton said complacently. Henry began to pace in front of the small altar.

'I pray so, for I hear tales . . . Did I not swear a holy vow to marry Elizabeth of York?'

'You did, and you shall marry her.'

'Yet I hear it said that Richard has developed an incestuous passion for the lady, and means to marry her himself. His own niece! Blood of Iesu!'

Morton cleared his throat. 'Indeed, the story reached my ears also. There's an obstacle to his ambition: his wife still lives.'

Henry made an impatient noise. He was trembling. 'When has he ever let the lives of others stand in his way?'

'Quite so,' Morton said, soothingly. 'So let us turn the rumour to our own advantage. It's well known she's ill. Doubtless he wishes her dead. It's only one step on to presume that he might wish to hasten her upon her way. Dr Fautherer shall go about his business, and soon the whole kingdom shall know that he has poisoned his wife in order to marry his niece. Two more brands of guilt upon him.

Child-murder, wife-murder, incest. It has a certain beauty, does it not?'

A shuddering breath came from Henry's mouth. 'As long as we are not too late. If he marries her, or even touches her . . . How can I marry a woman soiled by him?'

Morton was shaking his head. 'Think of it this way, sire. If he wishes to ruin her for you, it proves one thing.'

'Which is?'

'That he fears you.'

'Yes,' Richmond murmured. 'I would surely like him to fear me.'

'He will not marry her. Fautherer will see to it. It will be one more weapon in our armoury against him, that's all.'

Fautherer studied the distracted glow of Henry's eyes and saw envy, impatience, ambition and discontent in them. Fautherer felt coolly grateful that he had never been prey to such mundane emotions. He moved in the darkness without partiality. He *was* the darkness.

There was a messenger in the chapel doorway, a priest. Fautherer responded to his urgent signal and went to hear what he had to say, then passed soundlessly back to Morton's side.

'What is it?' snapped Tudor.

'We must make haste, sire. We are betrayed. Brittany's quarrel with England is ended. Richard has agreed to aid Brittany against France, in return for Duke Francis handing you over to him. And the Duke has agreed.'

Henry's face drained to yellow. Even Bishop Morton paled.

'What are we to do?'

'We must flee to France,' said Morton. 'France will aid us.'

'Horses are already waiting,' said Fautherer. 'Thank God we were warned in time.'

'It's foolish gossip,' said Katherine, straightening sheets and scattering drops of rose oil to freshen the air. Anne was a ghost against the pillow. Even her hair seemed spectral, a veil of reddish silk.

'All because Bess and I wore similar gowns at Christmas.' The Queen's voice was weak, torn with coughing. 'It seems so long ago now. I gave her that gown! She had nothing new to wear, and it was such beautiful material and so much left over; how could I not show her that kindness? Yet all they can construe from it is that Bess seeks to replace me!'

Kate glanced at Anne's other ladies, who were scattered about the chamber. Kate still felt an outsider among them. Although they were quick enough to run to her when they needed help, at other times they plainly thought themselves above her. They were perhaps a little jealous of Anne's trust in her. Kate tried to ignore their political jostling but Ursula took a keen interest and reported every murmur back to her.

A fragile hush lay on the room. Nan sat intently sewing. She couldn't bear Anne's illness and tried to keep busy at every moment, but Ursula was ever watchful. If anyone spoke it was in the faintest whisper, as if a sound would make Anne's soul flee on the spot. Kate's voice sounded loud to her own ears.

'I'd like to know who brings these stories in to you,' she said, pressing a cool cloth to Anne's forehead. 'You are meant to be resting.'

'I don't know,' said Anne. 'I hear people talking outside my door. The tales seep in to me. Nothing stays secret in this place.' She drew a rattling breath. Suddenly she reached up and clutched Kate's arm. 'I don't want to be sealed away from the truth. You say it's gossip, but what if it's true?'

Kate stiffened. Anger twisted her tongue. Martha had had a saying: you can only embroider upon cloth, not upon thin air. 'Your husband is the one to answer that, not me.'

The feverish eyes darkened. 'But he would say what I wished to hear.'

427

'You never used to distrust him.'

'No. No, I never did. Everything feels different now – fluid. My physicians have told him not to come to me in case he should catch my sickness; and when he does come, he looks at me so helplessly, as if he has no idea what to do.'

'He is a man. Of course he has no idea,' said Kate. Anne gave a skull-like smile.

'Richard should marry again,' she said. Her jaw trembled. 'But not her. Not her.'

Anne had never recovered from her son's death. She had succumbed to one malady after another, behind them all a single rolling cloud of illness that was slowly consuming her. Katherine had laboured for months to cure her. She had argued with the physicians, plied Anne with every healing herb she knew and cleansed her chambers of the smoky spirits that fed upon the dying. She had loosed all her arrows, and still the Queen faded. There was nothing left in a priestess's armoury but palliatives to ease distress.

It was spring. Richard had been king for less than two years, and was constantly besieged by ill-fortune. Spring, yet Kate felt her whole world had closed down to this dim stale chamber and the struggle to preserve Anne's life. She'd hardly had a moment to spare for Raphael. She had failed with Isabel, and hadn't been there for poor Edward of Middleham. If Anne died, too . . .

Anne let out a quick, unconscious sigh. Her eyes closed. She was asleep. Kate let her rest, watching her chest rise and fall narrowly, like a child's.

As the Queen slept, something dark came into the room and stood there.

Kate rose to her feet. Her heart was thudding urgently, yet none of the others in the room seemed to have noticed. They seemed far away, a courtly tableau frozen behind glass. She couldn't see the presence clearly, but she could feel it. The cloud of malevolence settled in the corner and watched.

How could she drive it out, without alarming Anne? Her hand crept up to her serpent pendant. She clutched the warm metal and silently called on the protection of friendly spirits. Faint green ripples moved the air. The candle flames danced and the watcher seemed to turn its attention to her, as if to say, *I know what you are doing and I'm not afraid*. After a time, very slowly, it vanished.

Anne's eyes flew open. 'What are they saying?' she gasped.

'My lady? You've been asleep. You're dreaming.'

'Are they tolling that bell for me?'

'There is no bell.'

Kate tried gently to push her down, but Anne rose under her hands with a terrible, bony strength. 'They are saying that I'm already dead!' she cried.

Somehow she struggled out of bed, got past Kate, and ran in her bedgown through the apartments and beyond, out into the marble-flagged corridors of Westminster Palace. Shocked, her ladies-in-waiting gave chase, calling out after her. No one could catch her. Kate was tantalizingly close as Anne slipped, sure-footed as a deer, down the curving steps into the main gallery. Not close enough. The sleeve of Anne's gown slipped through her fingers.

Richard was there, amid a knot of nobles standing beneath the array of tall, leaded windows. Kate stopped. The King looked up to see his wife flying barefoot towards him, her hair unbound. Startled, the other men parted to let her through. Kate saw astonishment on the faces of William Catesby and Thomas Stanley. Catesby was distressed, Stanley disapprovingly amused.

Richard stood frozen as his wife ran to him and clawed at the pleats of his doublet with luminous, sparrow-thin hands.

'Would you wish me to my grave early, putting it about that I am already dead? There's no need for your physicians to pour poison down my throat! I'm hastening to be with my Edward. How fast would you have me go? Don't toll the bells for me yet.'

She put her hands over her ears. Richard stared at her with horror plain in his face. For an instant, he caught Kate's eye; she looked back, dumb. Then his hands rose to grasp Anne's wrists and push them down.

'No one,' he said hoarsely, 'no one has put it about that you are dead, Anne. No bells are tolling. Who has told you this?'

'Someone.' She pulled away from him, her hands flying up in a helpless gesture. 'Someone who burns for me to die. I thought I had made my peace with you, for being a barren husk, a burden to you. I want no more of this world. The sooner I am called to join our son, the better.'

'Anne,' he said, 'you're not a burden. I have never said that to you.'

'I know what I am,' she whispered.

'Please. Go back to bed. I'll come to you.'

'No. Don't come.'

He lifted a wary hand towards her, but she turned away and walked back towards Kate with her head high, all fragile dignity, as if she trod on coals. Kate stood ready to wrap her in a robe that Nan had brought.

Leading Anne away, she glanced back at Richard and saw him rooted there with the same despairing expression. His eyes were edged with silver.

Anne slept, fading. Kate sat in an adjoining chamber, watching Ursula comb Nan's hair as they made ready for bed. Ursula combed with long, careful strokes, until Nan's hair was sleek and scattered with gold.

Kate sighed. 'Do you two ever wish you weren't in service? Always at the beck and call of others.'

Two faces turned to her in astonishment, glowing beautifully in the candlelight. Nan's eyes were wide with surprise, Ursula's dark and sharp. 'Why, madam?'

'Well, wouldn't you like a life of your own? To be free

to marry, to order your own affairs? I feel guilty. I don't wish to compel you to stay.'

Ursula looked at Kate with what she could only describe as pity. She smiled and frowned at the same time, shaking her head. 'Madam, we're with you because we choose to be. We love you. You can't question our devotion, surely?'

'No, no, of course not. I'm sorry. But if you met a young man . . .'

Ursula went on with her combing. She and Nan smiled at each other, and Kate saw something in the look she'd never seen before. They shared a life of which she knew nothing. She envied their closeness, felt foolishly arrogant for thinking their world revolved entirely around her.

'Everything we want is here,' said Ursula, and kissed Nan's head.

Raphael knew how ill Anne was. He'd barely seen Kate for weeks, and understood. When she came to him one night, seeking comfort, it was out of the blue and he found himself less happy to see her than usual, suspecting she was only seeking a shoulder to cry on. She looked exhausted. Drooping, she sat by the fireside in his small chamber and told him about Anne's outburst.

Raphael wanted to comfort her, but her tale made him angry. 'These are bitter rumours about the King,' he said. 'Are they so pernicious now that even his wife believes them?'

'She has nightmares,' said Kate. 'It's the fever.'

'But what provoked such a nightmare?'

'You're one to talk.'

Raphael bit his lip. 'Yes,' he said. 'But I can't say what causes mine, so how can I know what provoked hers?'

Kate's brilliant gaze held his. 'We love the King, and yet it's as if some outside force were trying to persuade us to hate him. Murder, poison . . .'

'Why? Are his enemies practising sorcery upon us?'

'I don't know,' she said. 'Perhaps they are.'

'I would have thought you'd have the answer, priestess of the hidden world.'

'I would have thought you would, since you're the one who weaves all the sinister dreams about him!' She rose and placed her hands on her hips. 'Raphael, why are you angry with me?'

He shook his head, ashamed. 'I'm not. I'm sorry. I'm angry with his enemies, and with whatever cruel fate has brought him so much misfortune.'

He took Kate in his arms, held her firm body against him and smelled the spicy fragrance of her hair. It was too long since they had been together. Sometimes he was close to cursing the King and Queen for taking up their whole lives, giving them no time to be lovers, let alone man and wife.

'Are you crying?' Kate asked gently. 'You are. What for?'

'For the Queen. Richard never shows it but he's distraught; he has been ever since his son died and Anne fell ill.'

He felt Kate's tension. She drew a short breath and asked, 'Do you think he has sought comfort from his niece?'

'What do you mean?'

'You know exactly what I mean.'

Raphael let out a sharp, annoyed sigh. 'If he had, who could blame him?'

He felt Kate shudder. 'You know something.' It was an accusation.

'No,' he said. 'He has always liked Bess. I have seen and heard no more than you. It's only gossip. Why are you troubled by it?'

'Because it hurts Anne! And if it's true, it will destroy her!' She pushed herself away from him. 'He has better friends than Bess. Still, I know he is often in her company, and with the full approval of her mother. Elizabeth Woodville would do anything for her daughter to become queen. *Anything*. Hateful woman. One moment she's trying

432

to destroy Richard, the next pushing her daughter at him.'

'I don't believe Richard would marry his own niece. What would be the point? She was declared a bastard, along with her brothers. What do you think?'

'I think you're being naive,' said Kate. 'I suspect that the beautiful Bessy is infatuated with him, and that he's flattered by her interest, thus giving his enemies another poisoned dart to hurl at him.'

She was shaking. Raphael held her again, trying to still the tremor. He kissed her neck. 'Let's not think about them any more,' he murmured.

Kate responded with a hunger that startled him.

Later, as they lay sated, a dream overtook him. He hadn't suffered such a dream for weeks. Why did it have to happen during this one, snatched night with Kate?

He'd fallen asleep pressed pleasantly against her, his arm over the warm valley of her waist, hoping she wouldn't rouse too soon and insist on returning to the Queen's bedside. The next he knew, he was floating, disembodied, in darkness.

He was in the Tower of London. He didn't know he was dreaming; it was real. The air was heavy and black, with a hint of bed hangings sketched upon it. Nothing was plain but for two faces, children's faces shining like those of cherubs against the dark, and looming over them, a threatening shape, hunched and terrible. An executioner.

The shape turned, and it was Richard.

His chiselled face was serene, lit with the beginnings of an inviting, conspiratorial smile. His eyes were luminous. A long dagger glinted moon-cold in his hand. With the same calm, malevolent joy he lifted first the older boy, then the younger, and, in turn, slit their throats.

Their faces contorted with bewilderment. Their mouths moved in mute pain, like drowning puppies. Blood gushed everywhere. Crimson flooded over their sheets, spraying Richard from head to foot so that he stood dripping with gore. Hands and face and dagger were blood soaked. There were no other colours in the scene, only black, white and red. And through the red veil, Richard was still smiling.

Raphael heaved himself out of sleep and lay gasping like a salmon dragged from a weir.

He opened his eyes to find a woman lying beside him, her face inches from his and her own eyes as wide as moons. In his confusion he had no idea who she was. It seemed a succubus lay with him, instilling nightmares so she could feed upon his terror.

There was a dreadful groaning noise in the room. He scrabbled away from her, fell off the bed and knelt on the stone-cold floor, staring at her, out of his mind. She rose up, her face white and terrible. Her black hair writhed over her shoulders.

'Raphael?' she said. Her voice was high with fear. 'Stop groaning! What's wrong?'

Her concern seemed malevolent, a mockery. She was the one who'd been feeding the horrible visions into him all along. He knew it.

'Get out,' he growled, and crossed himself. 'In Iesu's name, begone!'

'Raph, it's me, Kate. Wake up! Oh, Goddess . . .'

She scrabbled to light a lamp, couldn't reach and got out of bed to crouch over the wick. Light flamed up around her smooth, folded body, turning her bronze. She looked round, pushing her hair back behind one ear. Suddenly the dream let go of him and he realized he knew her.

Cold sweat sheeted over his body and he began to tremble as if with the rigours of fever. 'Oh, Lamb's blood,' he gasped. 'God help me.'

'You frightened me,' she said. 'Get back under the covers.'

'I'm sorry. It was so real.'

She climbed in next to him, and passed him a goblet of watered wine. The liquid was balm to his dry tongue. 'Raph, you're ice-cold. What dream this time?'

He could hardly get the words out. The nightmare clung

to him. Every time he recalled the images, it was as if he was still there.

Eventually Kate said shakily, 'You don't think this really happened, do you? You told me that . . . that you saw them.'

'Yes. I did. Dead of a fever, and their attendants in a flurry of panic.'

Her face looked sickly with genuine distress or with a mockery of it, he could no longer tell. Her every gesture seemed sinister.

'Then he didn't kill them. He can't have done. He was in York at the time.'

'I know!' Raphael cried savagely. 'That's not the point! I know full well he didn't murder them, but something, *something* is trying to make me think he did! In any case, he wouldn't have done it by his own hand. It's symbolic, I know that, but it won't stop. And it will keep on until I go mad! What does it mean?'

She touched his shoulder. He shook her off. Suddenly he couldn't bear her there, witnessing his distress, his weakness. How could she understand?

'Raph, it's all right. I'm here.'

'It's not all right,' he said softly. 'Kate, you'd better go. I am sure the Queen needs you.'

'She has other ladies. I can't leave you like this.'

'I want to be on my own.'

'But, Raph.'

'Please don't argue. Leave me.'

Her face now was wary, hurt, withdrawing. 'If you want, but—'

He couldn't find any softness for her; she seemed a stranger. Savagely he snapped, 'For God's sake, go!' and she slipped into her clothes and left, quick and wide-eyed, without a word.

In the days that followed, Anne was calm again. Against the royal physicians' advice, Richard came to see her, but the visits were difficult. Kate observed that he never knew what to say and almost feared to touch her. Repelled, she surmised, less by the illness itself than by Anne's eerie serenity. It was as if they'd disengaged from each other and were polite cousins again.

No, not always. Sometimes, although they said nothing, there was the ease of familiarity in their posture, the looseness of despair, and Kate sensed that volumes passed between them without words. At those times, she was bitten by jealousy. Then, in the slightest change of demeanour, Richard was obsidian again. Anne was already gone from him, and he knew it. She'd been slipping away since the moment of her son's death. Now it was plain that her husband had no claim upon her emotions, no relevance to her future.

That was what tormented Richard, Kate was sure. It frightened her, too.

One evening Anne was talkative, even cheerful and Kate dared to ask, 'You don't truly believe that Richard was trying to hasten your death, do you?'

'I believed it for a time. I was out of my mind, and the Devil is an opportunist. It must be sickening for my husband to see me lingering like this. If part of him wants it over, I can't blame him for that. But no, he has been nothing if not a friend to me.'

'A friend . . . only?' Her jealous hopes swam up, and made her ashamed.

'A brother, in truth. Richard has been my saviour on this earth, and the dearest of friends, but my true husband is Christ. It's always been so. Kate, you know it. It's why I can bear dying; the time is right. I know my son is in heaven. I shall go to him soon and welcome it.'

Kate was shaken by the confession. 'Weren't you and Richard ever in love?'

'You're sentimental, just like Isabel. Our father Warwick said that women shouldn't read, since it would only fill our heads with stories of courtly love and impossible dreams that would cause us nothing but unhappiness. He was right in wanting to protect us. Still, we couldn't help hearing minstrels singing, or blindfold our eyes to tapestries. Isabel was the romantic one. She was determined to believe Clarence was something he wasn't, and to adore him for it. I was lucky: I listened to my father and followed the hard path. I don't think I can love in that way. It's not within me. Those hopes died a long time ago, even before they married me to that sour-faced Lancastrian prince. No high-born woman expects romantic love, Kate. I have been lucky. I married someone who was a loving cousin and my dearest friend, someone I could trust to the ends of the earth. We shared faith and beliefs. We had a dear son. I couldn't ask for more.'

Katherine frowned. She felt ashamed for being tried by this when Anne was dying, yet couldn't stop herself. It was her only chance to know the truth.

'You don't love your husband?'

'You're not listening to me,' Anne said mildly. 'Of course I love him; how could we not be fond of each other? But if you are talking of passion . . .' She shook her head, indulging Kate's naivety. 'We've known each other too long, and suffered too much. It was never in my nature. He has been my rock. But Richard's passion lies elsewhere.'

'Where?' Kate turned hot and cold.

'With a disease-raddled harlot of a mistress called England.'

The day Anne died, the sky turned black, as if it knew.

The moon passed across the sun, turning it to a jet disk that burned and flared with diamonds. Day turned to dusk, and shimmered with strange multiple shadows. Kate heard people in the streets below the palace walls, crying out with wonder and terror. She shivered. Infected by a superstitious fear that the phenomenon could cause actual harm, she petitioned Auset to protect her mother.

Soon the inevitable sour rumours were making their

rounds. The eclipse was a sign from God; a sign of his black displeasure with King Richard III.

Anne lay in state within a bower of candles. The elementals that clustered around her made a blue glow, a melancholy but peaceful light. As quietly and firmly as she could, Katherine stopped the priests from exorcising them. The lamenting monks stood discreetly in the dark corners of the chamber, softening the air with their mournful chanting and incense.

Richard came and stood looking down at his wife. His hands were folded, his face gaunt. He was like a rope, weathered and drawn tight by grief. Kate wanted to comfort him. She would have done anything to be able to put her arms round him. The urge was a magnetic pull she could barely resist; but it was impossible. Grim, regal, armoured in robes of mourning black, with the flow of sable hair hiding his face, he seemed as distant as the moon. She could no more comfort the King than she could give a friendly hug to an archbishop. It was unthinkable. She dared not even speak, and avoided his eyes in case he should glance at her.

But he didn't even notice her. He was weeping.

He's lost everything, she thought, his supporters, his son, his wife. Now Anne's gone, I have no reason to stay with him . . . yet how can I leave him, or Raphael?

The thought of Raphael slipped another lead weight into her heart.

Presently she stood up and went out as quietly as she could, leaving Richard to pray alone. As she passed through the door into the desolate corridor beyond, she collided with Elizabeth of York. She felt the well-fleshed warmth of Elizabeth's bosom against hers, caught her musky perfume.

'How is he?' Lady Bess whispered, tilting her head to indicate Richard. She was a handsome girl, this daughter of Elizabeth Woodville, ripe and full of life; the opposite of Anne. The opposite of me, too, Kate thought. Compared to Bess she felt old and thin. In her colouring, build and

personality, Bess had none of her mother's icy imperious-
ness but a great deal of her father's florid energy.

'Desolate,' said Kate. She had never shown deference to
Bess, and Bess had never seemed to notice.

The full lower lip bunched a little. 'Naturally. It is still
a shock to him even though he wanted . . . I mean, even
though it was expected.'

'He did not want her to die,' Kate said harshly. 'You
should know better than to listen to such evil rumours.'

Elizabeth bridled. 'I am the last person to pay heed to
such scurrilous nonsense.' Her voice fell. She reminded
Kate of a boisterous, loving dog who would hurl itself at
you, regardless of whether your own demeanour was hostile or welcoming. It was a quality both foolish and endearing. 'Whatever enmity used to be between my mother and
the King is nothing to me. He has my heart. I cannot bear
to see him suffering.'

'Don't go in, my lady,' Kate said with a coolness that
Bess, again, did not notice. 'He needs to be left alone with
the Queen, Creator acquit her soul.'

Bess crossed herself. 'Of course. But I shall wait for him.
Of all the people in this wretched court, I am the only one
capable of consoling him.'

An unpleasant sensation trickled its way through Kate:
irritation at Bess's overflowing confidence, which was too
naive to be arrogance.

'I only hope he may prove consolable.' She lowered
her head, preparing to move away, when Bess touched
her arm.

'Lady Katherine, would you stay and be my lady-in-
waiting?'

Kate managed to swallow what would have been a loud
gasp. 'I'm honoured, my lady, but surely you have women
enough?'

Bess gave a winning, almost pleading smile. 'For my
present station, but perhaps not for my future.' She looked
meaningfully at the door to the chapel, where Richard

stood in darkness. Kate felt like lashing out with a fist and knocking her down. 'Besides, Anne liked you so very much. She said you were the best healer she ever knew, better than any physician, and that her sister Isabel would not have been without you in . . .' The round, handsome face flushed. She whispered coyly, 'In childbirth.'

Kate stood looking at her shoes, fighting an urge to laugh hysterically. Oh, lovely. Lady-in-waiting to Richard's second queen. And yet it was the only way to stay near him.

Somehow she forced a look of warmth onto her face. 'My lady, are you likely to be married soon?'

'I hope so.' Bess clasped her arm and pulled her aside, standing so close Kate felt her warm breath. She was very voluptuous. And Richard was not made of ice. Only towards me, Kate thought, hating him so bitterly she could have seized a sword and slain him as he mourned. 'I hope so. My mother says I was born to wear a crown, as she was.'

Kate could have said any number of vicious things that would have got her banished from court instantly. *So, for all your smiling charm, you will do anything to get a crown on your head; even bed your own uncle and dance on Anne's grave. You are more like your mother than I thought.*

Perhaps some of it showed in her expression. Bess hastened to justify herself. 'Lady Katherine, don't mistake me. My mother's reason is not mine. I'm his in heart, body and soul.'

'When did you fall in love with him?' Kate asked casually.

'I don't know.' Bess chewed her lower lip, turning it rose-red. 'I've always thought him handsome, haven't you? There's a light in him that people don't notice because he's quiet. Not like my father!' She started to laugh, then recollected herself, and stifled it. 'But once you see that glow in him, it shines brighter and brighter.'

Kate said coldly, 'Yet people are saying that he killed your brothers.'

Bess coloured. For a full ten seconds she said nothing. 'Do you know what they say of you, Lady Katherine? You have a reputation for saying things that no one else would even dare. Now I see it's true. My brothers were very ill. Lady Beaufort told me so herself. She's a right-eous and kindly woman and would not lie to me. She even mixed potions for them, and gave them to the good Dr Argentine to administer. People were trying to save them, not kill them, but the fever took them anyway, Creator acquit their sweet souls. It was not Richard's fault.'

'No,' said Kate. 'And does he love you?'

Bess caught her breath for a quick answer, then stopped herself with all her mother's poise. 'I hope that he will, once he has mourned his dear wife.'

'I suppose the devil you know is preferable to Henry Tudor.'

Bess gasped. 'Lady Katherine, you are wicked! I'd rather throw myself in a cage of starving graylix than marry a man I'd never met! I must have you with me. Please give me an answer.'

A dull mirth unfolded inside Kate like a scorpion's tail. She heard herself saying, 'Of course I will serve you, my lady. I'm honoured.'

'You are a good, good person,' Bess said sweetly, and kissed her cheek.

Woodenly Kate walked away, too numb and tired to feel anything. As she reached the far doorway, she heard a voice say, 'Bessy.' She looked round and saw Richard emerging from the chapel. His face, though sad, was trans-formed with pleasure. He was pressing his lips to Lady Elizabeth's hand, and she was curtseying and fluttering in a way that made Kate sick to her stomach.

After the dream of Richard soaked in blood, the visions began to torment Raphael in earnest. Almost every night, there was some mad pantomime awaiting him: Richard as a character upon a stage, stooped and deformed yet loping about with a terrifying, spidery energy; Richard with demonic eyes and a great mound upon his back, dripping poison into his wife's mouth, despoiling his niece while grinding the skulls of her two brothers into the earth beneath his boot. He saw a chronicler, who'd written reams in praise of Richard, tearing up his own words and replacing them with malicious condemnation to please Richard's enemies. Raphael knew what he was doing, and screamed his rage, but could not make himself heard.

Each morning he would wake exhausted, half-deranged. Somehow he struggled through his duties, dismissing the concerns of Francis Lovell, Will Shaw and others who remarked that he looked dreadful. Yes, literally, full of dread.

He broke his promise to Richard always to tell him of the dreams. How on earth could he trouble the King with this catalogue of wild imaginings? Once or twice was acceptable, but every night? Richard would only gain the impression that he was mad, possessed, or even mocking him for some sinister reason.

Richard had important affairs of state, Parliament and foreign policy to attend to. He had burdens enough. Raphael could do nothing but suffer in silence.

Worst of all was Kate.

Now she no longer had Anne to occupy her, she came to him every night, pleading with him to tell her what was wrong. He couldn't. Talking of it made things no better; if anything, it made them worse. Her concern made him feel guilty and desperate, because he could find no comfort, even in her. The last thing he could do was to let her stay with him at night. Certainly he had no love to give her, not even lust. All his energy was swallowed by the dreams, walking through them, trying to comprehend them, fighting them.

He began to fear sleep, and strove to stay awake, but lack of sleep for several nights only made things worse. At last he was forced to succumb. That was when he had the worst vision of all.

He was standing at the end of a long throne room. A dark vault enclosed the space, with rows of colourless windows running along both sides. At the far end he could just make out the shadow-shape of the throne on its dais, and knew the King sat there.

Cold and wrung-out with fear, Raphael began to walk the length of the chamber. He did so with a quietly gathering sense of dread. As he drew close, he looked up and saw the King gazing down upon him from the shadowy heights of the throne.

It was not Richard.

The face was gaunt and haughty. The eyes that gazed disdainfully from under heavy lids were yellow, like winter sun on snow, like a lizard's. A ripple of mousy hair fell from under a heavy velvet cap. Long hands clawed at the arms of the throne.

Raphael looked up at this alien figure, and felt his mind fragmenting. 'I have come to see the King,' he said. 'Where is he?'

'I am the King,' said the stranger.

'No, you're not. Where's Richard?'

The usurper smiled. His teeth were like brown needles. Then Raphael saw the people around him and knew them to be Richard's enemies: Bishop Morton, Thomas Stanley and his brother William, the Earl of Northumberland, Elizabeth Woodville. They looked subtly different and their clothes were strange, yet he recognized them. They were all laughing at him. Sitting on the throne next to Henry was Lady Bess, her plump beauty now oddly gaunt and strained; his Queen.

'Where's Richard?' he cried again.

'Richard is dead.'

'No.' Panic rose, because in the dream he knew it was true.

'Let me show you how he died,' said Henry Tudor. He

lifted a languid hand, and Raphael was sent spiralling into the pounding rush of a battlefield.

All around him was the metal stink of armour and blood. An endless, impossible struggle to reach an armoured figure with a gold coronet upon the helmet, battling as it fell under a deluge of blows. Raphael knew it was too late and was unable to reach him, but still he went on striving, anguish roaring from his throat, his own screams tearing him apart as he watched the last Plantagenet king fall, betrayed and butchered, and knew he could do nothing, nothing to save him.

Now I *was* terrified. Raphael's torment and the impossibility of helping him left me distraught. I only caught flashes of what he was experiencing, but it was plain enough. Our past, and his future.

This was the worst time for me. I avoided Fin, because I couldn't even share it with her. I was frightened, depressed and grief-stricken. I couldn't sleep. My dark lover Richard didn't come; instead it was Raphael's nightmares that visited me by night and brought me sweating and gasping out of my restless bed.

I switched on my desk light, sat down and tried to read instead. Still trembling but calmer now, I was trying to work out what the date would be for them, how much time they had left. Not much, not much. What would become of Kate and her graceful son, if Henry VII's cold gaze and that of his bishops fell upon them? In *my* reality, Henry had hunted down and slaughtered almost every one of Richard's relations, and on any pretext: from Richard's natural son John to defenceless old women.

I looked at pictures of old portraits, seals, letters, tombs. They put a flat, black and white distance between the immediacy of it. I tried to convince myself of Fin's words: it's over, it's history.

One photograph was of two carved figures upon a tomb: Henry VII and his Queen, Elizabeth of York, eldest daughter of Edward IV. Lying side by side they looked handsome, peaceful and saintly.

Had this paragon, the mother of Henry VIII, really

once come close to marrying Richard III? It seemed incredible.

Again, every author differed.

Richard's detractors portrayed Bess as a wilting victim, pursued by her ruthless, villainous uncle. Naturally she had recoiled from Richard's repellent advances and fled gratefully towards the hero, Henry Tudor.

His apologists showed an ambitious and forward young woman who was infatuated with her uncle and urged him towards a marriage he never wanted. The impulsion was all hers. A fact to be flatly denied and buried later, since no such stain could be allowed to attach to the character of Henry's queen.

Others said it was a relationship of mutual passion, consummated while Anne lay dying, and thwarted only by Richard's own councillors. It was they who advised him strongly against the match, saying the country would never accept it. Reluctantly he had put her aside. And she became the woman scorned, her love curdling to savage hatred and vengeance.

Who could know the truth?

Then I sat thinking of poor Kate and her anguish if Richard had turned, not to her, but to his niece. I didn't want to believe it of him.

And yet, as I sat looking at the stone effigies, there was a streak of delicious eroticism in the idea that Bess of York had never loved the husband beside whom she lay in virtuous peace. That she had once adored his enemy, the ultimate forbidden lover: Richard.

I sat back from the book and suddenly became aware that my face was saturated with tears. I felt calm now. It was as if a little of Kate's Goddess had woken in me. I was going to try something – one desperate, heartfelt attempt to communicate with them.

I lay down on the bed and began to meditate, slowing my breathing until I could feel myself hovering on the edge of sleep. Trance or dream, I'm still not sure. The world turned green around me and I found myself in a place I recognized, that I had visited in reality, the same, but subtly altered in its etheric form. I was floating through the underwater glow of a ruined church. Calm, and knowing exactly what must be said, as if Auset herself would speak through me, I waited.

Chapter Seventeen 1485: Bess

QUEEN ELIZABETH
Yet thou didst kill my children.

KING RICHARD
But in your daughter's womb I bury them
Where, in that nest of spicery, they will breed
Selves of themselves, to your recomforture.

Richard III Act IV scene 4

'How long has he been like this?' said Kate.

'All morning,' Will Shaw answered. It took a lot to destroy his usual jovial mood, but now he looked grey. 'He's not been right for days. He tries to hide it, but I always know.'

'He's had these fits for as long as I've known him,' Francis Lovell added. 'Never this bad, though. I could always wake him out of it before. I'm sorry, Lady Katherine. The last thing we wanted was to distress you. We don't know what to do.'

She stared down at Raphael writhing upon the bed, his eyes staring at scenes she couldn't imagine, his mouth twisted. Her tears fell on him.

'You were right to tell me,' she said. 'I should never have forgiven you if you hadn't.'

'Is he possessed?' said Francis, pallid with anxiety. 'Can you help him?'

'I don't know,' she said. 'I don't know.'

She tried to reach him. She trickled brews of soothing herbs onto his tongue, but he only choked and spat them out. In the end there was nothing she could do but sit there while the visions plagued him. He cried out, shouting at people she couldn't see. Torment wracked his body in fits. His eyes bulged. Sweat ran through his hair, veins snaked in his temples. She barely recognized him.

A priest and a physician came, sent by Richard. The first wanted to exorcise him, the second to restrain, purge and bleed him. Katherine drove them out with such fury that they turned crimson with shock, and fled.

The only people she allowed to stay were gentle Francis Lovell and Will Shaw. Lovell was upset, hovering anxiously at the foot of Raphael's bed. Shaw was a steadying presence. He was calm and practical, fetching and carrying for Kate. Nan crept in to help, mouse-quiet. Presently Ursula came, telling Kate that Lady Bess had summoned her. Kate sent her away with the message that a friend was seriously ill, and Lady Bess would have to wait.

Now she would be dismissed from court for certain, and she didn't care.

The visions let Raphael go at last, and he fell into a deep, heavy-breathing sleep.

Kate was exhausted. She made Francis and Will go and have supper, asking that they bring her back some left-overs. Alone with Raphael, she sat stroking his forehead, trying not to break down and begging Auset to help him.

A creak. The door opened, and light from the corridor fell through.

'I hope you've brought plenty, Will, and some decent wine,' she said.

'I am empty-handed, my lady,' said a voice that was not Shaw's.

The King came in and stood over Katherine, looking down at Raphael. She felt her limbs tensing, turning to iron. 'You sent away my physician and priest,' he said.

'Because the priest would have made him worse, and the physician would have killed him,' she said tightly. Every gesture he made only salted her wounds: the memory of his tender kiss upon Bess's hand, her flushed excitement, the web of rumours.

Richard sat on the edge of Raphael's bed and looked down at him. His knee was almost touching hers. 'He's one of my best and most loyal friends,' he said, taking Raphael's limp hand. 'It would be hard to bear if anything happened to him. What ails him?'

She found it difficult to answer. Her anger bled away. She saw Richard as someone who'd lost his family, and now feared losing a friend. He sat there, disconsolate, concerned and merely human.

'I'm not sure, Your Grace,' she said, wondering how much to tell him. 'He has suffered for years with nightmares.'

'Ah, his visions.' Richard's head dropped.

'You know about them?'

'He told me years ago. First was some dream that I had slaughtered Henry the Sixth. If he ever had a fair dream about me, he's kept it to himself.'

'And did he tell you . . .' No, it was unthinkable to mention his dream of the two Princes, which had disturbed him so violently that he'd driven her out. The memory was horrible. 'Anything of late?'

'Nothing.' Richard looked at her with tired eyes. 'But then, I have been somewhat preoccupied. Francis said he was raving, that he'd gone mad.'

'He appeared to be fighting some phantom battle,' said Kate. 'I can't tell what it was about until he wakes up and can explain it himself. Richard?'

'Yes, Kate?'

'You won't dismiss him from service because of this, will you?'

'Gods, of course not! If he can't return to work, I shall give him a fine estate and a good pension. He'll want for nothing. But all I desire is to see him fit and well again.'

A frown creased his forehead. He remained silent for

a time. Kate wondered what he was thinking about. His wife, his son, his brothers?

Presently Richard said, 'I should like to know what dream he had, and what it meant.'

'Why? It would be dangerous to think he was seeing into the future.'

'I don't know. I am clutching at straws. If he had a presentiment based on truth, perhaps it would help me to be forewarned. Still, he might only have envisioned something thoroughly predictable.'

'A battle?'

'The Tudor nobody has tried before; he will try again. I know how many enemies I have, Kate, and how many of them have gone over to the traitor. Every move I make causes the rattling of malicious tongues.' He was looking down somewhere in the direction of Raphael's hand, unfocused. 'Still, I never expected kingship to be easy. Why should it be easy? The question is, what degree of difficulty becomes the judgement of God?'

He pinched the bridge of his nose. He looked as if he needed to weep, but was too exhausted. His face paled, suddenly revealing a depth of pain that made her reel.

'Raphael's sickness represents the deterioration of everything around me, the manifestation of the shadow. Whatever demon has a grip upon me, he enacts its intentions.'

Kate looked at him in horror. She felt trapped in a crumbling abyss between them: Raphael raving; the King falling apart in a way that was quieter but as absolute.

He was losing everything. Betrayed by Buckingham, bereft of his wife and son. All support slipping away.

'What else has he dreamed of late?' Richard asked. His eyes and voice compelled her to answer.

'That you killed the two Princes, even though he knows full well you did not.'

'Ah,' he said. 'I don't know if Raphael dreams the future, but he does dream the truth.'

'No. They were ill. He told me. It wasn't your fault.'

451

'Not according to my conscience. What else? Did he see images of me slipping poison into Anne's mouth?'

'No,' said Kate, fighting sour tears.

'That's something.' His silence was so intense, so anguished that it was all she could do to stay near him.

'I am so sorry about Anne.' Her voice cracked. 'I did everything I could. You must blame me.'

He looked sideways at her, surprised. 'Blame? Of course not. Anne would not have lived so long, nor had such a gentle passing, without you. How could you think I blame you?'

'I always wonder if there was something else I could have done. My mother tells me it's foolish delusion to believe that healers of Auset should be infallible, but I can't help it.'

One corner of his mouth twisted upwards. 'A delusion shared by kings. Forgive me for sending the priest and the doctor – it was an act of desperation. If anyone can help Raphael, it's you. I should have had more faith.'

Kate, watching the King leaning over the bed, realized that he loved Raphael, a simple, unswerving love he held for all his close friends. Warmth swept over her, a strange recognition moved her. Made her envious, too.

'You should,' she said tiredly.

'Please help him,' he whispered. 'I beg you.'

They were silent for a time. Kate sensed a strange and gentle intimacy in sitting so close to him, united in concern. Poignant, because it was an illusion. She couldn't touch the King, and soon he would be gone and be unreachable again.

Raphael frowned in his sleep, and made a small, sharp moan.

'I heard that Lady Elizabeth has asked for you to serve her,' Richard said presently.

So, Bess had confided in him. She wondered if they spoke so intimately to each other, and if his hands strayed to explore her full, welcoming bosom and to stroke the sunflower hair under its gossamer veils of silk.

'Yes, she has,' said Kate. 'Apparently my reputation as a midwife is carolled the length and breadth of the kingdom. Would you mind?'

Lines tensed around his eyes. His lashes half-hid his eyes. 'Why should I mind?'

'Perhaps you'd sooner I left the court.'

Looking at Raphael, not at her, he said softly, 'Have we not had this conversation before? There is no need for you to leave.'

'Would I be serving your noble but bastard niece, or serving the Queen?'

Richard released his breath sharply. 'You have a scorpion tongue, Katherine.'

Kate bit the inside of her lip. No denial of the relationship. She took it as an admission. 'You used to praise my honesty. I have nothing to lose. No position, no influence, no political games to play.'

He looked at her, expressionless. 'There are always games to be played. Have you decided? You must be the only noblewoman in the realm who would dream of refusing a future queen, but still, you have the choice.'

So, he realized she might not relish the role, but did he understand why? It was burning the tip of her scorpion tongue to tell him the truth. *I cannot stand to see you marry again while I am taken for granted as servant to your wife, uncomplaining, humble in love. Not again. I am no martyr. My own pride would slay me!*

She didn't say it. The admission would be humiliating. And there was the risk that Raphael, although he appeared to be unconscious, might hear her.

'Lady Bess is a good and lovable girl, but she has no hold upon my affections,' said Kate. 'All I care for at this moment is Raphael. She can throw tantrums at my inattentiveness all she likes. I can't go to her, can't even think about her, until Raphael is well again. She can

453

have me dismissed from court, for all I care; he is all that matters.'

'You won't be dismissed.'

She looked at him. 'Why not?' she said coolly.

He was quiet. Colour came into his cheeks, then a steeliness that didn't quite mask his discomfort. 'You've become the heart of the place. Dame Grey is the opposite, like a door onto a freezing faerie realm that lies under perpetual winter. You are the hearth. I can't imagine my court without you.'

'In spite of my outrageous blasphemies and forbidden practises?'

'None of us is perfect,' he said flatly. 'You would be missed. *I* would miss you.'

Kate could find no sarcastic riposte to that. She said, lamely, 'Thank you, Your Grace, but you must miss me for a time.'

'Why?'

'Because I don't know how to heal Raphael. I feel helpless. All I can think to do is to take him to my mother.'

'To Derbyshire?'

'You have an impressive memory, sire.'

'Attention to detail, for which my councillors curse me. It's a hard journey for a sick man. There are good physicians . . .'

'This is nothing a physician can help. My mother's the only one I can turn to. May I take him?'

She was sure he would refuse. Perhaps she should have lied, and said it was a pilgrimage to Walsingham for a holy cure. He rose slowly, the creases of his robes falling back into place. 'The moment you deem him fit to travel, I'll order horses and an entourage to guard you on your way.'

To her shock, as he passed her, she felt him bend and drop a kiss onto the crown of her head. Lightning. In the next breath he said, 'Marry him, Kate. Few men are fortunate enough to enjoy such devoted love.'

A few minutes after Richard had left, Raphael opened his eyes. He looked ghastly, yellow as beeswax. Kate helped him sit up and gave him sips of watery wine to moisten his mouth. He seemed drained, but lucid at last.

'The King was here,' she said.

His eyes widened. 'What did you tell him?'

'The little I knew. That you seemed to be possessed by visions of battle. He's extremely concerned for you.'

Raphael groaned. His voice was shaky, and there was a wildness in his eyes that alarmed her. 'Creator's blood, the battle was the least of it. Such things I've seen, Kate. Am I mad? The world's shimmering and changing shape even as I look at it. The ways are so dark and long, like tunnels into the earth. I don't think I can come back.'

'Drink this,' she said. 'An infusion of calming herbs.'

She brought the goblet towards him but he batted her wrist aside, spilling half of it. 'Herbs won't make it go away! I've seen Richard's death!'

She jerked away from his anguish. 'Keep your voice down!'

'I must warn him.'

'No, Raphael. Not yet. Not until we understand what it means.'

At that – perhaps it was her sympathy that unravelled him – he gave a moan and squeezed his eyes shut upon a spill of tears. 'Kate, I've become a spectre. I've gone into the shadow world and I can't come back. I'm sorry, sorry.'

'What for?'

He clutched her hand. His fingers felt skeletal.

'I can be no lover and no husband to you. Forgive me.'

Staring at him, she felt her mouth squaring with denial. He was rejecting her. She was astonished. She had always thought that if they ever parted, it would be her decision, not his . . . but once her shock faded, she felt a strange clarity. He was right. How could they stay lovers, when he was half invalid, half mystic, and she his nurse? She'd never been honest, never admitted her fierce and shaming passion for another man, and this was her reward. Grief came. She mourned the end of a love that had been sweet and gentle . . . but she knew, also, that she and Raphael could never cease to love each other, any more than a sister and brother could cease.

'It's all right, sweetheart,' she said, crying. 'Don't fear any more. I'm taking you to Eleanor, and she'll know what to do.'

Auset help us, Kate thought. She had better.

Katherine was dreaming. She was sixteen again, labouring to bring forth Robin, every tendon straining until her eyesight turned red. Everything was painted scarlet: walls, bed hangings, her mother's skin. Eleanor laboured with her. In the dream the pain was blunt, and the scene held a strange ecstasy, as if she floated in serenity while the baby was expelled. Many times she'd seen Eleanor act as surrogate for another woman. Now she did so for her own daughter, gladly and without judgement. In the dream, Katherine looked in wonder on her mother's silently screaming face, wondering how she had the strength to take such pain while Kate merely floated.

She woke in a nun's cell. Their last lodging was an abbey half a day's ride from Lytton Dale. The mixed sense of loss and euphoria stayed with her, colouring the morning. She was glad to be going home. Nan and Ursula, though yawning and grumbling as they roused themselves, seemed in equally good heart.

The moment she stepped into the cloister, and saw Raphael's waxen visage as he walked towards her, her mood sank again. His face was losing its smooth-fleshed youthfulness, becoming thin; even his lips seemed drawn back against his teeth. Throughout their journey he'd been calm and lucid, resigned but wrung-out with exhaustion. She'd been glad of Will Shaw's earthy presence and his tireless good cheer. She had nothing left to offer Raphael herself.

Tentatively, she asked, 'How was your sleep?'

He looked at her and shook his head. 'No clear dreams. Only images.'

'Of what?'

'I can't tell. Lies and hatred.'

Shaw, who'd spent the night watching over Raphael, came into the cloister behind him bearing baggage. He gave Kate his usual quick, awkward bow of respect. 'I'll see the horses are saddled. Looks like a fine day.'

Summer was full, the afternoon fair as Katherine and Raphael rode towards the manor. All the way from London, the handful of liveried men Richard had sent with them had turned the heads of onlookers as they rode by. Will Shaw was steadfast at Raphael's side.

Eleanor came out to meet the party, with Martha and Thomas Copper, and Copper's son Tom, now a grown man. Katherine had written to her, saying only that she was bringing a friend in dire need of help. Eleanor's face was serene, but Kate saw the nuances, her brows arched a little in surprise to see outriders in the gleaming livery and the leopards and lilies of the King.

Kate was off her tireless Spanish mare and running into her mother's arms.

'Who is your sick friend?' Eleanor whispered.

'It's Raphael Hart.'

'Ohh. So that is Raphael? I haven't seen him since he was a boy . . . but yes, he hasn't changed.'

Kate turned. Raphael was still on horseback, looking around him with watery eyes and blinking against the sunlight. The welcoming shape of the manor, blending with the soft greens of the gardens that surrounded it, the falling flanks of the hills rich with woodlands – he absorbed everything with the look of a man who'd been snatched into faerie land.

'No colour in his face,' said Eleanor. 'What ails him?'

'A malady of the spirit, not the body,' Kate said. 'I've fought off priests wanting to exorcise him, doctors wanting to purge him. I think if he hadn't been the King's good friend, they would have cast him into some dungeon by now. But he's not possessed, not ill. He's a visionary, but the visions are driving him out of his mind. If we can't help him, who will?'

'Kate,' said Eleanor, wincing, and she realized she'd been pinching her mother's arms tighter and tighter as she spoke.

'Sorry,' she said, loosing her grip. 'Where's Robin?'

'In the stables, as usual. I asked him to stay out of sight for a while, in case you haven't told Raphael yet.'

'I haven't.' She shivered. 'It won't matter now, anyway.'

'Come in, love. Bring him inside. Tom will take care of your escort and their horses. Let Nan and Ursula go with Martha. No doubt they've much news to exchange.'

Raphael gathered himself enough to bow and give Lady Lytton a formal greeting. She asked him nothing, only welcomed him and led them through the great hall and up to her private solar. There she had food and drink brought, and left them to rest and refresh themselves. Alone, Kate and Raphael were polite and kind to each other, but he seemed a thousand miles distant.

After an hour or so, Eleanor returned.

'Raphael, your mother Edith was a close friend of mine. I cared for her until her death. She spoke of you often, and it was to my unending regret that I was unable to tell her you were alive.'

Muscles tensed in the corners of Raphael's mouth. He said in a low voice, 'Madam, the trouble that brings me to you now is the same as that which separated me from her. I was lost in visions and nightmares and didn't know who I was. By the time I remembered, or rather, allowed myself to remember, it was too late.'

He spoke with dignity. Eleanor nodded. 'You're honest. I appreciate that, since we'll get nowhere unless you *are* honest with me. Those conflicts of York and Lancaster made many orphans, and deprived me of my husband.'

'And they're not over.'

'Is this what troubles you? Speak candidly to me. I won't think you unmanly. Nothing you say will go beyond the three of us.'

Raphael took several breaths. Pain passed over his bleached face. 'I love the King,' he said. 'I have loved him since we were children. I've fought for him, served him, and been as loyal as a man could be. Yet my dreams have contained nothing but treason. I've dreamed of him committing bloody murders that he did not commit. I've dreamed that chroniclers were writing of him in the most iniquitous terms, as if to portray him as the very Devil. I saw . . . I saw another king on the throne, and the queen at his side was Bess, Elizabeth of York.'

Kate gasped. 'You didn't tell me that!'

'I couldn't.' His voice was like sand. 'I can hardly bear to think of it, let alone speak of it. Lady Eleanor, it's not just the dreams themselves. It's the tone of them. They are like grey nightmares, full of sinister revelation, as if all the demons of hell are about to erupt from the air and drag me down with them. Terrible fear. So yes, I saw this cold-eyed scrawny Lancastrian king on the throne, and I knew he'd killed Richard and stolen his crown.'

'Was it Henry Tudor?' said Katherine.

'Yes. I've never seen him, but in the vision, I knew it was him.'

'But he stands no chance. That's what they say. He has a chaotic gathering of ruffians against a great warrior with a royal army!'

'I saw the battle,' Raphael said helplessly. 'I was in it! Some of Richard's greatest nobles will betray him and go to the enemy. I saw Richard cut down. Overwhelmed, cut down and slaughtered, crying of treason. I fought to my last breath to save him, and couldn't.'

He was shaking his head in despair. Kate seized his hands. 'Raph, this is your fear of what might happen, not reality!'

'Kate, shut up,' Eleanor said crisply.

'I'm not claiming to see the future,' said Raphael. 'I can't tell what it is. Should I warn the King, when I might only be troubling him with my own phantoms? Shall I just take myself away, and trouble him no more? I don't know what to do. I want it to stop, that's all. Just for it to stop!'

He pulled his hands out of Kate's. Her eyes smarted. She remembered how he'd told her their love was over, and how she'd felt guilty relief mixed with her misery. The visions had stolen all the confidence and serenity that had shaped his beauty. At this moment she only pitied him, and hated the feeling.

Eleanor was quiet, studying Raphael's face. She said, 'I can't give you a quick answer. To know what these visions mean, I shall have to come into them with you.' She held out her hand. 'Will you trust me, and come with me?'

Raphael began to look apprehensive. He gave a quick nod. 'There's no way to escape them except to go right through the heart of them.'

'Tonight,' said Eleanor. 'Rest this afternoon; sleep if you can. It will be a long night. If you're troubled by visitations, don't be afraid, only observe them, and report them to me. That's all you are now, Raphael, dear. My observer.'

Raphael had no dreams that afternoon. He slept easily in a warm, wood-panelled room and woke feeling calm and subdued, as if Eleanor truly had taken the burden from him.

It was early evening. He rose, dressed and went out into the garden, plucked an apple from the tree and ate it, cold dew and all. Tonight he must walk knowingly into the visions instead of fighting to escape, and not emerge until the truth was known. He was terrified. But for now there was peace, nothing to disturb the green lushness of the world. A thrush spilled its fluid song over him.

'Raphael?'

Kate was looking for him. He saw her in the distance, moving along the edge of the house behind banks of lavender. He withdrew into the orchard. Not that he didn't want her company, just a brief time alone, to prepare.

He avoided her for a while, watching her through curtains of foliage. She passed out of sight. The world felt deserted.

'Raphael!' Her voice came again, nearer. He stepped from the cover of foliage and saw her coming towards him in a leaf-green gown, her hair loose. 'Oh, there you are. I was worried—'

'That I'd fled?'

'That the faeries had taken you, actually. They're particularly undiscriminating around here.'

He laughed. She smiled, too, but her manner was serious. 'You haven't eaten, have you?'

'One small apple.'

'I don't suppose that matters. Good. Mother insists that we must fast before our journey. If you're hungry, I'm sorry, but we can eat afterwards.'

'I feel there will be no afterwards,' he said quietly.

Her lips thinned. 'Then you won't have to worry about eating, will you? Come and get ready. You'll need warmer clothes than that.'

They were walking back to the house, through the herb garden that lay behind the stables, when Raphael saw the lad. He crossed in front of them, giving Raphael a start of recognition. As they entered the stable yard itself, he appeared again, walking straight towards them.

Raphael's mouth dropped. It was Richard. A very young Richard: the same dark hair, grey eyes, strong clear face. For a moment he was sure he'd somehow stepped into the wrong world.

'A good evening to you, Lady Katherine, my lord,' he said as he passed them, giving a quick shy smile. When Raphael turned to see where he was going, he had vanished around a corner of the house.

461

'Who was that?'

Kate had stopped in her tracks. Her face was stony. 'That was Robin.'

'But he looks like . . . like . . .'

She flushed scarlet. Her eyes were hard, shining. 'He looks exactly like his father, yes.'

'His father?'

'Don't stand looking at me like a sheep. Who does he look like to you?'

'The King.'

'There you have it,' she snapped.

'I don't understand. Are you saying he actually is . . . ?'

'Yes, he really is Richard's son.'

Raphael stood dumb, feeling idiotic. 'But how is that possible? What's he doing here? Richard has never mentioned him. You're having some kind of jest with me. You know he has two natural children, don't you?'

'Yes, I'm aware of that.'

'Then you'll know he's kindness itself to them, gives them every kind of preferment. He couldn't have this boy and never mention him. It wouldn't be like him at all. I don't understand.'

Kate looked ready to strike him. Raphael's confusion began to swell into dread. 'Richard doesn't know Robin exists,' she said. 'I don't have to explain this to you!'

A current of foreboding was pushing its way through him. 'No, you don't. It's none of my business. I'm just very puzzled.'

'I knew you were bound to see him, if ever you came here.'

'Why should it matter if I saw him? Kate? Who is his mother?'

She opened her hands.

All he thought he had known of the world crumbled. He turned, ran and was brought up short by a dry-stone wall at the edge of the orchard. Reaching it he fell to his knees and dashed his head against the stones.

'That must have hurt,' Kate said, drily, over his shoulder. 'Don't try it twice.'

He turned and sat slumped against the wall. 'This is a dream. I thought I'd escaped.'

'You're wide awake. Look, real blood.'

He put his hand to his temple and looked numbly at the redness on his fingertips. 'How could you not tell me?'

She folded her arms tightly around herself. 'I've never told anyone.'

'But I was different! We were friends, lovers! We were going to be married – how could you not say something? You lied to me.'

'No. I wasn't required to lie, since you never actually asked me if I'd had a child by the King.'

He swung his hand at her, not really meaning to hit her, just lashing out at his own pain. She dodged easily, and looked at him with narrowing eyes.

'I don't believe you,' he said. 'You didn't know Richard until you came to Middleham. You'd never met him. You can't have—'

He realized that this was jealousy – not only of Richard, but of Kate. He'd always thought of Richard as *his*. Had even thought that Richard and Kate didn't much care for each other.

'Of course I'd met him. After Barnet, don't you remember? And I served Anne's sister, Isabel. Naturally he came to see his brother Clarence, usually to argue with him. I tried to avoid him on those occasions.'

Raphael was shaking his head. 'The boy I saw was older. Richard was a faithful husband, the world knows that.'

'It was before. When we were both very young. I didn't even know who he was.'

Raphael laughed, horrified. 'You slept with a man you didn't know?'

'I will not tolerate your judgement upon me! I am not your wife. You turned me aside. I don't belong to you, I owe you nothing, least of all an explanation! Raphael.'

She crouched down beside him in the long grass, her hand on his knee. 'I should have told you. Forgive me. Robin is there, and no one knows except a few in this house, and that's all there is to it.'

He was remembering something she'd once told him, a fragment of the truth. *'It was someone, once, long ago, when I was young and silly. We didn't love each other; we barely met. It was a foolish mistake.'*

He put his hand over his eyes. 'How could you not tell Richard?'

'Because I didn't want to be beholden to him for the rest of my life. Just another youthful mishap, a ruined woman. I am not ruined.'

He exhaled, suddenly suspicious, remembering. 'Gods. The times I saw you with him, and thought nothing of it.'

'There was nothing to think.'

'Is that so?'

'He sought my opinion sometimes, though I don't think we have ever agreed about anything. We were . . . friends.'

'Friends? Without any desire for each other? Without any tender feelings at all?'

Her eyelids fell. She looked away. That answered him.

'Christ, Kate, tell me the truth! You said you didn't love him.'

'I've tried my hardest not to. I haven't been as successful as I hoped.'

'Iesu's blood. All the time that I thought you loved me!'

'I do love you. But I have never been able to forget about Richard.'

'Is that why you can't leave each other alone?'

'It's why he and I are always arguing. It's why I've not been able to marry you.'

'Then,' he said venomously, 'we've both had a lucky escape.'

Kate looked icily at him. There was no remorse in her, and that made him almost hate her. 'Rail at me, be furious

464

with me – you've every right. But do it later. We have a journey to undertake. You set me aside, so I'm sure you can set your anger aside, for Richard's sake.'

He let the hand drop. A cold mass hardened inside him. Everything he had cared about was being stripped away and, strangely, it gave him courage. 'You're not who I thought you were, Kate. Now I know I was right to part from you. Now I'm glad.'

'Get up.' She spoke briskly, but her voice trembled. 'Here's my mother.'

He obeyed, defeated. Eleanor was coming through the trees, magnificent and forbidding, in a full cloak of blue-black velvet with a hood half-hiding her face. Twilight was chilling the sky from gold to grey.

She looked from Raphael to Kate. Her eyebrows lifted. 'What has happened?'

Kate gestured helplessly. 'He met Robin.'

'I see.'

'I know I should have told him. I know! You warned me often enough.'

'Well. It's done now.'

'Lady Lytton,' said Raphael. 'Forgive me, but after this I can't go upon this journey with you. Perhaps Katherine meant me not to find out until afterwards. I wish it had happened so, because I can't . . .'

'Raphael,' Eleanor said gently. 'Your distress will pass. You have found out now for a reason, which is that you will need the knowledge upon your journey. Come.'

Raphael looked at her in disbelief.

'Come with me,' Eleanor repeated, not to be disobeyed. 'Kate shall stay here, then you needn't be arguing all the way. You and I shall go alone.'

The cave of the Cauldron Hollow thrummed with power. Raphael looked about him, shivering. Everything seemed precisely cold and white. The day's warmth had not reached here. There was only the pale, sepulchral curve of the arch framing the cave, the flat silver of the river below, and a perfect opal moon.

Eleanor bade him sit with her in the centre of the cave before a stump of stone. On the stump she set candles, a wreath of nightshade and celandine, and a bowl of dark liquid that she'd carried carefully from the house. An altar.

Raphael looked around uneasily, saw the crude black goddess-figure sitting in her niche in the back wall. Eleanor was no longer Kate's friendly if regal mother; she was a priestess. She was serious and self-contained; all business. He felt reassured by that. Fear streamed through him, but he watched it from a distance. He was going to give himself up to whatever Eleanor required.

'We call upon the protection of the guardians here present to watch over us on our journey,' murmured Eleanor. 'We call upon Auset, Dark Mother of All, to be present. Welcome, Great Mother, blessed art thou. Be our protection and our channel, unlock the mysteries of your faithful son Raphael.'

He no longer felt darkness at his back. Candlelight and Eleanor's words made an impenetrable sacred sphere around them. Beyond it, the world had turned blue.

'Drink,' said Eleanor, passing him the bowl. 'Just one mouthful.'

He obeyed. The liquid was foul, thick with Creator knew what deadly herbs and toadstools. Eleanor swallowed without expression, set the bowl down, and reached for his hand.

'Now we fly,' she said.

When he closed his eyes, he was in the hidden world. He was walking a thin precarious path, with mountain flanks falling away on either side. Huge toads clambered about on the rock before and behind him.

Eleanor began to cry out and shudder, as he had done when caught in visions of battle. Her hand nearly tore out of his, but he kept hold. She was in the thick of it.

He saw glimpses of the images that assailed her, but at a safe distance. She is living it for me, he thought, awed. All he had to do was follow the path until he met her at the other side.

He was standing at a fork, not knowing which way to take. Battle raged on either side, far away, seen through layers of gossamer. He hesitated until the insistence of Eleanor's grip made him take a step. The way branched again. He was looking at an infinite web of branches, all gleaming and shimmering with spectral colours.

He was meant to make a choice, and couldn't. Wordlessly he begged Auset to reveal what lay along each path. All she revealed was that the future would only become clear after he chose a path and set out upon it. And then there would be no turning back.

If I could just stay here, at the centre . . .

He opened his eyes to see dawn flushing the sky, the candles burned down to melted stumps. Eleanor was looking at him with dark, tired eyes. He felt as if seven years had passed in seven seconds. The night was almost gone.

'Now I see what you have been enduring,' she said

She'd taken the torment from him, at least for a while. For that, he could have worshipped her. He laughed weakly, but her face was heavy.

'I understand your distress,' she said. 'It was very confused. One thing I saw clearly, and that was King Richard cut down and slaughtered. Again and again I saw it, and couldn't help him.'

Raphael dropped his head. 'I'm sorry, good mother. I didn't mean you to be upset by this. But now you see. I'm not a prophet; I feel I'm seeing something that's already happened and therefore can't be changed. Richard is going to die, and I don't know what to do.'

'Then consider this,' Eleanor said slowly. 'Let us say you are right. It's something that has already happened, or is happening now; not to us, but alongside us, in a realm we cannot quite touch. Each path divides, and there is the one we decide to take, and the infinity of others we can never take. Nor can we cross over to them, nor see what would have happened if we had made a different decision. But you have crossed the wasteland, and seen something you were never meant to see. And this is . . . I don't know. Warning, preparation?'

'Or the gods laughing at me,' he said darkly.

'Or the gods showing you what must happen, because it is what always happens.'

'Are you telling me there's no hope? Just some ghastly joke, that I'm cursed to see Richard betrayed, slain and reviled after his death? And I am supposed to bear this knowledge – how?'

'By seeing that all knowledge is a gift. And that the path is not yours to change, dear.'

'Is that all you can tell me?'

'Your journey is not quite over yet. Go now.' Eleanor was holding out the wreath of drowsy-scented flowers. 'Pass beneath the archway, Briganta's Bridge. You will see a path, one of the ancient ways. It leads to Mag Tor. Climb up to the stones and leave these, an offering to the Goddess.'

He obeyed, leaving the cave and passing under the soaring arch. The path – a faintly shining indent in the grass – led him upwards through misty half-light. He was almost too tired for the climb, but forced himself, one foot in front of the other. The spire of stones loomed before him, the almost-human shapeless figure a monolith that held the brooding power of the earth. He shivered. Greater than him, greater than any king. He felt tiny.

Kate was waiting for him beneath the stacked rock. He gave the wreath to her, and she laid it at the Goddess's feet. She gave a pale smile, extending her hand to him. He took it. There was no anger in him any more.

'Can you forgive me?' she asked.

He nodded, looking at their joined hands. 'I don't blame you for loving Richard. And can you forgive me?'

'For what?'

'For abandoning you. It's not you, Kate. I feel as an ascetic must feel. Nothing of the flesh touches me any more. I must follow another road instead.'

She wiped moisture from her cheek. 'You're still like a dearest brother to me. As brother and sister, we can forgive each other anything.'

He grasped her hand tighter. 'Which way?'

She pointed downhill. A thin faint path wound away, marked here and there with a fragment of white stone. 'Follow the track where it takes us next.'

The path led them down into the wooded defile. Dawn gleamed through the veil of leaves. At the lowest point the track turned and wound along the valley floor. They were moving through a thick wood, with oak leaves massed around them. There was a green, eerie silence. Here it was damp and cold, the greens intensified by a slight mist. Kate could feel the cold drip of dew down her neck as they pushed forward through the foliage, following the path.

'This feels strange,' said Kate. 'This isn't Lytton Dale.'

There were diamonds of light. The oaks gave onto a clearing that glowed pale green and dew-gemmed in the dawn. Within it stood the ruins of a church, half-veiled by trees. There was a small lake to one side. Kate and Raphael looked at each other and went on, without speaking, towards the church.

Loneliness and desertion sighed within the stone shell. She expected to see elementals, but there were none. None tangible, at least. A stone tomb drew her. She moved towards it and ripped aside the cloak of ivy to reveal a plaque on which words were carved in precise, thin letters she couldn't read. She gave a soft cry.

'What is it?' said Raphael.

'I don't know,' she said. 'I feel that my son lies in there. Where is this place?'

'Eastwell Church,' said a voice.

A woman came out of the shadows. In this strange half-realm, her presence seemed natural. She was willowy, with long light brown hair, circles of glass held in gold frames over her eyes and nondescript clothes such as a peasant might wear in the fields. There was an eerie confidence about her, as if she belonged here. To Kate she was obviously the spirit of the place, a goddess or a muse.

'He was the finest king we ever had, Richard the Third,' said the woman. 'Shamefully betrayed. This is reputed to be the tomb of his natural son, Richard Plantagenet.'

Kate pressed her palms to the cold rough surface of the tomb. The cold spread all through her. 'My son's grave. I knew it. Good lady . . . how old will he be when he dies?'

'Upon your path, I don't know,' said the muse. 'Upon this path, he will be more than eighty. There is a legend that he fled here when the King his father was killed, took employment as a bricklayer and lived in obscurity for the rest of his life. Thus he avoided being executed by Henry the Seventh. It's a heart-rending story, too strange not to have some grain of truth in it.'

'Then he died in old age,' said Raphael. 'A long, peaceful life at least.'

'A life in hiding,' said Kate, her voice shaking. 'Never truly knowing his father, never receiving all that should have been his. Raph, if your visions are real, Richard has only a few months of life left.'

The air chilled her eyes. She stared down at the frigid tomb that contained the bones of her son. The whole of creation reverberated like the skin of a vast drum.

The muse's face became sombre with grief. 'Upon this path, his father died five centuries ago,' she said. 'Here, everything you know is long gone, ruined. To me, it's the present; but I can still weep for a past that I can't touch or change.'

Raphael went a step closer to the woman. He seemed

transfixed by her, as if he'd forgotten Kate was there. He asked unsteadily, 'Can you tell us what will happen?'

'Haven't you already seen it?'

'I've seen many terrible visions, but I can't fathom what they mean; what I'm supposed to do with these hellish premonitions.'

The muse reached across the corner of the tomb and laid her hand on his forearm. 'You're real,' she said softly. 'I can touch you. Raphael.' He looked questioningly at her and she went on, 'It's as Eleanor says. With every action, our world divides along different ways until there are infinite possible realities. Perhaps there are paths where Richard never was king, or was never born at all. Your path and mine are so close that I can only differentiate them in certain aspects. I think that's why you've been tormented by the echoes of my world, Raphael. Because they are so close, and you're sensitive.'

'I'd rather have heard nothing, seen nothing.'

'No, you wouldn't,' the muse said gently.

'I cannot stand by and see Richard die.'

'You may have no choice. I can't go back and change history, much as I would give anything to do so. You may have to stand by and watch it all unfold as it did in your worst nightmares, but powerless to make a difference.'

'No,' said Kate.

'All you've seen is true, Raphael. I could show you a hundred books that tell of it. He will be reviled after his death. His enemies will take every rumour and magnify it, blacken his name in order to justify their own seizure of power. They'll say he was hunchbacked which is an outwards sign of evil—'

'That is a complete lie!'

'But lies become legend. No one will see him any more as human, fallible or lovable in any way. He'll become an immortal villain, and an immortal hero.'

'A hero as well?' said Kate. 'Good lady, I don't understand.'

471

'In the times to come, some will begin to question the received wisdom – surely no one could be that evil? People of the north will never believe it, and will always love him. Scholars will set out to unearth the truth, and defend him. Some will even try to prove him a saint.'

'He's not that,' Kate said.

The muse smiled. Her teeth were small, white and uneven. For all her strange dress, she looked fully human. 'That's the point. There will only be extremes. And because of that, he will never be forgotten. Never forgotten.'

She spoke with complete conviction, an oracle. The imminence of loss overwhelmed Kate. She trembled, fighting tears. 'I don't want him to die,' she said. 'If he does, I have no reason to live.'

'But it's only his death in battle that guarantees his immortality,' said the muse. 'His brave death.'

'But my mother says the paths are not fixed,' Kate said fiercely. 'Not inevitable!'

'Then change it if you can,' said the muse. She looked from Raphael to Kate, imploring. 'I don't want to give any of us false hope by thinking that things could be different. But if you can, please . . .'

And she vanished, leaving only a sighing space of stone and ivy where she had stood. Kate and Raphael moved close together, awed, shaken by a sense of loss so great that Kate could barely encompass a fragment of it.

'Let us go back now,' she said.

'Do you want to?'

'What?'

Raphael's voice was dry, strange. 'We could walk from here into this unknown world and read our own story in history books. We wouldn't have to endure it any more. Leave Richard alive, Robin and Eleanor alive, and they'd always be alive in our memories. We wouldn't have to endure the pain of losing them. We know what's going to happen, Kate. We can't stop it. Why go back and live through each horrible moment of it? We could read books, and look back and think ah, that's how it was, and weep, but the pain would be bearable.'

'Read how our dear King Richard was evil and deformed, England's most wicked king? Is that what you want?'

He hesitated, face strained. 'It will happen anyway.'

'Not if we go back and change it.'

'But what if our attempts at changing things are what cause his death? How can we know? We are no one, Kate. We have no voice. No one who loved Richard will have a voice under the rule of his enemies.'

'You can't seriously consider leaving our lives behind. Running away? This isn't you speaking!'

'I don't know what my life is now,' he said. 'The whole world's changed. I didn't know you had a son. If you aren't the person I thought you were, then who am I?'

'I'm still the same,' she said desperately. 'So are you.'

He looked up at the sky through the broken roof. 'I feel drawn to this place. It's so peaceful. I want to stay and explore.'

Fear pinched her stomach. What if they couldn't leave and go back to the world they knew? What if she lost Raphael? She put her arm through his and said, 'Let us go back the way we came, and see what happens.'

'No, I want to go on.'

She clung to his arm as they emerged from the church, not trying to stop him, just to keep hold of him, to draw him back to her in some way. Raphael forged off along the bank of the lake, until trees on the other side of the church swallowed them again.

A sudden roaring noise made them both cry out and cower. An object passed overhead, making the trees shake, some gigantic demon, expelled from the smoky mouth of hell. Then all was quiet again. The birds began to sing loudly. They walked on and Kate saw a dryad, wrapping its green form around a tree, watching them as it slithered from branch to branch, a misty snake.

They stepped out of the wood onto a river bank. Eleanor was waiting for them.

Kate gasped out loud with relief. Raphael was silent. His head fell. When he looked up at her again, his eyes were calm.

'We shall have to go back to the King, and tell him everything that's happened,' he said.

'It might be better he doesn't know,' Kate said. 'What can it do but distress or anger him, and cloud his judgement?'

'But the choice, whether to heed my visions or not, should be his. Not ours. If we don't give him that choice, we're betraying him indeed.'

She nodded, pained but resigned. 'One thing, Raphael,' she added quickly. 'Don't tell him about Robin.'

'Kate, he deserves to know.'

'Yes, but it should be for me to tell him. Not you. Promise me, please.'

He hesitated. At last he said, 'I promise.'

'The court has been mad with rumours, all the time we were gone,' said Ursula, combing Kate's hair. 'The King is definitely going to marry his niece. Some are saying he's already got her with child.'

'What?' Kate spun round, so violently that she knocked the comb out of Ursula's hand.

'Lamb's blood, ma'am, don't blame me for it! I'm only reporting what I've heard. Crimson doesn't suit your complexion. Why are you so angry about it?'

'I'm not,' Kate said between clenched teeth. For a moment she saw herself slipping poison into Bess's wine. Violently and passionately she wanted to kill both Bess and the King.

Perhaps, if he died as the muse had said, it would be a relief. Better to grieve than be consumed alive by the bitter salts of jealousy.

'I'm sorry,' Kate said, mastering herself.

Ursula exhaled. 'No, I am. Nan confides in me. Your

tender feelings towards a certain person are probably more obvious than you realize. I didn't mean to upset you.'

'And I didn't mean to nearly knock you across the room. Well, I hope you and Nan keep your gossip about me firmly between the two of you.' Ursula coloured. 'What else?'

'They say that his own councillors are firmly set against the idea. Notably Ratcliffe and Catesby.'

'Because she's his niece, and declared illegitimate?' Kate said sharply.

'Because of the rumours that he poisoned his wife.'

Kate bit her lip, tasted iron. 'Never mind my hair. Curl it up quickly and pin that hennin upon it.'

'Where are you going?'

'To learn the truth.'

She looked in and saw a narrow slice of the room: the chequerboard floor, the steps to the throne dais, the flash of ruby, gold leaf and ebony, all washed in bronze lamplight. And Richard was there with Lady Bess. She was on the first step, he on the floor, so their eyes were on a level. As Kate watched, Richard leaned forward and kissed his niece on the lips.

The kiss was decorous, but welded Kate to the spot. She'd been passing, idly haunting the areas of the palace where she knew Richard sometimes walked if he couldn't sleep. She'd hoped to stumble upon him by chance, and now wished she hadn't.

Richard was whispering something to Bess. Her reaction was not what Kate expected. Her expression passed from confusion to desolation. Pulling away from him, she walked off abruptly, her head down, one hand cupping her face. She was coming towards Kate, almost running now. Kate pressed back behind the door frame but Bess scurried straight past, not even seeing her.

Richard, alone, stayed where he was for a few moments. Then he began to walk at a steady pace towards the door through which Lady Bess had passed.

Kate was too late to move. He'd already noticed her, but kept coming. She stood like a stone pillar, seeing no reason to run, or pretend she hadn't seen them. What did it matter? She felt as cold as snow, and if he upbraided her he might as well upbraid a cat or a serpent. She stared at him. He held her gaze until he was with her inside the unlit door arch. There he stopped and stood facing her.

At last he said, 'Well?'

'Raphael and I must speak to you, Your Grace.'

'Yes. I've asked him to come to me tomorrow. I've not had time today.'

'No, you are plainly very busy.'

Silence. They went on looking at each other, until he said, 'Is there something else?'

'Richard,' she said.

'I sense disapproval. Don't keep it to yourself; no one else in this kingdom has.'

'The rumours are true, then.'

'What rumours would these be? There are so many.'

'I thought it was a childish infatuation on her part. I didn't know . . .' She suffered an intense feeling of unreality. How had she come to be standing in a dark doorway, babbling nonsense to the King of England, while he stood listening, piercing her with those unfathomable eyes? 'Sire, if it's your wish, marry her and be happy. I'll be her lady-in-waiting, as I was Anne's. I'll serve and cherish her as I would anyone dear to you.'

She didn't know where the words came from, but Richard's reaction startled her. His eyes opened wide. He took her hand, his first two fingers folding into her palm, holding it tight. 'Kate,' he said. 'Bless you for that sweet sentiment, when all I've had is sour carping from every quarter. But I am not going to marry my niece. All you saw was me telling her so. I thought it only fair to apologize to her privately, before I dismiss these rumours publicly.'

Relief turned Katherine from stone to flame. She hoped he didn't see it.

'Did you . . . did you think of it?'

'Briefly. Foolishly.'

'She looked upset. She's in love with you.' And I shouldn't hate her for that, Kate thought.

Richard sighed. 'Bess and I were always fond of each other. I'm afraid that is ended now. We have both suffered loneliness and we mistook it for . . . A light dazzled us, obscuring reality for a short time. If she loved me, she was more in love with the idea of wearing a crown. She is her mother's daughter.'

Any relief Kate felt at hearing it was over was replaced by a maddening surge of frustration. She felt like screaming, *How could you turn to her when I was here*? Oh, because she was blonde, pliant and adoring, whereas I am Medusa with a scorpion tongue. Stiffly she said, 'If you have broken her heart, I shall be one of those who has to pick up the pieces.'

'I hope to God I haven't broken her heart.'

'But you probably have. And it's a shame she did not seek of me the advice that might have saved you both the most painful embarrassment.'

'What do you mean?'

'I mean, to prevent an untimely event. What if she's already with child?'

Seeing Richard's face, she wondered what she would have to do to place such amazement upon it a third time. 'Iesu's blood, Kate! What's wrong with you?'

'I'm merely being practical.'

'I have not touched her.'

'Oh. Then I apologize.'

'Once,' he murmured. He rested one hand against the wall and dropped his head.

'Once is sufficient,' Kate hissed. Coldness settled in her stomach, gelid.

'Kate, is it my imagination or are you are beginning to sound jealous?'

'I'm thinking of Bess. My mistress.'

She turned to go. He caught her elbow and held it so hard she couldn't move. 'You always get the truth out of me, so don't run away when I tell it. Once I went to her chambers, which I assure you I could not have done without the full collusion of her mother. I suppose I meant to lie with her. I suppose I desired her, or at least a welcoming body, and she was nothing if not eager. But when it came to it, I could not.'

'Why?'

He paused. His face was bleak. 'I thought I wanted her. She is fair, isn't she? Instead I found the idea repellent. I remembered her as a child. I could see too much of Edward and her mother in her.' He let her go and pushed a weary hand through his hair. 'That's all I could see, my little niece. Then I knew I could not marry her, not even to stop Henry Tudor having her. I realized I was not thinking at all. I haven't thought clearly since my son died. I was just acting blindly, because I no longer cared about anything. Aren't you ashamed of me?'

Her hand hovered. She sensed that her comforting touch would draw no reaction from him. How could they possibly explain Raphael's visions to him now?

'No. You were in pain.' Her voice went nearly to nothing. 'You could have spoken to me . . .'

'Now Bess is in pain. I shall have to send her away, find some worthy man for her to marry. Her mother will be furious and will probably begin conspiring against me yet again. I don't have to tell you what a wretched position this puts me in. All my own fault, or at least half my fault. Do you forgive me?'

She was astonished. 'You don't need me to forgive you.'

'Oh, I do.' He gave a wry, sad smile. 'No one else will.'

He stayed there looking at her for long seconds. She felt her heart thundering, the night turning like a velvet sphere. Then the moment passed. His face was shuttered, closed to complication. He bowed quickly to her, and was gone.

Bess wept in Kate's arms. She shook, hot as fever, soaking Kate's gown with the slime of her dripping nose and eyes.

'He has taken everything from me. Deprived me of uncle, lover, husband, throne – gods, he will be sorry for this. I thought I loved him. I was wrong. I hate him.'

Patiently Kate held her, murmuring comfort. If any other man had destroyed Bess's life, her heart would have bled with pity. As things were, she dared let no emotion seep through her shell.

'Can you – can you do anything for me, Kate?' asked Bess.

'What do you mean?'

'You know. Everyone knows what you are.'

'Then everyone knows that it is forbidden to use influence, Bess.'

'This is different. Help me. I want him to feel the pain I am in.'

'My lady, he already does.'

'Then I want him to hurt more!'

'I can't,' Kate answered thinly. 'Not in that way.'

'If you won't help me, my mother shall! She will write to Henry Tudor. I am not a bastard, Kate. I'm the rightful queen. Tudor can rule only through me. If Richard won't have me, a better man shall.'

Then her face dissolved, and she fell on Kate's breast again. Bess sobbed, oblivious to the secret feelings of her comforter, unaware of Kate's face as she rested her chin atop the golden hair: the fixed smile, the eyes of iced glass.

The King's face looked drawn. He'd been forced to make a humiliating speech before Parliament, denying that the intention of marrying his niece had ever entered his head.

Meanwhile, his councillors – according to the customary virulent rumours – had sat with narrowed eyes, knowing full well to the contrary.

Now, quiet and low in spirits, he listened intently as Raphael told him everything. They were in a private court-yard garden, the sun hot upon them. Richard sat on a stone bench, idly drawing on the ground with the point of a sword as Raphael spoke.

'Your Grace, I crave your pardon,' he said at the end. 'I wouldn't have wasted your time with mad imaginings and nightmares for the world. But I feel what I've seen to be true. It's already happened, is happening now and will happen again, a story that never stops unfolding. If you banish me for this, I don't blame you, but at least I've told you all I know. That burden is off me.'

Richard reached up and laid his hand on Raphael's shoulder. 'I'm glad you told me, my friend. I am fore-warned.'

Raphael found himself startled that Richard had taken him seriously. 'You believe me?'

'You may have misinterpreted certain things. That's entirely possible. Still, on the whole I can't dismiss what you've said.'

'Why?'

'Because a good deal of what you've told me is already happening. The Welsh pretender Tudor is on the march. With marvellous impudence, he comes to claim Bess as his queen. Since Lord Stanley is married to Tudor's mother, despite all my threats and incentives I don't know which way he will jump. Morton loathes me and is fully two years into his whispering campaign against me. Everything you have seen is the logical consequence of what's already in motion; but still, you are an inspired visionary. I'm glad you are on my side and not Tudor's, although, if you were, you might be having sweet dreams instead.'

'Don't say that.'

'Everything has been weighted against me from the beginning. I did what was needful and I'd do it again. I've no regrets. There's nothing left to bind me to earth, after all.'

His tone of resignation alarmed Raphael. 'You won't just give in to Tudor?'

'Did I say that?' The King gave a thin, shining smile. 'Win or lose, I'll give him the battle to end all battles.'

In Raphael's heart, a flame of excitement leaped. 'I'll be at your side.'

'You've been ill.'

'No. Not ill. I'm fully fit, and raging to fight.'

'Then I'll argue no more. One thing more, this battle you saw . . .'

Raphael had described as much as he could, the placing of the troops, the order of battle, only to realize it was all frighteningly vague. 'I'm sorry I can't tell you more. It was so powerful at the time, but when I try to recall the detail, it all falls into confusion.'

'Well, it's not been fought yet. What you have been able to tell me sounds quite feasible, but I don't want to know, or delude myself into thinking that I know, exactly what will happen. What if I changed strategy because of what you told me, and it was the wrong choice?'

'That's what Kate said.' Raphael gazed at Richard, thinking of Kate and Robin. It was so unfair to have this knowledge when Richard was oblivious, but he kept his painful promise.

'I'll take things as I find them, and make decisions accordingly,' said the King. He made to rise.

Raphael said quickly, 'There's something more.'

'Yes?'

'After all the bad dreams, there was a better one. You left us too soon but you were never, ever forgotten. Plays and unending books were written about you. Hundreds of years in the future they are still arguing over you, long after other kings are forgotten. And you still have lovers and defenders who never forget you. Even those who are determined to blacken you can never forget you.'

The dark eyebrows rose, cynically amused. 'Truly?'

'You will die, but become immortal.'

Richard sat gazing at him, his face contemplative. He was strangely tranquil, considering what Raphael had told him. 'Which fate is to be preferred? Violent death followed by immortality, or a long happy descent into obscurity? The first is more fitting to a Plantagenet king.'

'No. Entirely unique to you.'

'You're a strange creature, Sir Raphael. When I found you in the hedge, are you sure you hadn't been dropped there from the faerie realm?'

Later, as Raphael was walking past the chapel on his way to bed, he glanced in and saw the King there. He was on his knees, praying. Candle flames glinted in their dozens on solid gold and jewels. Around Richard himself they made an aurora, less a halo than an otherwordly glow, like a marsh light, spectral and deathly.

Chapter Eighteen 1485: Tudor

KING RICHARD
> Give me another horse! Bind up my wounds!
> Have mercy, Jesu! – Soft! I did but dream.
> O coward conscience, how dost thou afflict me!
> The lights burn blue. It is now dead midnight.

Richard III Act V scene 3

Summer lay heavy and motionless on the land.

Under a thick caul of heat the earth baked and cracked. Cattle tramped the mud of drying streams, tormented by clouds of flies. Leaves curled, crops withered. Shimmering elementals soured the milk. Hounds lay panting in the sticky ochre heat, even graylix were too lethargic to growl at anyone who approached their cages.

In towns and villages, people were succumbing to a cruel fever that basted them in salt rivers of their own sweat. Some survived, many died. August wrapped the land in a baking, airless shroud of fear.

In Wales, the air was fresher. Henry Tudor, Earl of Richmond, was on the march. He had landed at Milford Haven, kissing the wet sand while his priests gave thanks for a safe crossing. The sun was setting, turning the beach to a wet golden mirror as he prayed, while above them in the hills the beacons began to flash the news of his landing in chains of fire.

Tudor wound his way up the coast road, then inland towards the hills. Dr Fautherer rode with him in Bishop Morton's train. The chatter of voices around them was mainly French, with some Scottish and now Welsh voices mingling with them daily. As yet, their force was tiny. Yet Fautherer knew, with his usual dark instinct, that this didn't matter.

Richmond was becoming a messiah for the Welsh. He had experienced commanders including the Earls of Oxford and Pembroke. Margaret Beaufort, Henry's doting parent, had been hard at work raising money and allies in England. Her husband Lord Stanley had pledged his secret support. All southern England was poised to rise against Richard.

Most importantly, the hosts of heaven marched with Henry Tudor. Morton had encouraged Tudor to believe it with a passion.

The little force wound their way between the mountains. Above them, great slopes towered, touching the clouds. Mist rolled down over the stones. The landscape was immense, grey stroked with green. Against it, the giant red dragon snapping above their heads was garish, as threatening as fire.

Fautherer took in everything with a clear cold eye. The grandeur, and the rabble of mercenaries that disturbed it. They passed the mountains and came into a wild land of hills, the Welsh marches, the border with England. Through these lands once ruled by the Duke of Buckingham and now controlled by the Stanleys, Henry Tudor passed unopposed.

When news of the sweating sickness reached them, Fautherer saw Tudor's thin face grow long with anxiety. He would have to learn to hide that vulnerable streak, Fautherer thought. Henry was young, however, and was learning. The expression was gone in an instant, replaced by inscrutable heavy-eyed calm.

'We have nothing to fear from it,' said Bishop Morton. He swatted a fly away from his face with a fat hand. Beside the road, petitmorts were feasting on a dead sheep.

'Indeed not, Your Grace?' Richmond said in a thin voice.

'England is sick, Your Majesty,' said Morton. Their king-in-waiting planned to adopt a loftier address than that afforded to mere dukes and archbishops, something to separate him. His followers flattered him with it, bolstering both his ambitions and their own. 'Ailing in body and in spirit. It's God's anger that lies on the land.'

'Yes, of course.' Richmond was nodding. Fautherer and all those around him murmured keen assent.

'The cause of the sickness is King Richard, the Hog.'

'Do not call him king, I pray you. Hog by all means, but never king.'

'Certainly not for much longer,' said Morton, unperturbed by his own slip of the tongue. 'Once we have cut out the canker, and placed the true king on the throne, sire, God will be pleased, and the land will heal.'

'Amen,' said Tudor. Then, thoughtfully, 'I am already king. If Richard opposes me, he commits treason.'

Dr Fautherer smirked. He approved of such twisted logic.

Richard was in Nottingham, and had been there since June. Raphael was with him, feeling much older, sadder and wiser, but no longer tormented. It had been a pleasant summer, with nobles freely enjoying the King's hospitality, and hunting and hawking in Sherwood. Pleasant, but for the unceasing preparations for war.

Henry Tudor was expected to invade at any time. Ever efficient and self-controlled, the King sent out his orders: his officers to muster all able-bodied men; every knight, squire and gentleman to answer the call to arms. Nobles were strictly enjoined to set aside their own quarrels and aid the King. Sometimes the tone of the commands held icy threats. England bred so many traitors that he no longer fully trusted anyone. There were many in the Midlands who still revered those whom Richard had executed – Hastings, Buckingham, Grey – and resented him for it. And yet, thought Raphael, no one ever seemed grateful for his acts of clemency. He wondered if the trouble was not that Richard had been too harsh, but that he'd been too merciful.

In London, Robert Brackenbury commanded a large force to protect the Tower. Lord Stanley had gone to muster the men of the north-west, Lovell to superintend the naval defence of the south coast. From Nottingham, the heart of the kingdom, Richard could keep an eye on all quarters, and gather men quickly. He made his preparations, and waited.

Raphael knew that Richard both loved and hated Nottingham. He felt the same. There was a soothing majesty in the great salt-white edifice, the plashing of its waterwheels, Sherwood's shimmering tide of trees. But he could never come here without thinking of Kate. How they'd raced their horses through the forest and been so happy, only to return to the terrible anguish of the King and Queen at the news of their son's death.

They were hawking; the King and a handful of his friends. Raphael and Will Shaw had charge of the hawks and for a time they could forget everything in the pleasure of watching the sleek birds. Their flight across the sweltering blue of the sky brought a dream-like peace. Raphael still missed Kate, but found he could bear it.

He felt like an empty vessel. No more visions now. It was as if Eleanor had purged him. Kate had returned to her mother. Lady Bess had been sent out of harm's way to Sheriff Hutton Castle. Plans were in motion for Richard to marry a Portuguese princess, though he had shown only resigned indifference to the prospect.

He seemed more eager for Tudor's threatened invasion, as if the chance of war were a welcome barrier between him and marriage to a stranger. In none of Raphael's visions had he ever seen Richard with a new queen. Only alone and betrayed.

Even with hawking to distract him, Raphael found himself thinking of Kate again. Every time the pain came there was a counter to it; that he'd had no choice. Now he was glad, because she had lied to him. Lied for years. Never told him she had a natural son. Worse, never admitted that she and Richard had once been lovers. If she'd told him at the very beginning, he might have come to terms with it. Instead, she'd left it far too late.

It was almost as if she'd intruded on territory that Raphael had believed to be his alone. Not that of the physical plane, but of intimacy, of secrets. She'd shared something private with Richard, and that had made Raphael humiliatingly resentful of them both.

He couldn't look at her any more without imagining her in Richard's arms. Lying with him, the Duke of Gloucester, without even knowing or caring who he was! It seemed a form of sacrilege.

He wasn't angry with her. He no longer felt any violent emotion about her. It was sad their paths had divided, but his path lay with Richard, and always had, to the bitter end. It was easier to forgive Richard. As the priests said, men blundered into sin, but women led them there, knowingly.

When he looked at the King, however, he never thought of Kate. He didn't even picture Anne at his side. Richard had always seemed a creature alone, like a hawk silhouetted against a bone-freezing white sky. Since Anne had died he had worn only black. It was rich mourning garb, not austere. Clothes of expensive softness, damask and sable fur, midnight velvets sewn with jet, embroidered with black silk, dark oily pearls.

When Richard stood close to Raphael his presence was as real and as warm as that of any sleek-feathered bird of prey; all warmth and energy, and the familiar smile and tilt of his head as he spoke. He was alive and vigorous, the most vividly charismatic person Raphael had ever known. Alive now . . . but the grains of sand were falling, and Raphael had seen the bleak shape of the future.

A messenger came riding into the glade, in shirt sleeves and sweating nearly as hard as his blowing bay horse. He threw himself onto his knees at the King's feet and gasped out his message. 'Your Grace, I'm sent from the constable of

Pembroke. Henry Tudor's landed in Wales. He's marching towards England.'

The King lifted his head. There was no anger in his face, rather a look of relief. His eyes were intently narrowed. All he said was, 'Good.'

Above Redmore Plain the sky darkened. It glowed violet, bluest violet, smudged with bars of cloud. On the humped back of Ambion Hill the encampment slept, waiting. The wind fell and banners hung as ragged and blue as the night. Silence rolled in like fog.

Outside was the grating chirrup of frogs, the owl's haunting cry. In the King's tent a lamp burned, pallid as the gaunt face that reflected it. The King had talked to Raphael for hours, spilling anguished secrets that pierced Raphael to the core, for there was not a shaving of self-pity in them.

In their preparations for battle, Raphael had only seen Richard lose his temper once, when messengers came to him with the news that Tudor had entered Shrewsbury unopposed. Then he had raged, in a low savage voice that made everyone around him quail. He rarely showed such passion, but it was there deep inside, a slow-burning energy that drove him. With the same leaden resolve, he'd ordered the arrest of Lord Strange, Thomas Stanley's son. A hostage, to ensure the cooperation of a man who could not be trusted.

The battle was hours away but Richard could not sleep. He talked instead, beautiful as Lucifer, holding Raphael in thrall. 'Have I been so bad a king? . . . For there is a shadow in me, a great and dreadful shadow that would blot out the entire world with its clawed wings if it were left unchecked. And this has not been planted in me by enemies. They've glimpsed it, and that's why they are afraid of me, but they didn't put it there. It was born within me, and awoken when I was a child . . . Let me tell you about the waking of the shadow.'

Raphael had never known him talk so much, nor so

freely. He spoke of the hidden world, of an encounter with a sorceress and a witch-child who had terrified him and set him fleeing down the unlit paths of his life. Raphael wished the night would not end. Beyond it was no future, only a portcullis slamming down – for himself as well as for Richard.

'For all I've done, for all I am, and for all the sins of my family, I am punished,' the King said softly, looking out into the night. 'I am punished. I've spun a web of soot and barbs. And now, the final act.'

Around them, fate gathered, filled the heavens and began slowly to spin about them. The camp was waking. Raphael could hear the clatter of hammers on steel and men's tired, grumbling voices. The night was almost over. His last night with the King. There was nothing to say; all words melted to nothingness. Richard rested his hand on Raphael's shoulder and he could do nothing but stand there, wordless, watching two tiny figures toiling towards them up the hill.

One of them was a woman.

'Oh, God,' Raphael breathed. He found the edge of the tent flap and let it fall to conceal them. 'Your Grace . . . It's Kate.'

Katherine looked up and saw the light spilling from the King's pavilion, like fire through a crack in stone. The sky glowed behind the hump of the ridge. All around her the camp was spread out, fires glowing, the tents and horses solid shadows mingled with the night. Its murmur was a mere background. With her hand firmly through Robin's arm – he was too old for hand-holding – she stopped. The pavilion with its banners and undulating walls looked like an unassailable castle. She couldn't imagine entering it. Couldn't imagine standing in front of the King and telling him . . . Her tension began to ebb into disappointment. She realized she was simply going to walk away, back into the darkness she'd come from.

'Mama . . .' Robin's voice was very faint, questioning, as her hand began to pull at his.

'Lady Katherine?'

One of Richard's esquires was standing in front of her, a cheerful young man named Geoffrey. 'My lady, why are you here? This is no place for you.'

Steadily she said, 'Would you ask Francis Lovell if the King will see me? It's important.'

The esquire frowned, but didn't argue. With a slight bow, he turned. 'Of course, my lady. I'll escort you there and bring an answer as quickly as I may.'

Robin had snatched his arm out of her grasp as Geoffrey met them. He wanted to appear a man, not a child. She understood. He was, after all, very nearly grown. At his age, Anne Neville had been married, Margaret Beaufort the mother of an infant Henry. Her own hands felt like slippery ice. They climbed, and stood waiting outside the cloth-of-gold walls. Three minutes stretched to feel like an hour.

Her son looked at her with dark, suspicious eyes. 'Are we really going to see the King?'

'I don't know, Robin. He may be too busy.'

On the journey from Derbyshire he'd been trusting and excited, so thrilled to be travelling with his mother that he hadn't questioned her at first. It was a good ten minutes into the journey before he'd asked, 'Where are we going?'

'I'm taking you to meet your father.'

'Why?' He'd asked the question, not childishly, but with a weight of meaning behind it: *Why now? Why at all? With what intention?* He had a right to know, but she hadn't been able to answer. There were no words in her dry mouth.

He had accepted her silence for a few seconds. Then, quietly but more insistently, he had asked, 'Who is he? Plantagenet. Someone royal? Someone close to the King?'

'I'm afraid you'll not believe me if I tell you,' she said. 'I can best tell you by showing you. You must have looked at yourself in a mirror?'

He had bristled. 'I'm not a girl.'

'So you don't know what you look like?' she'd said sardonically.

'Well . . . I've seen my face in water, or reflected in a shield sometimes. Or in passing, in my grandmother's chamber.'

She smiled at his self-consciousness. 'That will do the trick. I guarantee, then, that when you see your father, you will know.'

'I don't know why you must be so mysterious about it,' he'd said. He'd feigned impatience while a glimmer of thrilled anticipation lit his eyes. Kate, though, felt no joy. The last thing she wanted was for Robin to be disappointed. Now, standing cold in the encampment and dreading the King's rejection, she wished she were anywhere but here.

Robin whispered, 'My father is in the King's service then?' He still hadn't guessed. To him, the obvious was not obvious, since it was clearly impossible. 'A cousin, a royal duke?'

As he spoke, Geoffrey came out, followed by another man, not Francis Lovell, but Raphael. He looked tired, his expression grim. They regarded each other as if they were strangers. His lips twitched, more grimace than smile, as if her presence were unwelcome but inevitable.

'Kate, you shouldn't be here.'

'I know, but I am.'

'He'll see you. But he's tired. He's hardly slept, and we're arming before dawn. He shouldn't be burdened with more troubles tonight.'

She was amazed to feel a trickle of jealousy. Raphael had been with the King all night and yet resented her taking even ten minutes of his time.

'According to your predictions, I shall have no other chance to burden him.'

Raphael lowered his eyes, but made no retort. He seemed a different person. Without comment he held open the wide flap of the pavilion for her and she went in.

After Kate went in to the King, Raphael walked among the tents like an exile, breathing the ripe scents of horses, leather, smoke. The clatter of preparation was growing. He'd felt a breath of annoyance that Kate had come, but even that had faded. He was the one who'd tried to persuade her to tell the King about Robin. Richard had a right to meet his son, if only once. Nothing seemed quite real. He felt that he walked in a vision, or in two mirrored worlds which overlapped.

A hand fell on him, making him start. Raphael found himself looking into the grave, kindly face of the Duke of Norfolk. He was already in armour. 'Well rested, Sir Raphael? How goes it with the King?'

'As well as it may, given our circumstances. He hasn't slept.'

'I'll go to him.'

'I'd give him a few minutes, Your Grace,' Raphael said quietly. 'He's speaking with someone.'

'As you say. But we must make ready, if we're to win the day. There's little time.'

Raphael looked into the grandfatherly face. '*You* will not let him down,' he said, with solid conviction. Tears pricked his eyes. 'You, of all people, will not betray him.'

'You speak the truth there,' John Howard said. 'Some worthless curs may be considering betrayal, there's many I'd not trust as Dick is forced to, but *I'll* fight and die beside him. A curse upon the traitors. A curse upon them. Go forth with courage, lad, eh?'

The Duke went on his way, and Raphael walked on as if quietly possessed. Strange instinct guided his feet to the tent of the Earl of Northumberland.

None of his esquires were in evidence to challenge Raphael, it was as if an enchanted sleep lay upon the world. The Earl, Henry Percy, was in a loose grey robe that gave him more than ever the look of a wading bird. His head was bent over a scroll of paper and he looked haggard with worry.

'You will betray him today,' said Raphael.

'What?' Northumberland's head jerked up.

'I have seen your fate. You were always jealous of Richard. You pretend to support him, but intend to fail him. You hope that Henry, instead, will favour you.'

'I don't know who you are, young man, but if you don't leave—'

'Sometimes people can sense their own future, a path they could have changed but chose not to. You have a hatred of crowds. Riots distress you.'

The Earl's face turned sickly white. A lump bobbed in the long, curved throat. 'How did you know that?'

'Anyone can sense their own future if they are set upon a particular path. If you betray King Richard today, you will think you have a fair future. Henry will restore you to favour. In time, he will set you to collect taxes for him. No one loves a tax collector, any more than they will forget Richard. A furious crowd will pull you from your horse and murder you.'

Livid eyes glared at him, pale as egg white and ghastly with fear. He wondered what Percy was seeing: a madman, or an angelic messenger? The Earl's mouth worked. 'This is sorcery. How do you know this?'

When Raphael smiled, the Earl crossed himself, his hand trembling.

'I saw it in a dream.'

There were fine rugs underfoot and laid over canvas, lamps glowing in the grass-scented twilight. Richard stood near an altar on which shone a gold icon of the Virgin, embowered in candlelight. He wore a white shirt and a soft dark robe, his hair shining on his shoulders. His hands were folded in front of him and his face was ghostly but composed. There

493

was something unnerving about him, as if he'd risen from the dead.

She'd almost forgotten Robin was with her, until he let out a loud gasp. He'd seen.

'Katherine?' said Richard. 'Why . . . ?'

She went quickly to him, knelt and kissed his hand. His skin felt as lifeless as her own.

'Your Grace, may I present my son, Robin of Lytton Dale?' Robin had dropped to his knees, apparently overcome. It seemed to have hit him very suddenly that they were actually in the presence of the King. His cheerful curiosity had dissolved into awe. 'We call him Robin,' she added. 'His real name is Richard.'

The King looked more than ever like a ghost. He stared from her to the boy, then went to him, placed his fingers beneath Robin's chin and lifted the face to meet his.

'Oh, dear Iesu,' he said.

He looked, Kate thought, enraged. She didn't blame him. Now he was gazing at her with plain distress in his face and she thought that Raphael had been right. She should not have come.

'Get up, lad, there's no need to be afraid of me.' Richard's voice was raw, but not unkind. Robin rose, trembling, to his feet. 'How old are you?'

'F – fifteen, Your Grace.'

'And a well-made, handsome young man. A credit to your mother.' Richard kept staring from her son to Kate. She wondered what he saw; perhaps a stony-visaged woman who'd deceived him?

'Thank you, sire.'

'Kate, why have you—' He stopped. He looked drained, as if this last shock had completely undone him. Then he went on as if struggling for something to say, 'Robin, did you know I was your father?'

Gathering courage, Robin answered clearly. 'No, sire. She said I would not believe it unless I saw you. She

494

was right. She told me only that you were a great man, a Plantagenet.'

'That was a kind description of me. Have you had a happy life, a good education?'

'Yes, sire.'

'He was brought up in my mother's household,' said Kate. 'He's lacked for nothing there.'

'I don't doubt it.' Richard went on asking him questions in the same ravaged yet warm tone, moving as he did so to rummage in a large, bound chest that stood to one side of the tent. Robin gave dignified answers. He spoke of his hawk, his duties on the estate. Kate was relieved that he, at least, was the one thing she could be proud of.

After a few moments, Richard came to him with a purse of black leather. He dropped into it several large gold coins, followed by a badge: a white boar made of sparkling stones set in heavy silver, with sapphire eyes.

Kate wanted to refuse it, but said nothing. She let Robin receive the gift. Richard touched one hand to the boy's forehead, and sighed.

'Lad, I'm going to be in the midst of a battle in a few hours. If I win, come back to me and you will receive everything that a son should receive of his father. However, if I lose . . .' He put his hand on Robin's shoulder, gazing closely at him. 'If I lose, my enemy is likely to hunt down and destroy every blood relation of mine. Being my son will put you in terrible danger. If that happens, flee as far from here as you can and never reveal your identity to anyone.'

Starkly, Kate saw the grave in the ruined church. Rustling green leaves and desolation. The man that lay there had lived a peaceful life to a great old age. Was that such a terrible fate?

'If I fought with you, you wouldn't lose,' said Robin, with more bravado than conviction.

Richard laughed. 'Ever fought a battle? No. You can go

with the priests and clerks and watch from a safe distance. Be my eyewitness. Will you do that?'

'Of course, sire, if it please you.'

'Good. Go now. Geoffrey and Raphael will take care of you. I wish to have words with your mother.'

Robin bowed again and left, his eyes swimming. Kate watched him go. She was almost past caring what the King said to her now. She'd done what she came to do.

She looked at the ground. Suddenly Richard was in front of her, so close he made her jump.

'Why bring him to me now?' His voice was low, rough with anguish.

'To give you something to live for!'

'Or to undo me completely. I marvel that Lady Beaufort didn't think of such a scheme herself.'

Kate stood dumb, chewing the edge of her tongue. She hadn't expected Richard to react so passionately, but what *had* she expected?

'The last thing I wanted was to distress you on the eve of battle.'

'Well, we often achieve what we did not intend.'

A spring-water chill dropped through her. Perhaps in Raphael's otherworld, it was this, that had distracted Richard so much he'd lost . . .

She said stiffly, 'I thought this would give you joy, not grief.'

'How could you not tell me?' He opened his arms and the black robe with its long sleeves billowed. He looked like a denizen of the night. 'How could you never, in all these years, tell me?'

Her throat closed. 'Pride.'

'You know I would have helped you.'

'I wanted no help! No payment. What would have been the point? Robin just another noble bastard, and I a cast-off, to be kept away and yet controlled in how I may or may not order my child's life? We did not want him taken away from us!'

'All the chances you have had to tell me . . . you kept it secret.' He groaned. 'I have to admire your fortitude. You are a well of secrets, indeed. Did anyone know?'

'Only my beloved and long-suffering mother. Oh, and the Countess of Warwick.'

'Anne's *mother* knew? How?'

'She was there often enough to learn of my plight. She advised my mother on how best to deal with it. Robin was brought up as the natural child of a serving woman. By the time I told him he was mine, he'd already guessed.'

'He must have been upset.'

'At the deceit?'

'Yes.'

'No. He's a bright boy. He understood, and was pleased.'

'As sanguine as he was to learn that I fathered him? He seemed less surprised than I would have expected.' Richard's tone was gentler. 'A composed boy.'

'Perhaps it wasn't a great surprise. I suppose any child who doesn't know its parent likes to imagine that they are the son of a king, or the lost daughter of a queen. How better to make a sweet romance of your own life?'

'Still, I'm only flesh and blood, Creator knows, and more riddled with wickedness than most of my peers, if you would listen to the rumours. I can think of nothing to say, Kate. I stand on the eve of the destruction of my kingdom, thinking that the universe has been so thoroughly wrenched inside out that nothing more can happen, and you slip in and change the world again. *How could you have not said anything?*'

'But what was I to do?' she snapped. 'I couldn't speak while your wife lived. Distressed and hurt Anne to no good end?'

'She was a gentle and tolerant soul. It wouldn't be first sin of mine she'd forgiven.'

'So she had enough to tolerate, without me adding to it,' Kate said under her breath. 'I had no wish to be seen as another youthful indiscretion, a mishap to be paid for her trouble, hustled away to a nunnery or quickly married off to some squire who didn't mind damaged goods. Damn that for a way to exist!'

'Iesu.' He stepped back, pinning her with unblinking, astonished eyes. 'Yes. I understand. I would like to think I would not have treated you in that way, but—'

'But you would. The world would. So there it is. You have a handsome, healthy son you didn't know about. I hope that when you've stopped railing at me, you will be pleased.'

He cupped his elbows, lowered his head. His dark hair fell forward. A thought went fleetingly through her that she would never touch it again; and even knowing that, she didn't dare try. A barrier stood around the King like an aura of glass, flaming, untouchable.

'Kate, dearest friend, pleased is not the word. I cannot speak. I should be overjoyed. I am. Or I would be, if it were not on this night of all nights. If I weren't so aware of Anne and my Edward already out there in the dark, little blue flames waiting for me to join them. Perhaps the joy is sharper for that, so it cuts me instead of soothing. It's more likely to make me weep than laugh. And I can't afford to weep before battle. Afterwards, that's the time, but not now.'

'I was afraid to wait until afterwards.' Her voice nearly failed her.

'So little faith in me?'

'No, but I travelled far enough with Raphael to share his fear.'

'Don't fear anything, Kate.' He spoke gently, looking straight at her. 'Whatever happens is the Almighty's will.'

'I don't believe that.'

'I don't have to remind you of your promise, I hope, not to use sorcery on my behalf?'

'I shouldn't break my promise unless you released me from it, sire,' she said tightly. 'I only hope that your enemy has extracted a similar promise from any sorcerers on his side.'

'Sharp as ever.'

'Of course, there'd be none of my sisterhood among Tudor's supporters. One of his first acts would be to destroy us. I'm sure he can't wait. You may not approve of us, but you have protected us. You are our only hope of survival. Yet you will not let us aid you in return.' She moved closer to him, as close as she dared. Although Richard stood with folded arms making a barrier, all his attention was on her. 'If Tudor wins, it will be the end of us, the sisterhood who tend the land. He has the support of churchmen who have been trying to destroy us for years, sometimes with the monarch's approval and sometimes without. Henry the Sixth encouraged them, your brother Edward was more kindly, but too lackadaisical actually to forbid their activities. I misread you. I thought you'd be on the priests' side and yet you have curtailed them. I don't know why, but I'm grateful. But now they can't wait for Tudor to unleash them again.'

His eyes were deep, dark slots. 'Kate, you have no need to lecture your king on this matter.'

'But I'm not saying it for selfish reasons. I'm sorry there isn't time to make you understand. Auset – the Dark Mother – she's the spirit of the land, the heart underground that gives us food, life, everything . . .'

His eyes widened as if he had, after all, understood. 'The sweating sickness.'

'Sickness, discontent, betrayal. Symptoms of the disease, all of it. If we withdraw from her, she withdraws from us. Everything that's afflicting the kingdom is the struggle of the ancient heart of the earth to be heard. If she isn't nurtured, if she's ignored, she'll wither away.'

He turned from her. He swayed, but caught himself on the back of a chair. 'If it's blood sacrifice she wants, no doubt there will be many before the sun is high. Is that it – a sacrificed king, so that the land can heal?'

Her eyes blurred. 'That's not what I said.' She denied it, but a boulder of dread rolled through her. Perhaps that was exactly what the Dark Mother did want. The spilled blood of a king, in payment for the desecration that was to come. Was that all Richard was, a sacrifice to hungry powers? She felt the earth tilting beneath her, leaning towards an unwelcome dawn.

He said, 'I should be glad to debate this with you, Kate, if we were sitting in the garden of some palace on a summer's evening, with nothing to disturb our peace. But I'm standing on the edge of an abyss and it makes me a poor philosopher. All I wish you to understand is that this battle must be decided fairly. That is, by my own strength or weakness, not yours.'

'I understand.' She swallowed the ocean of words that wanted to flow out. He was a warrior. In the face of battle, she would have no time for this, either. 'I never intended to interfere, and I won't.'

'I know your intentions are good.' The hint of a smile on his mouth was like light falling on her. 'You've been the kindest of friends to me, although I've done nothing to deserve it.'

'I suppose I never gave you a chance to deserve it. I've been a thorn in your side.'

'The sort that only hurts if you tear it out.' He turned towards the tent flap. 'Thank you for bringing Robin to me. I'm glad I saw him, if only once. If I win, bring him to me in Leicester. If not . . . keep him safe.'

His stance altered subtly, directing her to leave. He was saying goodbye. She stiffened, feeling desperate, hating to leave him, but knowing she must. He was a king steeling himself for a life or death battle and couldn't afford sentiment. She hadn't expected it. Even that small acknowledgement of friendship was more than she'd looked for.

'All the blessings of the Dark Mother be with you,' she said. 'Creator bless you and guard you.'

He nodded silent thanks. His whole life was in the

strained pallor of his face. He stood on the lip of the abyss, calmly ready to leap in. He looked deathly yet radiant, like an immortal.

'Raphael told me something strange,' he said. 'Even if my enemy wins the day, I'll be avenged. My name will never be forgotten. I suppose even infamy is preferable to obscurity. I pray you, remember me kindly, Kate, for few others will.'

She passed out of the tent and let the flap fall, cutting off her last sight of him. The night seemed immense; its cold breath filled her. She stood dry-eyed but breathing hard, as if the whole sky had crammed itself into her chest.

The steel curtain slams down. Richard is gone from us.

The end is coming and I'm afraid. I don't want to live through it but I must. The image of that last battle charge, that final rash gamble, his death plunge. One night it actually wakes me up with a jerk, like a falling sensation just as you're dozing off. I'm gasping in denial. *No, no, don't do it . . .*

It's over. Yet I can draw him back, into my mind, my dreams, my writing. Into my bedroom where he visits me with a dark, hot fever, but never with any answers.

Fin and I sit on her bed together, drinking. I am dreamy, idly describing the spiral paths of my parallel world. Fin is sharply analytical.

'Why am I so fascinated by him?' I ask. 'It's because of that streak of uncertainty. Because he's *not* a saint.'

'Would you still love him if he were definitely guilty?'

I half-choke on my merlot. 'Love?'

'Whatever you want to call it. Answer me. Do you, and do his adherents, need him to be innocent of child-murder so that you can love him with a clear conscience?'

'Well . . .'

'Which came first, the discovery of a terrible injustice followed by devotion? I put it to you that it was the other way round. Fascination first, and the quest to prove innocence after the fact.'

'Not guilty!' I say. 'No, Fin, I've never tried to prove anything. Why should he have been a saint, when none

502

of his family were? Perhaps he was innocent, perhaps he made one terrible mistake. It doesn't matter. I don't think I should tie myself in knots trying to exonerate him; just accept who he was. Only we don't know who he was, really.'

'And that's the attraction,' Fin agrees. 'The mystery, the darkness. And why not?'

We clink our glasses in a toast.

In the next breath she says, 'I know exactly who he is.'

'Oh?'

'You're quite right in saying you can't touch the real Richard. Your nocturnal visitor isn't the real Richard. He is the other half of you.'

My mouth falls open. Light dawns. 'Ah. My . . . animus?'

'Yes, but subtler than that. He is your daemon lover, my dear. The shadow-self in your soul. Your ideal lover, your inspiration, your muse. He visits your dreams and daydreams.'

'Relentlessly!'

'You've projected your daemon onto a real figure, as everyone does; but he's all yours. It's true, the daemon doesn't always appear in a virtuous guise; he may be dangerous, a vampire or a charismatic villain that you can't resist. That's essential, because he's trying to teach you something; to challenge as well as to delight. He inhabits the mysterious land of the psyche and shines the light of wisdom into the dark corners. Don't reject him. He's a messenger from your soul.'

I smile, thinking she is Eleanor to my Raphael. 'I don't want him to leave me, ever.'

'He won't,' says Fin.

Chapter Nineteen 1485: Plantagenet

CATESBY
> Rescue, my lord of Norfolk, rescue, rescue!
> The King enacts more wonders than a man,
> Daring an opposite to every danger.
> His horse is slain, and all on foot he fights,
> Seeking for Richmond in the throat of death.
> Rescue, fair lord, or else the day is lost!

Richard III Act V scene 4

At first the armour felt deceptively comfortable. The satin lining of Raphael's arming doublet was an echo of luxury, sliding coolly against his skin as Will Shaw began to tie his armour onto him, plate by plate. He shivered a little, but within moments he was beginning to sweat, like a crab in its shell. The King's pavilion was full of knights arming. Catesby and Ratcliffe, Robert Percy and Robert Ashton and all the other men of Richard's faithful household. William Catesby looked out of place in armour. He had the aspect of a lawyer, not a soldier.

When he'd finished, Will gave a lop-sided grin and patted his arm. 'Raffel, y'look like St George.'

'Appropriate, as it's a dragon coming to fight us.'

'Nah,' sneered Will. 'A hatchling horned toad, maybe.'

Raphael was calmer than he'd expected. This felt nothing like the dream. There was an atmosphere of tense urgency but each moment was real and solidly placed in time. Nothing nightmarish, just a feeling of intense tiredness, and anxiety coiled so tight in his stomach that he felt weightless.

An air of chaos lay on the camp, an ill omen. Henry

Tudor's side had armed earlier than expected. A tiny round priest, in a panic, was saying that the bread and wine for Mass had been misplaced; some boy must have stolen them, and would burn in hell for his misdeed. He was sweating and trembling before the King, but Richard seemed unmoved. He looked straight into the priest's eyes, his face grave and drawn. When he spoke the priest jumped, even though the voice was gentle.

'It doesn't matter. There will be no Mass.'

There was a clamour of protest. William Catesby said, 'Sire – if you go into battle without Mass, your soul . . .'

'And we can't breakfast until we've heard Mass, either,' Francis Lovell added prosaically.

'There isn't time. If I win, I'll hear Mass after. If not, there is no point in appealing to God; my fate is decided.' Richard turned, beckoning to his esquires. Raphael thought the priest was relieved as much as mortified. He shrank away from the King. There was something terrifying about him in the grey dawn, as if he'd entered the hidden world and emerged a spectre.

Raphael thought that was exactly what had happened to him.

He and Will left the King's tent and went to inspect the graylix. Other men had charge of them now, it was years since he'd handled them. The thought of their huge, dusty black heads and uncompromising faces, even their stench, stirred nostalgia in him.

Reaching the cages, he found their keepers distraught.

'We found seven of them dead this morning, sir,' said the chief handler, a gruffly spoken man with round, pouched eyes. 'Three and a half couple we've lost. Only one and a half couple left, and they're grievous sick. Poisoned. There were scraps of meat left—'

'By the enemy?' The news disturbed Raphael. His tension flared into frightening anger.

'I hope by the enemy. No one loves them, but I'm sure there's none of our own side would harm them.'

'And how the devil did the enemy creep up to their cages? Did you set no one to watch?'

'We did, sir. I'm sorry, sir.' The keeper drew away, miserable. 'We don't know how it happened.'

'Someone was sleeping when he should have been watching.'

The keepers looked on aghast as he went to the nearest cage and opened it. The beast inside snarled at him but was too weak to attack. He saw the bloody foam on its mouth, the yellowness of the accusing eyes. The stench of its laboured breath was foul. Reaching a hand to caress the huge skull, he felt its fever-heat and shudders of pain.

'Get me a crossbow,' he said. A boy obeyed. Raphael shot the graylix where it lay, ending its misery. He dealt with the other two in turn and then stood numb, with the keepers inarticulate around him.

He remembered the beasts as they'd been yesterday, hauling upon their chains as, two by two, they had magnificently preceded King Richard's army out of Leicester. A sign of royal might, heraldic creatures brought to life amidst the mass of standard bearers, trumpeters and priests bearing banners and crosses. Now, nothing but meat.

This had not been part of his vision.

'I'll tell the King of this,' Raphael said harshly, and saw the men's faces turn haggard. His own severity shocked him. 'Whoever let it happen will pay.'

Richard was ready, as bright as a leaping salmon. The armour was a silver aura on him; he moved as if it weighed nothing. He was smiling. In that moment he looked invincible. As Raphael walked towards him, he saw Francis lift the King's helmet and settle it onto his head. Round it was a gold coronet, spiked with blood-drop rubies.

At that, the first flash of fear went through him. Yes, this had happened before. This was all going as it had in the dream, every step, like a choreographed dance, and there wasn't a single thing he could do to change anything.

A moment later the feeling evaporated. He couldn't

recapture it. The vision became an irrelevant blur. No, this was real and nothing was preordained . . . His head span with the paradox and he envied the men around him who'd never been so afflicted. Richard's commanders surrounded him: Norfolk and his son Surrey; Robert Brackenbury; Richard's nephew the Earl of Lincoln.

'Dick, must you wear it?' Ratcliffe was saying. His heavy face looked rough from lack of sleep. 'It'll mark you as a target for every enemy soldier on the battlefield.'

Richard's face was serene yet dangerous, like that of a firehawk. There was no arguing with him.

'It will mark who I am, and show that I'm not afraid to be so marked. I'll fight and die a crowned king. One thing they'll not say of me is that I was a coward. Raphael? What's wrong?'

He didn't want to trouble the King now, but everyone was looking at him. He spoke quickly. 'Our graylix pack is dead, Your Grace. They were poisoned last night.'

Richard's reaction was minimal. His face gathered more shadows. 'The culprit?'

'Unknown.'

'Perhaps the same who has left a note for the Duke of Norfolk, warning him not to fight for me.' He exhaled. 'Another ill omen. A spy from the enemy or a traitor among our own, I wonder?'

Francis began, 'If any were so treacherous, they should be—' but Richard spoke across him.

'There are many who might incline to being so treacherous. A grim state of affairs, isn't it?' he said drily. 'Where's George Stanley?'

'Held under guard in his tent,' said Francis.

'Have him brought to the battlefield, where I can keep close watch upon him. Have word sent yet again to Lord Thomas and his brother William, reminding them that I hold their son and nephew hostage as surety of their support. They know the rest.'

'Yes, sire.'

Richard's face changed. Warmth came to it and he looked in turn at every man within the cloth-of-gold walls. 'And my dear faithful friends, who have stayed with me to the last. Today will see either the end of my reign or the beginning.'

When Richard's gaze fell upon him, Raphael couldn't speak. It might be the last time, the last quiet moment of friendship. The whirl of destiny filled him, too great for his frame to contain. He must swallow the feeling, think only of practical matters: that he had all his weapons to hand; that his horse was properly caparisoned; that the cramping of his guts was not beyond control . . .

'Come then, gentlemen. To arms.'

A fresh sky held the promise of heat. From the summit of the hill, the King's party held the advantage and a superb view of the landscape around them. There were villages tucked into folded fields, the spires of churches. Woodland spilled dark as holly into the folds.

The hem of the hill dropped away into a marsh. Mist hung there, damp and mysterious. The marsh formed a barrier of sorts, protecting the King's troops and limiting Tudor's path of attack.

Richard's horse was the grey charger called Fame of York, his favourite, a solidly handsome stallion covered in smoky silver dapples, the mane and tail like rippled cloud. Housed in armour and heraldry, the charger appeared to be beaten from steel.

Raphael's own mount was a dark liver-chestnut called Red Briar, an intractable beast that pulled like an ox. Others thought him mad to take the horse on, but he had always had an affinity for the wayward, the outcast. On a good day he could cajole the animal to go sweetly for him. Will Shaw was on foot beside him, in half-armour, looking faintly bemused at their situation.

A large company of knights surrounded the King – steel and gold. The leopards and lilies of England flew bravely above them. The confiding closeness Raphael had shared with Richard was gone with the dew. He was their commander, untouchable, a figure of burning silver glass.

The constant ebb of sound thickened the air: the clatter of armour, horses neighing and fidgeting. Below them on the forward slope of Ambion Hill stood the scarlet forest of the Duke of Norfolk's army. Behind them was the rearguard under the Earl of Northumberland. They stood high above the enemy, but the narrowness of the hill had forced Richard to place his troops in tandem, rather than spreading them out impressively.

Raphael knew, at last, that nothing he'd seen in his vision mattered. Even if he'd seen every detail, and every detail was precisely accurate, it would make no difference. He could not tell Richard what to do. The matter was out of his hands. He looked up at the sky with a sense of relinquishment.

'Any word from the Stanleys?' Richard asked. His visor was raised.

Raphael looked about, and could just see the two armies at a distance; the bristle of their lances, at least. To the north, Lord Stanley, whom Kate had so loathed. To the south, his brother William.

'They greet you well, sire,' said one of the heralds, looking angry, 'and say they have come defensibly arrayed, as you asked, ready to do battle.'

'But on whose behalf?' Richard said grimly. Turning in the saddle, he looked back at his hostage George Stanley, who stood on foot between his guards. The puppyish face was loose with fear; Richard's face hard, terrible. Raphael shivered, glad he was not in Strange's position.

Out across the marsh, Henry Tudor's army was approaching. Raphael caught his breath. Seen through the marsh vapours where the sun had not quite reached they were shapes in a mist. An army of the dead, moving through the blue and purple of the hidden world with a terrible, rustling thunder.

Richard looked upon the shooting-star banners of Tudor's commander, the Earl of Oxford, and let go a thin breath, almost a hiss. Raphael saw other banners he knew: Sir John Cheyney the giant, Sir William Brandon, Jasper Tudor, Edward Woodville. The traitors were flaunting their badges for all to see. In the centre floated the green, white and red of Tudor's dragon, unspeakably presumptuous.

'What makes him so arrogant,' Richard said quietly, 'if not sure knowledge of treachery against me?'

Catesby cleared his throat. 'I don't see either Stanley rushing to reinforce him.'

'Well, that's interesting. If Thomas Stanley sits on the fence any longer, it will cut him in half. Send word to him again to engage on our side on pain of his son's death.'

'Look at them,' said Francis. 'The finest ruffians Tudor could skim out of French and Norman jails. Queen Marguerite would be proud.'

The sun touched the enemy troops, showing not an army of ghosts but a rabble of brigands. Even at this distance they looked rough and violent like walking dead with nothing to lose. The Earl of Oxford himself was clearly visible in his golden armour. Raphael felt icy fury to see them. As they heeled around the fringe of the marsh and began to move face-on to Norfolk's front line, he saw the counterpoise of a familiar struggle. Beasts shouldering forward, handlers hauling them back.

'They have graylix!'

'So I see,' Richard answered, sounding angry now. 'And by what royal licence do they hold them?'

'Oxford's?' Ratcliffe said gruffly.

'Long revoked, even before Barnet.'

The first cannon fire shook the ground. Raphael's horse jumped under him, threw up its head and stood shivering. Sweat foamed on the dark coat. The crack of Norfolk's guns began to fracture the air: bombards, serpentines, harquebusiers. All around him, horses were shying, knights manfully struggling for control. Sharp smoke drifted. Like a dull echo, Henry Tudor's lines returned fire.

At such range, little harm was done. Before the fire of slow unwieldy guns faded, the archers let fly. The chilling rattle of arrows unfolded like a storm of deadly birds, wave upon wave. Tudor's retaliation formed an intersecting curve, a rain of thorns.

Raphael saw men begin to fall. His heart jumped to a higher rhythm. He was breathing fast in a maelstrom of excitement and fear. This was it, the final day, no going back. It might be his last hour; Richard's last hour.

Screams. Graylix were charging in among Norfolk's archers, causing havoc. He'd counted six couple while they were still on the leash. Arrows exhausted, the archers began to draw other weapons, swords, axes, billhooks. He could track the path of each graylix by the panicked eddies of men, mark where each was slain when the movement ceased.

A trumpet brayed; Norfolk was sounding the advance. Lines of men began to descend upon the Earl of Oxford, but the graylix attack had weakened Norfolk's front line and they were struggling to re-form, the captains yelling themselves hoarse.

Richard had superior numbers. It looked as if Oxford would be crushed by the sheer weight of men pouring down the hill. In a roaring crescendo, the two waves of soldiers crashed. Yells and screams ruptured the heavens.

Rapidly it appeared they had underestimated the pretender.

Oxford's little army stood solid under the onslaught. He aimed them like a wedge into the centre of Norfolk's vanguard and the whole line began to sag, men falling away like coral beads from a broken necklace.

A number of Norfolk's men had been carried off course by their own momentum down the incline of the hill, and couldn't find a way back into the melee. Raphael saw some throwing their weapons down and slinking away. Once

511

a few started, the impulse to flee seemed to spread like plague.

Richard was yelling, 'Send to Lord Stanley that if he does not throw his strength in with mine—'

Then they all saw the worst happening: Sir William Stanley's men were charging, openly attacking Norfolk's flank. His brother Thomas still held back, uncommitted, but little groups of men were peeling from his lines and trotting to join Henry Tudor's.

Behind Richard's troops, the Earl of Northumberland's army was ghost-silent. Raphael was astonished, when he glanced round, to see they were still there. He would not have been surprised to find they had silently quit the field. He remembered the Earl's nervous pallor in the candle-gloom of his tent, the convulsive bobbing of his larynx.

A messenger, one of many Richard had sent to Thomas Stanley, came riding back so hard that his horse stumbled. 'Your Grace,' the youth gasped, losing his voice. 'Lord Stanley replies that he has other sons.'

There was a dreadful, deathly pause, filled with the steady roar of violence. Richard turned his horse, rode up to George Stanley and loomed over him. 'Did you hear that, my lord?' said the King to the hostage. 'Other sons. Notably, a step-son he would like to see upon the throne, at any price.' The eyes of George Stanley grew huge; he was sweating so hard that his face seemed to run like a melting candle. Returning to his position, Richard pointed back at him with a gauntleted hand and said, brisk and cold, 'Kill him.'

Then the King dismounted from his horse and beckoned to Percy, Ashton, a couple of other knights and his stand-ard bearer. 'You five, come with me. The rest, hold the hill.'

Richard strode away, axe in hand, straight into the thick of battle. Raphael stared after him in disbelief and frustration. His instinct was to follow, but that meant disobedience.

Some of Richard's men were looking at each other in confusion. 'Does he mean us to kill Strange now?' said Ratcliffe.

'Dispatch him,' said Catesby, businesslike. 'It's the King's command.'

'My lords – please . . .' George Stanley's plea was like a child's, heart-rending.

'Take him off the field,' Lovell said hoarsely. 'Richard spoke in anger. If he really meant it, we'll do it later.'

'On your head be it, then,' Catesby answered, but sounded glad the decision had been taken from him. Strange was led away by his escort, almost collapsing with relief at his reprieve.

Down in the field, the circle of gold upon Richard's head was clearly visible. Dazzles of ruby light leaped from it. He fought on foot like some armoured angel, drawing men to his standard, putting fresh resolve and energy into them. Raphael watched in anxiety. The sun was mounting the sky and its beams fell hotly on the steel of his armour, roasting him.

William Stanley was wearing away at Norfolk's flank. The fighting laboured on, and Oxford would not give ground, and still neither Thomas Stanley nor Northumberland made a move to help. Down in the tide of battle, Richard vanished.

Raphael gathered Red Briar's reins, ready to charge to his own death if need be. His mouth was bone dry, bitter with the salt sweat running down his face.

Richard reappeared, surfacing from the chaos like a mermaid out of the waves. His knights and standard followed. His surcoat was torn and bloody and, as he wrenched off his helmet, Raphael saw his hair was soaked to black curls with his own sweat, his lips cracked and trickling blood, his expression anguished.

'Norfolk,' he said. His voice was raw, broken. 'My lord of Norfolk is dead.'

He gave Lovell the helmet, reeled a little way down the

side of the hill to a spring that flowed out of the rocks, and put his face into the water. Hesitantly, Raphael started after him, then halted when he realized Richard was not only quenching his thirst but hiding his pain.

The unthinkable was happening. They were losing.

When Richard rose again and came back to them, his eyes were black with rage. Sweat and water ran from him. 'My horse,' he said.

Will Shaw, who had been holding Fame of York, quickly brought the great stallion to him and held his bridle while Richard mounted.

'Dickon,' said Francis, in pain. 'This is your chance to flee. Save yourself and fight another day.'

Richard smiled. It was the darkest, coldest smile Raphael had ever seen. This was worse than his vision. A thousand times worse. 'There won't be another day, dearest friend. If I quit the field now, not a man here will ever fight for me again.'

'That's not so.'

'I said I would live or die this day King of England,' Richard replied simply. 'Do you see yonder banner with its impertinent red dragon?'

Raphael stared down the slope and saw the knot of men that was Henry Tudor and his bodyguard. They stood apart, on a small rise that kept them clear of the boggy ground, observing the battle from a safe distance.

'The self-styled Earl of Richmond has so far not set foot on the battlefield. If he won't grace us with his courage, let us take the battle to him.'

'Dick, for God's sake—'

The King's voice rose, hoarse, passionate. 'We have a clear path to him. We'll go now, before it closes again.'

'You'll have to ride in front of William Stanley!'

'It's our only chance to end this. Either Tudor dies, or I do.'

Raphael was now breathing so hard his lungs were sand. He held Red Briar hard with one hand and positioned his lance. Its bright tip flew its pennon above his head. He was going with the King.

'I see Raphael is ready,' Richard said drily. 'Francis, hold our position here. The rest of my household . . .'

Not a single man hesitated. Their unquestioning devotion moved Raphael. He glanced round at their resolute figures and saw Will Shaw mounting a horse that he must have begged off someone. Raphael shook his head, but Will shrugged and Raphael looked away, unable to argue.

It was only as Richard began the charge and sent Fame of York leaping over the rutted ground, the horse blowing and arching his neck, drops of foam flying from his mouth, great hooves splaying eagerly over the ground, that a coil of horrible knowledge unwound inside Raphael. This was the moment. It was all as in his vision after all. This was the decision that would undo Richard. One bold, brave, desperate mistake.

And it was too late. In an earthquake of hooves and a flight of bright standards, they were charging down the hill. Red Briar was pulling hard, almost overtaking the King, leaping rocks and tussocks. Raphael's arms ached and his chain mail chafed at the vulnerable angles of his armpits and groin. The sun dazzled through his visor, turning each drop of sweat that fell into a blinding diamond.

He saw the impudent dragon swelling, billowing. A wall of steel men stood between Richard and his prey. Nightmare and reality meshed. Raphael could no more turn back, nor change fate, than he could have arrested himself in mid-fall from a cliff.

He stood up in his stirrups and roared.

'King Richard! York! England!'

Katherine had taken Robin to a safe hill to watch the battle, but he soon ran from her, craning his neck to see more. Suddenly he was out of sight among the other watchers. By the time she'd woven her way through them, there was no sign of him.

Panic: a wave of it slammed the breath from her. She had a dreadful conviction that he'd given her the slip on purpose and gone to join the fighting.

'Robin,' she called, sharp and loud. No answer. The day was hot, shimmering 'Robin!'

A shape moved, yards ahead of her, hidden by bushes. Gathering up her skirts, she ran towards it. It was gone; wildly she looked about her, saw green woods and meadows on one side, and on the other the shifting colours of the battle. Nothing. Kate paused then ran on again. 'Robin!'

She came upon another knot of spectators, standing on a little rise with a copse of trees behind them. A loose group of priests and clergy, some mounted, others on foot. She didn't recognize them. They had the gaunt hard look of travellers, and she realized they were from Tudor's side.

'Have you seen,' she gasped, not caring who they were, 'have you seen a boy, fifteen, dark hair?'

The men turned, looking down at her from the great height of their mounts. One of them, she saw in dismay, was Bishop Morton. He gave her a dismissive glance and looked away without interest. She doubted he remembered ever seeing her before. Another said, 'No, my lady.' They turned away, all except one.

She knew the carved face with its pale, piercing eyes. It was Dr Fautherer. He went on gazing at her, as if beckoning her to him.

'No, my lady, we have seen no boy. Who is he?'

His eyes judged her, stripping her raw.

'My – I'm charged with looking after him.'

'This is a rash place to bring a child.'

'I haven't time to disagree with you,' she said. 'If you would let me pass?'

He came closer. She had the unpleasant sensation that his mind was crawling into hers. 'Allow me to help you find him.'

Katherine drew back, shaking her head. The last thing she needed was for Fautherer to find Robin. Then Tudor would know that Richard had a son. She didn't know how to refuse and could only think to stall him, while Robin ran ever further away.

'Sir, there's no need. He'll turn up.'

'Youthful high spirits,' Fautherer said, nodding in sympathy. 'Still, I'll go along with you.'

Miserably, she picked her way over the tangled grass with the gaunt priest at her side. She went slowly, hoping she wouldn't see Robin after all.

'The battle goes ill for Richard,' Fautherer remarked.

'Does it?' she whispered. She'd hardly been able to watch the melee seething across the hillside.

'See how Norfolk's line sags and wavers. There are many who hate Richard so passionately they'd rather see an ape crowned than endure his reign any longer.'

'You mean your friends, the Stanleys?' she said furiously. 'They're fools. They don't know him. All they care about is their own gain!'

Fautherer smiled. 'Perhaps, but that doesn't matter. All that matters is who wins.'

The world darkened; the battle became soundless, a pageant behind glass. All the times she had entered the hidden world, Katherine had never encountered anything that she could have described as evil, but in Dr Fautherer's presence she felt it. Pure evil.

'There is a new order coming,' he said. 'Your time is over. You've lingered for centuries longer than you should have done. Creator, it's as if the Druids still walked these islands! What you see upon that field is justice being done. The victory of light over dark. That is what my patrons believe, at least.'

'And you don't?'

'I have no opinion. I am only here to upset the order.'

Kate stopped. She stared at him. She saw through Fautherer, as he seemed to see through her. What she saw made her recoil.

'What are you?' she whispered.

*   *   *

Richard and his retinue smashed into the armoured wall and it broke, like a skin of ice, plunging them deep into the current. Raphael was flung from rarefied air into the thick of battle. Tudor's renegades seethed about them, roaring with pain as they went down under the huge hooves of the chargers. The King's men were striking out furiously on every side. Raphael felt a foot soldier trying to drag him from the saddle and swung his sword in outrage and thrust it through the open face of the man's sallet, straight into his skull, as if skewering the flesh within a clam. Blood hosed over him, bright red. Frenzied and fearless, he dragged the blade out and looked for the next adversary.

Fame of York was terrifying: huge, blood-soaked, blowing hard, a demon-horse. Men were falling out of the charger's path, blood spilling from throats or limbs. Richard hacked through them as if they were straw. He seemed more than human – possessed. Raphael saw amazed terror on the faces of his opponents and desperation. They hadn't been ready for a king so ferocious, so deadly, so devoid of fear. Mud flew. The choke of blood, sweat and metal filled the air.

Richard reached Henry's standard bearer and cut him down with a single heavy blow. The dragon standard billowed down like a fallen sail, entangling men beneath it.

Then Raphael caught a glimpse of Henry Tudor. He looked small even in his silver-white armour, and was struggling to control the brown horse leaping about beneath him. The raised visor revealed a pale, nondescript face with eyes like a startled hare. He was staring at Richard, who was struggling closer and closer to him, as if transfixed.

Tudor's bodyguard closed around him. The giant, Sir John Cheyney, came riding forward on the mightiest horse Raphael had ever seen. He towered over everyone, all dully shining steel like some plated monster. Richard looked tiny before him, yet he was charging to engage as if Sir John were no more than another scrawny foreign mercenary.

He has no fear at all, Raphael thought. Gathering the reins, he urged Red Briar forward, hacking his way through to the King's aid.

Will Shaw had got ahead of the King and was fighting furiously, striking down foot soldiers on every side. His sally took him into John Cheyney's path. It happened in a moment, even as Raphael reached Will's side. Cheyney swung with a massive axe and struck Will from his horse as if swatting a wasp. Raphael cried out. The moment was quick, glass-sharp: Will falling, blood spouting from his neck. He hit the ground with a grunt. The giant knight's axe swooped towards Raphael and he was petrified, unable to do anything but duck, feeling the hiss of air a breath away, and wait for the return blow that would dispatch him after his friend.

Then Richard was there, silver and fierce as the sun. His own axe bit into the giant's breastplate with a thick noise, like a meat cleaver into bone. Cheyney doubled over and rolled heavily out of the saddle. His horse, startled, barged into Richard's, and Fame of York stumbled backwards, put his hind hooves into the edge of the marsh, and fell.

Raphael's heart was thundering as if it would explode. He threw himself off Red Briar and stumbled to Richard's side. As he did so, he looked up and saw his nightmare brought to life, the path ending in the abyss, as the kindly gods had tried to warn him – William Stanley's soldiers were pouring down towards them, to overwhelm Richard's little force and make an end.

Richard's beloved knights were defending desperately – falling, dying. Raphael was attacked before he could reach the King. Foot soldiers were all around him, striking at him. The last thing he saw was their pinched, pocked faces. He went down under agonizing blows, choking, drowning, down into darkness . . .

He was floating in another place. Everything was mist-grey and indistinct. He could see the faint outlines of a church or cloister around him. Great tombs, a sense of sepulchral age. The muse was there. He saw first her veil of brown hair and then her sad, thoughtful face as she turned her head to look at him.

'He is the sacrifice,' she said. 'It can't change.'

He saw the taut pain in her eyes, the falling tears, yet she gave a sad smile. Another being was with them, a bony ghost of a man with a haunted, suspicious face. He looked twenty years older, but Raphael recognized him as Henry Tudor.

'Here is your consolation,' said the muse.

Raphael tried to speak. No sound would come out, but she answered his silent question anyway.

'No one will ever love him. Henry will die unmourned. Richard will live forever.'

In a hideous jerk, he came back to consciousness. His attackers must have thought him dead and left him. Mud and water oozed around him. A roar of sound scoured his ears. Every inch of him felt bruised. He was still in the marsh with Fame of York struggling beside him. The charger's mouth was open, nostrils working like bellows.

Beyond rational thought, Raphael staggered to his feet, seized the grey's bridle and began urging him to his feet. Fame of York struggled, like a fly mired in honey. Then, with a sucking rush that nearly dragged Raphael over, he fought free.

Richard was ten feet away, fighting back to back with Robert Percy, as Raphael brought his charger back to him.

Richard slew his opponent, said, 'Bless you, good friend,' and swung back up into the saddle. The words were brief, rough with exhaustion, but held a depthless well of feeling.

Of Red Briar, there was no sign. Raphael stood, his feet apart, on the destroyed grass, dwarfed by the mounted King. He clutched his lead-heavy sword two-handed and looked around for the next attack.

A crimson-coated foot soldier was suddenly crashing past him in flight, yelling, 'Northumberland!'

The air shuddered with yells and the sound of furious fighting nearby. Panting, Raphael looked up and saw streams of men pouring over and round the tilted slope of Ambion Hill. Northumberland had thrown his rearguard into the maelstrom at last. His forces crashed at an angle into William Stanley's men.

Raphael beheld his vision subverted, fate shattered, forking like lightning upon an unpredicted path. Half of Stanley's traitorous force had turned to defend itself; the other half was in flight, men flinging down weapons as they went. Richard's cavalry, held in reserve, now entered the fray, bearing down upon Henry Tudor's beleaguered position. As they rammed home, the last stand of Oxford and William Stanley roiled into a cauldron of screaming horses and dying men.

'He listened,' Raphael said under his breath. 'Northumberland listened to me!'

It was only now he realized that Richard hadn't positioned his cavalry as he had in the vision. Instead, he'd placed them where they could better help him, with a clear route to come to his aid.

Henry Tudor was naked, his bodyguard pared to nothing. Raphael saw him carried back and forth as he fought to keep his horse from bolting. He looked paralysed, a small figure shrinking in armour too big for him. Raphael saw his watery eyes, his face melting with sweat. It was hard to pity him. He had brought this upon himself.

Then Tudor saw Richard coming, an armoured seraph rayed with silver fire. The last of his defenders hit the ground in streams of gore. Henry visibly quailed and shrank. Breaking, he gathered himself for flight, so that he was turning flank-on as Richard reached him. Henry hauled on the reins, panicking madly as he struggled to defend himself. For a few seconds his eyes were full of a jaundiced light, more terror than hatred. One wild sword-blow aimed at Richard missed entirely, throwing the pretender off balance. Fame of York collided with the brown horse, shoulder to shoulder. Richard's axe hacked through Tudor's breastplate.

The self-styled Earl of Richmond hit the ground with a surprised grunt.

The fighting washed away like a wave upon sand. Tudor's supporters knew the day was lost. Most were in flight, leaving nothing but their discarded, bloody surcoats. No one wanted to be caught in the pretender's livery. Once news spread of Tudor's fall, there was nothing to fight for.

Richard slid down from his exhausted mount and leaned on his sword. He stood like a statue, dented and bloody. When he pulled off his helm he was drenched underneath, as if he'd emerged from a waterfall.

Gradually his knights and servants flocked to him and he embraced them each in turn. Now they would begin the account, Raphael thought, of who lived and who had died. The standard bearer came and the King's leopards and lilies billowed high. Peace descended, but it was uneasy, the atmosphere still rent by echoes of violence. Corpses lay everywhere.

Richard said quietly, 'Creator bless and acquit the friends who died for me this day. Who have we lost?'

'I'm still here.' It was Francis Lovell, who'd come down from his position on Ambion Hill with the cavalry. He walked unsteadily towards the King, leading his horse. 'Ratcliffe is slain, Catesby wounded but alive. Will Shaw's slain, Geoffrey and Marmaduke Constable alive. Of the others, I can't say.'

'And here's Raphael, thank God,' said Richard. His eyes were bruised, the whites bloodshot, the irises as clear as water.

'I couldn't save Will,' said Raphael, and felt a chasm open in his chest. Will Shaw had always been there. He couldn't begin to imagine his absence, let alone feel it. He was drained. There were knives in his joints, and the sun's heat slowly broiled him in his own juices; but he felt a wondrous calm. All his nightmares were purged. It was over. He suddenly thought of Kate, with regret and new hope.

Richard acknowledged the loss with a nod. 'Let the corpses be gathered and borne to Leicester with all the honour due to them.'

'Even that?' said Lovell, looking over at the twisted heap that had been the pretender, Richmond.

'Even Henry Tudor. If only for his nerve.' Richard gave a faint smile. It was like light falling, leavening the atmosphere. 'What of the Stanleys?'

His standard bearer answered. 'William was killed. Thomas is captured.'

'Good. Good.' He fell quiet, then said softly, 'This is England's victory, not mine.'

'Amen,' said Francis.

'Well, my lords, there's much to do. I'll need a messenger to post to Nottingham with news of the battle.'

'I'll go,' said Raphael, without pause.

'No, you won't.' Richard looked piercingly at him. 'Raphael, you've done enough. More than enough.'

'I'm not tired,' he said. 'I could ride a thousand miles for you.'

Richard shook his head, smiling. 'Is there no stopping you?'

'No, sire.'

Richard came to him and held him with both vambraces resting on Raphael's shoulders. 'Raphael, I listened to you. That's what saved the day. You don't have to go to Nottingham.'

'But I want to be the one to tell them. Give me a fresh horse. I'll rest when I get there.'

'Christ. If you insist. I could wish for no better messenger. But not without food and a change of clothes.' Richard moved away from him, addressing the others. 'Gentlemen, the day is done. Let us return to Leicester. We must mourn our friends, and decide how best to deal with those traitors who live. Pray with me.'

As they lowered their heads in prayer, Raphael saw, although no one else seemed to see it, a silver pard stalking the battlefield, its head rayed like the sun. It reared with its paws upon Richard's shoulders, touched its tongue to his forehead, and vanished.

The cry went up, one or two voices at first, then a swelling roar, spiralling out across the battlefield. 'God save King Richard! *King Richard!*'

'What are you?' asked Kate. She looked straight into Fautherer's eyes and saw nothing there. It was like looking into a skull. Heat shimmered too bright, blinding her. 'What are you?'

'Fire spreads best with the aid of wind,' he answered. 'Silt stirs from the river bed in the presence of a current. How can poison circle the body without a beating heart to drive it?'

Her eyesight was turning dark. The sounds of battle washed over her, but she couldn't bear to watch. If Richard fell, life would end. 'You came to destroy him. You, the spreader of malicious rumours . . .'

'No,' replied the whispering voice. 'I am the result, not the cause. And I grow ever in strength.'

He was a luminous figure, floating in a sooty penumbra. Kate felt all her certainty about the world being swept away. She stared at Dr Fautherer and knew he was not human. *Not human*. She stood in the face of a being utterly unknown, something insidiously passive and yet so malevolent that her soul shrivelled from it in revulsion.

'Mama?'

It was a boy's voice, calling from some yards away.

'Mama!'

She felt a light touch on her elbow. In the same moment, Dr Fautherer vanished.

He was simply gone. Kate blinked. The summer world reshaped around her and was all birdsong and vibrant greens again. Wild roses and woodbine twined in the undergrowth.

'Look!' cried Robin. 'Did you see? They've raised the King's banner over Tudor's rotten corpse!'

Kate turned slowly as if waking from sleep. She forced herself to look. The fighting had stopped. Soldiers were milling about or quitting the field as swiftly as they could. The figures were tiny, but she saw the gold circle of Richard's crown, his standards vaunting against the hill, streams of men in silver and bronze centring upon him.

'Oh, love.' She caught Robin's arm.

'He's alive, he's alive.'

'Oh, thank the Mother of All, thank the Creator. Now let's hear them bleat about who had God on his side!'

'You never doubted him, did you?' Robin sounded indignant.

'Well, we can never be absolutely sure.'

'I knew he would win.' There was a fierce light in her son's eyes. For his sake, more than her own, she could have wept with gratitude for his happiness. They embraced, crying together. Even in that moment, her son seemed more than ever a stranger; nothing to do with her any more.

Chapter Twenty 1485: Auset

Richard was not, to his cost, a political animal. His penchant for direct action in place of patient diplomacy brought him to die in a battle that should never have taken place.

Anthony Cheetham, *The Life and Times of Richard III*

The spire of Leicester cathedral impaled the sky. Around the skirts of the guildhall crowds thronged: onlookers and gossips, nuns and friars, merchants with bright robes swaying around their broad forms. Katherine forced her way between them. Robin had run ahead of her in his excitement, met with some of Richard's men, and was long gone; already with the King, she surmised. She couldn't blame him. He'd grown up independent of her, and had no reason to cling to her now. She would not have wanted it.

There were horses everywhere; the streets were caked with their dung and with their ripe, reassuring smell. Soldiers in the liveries of the winning side strutted about. Whether they'd fought bravely, wept in terror or stood idle on the battlefield, they were now all alike in triumph, swigging the gifts of ale the townspeople offered, boasting, heads thrown back in laughter.

A few yards from the door of the guildhall she came face to face with George Stanley, Lord Thomas's son; the threatened husband who had made her flee onto a wayward path. It seemed an age ago now. Kate harboured no resentment. He stood with other prisoners, awaiting Richard's judgement. He looked old, his hair thinning; but there was still something of the puppy in his eyes as he caught her gaze and looked frantically upon her.

'Lord Strange?' she murmured.

'Lady Katherine,' he said, and stammered mutely for several seconds. 'Would – would you do me one kindness, my lady?' She stared, then gave a wary nod. He pushed a sealed letter into her hand. 'See that my dear wife gets this. My last loving wishes to her. It's her I fear for, not myself.'

He looked desperate. She pushed the letter into her sleeve and he said, 'Thank you. Fare you well, my lady.'

Shaken, she gathered her skirts and went on. There was no sign of Raphael anywhere. Her anxiety pressed towards panic. She squeezed her way up to the door, and was stopped. Then Francis Lovell saw her, and let her through. He looked wrecked with fatigue, but was smiling.

'Is Raphael here?' she asked.

'No.' Seeing the alarm rising in her eyes, he added hurriedly, 'He's alive, my lady. He's gone to Nottingham with dispatches from the King.'

'Oh.' Her terror leaped and fell away in the same breath. 'The King sent him to Nottingham, after such a battle?'

'No. Raphael insisted. I don't know what more he thinks he has to prove, but there was no stopping him.'

'Idiot!' she said. 'And my . . . my son, Robin?'

At that, Lovell regarded her with dry amusement, not unkindly, but for just a little too long. Perhaps he didn't mean to, but plainly couldn't stop himself. Colouring, she said, 'I suppose the world knows.'

'The King has seen him, and sent him, I believe, with a number of his personal esquires to dine in the town.'

'And will Richard . . . will the King want to see me?'

'Of course,' he said. 'If you don't mind waiting, my lady, I'll tell him you're here.'

'Thanks, Francis. Bless you.'

The guildhall was a cool dim refuge from the street. There were knots of men standing about, talking earnestly as they waited for the doors to the inner chamber to open. Within, the city fathers had created a makeshift throne room for the triumphant King. He is behind those doors, Katherine thought. A thread of extreme emotion pulled at her, painful and thrilling. She looked at the closed doors and at the dozens of petitioners waiting for audience, and her heart sank. It would take him the rest of the day and half the night to see them all; he never turned anyone away.

They were looking at her, the men, some with slit-eyed interest, others with disapproval. She felt uncomfortable. How long must she wait?

The doors were thrown open and out came Thomas Stanley, chained fast between half a dozen of Richard's officers. Their demeanour was grim. Lord Stanley's face was the colour of a ripe plum, his eyes straining from their sockets. He strode along between his captors, practically dragging them with him like a graylix hauling at the chain.

'Eager for the axe, this one,' said one of the officers. Over his shoulder he called, 'Make haste to the market-place if you want to see traitors' heads rolling!'

The antechamber crowd fell back. A hush dropped upon them. Into it, an esquire said softly, 'Katherine Lytton?' and she was being ushered into the hall, the indignant others shut out.

Kate stopped, with a brief strange feeling that the King within would not be Richard but a stranger, Henry Tudor, and all of it a dream. The floor was a lake lying before her: an expanse lozenged in black and gold. At the far side was Richard, seated on a narrow dark throne. Velvet robes of plum and black trimmed with ermine fell about his upright frame; a cloak of crimson lined with white damask pooled on the oak of the dais. Above him a cloth-of-gold canopy had been raised and the walls hung about with royal heraldry. His face was as impartial as an archangel's: long and luminous, with narrow dark flames for eyes. He was fingering a ring with a huge ruby on his the middle finger.

He had just sent Lord Stanley to his execution. Others with him, she had no doubt. Across the chasm of the floor, he looked at her with an empty, brooding expression. Her mouth was arid; she had no idea what to say. Just curtsey, she told herself, congratulate him on his noble victory, and apologize for Robin coming ahead of me – and leave.

She saw his lieutenants around him: William Catesby, Rob Percy and Marmaduke Constable, the lords Surrey, Lincoln, Northumberland and all the others who'd been loyal to him. She accounted who was missing: Ratcliffe, among others. She hadn't realized she would miss his steadfast presence until he was gone.

The tingling heat of their attention was heavy on her. She felt excruciatingly self-conscious, but only one person among them mattered.

Katherine began to walk towards King Richard. The closer she drew the higher above her he seemed on the stepped dais; a position contrived to impress his authority upon all those who had supported him, but especially upon those who had opposed him.

The walk was dream-like but over in seconds, and two steps from him, her composure deserted her. She wasn't curtseying but falling to her knees on the steps and taking his outstretched hand. Not dropping a dry kiss on his fingers as she'd intended, but pressing her mouth to his palm then holding it hard to her cheek. She leaned on his thigh, her eyes leaking slippery brine to soak his hand, his sleeve and velvet-encased leg. She couldn't stop crying. He was alive.

All she wished through the blur was that his attendants would vanish. Hateful, to have them witnessing her collapse. At any moment, someone would lift her gently away and take her out, conveying His Grace's thanks, and it would be over.

Richard sat still for a moment, startled. Then he leaned

forward. 'Kate,' he said softly. His hair, brushing her cheek, smelled clean. She felt the weight of his head resting on hers, his hands moving over her arms and shoulders. Mole-blind she climbed into the embrace.

She felt his mouth against her temple and the pressure of his fingers around her arms. He was rising, drawing her to her feet with him; not pushing her away but encircling her. Her arms quested up beneath his cloak until she could hold tight to him. Beneath the layers of fabric his body felt lean and spare, as she remembered it. His arms were so hard around her she could barely breathe. There was no taint of the battle left on him, only the echo of soap and rosemary, the fragrant dusty scent of velvet. They kissed, opening starved mouths to each other's heat. Only briefly, for it was like fire on oil, but enough to sear away her belief that he'd been indifferent to her all these years.

She wasn't sure how long they remained there. She became aware at last of a muttering and subtle throat-clearing from the onlookers. Perhaps it would pass into legend, that the King Richard had passionately embraced an obscure noblewoman in public. God knew what rumours would be started. She didn't care. Richard plainly didn't.

'Kate,' he whispered, drawing back enough to look at her. His voice was unsteady. 'Will you wait for me? I have a thousand people to see. I don't expect you to stand about here through this tedious business, but if you will go with Geoffrey, he'll take you to the inn where we're lodged, the White Boar. You can rest there. It's a lot to ask, but I must speak to you.'

She slipped back, out of his arms. They stood hot and discomforted, trying to retrieve dignity. 'My son came to you without me. I apologize for him but he's young, excitable—'

'Nothing to apologize for. He's in good hands. He's gone with some squires of mine to eat, and no doubt to be regaled with tales of the battle.'

'He'd better not speak of it to me,' Kate said with feeling. 'To hell with all battles!'

'Amen,' said Richard. He dabbed at her eyes and nose with the fine damask lining of his cloak. 'They'll look after him. Will you wait?'

'If you will do one thing for me.'

'Name it.'

'Spare George Stanley's life.'

'It's done.'

'Then yes,' she said. 'Yes, I'll wait.'

Richard's chamber at the White Boar was plain, but fairly furnished. There was a great bed with hangings of crimson and sapphire, figured with fleur-de-lys in gold. A fire in a huge grate bathed the dark oak walls with rusty warmth. There was a separate privy with a seat of polished walnut, and, set behind a screen, bowls of water fragrant with floating rose petals. Kate sat in a chair by the fire, sipping claret and feeling mortally embarrassed as Geoffrey and a couple of young pages came and went, rendering the room perfect for the King.

A lot to ask, Richard had said. Despite the impeccable deference of his attendants, she felt like a whore. That was what the situation made her. It didn't matter if she and the King talked and only talked all night, in their eyes, she was there for only one reason.

She threw George Stanley's letter on the fire. Thank God and the Serpent Mother, there was no need to send it now.

Kate started up, hearing voices and footsteps in the corridor outside. Richard came in, half a dozen attendants with him. Suddenly the room was full of bustle, male energy, with Richard's presence shining in their midst.

Kate moved discreetly to the window and stood there, rigid, with her back to them. She heard Percy's cheerful voice, and Lovell's, and thought they would never leave.

531

She heard Richard hurrying them up, and could only imagine their smiles as they finally left the room.

'Kate,' he said.

She turned, and they were alone. His cloak and royal robes had been discarded; he stood in his shirt sleeves. They went quickly towards each other, meeting halfway between the foot of the bed and the hearth. His body felt burning hot through the cloth of the shirt. Tightly they clasped each other, like lovers who'd never expected to meet again.

'You waited for me,' he breathed. He kissed her throat; she arched her back, gasping in surprise and pleasure. More intimate than the mouth, it seemed. Her hands went into his hair, clasping handfuls of silk in an ecstasy of relief, relief that she could touch him at last.

He paused, his arms loosening, his mouth resting near her ear. She could feel his heart pounding beneath his breastbone.

'Oh gods, sweet Kate,' he said. 'This day has gone on forever. I'm so tired. I don't think there's any inch of me that doesn't ache.'

'And you're here. You won,' she whispered. 'You wouldn't ache if you were dead.'

'Yes.' His mouth touched her cheekbone, hot, flower-sweet. 'Not all pain is unpleasant. You should know that your son, our son, is still happily in the care of my trusted friends.'

'On his way to becoming a knight and forgetting his mother.' She sighed. 'I don't mind. I'm glad.'

'And I'm glad you brought him to me. Thank you, thank you. Beyond that, I have no idea what I wanted to say to you. Forgive me.'

'I didn't think we were here to talk.'

His lips folded into hers, parting them, and the sweet current of fire flowed. She felt him shaking. He drew back and his eyes, so close to hers, were grey lakes in a dark forest, an unexpected sombre surprise of light. 'Are you sure, Kate?'

She was touched that he asked, even though there was no need. She pressed hard against him. Beneath the frustrating layers of her skirts she was hot, starving for him to be inside her. All she wanted was his flesh against hers. 'Our reputations are in tatters anyway. Don't stop.'

'You will see some terrible bruises.'

'Show me. I'll soothe them with my lips.'

'Oh,' he breathed. 'I can't dissuade you, then. Thank God.' He was plucking at the fastenings of her gown, awkward in his haste. She gasped, laughing.

He'd been so distant, as if no more made of flesh than a carved saint. The change overwhelmed her. He was a great shadowy wing covering her, pulling her under. The current rushed and pounded in her ears.

'Yes,' she whispered. 'Don't mind anything else. Celebrate life.'

He rose from the bed and went to stir the fire, feeding logs into its slumbering heart. Kate propped herself on one elbow to watch him. The lean body, hard with muscle and flowered by battle-blows, flowed with firelight. He no longer seemed a king, only her lover. She was pleased he did this chore himself without a thought, rather than call for the page. He loved luxury, but was no spoiled prince. He'd always been a soldier, used to the hardest life could offer. When he came back to her, he brought a glass of claret. They both drank from it, sitting close and naked beneath the sheets.

'All this time I thought you didn't like me,' he said, smiling.

'Not like you?' She gave a small sigh. 'Hm. The trouble wasn't that I liked you too little, but that I liked you rather too much.'

'I would never have guessed. I sometimes thought . . . but then I'd always think I was mistaken. And I, if you knew how I've longed for this, Kate . . . gods – burned for years, ever since that first time.'

Kate expelled an incredulous laugh. 'You never said anything. There was a glimmer, a few times – the time you gave me the mare – but always gone so fast I was sure I'd deluded myself. You were like blind rock!'

'How could I speak? I was a married man, Kate, and you promised to Raphael.'

'That wouldn't have stopped King Edward. Oh, you are certainly not like him.'

'In my heart, worse than him,' he murmured. 'But only for you. After Anne died, I was too sad, too oppressed to speak to you. I couldn't even think of it. What was the point, when I was facing death? You were always beyond my reach.'

'Me, beyond *your* reach?'

He gripped her suddenly, and hard. 'Katherine, I'm so tired of being alone.'

'You're not alone.' She held him, her hands folding behind his head, fingers in his hair. 'I'll always serve you loyally.'

He groaned. 'Oh, not service, I didn't mean that.' The words came out with aching difficulty. 'Sweetheart. I would like you with me – as my wife.'

Heat flashed through her. Terror. A thousand curling threads of thought. Complete joy and leaden denial.

'Then would I also be the . . . Queen?'

'Such a fate usually falls to the King's wife, yes.'

She couldn't hold the words in. 'No. No, I couldn't. I don't know what to say. I can't be the Queen.'

'I asked you to marry *me*. Never mind what I am.'

'And it's you I want, but not the things that go with it.'

He raised his head and looked at her, his expression tinged with the first fading of dismay. 'However, I can't stop being what I am. It would not be so terrible, Kate. Would it?'

She saw her own skin turn crimson with the flush of panic. She loved him so completely she would have cheerfully walked through hell for him, but what he was

534

asking was something else entirely. 'You'll have to marry that Portuguese princess. What was her name?'

'I can't remember,' Richard said through his teeth.

'You'll have to, when you've cooled down and thought about it.'

He groaned and put his hand over his eyes. 'I want no foreign princess. I want someone I know, love and trust with my life!'

'I wouldn't be accepted. They'd revile me as they did Elizabeth Woodville. My blood's less than hers.'

'No,' he said fiercely. 'There's nothing wrong with your ancestry, Kate, it's as old and noble as my father's and my mother's. No doubt we're cousins, at some distance. In any case, it doesn't matter. Parliament could declare Robin legitimate, and he'd be my heir.'

That was too much to take in, and only increased her panic. Furiously she said, 'And if I told you I'm of no blood at all? If I said that my mother had no children of her own, that none ever came? That she took in a village girl, sad and desperate, who'd been got with child by the village cowherd, himself the bastard son of our old priest? That my mother gave the girl a home, hid her shame and brought up the child as her own? If I said that the woman who birthed me is lady-in-waiting to my mother? And that I've seen the man at a distance. A decent hard worker, they say, no malice in him, only the weakness that afflicts us all? But that the man I consider my true father was John Lytton, no other.' She was crying. She turned her face into his shoulder to hide it.

'*Are* you telling me that?' he asked after a time, very soft. 'It still doesn't matter.'

She sucked in a deep breath. 'But it would. Someone would find out and do to us what . . . what you did to Edward.'

Now his arms around her lost their tension. He lay back in thought, weighing what she'd said and what it meant, whether it was a refusal or a test. She didn't even know herself, only that she was shaken, and frightened, and could not face what it all meant.

Not in a thousand years could she envisage being Queen. And Robin – would he welcome being burdened with the throne, instead of having the freedom to order his own life? And this matter, and that . . .

In the morning, she knew, Richard would again be a stranger to her.

She waited until he slept. Exhausted from the battle, he did so deeply. Then she slipped out of his relaxed embrace, dressed as best she could with no one to help fasten her gown, slipped past his sleeping attendants, and went silently into the night.

Eleanor was surprised when Kate came home, dishevelled, without a single one of the attendants who'd accompanied her and Robin to Leicestershire. Her lovely Spanish mare looked worn out. Kate had ridden her hard, which was not like her. Kate's own demeanour was ominously subdued.

She insisted on stabling the mare herself. Eleanor leaned on the stable door, watching her as she groomed and fed the animal as if to atone for having asked too much of her.

'Dear, what's happened?' Eleanor asked.

'Have messengers come?'

'Yes, one came this morning. They said King Richard was victorious. Martha and I cried. That's all we could do, cry with relief.'

'Did they tell you that he had Thomas Stanley executed?'

'Yes,' said Eleanor. Again the pang – not quite grief, just dull regret.

'I'm sorry, Mama. I know you had a tender spot for him. A sentiment I found entirely inexplicable, but, still, I know the news must have hurt you.'

'I was sorry to hear it. However, I don't see what else Richard could have done. Thomas brought it upon himself. A shame Richard didn't also cut the head from that bloody woman Thomas married. What of his son?'

A faint smile twitched on her lips, and was gone. 'George? Richard spared him.'

'Good. I doubt he has the fire to start another rebellion to avenge his father. I hope not. Let us pray Auset that this brings peace.'

'You don't blame Richard, then?' said Kate. 'I would hate to think this had turned you against him.'

'It hasn't,' said Eleanor. 'But what's happened?'

'He has Robin.'

'Ah.' Another wisp of sorrow, but not as keen as Eleanor had expected. Kate's news seemed inevitable. 'So clearly he had no doubt that Robin was his.'

Kate laughed. 'How could anyone doubt it? Richard raged at me for not telling him, but once that was done, he was overjoyed. I suppose he'll take him as a ward of the royal court and we'll see him no more.'

'Is that what Robin wants?'

'Mama, you have never seen a creature as thrilled as Robin was to learn who his father was. He was gone from me like a trout in a beck. He has a wonderful future now. I would not take that from him.'

'Is that why you're so sad?'

Kate rose from rubbing the mare's legs and looked at her. Her posture was one of resigned exhaustion. Her eyes were brilliant in the darkness. 'Mama, I'm not sad.'

'Whatever has made you flee in such disarray? I wish you would tell me.'

'There's nothing to tell.'

'Then why have you come home?'

Kate's demeanour changed subtly; her shoulders went back and the misery fell away from her. 'Because it's the path I have chosen. I've come to take up my duties as your heir, *Mater Superior*.'

Kate was in a hedgerow, picking herbs. The moon shone full upon her. She took the tender stalks at their maximum potency, while the tide of their silvery energy waxed with the moon's pull. Her mother's grey cat followed her. Around her the world was charcoal and silver; dew-moist and fecund, but cool. Every scent and every fall of light woke a memory. Her father, smiling and kissing her as he rode away to yet another battle. Playing hide and seek with Nan. Her sweet mare, Mab. Processions of softly chanting sisters, making their way to Briganta's Cave, lit by lanterns that might make onlookers think they'd seen a procession of faerie folk.

Seducing a sweet and hapless stranger.

She thought of how Richard had once accused Elizabeth Woodville and her mother Jacquetta of trapping Edward into marriage by sorcery. As if Edward could not simply have been following his heart, and made the decision – however ill-considered – by himself.

Did Richard really believe that? Had he forgotten what Kate was when he asked her to marry him? Or did he hope or expect that she'd forsake all she had been?

No, Kate thought, harvesting her plants with vigour. Her basket was full. She closed her eyes tightly. She'd given her answer. Couldn't turn from her true self, even for him. She swayed on her knees. Her skirts were soaked. The cat came pushing at her, forcing its way between her arms and lap. She pressed her cheek against the wet fur. Somewhere in the distance, a voice was calling her name – she ignored it. Instead she hugged the cat – as if it could fill the void – until it objected and wriggled free.

He was alive. That was all she and Raphael had worked for. Nothing else was possible, had ever been possible.

It was past midnight when she went back to the house. Strangely, Martha was still up, she and two cookmaids busy in the kitchen. Martha leaped from her skin when she heard Kate, and whipped round, glaring at her with mouse-bright eyes.

'Why are you about so late?' Kate said, placing her overflowing basket on the table.

'Oh, thank heavens you're back! Did you not hear me shouting?'

'I was out in the meadows.'

'Go to your mother immediately. She's in the great hall.' Martha came storming forward and started fussing at Kate's hair. 'How did you get into such a state?'

Kate caught her hands and pushed them down impatiently. 'What's so important?'

Martha drew a deep breath. 'You can't go looking like this – but you must go at once. What am I to do with you?'

Kate looked down at herself. She was wearing a plain grey dress, black from the knees down with damp. She pulled the kerchief from her head and shook her hair loose. 'Stop fussing. Mother will have to take me as she finds me.'

She went with measured steps, determined not to rush. All she could think was that her mother had somehow found out what had happened in Leicester. Gossip always seeped through in the end. Or perhaps Raphael had arrived. It was impossible that someone would not have told him, as soon as he'd returned from Nottingham, that she had spent the night with the King. Perhaps he'd come to berate her and tell Eleanor the worst.

The hall was a glowing tableau, soft red and amber. In the flickering light, facing her, she saw her mother sitting in her tall chair by the hearth, magnificent in russet silk, with drops of gold shining on the hennin that covered her hair, every inch the lady of the house. The chair facing Eleanor contained a man who had his back to Kate. She could see nothing of him except one elbow. There was an aura of polite ease between them, as if he and Eleanor had been talking for some time. No one else was there.

Seeing her daughter, Eleanor rose. 'Katherine, you have a visitor.'

She walked towards them. The man stood up and turned to greet her. It was Richard.

Never in a hundred lifetimes had she expected him to come after her. She stood idiotically dumb. Her first thought was that he must be here for some other reason, not for her.

He was plainly dressed, in breeches and doublet of a bitter-brown colour over a white shirt and wearing long black boots chased with bronze. Fire painted his hair with a curve of red amid the black. He looked astonishing. All the breath went out of her.

'Kate,' said Eleanor in a light, firm tone. Kate had never seen her nervous before; in other circumstances, it would have been amusing. 'Greet our guest according to his high estate. This is the King.'

'I know,' she answered tightly.

But as she began to curtsey, Richard said, 'No, no, forget formality. We know each other well enough.' Sombre-faced, he kissed her hand. His skin was warm from the fire and she felt the heat of mortification spreading through her. Eleanor regarded her with shrewd eyes. What on earth had they been talking about?

Kate managed to say, 'Excuse my dress, Your Grace, but I was working – gardening.'

'At midnight?'

'Certain plants can only be—'

'You would look fair in rags,' he said quietly. 'You never were of an idle disposition, my lady.'

Eleanor said, 'Katherine, His Grace the King has informed me that he wishes to speak with you privately. Are you willing?'

Her breath was unsteady. She didn't want her mother to leave. Alone, she feared that Richard would be furious, or cold, or menacing as she knew he could be. What was there to say? Slipping away in silence had been the only answer. To be forced to defend her decision was unbearable.

'If I have your permission, my lady Mother,' she murmured.

'Then I'll leave you. There is wine. Call Martha or

Thomas if you require anything else. If you will grant me leave to withdraw, sire.'

With another meaningful look at her daughter, Eleanor glided out.

Now Kate was shaking so hard she could hardly move. Her hands twining together were clammy. Richard leaned on the carved chair back, regarding her without expression.

'This is a beautiful house, and your mother is very gracious.'

'Despite being embarrassed that she couldn't find me.'

'My father-in-law Warwick would have blustered and made a great issue of it. "Madam, can you not find your own daughter?"'

Kate gave a faint smile. 'You'd never be so ungracious.'

'Were you hiding from me?'

'No. I didn't know you were here until I came in.'

'Why did you leave Leicester?'

She felt that his eyes, as he asked the question, would scorch the flesh from her bones. She chewed at her lower lip. 'I panicked.'

'At what?'

'At what you asked.'

A line creased his forehead. He looked angry and hurt. It took a brave woman to reject a king, and Kate didn't feel brave at all. 'And what's this? Your answer? Or a test of my determination?'

She stood twisting her fingers together, then forced her hands down to her sides. In truth, knowing he had pursued her made her feel weirdly ecstatic. He has power over me, she thought, but I have power over him, too.

'It wasn't my intention to test you,' she said. 'Just to vanish quietly.'

'Didn't you expect me to follow you?'

'No,' she said. 'In all honesty, I didn't.'

He shook his head in frustration. 'I thought it was plain that – I thought we both understood – How could you think I'd let you go without a word?' He came forward and seized her left wrist, making her start. 'Did you really think I'd not come after you? I forsook all my duties, when I could least afford to do so, to come here. All I could think of was finding you. If you set out to bewitch me, it's worked.'

'I haven't bewitched you. No more than you've done to me.'

'And what was that night? I thought we shared the same feelings. If I was wrong, that was a display of passion so remarkable that I mistook it for love.'

She lowered her chin. 'You didn't mistake anything. We spent years forbidden to touch each other . . .'

He put his fingers to her cheek. 'Is it forbidden again?'

'No.' She caught his hand to keep it pressed against her cheek. To go through this again, when she'd thought it was over, was torture.

'If you think I only took advantage of you and would have discarded you at dawn, you deal me a great insult.'

'I didn't think that. Beloved.'

'Then why run away? Is the idea of marrying me so abhorrent? Of course! I poisoned my wife so I could marry my niece – what sane woman would have me? Still, I should like the courtesy of an explanation.'

'That's unfair! You know full well I never gave credence to those rumours. But you asked with your heart – if not with an organ somewhat lower down. By morning you would have had to consider it with your intellect. You would have realized it's not possible.'

He dropped her hands and paced the flagstones. A huge shadow spread from his feet and leaped upon the wall.

'Tell me why it's not possible.'

'They – they won't allow it!'

'Who?'

'Oh, your councillors, your bishops, all those to whom you must answer! They'll dissuade you in the end. You must do your duty – marry a foreign princess or whatever is best for your kingdom.'

He came towards her again and stopped, arms folded. 'I

told you, I don't want a stranger thrust into my bed, some poor girl torn from her homeland and probably as reluctant as I am. I want you, Kate. In this one thing I'll do as Edward did and marry as I desire.'

She tried to blink away the scratch of tears. 'And they'll tell you that equal disaster will follow from it. I'll be no more popular that Elizabeth was! What if they found out—'

'That you were a foundling?' His face was stony. 'There's no need for them to find out. For all the world knows, you're a woman of perfectly sound birth. And if rumours escape, I'll deny them.'

'You've certainly had plenty of practise.'

That hit home. He flinched. His eyes turned darker, frozen basalt. 'Then it can hardly make things any worse.'

'I'm sorry,' she said helplessly. 'I shouldn't have said that.'

His eyebrows flicked upwards. 'Truth is cruel.'

'In fact, there's nothing to find out. Lord and Lady Lytton are my true parents.'

He shouted, making her jump. 'Then why tell me . . . ?'

'I didn't. I said, what if I *were* to tell you? My mother took in so many unwanted babes, I often suspected I might be one of them. But she assures me that I am her true daughter. She wouldn't lie to me.'

'I'm glad, but it wouldn't have mattered. Test me if you must, but there's no need.'

'I'm still of lower birth than Elizabeth Woodville.'

'That's untrue, and if you compare yourself once more to that woman, I shall leave. Have you a large and grasping family, waiting to seize all the wealth and power they can lay hands on?'

'No.'

'Are you manipulating your way to wearing a crown?'

'No!'

'That's one of the reasons I trust you. You're too far the other way, if anything. The very mention of it made you flee like a startled colt.'

'Yes, I was afraid,' she said. 'But I was also being realistic. If you were a knight or a shepherd, I'd not hesitate; but then you wouldn't be the same person, so who can say?'

'I'm damned either way, then. Tell me the worst. Are you still in love with Raphael Hart? Have you some promise to him, plight-troth, hope of marriage?'

She shook her head. Tears got the better of her for a moment. 'No, we never made a formal promise. All that was between us ended forever once he learned about Robin. Raphael is a good, gentle soul, but he isn't you. In another life I could have been content with him, if I had never met you. But I did meet you. And that's why I never married him.'

She heard Richard's soft breath, in and out. 'I feared you fled because you realized you didn't love me, had perhaps decided I was some kind of tyrant after all. Yet you don't seem to be telling me that.'

'No, I'm not. I love you so much I'm terrified.'

'Kate, are you intent on making me beg? Stay with me, love, please. What have I defeated the Welsh pretender for, if I lose you?'

He sounded desolate. 'You're not considering the greatest obstacle of all!' she exclaimed. 'I'm not an ordinary woman. I'm a witch, a sorceress – not in rumour, but in reality. I'm bound to the Dark Mother and one day I'll replace Eleanor as head of the Motherlodge. I'll be to the guardians of the hidden world as you are to the outer world, if you like. Their queen and their servant. I can't give that up. It's what I am.'

The look on his face told her that he hadn't considered it for a second. Her heart fell. Although she'd never admitted it to herself, some obscure part of her had hoped he'd have an answer.

'Did you expect me to turn my back on it?' she went on. '*They* will expect it, your bishops and Parliament, every single one of your subjects. The King must marry a good, biddable Christian woman, and I am none of those things.

Not good, not biddable, not Christian. Not that I disbelieve in your Creator. If the Church says he's there, who am I to argue? But I follow a different way. They won't approve of me anyway, but they'll certainly expect me to forsake all I am and play the pious queen.' She shuddered. 'Perhaps they'll demand some horrible ceremony of repentance and conversion.'

'Kate . . .'

'I can't do it. I can't take an oath of devotion to God at my coronation. I can't submit myself to "churching" when I've had a child, since I don't believe that childbirth makes women unclean. I can't do any of it. That's why it's impossible for us to marry. I have duties too! They will take up a great deal of my time and that's why I came home: to take up my responsibilities.'

Richard said quietly, 'God Almighty.'

For a long time, neither of them spoke. He moved about the hall with a dark silhouette haunting him. She leaned on the back of the chair where he'd been sitting. It was all that kept her on her feet.

Eventually he said, 'You were right. I should have let you go. It would have been cleaner, less painful.'

'Yes.'

'What am I to do, then? Go back to London and marry some stranger whom I'll never love, while you and I never meet again?'

'You see I'm right, at last.' Kate turned towards him, tasting the salt trickling into her mouth. Richard sat down on a bench by the far wall. The light made great black wings of shadow behind him.

'Yes.' His voice was hollow. 'Everything you've said is true, but it's more, and worse. We've cheated fate and so we can't ever be happy. You're right to decline, Kate, but not for the reasons you've given. I'm not loved as a king and I doubt I ever will be.'

'That's not true!'

'Let me finish. The hidden world claimed me long ago.

I suppose that is why I'm drawn to you. I've fought it all my life with devotion and prayer, but nothing I've done has defeated the darkness. Each time I try, it comes back in greater strength. I sold my soul to the Devil in order to seize power and keep it. Everything Raphael dreamed of me was the truth, or at least held the seed of truth. That's why I was never angry with him, never sent him away or accused him of treason.'

'Raphael loves you,' she said faintly.

'I know. He showed his love by telling me the truth. It's as if he said that I should have died, my corpse been stripped naked, defiled and spat upon, my name blackened for all time; then my debt would have been paid. If God sent a messenger, it was Raphael, not Henry Tudor. Instead, I've an even greater punishment waiting. If this is all I am – deceiver, usurper, murderer – I don't glory in it. I'm cursed with it, cast out of heaven with Lucifer.'

'Do you believe that?'

'I'm not sure "believe" is the right word. But I give it serious consideration in my darkest moments.'

'Does it frighten you?'

She moved towards him. His black wings flared upwards. He looked all he had said, darkly beautiful as Lucifer, dignified in damnation, untouchable. Yet she touched him; she knelt at his feet and laid her hands along his forearm.

Richard turned his head and looked down at her. 'Any other woman would have fled my presence by now. Yet you ask if *I'm* afraid?'

'Are you?'

'Yes. Terrified. Never of battle, only of what lies in the hidden world, and what will happen when it claims me at last.'

'You once entered the hidden world by chance, and have been fleeing from it ever since.'

'Did Raphael tell you that? Nothing stays secret.'

'No. I was there, remember?'

Anxiety etched lines in his blanched face. 'By chance? I

doubt it. And yes, I know it was you and your mother I met there. I was a child, utterly undone by fear. I thought the Church would shield me, but it's been a ragged veil against the shadow. I wonder if my loathing of the Woodvilles' depravity and my punishment of Eliza Shore was only an attempt to purge some darkness I feared inside myself. Fruitless.'

'There was no need to be afraid,' Kate said with feeling.

'Easy for you to say. You were so confident there.'

'You're not afraid of us now, surely? You know us.'

'Sometimes, sweet Morgana. Not in the outer world, but I still fear what you may become in that other place, as I fear for my own soul. That time we met and lay together, didn't you wonder why I left so abruptly?'

Her lips formed a thin smile. 'Not really.'

'You took me to the threshold of that godless realm again. The land of faeries and demons. It was all so sweet, until I woke and realized I'd been bewitched.'

'Or thought you had,' she said sourly. 'Yet you have protected the Motherlodge.'

'That was to appease the darkness, I think.'

'Only that? Not out of some secret sympathy with us, that you can't even confess to yourself? Love, admit it. You're one of us.'

He turned away. 'You grow to manhood and learn to mask the fear,' he said, very quietly now. 'It took me years to trust you. Now, I wonder. Do I want you with me only to tame you, to feel that I control the demons that haunt me? Do I love you because only a faerie wife could love me in return? You know one of your own, after all. My soul was marked for the Devil and you claimed it when I was seven. I am talking superstitious nonsense, I know, but deep inside, I feel it to be true. As you say, it's impossible.'

He rose. She stood up with him, her heart beating in painful alarm.

'Where are you going?'

'To rouse my men, and leave. Thank your mother for her hospitality.'

'You can't go.' She'd spent all this time persuading him to leave her; now he was doing just that, she was horrified. 'It's too late.'

'If I stay, I'll not be able to sleep.'

'Don't sleep, then.'

In response, he rested his cheek against her hair. 'What do you mean?'

'Let there be one last night.'

He groaned. She felt the tremor go right through him. 'Worsen the torment? After the confession I've just made, you'd still lie with me? You are a witch, for certain.'

'Of course I would. I'm the Whore of Babylon.' She pushed her hands into his hair and clenched her fingers, holding him. 'But I didn't mean that. You've misunderstood everything. Face your fear. Spend the night with me in the hidden world.'

All this, and I still haven't touched the truth. I've touched something, though, if only inside myself. The mystery of it was beautiful.

I'm here at Bosworth Field again. Nothing has changed. The same steady wind is breathing through me, and the same brooding peace lies folded over the landscape. The history books still tell the same story.

I place a white rose upon the stone where Richard fell. It always chokes me; I don't know why. He fought to the death with no thought for his own safety; he was hideously betrayed; he was so young, barely given a chance to begin his reign. They trussed his body naked and spat upon him as he was carried without dignity into Leicester. Thus revealing more about themselves than they did about Richard. Almost alone among English kings, he has no grave.

We try to atone.

Perhaps in another world, they place red roses on the spot where the pretender fell. I doubt it. For them the name Tudor would have made no greater mark on history than the name Warbeck, or Simnel; just a name to make schoolchildren groan.

Shakespeare's play has to end as it does. Such glorious wickedness cannot be seen to go unpunished. But, oh, because the character is to be punished, he is granted full licence to be so gloriously wicked.

And reality. The fascination is not because he was a devil, not because he was a saint, but because he *was*. Richard is seen through a prism, flowing and changing.

Different colours float over him according to which angle you choose, ruby and violet and indigo, pulled by the distortions of the glass; enticing, but never quite clear.

Someone is coming towards me. Over the shoulder of the hill and down the broad quilt of grass he comes, blurred and shimmering as if he moves through the mirage barrier of the otherworld. He looks about, bemused. The wind lifts his hair. He's dressed strangely, but that won't mark him out. People only smile, thinking he's part of some medieval re-enactment group.

I rise, white roses falling from my lap, to greet him. At last.

Chapter Twenty-one 1485: Muse

Don't you see yon narrow, narrow road
So thick beset with thorns and briars?
That is the road to righteousness
Though after it but few enquire.
Don't you see yon broad, broad road
That lies across the lily leaven?
That is the road to wickedness
Though some call it the road to heaven.
Don't you see yon bonnie, bonnie road
That lies across the ferny brae?
That is the road to fair Elfland
Where you and I this night must go.

Thomas the Rhymer

Richard recognized the cave: the low, rounded mouth, overhung by a wild fringe of grass and foliage, the misty black interior. It had featured in so many dreadful dreams. He had always been drawn towards it, his heart pulsing with greater force the closer he went; and then running, running while the woman and the child stood like spectres, watching him. Never, in the dream, had he been able to face what lay inside.

Now his skin felt icy. He noted the familiar, gathering rhythm of fear. A hundred battles, a thousand charges against a wall of armoured men could not hold a whisker of fear to compare with this. Yet it was only a peaceful walk by night along a river bank, with the moon and stars bleaching the pale rock and shards of limestone crunching beneath their feet. A gentle climb, and then the broken arch of stone receiving them like an ancient gateway.

Katherine went ahead, graceful as a goddess with her dark hair hanging down her back. This was her domain. Following her, he felt as vulnerable as a child. He had no knights of the body, no attendants. No one even knew where he was. With all the trappings of kingship stripped away, he was only a man; his soul naked.

The cave was a temple. Katherine went straight in, ducking a little. The lantern she carried scooped out the darkness and revealed a dry, bleached-gold space with a stump of rock in the centre. It looked primitive, pagan, yet not sinister. Before he could allow himself a chance to hesitate, Richard followed her.

She began to light candles on the rough altar. Flame writhed on a lump of pitted black rock set in a niche on the rear wall. It was a crude statue; all female curves with a terrible, featureless visage rearing from its shoulders. Its blackness was startling against the white limestone.

'She is Auset,' said Kate. 'Isis, Tara, Callieach, the Black Virgin. She has many names, but if it makes you easier in your mind, address her as the Mother of God.'

'She bears little resemblance to the Madonna.' The cave spun their voices into loud, echoing whispers.

'More than you think, perhaps.' Kate bent to light amber resin in a censer. Fragrant clouds wreathed round her, musky and evocative. 'In the beginning, as our legend goes, there was only the Dark Mother. She is complete in herself, able to give birth without a male counterpart. Think of it in this way. It's her son who goes out into the world, fiery and wrathful and smiting unbelievers. The Mother remains in her seat of earth, biding her time and occasionally rolling her eyes at his excesses.'

There was distinct amusement in her tone. Richard half-smiled. In other circumstances, it would have seemed she was speaking the grossest heresy. Here, though, he knew he had stepped into another world entirely. It was her realm, where her theology was solid and true.

He said quietly, 'Kate, the time – that first time I entered the hidden world, I saw this cave, or one so like it I can see no difference. But it wasn't here. I was in Ludlow.' The memory still disturbed him. 'Ludlow. Many days ride from here!'

Unperturbed, she looked at him with large, dark-edged eyes. God, her wondrous eyes were just the same as when he'd thought her an elf-child. Chills seeped through him. 'As I have told you before, the hidden world is not only in one place. It's everywhere. It has no map and no logic. If we were meant to meet you, it's perfectly feasible that we were here and you in Ludlow.'

'As if we met in a dream.'

'Yes, but a dream as solid as reality.'

'I think I'm expecting too much to understand what happened.'

As he spoke, something came into the cave.

A whirl of cold air, nothing visible. He was suddenly transfixed by an awareness of eyes upon him. An intense, mocking scrutiny. Despite his iron efforts to stay calm, his breathing turned quick and shallow,

'It's nothing,' Kate said easily. 'A nosy elemental. We will attract them, but they will protect us, so it's a fair exchange. They're friends.'

Richard stood chilled and shaking, watching her arrange the small altar to her satisfaction. This was against all he'd been brought up to believe. Elementals came creeping up from the godless faerie realm, the Devil's garden. Priests were always called to drive them out. Yet Kate and her sisterhood welcomed and worked with them.

He swallowed and said, 'I don't know if this is proof that you worship the Devil or simply proof that we don't understand you.'

'Unfortunately, people's fear of what they don't understand leads them to destroy it. And to justify destroying it, they must put about that it's evil.' She shrugged. 'Come, sit down. Try to forget any notion that this is either good or evil, or that it needs to be.' She placed two age-worn tapestry cushions on the floor before the altar. One showed a graylix, one a silver pard. 'Don't kneel. We don't abase ourselves.' Grinning, she added, 'Only in the direst circumstances.'

Hesitantly, he sat cross-legged beside her. 'I don't see what this will achieve.'

She put her hand on his arm. 'You're as tense as a priest forced to walk down Cock's Lane.'

He laughed out loud. 'Your analogy is perfect: the horror of the depravity and the temptation of falling into it.'

'That's it. Horror and temptation. Don't look away from them. Trust yourself. Have you something to give as an offering?'

'Offering?'

'It needn't be a slaughtered lamb. Just a gift, a token. A thread from your doublet – anything.' Leaning forward, she opened a pouch and tipped a handful of walnuts into an empty gold-rimmed bowl. 'Auset, Great Mother of All, we bring you these tokens of our love and we ask you to stand before us, as we stand before you, in perfect love and perfect trust.'

Richard paused, uncertain. Then, quickly, he took a chain from around his neck. From it hung a silver cross, its pointed arms curled around rubies. It looked like a little sword. He set it upon the walnuts and let the chain pour in after it. There it lay, shining.

'What should I ask of her?'

'Ask for clear sight,' said Kate.

He did so, silently. Closing his eyes, he made a wordless invocation to the Dark Mother. *Let the darkness come, then, and do its worst. I'll ask no protection of God. If the Devil claims me, so be it: I'll pay my debt and I'll do so without fear. Only let me see the truth.*

When he opened his eyes, the world had turned slate-blue and Kate had vanished.

Richard rose to his feet in confusion. If he'd been nervous before, it was nothing to the terror he felt now. It wasn't a fear of losing his life, but of losing his sanity. His soul. The candle flames on the altar burned dim and blue, everything was swathed in a limpid blue mist. He was in the hidden world.

He'd thought Kate would be with him. He hadn't expected to find himself here alone. She'd given him no instructions for waking from this dream. He looked for his cross, meaning to take it for protection. The offering bowl was empty.

Ice-cold, he went to the cave mouth. Bluish twilight awaited him. As he stepped out he found no river bank below, instead a marsh lay spread before him, the marsh of countless nightmares, gleaming, waiting. Wan lights danced here and there. Shadows moved between the tussocks, prowling. Smoke and eyes. The whole place was softly alive and watching him.

Raising his head he walked steadily forward, passing beneath the arch of Briganta's Bridge, until the ground began to squelch under his feet. He stood on the very edge of the marsh. The marsh in which . . .

In which, in another life, Henry Tudor's men had butchered him. He felt the echo of memory: the last chopping blows and the breath bursting harshly out of him, 'Treason, treason!' He felt he was dead, after all, and in the underworld.

This was the place he'd dreaded all his life. He was here again, as he'd always known he would be, bone-cold and desolate, but knowing he could not be anywhere else. This was inevitable. As resignation came, his fear fell to a dull background ache.

There was something moving out on the marsh. Something huge was coming towards him. He watched, lips parting in wonder. A charcoal bulk, stuck with spars and spider's webs of rigging, pitching as it came, sailing the marsh as if through clear sea.

A black ghost ship. Coming for him.

He thought it would plough him down where he stood,

yet he couldn't move out of its path. As it hoved closer, he saw that it was not a ship at all but a living creature, a gigantic sea-monster, leviathan. It veered broadside on and he saw moisture coursing down its dark, sheened sides. Its spars were the spines of the bony fans that splayed from its neck, with cobweb membranes stretched between them. Its head was a wedge poised high in the gloom. Tar black, it loomed above him and he tried to back away, only to find himself sinking, thigh deep, in the ooze.

He stumbled back into the sucking mud. Between them, marsh and serpent would consume him. He struggled to breathe. Then his feet touched a resilient surface and he was being dragged forward, lifted. The monster had forced her paw beneath him and he had no choice but to cling on to the plated limb. She lurched, turning. He climbed as if scaling the side of a ship, gained her shoulder and then the broad span of her ridged spine and ribs.

Her fins cracked like sails, folding and unfolding. The leviathan completed her ponderous half-circle and began to take him away from shore. Away from Kate. Looking back, he couldn't even see the cave.

There was open sea around him, a disc of calm rippling water, black in the night, encircled by a wall of fog that moved with the sea-monster. No boundaries. Above, the moon was a dull green eye staring down.

He was on the English Channel, going into exile. That had been their life, he and his brothers. Fleeing in defeat, storming back to triumph. Washing in and out like the tide. A strange life, but all he knew. It seemed a million years ago.

Edward, George and Edmund were long gone. Richard was all that remained. He felt stranded in life, left behind. He yearned to join them.

He heard a sound behind him. A whisper of cold, the faintest rustle of movement, and something . . . breathing.

Richard flung himself forward, rolled on the scaled surface, and came back to his feet with his dagger in his hand.

His only weapon. The creature that faced him was a demon no taller than him. Its body was fire, its face dazzling, and above its shoulders rose two huge curving wings, black and shot through with peacock colours.

A voice came from the being, rumbling from the palely blinding mask. 'You know me.'

'No, sir, I don't.'

'Then let me come closer.'

The demon lunged. Richard ducked the sweep of its pinions and thrust up at the abdomen. His wrist was stopped as if he'd hit stone. The pain made him curse. The demon had him in a vicious grip and was forcing his arm up, up.

With his free hand, Richard struck out and met strangely insubstantial flesh. His hand was on the burning-cold face, forcing the chin back, fingers seeking the eye sockets. His assailant uttered a sibilant gasp. Then it gave a vicious squeeze of its hand, and Richard's fingers sprang open. The dagger skidded away, down the curved flank of the beast and was lost. He heard the *plop* as it hit the water.

He jerked out of the demon's grasp. It was years since he'd fought bare-handed. The moves came back easily, but the creature would not play. Like sails, its great wings carried it beyond his blows, or buffered them.

The leviathan's mounded back was unstable and treacherous. Wrestling, they slithered upon it. His attacker's strength and agility were too great. It ran him back against the serpent's thick neck, which rose like a mast cut from a massive tree, and there it held him.

It seemed intent on smothering him. They held each other in stasis and, as the terrible face came closer, its odourless breath filled him like the wind. It was drinking his soul. Above them, its great wings cracked on the air.

The dance went on. Its hands were on his throat. Richard felt himself failing, as much through horror as exhaustion. He saw the black void of the sea waiting for him. This was the end, the last stand against the Devil.

With a grunt of desperate effort, Richard jerked up and broke its grip. He got one arm free, and the demon was suddenly half-doubled beneath him. The chance was brief. He brought his fist down with a crack on one of the wing bones and felt it break like a bird's.

As he did so, he felt pain flaring in his own shoulder. Breathtaking agony.

Then he understood.

The shock of the pain made him stagger back. The demon drew itself up and stood in mirror pose. The broken wing rose to its former arch, healing. Even as his own pain faded, the sight made Richard desperate. In the pause, he launched himself at the demon and bore it backwards until he had it pinned over the leviathan's heaving shoulder blade.

As he held it there beneath him, it felt suddenly frail, as if its strength had faded. The fire was gone out of it; the body was dark. One wing-tip came free and fluttered out over the water. Its face, close to his, was ghostly with deep black eyes.

It was his own face.

Behind it, far below, Richard saw the hungry shimmer of the sea. He meant to throw it into the depths. Then his shadow would be gone forever. But as he tried, it clung to him like a lover. He hesitated and could not bring himself to do it. It was wrong, wrong. His hands slid under its feathery wings. He was breathing hard, the breath jerking out of his chest.

'Embrace me,' whispered the demon. It kissed him with its mouth on the corner of his. They were mirror images, sliding into each other.

He could not keep a grip on the slope of the monster's shoulder. They were slipping, the momentum accelerating. They fell together, hitting the water with a smack and descending through fierce clouds of bubbles, drowning. Richard embraced the shadow, his mouth full of feathers and salt water.

The creature was silk in his arms, then seaweed, then

water. He was alone. All was still, silent, and utterly clear at last.

The sea erupted.

Richard was hurled upwards on a breaking wave. Choking, he landed on his back on dry ground. The sea-serpent filled the sky. He looked up in awe at her long, equine head, the tendrils drooping from her muzzle, the huge black eyes under fierce ridges of bone. Salt water coursed down the long, plated neck. He felt no desire to fight her, no fear either. Only wonder, as if in a strange dream. The huge head dipped, and looked at him with eyes that had seen everything.

He rose to his feet and bowed to her. He pulled off his soaked shirt and felt salt drying on his bare torso. Following the tilt of her head he looked round, and saw the rounded mass of a hill.

A spiral path took him to the summit. All around him lay the landscape of the hidden world, blue and mysterious. He recognized the scarps and tors of Kate's demesne, but everything looked subtly different. The maze-like loops of the path had a spectral sheen. Upon the hill itself there was nothing but a slab of slate, like a tomb.

He stood at one end of the slab. At the other end, facing him, there appeared three figures: his brother Edward, as lean and golden as he'd been in his prime; on either side of him, a son, blond and rosy with the moody pale eyes of their mother. There was a mistiness about them, an aura, like light shining through the finest rain. They stood at the far end of the tomb-like slab and gazed at him. Behind them he saw other ghost-figures: Warwick the Kingmaker, George and Isabel, Anne hand in hand with a small boy. But they were insubstantial. Only Edward and the two princes were solid.

Richard took a step towards them, and stopped. He could go no closer. His eyes burned.

'Edward? Dearest brother. I never thought I would see you again.'

Edward spoke. 'We are gone but you still live. I left my children in your care and they came to grief.'

'I have wept for it every day since,' Richard said dully.

'I want no vengeance greater than the punishment that you impose upon yourself.'

'I do not expect your forgiveness, but I beg it anyway.'

'And I beg yours,' Edward said softly, 'for abruptly leaving a situation hopelessly unresolved.'

'It was hard to forgive you for dying. Still, I did so, long ago. You've no need to ask me that. The actions that followed . . . I had no choice.'

'I know,' said the spectral Edward. 'What other lesson have we ever had, but to seize control at any cost? In your position I would have done the same.'

'In truth?'

'In very truth. I am no worse than you, Richard, and no better. And the same goes for my sons. At least they kept intact the relative innocence of childhood.'

'Whatever forces caused our death, we bear no malice,' said the elder Prince. His eyes stayed expressionless.

The younger boy spoke, his voice high and clear. 'Shall you play ball with us, Uncle?'

He seemed to come forward; Richard could only stand paralysed. He felt tears running freely down his face. Perhaps Edward pulled the boy back, because when Richard blinked, he was still at his father's side as if he hadn't moved at all.

'No malice, no unkind thought, nothing but the fondest affection,' Edward said sombrely. 'I love you, Dickon, as I hope you still love me. It is for higher powers to forgive what we have done.'

Richard whispered, 'Have you – seen God?'

'It's not as you think,' his brother answered cryptically. 'You look towards heaven and ignore the earth at your peril. For that reason and every other, we are glad you won your battle.' He smiled. 'I would not have seen you lose for anything. I know this: your enemy would have hunted and slain every last one of our blood relations in time, even to the frailest old woman. We all have a shadow, Richard. If there's no shadow, there's no light.'

And his brother and nephews made obeisance to him – his own brother, Edward the Sun in Splendour. In the background, all the ghosts of his past went on their knees. Richard closed his eyes and turned away. He did not want to think that this was generated by his own dreaming mind.

When he looked up again, the spectres were gone. In their place, a woman stood before him. She was not ghost-like, but earthy and real.

She was no beauty, but big and coarse, her plump rolls of fat sheathed in a robe of some nondescript stuff that might have been ancient leather or dead leaves. Scales tiled her skin and her face was hog-like, haloed by coarse black hair.

Around her neck hung his cross. With one hand she cracked a walnut shell and ate the meat. Richard laughed, infected with a weird delight at her self-possession.

'Do you know me?' The voice was a purr, rumbling deep through him.

'I think so, Great Mother.'

'That's good. Few recognize me these days. Or if they do, they turn their backs upon me in horror.' She took a few swaying steps nearer. 'Do you fear me?'

'No,' he said. 'Yes.'

'I am the earth. The earth is not from the Devil. Your shadow is not from the Devil. It only played devil's advocate for as long as you set it outside yourself.'

'It's inside me now.'

'Good. That's the way of things, dark and light in one being. Try to cut yourself in half and disaster follows. You are the anointed King.'

'Still?'

'Still.'

'Many curse me for it,' Richard said quietly. 'But I had

no choice. If you set me down two years in the past, I'd act no differently.'

The thick nose wrinkled. A powerful scent came from her, like wet earth, decaying leaves, sea wind, and the musk of sex. 'So you acted as much through dark as light. How then do you differ from any other human? Though many may hate and envy you for it, you are beyond good and evil. Attend.' She lifted a large brown hand. 'You are the anointed King, divine guardian of the land and wedded to the land. Many kings of late have forgotten this. Those of the future will lose the knowledge altogether, unless you revive it. They will enforce the spiritual or wallow in the material. In doing so they will neglect the heart, and cut themselves off from their true source of power and their true duty. They will oppress my daughters who struggle to keep the flame alive. All that serpent energy they'll despise, discard and waste, and never know what they've lost! If they continue in that wise, they'll starve the land to death, for I'll go deep underground and leave only a mantle of stones for men to till their feeble crops upon. All my daughters and sons will be enslaved to feed the power of the Church. All their vigour and wisdom wasted. Those who rebel, or are even suspected of giving succour to their old mother, shall be hanged and burned.'

'Not in my reign.'

'No? It has happened on other paths a shade away from this. You've been close, putting your own shadow onto others.'

He thought, reluctantly, of Eliza Shore. Of the way he'd fled the enticing and dangerous temptation of Kate.

'You became king for a reason,' she went on. 'The potential to see beyond the material, the political, and into the bones of the earth. No other in your time could have done this. You can remember and restore the true meaning of kingship. Restore your Plantagenet legacy. Bring the spirits of earth back into the light. Will you take this duty upon you?'

He fell to his knees. The slab bruised him to the bone. 'To do this, I must relinquish all I have believed.'

'Not all.' The Goddess sighed. 'Not to relinquish anything; just to accept all that is.'

'And I know what you say to me is the truth.' His voice was rough.

'Yes. The truth that none dares utter.'

It was painful, the final sloughing and falling away of the armour. A shell cracking, light spilling through, smooth rawness beneath. But it was over quickly. Then he felt an intense calmness. 'Yes, Great Mother. I welcome it. I swear by all I hold sacred to take this duty upon me until death.'

The Goddess came to him. Her heavy stride shook the ground. When she moved, her robe split and fell away like a seed husk to reveal multi-coloured skirts aglow with fruits and flowers. Over them was a mantle, black and full of stars. He saw that her hair was woven with corn stalks and crowned with two vipers that held the moon between them. In her hands she held a vessel of bright pearl.

'I anoint you King with the power of the elements. Earth,' she smeared soil on him, drawing symbols on his forehead and naked chest, 'water, fire.' A mixture of blood and brine were poured on his head from the vessel. A fiery brand that she produced from nowhere seared runes on his skin. She was making him anew, and with more power than any archbishop could endow, a primal, immortal power. 'With air,' she said, and, leaning down, put her mouth to his and breathed into him.

Autumn storms went through him.

'You are the divine King and therefore wedded to the land. King, only through your marriage to her.' She gave him her hand to steady him as he rose to his feet. 'Let us seal the covenant. Share with me.'

She gave him an apple, from which she'd already taken a large bite. Juice oozed pink from it. He ate the red fruit. The food of faerie land. After that, he knew, there was no going back.

'I am Nature,' she said, 'the universal Mother, mistress of all the elements, queen of the dead, queen also of the immortals, the single manifestation of all the gods and goddesses that are. Only remember, and keep these words of mine locked tight in your heart, that from now onwards until the very last day of your life you are dedicated to my service.'

'Yes.' He went into her arms as if falling. All the energy went out of him and there was a sensation of utter peace, of sinking into the warmth of the earth.

He opened his eyes and it was not Auset who held him in her arms, but Kate.

They were on Bride Cloud. The distant moors and the wooded griffes of the demesne lay folded in eerie mist. Dawn had come early and sweet, shining on the river far below them. He heard the gentle rush of waterfalls.

'Were you there all the time?' he asked.

'Leave it part of the mystery.' Her smile was tired and glowing. 'Well, did she give you clear sight?'

Richard sighed and raised one hand to shield his eyes against the rising sun. 'So clear I'm dazzled,' he said.

Summer heat came early, creating a delicious balance between the chill of dawn and the basking warmth to come. Katherine threw off her gown and waded naked into the Melandra to bathe. The cold made her gasp. The river was pale, blazing gold. Never had Lytton Dale seemed more alive, so full of delicate colours. She was beyond inhibition, like a naiad. She was aware of Richard's eyes on her, on her slim curves, the banner of black hair down to her waist. His attention was a caress.

A minute later, Richard joined her. She smiled at him walking naked across the stony shore. His narrow body had a preternatural purity and symmetry in the rising light, like ivory silk. Ten years had fallen from him. He looked no more than twenty.

She laughed at the shocked cry he gave on entering the

water. They splashed each other like children in Eden. Then they kissed, sinking deep under the surface. Their hair floated in fronds. It was a strange kind of baptism. Rebirth.

Drying themselves in the sun and tenderly warming each other, the grass was a rough bed beneath them. The world shimmered, kingfisher-bright. How they had each had the will to hold back from this for so long, she would never know.

'The things I saw,' he said as they dressed at last, dragging garments over still-damp skin. 'I would like to tell you of it . . . later. For now, I can't speak.'

'I saw some of it,' she said, looking searchingly at him. She couldn't take her eyes off him. 'But not all. Much of the journey was for you alone.'

He came to her and placed his hands on her arms. 'Is your answer still the same?'

'My answer?'

'Let's imagine we've washed away everything that was said before. Katherine, have mercy on this weary old soldier. Please be my wife.'

She rested her head against his shoulder. The question was as wondrously terrifying as it had been the first time. She gave a sob. It was the hardest future she could possibly choose.

He dropped suddenly to the ground in front of her. 'Kate, I'm on my knees. Please. I can't be alone any more. There's no one else I want beside me but you.'

She looked at his haunted face, his tears falling. She knelt down with him and put her arms around him. They clung to each other.

'They will say you married a witch.' The words came out in a sob of awful amusement.

'Then I'll only be doing as they expect of me.'

'Worse. They will say that I was your mistress all the time you were married to Anne. They'll say that I helped you poison her.'

'Oh God, Katy, don't. Do you think such evil lies in their hearts, to think such evil of us? We'll survive it. Answer me.' Now she couldn't speak. He spoke into her ear, barely audible. 'And the thing that can never be mentioned. The Princes, my nephews. Is that why you can't say yes to me? I don't blame you, sweetheart. Only tell me the truth.'

Kate pulled back, smearing moisture out of her eyes. 'Love, I know who killed them. Bess told me.'

'Bess?' His face became streaked stone. 'She knew nothing!'

'She didn't even realize what she was telling me. She said that kind Lady Beaufort sent potions to them by their doctor. Beaufort poisoned them, Richard.'

She wasn't sure how she'd expected him to react: rage, disbelief, ghastly joy. Instead the hard lines of his face relaxed. 'Try to understand, Kate. They were in my care. The responsibility was mine. If Lady Beaufort did that, she couldn't have done so without my having facilitated it by the fact that they were imprisoned.'

'But you did not—'

'Don't try to absolve me of it. Take it that I'm guilty. Can you still love me?'

She nodded helplessly. 'Yes, whatever you've done. I take the shadow as well as the light. Will you punish her?'

'How can I punish Margaret Beaufort any more than I've punished myself? Any more than we've both been punished by the death of a son?' he said. 'I'm glad she shares that pain. One son each. Does that mean we've atoned? If this one, terrible thing is not stopping you, Kate, what is?'

'Everything I said yesterday. I will not repent, I will not convert. They must take me as I am, or not at all.'

'They shall.'

'What if they revile me?'

'They will love you,' he said with a confidence that touched her. 'People know a kind and good soul when they see one, Kate. Perhaps through that love there will be reconciliation, and they will look more gently upon me at last, so that I can fulfil my duties as I wish. A new beginning. That's what we were shown in the hidden world. I won't let you go until you say yes.'

'We're already married in the hidden world,' she said.

'Well, we shall have to do so again in public, with some pomp and ceremony, or no one will believe us.'

'You understand, don't you?' she said, looking at him. 'I'm the high priestess, the avatar of the Goddess. As in the ancient times. That's how you're joined to me; not just as man to woman, but as the King to the land.'

'Yes,' said Richard. 'To bring the strength back to the land, which, God knows, she sorely needs. I know it won't be easy, Kate, but all I can do to make you happy, I shall do. Only please give me a clear answer.'

She took a long breath and said, 'Yes.'

In Eleanor's presence, Richard became King again. He seemed to acquire the gravity of kingship as if gathering up a trail of garments he'd discarded on his way to the cave. He was immaculately dressed, the last man to have swum as naked as a savage in the river, or caressed her daughter in the grass while the sun dried their skin. A dark jacket glinting with jewels, a soft velvet cap on his polished hair, his gentlemen attendants waiting discreetly in the background. His whole demeanour had changed. He was magnetic, untouchable.

Katherine noticed the grey lines of dried mud on his boots, and smiled to herself.

'Union between the outer and inner worlds,' Eleanor said thoughtfully. Kate noted that she and Richard spoke to each other as respectful equals. 'A chance to bring the Motherlodge into the light. So that we can follow our path freely and without persecution.'

'That's what I hope.' Richard looked sombre. 'I shall have a glorious battle on my hands.'

'The Church.'

His eyes narrowed, gleaming. 'It's not designed to please the Pope. He's been leaning on the priesthood for years to abolish the Motherlodge across Europe.'

'If in the end you bow to him, this is all for nothing.'

'I'll not bow to him,' said Richard. 'The difficulty will be to coerce the bishops gently to heel. The last thing I want is to alienate them and have it all end in a disastrous conflict.'

'Goddess,' Kate breathed, and put her head in her hand. 'That's just the danger. That we'll push too hard and give them the very excuse they need to crush us. It's impossible, isn't it?'

'Hard,' said Eleanor, 'but not impossible. If anyone can effect it, it's you, love.'

Richard said softly, 'If this means I have to break with the Pope, I will. The joining of the King of the outer world with the Queen-to-be of the hidden must be seen as a natural and desirable outcome, as we know it to be. However, it will require you to coax them gently to it, Kate, not me to force them. And you will.'

'Thank you for your faith in me.' She squared herself, feeling more composed. Broad shoulders for the impossible responsibility.

Richard sat forward and said to Eleanor, 'Madam, would you be so kind as to have someone send for your village priest?'

'Of course, sire.'

While Eleanor went aside to speak to Thomas Copper, Kate leaned close to Richard and whispered, 'Why do you want the priest?'

'To ask if he can marry us today.'

A delicious mixture of fear and excitement coiled through her. 'Why the hurry?'

He put his lips to her ear. 'Because I want to lie with you tonight, and it would not be seemly to do so under your mother's roof unless we are married.'

'I see.'

His hand tightened on hers. 'And so that you can't change your mind. We'll have a great celebration at court, even another ceremony to please our subjects; but if we're already married, none can interfere or divide us. Tomorrow I must set out to London. I'm not going without you.'

Her memory roused. 'Oh, Richard . . .'

'Yes, Kate?' He smiled at her.

'Do you remember the elemental I took from you, that was feeding upon your strength?'

He looked startled, as if he'd expected her to speak of the wedding or the journey. 'I can't imagine why you choose this moment to remind me of it, but yes.'

'Anything may emanate an essence of itself. Rocks, earth, fire, water, illness and death, weather, even an atmosphere of joy or anger. Usually they dissipate in their own time, but if they become powerful enough, they are half-sentient.'

'No more wit than a horned toad, you said.'

'I was wrong,' Kate said, so eager to tell him that she felt she was making no sense. 'There was one close to you, working for your enemies – Dr Fautherer.'

'What?' His voice hardened.

She told him what she'd seen on the battlefield. 'He appeared human, but was not. Once you had won the day, he had no more reason to exist. I saw him vanish.'

'If not human . . . what was he?'

'I don't know where he came from, or where he went,' she said, soft against his shoulder. 'But I believe I know what he was. The pestilence of rumour. He created it, multiplied it and fed upon it.'

He took this in thoughtfully and did not contradict her. 'Are you suggesting that Margaret Beaufort and Bishop Morton worked sorcery against me?'

'More than that. I don't think they were powerful enough to create him. Rather, he was naturally attracted to them. He was the embodiment of all the forces that worked against you. The face of all those cruel tongues and vile rumours.'

She felt him breathe in then exhale. 'Then there must

have been something of me in him too. They weren't all without foundation.'

'But I'm trying to say that since Fautherer is gone, I can hope that you're right. We cheated fate, so the bane is gone. There might be a new beginning after all.'

He was laughing, kissing her. 'And that aside from the fact that it will not be Tudor who commissions the history books, but Richard.'

Dawn found Katherine in her mother's herb garden, gathering a posy to take back to Richard. She'd left him asleep, but the first soft bloom of morning had enticed her outside with the promise of dew and birdsong. She needed this time alone to think over what had happened to her. To believe it.

She thought, idly, that it would be pleasant to have a daughter. Essential, in fact. She needed a daughter as Richard needed a son. Her own heir to the hidden world.

There was a man in the distance, on horseback, riding towards the house. She watched as he came closer and saw her. He leaped from the saddle and came running across wet silvery swathes of grass towards her. It was Raphael. Kate stood idiotically frozen with the flowers in her hand, as he ran to her, his brown hair flowing back over his shoulders.

'Kate,' he said. 'Thank God I've found you. Everything I said to you – please pardon me for it. I wasn't myself.'

He seized her hand and was pressing it to his lips.

'Raphael, it's all right.'

'I meant to be formal,' he said. 'Courteous. But when I saw you . . . I still love you. Forget everything I said. Marry me.'

Her flowers fell to the grass. She let out a breath, a sob of pain.

'Raphael . . . love, it's too late. I'm already married.'

'You can't be.' His face was a map of disbelief. He

shook his head, his irises becoming white-ringed. 'Married when? How?'

Kate felt close to falling apart. 'You must know that the King is here.' He said nothing. 'You probably heard gossip that I was with him, the night after the battle.'

He averted his face and stared at a bank of rosemary. 'Yes, I heard. I didn't want to believe it. I was . . . jealous.'

'Is that why you came here? He asked me that night. I fled. Can you imagine me, swanning about like Elizabeth Woodville?'

'I can, actually.'

'Thank you. He came after me and now it's done. I'm sorry.'

'When was it done?'

She half-smiled, remembering. 'Last evening, in our village church. We had the Christian ceremony inside, and the old ceremony in the meadow beneath Mag Tor.'

Raphael laughed. 'Richard stood in a pagan circle, and jumped the broomstick with you?'

'He did. All the village came.' She thought of the glowing amber sunset that had flooded the church, the gorgeous warmth of the evening, the wreath of flowers they'd placed upon her hair. The village would talk of it forever more. King Richard had married their Lady's daughter in their tiny church. The event would pass into legend.

'Ask my mother if you don't believe me.' She glanced up at a leaded window, glittering in the first rays of sunlight. 'Ask him.'

All the fire went out of Raphael. He met her eyes, bleak and calm. 'Would it have made a difference if I hadn't come too late? If I hadn't gone to Nottingham?'

'No, love.'

His hands went to his face, fell. 'This is my fault.'

She frowned. 'That you've lost me? Oh, Raphael. We can't help how we love. I know how Richard lives, that he's never still and that if there are any more battles, he will insist on being in the thick of them. The idea of being his queen terrifies me. But I can't let the fear stop me. He has an heir again, a reason to live. We might do some good.'

'Well.' He was silent for a minute. When he spoke again, he was all stony dignity. 'Well, I'm glad for you. I'm glad, Katherine. Your Grace.'

'Gods, don't call me that.'

He smiled. 'I must, from now on.'

'Won't you come in?' She took his hand. 'Come in and see him.'

He hesitated, then said quietly, 'No.'

'But you must. Why not?'

He began to walk away. Desperate to say anything to keep him there, she ran after him and stopped him. 'I've so much to tell you . . .'

She told him about Fautherer, but when she'd finished he acknowledged what she'd said with a nod, and went on his way again.

'Where are you going?' Kate was distressed, but he only shook his head.

'Bear him my heart's love. But I said farewell to him before the battle.'

Raphael walked steadily, following the ancient path. Around the circle of the churchyard, out along the river bank towards Old Mag Heads, mounting the shale-treacherous hillside towards Mag Tor. His walk had the hypnotic rhythm of dancing round a sacred circle.

His fervour had burned away now. For a time he'd raged to himself: that he'd been so stupid as to lose Kate; that Richard whom he'd loved and served all his life had thanked him by stealing her. He couldn't stay. Couldn't return to London with them. It would have made him demented to see them together, the raven-haired King and Queen of witches with their beautiful grey-eyed son between them. A storm had roiled through him, madly seeking escape, winding ever tighter because he could find no way to express it. What should he do? Roar, take a heavy sword and slash every tapestry within Lytton Hall to shreds? Slay the King, then Kate, and then himself?

No. The storm passed. Some wayward instinct had taken him to Nottingham, when he could have stayed in Leicester and tried to win her back. Instead, he'd only made it easier for Kate to follow her heart.

Three times widdershins around Mag Tor, looking all the time at the tumbled stack of rocks spiralling above him, entreating the blind, preadamite mass for protection. Then down the narrow track into the griffe. The woods swallowed him, blue-green as an ocean.

The trees parted in a series of watery veils. He strode on through a world that seemed a little harsher and colder than the one he'd left. He barely recognized the battle-field, but knew where he was. The contours resolved. Even cloaked in different vegetation, they were all too familiar.

His path ended at a small standing stone, which drew him as if it marked the centre of creation. He saw a young woman there. She was placing a white rose at its foot, her head bowed and her long hair, the pale brown of beech leaves, covering her. As he approached, she stood up with white roses falling out of her lap and waited for him. It was the muse.

They met and embraced without a word. She greeted him with a kiss full on the mouth. Desolation faded.

'My angel Raphael,' she said, stroking his face.

'I found you,' he answered. 'My lady . . . your name?'

'August.'

'It sounds like the name of a goddess. The month of death and rebirth. Do you know what has happened?'

'Yes,' she said, smiling. 'I've seen everything. But you know what happened here, also?'

Together they stood with their arms around each other and looked at the mournful stone, the white rose stems scattered upon it. The sight of it stopped him breathing.

He'd lived both lives, both paths at once: one where Tudor was dust, and this . . .

'I think they've put it in the wrong place,' he said.

'Without a doubt,' she answered. 'It doesn't matter. The thought is there.'

'I wanted to see a world where he died,' Raphael said after a time. 'To know how the emptiness I saw in my visions felt.'

'To torment yourself?'

'No, just to see if I could endure it. I knew that night in his tent would be the last of our friendship. As in that world, so in this. If he'd died, would Kate and I fallen into each other's arms and comforted each other? I devoted my whole life to averting his death, and in return he took her from me.'

'Then you truly gave him everything,' said the muse, 'which is what you wanted.'

'I would have given him my life!'

'I know. But you're still here. And so am I.'

'Do they remember him, here in your land, Lady August?'

'Oh, yes.' She gave a quiet laugh. 'And still some love him and some hate him; but no one forgets him. My friend once told me a tale . . .' She spoke of a sacred king, mutilated, blamed and sacrificed.

'And did his death heal this land?' Raphael asked.

'I would like to believe so, Raphael. I don't want to think it was just a story to comfort ourselves; we have to make it meaningful. Still, the healing's been unbearably slow. But now there's been a rebirth at last, and Eleanor was right: the future is not set in stone. Will he be half-forgotten in your world, because he ruled well and lived to old age and left fine Plantagenet sons and daughters behind him? Or will the good he does in life prove more important than lasting fame?'

'He'll never be forgotten,' Raphael said emphatically. 'I don't know why I never saw visions beyond his death.'

'Because you were seeing this world, not your own,'

she answered. 'The paths divide here. Don't abandon him, Raphael. You have a future now.'

He felt all the tense misery go out of him then. The muse's arms were so warm, her body lithe against his. He felt a desire he had not felt for months. 'You're right,' he said. 'God knows, he deserves some happiness after everything. I can't deny him and Kate that, or their son a father. It's what I was meant to do. To see the two people I most love, happy.'

'Then you've won.'

He smiled. 'And I'm glad. I can't feel bitter about it. I don't.'

'And how does this world feel to you?' the muse asked gently.

'Bleak,' he said.

'It is, Raphael. It's bleak.' She stroked his cheek and looked at him, warm and serious. 'Take me to a world where he didn't die.'

Freda Warrington is the author of the bestselling BLACK-BIRD fantasy novels. She has also written dark fantasies, including a sequel to DRACULA which won the Dracula Society's award for Best Gothic Novel. Her novel THE AMBER CITADEL, part of THE JEWELFIRE TRILOGY, was nominated for the British Fantasy Society's Best Novel award. Freda was born in Leicester and grew up in the beautiful Charnwood Forest area which inspired her feeling for atmosphere, nature and the mysterious side of life. She has worked as a graphic designer and medical illustrator but her main love has always been writing. She still lives near Charnwood (in the shadow of a medieval castle) where she enjoys art, all things Gothic and stained-glass work. For more information, please visit her Website on http://members.aol.com/FredaMike/index.html

POCKET
BOOKS

ISOLDE I

Queen of the Western Isle

Rosalind Miles

The first in a magnificent new Arthurian trilogy from Rosalind Miles,
author of the bestselling *Guenevere*.

Only daughter of Ireland's ruling queen, Isolde has always known that
she will take over the rule of the sacred Island of the West when her time
comes. Until then she practises her skills as a healer and struggles to hold
back her mother, a passionate, headstrong woman under the sway of her
champion, Sir Marhaus, who is determined to make war.

Attacking Cornwall, Sir Marhaus wounds the king's nephew, Sir Tristan
of Lyonesse, so badly that he can only be saved by Isolde, the most noted
healer of the isles. And when the King of Cornwall decides to marry
Isolde, unaware of the young couple's growing love, the stage is set for the
mythic tale of star-crossed lovers that the world knows so well.

Set in Ireland, Cornwall and Camelot, *Isolde* offers a compelling new
version of the familiar legend rich in Celtic magic and mythology, yet
firmly grounded in the well-loved Arthurian world. Merlin, Arthur,
Guenevere, and all their knights appear once again to delight those who
enjoyed Rosalind Miles's previous forays into this enchanted terrain.

ISBN: 0 671 03721 8
PRICE £6.99

POCKET
BOOKS

THE TINNER'S CORPSE

Bernard Knight

When Crowner John is summoned to the bleak Devonshire
moors to investigate the murder of a tin miner, he has little
idea how difficult this new investigation will prove to be.
A decapitated body, a missing tinner, a disgruntled band of
miners and a mad Saxon. How on earth can Crowner John
sort all this out? Surely things can't get any worse?

PRICE £5.99
ISBN 0 671 02966 5

THE GRIM REAPER

Bernard Knight

May 1195, and Sir John de Wolfe is faced with a strange series of
serial murders, the common factor is that an appropriate Biblical
text is left at each murder scene. This means that a literate and
Bible-learned killer is involved – which, in an age where only
1% of the population can read or write – can only be a priest.
There are seventeen parish churches in Exeter, so the killer could
be any one of about a hundred clerics. Crowner John sets about
to discover the identity of the homicidal priest.

ISBN 0 671 02967 3
PRICE £6.99

POCKET BOOKS

This book and other Pocket titles are available from your bookshop or can be ordered direct from the publisher.

Guenevere:

0 671 01812 4	**The Queen of the Summer Country**	Rosalind Miles	£6.99
0 671 01813 2	**The Knight of the Sacred Lake**	Rosalind Miles	£6.99
0 671 01814 0	**The Child of the Holy Grail**	Rosalind Miles	£6.99
0 671 03721 8	**Isolde**	Rosalind Miles	£6.99

Stone of Light:

0 671 77371 2	**Nefer the Silent**	Christian Jacq	£6.99
0 671 77374 7	**The Wise Woman**	Christian Jacq	£6,99
0 671 77375 5	**Paneb the Ardent**	Christian Jacq	£6.99
0 671 77376 3	**The Place of Truth**	Christian Jacq	£6.99
0 671 51673 6	**The Sanctuary Seeker**	Bernard Knight	£5.99
0 671 51674 4	**The Poisoned Chalice**	Bernard Knight	£5.99
0 671 51675 2	**Crowner's Quest**	Bernard Knight	£5.99
0 671 02965 7	**The Awful Secret**	Bernard Knight	£5.99
0 671 02966 5	**The Tinner's Corpse**	Bernard Knight	£5.99
0 671 02967 3	**The Grim Reaper**	Bernard Knight	£6.99

Please send cheque or postal order for the value of the book; free postage and packing within the UK; OVERSEAS including Republic of Ireland £1 per book.

OR: Please debit this amount from my

VISA/ACCESS/MASTERCARD . . . .

CARD NO: . . . .

EXPIRY DATE . . . .

AMOUNT £ . . . .

NAME . . . .

ADDRESS . . . .

. . . .

. . . .

SIGNATURE . . . .

Send orders to: SIMON & SCHUSTER CASH SALES
PO Box 29, Douglas, Isle of Man, IM99 1BQ
Tel: 01624 675137, Fax: 01624 670923
www.bookpost.co.uk

Please allow 14 days for delivery. Prices and availability subject to change without notice